Purgatory's
Shore

Purgatory's Shore

Taylor Anderson

ACE
NEW YORK

ACE
Published by Berkley
An imprint of Penguin Random House LLC
penguinrandomhouse.com

Library of Congress Cataloging-in-Publication Data

Names: Anderson, Taylor, 1963– author.
Title: Purgatory's shore / Taylor Anderson.
Description: New York : Ace, [2021] | Series: The Artillerymen Series
Identifiers: LCCN 2021008728 (print) | LCCN 2021008729 (ebook) |
ISBN 9780593200711 (hardcover) | ISBN 9780593200735 (ebook)
Classification: LCC PS3601.N5475 P87 2021 (print) |
LCC PS3601.N5475 (ebook) | DDC 813/.6—dc23
LC record available at https://lccn.loc.gov/2021008728
LC ebook record available at https://lccn.loc.gov/2021008729

Printed in the United States of America
1st Printing

Book design by Daniel Brount
Interior art: Smoke background © swp23/Shutterstock.com

To:
All my pals in the 1st Section
C Company
3rd US Artillery
(You know who you are.)

THE YUCATÁN, HOLY DOMINION, AND BEYOND

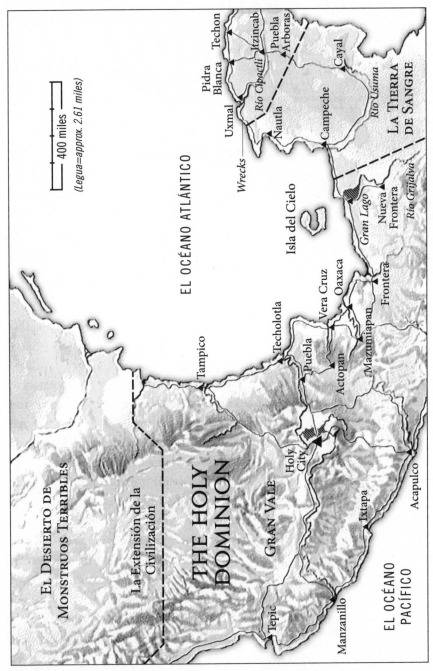

Drawn from the embroidered atlas in Uxmal. Important roads including the coastal "Camino Militar" are depicted, as far as their extent is known. Larger cities are symbolized thus: ▲

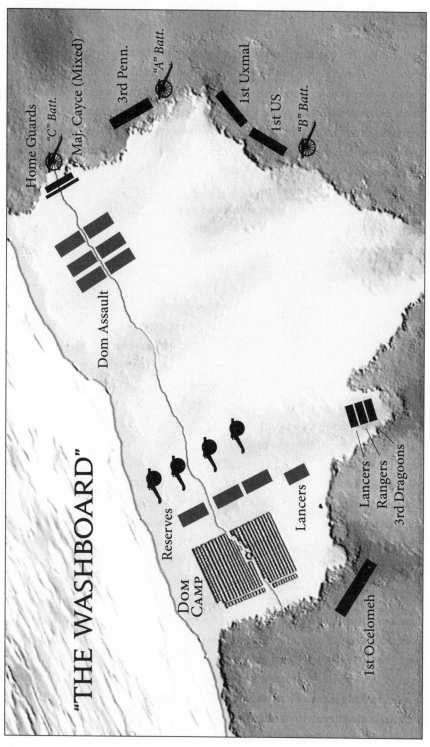

"THE WASHBOARD"

Home Guards

"C" Batt.

Maj. Cayce (Mixed)

3rd Penn.

"A" Batt.

1st Uxmal

1st US

"B" Batt.

Dom Assault

Reserves

Dom CAMP

Lancers

Lancers

Rangers

3rd Dragoons

1st Ocelomeh

US Battery (6 guns)   Dom Battery (5 guns)

I'm now as certain as it's possible to be that innumerable "Earths," perhaps entire universes, simultaneously coexist in the cosmos. That would explain a great many things, such as where various peoples and species (some sentient, others not) we find on "this" far different Earth originally came from, though the means (or purpose?) by which they—or we—were transported here through the ages remains frustratingly elusive.

And "this" Earth remains as strange to me as are many of its inhabitants, perhaps influenced by indistinct but profound changes in the prehistoric past? It teems with descendants of creatures long extinct where we came from, and quite a few others that either came here like ourselves or sprang into being independent of our own fossil record. However different, it's clearly "an" Earth because, aside from a few puzzling exceptions, the geography is roughly the same, though shorelines reflect a generally lower sea level. It's my belief this is due to another (or a lingering) ice age, the Arctic and Antarctic expanses vastly expanded and hoarding more of the planet's water. Indeed, with the exception of equatorial regions, temperatures all over the world are noticeably lower as well.

But this is no scientific treatise, any more than my multivolume The Worlds I've Wondered—*first published by the University of New Glasgow Press in 1956—pretended to be. In those books, I chiefly documented the adventures of myself and many others, essentially chased to this world aboard the decrepit US Asiatic Fleet destroyer USS* Walker *by the marauding Japanese. These volumes,* Lands and Peoples, *relate the often tragic sagas of others we've come to know, based as closely on their histories as possible. In many cases, their early experiences directly influenced ours, but I'll leave the reader to draw those connections.*

Therefore, I shall begin with the tale of a group that arrived on this world almost exactly a century before us, whom we first referred to as the "1847 Americans."

Excerpt from the Foreword to Courtney Bradford's
Lands and Peoples—Destiny of the Damned, Vol. I,
Library of Alex-aandra Press, 1959

PURGATORY'S SHORE

CHAPTER 1

The world was shades of gray, reminding Captain Lewis Cayce—formerly of C Battery, 3rd United States Artillery Regiment—of different kinds of lead. The sea to the north of the Yucatán Peninsula was the blue-gray color of molten lead when it got too hot, and the sky had the chalky gray-white look of a corroded musket ball. The comparison struck Lewis Cayce as he leaned on the weathered windward rail of a wretched old barque-rigged whaler named *Mary Riggs*, wallowing down toward Vera Cruz, Mexico. There'd been more real lead in the air around him over the last year than he cared to remember, and a bloody-fingered surgeon had even plucked a particularly shiny wafer of it from his side after the Battle of Monterrey. Now that he was heading back to the fighting, to join General Winfield Scott's push inland from Vera Cruz, he'd soon be exposed to a great deal more. Staring grimly across the choppy sea at three other ships straggling along in company, he decided the sea and sky were a portent.

Mary Riggs's closest companion was USS *Isidra*, a neat little former Mexican side-wheel steamer captured at Frontera on the Grijalva River. She was crowded with regular infantry, officers' horses and personal baggage, as well as most of the senior officers responsible for men on the other ships. USS *Commissary* was a government transport, loaded with munitions, supplies, and volunteer infantry. *Xenophon* had joined them en route and looked like another old whaler. Lewis suspected her cargo and circumstances were much the same as *Mary Riggs*'s.

Worn down by decades of yearslong voyages, storms, and hard use associated with her former occupation, *Mary Riggs* was destined for the breakers or abandonment when she was purchased cheaply by a group of New Orleans investors at the outbreak of war between Mexico and the United States. There was money to be made by a transport for hire to the army, and she was hastily reconfigured to carry horses. She'd done that several times already, but this time she'd been loaded with far too many, as well as a half dozen cannon, limbers, several caissons, and a pair of forge wagons—*before* being packed to the bulwarks with four hundred men. She reeked unimaginably, the stench of her earlier life almost—but not quite—overwhelmed by the new combination of the manure and sweat of terrified horses, 430 (counting the crew) unwashed bodies, stale tobacco smoke, and most crushing of all, the waste and vomit of too many passengers as unused to the sea as the horses. At least here, by the windward rail of the laboring ship, the air Lewis breathed was slightly fresher.

He wasn't sick himself, being more accustomed to seafaring than most soldiers. He'd traveled up and down the East Coast several times in his career, and all the way to Europe with his former commander, Samuel Ringgold, a decade before. Perhaps a lifetime on horseback reinforced a certain resistance to the sickening motion of a ship as well. Besides, he'd already seen enough of this war, since its brutal beginning on the sandy, cordgrass plain of Palo Alto, that few things could turn his stomach anymore. But that was him. Most aboard the pitching vessel, leaning hard under a press of dingy canvas, were new recruits, and many were youngsters, as new to war as they were the sea, so he idly wondered why he had such a stretch of the coveted rail to himself. The fighting in Northern Mexico had hardened him in various ways, dulling what many old West Point classmates would've described as a general cheerfulness, but it hadn't turned him aloof. Quite the contrary. Having watched a number of dear friends die (including Major Ringgold, whom he'd deeply respected) made him appreciate those who remained all the more. That's what he thought, at least. But even he recognized those losses might've made him less anxious to make *new* friends, and it was possible that disposition was detectable by others.

Still, besides the fact his gold-edged shoulder boards and black knee boots were the only indication he was an officer (he didn't even own a frock coat anymore and preferred the dark blue enlisted fatigue jacket above sky-blue trousers), he assumed his isolation was due to his being the most senior army officer aboard—while not technically having a command. Half the troops in *Mary Riggs* were artillerymen who, besides their dark blue wheel hats (standard issue for all branches), wore sky-blue uniforms with yellow trim. Many had stitched nonregulation red bands around their hats and stripes down their trouser legs, aping the now famous "flying" horse artillery Lewis had belonged to, but they were "foot" artillery, mostly trained on massive coast defense guns. Some with longer service were probably familiar with lightweight field artillery, but few would've practiced the tactics of rapid maneuver and concentration of fire that Major Ringgold pioneered and had proven so successful. Even more strangely from Lewis's point of view, they may not even *serve* as artillerymen when they joined General Scott. Some might be sent as replacements to artillery units already in the field, but they'd all been equipped with .69 caliber Model 1816 muskets and more thoroughly trained as infantry.

Then there were the two hundred dragoons, armed with pistols and sabers and the odd-looking .52 caliber Model 1843 breechloading Hall carbines. Lewis was impressed by the volume of fire Halls could acheive, and even their short-range accuracy (much better than musketoons for mounted men), but they'd earned a reputation as troublesome, underpowered weapons. Men who carried them typically loved them or hated them—much like dragoons themselves were regarded by the rest of the army. They wore the same dark blue jackets as Lewis except theirs were trimmed with yellow instead of the horse artillery red Lewis still stubbornly wore. He didn't command them either.

Unknown to him, the real reasons he remained alone with his thoughts had more to do with the intensity of his gray-eyed gaze and the scorn it focused on the ship full of officers a quarter mile away, as well as the unconsciously unhappy frown within the short brown beard on his face. He was physically intimidating as well: taller than average, with wide, strong shoulders straining the seams of his jacket. Yet despite all that, nothing travels faster than rumors and speculation among bored and miserable soldiers, and virtually every man aboard *Mary Riggs* already knew who he was and at least a version of what he'd seen. There were few veterans among them, and only a handful who'd already fought Mexicans. Some Noncommissioned Officers (NCOs) had campaigned against Seminoles in Florida, and a few older European immigrants might've faced (or fought for) Napoleon in their youth, but most of these men had been shopkeepers, farmers, recent immigrants, even quite literally gutter sweepings drawn to the regular army by enlistment bonuses when the current war began. All were volunteers, but unlike volunteer regiments specifically raised for the war, they weren't dreamy-eyed patriots looking for honor or glory or entranced by some notion it was the "manifest destiny" of Americans to spread their enlightened ideals (and themselves) across a continent. Most were in it for regular meals.

That didn't mean they'd be bad soldiers. The United States' tiny standing army and increasingly professional officer corps had fought magnificently so far, but until recently it was composed of men with long service, even among the enlisted ranks, who probably *had* absorbed many of the ideals their country—native or adopted—was fighting for. These newer recruits, really part of "America" yet or not, were "regulars" now as well. And with all the hard training, sometimes seasoned with genuine abuse, their lot was no worse than that of soldiers in other armies of the world. Just as important, they hadn't been *forced* to join. So most became good soldiers, proud of their regular status and loyal to one another—if not always yet the country they fought for. Some, especially foreigners, thought of themselves more as paid mercenaries than Americans, but that sometimes made them *better* soldiers, determined to prove they were Americans after all. In any event, as regulars, they were supposed to be professionals, and they were prepared to hold themselves to a higher standard than the short-term volunteer units they mocked. That made them . . . professionally curious . . . about what they were likely to face, so Captain Lewis Cayce had been the subject of much discussion among them—while his uninviting countenance made even the few junior officers aboard hesitant to approach him.

There were exceptions. One was another full-bearded man (though his whiskers were streaked with gray), who seemed acquainted with Cayce and stopped to speak from time to time but never lingered. He was just as tall, if not as heavily built, and would've passed for a civilian if not for his own battered wheel hat (with the folding neck flap removed) and sky-blue military vest he wore over a black-striped shirt. Dark corduroy trousers were tucked into the tops of brown knee boots similar to the black ones Lewis wore. Word was he and several more men aboard were Texas Rangers who, like Captain Cayce, had been in Northern Mexico with Zachary Taylor. Many wondered about their presence, since rumor had it General Scott didn't like their bloodthirsty reputation.

Another exception was a young dragoon lieutenant who—after three days at sea—finally seemed to gather the courage to approach the brooding artilleryman.

"If I may be so bold, sir," came a somewhat anxious voice, suddenly at Lewis's side, "aren't you excited to get back to the war?"

The words jolted Lewis from his dark reverie, and he looked momentarily stricken before turning, almost thankfully, to face his visitor. Dressed in the stylishly tight junior officer's frock coat, he looked ridiculously thin and boyish, even with the pillow quilting under a single row of glistening buttons intended to make his chest look bigger. Wispy blond side whiskers had formed on his cheeks, a premature attempt to emulate those so many of the men sported, occasionally to outrageous excess. The youngster belatedly saluted. "Second Lieutenant Coryon Burton, sir. North Carolina. Class of 'forty-six."

Lewis returned the salute, still leaning on the rail. "Captain Cayce," he replied. "Of Tennessee, originally. Now just the army," he added wryly. That was certainly true. A West Point Class of 1830 graduate, he'd been in the army almost half his thirty-eight years. Peacetime promotion came very slowly, and he'd still been a first lieutenant when the war began.

"Yes sir, I know," the youth blurted. "All the fellows are talking about you." His accent softened the words under the excited tone, and Lewis vaguely envied him that. His own birth accent had almost entirely vanished.

"*All* the fellows?" Lewis asked, amused, as Burton began to redden. "I wonder what they say."

"Nothing bad," the young dragoon quickly assured. "They, ah, that is to say, it seems to be the consensus that you're a hero."

Lewis grunted and glanced around. "Is it indeed? *I* haven't told anyone so. I haven't even spoken to any of them. Even the artillery lieutenants aboard."

That had struck Lewis odd, that neither young artillery officer had presented himself out of courtesy. They weren't required to, since he wasn't their commander and they were all—essentially—just passengers on the same ship for now, but it wasn't good manners.

"I . . . can't speak for the others, sir, but . . ." Burton glanced meaningfully at the red trim on Lewis's jacket. "Just as there is rivalry between dragoons and Mounted Rifles, there exists a certain friction between mounted and foot artillery. It might also be . . ." The boy flushed again. "I can say for *myself* that your glorious experiences in battle have given me much to think about. Much to look forward to," he quickly added, "but also to question—whether I can perform as you did."

Lewis shook his head. "I saw little glory in Mexico and I'm certainly no 'hero.' I might congratulate myself for my survival, but not any extraordinary deeds."

"No more than anyone else who was there, is that it, Lewis?" came a growling voice on the other side of the dragoon lieutenant, who was startled to see the tall Ranger there.

"That's Captain Giles Anson of the Texas Mounted Volunteers, also known as 'Rangers'—among other things. Lieutenant Coryon Burton," Lewis announced by way of introduction.

"At your service, sir!" Burton exclaimed.

Anson smiled and nodded, but looked intently back at Lewis. "Palo Alto an' Resaca de la Palma were 'glorious' for us, I suppose." He glanced back at Burton. "Maybe even miraculous, considering how inexperienced an' outnumbered we were, an' only Ringgold's an' Duncan's artillery seemed to know what they were doin'. That miracle cost us Ringgold an' some other fine fellas, but bought us a lightly contested advance—aside from skirmishin', sickness, an' accidents," he inserted darkly, "all the way from Matamoros to Monterrey. Things were . . . different there, an' everyone was called to be a hero in *that* fight." He smiled oddly at Lewis. "Captain Cayce too."

Lewis looked back out to sea. *Isidra* was steaming easily enough, and even *Commissary* appeared to ride comfortably, but *Xenophon* was wallowing and bashing her way along just as roughly as *Mary Riggs*.

Much of the Battle of Monterrey had been fought *in* the city, house to house, rooftop to rooftop, even through the walls. Lewis had never seen anything like it. Never *imagined* something so brutal and desperate. His main contribution, after initially being attached to Duncan's Battery of the

2nd US to support an assault on Fort Libertad atop "Independence Hill"—in which Anson also participated—was to push a section of guns right down the rubbled, corpse-strewn streets of the city.

"He was wounded there, you know," Anson told Burton as if in confidence. "Me too, which is why we missed the more recent 'glorious' festivities at Buena Vista, or the Siege of Vera Cruz. Otherwise, we'd've been involved in one or the other." He chuckled. "The 'one' for me, most likely, an' 'the other' for Captain Cayce. General Taylor likes Texans better than General Scott, though 'Old Fuss an' Feathers' is startin' to learn he needs us after all. That's fine," he continued. "We need him too. Taylor's had most of his army taken away, an' there'll be *much* more fightin' on the road from Vera Cruz to the halls of the Montezuma."

With that, he nodded a bow and strode down the leaning, bounding deck and squeezed through the miserable soldiers sitting on it, surrounding four other men dressed much like he was near the base of the main mast. Lewis didn't know their names but had seen them all before. One was as massive and hairy as a bear, with a voice rather like one as well. Another was clearly Mexican himself, with a huge mustache and bristly black side whiskers. The last was a tall, slim youth, also apparently of Mexican descent, but with no facial hair and almost delicate features. He was always with Anson and served as his aide. There was even a slight resemblance. Lewis knew most of Anson's family, including his wife, were murdered by marauding Mexican soldiers during Texas's war for independence. Anson was with Sam Houston's army at the time. Lewis had no close family and could only imagine how devastated the Ranger must've been. It certainly helped explain his implacable attitude toward the enemy. At least to a degree. Lewis suspected the boy was a surviving son or nephew.

"A hard man," he murmured, watching Anson go. "But valuable in a fight." He cleared his throat and tried to smile at Burton. "And though not the only man aboard 'excited' to go to war, perhaps the only one anxious to return to it." His brow furrowed. "I don't mean he's looking forward to it; there's a distinction. . . ." He shook his head and sighed. "Of some sort. I can't really explain it. Captain Anson isn't a cruel man, but he's performed cruel deeds on occasion." He cleared his throat and bestowed his first genuine smile on Burton. "He's a Texan, after all. They have a more bitter history with Mexico—and President Santa Anna—than the rest of us. Don't let it bother you," he advised. "You'll likely never see him again after we disembark at Vera Cruz."

Coryon Burton's boldness—and Anson's departure—seemed to have encouraged others. Two more young men approached, both dressed like Burton, but looking a little ill under the slightly fuller side whiskers they'd accomplished. The first was presented as Second Lieutenant Justinian Olayne, R Company, 1st Artillery, and the second was Second Lieutenant Clifford Swain of the Mounted Rifles. Lewis was surprised to see the embroidered silver eagle on his stiffly stuffed wheel hat with an R on the shield.

"Are there many riflemen aboard, Lieutenant Swain?" Lewis asked. The Rifles were virtually indistinguishable from dragoons in dress, except for dark blue trousers with black seam stripes. Lewis hadn't noticed them, and with virtually everyone abovedeck sitting now . . .

"Not many, sir. Most are in *Isidra* with the regular infantry—which is how we'll serve, I understand," he replied morosely. "There's a painful shortage of American horses in Mexico, and since the Rifles already there lost most of theirs to a storm at sea, we'll all be afoot when we get there."

"And how many men are here?" Lewis pressed.

Swain gulped embarrassment. "Just twenty, sir, and only me for an officer. The spillovers from *Isidra*."

"Very well." Lewis looked at Olayne. "You have two companies of foot artillery and only one officer?"

"I do," Olayne replied with a faint Irish accent. "But there's three officers, sir, counting yourself."

Lewis smiled. "Indeed. And the other?"

Olayne shook his head. "Down with the seasickness as bad as any aboard. I fear he'd drown himself if he had the strength to creep up on deck."

Lewis forced himself not to laugh. It really wasn't funny. He tilted his head toward the setting sun. "Well, perhaps he'll survive another three days or so. We've made our turn west. Captain Holland tells me we should anchor off Vera Cruz by then. Personally, I suspect it'll be the morning of the fourth day. Holland strikes me as the careful sort, uninclined to approach strange shores after dark, but . . ." He paused and pointed. "Look to the south, past the other ships. You can just barely see it when we crest the waves."

The three young men waited, straining their eyes, and were finally rewarded with a view of a distant, hazy shoreline. "Is that Mexico?" Coryon Burton asked, slightly hushed.

Lewis had to remind himself that, officers or not, his companions were still basically just boys. Any land beyond their limited travels, particularly that of an enemy, would be strange and exotic. "Yes, in a sense, though that's what they call the Yucatán, and it's an independent republic."

"Whose side are they on?" Burton asked.

"An interesting question," Lewis hedged. "Before joining the Union—and the current war began—Texas used its little navy to help Yucatán break from Mexico, and the two republics were allies. But the indigenous Maya, with the assistance of the British—after the British helped Mexico against Yucatán and Texas—have rebelled, and Yucatán has requested Mexican aid to subdue the uprising." He shook his head. "The British do love to stir the pot."

"As does Mr. Polk," Justinian Olayne agreed. Lewis frowned. He never discussed domestic politics and didn't think professional officers should, whether they agreed with them or not. Olayne caught his look. "I only meant that it seems *all* political leaders appear to enjoy baiting the bear of war, only to scurry behind the soldier when the bear decides to bite."

Lewis still frowned but couldn't really argue with that. "In any event," he said, "I don't know whether we'd be welcome there or not."

"I've seen Yucatán on a map!" Lieutenant Swain exclaimed excitedly, loosening the slight tension. "It pokes up into the Gulf, like Florida pokes downward!"

Lewis smiled, suddenly enjoying himself. He'd forgotten how much he'd missed simple, casual conversation. "Very much like that." He tilted his head to the west again, only this time glancing that way as well. He was startled to see that, while the sky around the blurry sunset remained a milky, yellow gray, a stark, brooding darkness was growing in the south-southwest. There was also a distant sail. "Excuse me, gentlemen, I'll be back." He smirked. "Save my place by the rail, if you please." Turning aft, he threaded his way between and around the uncomfortable forms cluttering the deck. Most wore everything they owned in the world: bulging knapsacks and blankets, coats rolled up inside, as well as their buff-strapped cartridge boxes and weapons, of course. Lewis noted the salt air was starting to redden their bright musket barrels. No one looked up as he passed, and he didn't blame them. If they did, they'd have to "notice" him and stand and salute. Lewis pressed on, mindful of the occasional slick streak of vomit.

The state of the deck reflected no disgrace on Captain Eric Holland and his ship, or even the NCOs responsible for detailing parties to deal with the mess. Vomit was an endless, constant occurrence, impossible to stop and just as hopeless to keep up with. Lewis finally joined *Mary Riggs*'s thin, rather rough-looking commander standing by the helmsman at the wheel. Unlike most, Holland was clean-shaven and wore his hair long and unbound. The elements had made him look close to eighty, though as spry as he was, he couldn't possibly be that old.

"Aye," he said, noting Lewis's arrival with something like approval. "I expected to see you soon enough." He nodded out at the crowd of soldiers. "You're the only one of that misbegotten lot aware of events around him."

Lewis considered that unfair and inaccurate. He hadn't been aware of much at all, shortly before. "There seems to be rough weather ahead," he said. "And an unknown sail."

Captain Holland nodded. "Aye. The lookouts've been cautioned against shoutin' things out"—he grinned—"that might upset the passengers. God knows most're unhappy enough already." He gestured forward. "As to the first, I don't expect a storm. The glass is actually risin'"—he pressed his forehead—"an' I feel it in my head. There's a southeasterly wind, sure—which is rarely a pleasant thing—but it serves our purpose an' should push those ill-lookin' clouds to the north an' away." He squinted. If anything, the dark smudge on the horizon had grown. "I'd generally think so at any rate, but the weather obeys no command, an' damn few of the rules it makes for itself. All we can do is take our best guess," he added with a little less certainty. "As for the sail?" He shrugged. "Your guess is as good as mine, though with the navy so active I doubt it's hostile. There's little we can do if it is. Only *Isidra*'s armed; a dozen twelve pounders if I'm not mistaken, an' those only carronades." No one would be fooled by the gunports painted on the sides of the old whalers. "She'd be better off usin' her engine to run," Holland continued, then chuckled darkly. "As for *Mary Riggs*, *Xenophon*, an' *Commissary* . . . we might see the foe off with a broadside of puke."

A sailor slid down a backstay from the maintop as nimble as an ape and hopped around the men to join them. He was barefoot, and Lewis sympathized with the extra care he took. "She's British, Cap'n," the man confided lowly. Holland relaxed, but his craggy brows knitted in anger. "We're safe from her, at least—though if it were up to me, we'd be fightin' England again instead of Mexico!" He cocked an eye at Lewis. "We nearly were, over Oregon, an' like as not you'd prefer that as well. As for me . . . I was a bo-sun's mate in USS *Essex* at Valparaiso, with Porter, God bless 'im. March twenty-eighth, thirty-two years past, last month. That was a foul, bloody day. God damn the British," he seethed before glancing at the distant *Isidra*. "An' god*damn* carronades!"

Lewis touched the downward-pointing, almost useless brim of his 1839 pattern "wheel" hat. Infantry liked the round-topped, vaguely mushroom-shaped hats since they could rotate the flat brims around to the left to pro-tect their faces from the vent jets of muskets beside them in line, but otherwise they wouldn't even keep the sun out of your eyes—not even off your nose. Lewis's nose had remained red and peeling ever since the hats were adopted. "Thank you for your courtesy, Captain Holland. I'll take my leave."

Holland nodded. "Aye. We may be as different as fish from fowl, but I know a man who takes pride in his work—whether he likes it or not. Such men deserve my respect." He frowned, staring forward past Lewis, whom he'd essentially now dismissed from his mind. "Damned if that wicked line of clouds ain't growin'," he told the helmsman. "We'll have to shorten sail before dark."

Lewis left Captain Holland to run his ship and rejoined the lieutenants by the rail. The distant sail became a ship—clearly now flying the Union Jack—tacking south across their path. Lewis wasn't a sailor, but knew the British captain would soon slant back to the north. He wouldn't want to be much closer to shore, especially as the haze-filtered sun vanished on the horizon and the darkening sky turned ever more menacing. Dull ripples of lightning pulsed in the clouds. Signal flags flashed up the halyards on *Isidra*, likely the last they'd see that night, instructing all ships to maintain their heading but shorten sail. Sailors scampered up the shrouds to reef the canvas as Holland directed, voice surprisingly loud even without a speak-ing trumpet. Some of the soldiers on deck looked around with interest, watching the activity. Most merely sat, made insensible by misery.

"A hell of a way to go to war," Lewis sympathized.

"I agree wholeheartedly with that!" said Olayne, gulping and looking little better than the men as he waved at the sea beyond the rail. "You don't suppose it can get *worse* than this, do you?"

Lewis finally laughed. He couldn't help it. "I'm sorry to tell you, but it certainly can. *Much* worse. This isn't bad at all, now."

"My God."

They watched the strange ship for a while, making its oblique approach, commenting on its features. It was a tall three-master, black hulled with a broad yellow stripe down its side, much faster and more weatherly than *Mary Riggs*. There was no commissioning pennant, and Lewis suspected she'd been a frigate, sold out of service, now in her declining years as well. Sails flashed and turned as she heaved over and took the wind on her starboard beam, coming up and across ahead of them. Signal flags broke out in her mizzen top, streaming dull in the failing light, but Captain Holland saw them and cursed loud enough for all to hear. "She's 'carryin' dispatches'— nice way to say 'To hell with you. We won't stop to speak.' I'll warrant she's really takin' European diplomats and moneymen, along with their squallin' broods, away from the war an' fever that comes to Vera Cruz in spring." Derisive laughter met that opinion, though Lewis didn't think that was funny either. Fever was no joke, and the army he'd been with in Northern Mexico had lost more men to disease than Mexican steel and lead. "Oh, isn't that lovely!" Holland ranted even louder at an additional hoist. "They all wish us joy on our adventure in Mexico!"

Sailors, even some soldiers, braved the blowing spray and gathered in the bow to jeer as the British ship swept by in their path, hardly a cable away, but the wind was freshening and they'd never be heard.

"At least the men seem keen enough to take offense," Burton observed.

"Those who can move," Lewis agreed, his estimation of Holland rising. Unlike most, he knew the second signal merely warned of the weather and wished them good luck. But few things brought people together, Americans and foreigners alike, better than a jab at the British. Holland had seized the opportunity to take the men's minds off their wretchedness and fear, and Lewis only wished he'd thought of something similar himself. It dawned on him then that he'd probably failed the men in other ways. What difference did it make that the junior officers hadn't come to him sooner? Regardless of protocol, he should've gone to them and *taken* charge, *forced* them to organize diversions for their men, even if they'd only been make-work details. But just as the men had largely been in their own desolate, uncomfortable little worlds, so had he.

As Captain Anson said, Lewis had been wounded at Monterrey: a musket ball in his lower chest. Only distance, inferior Mexican gunpowder, or divine providence stopped the ball from passing through the ribs it broke and cracking his liver open. So sure it had and he would die, Lewis took mad chances, exposing himself stupidly until the end of the battle—and he discovered the wound wasn't as bad as he'd feared. *That* had been part of the source of his "heroism," as he prayed for another ball to give him a quick, clean death so he could avoid the lingering suffering he'd watched Major Ringgold endure. And in any event, he had to withstand it anyway. Relatively minor as it was, the wound turned septic due to all the filthy uniform fragments the ball carried under the skin, and Lewis nearly died. His chest still hurt, and the wound remained partially open, disgorging pus and rotten fibers of wool or cotton in addition to slivers of bone and tiny flakes of lead. Sometimes he wondered if it would ever heal—and if his mind had been damaged as badly.

In spite of the pain and certainty he'd die, he'd *become* the battle to a shocking degree, like the lightning in a storm, even loving it in some strange way as if only then and there had he achieved his destiny, no matter how brief it may be. He hadn't become a berserker, mindlessly flailing about; if anything, he turned colder, more thoughtful, but instantly decisive and infinitely more lethal as he saw things more clearly than he ever had, directing his bleeding section of guns relentlessly forward, even replacing a fallen gunner and aiming one of the weapons himself, almost gleefully blasting down adobe walls and annihilating clots of troops that tried to assemble in his path. Soon, he had only enough bloody, exhausted men to crew a single gun, but he wouldn't have stopped even then. Less than two blocks from the Central Plaza, a messenger—Captain Anson, in fact—grabbed him from behind, dodged his weak saber slash, and angrily told him there was a truce. To this day, Lewis wasn't sure what he would've done if he hadn't collapsed from loss of blood. Would he have kept pressing on? Would he have slashed at the Ranger again? He honestly didn't know, and that even more than his fear of suffering had left him oddly ashamed and hesitant to go to battle again. Not out of fear of Mexican musket balls, but because of how much he liked it. Afraid he might prove himself as much a monster as he sometimes thought Captain Anson was. It had made him withdraw, kept him from asserting the leadership he should have over these unknowing, unsuspecting boys.

"You have musicians aboard, do you not?" he suddenly asked. The young officers looked at each other.

"Besides buglers? Fifers and drummers, of course. Two each for the artillery companies, and a trio of fifers for the dragoons."

"None for the Rifles," Lieutenant Swain lamented, "though one of the men has a fiddle."

"But enough to provide some music for the men?" Lewis pressed.

Burton's eyes widened. "Of course! That's just the thing!"

"Ask Captain Holland's permission," Lewis cautioned. "He may have good reason to object. If not, assemble the musicians in the waist of the ship so those belowdecks can hear them as well. We'll see if a little entertainment helps pass the time."

The four ships churned on through the deepening gloom, and even as the wind began to rise and whip inconsistently and flickering, muttering clouds built in power and size, the martial skirl of fifes and thunder of drums seemed to challenge the natural powers as boldly—and feebly—as Homer's Ulysses. Eventually, male voices rose in bawdy mockery as well, first in *Mary Riggs*, then *Xenophon*, whose people must've heard and been inspired. For what seemed a pathetically short time, in retrospect, the voyage turned less hellish for the sick, and the rest were distracted from their grinding fear or boredom. Lewis would also later reflect that the resultant animation might've saved many lives because men were more alert, more ready to move, when—now ignored by those who'd been in their power—the heavens or some other elemental force, perhaps even God Himself, somehow took offense.

"Stand by to wear ship! Quickly now, for your lives! We're comin' about!" Captain Holland roared through a japanned speaking trumpet, voice rising over and crushing the music and singing. "Down helm," he cried to the helmsman, who, sensing his captain's urgency, actually spun the wheel. "Helm's alee!" he shouted as the ship heaved over to port and began a radical turn to starboard. Sailors slammed through the soldiers to perform their next tasks without commands, hauling in the main course sheet and easing the headsails, but Holland gave orders anyway. "Top men aloft! We'll have the topsails off her, fast as you can! You soldiers, make way by the shrouds, goddamn you! Secure your gear. Secure yourselves!" He was barely ten paces from Lewis but pointed the trumpet directly at him, and their eyes met when he continued, "Get any man up from below who can move!"

LEWIS HAD NO idea what was amiss, but knew this was no joke. Worse, he couldn't imagine why Holland would want *more* men on deck. The ship was well ballasted with horses, guns, and supplies, but if a blow was coming—the only possible explanation for these frantic preparations—why make *Mary Riggs* more top-heavy? The only answer was obvious. Holland thought the ship would founder. Pandemonium had erupted as sailors raced up the ratlines and soldiers loudly scurried to rails, the capstan, windlass—anything they could grasp. "Get your men up," Lewis shouted at the lieutenants still standing by while he looked to the west. If they were turning away from it, that had to be the direction of the threat—where those malevolent clouds had been. At first he saw nothing in the near-total blackness, then jagged ribbons of lightning rushed all across the horizon, lacing through the sky like thousands of silvery capillaries on some monstrous, greenish-black eye. More lighting, almost blue, then yellow, pulsed inside the terrible cloud—and Lewis saw what so alarmed Captain Holland. The thing was *close*, impossibly so, implying a tremendous velocity—wind like they'd never seen—pushing a rain squall heavy enough to whiten the sea at its feet as it thundered down upon them.

"My God." He turned to the lieutenants, still rooted. "Go! You haven't a moment to lose—and don't go below yourselves. Just shout down for everyone to come on deck, then report back here, understood?"

Justinian Olayne and Coryon Burton rushed into motion, but Clifford Swain hesitated. "Do you think we're going to be drowned?" he cried.

"Of course not, here on deck," Lewis lied, "but if the horses break loose, they'll kill everyone below." It was all he could think of to say. If the ship went down, everyone below would go with her. And he honestly doubted it would make much difference to those on deck. Few soldiers could swim—he couldn't—and most had put all their heavy gear *on* when the alarm was sounded. They'd sink like stones. The ship's fragile longboat wouldn't carry many, and would never survive the destruction of the ship in any event. A few might cling to shattered debris. But Lewis's last glimpse of land put it over ten miles away.

Swain stood still and Lewis patted his arm. There was nothing the boy could add to what others were already doing. "That's all right. Stay here where Burton and Olayne can find you. I'll be back after a word with the captain." Lewis stepped toward the helm, noting that whatever troops hadn't found part of the ship to grasp were now clinging to one another.

"Rise tacks and sheets!" bellowed Holland's burly mate, Mr. Sessions, pacing forward.

"Let go and haul!" Holland shouted before turning to stare behind them as the wind came around on the starboard quarter. It was a fitful wind now, however, increasingly uncertain. He shook his head. "Ease the headsails to run with the wind and take in everything but the forecourse. Fast as you can, lads!"

A lightning-lit glance to the south showed Lewis that *Commissary* and *Xenophon* had both come about as well, but *Isidra* was steaming onward, sparks gushing from her single funnel past sails tightly furled to the yards, her captain apparently intent on taking the storm head-on, under power.

"What'll happen?" Lewis shouted at Holland over the rising west wind when he thought he was close enough to be heard.

"Down *now*, damn you!" Holland roared into the rigging. A few men were still struggling to secure the flapping fore topsail. He looked at Lewis, eyes wide with more incredulity than fear.

"I've no idea!"

They both turned aft as the first blow struck in the form of hail the size of musket balls. Men screamed as hard, icy projectiles slashed them like double loads of canister from the sky. Lewis's wool uniform, even his ridiculous wheel hat, afforded him some protection, but the sheer suddenness and violence of the assault stunned him, even as his hands and face felt like buzzards were brutally pecking and snatching great gobbets of flesh. It wasn't quite that bad. Big as musket balls or not, the hailstones had little mass. They could cut but not kill. Most couldn't, at least. Occasional giants the size of roundshot crashed into the deck, blasting apart in stinging, lacerating fragments. A few of those hit men, breaking bones and crushing skulls. Lewis peeked under the little visor that actually deflected a smaller pellet from his eye and saw Holland, bareheaded, standing grim and bloody at the wheel, the helmsman sprawled at his feet. "Hold on!" the man bellowed, just as rain and wind as dense and hard and solid as a wall of water slammed *Mary Riggs*.

Lewis had no time to grasp anything and was blown to the deck, where he slid and tumbled before fetching up against a skylight, the glass panes shattered. He raised his head against the battering rain to see men literally swept over the side, either by the thundering wind or the inches-deep sluice of water already roaring out the scuppers. They must've screamed, but he never heard them. He *did* hear a great snapping, crackling noise as back-stays parted, timbers screeched, and all three of the ship's towering masts crashed down forward, smashing screaming men under tons of wood, cordage, and canvas, breaking arms and heads with blocks, and snapping lines. *How many men just died because I called them up from below?* he thought. *No more than will drown when the ship goes down,* he realized. In an instant, *Mary Riggs* had been entirely dismasted, the entangling wreckage blown forward into the sea pulling her around broadside and helpless against the wind and ferocious deluge. She heaved hard over, and Lewis felt himself tumbling across the deck toward the sea.

Then, in a heartbeat, everything changed.

Lewis was no longer sliding, and the rain had stopped. Even the wind had dropped to nothing in the space of a breath. He couldn't tell for certain, but didn't believe he saw the sea below him anymore, and utter blackness yawned. It was as if some giant hand now held the ship immobile, poised to drop it in an infinite void. The same unnaturally turbulent sky still brooded overhead, but its violence had been arrested, and it was just as unnaturally still. Even the streaks of lightning had slowed to a glaring halt in the glowing, greenish heavens. That's when Lewis noted another kind of glow, somewhat bluish, completely enveloping everything around him, even the ship itself. It was brightest on the ironwork and soldiers' muskets, but brass and pewter buttons, beltplates—anything metal—seemed similarly affected. Like Saint Elmo's fire, it had to be an electrical phenomenon. Lewis was fascinated by electricity—the Morse electrical telegraph was just one of many wondrous new applications—and knew enough about it to understand water conducted it, sometimes dangerously so. That could explain why everything glowed, he supposed. Nothing could explain . . . anything else, and most disconcertingly, how the rain just hung there in the air; large, densely spaced raindrops inexplicably suspended as if time itself had ground to a stop.

There was no sound, no . . . natural movement around the ship at all, for long, terrible moments. Somewhat to his surprise, however, Lewis found *he* could still move, and he waved his hand in front of his face in wonder, half expecting the raindrops to scatter as he brushed them aside, but they only further wet his skin. His eyes focused on the jumble of wreckage around the stump of the mainmast and saw two of Anson's Rangers, the giant holding the youth. The boy's wheel hat had fallen away, and though the slick black hair it released wasn't particularly long, the way it lay, the shape of the head, the neck, the large brown eyes staring at the raindrops with the same amazement Lewis felt, all suddenly convinced him that Anson's son or nephew was really a daughter or niece.

That couldn't have mattered less at the moment, because movement and sound aboard *Mary Riggs* had only been stilled by shock. The muffled shrieks of horses erupted from below, and men cried out in terror and agony as they tried to crawl from under fallen sails and spars—only to see the raindrops. They shouted anew with a wholly different kind of terror, and a growing agony Lewis shared. He remembered Holland's comment about the barometer as an irresistible pressure began to build, mashing his eyes into his head and trying to crush his skull and chest. He vomited in standing water full of floating hail and tried to take a gasping breath, but his chest simply wouldn't expand. All around him, men—and one now very frightened young woman—were doing the same. The screams abruptly tapered off as men and horses lost the air to voice them.

Then he was falling—or thought he was—and he scrabbled for a shattered section of the broken mizzen top as his vision began to darken from lack of air. His last conscious thought would've been focused entirely on that tangled heap of wreckage if his lungs hadn't suddenly sucked in a gasping breath. Others did the same and the deck around him sounded with more panting, gasping, coughing, and moaning—before the terrible pressure reversed itself and a nauseating, agonizing, screeching sound quickly built. Rolling over on the deck, he wrapped his arms around his head to stifle it, but it only grew, like it was coming from inside his skull. His head began to feel like a shrieking kettle, and he imagined jets of steam roaring and squealing from his nose and ears as he clutched his head even tighter, afraid it would burst.

He was falling again, he was certain, just as the suspended raindrops thundered down in a final fury. The giant hand had released the ship to drop in to the void at last. Piercing screams of terror accompanied the fall; one was his, most likely. But there was a bottom to the void after all, and

Mary Riggs abruptly met it with a stunning, jarring crash, half collapsing amid a thunderous roar of shattering timbers, screaming men, and shrieking horses. Before the wreck completely settled, cascading water, hailstones, debris, and other men swept Lewis along to resume his slide across the still-tilted deck. He went over the side with the rest, plummeting into darkness, and remembered nothing more.

CHAPTER 2

C aptain Cayce! Captain Cayce! Oh, please wake up! We need you rather badly!"

Lewis's mind rejected what he was hearing. It sounded like the young dragoon lieutenant. Coryon Burton, wasn't it? Of North Carolina. Class of '46. *But that's impossible. I'm dead. We're all dead, swallowed by the void.*

"He's alive," came another impossible voice—Giles Anson's. "And none of his arms or legs seem broken. Probably bumped his head. Maybe he fell on it? Without a surgeon, who knows what's wrong with him if he won't wake up."

"I can't wake up," Lewis managed to protest through painful lips. "None of us can."

"Aye, he's comin' around," came a gruff, slightly Scottish voice. "You, Private Willis, pour some water on his face. He probably can't even open his eyes with all that dried blood gluin' 'em shut."

"But Sergeant McNabb!" objected a harsh, squeaky voice, apparently Private Willis, "we ain't found any fresh water yet, an' all I got's in my canteen!"

"Do as ye're told, damn ye! There's plenty o' water in the ship—if we can get to it before all the started butts leak it out."

Lewis sensed movement beside him and a sudden coolness on his face. Gentle fingers massaged his eyes and he cracked one open. The sky was bright pink until he blinked several times to clear the blood. It looked perfectly ordinary then; bright blue with the sun creeping into view overhead. But that was the only thing right. The deck below him didn't move because it wasn't a deck and the sun was beginning to glare through tall, straight trees, many of which had their branches savagely ripped from the near side of their trunks. Colorful birds—Lewis assumed they were birds, though they were shaped very strangely—flitted through the trees, cawing raucously. Those of different species didn't seem to get along very well, and there was constant skirmishing. That didn't matter. Realistically, the only birds Lewis should've seen were gulls.

Giles Anson leaned into Lewis's view, festooned with all the weapons he generally carried in the field. A pair of Colt Paterson revolvers were in belt holsters at his side, and a Model 1838 flintlock pistol was thrust into his belt. An 1817 flintlock rifle, a fine, .54 caliber weapon like Lieutenant Swain's Mounted Rifles carried, was slung over one shoulder and a pair of tooled, privately made pommel holsters were draped over the other. Knowing the Ranger as he did, Lewis wasn't surprised the man had immediately collected his weapons. Anson nodded with apparent relief and produced a genuine smile. "See there, Lewis? You *can* wake up." A more customary ironic smile replaced the first one. "Might wish you hadn't, though."

Lewis groaned and picked clumps of dried blood from his eyelashes, still knitting the other eye closed, while a man behind helped raise him to a sitting position. He'd expected to find himself sitting on sand for some reason, but realized he was on a bed of dry, ferny-looking leaves with spines as rigid as pine needles. That didn't make any sense. "I thought I was dead," he confessed hoarsely, "but even in hell, I doubt I'd hurt this much." His other eye clear, he gently probed his scalp under blood-matted hair. "And either I didn't feel what hit me when we were wrecked—I assume we were wrecked?—or I did fall on my head." He looked up at Anson and Burton. "But not in the water?"

"Give him a drink, ye fool," came Sergeant McNabb's voice. Lewis looked at him and beheld a virtual stereotype of his breed. Tough, craggy-faced, probably in his forties, McNabb wasn't particularly imposing, but his rank in the regular foot artillery meant he'd been in long enough to develop sufficient skill, personality, and experience to deal with much larger men. Private Willis, also one of Lieutenant Olayne's 1st Artillerymen, looked like he sounded: a short, wiry youngster, wearing a put-upon expression in addition to all his gear. Beyond them, and a cluster of other armed men (1816 muskets, bayonets, and short swords for the artillerymen, .54 caliber 1817s for the Rifles, and .52 caliber breechloading Hall carbines hanging from white leather straps and iron clips on the dragoons), stood a densely wooded forest of tall, straight-trunked trees. Lewis blinked. Private Willis handed over a gray, stamped-steel canteen.

Lewis took a small sip and nodded his thanks. "I have a glaringly obvious question, I suppose," he managed with a firmer voice.

"Think you can stand?" Anson asked.

"I must."

Anson and Lieutenant Burton grasped his arms and hauled him to his feet. His legs supported him, but a wave of painful vertigo left him swaying for a moment before the dizziness, at least, began to pass. Gently, the men still holding his arms guided him around to look behind. "My God," Lewis Cayce muttered.

He'd assumed the men had carried him inshore from whatever coast they'd struck, but the wreck of *Mary Riggs* was in this strange forest as well, far from any sound of the sea. Dizziness threatened to take him again as Lewis contemplated the impossibility of that.

Anson knew what he was thinking. "Do you remember falling? All the rest of us do, an' apparently the ship fell with us." He gestured at the stripped branches on trees, extending fifteen or twenty feet up. Somehow, that felt about right. Anson pointed back at *Mary Riggs*. "That"—he hesitated—"peculiar storm must've carried us inland on a wave surge of some kind, leavin' the ship—us—here as it receded." Lewis glanced at the ferny needles at his feet. They were damp, but unscoured by a flood. "You'll note the lighter-built upper hull o' the ship, weighted with all our people an' broken masts, collapsed downward," Anson continued. "Probably cushioned our landin' a bit, but I expect anyone still on the deck below was crushed. The lower hold an' hull look a little ruptured, but seem essentially intact."

Lewis had registered the diminished but still poignant cries and murmurs of injured men, much like he would've heard at a field hospital after a battle, but now he identified the pitiful, muffled sounds only hurt and terrified horses made, coming from the cracked timbers enclosing the hold.

There'd been *seventy* horses crammed in there, including his own beloved chestnut mare, Arete. He shook loose from Anson and Burton and glared at them. "I . . . apologize for my indisposition, but the day appears relatively advanced." He gestured around. "I see you've ensured our men are under arms—which is good, since this can only be Yucatán and, officially hostile or not, the enemy could be present. But I also see a lot of men doing nothing—and virtually no effort to access the wreck."

Anson scowled, but Coryon Burton nodded enthusiastically. "That's why we need *you*, sir," he began, redirecting Lewis's attention to a clot of men involved in a hot debate. Lewis was relieved to see Lieutenants Olayne and Swain alive, if just as battered as he, but they and a cluster of NCOs were arguing loudly with a larger group of sailors around a bruised and bloodied Captain Holland.

"I may be a captain," Anson said sourly, sarcastically, "but I'm only a 'volunteer' with four men in the eyes o' your Lieutenant Olayne. He's done a few things right, but I think his first taste of authority has overwhelmed him an' he's havin' trouble gettin' confused 'n' scared men to cooperate. He wants to tear into the ship, but Captain Holland won't have it." He coughed. "Some o' his sailors've got some rum in 'em, an' maybe a bit embarrassed, are backin' Holland to the hilt."

"I see," Lewis replied stiffly through another wave of dizziness, but he stepped toward the growing argument as briskly as he dared. "What's the meaning of this?" he demanded loudly.

"Captain Cayce, thank God!" Olayne exclaimed. "I've been trying to form details to break into the ship for provisions and supplies—the ordinary routes from above are quite impossible—but *this* man"—he gestured at Holland—"has threatened violence if we attempt it!"

Lewis raised an eyebrow at the glowering Holland, but directed his gaze at Olayne. "Did you, in fact, refuse to take direction from Captain Anson?"

The young lieutenant was taken aback, startled by the question. "Well . . . of course. He's a volunteer officer. I can't give him orders, since he does outrank me, but neither can he give orders to a regular officer!"

"Wrong!" Lewis snapped. "And even if that were true, Captain Anson had his *federal* commission confirmed in my presence by General Zachary Taylor. His more recent promotion to captain came immediately after mine. That . . . two-minute seniority is the only reason *I* can command him instead of the other way around. Do I make myself clear?" Lewis took a breath. "On the other hand, since you seem to have taken the burden of command upon yourself, Lieutenant Olayne, I expect you've already set a perimeter around the wreck? Collected the dead for burial? Sent out scouts? Compiled a list of killed, injured, and missing?"

Coryon Burton coughed and Olayne stepped back, clearing his throat. "I've, uh, sent a few small parties out a short distance to search for water or warn of threats, but I thought getting in the ship was the most pressing concern."

Lewis looked at Holland. "Perhaps it is, but *you'll* see to those other things directly. Lieutenant Swain and his Rifles will provide security while you direct our artillerymen in constructing field fortifications around us as well." Still looking at Holland, he continued, "Use debris from the ship and the timbers the dragoons tear off her to strengthen those defenses."

"Now, wait just a god damn . . ." Holland started angrily, but Lewis held his hand up. To his astonishment, the man piped down. Gazing intently at Olayne, he lowered his voice. "The men—all of us—have been through a frightening ordeal, but we . . ." He glanced around. There were a couple more young dragoon officers present whom he hadn't met, and aside from the grizzled artillery sergeant, he didn't know any of the NCOs. "We aren't well acquainted, and I regret that, but we'll get to know each other soon enough. For the moment, however, our first concern is to conquer our fear and reestablish order and discipline. We can't allow the men to dwell on what's happened, particularly since we have no answers for them. Give them something familiar to cling to—their duty—and keep their minds and bodies occupied. Dismissed."

Olayne's expression hardened into one of respect and determination before he and Lieutenant Swain, followed by the rest, spontaneously saluted and returned to their duty as well.

"Nicely done," Anson remarked as the officers paced away and NCOs began barking for attention.

"Aye," Holland grudgingly agreed, "an' right for my men as well." He frowned. "But I'll argue the same with you as I did with those young gentlemen; I won't have my ship broken open! We'll help clear the topsides to get your precious horses out, but the hull's still basically sound, an' we might still need the ship."

Lewis shook his head. "I understand how you feel, Captain Holland. I'd feel much the same myself. But if you step only a short distance away and take a broader, more objective view, so to speak, you'll see your ship's badly hogged and her back's broken. I'm no sailor, but like most artillery graduates of the military academy, I'm something of an engineer. Even if we somehow managed to drag what's left of *Mary Riggs* back to the sea, wherever and however far that may be"—he shrugged—"frankly impossible. Even with every horse inside her and every man pulling together, I assure you she'll never swim again." He took a deep breath. "And while we stand here arguing, the horses inside are suffering and dying, and there might be men in there as well. Aside from all that, we're likely on a hostile shore, and we need all the cannon, ammunition, and other supplies, not to mention provisions, out at once. We can't even move from this spot until we're as organized and well equipped as possible. Do you understand?"

Holland wiped a grimy, blood-caked hand across his forehead. "Aye," he murmured softly. "Aye," he repeated more firmly, but gave Lewis a disconcerting look before turning to the twenty-odd sailors still behind him. About a third were black, or at least dark-skinned, so they might be Indians or even Mexicans themselves. Lewis figured more than a dozen must've been lost when the masts toppled, either crushed or thrown in the sea. "Fetch tools an' work with Lieutenant Burton's horse soldiers to free their beasts—if any survived in better shape than our poor ship. We may even free a few shipmates." With the air of men who'd rather fight all the soldiers than help them break the wreck, the sailors began to disperse. Some grasped trailing lines and climbed back up on it while others moved in the direction of a bellowing dragoon sergeant. Lewis turned to Lieutenant Burton. "How many . . ."

"A hundred and twenty dragoons, fit for duty," Burton answered without hesitation. "Twenty more injured to various degrees." He cleared his throat. "We *have* begun gathering the dead, but just from the dragoons almost sixty are missing or lost."

Lewis nodded, impressed again by the young officer. "Very well. You're in charge of the wrecking detail, but make sure your NCOs take direction from our nautical friends; they'll have a better idea how to take their ship apart. Consider Captain Anson your company commander for the time being. The sailors will constitute Captain Holland's company."

"Will the sailors be armed?" Burton asked.

"Yes, if Captain Holland will vouch for their proficiency."

"*All* of them?" Burton pressed, looking meaningfully at several darkskinned men already back on the ship.

Lewis frowned, now somewhat disappointed in the young dragoon. "Leave that to Captain Holland's discretion. He knows his men better than we do."

"Will the artillerymen stay under Lieutenant Olayne?" Anson asked with a smile.

"Of course. Especially since it appears his seasick companion wasn't among the survivors. And not only is he an active officer—now that he's ashore—I suspect he's learned a lesson. He just needs direction, and I'll see to that."

The gathering that had seemed destined to deteriorate into a brawl—and the resultant chaos and panic that would ensue when it was seen all control was lost—broke up amicably, directed to new purpose by shouting NCOs and Captain Holland's surviving mates. Lewis knew how devastating chaos and panic could be, having seen it wreck a superior Mexican army at Resaca de la Palma, and breathed an inner sigh of relief. Soon, there came the sound of shouts and rending timbers as more men crawled over the collapsed upperworks, throwing down debris, while others attacked the hull planks, prying them off the stout ribs beneath. Artillerymen had stacked their muskets to carry heavy timbers toward a slowly forming breastworks. Others trimmed limbs and brush with their Roman-gladius-shaped short swords, the only thing Lewis ever really considered the weapons good for.

For a while then, only Lewis, Anson, and Holland stood together, though Lewis noted Anson's "aide" a little to the side, glancing nervously at him from time to time. *His daughter, I think,* Lewis told himself, remembering more of the sparse details Giles Anson had shared about his former life, *and likely the only family he has left.* Lewis would say nothing. Unknown to the public, there'd *always* been women hiding in the ranks of the American Army, dressing and behaving as men. Some followed husbands and lovers, even fighting and dying beside them. Others of a different sort endured army life strictly for money, maintaining a periodic monopoly on certain services among an exclusive and captive, often protectively appreciative clientele. The practice wasn't widespread, but was more common than any civilian would believe. Observant officers knew about it, but few took notice unless they had to. It often came down to whether the affected unit would be better or worse with or without its female influence. If the former, well, any unit's performance reflected on its commander. If the latter . . . when women were "officially" discovered lurking in the ranks due to their behavior or appearance (often unconcealable pregnancy), or when a surgeon attended an injury, they were dismissed to fend for themselves wherever their unit was at the time. The fortunate ones might take up with camp followers or sutlers, always close by an army on the move. The irony was, when women joined a fight in extraordinary circumstances, like "Molly Pitcher," for example, they were celebrated.

Could I leave my only surviving child behind, even to go to war, after losing her mother and brothers to the very people I'm fighting now? Lewis asked himself. He didn't know. Looking at her now, he had another thought. And perhaps the girl hadn't really given him a choice. He sighed and spoke. "I came here without a command of my own, expecting to wind up scouting gun positions or shuffling paperwork on somebody's staff."

"Well"—Anson chuckled darkly—"you have a command now—for however long it lasts."

"It may be longer than you think," Holland warned.

Lewis looked at the sailor in surprise, but Anson said, "As soon as we're organized, I'll lead a scout to the coast. It must be north, an' it can't be far. We'll find one of our other ships lyin' offshore."

Holland shook his head. "I don't think you understand." He raised a tarnished sextant he'd been holding. "I can't make our exact position without a horizon, but I'm tellin' you no wind or wave from the west carried us four or five leagues to the *south*. Not in the short time we were in its grip. It may've seemed an eternity, but . . . whatever happened lasted only moments. It's more like . . ." Holland shrugged. "I've been a sailor for forty-five years. I know these waters, and I know the sea. I know almost *exactly* where we were and could point to the very spot on the chart in my crushed cabin. We *can't've* been heaved onto the land we knew. It's more . . . like the shallows north of Yucatán came up from the sea beneath us."

"That's . . . ridiculous," Lewis said softly. "And I'll ask you to keep such wild notions to yourself," he quickly added.

"Wild, aye," Holland snapped, but he kept his voice down. "Yet true enough as far as where we *can't* be."

"But"—Lewis waved around at the trees—"*these* don't grow on the bottom of the sea!"

Anson looked thoughtful. "I've been to Yucatán before, with a diplomatic mission after the Battle of Campeche." He snorted at Lewis. "Yes, me.

Diplomats need protection, after all. That was a good ways from . . . where we must be," he confessed, "but I never heard tell of trees like these. They're more like the piney woods in East Texas—only taller an' thicker."

"Then we're obviously somewhere else!" Lewis exclaimed impatiently. "An island or something."

"There's *no such island* near where we were!" Holland insisted, then rolled his eyes at Anson. "An' o' course there're no trees like these—or any others—on the bottom of the sea." His expression turned haunted. "But while we debate where we are, you've already forgotten how we got here. In all my years . . . I've weathered fiercer blows, aye, an' been dismasted too, but no storm ever done anything like the *other* things this one did. I . . . fear it could've thrown us on whatever shore it chose to."

Lewis's blood-crusty eyes narrowed at the sailor. "Superstitious nonsense," he murmured without conviction. "Weather makes no choices."

Anson was scratching the bushy beard on his chin. "What the devil are you sayin'?"

Holland looked speculatively at his ship as a long timber was wrenched away, pulling shrieking spikes from the ribs. Horses squealed in excitement and pain as daylight entered the hull. "The Devil's as good an explanation as any," he muttered. "An' I'll warrant if you do find one of our consorts, it won't be anchored offshore. It'll be lyin' among these same god damn trees, as sprawled out an' broken as my *Mary Riggs*."

CHAPTER 3

E nough of this, let's go back," groused the young artilleryman, trudging southwest along a well-used trail through the forest ahead of Private Felix Meder of the Mounted Rifles.

"A little farther," Felix said. "I can't make sense of the tracks on this path—it's too dry—but it's almost as big and straight as a road. It has to go somewhere."

Felix didn't know the artilleryman with the strong British accent—identified only as "Private Hudgens" when they were arbitrarily paired—but though he seemed a little jaded, he wasn't a malingerer. They'd already explored quite a distance from the wreck, and he was understandably reluctant to continue. Now he glanced back and sighed dejectedly, slinging the musket he'd been carrying at the ready. "Fancy yourself a yankee frontiersman, do you? Tracking your wily prey through the dark forest with that bloody rifle? There may be Mexicans in these woods, but you'll find no savage red men." He patted the musket. "Mexicans are civilized folk and fight like Froggies. I'd sooner have this. Get off three shots to your one."

Felix sighed in turn. Perhaps he was a "yankee," though his parents had immigrated to Ohio from Munich a year before he was born. And he *had* grown up in the woods with a squirrel rifle, steeped in tales of the frontiersmen who opened the country around the family farm a couple of generations before. He revealed none of this and didn't point out that he was at least three times as likely to *hit* his target with the rifle as the other man was with a musket, and at three times the distance as well. Not that distance meant much in these woods. "Your own lieutenant sent us to find water," Felix pointed out.

"Aye"—Hudgens snorted—"an' have a look about. I only hope Captain Cayce has woke up an' taken charge. Word is, he's a man of experience. Olayne's even sillier than most young officers, born without the brains of a goose." He chuckled. "An' he was flustered as a new-hatched goose when he chose a half dozen pairs o' fellows to have a scout." He glared back at Felix. "But he only picked *us* because we had dry powder, all our kit, an' *you* looked so bloody bored. *Bored*, damn you, after what happened, an' I had the bad luck to be by you!"

"I wasn't bored," Felix almost whispered. He'd actually been in a kind of shock and had gathered his gear and made himself and his weapon ready without a conscious thought. Personally, he was glad Olayne had given him something to do.

"Well," Hudgens stated, stopping and turning around, "even the lieutenant never meant us to trek for miles, for the rest o' the day. There's not a drop o' water this way, nor even a dried-up stream. Aside from these damned trees, this is the flattest ground I ever trod. *I'm* bored now, an' tired an' hungry too. You seem a good lad, for a horse rifleman, an' we've had our stroll. Time to go back."

Felix considered. He wasn't in charge, of course, and suspected the other man had at least five years on his own nineteen. But since neither wanted to be alone, turning back required his consent. That kind of put him in charge, in a way. "Just a bit farther, like I said." He tilted his head to the sky. "We haven't seen any animals, not even a squirrel, but have you noticed all the strange birds overhead?"

Hudgens scowled. "Aye," he admitted. "Me old man was a fiend for birds an' such. Dragged me through the salt marshes near every day when I was a nipper, like he was tryin' to drown me. But I reckon it made me take notice o' birds, an' I never seen any like these. Some are straightforward, despite differences you'd expect in a strange land, but most look more like *lizards* to me. Or some kind o' damn bloody bat."

"Some could be bats," Felix conceded. "I've only ever seen one, trapped in the loft of a barn. It didn't look like these. It could've been a different

kind. But whatever *any* of them are, they all seem to be flitting *that* way."
He pointed the muzzle of his rifle down the trail.

"We're just pushin' 'em."

Felix shook his head. "No, they're flying that way from behind us too,
ignoring us. Something's drawing them. Maybe it's water."

Hudgens tilted his wheel hat back and grimaced, rubbing his forehead.
Then lifted his canteen as if evaluating the weight. If the water butts in the
ship were broken, and it was likely they were, things would get very thirsty.
He might consider Olayne a fool, but seemed to agree with his instinct to find
water. "Could be, I reckon. Very well. Just a few hundred more paces. Agreed?"

Felix paused, then nodded. "Agreed."

They didn't go much farther at all before both of them noticed more sky
leaking down through the trees ahead. Hudgens started to quicken his
pace, but Felix held him back.

"What?"

"This is wrong," Felix cautioned.

"What do you mean?"

"Listen."

The raucous sound of the birds in the woods had increased tremendously all around, but the noise was even louder ahead. If they'd come to a
water hole or stream, the flying creatures acted just as excited to find it. Or
perhaps there was a village with an abundance of refuse the birds liked—
but villagers might not be friendly. Sure that Hudgens was on his guard
now, taking his musket in hand, Felix released him, and they crept slowly
forward, side by side. The first thing that gave them a dreadful inkling of
what they'd find was a splintered spar, wrapped in ragged canvas. Spider-
webs of frayed cables began to festoon the trees. Then they saw the trees
themselves had suffered like those around *Mary Riggs*.

"Lord protect us!" Hudgens hissed, whipping his musket to his shoulder. He didn't fire. Hundreds of colorful birds—and not birds—crawled on
a human corpse lying in the ferny needles near the path, ripping clothing
and tearing bloody gobbets of flesh. The things were utterly absorbed in
their meal, pausing only to fight over the choicest morsels. And beyond that
first horrible sight, Felix and Hudgens found another, and another, until
they came to a clearing created by the far more shattered wreckage of another ship, surrounded by what looked like *hundreds* of bodies, all buried
in colorful, riotous mounds of feasting creatures.

"Lord have pity on 'em," Hudgens murmured. "It's *Xenophon!*"

"How can you tell?" Felix whispered sickly. "The ship's . . . upside down!" It was true, for the most part. The vessel had impacted at least as hard as *Mary Riggs*, but also broken in half. The bow was perfectly inverted and even more collapsed than the other ship after all the ballast and cargo crashed down and blew out the sides of the hull. Anyone in it or on it would've been mashed to paste. The stern was a splintered chaos of ragged timbers splayed out around flattened, whalelike ribs, and the rudder dangled from the sheared-off trunk of a broken tree. Felix fought an urge to vomit. He'd never seen anything so violently destroyed before—and that included the bodies being ravenously devoured.

"I lived near Southampton an' watched ships come an' go most o' me life, didn't I?" Hudgens hissed angrily. "Even as she is I can tell she was another old whaler, an' that makes her *Xenophon*. Aye, an' the blow must've overturned her before she fell." He shook his head and practically shivered. "Thank God for Captain Holland or we'd've ended the same."

Even as they stood there—live versions of the things the flying creatures ate with such frenetic relish—they were ignored because they were upright and moving. But that might've caught the attention of other things. Something almost as tall as a man suddenly rose up from within the thunderous flock of carrion eaters and stared directly at them.

"That's no bird!" Felix exclaimed with a rising voice. Its shape and posture might've resembled a bird's, and it was covered with a kind of feathery brown-and-white fur with a short dark crest and tail plumage, but it had powerful arms with long, vicious claws on its hands in place of wings. Its tail was long and whiplike before spiky plumage flared near the tip. The biggest, most horrifying difference, however, was the head. Bobbing like a grackle's on the end of a relatively narrow neck was a head straight out of a nightmare. Large, reptilian eyes glared down either side of a long, narrow snout, jaws bristling with jagged, bloody teeth.

"No, it ain't," Hudgens agreed, taking a small step back. The creature uttered a rasping, guttural bark that cut through the noise of the feeding flyers, and two more just like it raised their frightening heads to regard the newcomers as well. "*Bloody* hell," the artilleryman breathed, obviously frightened but amazingly calm. "We sure found *somethin'*—if we get back to report it."

Bolstered by his companion's composure, Felix took a step back as well, murmuring, "Whatever you do, don't run." There'd still been black bears in Ohio when he first began to traipse the woods, and though he'd never seen one, men had always told him it was sure to chase him if he ran. That made perfect sense. He'd seen cats chase big dogs when they ran. Conventional wisdom agreed that if he couldn't kill the bear (always preferable in the Ohio of his youth), he should simply ease away. If pursued, he should roar and growl and make himself appear as big and aggressive as possible—and prepare to fight for his life. Often, that would discourage a bear, unless it was a sow with cubs. In that case, there was no telling how it would react. Of course, whatever these things were, they weren't bears. Running still seemed stupid.

The trio of monsters watched them intently as they picked their way back through the shattered trees and rapidly disappearing corpses, all while flying things swooped around them, lighting among others with challenging cries or squirting streams of yellowish shit. They'd almost retreated to the first body they discovered, and one of the monsters had tired of watching them and returned to its meal when Hudgens suddenly stumbled and fell on his backside—right on the edge of the feeding frenzy. The obsessed little diners exploded into flight amid indignant shrieks, snapping and clawing at both men as they took to the air. Hudgens cried out in anger and pain as several attacked his face and he flailed at them with his musket. This regained the full attention of all three larger monsters. Perhaps his shout and thrashing convinced them he was injured. Exploding through their own clouds of greedy scavengers, they came at a trot.

"Jesus!" Hudgens shouted, leveling his weapon. *Klaksh—boom!* The musket roared and downy fuzz sprayed off the side of one of the charging creatures. It squealed and nipped at the graze even as the loud shot sent *thousands* of colorful carrion eaters thundering into the sky. Hudgens was already tearing at a paper cartridge with his teeth as Felix hauled him up. "Should've frightened 'em off like that when we first arrived," he snapped furiously, likely embarrassed as well, as he primed his piece with a small portion of powder from the cartridge before pouring the rest down the .69 caliber barrel and stuffing the paper-wrapped ball down after it with his fingers. He was just drawing his shiny steel ramrod when the flock of swirling bird-things cleared enough for the men to see they hadn't frightened the bigger monsters at all and they were right *there*.

Felix already had his rifle shouldered and squeezed the trigger as the closest beast coiled to pounce as it ran. The smaller, more finely tuned lock on his lovingly maintained .54 caliber 1817 rifle snapped and ignited the charge with no discernible delay. With a distinctive *crack*, its ball struck the creature right in the nose, exiting the palate in a shower of blood and teeth before continuing on to blow a spray of bone and brains out the back of the monster's head. It fell writhing on the ground, kicking and flailing its long, bristly tail. The other two monsters paused, both at the sight of their dying pack member, as well as—possibly—the different sound the rifle made. Felix didn't have time to think about that since they didn't hesitate long. Both snarled and leaped.

Cursing loudly, Hudgens slammed the ball down his barrel and threw his ramrod at a rushing beast before raising his musket again. Felix was essentially disarmed except for the club his rifle had become. Mounted riflemen were issued the same 1840 sabers as dragoons, but they were ridiculously cumbersome and virtually useless (he'd thought) for a trek through the woods on foot. And Private Hudgens was right; rifles did take longer to properly load. Felix could've done as the artilleryman had and dispensed with the cloth patch that took the rifling to spin the ball if he had a few more seconds, but the creature was on him like lightning, hurling him to the ground, slathering teeth grinding on the stock and barrel Felix only barely managed to slam between its jaws before they tore his face or throat away. He heard the *boom* of Hudgens's musket and a screech, but then there was more cursing and a cry of outraged pain.

Felix tried to push the monster off him, but it was incredibly strong and had to weigh almost as much as he. Worse, even as it clutched him with one arm, the curved claws piercing his wool jacket and flesh of his shoulder, the claws on the other hand were raking his chest. So far only one had painfully slashed him, the others defeated by chance and the heavy leather cartridge box strap. The thing had other claws, however, and it cocked a leg forward to deploy one on the inside of its ankle that looked like an oversize fishhook. Felix screamed as it tore into the flesh of his thigh, instinctively knowing it would rip downward and fillet the muscle from his leg. He'd be finished, then. With a desperate, gasping effort, he heaved the thing to the side and bashed its face with his rifle butt. Shattered teeth flew as it tumbled away and he managed to stand.

For just an instant, Felix saw Private Hudgens. He'd discarded his musket and had his short, gladius-like sword in one hand, his bayonet in the other. The points of both were bloody. He was limping, but so was his attacker as they cautiously circled each other. Felix's opponent stood and prepared to lunge again. He wished he had a bayonet, but riflemen were trained to keep their distance and were emphatically *not* supposed to get into situations like this. That was deemed sufficient reason not to issue them bayonets.

Situations like this! Felix snorted almost hysterically to himself, bringing his rifle back over his right shoulder—*God, it hurts!*—and taking a stance, left elbow forward, ready to smash the iron buttplate into the monster's head like a pile driver. It gurgled at him and shifted, muscles tensing.

There was a *fluppering* sound, followed by a *thunk!*, and Felix was amazed to see what could only be a large-diameter arrow with oddly oversize fletching protruding from the monster's side. The beast shrieked and snapped at the shaft, just as another arrow struck very close to the first. Foamy orange blood spewed from the creature's nostrils, and it hacked out a clump of lung. Wheeling away, it took three bounding steps before collapsing and kicking as more blood exploded from its mouth. Felix turned to Private Hudgens, who fell to one knee, gasping from pain, exertion, terror . . . and now what? His attacker lay with four long arrows in its chest.

"There are more of you after all. Well fought!" came a strange voice speaking English, but with an equally strange accent. Perhaps a dozen dark-skinned men with long black hair began emerging from the gloom of the forest. All wore soft leather tunics, leggings, and moccasins, but most also had bright-colored breechcloths of finely woven fabric. About half were armed with bows taller than they were, each with deadly arrows nocked. The rest carried spears as long as the bows, brandished just as menacingly. The points on the weapons were four to six inches long, cunningly knapped from greenish obsidian as clear as lightly colored glass.

"Savage red men after all, it seems," Hudgens gasped, "an' glad I am to see 'em too—I hope." His breath caught then, as did Felix's, when two more men approached, clearly escorting another . . . being. It was the same height as the men, about five three or so, dressed much like them, except the leather was less weathered and soiled and the seams were decorated with small bones, shells, and a riot of feathers. The breechcloth was bright green. What most caught their attention and astounded them—aside from the fact it wore a long-bladed basket-hilt rapier at its side and carried what looked like a British-style musket of an older type than the Mexican Army used—was this "person" looked for all the world like an upright cat. Its sky-blue eyes were proportionately larger than a cat's, and more rounded ears were lower on the sides of its head, but except for darker and lighter patches on its face, it was covered in dark tan fur. And then there was the long, fluffy tail, of course, swishing rapidly from side to side behind it.

"God in heaven, what *is* that? Where the *devil* have we found ourselves?" Hudgens whispered, words nearly overwhelmed by the returning cloud of birds.

Felix was struck nearly speechless, terror and dread rising again, heart pounding in his ears. "Are you . . ." he managed fearfully, then had to clear his tight throat to continue. "Are you a demon? Are we dead and gone to hell?"

The cat-thing's face around its eyes never changed, but it blinked rapidly and formed what could only be a grin. Rather disconcerting itself, considering the long, sharp canines it revealed.

"I'll leave you to decide if you're in hell or not, but you're not dead," the cat-creature replied with a stern but surprisingly soft voice, touched with what sounded like amusement. "And I'm no demon. At least not to my friends. Hopefully, you'll be among them."

"You speak English!" Felix said harshly, accusingly, as if that were further proof the creature was a demon.

It took a breath, and Felix noted that its chest swelled like a woman's, with female breasts under the buckskin tunic. "I speak several languages. English is one I had not used much for . . . a number of years." She—it had to be a she—rapidly blinked her eyes and made a *kakking* sound. "And *you* speak English, as did the other few survivors we managed to rescue before the monsters began to swarm. How interesting. Does that make *you* demons?" She cocked her head to the side as if awaiting a response before continuing. "Allow me to introduce myself; I'm Varaa-Choon, warmaster to the great Jaguar King Har-Kaaska." She gestured around her. "These are my warriors, my 'Ocelomeh.' We offer you aid in this terrible world, at least until you learn more of it, just as we did eleven others we found alive."

"You *saved* people here?" Felix blurted.

"We just saved you," Varaa-Choon reminded, eyes narrowing slightly. "Some of the others were badly injured and may still die. All were hurt worse than you, even after your fight with the garaaches."

"Garaaches," Felix murmured, kicking the dead monster that almost killed him. So spellbound had he been, it took the sudden movement to re-mind him of his leg and shoulder wounds. He hissed at the pain.

"Garaaches and other things. Few of the greater dragons roam the dense forest, particularly during this dry time. Their preferred prey stays closer to water, and the trees restrict their movement." She gestured in the direction of the broken ship, and her tail whipped more rapidly behind her. "With the smell of so much meat on the wind, however, more dangerous things will come. We must be gone. Wild garaaches will avoid the scent of so many of us, but it doesn't deter the tribal kind, or the greater dragons. Bind their injuries so we can move," Varaa-Choon told the men around them, who lowered their weapons and approached. It was Felix's first indication the Ocelomeh understood English as well. Private Hudgens quickly scooped up his musket and took a limping step back.

"You won't be disarmed as long as you offer no violence," Varaa-Choon hastened to assure them, then added matter-of-factly, "You'll be killed at once if you do." Private Hudgens reluctantly stood while a pair of men knelt to examine his bloody foot. Apparently the . . . "garaache" had hooked his shoe with a claw and torn it off, badly gouging the flesh underneath. Two other men inspected Felix, cutting his trouser leg and peeling his jacket back so they could view his other wounds. All the while, they carried on a rapid conversation in a language Felix couldn't identify. Varaa-Choon was looking at the wreck of *Xenophon*. "Once the predators are done, we'll re-turn and pick the bones of your ship more thoroughly. Others we saved told us you were at war with the people of the land you thought this was."

"Its president, not the people," Felix loyally countered.

Varaa-Choon snorted. "You make such distinctions? Your world must be *much* different from ours," she added cryptically. "In any event, I'm also told there are weapons in the wreck—powder and shot, perhaps even can-non. We'll come back when it's safe."

Felix was more and more confused by the strange warmaster, and virtu-ally every word she said. The situation, the creatures that attacked them and the wounds they inflicted, Varaa-Choon herself . . . all left Felix in a kind of growing shock. But what was all this about *different worlds*? It was too much. He was a good Lutheran boy from Ohio and still couldn't banish the conviction he was in some kind of hell, or at least trapped in a terrible nightmare.

But Varaa-Choon obviously assumes Private Hudgens and I are survi-

vors of this *wreck, and don't even know about* Mary Riggs. *What of the other ships that were with us? Are they lying shattered in the forest as well, their people being eaten?* Utterly bewildered, Felix didn't know what to do. His instinct for secrecy in an enemy land was to keep his mouth shut, but these people weren't acting like enemies. One warrior had just handed him his gnawed-on rifle! *Maybe they're Maya Indians,* Felix thought. *They have to be, don't they? Aren't some of them fighting Mexico too? But what of this "Varaa-Choon" creature? She isn't only a different race of human; she isn't human at all. What does that leave, besides demons? Then there was her comment about "more dangerous things," and "greater dragons." What are they? More important, are they or these "Ocelomeh" more dangerous to our comrades at* Mary Riggs?

He caught Private Hudgens looking searchingly at him, apparently consumed by the same doubts and fears. Felix sighed and pointed at the seething hell around *Xenophon's* corpse, then shrugged as if asking the older man what to do. The artilleryman shrugged back. Taking a chance, Felix began reloading his rifle even while the Ocelomeh continued working on him. Private Hudgens nodded slightly and did the same with his musket. Far from trying to stop them, one of the buckskin-clad warriors retrieved Hudgens's ramrod and handed it back. Varaa-Choon said nothing, but it was clear she was growing agitated; not at them, but at the time it was taking to treat them. The sun was quickly dropping below the tops of the trees, and a heavy gloom was descending.

"My name is Private Felix Meder of the United States Mounted Rifles," Felix told Varaa-Choon very formally. "My companion is Private Hudgens, of the First United States Artillery."

"Elijah Hudgens," the artilleryman supplied, giving him a slight, grave nod.

Felix nodded back, then looked at Varaa-Choon and spoke again, as much for Hudgens—so the other man would know his thinking—as for Varaa-Choon. "We appreciate all you've done for us, but can't allow that to happen to the others." He indicated the seething wreck a short distance through the trees. "Even if they've protected themselves, what if they send searchers looking for us? We have to warn them," he ended firmly.

"What others?" Varaa-Choon immediately demanded.

Still afraid he was betraying a sacred trust but convinced he must, Felix quickly explained where he and Hudgens came from. Varaa-Choon managed to look thoughtful, staring at a patch of lizardbird-crowded sky while her warriors finished treating the two men.

"About four miles, you say?" she asked. "But *many* more survivors? Probably too much activity for the lizardbirds, and they didn't draw in the larger things," she told one of her companions. "Do you think they'll have fortified themselves? Buried the dead?" she asked Felix.

Suspicious again, Felix nodded. "This was potentially hostile territory, even . . . where we came from. Yes, the dead were being buried when we left, and the survivors were preparing defenses. There are some"—he paused—"experienced officers there." He hoped that was the case. Anson seemed tough enough, but was apparently unwilling to take charge. Olayne knew what to do, just not how to do it. Perhaps Captain Cayce had come around? With the help of Swain and Burton, maybe others, even Olayne should make the impromptu camp relatively secure—against things they understood. But what about things they didn't?

Varaa-Choon finally shook her head. "Night is coming. I see better in the dark than my warriors and can warn them, but they still have to see to fight."

"It's only an hour's brisk walk to the ship," Felix objected. "We have to warn our people!"

"In an hour, it will be *quite* dark in these woods, and *you*'ll be walking nowhere briskly in your condition," Varaa-Choon countered, blinking in a way that seemed to emphasize what she'd said. "You'd never make it with your wounds, and without quick, proper treatment, they'll turn bad anyway. You have no idea how quickly fevers strike on this world without anti-sepsis medicine."

Another reference to a "different world." What does she mean? Felix wondered feverishly while Varaa-Choon gestured around at her companions.

"Some of *us* could get there, but not with the two of you along. How well would we be received without you? Here, we were saviors and the situation was clear. But meeting armed and frightened men with fingers on their triggers, who've possibly already encountered *other* things to frighten them further . . . No, even if they didn't shoot at us, *we'd* be relying on unknown strangers to shelter us through the night." She regarded Felix with those huge, blue eyes. "Night is *very* dangerous for small groups in this land."

The idea that this place could be more dangerous than it already was made Felix gulp. Still, "Then I'll go back alone. I'll tell them about you and they won't shoot!"

"Very noble, but you would die—*after* you've been in our care," Varaa-Choon said simply. "Not the best message to send them either, I think. No, if they prepare, they should do well enough." She grinned. "And they'll have accomplished something. More than most who come to this world—and perhaps more than they would where they came from, eh?" she added cryptically, glancing at Hudgens and back at Felix. "You young fellows as well."

"We go back to the sanctuary, then. Take them to Father Orno like the others?" asked one of the men who'd escorted her in. He looked bigger and older than the rest, but his hair was still jet-black.

"Sanctuary?" Hudgens asked.

"A refuge of sorts for traveling Ocelomeh. Quite well hidden and protected. You're lucky there was one so near and we were in it when you fell to this world," Varaa absently explained before looking at her companion. "Father Orno will want to hear another account of your arrival." She paused. "Strange that he chose to accompany us on this survey. Almost as if . . ." She shook her head. "Yes, the sanctuary for tonight," Varaa-Choon said. "Tomorrow . . . we will see."

CHAPTER 4

B y the time the sun slipped beneath the trees and even the shattered
clearing surrendered to darkness, the port (northern) side of the increasingly skeletal corpse of *Mary Riggs* had become the southern
bastion of a large, waist-high stockade, constructed of fallen trees and the
ship's own salvaged timbers. Forty-six horses had been taken from the
wreck in good condition, Arete among them, to Lewis's relief, and eleven
others had sound legs and should recover. The rest were either dead or had
to be destroyed. Details buried 106 men, but dead horses were dragged out
through the "gate" and about seventy-five yards into the forest. No one
wanted to eat them—they'd recovered their provisions of salt pork and
biscuit—but Lewis hesitated to have them burned. A sufficient fire to do the
job would make a beacon at night and smoke by day, equally visible to
friend or foe. Besides, after the dampness of . . . whatever happened to
them . . . dried up during the day, he'd realized the forest around them was
a tinderbox. He preferred to just leave the dead horses since he didn't intend
to linger long.

They'd finish unloading the ship by morning and prepare to make for
the coast all together as soon as the next day, or the next, after a strong force
scouted the route. Lewis would risk no more men wandering about in pairs.
Half of those Olayne sent out hadn't returned. Hopefully, they were simply

lost and would find their way back. The other half had little to report besides the bizarre bird-things they'd all seen, which grew increasingly aggressive as the day wore on. Some had seen shadowy figures following or pacing them through the woods, but could provide no more details. Pickets placed outside the stockade—but well in sight of it—reported the same. Some were frightened by what their stressed and rampant imaginations made them *think* they saw, and Lewis was amazed none of them had fired on the shapes. In the meantime, dragoons had replaced the artillerymen at the breastworks and tired gunners now labored to heave the six shiny new Model 1841 6pdrs, their limbers, caissons, and other artillery vehicles, out of the wreck by lantern light. He smiled to hear Sergeant McNabb's appraisal of the weapons hauled into the gathering night, his native speech rising closer to the surface than Lewis had heard before:

"Oh, would ye *look* at that one, then! Such a beauty she is, sparklin' like the golden moon himself! I've trained on small guns, aye, as have many of ye, but they were sad, decrepit things from the second war for independence. It was enough to make ye weep an' wonder whatever they might be good for. But *these* lovely ladies! They're bigger but not much heavier, an' look how ingeniously Mr. Mordechai devised these lovely trails! A single man could lift it. *Get yer filthy grabbers off the brass of her barrel,* damn your *bones,* Mr. Finlay! Clap on to the spokes like a Christian! That's why they paint the bloody things, an' the whole bloody carriage too, to keep bog trotters like you from stainin' her fine, shiny barrel with yer greasy damn fingers!"

McNabb's caustic but good-natured diatribe went on like that, mixing humorous abuse on the men with loving admiration of the guns, as one by one he supervised their excavation and emplacement around the perimeter, each loaded with a round of canister and hastily crewed by men who at least knew how to fire it. Few were acquainted with the Hidden's Patent percussion lock they were equipped with, however, and Lewis had to explain.

"It's just a bloody great percussion cap, like the damn dragoons use on their carbines," McNabb had said, holding one up when the first ammunition chest was opened for inspection.

"The new Model 'forty-two muskets use them as well," Lewis had confirmed, "though I haven't actually seen one. They say they're to be rifled to fire hollow-base projectiles based on Minié's principles, and fitted with long-range sights. In any event, percussion caps are the future, though I think the new friction primers might serve better for artillery."

McNabb had continued to stare dubiously at the object, shaped like a top hat and almost as big as a button, the "brim" of the hat jaggedly serrated like a sunburst. "Whatever was wrong with slow-match an' linstocks, even portfires?"

Lewis had smiled. "Nothing, except you have to light them before you can use them, and that's not always easily or quickly done. And quicker ignition means improved accuracy against moving targets."

McNabb had seemed to agree with that, but continued to frown at the cap. "Do we have any friction primers?"

Now the moon was full and bright, and the temperature, never brutal during the day, remained balmy. Still, though no one was cold, mosquitoes were a growing problem. Lewis had denied requests to light fires to smoke the pests for the same reasons he'd prohibited a pyre for the horses. The only dubious relief the men got was by huddling near men with pipes or cigars, and even they'd been cautioned to be careful. Against Captain Holland's objection, Lewis actually insisted the cooks make a fire, however, to feed the men. After all they'd been through, a cooked meal of whatever quality would go a long way toward raising their spirits.

"I see you found your hat," Captain Giles Anson observed, joining him, Holland, Burton, Swain, and another dragoon lieutenant named Edgar Dwyer from New York, where they'd gathered for an "officers' meeting" called by word of mouth. Lewis wanted no bugles. They'd been watching the loud, sweaty work inside the wreck while they waited. Anson was enjoying a large cigar and now benevolently blew clouds of smoke at the other officers. Most smiled appreciatively, but Coryon Burton pretended to gag.

"Yes," Lewis said, taking the battered thing off and looking at it. He'd also washed the blood from his hair and face when he sat for a couple of stitches in his scalp applied by the giant, bearlike Ranger named Corporal Bandy Beeryman. Lewis discovered during an interesting conversation—closely watched by Anson's "aide"—that the big, surprisingly soft-spoken man had done a lot of "doctorin'" and was appropriately known to his colleagues as "Boogerbear." In any event, though Lewis looked better than he had earlier in the day, he still felt like hell. "Whoever designed these ridiculous hats must've thought they looked dashing," he continued dubiously, "and I never dreamed I'd be glad to wear one. But the padding in the top probably saved my skull." He put it back on. "I suppose I'd hate to lose it now."

Lieutenant Olayne finally stepped up, the only other surviving officer, and shyly handed Lewis a shiny steel scabbard protecting a Model 1840 artillery saber, wrapped in a white belt and rectangular eagle buckle. "Thank you, Lieutenant!" Lewis said, genuinely glad to see the weapon. It was an Ames-made officer's version of the standard horse artillery saber. Lewis had purchased it himself and had a few embellishments added. The blade was acid-etched with the customary large US surrounded by floral and martial panoplies, but the grip was covered with coarse sharkskin to prevent it turning or slipping in his hand, and the brass guard and pommel had been tastefully engraved around his cursive initials. Despite the fact it had seen a fair amount of use and the golden sword knot was battered and frayed, he kept the blade's edge much sharper than most officers took the effort to do. Next to his horse, Arete, it was probably his most prized possession.

"Sergeant McNabb found your baggage," Olayne confessed, also handing over a set of scuffed black leather pommel holsters, protecting a pair of .54 caliber Robert Johnson contract M1836 pistols. They were well-made weapons, and Lewis was surprisingly good with them considering they were smoothbores without rear sights, but they didn't mean as much to him as the saber. "I'm afraid your trunk was shattered, however, and most of your things damaged by water. Perhaps your clothing will still serve when it's been dried. Some of the lads are trying to salvage the other officer's clothing as well." He managed a tentative smile. "Your Ringgold saddle is safe"—dragoons and mounted riflemen mostly rode Grimsleys, and Ringgold saddles were expensive and rare—"and Private Willis is oiling the leather."

Lewis chuckled, remembering the scrawny little soldier who didn't want to share his water. "As punishment for something?"

"Sir? No sir. You need an orderly, and Sergeant McNabb said he volunteered."

"Did he indeed?"

Lewis turned to the others, evaluating their lantern-lit expressions. All were exhausted and aside from Captain Anson and perhaps Captain Holland, were visibly doing their best to control their anxiety. Not that Anson and Holland *weren't* afraid—Lewis certainly was, and assumed they were

as well—but they had experience leading men in battle or against the elements. They'd learned, of necessity, how to suppress or hide their fear.
"Well, gentlemen," he began wryly, attempting to lighten the mood, "we
seem to be in good shape, all things considered. Our position is more secure, and the men have returned to their duty to the extent they're already
trading barbs about their respective service branches." He nodded at Lieutenant Coryon Burton. "One of the dragoons, Private Buisine, is apparently
a closely shaved squirrel." He waited while the chuckles came and went.
"You may have seen him scurry to the top of one of the closest undamaged
trees."

"Aye!" Holland exclaimed with real admiration. "Higher than *Mary
Riggs*'s mainmast was. He'll make a fine topman when he has his fill of
horses."

"In any event," Lewis continued, "he scanned the horizon in all directions as best he could and never saw the sea, though he was sure the forest
does end just a few miles to the north. No doubt the sea is below the treetop
'horizon.'" They all took that as good news, continuing by apparently universal consent to avoid the searing question of *how* they got "a few miles"
from the sea in the first place. Lewis pursed his lips. "Due to how flat the
top of the forest seemed in other directions, Private Buisine concluded the
ground below must be equally flat. Captain Anson confirmed that's consistent with what he knows of the northern Yucatán, though he remains as
mystified by the forest as Captain Holland." He paused. "Buisine did note
some anomalies, some distant hills or knobs, one of which appeared in his
glass to have been made of shaped stones. And several were shrouded in a
haze of wood smoke, so there *are* inhabitants nearby. We must be cautious.
We've no idea whose side, if any, they're on." Gratefully accepting a cigar
from Anson, he lit it from the other man's and puffed it to life.

"Tomorrow the Rangers and a squad of dragoons will scout to the north
for the best route to the coast. Hopefully, they'll find our friends anchored
there, or a friendly settlement where we can wait for transport."

"Even an unfriendly settlement could be induced to change its tune,"
Coryon Burton observed. "We have a full battery of guns and a couple hundred well-armed men." He glanced around at the growing frowns. "*They*
won't know how unfit to fight we are," he insisted. "The locals won't resist
us, and there can't be enough Mexican troops in the vicinity to do so."

Lewis wasn't so sure, but nodded. "Friendly or not, they won't be molested," he warned mildly, but no one could doubt his resolve. "That's the plan. I suppose things could've been much worse indeed, and we should thank God they weren't."

"It couldn't have been worse for my poor ship, the hundred an' six men we buried, an' the forty-two we can't find"—Holland snorted—"but for the two hundred an' eighty-two of us left, aye, I reckon you're right."

Lewis sobered. "Those are the final numbers?"

"My purser, Mr. Finlay, is a villainous thief, like all such creatures, an' unfit for the labors that've occupied the rest of us," Holland explained, then chuckled. "Sergeant McNabb threw him out of the ship! But in addition to startin' an inventory of our stores, he seemed the logical choice to count everything else. Includin' those we've lost."

"His numbers came from the acting adjutants appointed for the various companies while you were . . . indisposed, sir," supplied Lieutenant Swain. "Obviously, those numbers might . . . rearrange themselves since some of the injured may die, and the missing scouts are still listed among the living."

"Pray they remain so," Olayne murmured. He'd sent them out and had been right to do so, but his initial confusion prevented him from giving them better instructions and limiting the scope of their explorations. He'd confessed as much to Lewis, who'd consoled him that at least he'd *tried* to restore order and purpose, but Olayne was still struck by the losses his first brief "command" may have incurred.

"That's enough, gentlemen," Lewis said. "If there are no questions, we should get back to work. Captain Holland, please have your Mr. Sessions get with these officers or the adjutants they appointed to establish the same kind of watch your sailors observed while we were under way so at least some of them can get some sleep."

"Aye, Captain Cayce, though I'll warn you: it's a bit less restful than your soldiers are used to."

"I know," Lewis snapped with fatigue-induced annoyance before he could catch himself. "That's why I asked you to do it. I want half the men up at all times, on guard or working." He sighed and drew on his cigar again. "My apologies, sir, but we have much to do, and none of us will get as much rest as we'd like, no matter how much we need it."

The dragoon private named Buisine had trotted up, waiting to be no-ticed, clutching his saber beside him so it wouldn't drag or trip him. His other hand kept the Hall carbine, suspended from its strap and hook, from doing the same. If Buisine was any indication, keeping himself armed with everything but his pistols, the men were still on edge.

"What is it, Private?" Burton asked as the other officers began to disperse.

"It's the horses, sir, actin' mighty antsy. Sergeant Hayne sent me to tell you."

Now that it was brought to his attention, Lewis—and Anson as well—realized the trooper was right. The horses had all been picketed along the curve of the dead ship's frames, leaving only a gap for those still hauling crates and barrels from the hull. Lewis's Arete was nearby, still fairly placid, but the horses closest to the bow—closest to where they'd ultimately heaped the dead ones—were growing increasingly alarmed.

"I told him it was probably scavengers, out at the dead pile," Buisine suggested helpfully. "All them nasty, damned birds flocked over there once we cleaned up the camp."

"That's most likely true," Lewis agreed, hooking the buff saber belt around his waist and tossing the pommel holsters over his shoulder like Anson always carried his, "but we'll have a look. Sergeant McNabb," he called into the hull. "You stationed a gun near the bow?"

"Aye, sir," came the muffled response. "My very favorite one, she was. Survived the wreck without the slightest scratch. Loaded proper with canister too, like you said, as soon as we put her in place."

"Crawl up out of there and come along. Bring a reliable gun crew—I assume you've identified one by now?—and fetch those lanterns along as well." Lewis turned to Anson as the whole group of officers and artillerymen Lewis summoned made their way toward the section of the palisade behind which the horses were growing *very* upset. "In your travels, did you acquaint yourself with the predators we might expect hereabouts?"

Anson hesitated, then murmured, "Let's ask . . . my son. *Leon* is his name," he stressed, beginning to talk faster, displaying a diffidence Lewis had never seen in him. "He don't say much, bein' a little self-conscious about a voice that won't break, but he ain't shy in a fight," he stated firmly. "He's had his growth as well; is near as tall as me. Just hasn't filled out yet. Private Anson," he called loudly, but his "aide" was practically beside him, as always, a challenging, dark-eyed gaze fixed on Lewis. "You have an eye for beasts, an' you rode the back country when we were . . . near here," he said. "Did you hear Captain Cayce's question?"

"We've never been *here* before, Father. Not even close," said "Leon" with total conviction. Despite what Captain Anson said, the voice was a little husky and could've easily been a boy's. Lewis was even more certain it wasn't. "Either way, the only critter I can think of that might scare the horses is a jaguar." She paused. "You know what a jaguar is, Captain Cayce?"

"It's something like a puma, isn't it?"

"Yeah, only bigger."

The horses were squealing in terror now, pulling hard against the ribs of the ship where they were secured, kicking violently at each other and nothing at all. A couple of dragoons were moving to calm them, but Sergeant Hayne roared, "Get back from there, you fools! They'll kick your little brains out!"

"What have you seen, Sergeant?" Lewis demanded as they joined him. He hadn't been worried about a puma or jaguar. A shot in the night should see it off. He'd been most concerned that enemies might be sneaking up. But the horses were going berserk. They'd never do that because of people.

"Nothin', sir. Can't see nothin' out there. The moon's bright enough, but there's too many trees between us an' the dead pile."

"*I* seen somethin', Sergeant!" cried one of the men by the palisade, carbine at the ready.

"Private Priddy *thought* he seen somethin'," Hayne said, rolling his eyes, "big as a horse itself."

"It *was!*"

Lewis peered into the darkness. The sergeant was right; the trees were in the way and there was too much noise to hear anything. "We'll just have to take a look, won't we? Bring those lanterns closer. Lieutenant Olayne, send for more of your men with muskets and post this gun crew." He removed his pistols and a small priming flask from the pommel holsters, double-checking each weapon with the ingenious swiveling ramrod under the barrel to ensure it was loaded. Finally, he dusted the priming pans with a small measure of fine-grained gunpowder from the flask before thrusting one into his belt. "I hope the damp didn't get to them. It seems not. I keep them loaded, but not primed," he explained, draping the holsters on the palisade.

Anson patted the holsters still on his shoulder. "These're always loaded *and* primed."

"Lieutenant Burton," Lewis said louder. "Half a dozen dragoons, if you please, but you remain with Olayne. I want steady officers behind me who won't let their men shoot at shadows."

"You're going out there yourself, sir?" Lieutenant Swain asked.

"I am."

"Then I'd like to come." Swain's few riflemen were scattered along the palisade.

"Very well."

Anson said nothing, but moved to stand by Lewis as the rest of their party formed. Lewis had expected as much. They weren't friends, but they knew and trusted each other. Besides, if something happened to Lewis, Anson would be back where he was that morning: burdened with the highest rank but unwilling to command. Lewis considered him the best (and most ruthless) irregular cavalry leader any commander—who could control him—could want. That's why he put him in charge of all the mounted troops. But Anson had no idea how to employ a mixed force like they had. Lewis was sure if they confronted a serious threat, Anson would protect him better than all the dragoons. "Let's go," he said, climbing over the shattered timbers. "Spread out once you're across, a lantern for every other man."

"Be careful, sir," Coryon Burton urged.

Lewis glanced back and smiled, surprisingly moved, as he motioned the detachment forward. He was disapprovingly *un*surprised to see "Leon" Anson beside her father. He wouldn't make an issue of it. Not now. He needed Anson's support and didn't want an argument. Anything that undermined the fragile unity they'd achieved was foolish. Besides, he already felt foolish enough, advancing in the dark with lanterns lighting them up while largely ruining their ability to see what they were looking for. He didn't think human enemies were frightening the horses, however, and expected whatever it was would flee as they approached.

"Probably more of those dreadful birds," Swain almost whispered. "Some were the size of turkey vultures, but very strangely shaped and colored. The horses can't see them in the dark, but they hear them—and smell all the blood from the dead horses they've torn open." Lewis suspected Swain was right.

The shrieking and neighing of frightened horses still echoed in the woods, but as they moved away, they heard other things ahead. There was an intense, urgent grunting, growling, and crunching, mixed with an outraged or protesting cluckering sound, like packs of hogs, dogs, and chickens all contending over the same slops in some macabre farmyard.

"Lord, what a ruckus," a dragoon murmured nervously, hoisting his lantern higher.

"Yes," Lewis agreed, "but I believe we can rest assured they *are* animals, after all."

There were ten of them, half with lanterns and pistols, the other half with Hall carbines at the ready, or in Swain's case, an 1817 rifle. Like Lewis, "Leon" carried a lantern, but also one of the ingenious Colt's revolvers. In addition to their five-shot capacity, Lewis admired the long-barreled but otherwise compact weapons for their remarkable accuracy. And if the .36 caliber balls they spat only rarely quickly killed a man, they'd take him out of the fight as efficiently as larger projectiles. Captain Anson had possessed a pair openly holstered on his belt for as long as Lewis had known him. Apparently, his three other Rangers were similarly armed. It made Lewis briefly wonder what Anson carried so protectively in the pommel holsters over his shoulder.

Now, as they crept carefully closer and the dark mound of carcasses began to take shape, so did the shadowy forms and light-reflecting eyes of unknown creatures feasting on it. Instead of running from the light, the forms only gorged more desperately, the revolting sounds growing more hurried and distinct. An unearthly screech erupted from the mound, and Swain exclaimed, "My God, one of those horses is still alive!"

"That was no horse, boy," Captain Anson countered darkly, teeth clenched. Lewis knew him well enough to recognize his tension, and that the "boy" crack wasn't deliberate. "That was a challenge."

"From what?" hissed another dragoon.

"Let's find out," Lewis told them all. "Be ready. If our presence alone doesn't frighten them away, we'll fire into them. That should do it. One quick volley on my command, mind you," he cautioned. "I want no drawn-out shooting to help an enemy pinpoint our position."

A shadow that had remained still until now suddenly shifted, and Lewis realized—as dragoon Private Priddy claimed—it *was* as big as a horse. Bigger, actually, rising from its meal to stand half again taller. Other creatures with impossible, nightmare shapes bolted, but they weren't running from Lewis and his little squad. They fled from the giant beast suddenly aroused in their midst. Snarling fiercely, it lunged at the interlopers across the heap of mangled flesh.

Lewis had never seen anything like it, never *heard* of a creature outside of myth even remotely resembling this monstrosity. It leaped into the lantern light as lightly as a crow over a stone, pausing only to gather itself. Great, bloody, dagger-toothed jaws gaped wide, and it roared a thunderous warning at things it probably supposed were here to snatch its feast. For perhaps a second—the longest, most vivid second Lewis ever experienced— he saw the monster plainly. Its bearing was more like the swift, snake- and lizard-eating ground birds he'd seen in Texas and Northern Mexico than any crow, and it stood ten feet tall, from its clawed, three-toed feet to the top of its horrifying, bristly crested head. Large, luminous orange eyes glared directly forward at them down the long, arched, but concave-sided snout. Powerful arms and hands, each with two clawed fingers and presumably a thumb of sorts, still effortlessly grasped the gnawed foreleg and shoulder of a horse. The whole thing was so splashed with drying, darkening blood that the true color of its matted, somewhat feathery fur was impossible to distinguish in the lantern light.

That was the only insight Lewis gathered before, without his command, virtually everyone fired at it. The smoky flash and *boom* of several carbines and a couple of pistols made the thing blink and recoil slightly, but even if every shot hit, Lewis doubted they'd seriously injured it. He'd avidly read the journals of the "Corps of Discovery" sent up the Missouri to explore the Louisiana Purchase and vividly recalled accounts of how many desperate shots it often required to dispatch "White" or "Grizzled" bears. Not only was this monster four or five times more massive than any bear; they weren't sufficiently armed. Pistols would probably only anger it, and the breechloading Hall carbines, while quick to load, leaked a lot of the force of their charge and were notoriously underpowered.

The monster bellowed, perhaps in some pain but certainly indignation, and lunged forward again. "Back to the palisade!" Lewis cried, dropping his lantern and uselessly drawing his saber. Both his pistols were still loaded, but they were equally useless. Everyone already *had* run, except Anson, "Leon," and Swain. The two Rangers fired their revolvers, the noise and sting of hot little balls perhaps enough to give the thing slight pause, and Swain was aiming his 1817 rifle. It would do better than a Hall, but not enough. "Now!" Lewis roared. Together, they turned and fled.

The monster stomped the lantern Lewis dropped, the candle still fluttering until it was crushed. "Leon" had set hers on the ground, and the creature attacked it next, snapping jaws crumpling tin and shattering glass. The candle died, but molten wax splashed across a sensitive tongue. The thing squealed in pain and surprise, but its vision adapted quickly enough to see the figures sprinting for the palisade. With a steam whistle screech, it galloped in pursuit.

The dragoons were already hopping over the barricade, one still carrying his lantern. All were shouting for men to shoot toward the dead pile. Burton, Olayne, and a growing number of NCOs were bellowing terrible threats of what would happen to them if they did. Men started shouting encouragement when they saw Lewis and his companions, but their cries took on a note of terror when they saw the thing chasing them. Over the rasping gurgle of their quickly closing pursuer, Lewis heard a *thump* and a high-pitched "Arph!" He spun to see "Leon" had tripped over a shattered tree trunk and sprawled on the ground. Anson turned as well, but Lewis grabbed an upflung arm and started dragging. Girl or not, "Leon" was tall and well muscled and certainly no feather. The going got easier when Anson grabbed his daughter's other arm despite her angry demand that they "Let go! I'll carry myself, damn you!" Whether she could've regained her feet and escaped on her own at first was immaterial. She couldn't possibly do so now. Lewis and Anson raced the rest of the way like that, dragging their sputtering burden.

Still, the terrible beast would've caught all three if not for Lieutenant Swain—a very different Clifford Swain than had been so fearful in the face of disaster aboard *Mary Riggs*. Seeing what happened and how close the monster was, he stepped between them without a thought and raised his rifle again. His gasping breath affected his aim, but the target was very large and close. With a bright orange flash and distinctive *crack!* his ball hit the thing in the snout and caromed down its concave surface to blow its left eye out in a viscous spray of gore. The monster screeched and whirled as if attacked from its blinded side, but its great long tail, like a whip the size of *Mary Riggs*'s main yard, slammed into Swain with a sickening, crunching *thwap*, batting him thirty yards through the air. Regardless how insignificant, the monster felt the strike and whirled back the other way, snapping at air.

In the meantime, Lewis and Anson had thrown "Leon" over the breastworks. Even as they climbed over themselves, Lewis roared, "Open fire!" A ragged volley of carbine and musket fire slashed at the thing, and it screeched again, rounding on this new irritation. Back with their comrades, even the dragoons who'd run stood their ground, shooting and reloading twice as fast as the men with muskets. And the volume of fire was telling. The thing was furious and in agony, but now also afraid. It finally tried to get away from the crackling, flaring, painful thing it chased and whirled to run—just as Olayne shouted, "Fire!" Sergeant McNabb yanked his lanyard, and the hammer on the Hidden's lock clapped down on the cap, priming his "favorite" 6pdr. The field piece stabbed the night with an eight-foot jet of flame and an earth-shaking blast as it leaped back, sending its load of canister—forty-eight 1.15" balls weighing almost a quarter pound apiece—at the monster. Less than thirty yards away, all of them hit in a very tight pattern across its back and churned a three-foot section of spine into a bloody, salt-like gruel before most of the projectiles came to rest in its vitals. As if it had only been some kind of hellish marionette and a vengeful, thunderous god snipped its strings, the monster crashed to the ground. One hind leg stretched rigidly out and quivered for a moment before it dropped and the thing lay still.

A few more musket balls, fired as much by fear as gunpowder, slapped into the motionless corpse while Lewis shouted to cease fire. Stunned NCOs took up his cry. Leaning back against the barricade, gasping from exertion, Lewis appreciatively accepted one of the several canteens offered to him and took a long gulp. He watched Anson try to help his daughter up, but she angrily shook off his hand and stalked away toward the horses, now quickly calming down. Compared to the scent and sound of monsters, gunsmoke and even cannon fire almost seemed to have soothed them. Perhaps it had. *I hope it had the same effect on the men,* Lewis thought. But frightened voices were rising again as the imperative of action faded and shock set in. Lewis heard the word "dragon" several times. No one ever heard there were dragons in Yucatán. "Lieutenant Burton, get these men silenced and organized at once. Form details to get some fires lit as well. Large ones. Ensure the ground is sufficiently cleared around them, of course, and detail men with shovels to watch them closely."

"But the enemy . . ."

"I'm more concerned about big, furry lizards than Mexicans and forest fires at the moment," Lewis countered, then raised his voice to carry. "Fires will keep them away, or make them fine targets."

"Aye, an' they'll see what we done t'th'other," rejoined a satisfied voice.

Others growled agreement. It was better than nothing. "Reload that gun, Sergeant McNabb!" Lewis continued. "Lieutenant Olayne, I think now would be a good time to confirm the crews manning the other guns are as ready as this one was."

"Yes sir," Olayne replied after a short hesitation, then trotted down the line. Lewis's apparent confidence and barrage of orders seemed to have suppressed the growing unease, and the rising shouts of NCOs helped even more. Lewis turned to look out at the dead monster as Anson, then Captain Holland, stepped up beside him. Instead of acknowledging them, he called to Sergeant Hayne. "Take some men to get Lieutenant Swain." His tone left no room for debate. "I'm sure he's dead," he said lowly, dismally, aside to Anson and Holland. "I heard every bone in his body break."

"A hell of a thing," Holland commiserated.

"I owe him my life, for my daughter's," Anson simply said, abandoning his deception at a volume only they could hear. *Of* course *Holland knows "Leon" is a woman,* Lewis realized. "As I owe it to you, Captain Lewis," Anson went on. "You saved her, an' Lieutenant Swain saved the rest of us."

"She doesn't seem particularly appreciative," Lewis retorted, abandoning the fiction of "Leon's" gender as readily as Anson, with him and Holland at least.

"She'll come around. She's only mad she *had* to be saved. Considers herself as able as any man and'll blame herself for Mr. Swain's death." He frowned. "She's had a hard road. My fault."

Lewis was naturally curious but wouldn't pursue it now. Instead, he said, "Then she should know it made no difference to Lieutenant Swain who or what she is. I doubt he had any idea. He defended comrades he hardly knew, without thought, because it was his duty. I wish I'd made the effort to get to know *him* better, before he gave his life for us," Lewis added regretfully.

"It *was* a remarkably standoffish bunch in *Mary Riggs* before the wreck," Holland noted. "But I think Mr. Swain recognized the leader you are—as I've begun to—an' knew we need a good one to survive whatever mess we're in. He protected you for the rest of us."

"Nonsense," Lewis objected.

Anson held up a hand. "What does it matter?" He glanced at Holland. "Despite all our earlier self-deludin' denial an' pretendin', we're—somehow—nowhere *near* where we should be. That's certain." He pointed over the barricade where men with lanterns were staring and poking at the dead monster. A fire was growing nearby, and the carcass looked even more lurid and outlandish. "Or that . . . whatever it is—might as well call it a 'dragon'—ain't where *it* should be. Given the bird-things and other critters, these woods, an' the fact we're higher an' drier than reason can explain, I suspect *we're* the ones who've been . . . misplaced."

"Aye," Holland agreed sourly. "There's more wrong with all this than anything I could imagine." He suddenly grinned at Lewis. "I only thank God *you're* in charge."

"Why?" Lewis demanded angrily.

Anson shrugged. "Holland's right. So was Mr. Swain. I saw it myself at Monterrey, now here. You don't just twist your hands an' dither. You lead."

"Right," Lewis countered. "I 'led' Lieutenant Swain to his death. We never should've left the palisade."

"Maybe," Anson conceded. "Or that dragon could've decided to sample live horses in the night, killing *more* men, deafened and distracted by our own maddened animals. Or the horses might've finally just broke loose in their panic, bustin' themselves up an' tramplin' half a dozen fellas. But you'll never *know*, because you acted." He sighed. "I'm sure Captain Holland'll agree, an' if they don't teach this at West Point, they should: makin' any decision, even the wrong one, is *always* better than makin' none." He snorted. "Second worst in a crisis is a slow one, which turns to none as well." He looked away, staring into the past. "You remember I had a limp when Leonor an' I showed up at Fort Texas to meet Boogerbear an' Sal an' join up with Jack Hayes?"

Lewis nodded vaguely. "I was there when you reported."

"We'd stopped at a stream a few days before, to water our horses. Just the two of us," Anson said. "Lookin' up the other side, we saw six mounted Comanches, just as surprised as us, but already raisin' their weapons. Bows, mostly, but one had a Mexican 'scopet. That's a kind of musket," he added for Holland's benefit. "Anyway, without even thinkin', Leonor and I both pulled our revolvers and charged, shootin' mostly wild. Leonor's horse took a rushed, weak arrow in the neck that didn't cause much harm. I took a graze from the 'scopet ball across the top of my thigh. But the Comanches were already runnin' before we were across the stream. I've no idea if we even hit one." He shook his head. "Doesn't matter. They were prob'ly raidin' for horses, an' no horse is worth their life." He patted one of the Colt's Paterson revolvers at his side. "An' they respect these little fellas. But it came down to the fact they'd shot their bolt an' we hadn't. Comanches're dangerous and bloodthirsty as that dragon, I expect, but they ain't fools. An' we weren't fool enough to chase 'em. 'Good riddance,' we said, an' tended our hurts.

"The point is, though, as soon as we saw 'em, we had exactly two choices; fight or run. Doin' nothin' is *never* a choice, by definition, an' we'd both be dead. Leonor an' I both realized later that it never even occurred to us to run. Not because we weren't scared, but because we know Comanches. If we hadn't put 'em on the defensive an' hurried their fire, they would've had *whole seconds* to take careful aim an' shoot us or our horses. Even if they all missed—damned unlikely—they would've chased us. Now, whether their horses are actually better or not, Comanches'll get more out of 'em an' they'll always run you down." He paused and lit a cigar he'd fished from his vest. "So it would've been a runnin' fight at best, maybe even endin' the same if we found a place to turn on 'em, but they would've had more and longer chances to hurt or kill us first."

He looked intently at Lewis. "We made an *instinctive* decision, forcin' them Comanches to do the same." He shrugged. "Likely turned out best for all concerned. Tonight?" He patted his long-healed thigh. "Tonight we got hurt, an' lost Lieutenant Swain"—he gestured over the palisade where the body was being carried in and more men—quite watchful—had gathered around the monster's corpse—"but you didn't 'do nothin'" when the trouble started, an' you didn't 'do nothin'" when my girl fell in front of that beast. Now you ain't lettin' the men 'do nothin'" but dwell on their fears. You act an' you lead. An' best choice or worst, it *was* a choice to *confront* a problem even if you didn't understand it." He took a long draw on his cigar, exhaling the smoke at the monster like a small re-creation of the blast of canister that cut it down. "Now, *that* 'Comanche' will trouble us no more, an' the men are better prepared to face another."

"He's right, Captain Lewis." Holland nodded. "An' sometimes, like last night, when that wicked storm fell on us, there isn't a 'right' choice except doin' your duty as best you can—an' pray. That's what I did, an' you've done the first, at least, ever since you came to your senses. That's enough for me, an' the men've been steadied to see it."

Lewis sighed. He was exhausted, heartsick, and sore. Scared too. He'd even aggravated the old wound in his side that never seemed to heal. "Go to . . . your son, Captain Anson," he said, resuming the fiction. "Angry at himself—and us—or not, he had a terrible fright."

Anson frowned. "Sure, but she won't thank us for sympathy. Maybe someday . . ." He shook his head. "Someday she'll tell you herself, if she wants." He threw down his cigar and stamped it out. "But I'll go find her, an' try to get some sleep. I expect another busy day tomorrow."

"Count on it," Lewis agreed.

CHAPTER 5

Captain Anson and Lieutenant Dwyer prepared to lead the three Rangers, six dragoons, and six mounted riflemen through the "gate" in the palisade about an hour after dawn. Sal Hernandez, Anson's expert on horses, had selected the eighteen steadiest of the fifty now determined to be fit. Fifty was more than they thought they had yesterday, but Anson was taking an awfully large percentage. Lewis would've preferred he take six more—to pull a gun and carry its crew. It seemed only a cannon could be relied on to swiftly dispatch a dragon. Unfortunately, since they didn't know if they'd find a road, a gun might severely hamper the scout. Besides, though Lewis was now confident Olayne's foot artillerymen were reasonably proficient with the battery at their disposal, they weren't *horse artillerymen*, relentlessly trained and drilled to swiftly maneuver a team of horses and three thousand pounds of gun and limber, then accurately fire at a potentially moving target. As advanced as these new 6pdrs were, and the new 12pdr field howitzers that fit the same carriages, it was the "shoot and scoot" tactics that allowed American artillery to dominate its generally static Mexican counterpart and wreak such havoc on enemy infantry and cavalry. *Only* that training would make a gun on the march an asset instead of a hindrance against a rampaging monster at close range.

"I'd like to tell you to start back by midday if you haven't found anything," Lewis wryly told the mounted officers, "but you'll have to use your discretion." They weren't only looking for the coast. An exposed beach would be no improvement over their current situation. They needed a settlement of some kind and a reasonable route they all could take to get there. "And I don't want you sending couriers back. That'll only expose them to excessive hazards and diminish your force. But mark your progress, blaze trees as you go, and come back together by tomorrow evening at the latest. If you don't, we *will* come looking the following morning." He said that more for Lieutenant Dwyer's benefit, as much to reassure him as to put it in his mind that others would be at risk if they tarried unnecessarily. Anson knew what he was doing, but if something happened to him, Dwyer must understand as well.

"In any event," Lewis concluded, "good luck and be careful. We can't spare anyone else." He said the last with a glance at a party of Swain's riflemen, digging his grave, adding to the long line of fresh mounds and crosses.

"You're just worried about your horse," Anson retorted with a grin. His own bay gelding, Colonel Fannin (what a name for a horse, and Lewis doubted it was complimentary), had survived, but Leonor's hadn't been so lucky. Lewis insisted she take Arete, still unsure why. Partially, likely, it was an expression of esteem for her father. They might not be friends, exactly, but the man's solid, objective support had been crucial thus far. He might also have meant it as a peace offering to the fiery Leonor, still outwardly angry at them both. *And why should that matter to me?* he asked himself, unaware his gaze had settled appraisingly on the girl. Her short black hair, dark eyes, and olive skin came from her Mexican mother, but her height and build and some of her features, though much softer, were straight from Giles Anson. Really evaluating her as a woman for the first time, Lewis realized she was actually very pretty and wondered how she'd ever fooled anyone. Then again, she always wore her sky-blue vest tightly buttoned and acted, spoke, and carried herself, even now, lounging on Lewis's Ringgold saddle, amazingly like a man. Lewis shook his head, supposing that came from being raised like a man for the last eleven years.

He cleared his throat and looked back at Anson. "That's right," he lightly agreed. "Arete's the finest horse here, and I think of her like a daughter sometimes," he added significantly.

Anson nodded understanding and applied his spurs. Colonel Fannin groaned in protest and reluctantly broke into a fast walk. The others followed and the column snaked around the palisade to where it came in contact with the shattered stern of the ship before turning north, widely avoiding the dead pile. Moments later, they were swallowed by the forest.

Lewis took a deep breath, pressed a hand to his aching side, and went to have a daylight look at the dead monster. A crowd was gathered around it again, mostly dragoons. All were armed. Olayne already had half his artillerymen drilling on the guns, the other half still sorting equipment and supplies. Lewis was about to ask the men if they had something better to do when he recognized his hypocrisy. He'd come to gawk as well.

"You too?" Captain Holland asked, amused, falling in step beside him. There were also a couple of sailors and an indignant-looking Lieutenant Burton, clearly coming to send his men to their duties. Lewis shook his head at him and smiled. A scrawny little artilleryman, musket slung and bouncing against his back, was bringing up the rear, studiously staring at a large, sloshing mug as he hurried along. Lewis stopped short of the group around the carcass and waited. The man glanced up, surprised, almost dumping the mug on Lewis.

"Which I been *tryin'* to get this coffee to you, sir," he accused.

"You're Private Willis," Lewis stated, taking the cup and raising it to his lips. The steam felt good on his face, and the coffee—extra strong—felt even better going down.

"I am. Detailed to be your orderly," Willis added sourly.

Lewis nodded. "Then you'll have easy duty. I don't require much."

"That's what I was hopin'," Willis said with open relief.

Coryon Burton glared at him. "Sir, if you prefer . . ."

Lewis chuckled. "No. Private Willis is only being honest, so I'll return the courtesy. I *don't* require much, and grumbling is a soldier's right. But he'll perform what few chores I ask to my perfect satisfaction, or his 'easy duty' will abruptly cease."

Willis gulped and Lewis turned to Captain Holland, holding up his cup. "They've found more sound water butts?"

"'Sound' ain't the word I'd use," Holland replied, "but we saved enough that I reckon we've got days to find water rather than the hours we feared yesterday. After last night, coffee for all hands seemed appropriate." The man sounded as vital as ever, but his face seemed to have added another brutal decade since the day before. Lewis started to step toward the dead monster again, which was looking—and smelling—even more horrible in daylight, but stopped when he heard snatches of what the soldiers around it were saying:

"It's some kinda giant freak alligator. We got alligators in Loosy-anna," one man said.

"Alabama too," agreed another.

"It ain't no alligator!" a third objected.

"Well . . . maybe not like I seen before, but it's still just a big damn lizard. That's a lizard's head if there ever was one."

"I say it's a lizard too," proclaimed another onlooker.

"Lizards don't have fur."

"That ain't fur. More like fuzzy feathers on a goose chick, only longer."

"An' different colored."

"Lizards don't have feathers neither."

"These ones do."

Lewis finally cleared his throat, and the men all stiffened. "Sir!" exclaimed one with corporal stripes. "Lieutenant Burton," he added. "We're back from down at the dead pile, like you sent us."

"I sent you at *dawn* and expected a report long since!"

"Sorry, sir," the corporal apologized. "I reckon we *were* kinda slow creepin' up on it." He waved at the dead monster. "Then we got distracted comin' back."

"Very well," Burton conceded impatiently, "what did you see?"

The corporal hesitated, looking at the others. "Well, you wouldn't credit it, an' I don't rightly know I do, but we *thought* we saw another critter kinda like this, only man-size, lift off an' go flappin' up through the trees!"

"It was bright colored, like a parrot," another man put in. Several nodded agreement.

"Scared it off, though," the corporal concluded. "Prob'ly about a hundred smaller flyin' things too. Some other critters run off, but we didn't see much o' them." He shrugged. "That was it."

"What do you mean?" Lewis asked.

"I mean that's all was there. The dead pile's *gone*. Just bones scattered everywhere, broke up an' chewed. Just the leavin's, like when you shoot a deer when it's warm an' don't find it till the next day. Coyotes don't even leave fur, most times. Just gnawed-up bones on a dark spot in the grass."

"There were close to *forty* horses there," Burton murmured in wonder.

Lewis glanced down at the dead monster. "Clearly, this wasn't the only large creature to visit last night."

"No sir," one of the dragoons piped up. "There was even bigger tracks. Don't know how many, 'cause it's all churned up, but sure as sure, more like this 'un."

"It *ain't* a lizard!" protested the man who'd talked about feathers.

"Is too. An' I bet there was a thousand o' them lizardbirds."

"Lizardbirds. I like that," Holland agreed. "Simplest, most intuitive description of 'em, I suppose."

Lewis looked at him. "But the horses never had another fit."

Holland nodded toward the west. "The wind shifted. That kept the horses calm, an' the smoke an' firelight, the smell of this dead bugger here, maybe even the noise of our fight with him, kept the rest away."

Lewis frowned. "You men, get inside the palisade and get to work. The dragoons will be relieving the artillerymen in the wreck soon."

"You too," Holland told the sailors.

"Yes sir," they all chorused, including Willis, and headed for the gate.

Lewis was still looking at the monster with Holland and Burton. "So," he said disgustedly, "if I'd just allowed the fires, or the wind had shifted earlier, Lieutenant Swain would still be alive."

"Most likely," Holland agreed. "But *nobody* knew *anything* yesterday. You did your best with the *nothin'* you knew, an' a lot of good came from it." He snorted at Lewis's expression. "What? You think a *sailor* would've made better choices last night? An' like I said, Lieutenant Swain—rest his soul—didn't die in vain. The attack opened our eyes, an' now we can proceed more carefully . . . more appropriately. Another thing." He nodded in the direction the soldiers and sailors had gone. "You heard those fellas, talkin' about 'alligators' an' 'lizards,' but the only thing really spooked 'em was one might've jumped up an' flown away." He kicked the huge beast before them and actually shuddered. "Jesus, that gives *me* the shivers. Still, they might even decide this was a 'dragon,' like Mr. Anson, but they didn't go on about 'demons' an' 'devils'—like I have in *my* head." He looked squarely at Lewis. "I'm through with that because we *killed this damn thing* and I've a notion no mortal man's gonna be killin' demons an' devils. The rest'll feel the same, an' that'll make a difference. Those fellas might've sounded a little scared—they've a right to, by God—but they weren't terrified an' about to break like last night. Mr. Swain showed us the beasties can kill us, an' that's a terrible thing to be sure. But the sea could'a killed me any day of my life. The Mexicans might kill you soldiers if you ever get where you're going." His expression hardened. "But as long as I can fight the sea an' you soldiers can fight your enemies, *as long as our monsters* can *be killed*, we ain't helpless, see? Only helpless turns to hopeless, an' Mr. Swain—and you, Captain Lewis—showed us we ain't helpless a'tall."

Lieutenant Burton was openly staring at Captain Holland in near amazement. Like every graduate of the military academy, he'd been immersed in math, history, engineering, and "natural and experimental philosophy." The latter encompassing everything from astronomy and magnetism to drawing and geography. Tactics were taught, of course, but even they drew heavily on history—and classical philosophy.

Lewis managed a small smile. "Well said, Captain Holland. I never dreamed sailors could be so philosophical."

"There's nothin' more philosophical than sailors, whether they've read Plato or not."

"Plato *did* liken philosophers to ships' navigators," Burton allowed.

Lewis actually grinned. "But was he a sailor?"

"I misremember," Holland said. "He talked like one. So did Socrates."

In spite of the trauma of the night before, the day proceeded in a remarkably ordinary fashion. The sky was clear, and the air, though humid, wasn't terribly hot. Men either continued to labor, grouping equipment and supplies for transport, or they drilled. All the men under Lewis's practical command, even most of the sailors, were proficient with muskets, and they had a lot of them. Part of *Mary Riggs*'s cargo had been four hundred of the newer M1835 Springfields, in crates, destined for General Scott's army. They were the same .69 caliber and functionally identical to the M1816 variations already carried by Olayne's artillerymen, but were newer, more robust, and somewhat better shaped. Perhaps most significant, they'd been built to standards exacting enough to permit almost perfect parts interchangeability.

They weren't needed at present, however, because the sailors could be issued weapons recovered from the fallen. The arming of "colored" sailors precipitated some grumbling (though not from Burton this time), until Lewis angrily reminded the men of their circumstances and how important it was to remain united and use every willing hand. Resistance vanished surprisingly quickly. Testing Burton further, Lewis required the dragoons to familiarize everyone, including the sailors, with their Hall carbines because there were extras of those as well. Burton made no objection. Finally, Lewis ordered Olayne to run an ongoing, rotating school of the piece at each of their six cannon positions, requiring him to use the howitzer drill he preferred. (Much as Lewis had admired him, Major Ringgold had prescribed different drills for guns and howitzers, some of the men's duties reversed for no good reason Lewis could see.) Captain Holland's remarks about "helpless turning to hopeless" had made a deep impression, and Lewis was determined that no man would find himself helpless if there was *any* manner of weapon at hand, no matter what horrors emerged from the woods.

And even the horror quickly faded as the day wore on. Constant labor and activity tired the men's bodies and occupied their minds. The term "lizardbirds" quickly caught on to describe the odd little flying things that capered in the trees, screeching and cawing and contending with "ordinary" birds just as aggressive as themselves. And the men used the term derisively, not in fear, just as they'd say "buzzard." The rising stench of the dead "dragon" became unreasonable by afternoon, but it remained constant proof the frightening things could be killed. Occasionally, a vagrant breeze carried the scent to the remaining horses. They rebelled again at first, but eventually grew accustomed to, if not comfortable with, it. Lewis wanted it gone but wasn't about to try to move it with horses. By evening, he decided to burn it. Despite his concern about the dry conditions, it was simply understood there'd be watch fires after dark and fatigue parties had been dragging up brush all day. Lewis directed that a wide clearing be made around the corpse and more wood heaped upon it. All the long timbers they could tear off the wreck had gone into the palisade, so when the nearby brush was finally exhausted, Captain Holland set his sailors to gathering smaller debris: broken crates and barrels, the main and mizzen top platforms, the ship's wheel, even the shattered furniture and fittings retrieved from his cabin after they pried the collapsed deck off. There'd be enough wood to last the night and even burn the monster, but they'd have to venture farther afield if they stayed there longer.

Lewis was exhausted again, his side aching more than ever, when he sat on one of a dozen or so recovered camp stools and waited for night to fall. It was the first time he'd been off his feet all day, and they ached badly as well. He hadn't carried heavy hull planks or exerted himself in that line, but he'd been everywhere, supervising or observing everything, as much to help as just be seen. He'd assisted with Olayne's artillery schools, mostly describing the differences between foot and horse tactics, finding eager listeners. Many were interested to hear about the battles of Palo Alto, Resaca de la Palma, Monterrey, and the dozens of smaller actions and skirmishes along the way, so he used that interest to keep pressing the advantages of rapid maneuver, deployment, and expert gunnery. He knew Olayne was anxious to learn more. He suspected some, like Sergeant McNabb, already *did* know more.

In any event, he'd tired his voice as well and now waited for dark with a measure of dread, worried about Captain Anson and his party. He wished he could've sat up on the bones of the wreck, to see farther—and especially to the north, where the scout had gone—but there simply wasn't a place to do so safely anymore.

"Her whole rotten frame'll collapse without hull timbers to stiffen it." Captain Holland sighed wearily as if reading Lewis's thoughts, easing onto a stool beside him. He snorted. "It'll probably go down slow an' creaky, like I just did."

A throat cleared behind them, and they turned to see Private Willis holding a pair of steaming plates. "Which I brung supper," he announced in a tone suggesting the effort almost killed him. The cook fire had burned through the day, wood smoke from local tree branches tarry and dark and hard to breathe, like pinyon pine, but now welcome because it discouraged mosquitoes. "Supper for *both* of you," Willis stressed resentfully, "even though I ain't no *sailor's* orderly."

"Heaven forbid," Lewis acknowledged, receiving the plate of slimy salt pork mixed with beans.

"Obliged," Holland said. Willis nodded, oblivious to the sarcasm. "Does there happen to be a fork? Or spoon?" Holland pressed. Willis started, as if he'd forgotten, then pulled a pair of bone-handled spoons from his pocket. Wiping each on his filthy trousers, he handed them over. "If there ain't nothin' else, I'll get *me* somethin' to eat."

Lewis waved the spoon. "Go ahead. After you do, rig a place for me to sleep, if you can. I hope to get some tonight."

"Which that's what them four big tents are for. Dry storage an' officers' cots," Willis complained. "I helped set 'em up, an' don't even get to sleep in one."

"Doesn't seem fair, does it, Private?"

"No sir."

"Well, I'm sure you'll manage." There wasn't room within the palisade for wedge tents for all the men, but with the weather like it was, few would want them anyway. And it looked to Lewis like sufficient shelter from any possible rain had been rigged from sails if it was needed. "Report to Sergeant McNabb and see if he has other duties for you. Otherwise, I'll see you in the morning."

Willis sulked away, and Holland shook his head at his back. "Strange man."

Lewis scooped steaming slop from his plate and ate it before glancing at Holland. "He doesn't strike me as a very enthusiastic soldier. Clearly, he's even less keen to be a servant."

"Why put up with his sass? Throw him back an' pick another."

Lewis chuckled. "Better a bad servant than a bad soldier. Besides, his 'sass,' as you call it, amuses me. Particularly under the circumstances." His expression turned dark. "I'm even rather sympathetic when it comes to discontented servants. There's no real comparison, of course, but my father owned several slaves to work his Tennessee farm, and we disagreed so strongly about the very continued existence of slavery that we didn't exchange a word for the last five years of his life. My mother was long dead when he passed, and I immediately freed his slaves and sold the farm."

"A Whig soldier from Tennessee," Holland wondered aloud, "fightin' a war for a Democrat president—from Tennessee, no less."

"Perhaps a Whig," Lewis confessed uncomfortably, reluctant to talk politics even with a sailor, "but not the anti-Masonic sort."

Holland fingered the golden square and compass hanging from his watch fob and accepted that. "Still, I wondered about your willingness to arm my colored sailors. My opinion on slavery's a bit mixed since I've seen every sort. It's been with us since the beginnin' of time an' still is— regardless of race—across most of the world. And I've seen a *lot* of the world." He ate for a moment before continuing. "In ancient times, an' even today, conquered people're enslaved in war. Seems kindlier to work a man than kill him, I reckon, an' a lot of those slaves get absorbed by the conquerin' power. Become part of it. Most Injins adopt the captives they let live. But I never skippered no damn blackbirder, an' I'm against takin' slaves for commercial reasons, or a man's *race* bein' the justification for it. A man's a man, no matter what color he is, an' any man who sails with me'll

Mexico, along with its slow drip, drip, drip of blood, only intensified the antagonism.

Well, Leonor simmered, growing angry now, *Lewis wasn't there. He didn't see. Didn't have happen to him . . . what I did.* Of course *Father hates Mexican soldiers, and so do I.*

The fact her mother had been Mexican and she and her brothers were half never affected her passion for revenge. They'd *all* been Texans— Texians, then—regardless of their heritage, and the things Santa Anna's *soldados* did . . . And now they were fighting Santa Anna again. *What did Lewis Cayce expect?*

Dwyer's horse suddenly screeched and hopped, nearly flinging the young dragoon into a tree. He managed to keep his mount but immediately fumbled for his carbine while Boogerbear, Sal Hernandez, and some of the other men surged forward, raising their weapons as well.

"Hold your fire, damn you!" Captain Anson hissed. He'd raised his own rifle but was just pointing it generally at a large moving shape the size of a freight wagon.

"What the hell?" Boogerbear rumbled.

Leonor realized with a thrill of terror she quickly subdued that the thing looked like a gigantic cross between a turtle and a horned toad. It was heavily armored, with spiky projections around its protective shell, and wore another equally formidable shell on its head like a helmet. Bony protrusions protected small, beady red eyes. Four short legs supported it, at right angles to its body, and a strikingly long, spike-studded tail whipped menacingly behind it as it raised its head and snuffled the air.

"It can't see us," Dwyer whispered shakily. "Not well, at any rate."

"It might hear us, you fool," Anson hissed back. "Or *smell* us. Be silent. The rest of you, back away an' give it a wide berth."

They backed their nervous horses as carefully as they could, each snapping twig renewing the creature's belligerent attention, but soon they'd gained enough distance to go around. It utterly ignored them then, rooting violently along the base of a fallen tree, splintering rotten wood and greedily eating things in and around it. "That's why there's so little deadfall in the forest," Boogerbear lowly rasped. "Critters like that tear dead trees to shreds."

"'Critters like that'?" Dwyer softly, incredulously quoted. "Where have you seen 'critters like that' before?"

Boogerbear glanced at the dragoon and shrugged. "Not sayin' I have, but that's what it does. Good thing it don't see too good. Like a armadillo, it don't have to, I guess. What's gonna take ahold of it? Even the dragon that attacked the camp couldn't harm it much."

"What could?" murmured one of the riflemen in a nervous tone. No one replied, and they pressed on to the north.

The ground became more broken and they crossed a number of dry, rocky streambeds before they finally found a meager, stagnant pool of water. Flocks of lizardbirds exploded away as they approached, some clasping small fish in their jaws. The water looked foul and slimy and infested with bugs. Anson wouldn't even let the horses drink it. Not yet.

The forest began to thin, occasionally interspersed with grassy clearings, yet even as they finally smelled salt air and caught occasional glimmering glimpses of the sea they were reminded how fragile all their reasonable expectations had become because the clearings harbored the strangest beasts so far. Monstrous animals of different sorts as big as or bigger than a house grazed contentedly, also apparently oblivious to their presence. Some had long necks and tails, pulling and eating grass with great sweeping motions of disproportionately small heads, or plucking clusters of ferny leaves with piano key–like teeth from tree limbs high above. Others, lower to the ground but with heads just as excessively large, seemed to have no necks at all except for what was concealed under frilled and horny facial armor, like the "horned turtle," only smoother and without a segmented appearance. Captain Anson took his patrol wide of them as well.

"Buffalo act as peaceful as can be," he told them softly, "until somethin' gets close enough for 'em to notice."

Lieutenant Dwyer had had enough, and his voice carried a note of hysteria when he spoke. "Well, these aren't buffalo, any more than that . . . thing eating a damned tree in the forest. I don't know *what* they are. Does anyone? How could such creatures exist without someone knowing about them?!"

There were mutters of agreement, and Leonor even heard the usually unflappable Sal Hernandez grimly say, *"Estamos muertos y en el purgatorio."*

"I figure they're elephants," Boogerbear said reassuringly. "I seen drawin's of 'em once. In a book."

"Elephants like those things?" Dwyer demanded, almost shrill.

Boogerbear hesitated, then confessed, "Not *just* like 'em, but I guess there might be different kinds. Maybe these're the sorts from these parts."

"I don't think there's supposed to be elephants of *any* sort around here," Leonor said, carefully controlling her tone. *Damned if I'll get all squeaky, like Dwyer,* she insisted to herself. Boogerbear shrugged as if it made no difference to him.

Her father must've heard the exchange but rode on in silence a moment before turning in his saddle to respond to them all in a voice just as low and calm as Boogerbear's. "Yeah, the critters here are mighty strange. No question. I've never seen or heard of anything like 'em. But what's even stranger is it's a little past noon an' we've come about seven miles. No *wave* carried our ship that far overland, leavin' no sign of its passage." He gestured around at the undisturbed foliage and dry ground, obvious to them all. "*Of course* somethin's *very* damn wrong, so we better get hold of ourselves an' stay sharp-eyed an' thoughtful. We're surrounded by mysteries an' unknown threats. Focusin' on what things *ain't*—moderately self-evident by now—don't help us watch out for what *is*." He urged his horse ahead and continued briskly, "The sea's close, an' I suggest we concentrate on lookin' for signs of habitation. At least a proper road or trail that'll lead to such."

They were almost surprised when they found it; a rough, double-rutted pathway made by wagons or carts that extended as far to the east and west as they could see in the gloom of overhanging trees. They paid it little heed at the moment because the wind and surf were roaring loud and the white-capped sea was clearly visible beyond the final tree line. Most gripping of all, however, was the scene on the beach and in the water beyond. Another ship lay broken, right at the water's edge, foaming surf wrapping around and seething past to climb what would've been a picturesque white sand beach, if not for all the debris deposited there.

Leonor's heart plummeted at the sight until she saw living men, perhaps two or three hundred, and horses as well. Nearly all were moving about and doing things. A long line of motionless, sky-blue-clad bodies was stretched out on the sand, but other lines of men, in drawers and shirt-sleeves or naked, were knee-deep in the surf, handing kegs, crates, and other baggage out of the wreck and collecting it all in large heaps above the tide line. Cook fires smoldered in pits in the sand, and shelters had been rigged for other motionless men, but though there'd been no apparent effort to establish defensive works, two 12pdr field howitzers stood sentinel over the busy survivors.

Leonor knew little of ships, but even she could tell this had been the stores and personnel transport USS *Commissary*, her larger size and distinctive features still recognizable, if even more thoroughly smashed than *Mary Riggs*'s. Perhaps the sea had scattered her splintered flotsam considerably more, but it also looked like she'd somehow fallen *farther*. That made an odd kind of sense. Leonor couldn't be sure, of course, since the land was so generally flat, but it stood to reason sea level was lower than where *Mary Riggs* had come to rest. If the ships actually *had* somehow "fallen" from the same plane, *Commissary* would've come down harder, and it was a wonder there weren't even more human forms lying still in the sand, and any horses alive at all. What suddenly filled Leonor with hope, however, were the two other ships riding at anchor some distance away from shore. One was the steamer *Isidra*, a haze of coal smoke streaming downwind from her stack. The other could only be the former British frigate they'd seen right before the storm. Both were largely dismasted, though the frigate still had the lower sections of her foremast and mainmast. *Isidra* had no masts at all and was relying entirely on her engine. It looked like she'd found the other ship and brought her here under tow. Boats were plying back and forth between them, as well as between the ships and shore.

"Well," Captain Anson said with satisfaction, "not exactly a 'settlement,' but Captain Cayce should be satisfied to learn we're not entirely stranded, after all."

"That steamer can't carry everyone," Dwyer pointed out, probably coming to the same count Leonor made. *Close to six hundred men including those we left behind, but not counting those still afloat.*

"No, but it can fetch other ships."

An alarmed, wind-muffled shouting greeted the riders as they emerged onto the beach. A dozen or so infantrymen snatched bayonet-bristling muskets and black, white-strapped cartridge boxes from tripods and hurried in their direction, laboring through the fine, snowy sand and throwing little geysers from churning, hobnailed shoes.

"Hold up," called Leonor's father. "Those fellas seem a little on edge. We'll wait for 'em to come to us."

Captain Anson and his Rangers, including Leonor, had been the first to appear, and their irregular dress clearly left the approaching men unsure whether to point their muskets at them as they neared, but Dwyer's dragoons and the riflemen noticeably reassured them. They looked calm, though winded, by the time they came to a stop. The sergeant in charge promptly shouldered his musket and brought his left arm across his body to perform a proper salute. "Lieutenant," he said to Dwyer, eyes on Anson. "Sergeant Ulrich, B Company, Third Regiment of Pennsylvania Volunteer Infantry. Enlisted for the duration," he quickly added with a glance back at Dwyer. Leonor chuckled inwardly. In spite of everything, the sergeant's first impulse was to deter a regular officer's contempt for short-term volunteers whose enlistments invariably seemed to expire right before major actions. Dwyer and Anson returned the salute, fingers touching their small wheel-hat visors, palm out, and Leonor's father told the man who they were. Regardless of rank, Sergeant Ulrich seemed at a loss for who to address and compromised by glancing at both as he spoke. "Off one of the other ships, I guess? Please come with me. Colonel De Russy'll be glad to see you and hear your news."

"Lead the way," Anson said.

"Private Cox, you're with me," Ulrich told a tall, skinny, towheaded kid. "The rest of you, carry on." He glanced back at Anson. "Have to keep a guard up. Things . . ." He hesitated and frowned. "Things seem very queer hereabouts, and the lads're uneasy."

"You don't say?" Anson replied dryly. "Dismount," he told his small command. "We'll lead the horses from here." He stepped down himself, unconsciously removing the pommel holsters from his saddle and, like always, draping them over his shoulder. Drawing a lot of stares, combining relief, concern, and tired indifference from men working to salvage the wreck, they followed Sergeant Ulrich and Private Cox through the well-organized labor up to a place where the forest protruded farther onto the beach. There was another unmanned 12pdr and a large number of tents and other shelters rigged directly to the trees. Leonor noted with surprise there were two more horses wearing unfamiliar saddles, blankets, and saddle rolls, held by an infantryman. Then it dawned on her the equipment wasn't unfamiliar at all. *Those are* Mexican *horses!* A glance at her father told her he'd noticed as well, and his expression sharpened.

"Just a little farther," Sergeant Ulrich said. A broad fly had been erected under the trees, and quite a few men were seated on folding wooden chairs in a semicircle around a smallish table covered with bottles and a large porcelain pitcher.

"Stay here," Anson snapped at the men around him, tossing his horse's reins to one of the riflemen and advancing with Dwyer toward the others, several of whom rose at his approach. Disregarding the order, Boogerbear, Sal Hernandez, and Leonor followed as they always did. Most of the men under the fly were American officers, apparently sitting closer to the table in order of seniority, but there were also a couple of civilians. One was a slight, tired-looking man of about forty, wearing spectacles, a civilian vest, and matching trousers. The fabric was dark but seemed stained with blood. The once-fluffy cravat around his neck was crumpled and soiled. The other was very large and round, and despite the sweat running on red, pudgy cheeks above a bristly beard, he still wore a coat and was dressed all in black.

As suspected, there was also a young Mexican officer dressed in a medium blue tailcoat with scarlet collar, epaulettes, and cuffs, and dark blue breeches with scarlet seam stripes, tucked in a pair of black knee boots. To Leonor's surprise, the eyes regarding her were almost purple, like fire-blued steel, and the man's dark hair had a reddish tinge. By contrast, the enlisted companion behind him wore only fragments of military garb and looked half-black, half-Indian. Despite the obvious fact the officer, at least, had taken pains to make himself presentable, his face appeared haunted, and his uniform was anything but new and crisp. Leonor watched her father studiously ignore the Mexicans as he presented himself and Dwyer.

A heavyset officer with graying side whiskers and a wisp of black hair on his sweaty, uncovered head was wearing the shoulder boards of a lieutenant colonel. Smiling, he stood and shook Anson's and Dwyer's hands. "I'm Colonel Ruberdeau De Russy, congressional representative of the commonwealth of Pennsylvania. Perhaps you've heard of me," he added, smiling wider. "My beloved constituents call me 'Rube.'" Noting the blank stares, he sighed and tugged self-deprecatingly at his uniform. "I'm currently otherwise occupied, as you see, by Governor Shunk's appointment." He frowned. "I'm proud to serve my country, of course, but I fear dear Governor Shunk's true purpose was to whisk me off before the next election. I've considered challenging him. He's not a well man, you know." De Russy shook his head and beamed again. "But by God, what a relief it is to see you!" He gestured back at the rest of the party. "I assume you came ashore from one of the other ships? Was it *Xenophon* or *Mary Riggs*?" He waved up and down the coast. "Where does she lie?" He nodded out to sea. "I hope she's in better condition than *those* floating wrecks. I find this delay in reaching our destination most inconvenient!"

Lieutenant Dwyer could only stare at the man incredulously, realizing that no matter how well trained or professional these volunteer troops might be, politically appointed officers, often with no military experience at all, were one of the biggest problems with them.

Anson glanced quickly at the Mexicans, then cleared his voice. "I'm relieved to see you as well, Colonel De Russy. More than I can say. But I regret to inform you *Mary Riggs* is in no better shape than *Commissary*, an' *she* 'lies' onshore some distance to the south, nowhere near the water. Like you, we suffered casualties, an' had other . . . unexpected adventures. I don't know where *Xenophon* is, an' don't have any idea where *we* are. One thing's sure: this ain't the Yucatán shore we saw in the distance before that damn storm struck."

There was a babble of voices and De Russy sat back and scowled at the Mexican officer. "Oddly enough, that's what this fellow's been trying to tell us. My apologies, gentlemen. Allow me to present Alferez—which means 'Ensign,' I'm told—Ramon Lara, representing a detachment of a light mounted regiment. He came to parley, under a flag of truce," he warned the Ranger.

"This is *not* Yucatán!" the young man insisted in carefully precise English.

"Then where are we?" Anson demanded hotly. "Farther west? Where?"

"If I knew, I would tell you, but it cannot be to the west. All should be *la jungla* . . . jungle? Yes, jungle there. And here it *should* be . . . much different. This is nowhere I or any of my men know." He sighed. "At the request of the government of Yucatán," he said with a defiant glance at Anson, whom he apparently recognized as a Ranger, "my patrol was scouting the coastline for smugglers bringing arms to the rebels." He looked back at the others. "But we also were much to the south of here. *This* should be the bottom of the sea! An unnatural storm came suddenly upon us and swept up my entire command as if by a tornado! It carried us into the sky and dropped us to earth, but *not* where we were before." He looked back at Anson. "Six of my *soldados* and nine horses were killed. We could only mount all my men by distributing the baggage. But we too had further 'adventures' and were set upon by terrible monsters that could not be killed by bullets." He looked at De Russy. "We fled to the coast, and here we found you." He shrugged. "It appeared you had been ravaged by the same hellish storm. The same . . . *la tormenta.*" He frowned. "We may be enemies, but all are the enemies of hell. Seeing no alternative, I trusted that you would be honorable enough to respect a truce while we confer as common victims of El Diablo. The Devil."

"Nonsense!" cried a lieutenant. "Storms of hell? Monsters immune to bullets? This is the same madness that's taken many here!"

"You just came ashore, Lieutenant," De Russy rebuked him in a tired tone, completely unlike his greeting.

"You've seen the things the Mexican spoke of?" Anson asked.

"Not as such," De Russy demurred. "Some of the fellows, better woodsmen than I—and who isn't!—described disconcerting tracks. Other men fired on grotesque shadows annoying the dead last night." He bit his lip. "But that's only to be expected, isn't it?" He rolled his eyes upward. "And then there are these confounded birds, always swooping and nipping. Vicious little brutes! But no, we've been too busy saving ourselves and our equipment to mount a proper scout, and no one has precisely *seen* anything well enough to give a credible description"—his eyes narrowed at the impetuous lieutenant—"unless you credit the tales from the ships."

"They claim there are swarms of things in the water, like fish, that behave like small, insatiable sharks," interjected the smaller civilian."Some men killed in the storm were buried at sea, and the sailors swear they were torn to shreds before they even sank from sight." He nodded at the men working around the wreck. "Thank God whatever got them doesn't seem to take to shallow water." He looked back at Anson, shaking his head. "But other sailors claim to have seen bigger things in the distance, *huge* things, swimming like porpoises but with great, rainbow-colored fins." He pursed his lips. "The trauma of tragedy does things to the mind."

Standing with exhausted effort, he extended his hand as well. "Dr. Francis Newlin, at your service—though I hope you don't need me just now."

"Dr. Newlin's a civilian physician engaged by the officers of the Third Pennsylvania," put in a ruddy-faced major sitting by De Russy, "and thank God for him. He's better than the army quacks pretending to be so busy on *Isidra*. I brought a couple over this morning to help attend the hurt, but I fear their incompetence has only aggravated the doctor's fatigue. He came here at our request for refreshment when our Mexican visitors came to call."

"Speaking of 'refreshment,'" Anson strongly hinted.

De Russy looked stricken. "Oh my! Yes, of course, please forgive me! I find myself so distracted. Barca! Cool water for these officers and their men at once!" He looked apologetically at Anson. "Or wine, if you prefer . . . ?"

Anson shook his head, watching a young black man, little more than a boy in army dress, hurry to seize the big ceramic pitcher and a cluster of tin cups. "Just water, if you please."

"You brought no 'quacks,' Major Reed," Newlin admonished wearily, "only men of good will, insufficiently trained. I'm content with them as long as they do as I ask and learn from it. Still, I would've been utterly overwhelmed if not for Mademoiselle Mercure, and particularly Mistress Wilde. They're a better balm to the hurt than laudanum."

"Women? Here?" Lieutenant Dwyer asked, finally finding his voice after taking a cup of water from young Barca.

"A depressing number of the creatures, I fear," grumbled the other civilian from within his beard-covered face. Where De Russy was heavyset, this man was positively obese. "That British ship out there used to be the old fifty-gun *Tiger*. I'd wager she hasn't more than twenty guns now, since betting on a certainty isn't a sin. In any event, she was transporting European diplomats and merchants out of Vera Cruz. More to avoid fever than war, I'm sure, but there are certainly twenty or more women of all shapes and ages in her even now. The young ladies Dr. Newlin spoke of were indecently unaccompanied and brazenly resisted efforts to restrain them on the ship when they learned we had such dreadful casualties." He shook his head sadly. "Women these days." Looking back up, he introduced himself without bothering to stand. "Reverend Samuel Harkin, Congressman De Russy's guest. I can do nothing to alleviate our dear soldiers' aches and injuries, but can minister to them and recommend their immortal souls to Almighty God."

"Then maybe you ought to do that, an' bury the dead ones quick," Leonor practically snapped, surprising herself by speaking up. At least she'd used her "man voice," more than second nature now, but Reverend Harkin's tone and attitude stabbed her with a spike of annoyance. Chagrined to find everyone suddenly staring at her, she churned unapologetically on. "There *are* monsters in the woods, an' we've 'credibly' seen 'em. They *will* scavenge your dead if you don't get 'em decently in the ground before the smell attracts 'em in their hundreds. We've seen that too," she added grimly.

"My son's right," Captain Anson said, proceeding to give a quick, succinct, and dispassionate account of the wreck of *Mary Riggs* and its aftermath, the "dragon" that attacked the camp and killed Lieutenant Swain, and finally their journey here. Presenting the report in the same absolutely certain, matter-of-fact way he'd delivered others to General Zachary Taylor, De Russy—who paled noticeably throughout—had no choice but to believe it entirely.

"My God," De Russy murmured. "Yes, we must bury those poor fellows at once. I'd hoped to carry them to Vera Cruz, perhaps in *Xenophon* or *Mary Riggs*," he explained. "A false hope now. And *Isidra* can't even take *us*, or tow *Tiger* any farther, as I understand it. Her engine has been worked very hard." He took a deep, regretful breath, glancing around. "In light of Captain Anson's report, I'm less content to continue the plan already begun, but I don't see we have any choice."

"What plan is that?" asked Anson.

"Major Reed?" De Russy prompted, and the red-faced officer cleared his throat. Leonor could tell he wasn't happy. "*Isidra*'s not undamaged herself, but she's the only vessel that can continue on to Vera Cruz and report this disaster. Obviously, as Colonel De Russy said, she can't carry us all." He frowned. "Can't carry what she has already, it seems. Colonel Wicklow of the First Infantry is the senior officer present and has decided to put his troops, horses, and military supplies ashore so De Russy can establish an impregnable position where all can gather and wait in safety for the transports Wicklow will dispatch from the fleet at Vera Cruz." His expression soured. "This will, incidentally, make room for *Tiger*'s many passengers—and all their baggage, I presume. It wouldn't do to inconvenience or upset wealthy, influential Europeans," he added ironically. "With their history, I doubt Mexico would ally with the French, but Colonel Wicklow still imagines the British might join the war on their side." He spread his hands. "In any event, it shouldn't take more than a few weeks for sufficient transport for everyone to return."

"Weeks," Leonor murmured.

"An' you, Major Reed?" Anson asked. "How many officers is Colonel Wicklow leavin' us?"

Clearly ill at ease, Reed shook his head. "My apologies in advance, but Colonel Wicklow believes, and I quote: 'ably assisted by a few professional junior officers, Colonel De Russy should provide sufficient leadership for the volunteers and regulars entrusted to him.'" There were indignant sounds, and Reed glanced around in embarrassment, then focused on De Russy's disappointed expression. "Personally, I believe Colonel Wicklow is . . . misguided, and I'd prefer to remain here myself, but he wants his senior officers to build his staff at Vera Cruz and prepare for the men's arrival. As if that would've been done in any event," he added with a touch of bitterness. "So. Unless Major Philips is found safe with *Xenophon*, Captain Cayce is next in line of seniority." He sighed. "At least you have Cayce. I knew him before the war, and he's a good man."

De Russy shifted uncomfortably in his seat. "Yes. Well. I suppose we must manage. Thank you for your candor, Major Reed, and I appreciate your personal sentiments." He glanced around at the others. "But it looks as though we'll need to make more room for the regular infantry and their supplies, as well as more animals." He glanced at Anson, Dwyer, Boogerbear, Sal, and Leonor in front of him. "In addition to *Mary Riggs*'s survivors, of course. We'll have to see to moving them here, and search for *Xenophon*." He shook his head and blinked. "*Mary Riggs* truly is *miles* inland, you say?"

"Probably eight or so," Anson confirmed.

"Extraordinary," De Russy breathed. "Is that consistent with the distance you traveled, Ensign Lara?" he asked.

The young Mexican officer shook his head. "I believe we first found ourselves perhaps four or five *leguas* distant? About fifteen miles? It took us all of yesterday to reach the coast, then much of today, following the shore, to find you here."

"And you saw . . . monsters like those Captain Anson described?"

Lara drew in a deep breath, possibly surprised he'd been believed. "*Sí.* Yes. Many with the horns and long necks. Some like the 'dragon,' though not as large, but the ones we saw moved in groups. They were *very* frightening," he confessed, "since they seemed intelligent enough to coordinate their pursuit. I'm sure only our numbers and occasional shots kept them away."

"Did you ever pass a settlement? Find water?"

Lara hesitated. "Of all the things we saw, that may have been most disturbing. We came across ancient structures similar in ways to those we should expect here, but they were *not* all ruins—and not where they should be. One was recently abandoned and showed evidence of being sacked.

"We also passed a settlement of sorts on the banks of a stream a short distance to the west, but the people there were naked savages, and my men were afraid to approach them. Even the Indians in my detachment could barely understand one word in ten." He shook his head. "For that and other reasons, they seemed too strange to trust."

That admission struck Leonor harder than anything else Lara said, since it implied he trusted *them*—enemies—more than other people he saw in this land that should be his.

De Russy stared searchingly at the man. "Then I presume another reason you approached us was to surrender?"

Lara straightened in his chair. "No, Colonel. I will not surrender. I would, however, be pleased to maintain the current truce for our mutual benefit."

"How would that benefit us?" Anson growled.

Lara blinked at him, surprised by his vehemence. "Instead of the added uncertainty and possible nuisance of a hostile force in your proximity, you gain a friendly one of excellent horsemen who, while not familiar with where we are at present, are accustomed to life on *la frontera*."

"Extraordinary," De Russy repeated, then grunted. "I'll take it under advisement. Captain Anson, what are your views on my other priorities?"

Anson tore his gaze from the bold young Mexican and managed a nod at De Russy. "Sounds as good a plan as any, but inhabited by 'savages' or not, I recommend we find a town or something to fortify instead of this exposed beach. Captain Cayce built a fort around our wreck, an' it was a good thing he did. You should at least move a little inland an' cut trees to build a stronghold. You *will* need the protection," he said with certainty, "an' it'll give the men something to do. As for us"—he paused and pulled his watch from his vest and glanced at it before looking out from under the fly at the day—"I'd like to have a quick look at the settlement the . . . ensign described. Just myself, a couple of Rangers, an' half the mounted riflemen. At the same time, Captain Cayce needs to know we found you. It won't take near as long to get back as it did to get here. A party guided by Corporal Beeryman and the rest of the riflemen"—he gestured at Boogerbear—"*should* make it back before dark. At the same time, I agree with Alferez Lara that safety requires numbers. Have you any men or horses who can relieve Lieutenant Dwyer and his dragoons? They could use the time to find you a more defensible position nearby."

Leonor knew her father well enough to understand he wanted rid of Dwyer. He might be a good officer under ordinary circumstances, but he'd displayed both imprudence and fear. Not a good combination to lead a detachment back to *Mary Riggs*. Just as important, his men's Hall carbines might be excellent for combat against human enemies at close range, but were too underpowered to much discourage the dangerous creatures they'd seen.

De Russy made a moue. "I can certainly use your dragoons. I've no mounted men at all. I do have some horses, of course, and you can take your pick. They were intended for the dragoons or artillery in any event. For men, all I have are infantry. Perhaps a few know how to ride," he added doubtfully. "I'll ask for volunteers."

Leonor was sure more than a "few" could ride, but how many would willingly leave the illusory safety of this place?

"Thank you, sir."

"But what of you, Captain Anson?" Reverend Harkin grumbled. "Will your scout have sufficient numbers for safety?"

Anson grinned. "From what I've seen, I'd say not—if I was coverin' a lot of ground between two places the monsters are already gatherin' at. For spyin' on Lara's 'savages,' the half dozen I'll take may be too many."

"But *you* don't even know where you're going," interjected Dr. Newlin.

"Just gotta backtrack the Mexicans," said Boogerbear as if anyone should've thought of that. "Long as they're tellin' the truth."

De Russy looked at Ramon Lara. "Will you lead Captain Anson back and show him what you saw?"

Anson seemed taken aback, but Leonor seethed at the idea. Lara wasn't just a Mexican; he was a Mexican *soldier*. She shuddered.

"I will," Lara said slowly, "if Captain Anson will promise not to murder me."

"You'll be perfectly safe. From *him* at any rate," De Russy assured him. When he stood and spoke again, he was talking to everyone. "In the meantime, we'll continue salvaging what we can as the regular infantry comes ashore." He looked at Major Reed. "When does Colonel Wicklow plan to abandon . . ." He smiled ironically. "Leave us?"

"As soon as he can, sir. Morning at the latest."

"Very well. We all have a lot to do. Ensign Lara," he said to the Mexican as he also rose from his chair, "I'll give your offer of cooperation my utmost consideration. Perhaps I'll have an answer by the time you return. I'm sure Captain Anson will have a recommendation by then as well. One way or another."

CHAPTER 7

"Y ou don't say much," Alferez Ramon Lara cheerfully told Leonor. To her dismay, he'd chosen to fall back from where he'd been riding beside her father, pointing the way down the rough, rutted road they'd crossed earlier. The fact he was alone with them, having sent his companion to explain to his other men, didn't make Leonor any easier around him. His threadbare uniform was different from that worn by the men who'd killed her mother and two brothers, and done . . . the things they had to her, but that didn't make much difference either. It was close enough—*he* was close enough—that her skin crawled just to be around him. She couldn't have rationally explained it any easier than her father could. She didn't hate *Mexicans* any more than she could hate herself or her mother, or Sal Hernandez, whom she loved like a brother, but the uniform this Mexican wore made him a part of a separate, infinitely more barbaric species in her mind. She couldn't help it.

"You only have about twenty men," Leonor scornfully snapped.

Lara ignored her tone and shrugged. "You have a good eye for tracks. I have twenty-four." He raised his voice so Anson and the riflemen could hear. "Some will be joining us momentarily."

Anson whirled his horse around, and he and Leonor already had their Patersons pointed at Lara's face. He blinked, carefully keeping his hands away from his sword and pistol. "You Rangers have a reputation as killers, even down here. I admit I'm surprised to meet people who actually match the stories about them. But I told you about our reinforcements as a warning, not a threat. May I call my friends? There will only be four." He smiled at Leonor. "We will then be equal in numbers."

Anson hesitated, then nodded. Lara took a wooden whistle from inside his tunic, hanging from his neck, and blew a single, piercing blast. Several moments passed before four horsemen appeared, approaching quickly but cautiously through the trees. To Leonor, only one—a sergeant—looked more like a soldier than the Rangers themselves. They acted like soldiers, however, two neatly attaching themselves to the back of the small column, while the other two positioned themselves on the flanks.

"You see?" Lara said. "They are only here to help. They were not even close enough to watch us properly."

"We would've killed 'em if we saw 'em. You too," Leonor hissed.

Lara nodded somberly. "That's why I told them to hold back until I signaled."

Anson holstered his revolver and spat, before fishing a cigar from his vest and putting it in his mouth. He didn't light it. Turning, he started the column again. "I agreed there was safety in numbers, but not for what we're doing."

Lara nodded as he urged his horse up alongside the Ranger. "But you also said we were already too many for stealth. Better to be safe. We don't know if the savages at the village will be friendly, but we do know the monsters aren't." He lowered his voice and for the first time, sounded only like a young man, not a soldier. "I confess I'm afraid. Afraid of how we got here, of the monsters, the people and places we saw, and now I'm afraid of you Norte Americanos. All this has been too much for me, for my men, and most are not even real *soldados*, you know. Some *have* been at one time or another, but now? We're more like . . . *policia*. Provincial police. The war has been very far away for the most part, and my men were glad not to be in it." He shrugged again. "But we still had our duty, and so we were here. To be . . . taken up by whatever took us. I *swear* we know nothing more about how or why than you—and we're just as afraid as you *should* be unless you're insane."

Lara straightened in his saddle, and the soldier was back. "So. You didn't kill us and we won't kill you. We must work together against the things that will, at least until this *pesadilla*, this nightmare, is over."

Anson was nodding slightly, a scowl on his face. "For now. Later, we'll see."

Leonor caught his quick glance back at her and sent him a withering glare.

They followed the road another two miles before Lara took them off it to the south. "The road looks little used—I wonder why?—but it leads right into the village. We came around it, crossing upstream after watching the savages from a little rise. The same rise is on this side of the stream, and we should see them from there as well." The forest held a haze of wood smoke now and the echoing sounds of talking, chopping, and the occasional snap of large limbs being broken into firewood. They were very close. "We leave the horses here," Lara said, and his sergeant detailed two men to hold theirs while two riflemen did the same for Anson. Six of them crept up the rise, finally reaching the crest. From there, they crawled on their bellies through dead, ferny leaves, working their way far enough to see down into a small, rather picturesque coastal valley sprawled around the village and the creek flowing through it.

Leonor's first impression was it was actually two villages, on both sides of the stream, because each roughly four- to six-acre collection of about a hundred hide-covered wickiup-like structures was enclosed within an impressive oval stockade of outward-leaning sharpened stakes six to eight feet long. There were little garden plots of vegetables beyond the stakes, but nothing that would attract large predators. The stream itself was spanned between them by a sturdy-looking, rough-hewn bridge, large enough to accommodate the two-wheeled box carts parked in abundance, as well as— and her mind reeled at this—the large collection of apparently docile draft animals that looked for all the world—

"My God," murmured her father, "*real* armadillos, but two tons of 'em, apiece! They must use 'em like oxen!"

"So it would seem," Lara whispered back.

After a moment or two in which Leonor was sure her companions were considering the implications of that as well, she turned her attention to the human inhabitants. There weren't as many as she'd expected, and most were dark-skinned, almost naked women, going about evidently daily chores of trimming scraps of fat and flesh from absolutely enormous hides draped between huge tree trunks left standing for that purpose. Others, with children, crawled and scraped like ants on more large hides staked to the ground where midday sunlight would fill the clearing.

"They look like Injins," whispered one of the riflemen, glancing at Lara. "*Wild* Injins, I mean."

"He's right," Lara confirmed. "There *should* be Indios here, constituting the bulk of the Yucatán population. But 'wild' tribes like this . . . They're usually smaller and keep themselves remote." He nodded ironically toward the giant armadillos. "And they don't keep those."

"Yeah," Anson agreed. "Well, when you told us about 'em, I wondered how folks could just live in a place like this. I guess the stockade keeps big critters away." He frowned. "But smaller things could still get in. How do they deal with them?"

"Especially with so few menfolk around," the rifleman pointed out.

Leonor felt a touch of resentment, but realized he was right.

"I noticed that too," Anson said. There seemed to be only a handful of fighting-age men from both parts of the village combined, all gathered around a cluster of reassuringly normal-looking horses near the entrance to the largest hide-covered structure: a garishly painted dome within the closer, eastern stockade, about thirty yards across and ten high. Sulfurous yellow smoke wafted out a hole in the top. The men were clearly warriors, bodies painted all over in red with swirling designs highlighted in black or white. All carried bows longer than they were tall and rigid tube quivers of some kind of furry hide filled with long, large-diameter arrows with fluffy red, white, or black fletching. The effect of the cloud of fletching up behind their heads was interesting since each man had shaped his hair into a kind of high cockerel's crest, painted the same color as the fletching he used.

"Maybe they're all out huntin'," the rifleman suggested hopefully. "The critters we've seen . . . it'd be like goin' to war to kill 'em."

"Maybe," Anson allowed. Leonor didn't believe that any more than he did. "You're sure no one saw you when you passed by here?" Anson asked Lara.

"I can't know for certain. I didn't think so at the time." He was obviously growing concerned as well.

An entrance flap was whipped aside on the dome, and a large man, painted all in red with no other decoration, stepped into the late-afternoon sunlight. Only his crested hair, breechclout, and feather fletching were black. The men with similar fletching gathered around him with frighteningly excited yipping sounds, which all the others joined. Immediately after him, three other men emerged from the structure, and Anson's party was astounded to see that, though dark-skinned as well, they wore very European-style uniforms of a decidedly outdated fashion. The coats and breeches were bright yellow except for black facings and cuffs on the coats, set off by shiny silver buttons. One man, taller and broader than the others, wore his coat open (cuffs and facings covered with silver lace), exposing a stark white waistcoat. All wore black boots or leggings (it was impossible to tell at this distance), extending up past their knees, and placed large black tricorn hats on their heads as they moved to join the red-painted giant. Finally, the apparent officer's companions both carried muskets of some sort.

"Who the hell are *they*?" demanded Anson.

"I've no idea," Lara confessed. "Perhaps . . . Spanish lancers?" he speculated doubtfully. "But why would they be here?"

"I don't think that's what they are," Anson said, beginning to ease back a bit and motioning the others to follow, "but whoever they are, they're 'somebody' down there, and I don't think the warriors have gone huntin'. Not for animals. We better get back."

A rifle cracked loudly down in the woods behind them and lizardbirds exploded from the trees with rasping cries. The warriors and strangely uniformed soldiers stood rooted for an instant before bursting into motion as well, flowing toward an open gate in the stockade or mounting their horses.

"That's done it," Anson snapped, sliding quickly back and rising to his feet before bolting back the way they came, a revolver in his hand. The others followed, with Leonor bringing up the rear, also armed. There came another rifle shot and the *thump* of one of Lara's men's musketoons just before Anson burst in among the squealing horses and their holders.

"They just come on us!" one of the riflemen cried, almost hysterical. "We was talkin', quiet-like, us an' the Mex'kins, an' the first thing we seen was poor Doonie standin' there with a goddamn *spear* through his chest!" The other rifleman lay dead on the ground with one of the big, red-fletched arrows run completely through him. The black obsidian point was covered with blood and snapped in half. "I got the bastard who done it," the rifleman continued, pointing at a body with his rifle, "but there was more. My horse got stuck bad, an' maybe some o' the others. I took Doonie's rifle an' killed another one o' the devils. Jaime got one too, before one o' those arrow spears went through his arm!"

Men were quickly checking their horses and mounting up. Leonor reflected on the fact that the US and Mexican horse holders had learned each other's names and suspected that very fraternization was the reason they'd been surprised. Lara's sergeant—Espinoza—swiftly wrapped the shocking wound in the moaning "Jaime's" arm while Leonor grabbed the dropped rifle. "Let's go!" her father commanded. "At least one got away. Not that it matters," he added warningly. The unearthly yipping and shrieking of the unknown warriors was drawing closer. All were mounted now, and Leonor was grateful Arete hadn't been hurt—though she'd pried one of the huge arrows from the cantle of the Ringgold saddle.

"What about Doonie?" complained the rifleman who'd climbed on the dead man's horse as his own groaned loudly and fell to the forest floor, blood pulsing from around the heavy shaft in its side.

"Leave him," Anson snapped, "an' thank God you've got his horse or we'd be leavin' you too!" Spurring his animal forward, he galloped back the way they came, followed by the others. He didn't need Lara to show the way again.

"Even on foot they'll reach the road where we left it before we do," Leonor called ahead.

"I know," her father answered, "but we have to have the road. There ain't time to pick our way through the woods."

"We could go farther around before we strike the road," Lara suggested breathlessly, urging his horse closer to Anson's.

"An' they'll have time to catch us *there*. Won't work." He took several deep breaths while his horse went around a large tree and Lara caught back up. "Besides," he continued, "if they're doin' what I think, it might be *nothin'll* work, an' we'll have to run a gauntlet all the way back to the ship. Think about the road."

Lara was perplexed. "There was no fresh sign." He paused, considering. "For longer than we've been here."

"Right. Big as that village was, ain't that strange? A fine road nobody uses? Why? There's *somebody* at the other end they don't like."

"That makes sense," Lara conceded, then frowned. "How did you and"—he hesitated—"your son learn to think like this? To notice things so quickly and choose a course of action?"

"What? Oh." Anson shrugged. "Comanches taught us. If you ain't on your toes around them, you'll wind up slowly an' painfully dead." He jerked his thumb behind them. "I get the same feelin' from those guys."

"What does this 'feeling' tell you?"

Leonor had flashed through the trees to catch up, exhorting the rifleman who'd fired his weapon to reload and for the rest to see to their priming. Now she rode by her father, ready to add the rapid firepower of her revolvers to his. He glanced at her and nodded before replying to Lara. "I figure all their warriors but the bigwigs an' whoever those yellow fellas were—call 'em 'Yellows' for now—are already fightin' somebody else past our people, or were on their way to do it, usin' the woods to move so as not to alarm their enemy—or maybe walk into a trap. Who knows. Either way, with a gust of wind and a bolt of lightnin', here we are in the middle."

"And whoever they are angry at, they are angrier now at us. They might even think we came to side with their enemies," Lara guessed.

"Could be, knowin' our luck of late, an' . . . damn, I'm told it's sinful to be a pessimist, but there they are!"

Fifteen or twenty warriors were already lingering where they'd left the road, along with the three strange men in yellow uniforms. All were looking in their direction. "Spread out, an' at 'em!" Anson roared, spurring his horse to a gallop. Leonor had anticipated him and stayed glued to his side. The others missed a beat but thundered along as well. Surprised by their appearance or not, the Indians on the road were thrown into confusion by the boldness of the charge and furious fusillade of shots. Leonor and her father quickly expended all five chambers in their first pistols, miraculously even hitting a few men as they closed the distance. Both were better-than-average marksmen, but deliberately striking a specific target from the back of a lunging horse requires more divine intervention than skill. By the time they drew their second revolvers, however, they were shooting men they could almost touch as they smashed directly into them. Some scattered, but most tried to fight.

Leonor shot one painted man drawing his bow, then quickly shot another who tried to grab her horse right in the top of the head. An arrow whipped past her face, and she twisted in the saddle toward the source, only to see one of Lara's men blow the archer down with his musketoon—just before an arrow took him in the back. Screaming, he fell to the ground, and painted warriors converged on him with triumphant shrieks and bronze-bladed bolo-like knives. Leonor spurred Arete again, and the mare raced through a swarm of whistling arrows and unhesitatingly trampled the cluster of men who sent them. They were almost through, and there remained only the apparent war chief and his guards, as well as the men in yellow uniforms. All were mounted. More arrows flew from the guards while the war chief raised a heavy spiked club that might've been the tail of an adolescent specimen of the "horned turtle" they'd seen. The two apparently enlisted "Yellows" brought their muskets up.

Leonor's father had emptied both his Patersons, but instead of taking time to draw his more prized weapons from the ever-present pommel holsters, he brought his rifle to bear and killed one of the Yellows just as both of them fired. Both balls went wild, though one *vrooped* disconcertingly close past Leonor's ear before slapping into someone behind her with a dull *whap!* Anson charged right at the chief, whose red-painted face was hard to read, but seemed to reflect a mixture of apprehension and triumph as he urged his horse forward to meet Leonor's father, spiky club whirling over his head.

Anson's gelding was named Colonel Fannin for a reason. He was moody, often recalcitrant, and sometimes infuriatingly slow to get moving. But Anson prized him because he'd learned the horse's spirit didn't reflect his namesake at all. When the fight was on, he was all in. Now, instead of whipping past and presenting the chief with a target for a sweeping blow with his club—as he'd clearly expected—Anson directed Colonel Fannin to perform a maneuver they'd honed to perfection: swerving in to ram the other horse in the shoulder. It was really only a glancing blow, but the chief's horse staggered to the side and nearly fell. Unfortunately for the chief, Anson's real target was the man's near-side leg, which was crushed under Colonel Fannin's powerfully churning shoulder muscles. He screeched and dropped his club, and Anson pounded the side of his head with a brutal stoke of his rifle butt. The screech abruptly ceased, and the man toppled bonelessly to the ground.

Leonor was next, passing close to the Yellow officer. He still held an empty, smoking pistol, but had drawn a long narrow sword. Almost contemptuously, Leonor fired her last pistol ball and saw the look of astonishment cross the man's face when the bright yellow uniform exploded redly in the vicinity of his right collarbone. The sword twirled from his hand. Kicking Arete again, she thundered after her father.

More enemies were ahead, strung out along the road, and the closest started shooting arrows almost immediately. Leonor heard a cry behind her and turned to see one of the riflemen slump over in his saddle, a long, bloody point protruding from his back. "Get his rifle!" she cried to the Mexican behind him, who snatched the sling off the dead man's shoulder as he fell in the road. Her backward glimpse revealed chaos in their wake, but also that they hadn't all made it. There were only six of them now, and the fight wasn't over. Worse, she assumed all their guns but her rifle were empty.

Except for her father's *other* two pistols, of course. A rapid series of sharp, barking *booms*, far louder than a Paterson, proved that her father hadn't forgotten them either.

Ahead, through the fire and smoke Captain Anson spat from the monstrous revolver in his hand, Leonor saw painted warriors shouting in surprised terror and scrambling into the woods. The reaction was much like she'd seen the first time they unleashed repeating pistols on Comanches. Back home, the terror hadn't lasted once the Comanches realized Patersons weren't particularly lethal, but they did wound, and wounds were prone to fester, so they continued to respect them. The *new* Colt pistols her father so cherished were altogether different. Sent to him by an old friend and comrade named Samuel Walker, who'd helped Colt develop them, they were .44 caliber *six*-shooters instead of .36s. Equally important, each conical bullet was loaded atop up to four times as much powder, and the improved loading levers under the barrels made them easier to load. By any estimation, they were the most lethal handguns in the world, and Leonor's father now used his to clear the way as they galloped east.

The arrows stopped, and for critical moments, Anson, Leonor, Lara, Sergeant Espinoza, one rifleman, and one more of Lara's troopers—Espinoza had seen the wounded Jaime pulled down—were able to slow their blowing animals and reload their weapons. Anson's massive Walker Colts were back in the pommel holsters. The sun was getting low, and they were still a couple of miles from the American camp around the wreck of *Commissary*.

"*Escucha!*" Lara urged. Over the sound of the wind and nearby surf came the strident rumble of drums that American infantry still used to call its men to arms, continuing even as the first unmistakable crackle of muskets began. In mere moments, the crackle became an unbroken roar, punctuated by the rolling *poom!* of a howitzer.

"The camp's under attack!" Anson growled.

"A *big* attack," Leonor agreed darkly.

"It'll be the very devil gettin' to it now!" exclaimed the surviving rifle-man.

"*Dios nos ayudara,*" Sergeant Espinoza said flatly, and the trooper glared at him. "What's that mean?"

"He said 'God will help us,' Private," Anson said distractedly, still listening to the distant fight.

The rifleman blinked. "Oh. Well, I sure hope so."

More firing erupted to the right in the woods, much closer, and it began to seem all the land around them must be boiling with enemies—far more than could've come from one village.

"Did anyone see firearms in use by the men we fought?" Lara demanded.

"Just the Yellows," Leonor said.

"Then those must be *my* men out there, also under attack!" Lara started to urge his horse off the road toward the shooting, but Sergeant Espinoza blocked him, and Anson growled, "What's the matter with you? Are your men fools? They'll make for the ship, same as us."

"*Tiene razon, Alferez Lara,*" Espinoza told him. "*Nosotros debemos ir con los Americanos.*"

Reluctantly, Lara jerked a frustrated nod, and they continued on, gradually increasing their pace. They'd gone half a mile when another flurry of gunfire came from the woods and twelve riders abruptly galloped out on the road ahead of them, pushing a swarm of fluttering lizardbirds and other strange creatures on foot. They'd started spurring their horses into a sprint to the east when someone looked back and saw the party galloping up behind. He shouted, and the Mexicans held up. "Let us through, into the lead. We're all going to defend the ship," Lara called to them in Spanish, before glancing defiantly at Anson.

Anson shrugged as they passed to the front of the ragged, frightened column. Several men were wounded, and if this was all that remained, Lara's detachment had lost heavily that day. "I guess there's nothin' for it, Alferez Lara. Unarmed prisoners ain't any use in a fight, an' we've found a bigger one than we know, against monsters an' savages that shouldn't exist, in a hellish place nobody's ever seen." He frowned and glanced at Espinoza before looking back at Lara. "Maybe it *is* 'purgatorio,' like our friend Sal said, an' this is how it is for fightin' men. But whatever the hell's goin' on, we're all on the same side in this '*pesadilla*,' an' I'll tell De Russy so." The firing was intensifying up ahead. "If he's still alive."

They fought off a small attack from the woods after another of Lara's men was wounded by a rushed flurry of arrows, but they could tell by the calls and shouting in the forest that there were a *lot* of men in those trees. The next attack would have more weight. "Time to take to the beach," Anson grudgingly decided, and the mixed force followed him through a cut leading out on the sandy shore. The sun was down, leaving only gold-streaked clouds to the west and just enough light to see, for the first time, the results of the fighting they'd been hearing all the way back. *Commissary* looked much as she had, lying bleak and broken and deeper in the water as the tide came in, but though *Tiger* was still at anchor offshore, *Isidra* had stood away until she was only an indistinct shape on the darkening sea. Leonor couldn't understand that at all.

The beachhead itself had contracted considerably, and the men had—finally—erected breastworks, largely from wreckage but also the very crates and barrels of supplies and provisions they'd earlier worked so hard to consolidate. There was no shooting at the moment, and for a brief instant Leonor feared the savages had already overrun the place. Most of the tents were down, and she saw few standing horses. Bodies were everywhere, almost black against the still-startling white of the sand, and in the rapidly deepening half-light, many of the dead looked . . . very strange. Then her attention was drawn to the movement of other figures throwing hundreds of shovelfuls of sand on the breastworks, like an equal number of ant lions clearing their little traps. Most reassuring of all, a t'gallant mast had been taken from the ship and erected so that two flags might stream over the men below. The highest was that of the United States, with its thirteen stripes and twenty-eight stars. Below was the predominantly blue flag of Pennsylvania, with its draft horses and coat of arms, cradled by red banners with golden letters naming the 3rd Volunteer Regiment. "They're still there," she murmured, relieved beyond words.

"For now," her father agreed grimly. "We better join 'em durin' the lull."

But the "lull" was over. A hissing, animal roar rose from the shot-pocked tree line, and a black cloud of arrows soared over hundreds of shapes pouring out on the beach, surging like a wave at the makeshift breastworks. For an instant, Anson and his party paused, shaken by what they saw, for the attackers racing down on the American infantrymen weren't the same as those pursuing them. They weren't even people. To Leonor's disbelieving eyes, they looked like smaller versions of the terrible dragon that killed Lieutenant Swain. A steadier volley than those they heard earlier slammed into the monsters, scything them down, and a pair of howitzers coughed double loads of canister into the raging mass amid horrible, piercing squeals.

Arrows swept among Anson's party as well, making one of the horses scream with pain, and more enemies—human this time—swarmed out on the beach behind them. "To the breastworks!" Anson roared, pointing ahead, "right along the water's edge!"

Wet sand fountained behind the horses as they pounded forward at the edge of the surf. "Take 'em in!" Anson shouted at Leonor as he peeled around to bring up the rear, firing his pistols at their pursuers. Torn between her desire to aid her father and the sensibility of his command, Leonor charged on, Alferez Lara beside her. Luckily, Anson's shooting and the fact they were mounted and clearly fleeing pursuit prevented anyone behind the breastworks from firing at them as most jumped their horses right over the waist-high barricade. One of the Mexican horses balked and almost threw its man, but made the jump on a second try. That left only Anson and the other rifleman, whose horse had been mortally wounded and couldn't go on. The man slid off the dying animal and started to run. Anson wheeled, pistols empty once more, urging Colonel Fannin into a sprint. The big horse leaped the barricade just as the dismounted rifleman reached it, and an anxious volley flashed and clattered at the men running up behind them. Several fell, and the rest loosed arrows before darting away.

But the monsters making the frontal assault still came, several hundred smashing into the hasty works with obsidian-tipped spears and jagged flint-studded clubs, thrusting and bashing on and around bristling bayonets and musket barrels. The men with those muskets were almost all new to combat, and none had ever faced things like these: furry/feathery nightmare monsters that looked and moved like voracious, predatory birds— with the jaws, teeth, claws, and tails of some kind of terrible lizard—painted and festooned as garishly as the men Leonor had already been fighting. And they attacked like the very devils they resembled, stabbing and clubbing, biting and slashing, using all their weapons with savage effect. But veterans or not, the Pennsylvania Volunteers and regular infantry that had joined them resisted the onslaught with surprising tenacity and ferocity, even while wailing in terror or cursing in high-pitched tones. They fought the monsters like they never would any mere human opponent because the things *were* devils in their eyes and they were defending their souls as much as their lives.

"Get those horses under cover!" roared a harried-looking, wide-eyed Major Reed, waving his sword to the rear, where an odd kind of tall, one-sided fort had been erected from timbers, gratings, and what appeared to be whole sections of the dead ship's deck right near the water's edge, obviously meant to give cover to animals, wounded, and the people tending them. With *Isidra* steaming away, Leonor was surprised to see the regular officer still here. "You!" Reed cried to a cluster of frightened young drummers. "Take these horses back with the others. We've already lost too many, and they're terribly in the way!" Without pause, he turned to Alferez Lara. "Are you Mexican gentlemen here to fight with us? Very well. Some of you have lances, I see. Very useful here, if a bit long. Those with only musketoons can load behind the line and step up to fire—until a musket with a bayonet becomes available." Lara merely nodded and passed the instructions to his men.

With the lizard creatures right on top of them, the flocks of arrows had ceased. For the moment, as long as the infantry at the breastworks held, it was relatively safe behind it. Regarding Anson and Leonor as they reloaded their weapons, Reed finally took a breath. "I see you encountered some trouble yourselves. I frankly never expected you to return."

"I thought you'd gone when we saw only that British hulk still wallowin' offshore," Anson replied, noting the scowl on Reed's flash-lit face, "an' guessed we'd find this place overrun after we heard the fightin'." He gestured at the barricade, where some of the men had gained enough of a respite to start loading and firing their muskets.

"Lieutenant Dwyer's dragoons saved us," Reed said. "They left shortly after you to scout a place for a fort and discovered the demons assembling. Demons *and* men," he added meaningfully.

"We've met the men," Leonor told him. "These . . . lizards're somethin' new."

"In any event," Reed continued, "though poor Lieutenant Dwyer was killed by an arrow, the rest of his party gave warning, and we were able to begin assembling defenses." His scowl deepened. "Despite the fact no enemy *ship* seemed to threaten us, Colonel Wicklow was . . . alarmed by the nature of the threat reported and decided his first priority must be the safety of the civilians in his care."

"He ran like a rabbit," Leonor declared with contempt.

Reed glanced at her this time before continuing. "Neither I, nor the two admirable young ladies assisting Dr. Newlin, obeyed the colonel's order to return to the ship. I was merely disobedient, refusing to abandon these men to their fate. The ladies believed the colonel's excuse and stayed to extort his continued presence, hoping he'd consider *their* safety as well and never dreaming he'd actually leave them. They were disappointed. Even so, even in the face of this"—he waved his sword at the fighting, now murky with darkness and almost invisible except for stabbing flashes in the heavy smoke—"they've remained with Dr. Newlin, helping him deal with ghastly wounds." He blinked. "The monsters, perhaps the men out there as well, apparently . . . snatch bites from their victims as opportunity allows."

"What happened after that?" Anson asked impatiently.

"The first attack, by men, still caught us unprepared. They swept in and killed a good many fellows—especially the poor wounded—and chased off most of our horses. I think stealing horses was their primary aim, in fact"—he pointed his sword at the fighting, and his lips twisted—"to get them out before *these* things struck."

Anson had finished pressing lead balls down on the powder charges he'd poured in the cylinder of his second Paterson and returned the loading tool, dangling from a watch chain, back into a vest pocket before putting the barrel back on and driving the wedge in place. Even as he methodically pinched five small percussion caps and pushed them on the ripples at the back of the cylinder, he glanced back up at Reed. "So where do you want us?"

A howitzer boomed on the left, whistling canister swallowed by the shrieks of inhuman beasts, and Reed hesitated. "Here, if you please. Captain Beck of the First is a steady fellow and seems to have the left in hand. Colonel De Russy's supposed to be in the center, but I fear he's been somewhat . . . overwhelmed since the attack began. That fellow with him . . ."

"Reverend Harkin?" Leonor interrupted.

"Indeed. He was the first to declare our enemies 'demons,' and I fear that preyed heavily on Colonel De Russy's mind. I'd like to return to the center myself."

"Very well," Anson agreed, and to Reed's surprise, amid the fire and fury of battle, he chuckled. "Some of the Mexicans think we're fightin' demons too, in purgatory. I was startin' to believe it myself, but . . . well, if they can still kill us, an' we can kill them . . ." He shrugged. "Seems purgatory'd be harder to get out of than dyin'. But you tell De Russy when you see him, an' that preacher too, even if that *is* where we are, we're gonna have the place to ourselves before we're done." With that, he took his rifle from where it had been slung diagonally across his back and stepped up to join Alferez Lara behind the firing line.

Leonor glanced around, taking in the fight. The screaming and shooting and clashing of weapons reflecting back from the wall of trees was almost as loud as the Battle of Monterrey—with fewer cannon. Most surprising was how well these green infantrymen had stepped up to oppose such unexpectedly terrifying creatures. Then again, scared or not, with the sea at their back it wasn't like they could run. *I'm scared too,* she acknowledged to herself. *Not like a decade ago—I was only fourteen! But now I know how to fight.* She tossed Reed a sardonic salute along with a bitter, cryptic smile. "Well," she said, "devils, lizards—whatever they are—the worst they can do is kill us." Unslinging her own rifle and checking the priming, she walked to join her father.

CHAPTER 8

A musket flashed and cracked in the darkness, followed by another, and edgy riflemen and artillerymen shouted to one another behind the palisade around the wreck of *Mary Riggs*. "Hold your fire, damn you!" came Sergeant McNabb's distinctive roar, reinforced by the higher-pitched, more excited voices of Lieutenants Burton and Olayne.

"What the devil?" Lewis Cayce demanded loudly, standing with a wince. It seemed the longer he and Captain Holland sat listening to the muted booming and watching the pulsing light show of the distant battle—for battle it had to be—the worse his old wound ached.

"I reckon the lads're jumpy, is all," Holland reassured him as they strode past tense men in the direction of the shots.

"Of course they are," Lewis replied irritably, then confessed, "so am I. They're nervous as cats and tired nearly to death. And on top of everything else"—he jerked his thumb behind him—"they *still* can't sleep because they've been watching *somebody* fight *somebody* ever since the sun went down. I can't help thinking that's where Captain Anson is. I thought I was more worried than I should be when his party didn't return before dark. Now I expect I wasn't worried enough." They drew to a stop where Sergeant McNabb was holding two artillery privates by the button-down loops on their shoulders in front of Burton and Olayne. "These was them," McNabb accused, "shootin' at nothin', without orders!"

"It *wasn't* nothin'," one of the men complained indignantly. "We seen things movin'!"

"Is this true?" Olayne asked the other man, who cut his eyes accusingly at his companion.

"It is. But I never would'a fired if he didn't."

"Did it occur to either of you that we have *people* out there?" Burton demanded hotly, voice rising again. "You might've shot Captain Anson!"

"They didn't," called another distinctly gruff voice not far off in the trees in the direction the men had fired, "but they nearly got me—ol' Boogerbear, that is. Corporal Beeryman, I mean. I heard a ball zip past, not a foot from my head!"

"I bet it was mine," one of the miscreants gloated to the other. Sergeant McNabb shook them both.

"Come on in," Lewis said with relief, but there was no immediate response.

Finally, the big Ranger called in again. "Just one thing; Cap'n Anson an' some o' the others ain't here, but there's more of us than you'd expect. We picked up some strays, an' some new . . . acquaintances along the way back. I'll caution they might give a fella a start. If you soldiers'll take your fingers off your triggers an' angle your muskets up an' away, why, we'd be obliged to come in."

Mystified, Lewis gave the order. Just to be safe, Olayne had Sergeant McNabb call the men to attention and shoulder their arms. Shapes began to stir in the trees, the watchfires painting bizarre, sinister shadows beyond them, but the soldiers began to relax when the Rangers Boogerbear and Hernandez led the mounted men in, followed by two of the dragoons they left with, and two of the mounted riflemen. The latter rode double, carrying a pair of bandaged soldiers. Olayne gasped with relieved surprise when he recognized Felix Meder and Elijah Hudgens. "Those are men I sent to scout while you were indisposed, sir. I feared they were lost!" Behind them rode four infantrymen: a lieutenant in the usual dark blue single-breasted frock coat, and three privates wearing the same sky-blue wool as most everyone else except for the white herringbone trim on their jackets. Their presence seemed to prove Anson had at least made contact with one of the other ships. Lewis was anxious to talk to them—until he saw the dozen people and pair of . . . other beings . . . bringing up the rear, on foot.

His eyes took in what looked for all the world like nine Indians dressed remarkably like native hunters he'd seen as a youngster in Tennessee before the shameful Indian Removal Act displaced them westward. Just as much as the slavery issue, that turned Lewis against his father's political party and president. But even the strange hunter/warriors couldn't hold his attention away from the dark little man in the wide-brimmed hat and long, black, collarless frock coat closed with at least a dozen silver buttons. Most shocking of all, *he* was walking beside creatures *shaped* like men carrying muskets, but with fur and tails . . . and faces more feline than human. Lewis's mind reeled.

"It's a joke, a costume," Coryon Burton blurted defensively as the closest soldiers started reacting as well. Some cried out in surprise or fear, others in anger. One even tried to bring his musket to bear before he was slammed to the ground by McNabb.

"No," Lewis murmured as one of the creatures paused and regarded him intently with wide, blue eyes. "It's no joke, no costume. But I'm damned if I know what it is."

"'It' is Varaa-Choon," said the creature in careful but bizarrely accented English, "warmaster to the great Har-Kaaska, Jaguar King to these faithful Ocelomeh—'Jaguar Warriors'—accompanying me." It gestured at the "Indians." "We rescued your wounded men from marauding gaaraches, as well as some few survivors of another ship that fell to earth as yours did." It nodded at the man in the frock and hat. "Those others were more grievously injured and have already been started on their journey to Father Orno's city for treatment. All will be returned to you."

Lewis literally couldn't speak, and men were moving closer from all along the palisade, pushing and shoving to see while their mood grew more panicky by the moment. All the calm Lewis had worked so hard to establish had vanished like a puff of smoke. They'd endured too much: been swept from the sea to fall from the sky, been attacked by strange monsters, and now there were Indians and talking cats. It was just too much. They were afraid, and Lewis was uncomfortably aware that fearful men tend to kill things that scare them.

Boogerbear and Sal Hernandez, still mounted, grimly drew their pistols and slammed their horses into the growing mob, pushing it back, while the two bandaged men shouted to overcome the tumult. "It's true, it's true! They're *friends!*" the wounded rifleman cried. "I'm Felix Meder! Some of you *know* me, for God's sake! Private Hudgens and I found *Xenophon*, upside down and smashed, with lizard monsters—'gaaraches'—swarming all over it. They came for us, and we'd have been done for if these 'Ocelomeh' didn't save us!"

"That's how it is," Boogerbear roared. "Other critters, like lizardy Injins, were after *us*, the same that're attackin' the footslogger survivors of *Commissary* now—where we came from—an' these . . . Jaguaristas drove 'em off." His eyes latched onto Lewis. "They're here to talk to *you*, Cap'n Lewis, an' you better listen!"

"Get back to your posts, you buncha useless gawpers!" Sergeant McNabb bellowed, quickly (if less forcefully) echoed by other NCOs. Lieutenant Olayne, to his credit, had recovered even faster than Lewis and added his stern orders to those of the visiting infantry officer, and now even Captain Holland. Lewis, with a dull twinge of shame—*What's wrong with me, damn it?*—finally raised his own voice. "Go back where you were, men. Build up the watchfires. Nothing's changed *our* circumstances, and we must stay on guard. I'll talk to these visitors and learn what I can. Return to your posts, do your duty, and you'll soon know whatever I do."

There was grumbling, but Captain Cayce had earned the men's respect. Moreover, his actions and level-headed leadership since their arrival had earned him more hopeful trust than most of these inexperienced but hard-bitten soldiers ever bestowed on an officer. Perhaps that was inevitable; they were afraid and had to trust *somebody*, but Lewis had felt that fragile trust begin to grow through the day and played on it now, while promising himself not to abuse it. He *would* tell the men—all he could—when he knew it.

Gradually at first, then ushered more forcefully by NCOs, the crowd left a surprisingly large space around the visitors. It was as if, unable to kill this new, frightening thing, the men wanted away from it.

"That was close," Holland breathed in Lewis's ear as the mounted men stepped down from their horses. The dragoons and unwounded riflemen took charge of the animals, with the infantry privates in tow, likely anxious to begin spinning their own tale. Lewis had no problem with that. The story would be distorted, no doubt, but the gist would get around and form a foundation for him to build on while refuting things that became overblown and encouraging the "bright side" of things. *If there is a bright side.*

"Thank you, Captain Cayce," the blue-eyed . . . cat-person said, disconcerting Lewis again to hear English from its mouth. "Believe me, I understand your position. My people have experienced *many* strange encounters on this world over time!"

"Your people? 'This world'?" Lewis immediately pounced, but Varaa-Choon made a dismissive gesture.

"For the present, we must focus on more pressing concerns. I and those I help to lead really do come to you in peace and friendship. We need one another rather badly, I fear."

"Indeed?"

"Yes." Varaa-Choon paused. "First, allow me to present my companions. The other Mi-Anakka, the . . . other of my kind, is Consul Koaar-Taak. He's a, ah, 'subchief' of the nearest band of 'Jaguaristas,' as your man called them. An appropriate term, I suppose, since not all are warriors, but these warriors are all from his village." The creature sniffed. "Do I smell food? Would it be possible to feed my escort while we continue?"

Lieutenant Olayne seemed about to protest, but Burton had gathered his wits enough to call Sergeant Hayne. "With the captain's permission, assemble a detail and escort our guests to one of the mess areas. Don't let anyone pester them."

Hayne looked at Lewis, who nodded.

"Sir."

"Thank you again," Varaa-Choon said, blinking strangely at the little man in the hat. "I already named Father Orno, who is a 'Verdadero Cristiano,' a 'True Christian.' I gather from Private Meder and Private Hudgens most of you are as well."

Koaar-Taak was rapidly translating everything to the little priest. Lewis recognized a lot of Spanish, but it was mixed with something else.

"Christians, aye, but few bloody papists!" Hudgens muttered darkly as Boogerbear and Hernandez herded him, Meder, and the infantry lieutenant over to join them.

The cat-creature *kakked* a kind of laugh. "Father Orno may call himself a Jesuit, but you won't find him quite the 'papist' you imagine."

That only confused Lewis more. "Let's move away where we can talk." Turning, he led the way back to the skeleton of *Mary Riggs*, where he and Holland and Anson had their talk the night before. It seemed surreal. They'd thought then that they were finally getting a handle on things, at least for themselves, but now he realized they knew nothing at all. Calling to Private Willis, skulking surreptitiously closer, he told him to bring food. Mumbling to himself, Willis turned and snapped at men to help him. Leaning on one of the dead ship's cracked ribs while absently rubbing his own, Lewis first looked expectantly at the infantry officer, who quickly saluted. "Lieutenant James Manley, First Infantry, sir, dispatched by Colonel De Russy with three Third Pennsylvania Volunteers to contact you." He quickly and succinctly described the situation at the shore as it was when they left.

"What's goin' on there now?" Holland asked, gesturing at another flash on the horizon.

Manley pursed his lips. "A . . . battle, I presume." He looked almost imploringly at Boogerbear.

The big man snorted. "A battle sure enough, an' considerin' how many Injins—man an' lizard—we dodged comin' out, an' the way things were when we left—no defenses at all—I'm surprised De Russy's kept it goin' this long. Maybe he got some warnin'."

"We must hope he did," Lewis said brusquely, "but now you speak of 'lizard Indians'? What are those, and"—he glanced at Varaa-Choon—"what *other* surprises will there be?"

Now Varaa-Choon snorted. "The surprises will never cease. But regarding the 'lizard Indians,' the locals here long called them 'Lagartos del Diablo.' They're distressingly similar to creatures called 'Grik' that border . . ." Varaa-Choon paused. "My own far-away land. Many now call them Grik here as well."

"They're bigger and smarter than the gaaraches that injured Private Hudgens and me, and there are different tribes of them, like Indians," Private Meder supplied.

"And they sometimes ally with some of the more warlike Indios—'Indians,'" Varaa-Choon agreed darkly. "A combined force of Grik and Holcano Indians—who fancy themselves human cousins to Grik—was actually staging to make a long-planned attack against *our* allies at Father Orno's city of Uxmal when your ship on the beach appeared in their path. Such events are rare but not unknown, and there is always great plunder to be had . . . and meat. They couldn't resist attacking it, even at the expense of their previous plans."

"They *eat* people?" Burton gasped. "Just the lizards, surely."

"No," Varaa-Choon stated flatly, blinking rapidly. Lewis was beginning to think the blinking conveyed meaning, like human facial expressions. "I'm only being pragmatic when I say that was a good thing for *us* in the short term," Varaa-Choon continued, "since even as they die, your people weaken our enemies. In the long term, however, our enemies will quickly recover, *and* they'll have deadlier weapons. *Very* bad for us." Varaa-Choon looked intently at Lewis. "Based on my impression of Private Meder and Private Hudgens, I've come to offer a temporary alliance. Koaar has sent for all his Ocelomeh, and almost four hundred can join us before dawn. Travel by night is always hazardous, but less so for large groups. In any event it can't be helped. King Har-Kaaska will send more Ocelomeh when he learns of the need and though there are few warriors among the Uxmalos or other city dwellers, Father Orno assures me they will come as well."

Varaa-Choon paused significantly. "The problem, of course, is it will take too long for the Uxmalos or other Ocelomeh to arrive. The battle is happening *now*. For you to save your people and me to save those I protect from your weapons, we must move together against our very suddenly common enemy at once."

Lewis stared hard at the creature. "You honestly expect me . . ."

"Sir, they saved us! *She* saved us!" Private Meder blurted. "Those things out there . . . our people!"

"Silence, Private!" Burton barked, startling Father Orno, "or I'll have you bucked and gagged!"

Lewis would never allow that; he hated that sort of punishment. But he hardly even noticed the threat. "She," he murmured, recognizing for the first time that Varaa-Choon was actually quite clearly female. He'd been so overwhelmed by the rest of her appearance, the very fact of her . . . *Of course she's female*—his mind reeled, winging unbidden to Leonor Anson, *another* female warrior, certainly in danger if not already dead. Varaa-Choon seemed amused by Lewis's consternation, but blinked in apparent surprise when Lewis snapped angrily at her. "What makes you so certain De Russy will lose—and what did you mean by 'this world'?" he repeated adamantly.

"The primary assaulting force is Grik, not human, and they don't fight by half measures," Varaa-Choon informed him, tone milder than before. She did know what he was trying to cope with, or thought she did. "They breed and mature very quickly when they need to and food is plentiful, so fighting to the death is part of their culture. It's *expected*. They've pressed us long enough that their numbers have soared, and perhaps several thousands, from different tribes, will eventually be drawn to the fight. The gaaraches Private Meder spoke of will gather as well. They're merely young Grik, running wild and not yet attached to a tribe."

"A somewhat singular approach to child rearin'," Holland said softly.

"De Russy had three, four hundred troops. Maybe a couple hundred more if the infantry came ashore from *Isidra* like they planned," Booger-bear said.

"Six hundred at best, and a battery of howitzers," Lieutenant Manley agreed with a worried frown.

"And the men? The enemy Indians?" Captain Holland demanded. "How many are they?"

"That's our only hope," Koaar said, speaking for the first time, other than translating for Father Orno. "The Holcanos are more dangerous at a distance for the same reason we are: our bows." He said this despite the fact he, like Varaa-Choon, carried a musket. But all the human Ocelomeh carried longbows the English would envy, and very large arrows. "Grik aren't built to do well with bows and have to get close to fight with spears and other hand weapons." He blinked. "And their teeth and claws, of course." He raised his musket. "Sometimes I suspect that bows and other distance weapons are the only reason anyone but Grik can live on this world," he added somewhat dismally. "But the Holcanos are just as scattered as we are at present, preparing as they were to attack *us*. There are probably fewer than three or four hundred near enough to influence the fight."

"We have two hundred and ten men fit for duty," Olayne urgently reminded Lewis, "but almost a hundred we can't leave and can't take!"

"We'll leave enough Ocelomeh to protect your injured," Varaa assured. "You've fortified this place well, and it'll be simple to hold against most forest monsters."

Funny, Lewis thought. *Now that I know this warmaster is female, suddenly she's "Varaa" in my mind.*

"Four-to-one odds sound long to me," Holland grumped, looking at Boogerbear. "What do you think? You said these 'Grik' and 'Holcanos' chased you."

Boogerbear scratched his thick black beard. "Appears to me, it's four to one at *best,* an' that's if we fight right now. If they rub out those foot soldiers, the odds get worse. I've fought Comanches most o' my life, an' Holcanos don't scare me. But I never fought a single lizard before, much less thousands of 'em. On the other hand, Arista had twice as many men as us at Palo Alto, just as well armed, an' we whipped *him*. So I figure it's more how you do it than how many there are."

Varaa-Choon was nodding approval. "The principal war chief of the Holcanos calls himself 'Kisin.'" She snorted. "Kisin, indeed. He listens too much to the filth the Dominion feeds him. But I'm a better warmaster than he." She didn't seem to be bragging, only stating a fact. Lewis wanted to ask what she meant by "the Dominion," but she was already speaking to him. "So what's your decision? If we make this fight, you must move at once. We'll lead you along the shortest path to a road—your Mr. Boogerbear has seen it—and the bulk of Koaar's Ocelomeh will join us on the march. There's no guarantee your friends will last the night," she cautioned, "but even if they don't, right after they die is the *next*-best time to strike." Lewis was annoyed by Varaa-Choon's insensitivity, but accepted her pragmatism. Whatever its nature, an attacking force is always most disordered after a battle it thinks it has won. The strange female warmaster continued. "My next question is equally important. If you do choose to fight, will your men follow you? I *do* understand what they've been through. Koaar and I, and others, were merely victims of an ordinary shipwreck in this land, but our history is full of others who came to this world as you did. Can you *make* your people fight?"

Lewis saw Private Willis waiting impatiently at a distance with a cook and his helper, each holding three steaming mugs with spoon handles sticking out. Seemingly out of the blue, he said, "Private Meder, Private Hudgens, I congratulate you both on your survival. How are your wounds?"

"They do very well, sir," Hudgens begrudged, as if surprised himself. He nodded at Father Orno. "He fixed us up right."

"Good. All of you who just came in, go get something to eat as quick as you can. You too, Lieutenant Manley. Lieutenant Olayne, I want you to choose your very best gun's crews, enough for two sections, and have them prepare four guns to move in the fashion of flying artillery. I know you've grasped the fundamentals. Let's hope the men have too. Lieutenant Burton, you'll assemble everyone here directly. I promised them a report. Captain Holland, stay by me for a final word with our guests, if you please."

He looked at Varaa-Choon, Koaar-Taak, and Father Orno while the others left. The little priest seemed on edge, but earnest. Lewis's Spanish was poor, but he'd recognized enough of the parts of the conversation

Koaar translated to believe Father Orno received a good account. It was natural he'd be nervous about what Lewis would decide, since apparently, his people might be as much at risk as the shipwrecked Americans. Lewis finally sighed and shook his head at Varaa.

"I won't *make* these men march off to fight someone else's enemy. After what they've been through, I'm not sure I could if I wanted to." He took a breath. "I'll *ask* them to, though, because Corporal Beeryman and Lieutenant Manley confirmed your 'Grik' and 'Holcanos' are attacking our people, and that makes them our enemies too. That's what I'll say when I tell them everything else. After that?" He shrugged. "I *think* they'll fight because the lives of their countrymen are at stake. Many won't want to, but they'll go because others do and because they know it's right. Finally, after I tell them what you've been hinting at—about this somehow being a whole different *world* . . . I guess most will agree there isn't a choice." He frowned and remembered. "After all," he said lowly, "doing *something*—no matter what— is almost always better than doing nothing."

Varaa-Choon stroked the tan fur on the side of her face with nails almost like claws, blinking something Lewis would later learn conveyed respect. Very quickly, she told Lewis Cayce and Eric Holland enough to confirm their worst fears: that they *had* somehow fallen to another world of some kind. She capped it off with a revelation they hadn't even considered yet, however, and by far the most devastating. When she was finished, watching them closely, Holland cleared his throat and found his voice first. "Well, Lewis," he said, using the artilleryman's given name for the first time, "I reckon if it was me, when I talked to the lads, I'd leave that last bit off for now."

CHAPTER 9

THE BATTLE OF "FORT COMMISSARY"

Leonor Anson pounded a ball down the fouling-choked barrel of her rifle, primed the pan, then collapsed in the sand, exhausted and in pain. The monsters had pulled back again, dragging bodies (their own as well as American) into the darkness of the coastal forest. She lay like a corpse herself, panting, with men she didn't know—though she recognized the grimy face of the volunteer Private Cox, who'd led them to the officers when they first arrived. She didn't care, couldn't think, and couldn't remember when she'd last slept. All she'd been through over the last few days came to her only as brief mental images, and she tried to order them in her mind. There'd been the storm and shipwreck, then the dragon attack, followed by an all-day trek, a running fight, and now a nightlong battle against Indians of some sort and nightmarish monsters. Both her arms had been cruelly raked by claws when lizard warriors tried to drag her over the breastworks and eat her. An insanely sharp obsidian spear point had sliced the top of her left shoulder, narrowly missing ripping a gaping hole in her chest. She'd been saved by the infantrymen around her, whether they knew it or not, who fought with a manic ferocity and apparently boundless energy *beyond* their attackers', at times. Leonor wasn't fooled. She was proud of their defiance and inspired by their refusal to quit, but knew there'd eventually be an end to their strength. And courage—even fed by terror— had a limit.

There weren't many left to hold the flimsy barricade. Leonor had no il- lusions and knew they'd only lasted to see the first paintbrush streaks of another dawn because they were defending a relatively small enclosure the enemy couldn't swarm with all its might. And that equally exhausted en- emy had to pull back and rest from time to time as well. When they did, like now, blood-smeared men fell gasping to the ground, lying as still as the unheeded dead except for their heaving chests. There was still no true re- spite, because now the heavy arrows came, making it dangerous and often fatal for walking wounded to bring water and more ammunition, or drag their injured behind the heavy "fort" thrown together from *Commissary*'s timbers where Dr. Newlin and his helpers, including the curious foreign women, did their best for them.

Both Leonor's revolvers were so gummed with fouling they simply wouldn't function anymore in spite of the fact she—like her father—had twice retreated from the fighting to break the complicated pistols down and wash them out, drying them as best they could with shirttails and lubricat- ing them with pork slush from an overturned cookpot. Those were the only times she'd seen her father, more haggard and bedraggled each time, though she'd heard the distinctive bark of his Walker Colts at intervals suf- ficient to let her know about where he was, and that he was alive.

Fumbling at her side, Leonor drew the Paterson she feared she'd forced too hard, possibly damaging delicate internal parts. Shakily lifting her can- teen, she pulled out the stopper, hoping for a few drops to smear in strategic places to soften the fouling enough to shoot the last four chambers without spoiling the loads. It was hopeless. The canteen was as dry as her cracking lips. There was a *shooshing* sound beside her, and she turned her head to see Alferez Lara crawling toward her through the sand. *Slithering, like a snake.* She shuddered and felt an uncontrollable urge to jump up and run away. *But that's insane. Besides, he isn't really slithering.* She waited until he came up beside her and produced his own canteen. "Here," he offered. "There's little left, but enough to loosen your weapon and perhaps take a sip."

She was repelled by the thought of drinking after him, but she'd gladly use the water to soften the fouling on her pistol. She took the canteen and carefully dribbled its pitiful contents on the gummy, blackened Colt. "Why?" she murmured.

Lara shrugged. "One of the bullets in your *pistola maravillosa* might kill a lizard that's trying to kill me." He looked away. "And because you hate me. I don't want to die being hated."

Leonor snorted. "A few drops of water an' spit'll change that?"

"I hope so."

Leonor started working the hammer first, trying to draw it back, then gently encouraged the cylinder to turn. Finally, the hammer made it to the half-cock notch, and she turned the cylinder more briskly. Then she sighed. "It's nothin' personal against you, Alferez," she finally managed, "though it *is* mighty personal. I don't hate you as a man, right here, right now—I just hate Mexican soldiers. Can't help it."

Lara's . . . compelling eyes narrowed in his dark, handsome face. "*Solda-dos* . . . harmed you," he guessed.

"*Mexican 'soldados*,' yes," she hissed. "As bad as you can imagine."

Lara was silent a moment. "Then I'm very sorry."

Leonor shook her head, exasperated. "That's the crazy part. I know *you* got nothin' to be sorry for, but that don't change how I feel."

Lara chuckled dryly. "Very well. Then I must be content to die hated only for *what* I am, not who. That's worth a few drops of water and spit."

Leonor actually rolled her eyes and stifled a smile that tried to form. "Go away."

"No. I think the next attack will be very difficult," he said in all serious-ness, then grinned. "And I must remain close to the pistol ball that will save my life."

It dawned on Leonor then that if Alferez Lara, like Lewis Cayce, didn't already know she was a woman, she'd practically just confirmed it. *Well, my vest's open and my shirt's loose, so I guess it's easy to tell,* she considered bitterly, quickly buttoning her vest back up. Beyond doing that, she was just too tired, sore, and scared to try to reintroduce doubt, or even much care. *But Lewis made sure I had his horse, and now Lara wants to protect me. The hell with that!* "I guess I can take care of myself," she said frostily, lifting the pistol. "I killed more lizards last night than anybody but father, an' maybe the howitzers." She glared at Lara. "An' I've killed more *real* Mexi-can soldiers than you've ever seen in your fleabag, backwater post!"

Lara turned somber. "I doubt that. I was born in San Juan de Villaher-mosa, in Tabasco, which is not a 'fleabag,' and once raised its own rebellion against the current president of Mexico. Yet it was attacked by Americano *soldados* after I transferred home to command militia and recover from wounds I had at Resaca de la Palma. So I have no reason to love Americanos—and perhaps you almost killed me as well?"

Before Leonor could respond, the young black man dressed like a soldier—*his name's Barca,* Leonor recalled—sprinted through a sudden storm of arrows, a bulging knapsack under one arm and a sloshing bucket in his hand. A tinned cup dangling from a piece of twine rattled as he came. Leonor was glad none of the arrows came very close to the swift, agile youngster, even though the light was growing fast. More men were doing the same as Barca, all at once, farther down the line, and that probably distracted the archers enough for them all to make it. Plowing into the sand by Leonor and Lara, losing more precious water, Barca wiped his sweaty brow and flashed white teeth. "Here's water," he announced unnecessarily, pushing the bucket to Leonor. "Take a quick gulp and pass it along." He shook the knapsack at Private Cox, who stared dumbly back. "This is full of musket cartridges. Take a double handful and pass the rest along as well. Just make sure nobody drops their pipe in there!"

Lara grabbed some of the paper cartridges for his smoothbore musketoon, before Cox stirred and took the knapsack. Lara's weapon, like nearly all in the Mexican Army, was British made and .75 caliber. It had been cut down for mounted use from an "India Pattern Brown Bess." Though larger-bored than the .69 caliber American muskets, it would still shoot these only slightly looser-fitting projectiles. They wouldn't be very accurate, but then his weapon never had been. He could count on hitting a man-size target—somewhere—at fifty paces. Past a hundred, a man—or lizard—probably had more to fear from lightning. American muskets with tighter tolerances were much better, but only a rifleman could consistently kill at two or even three hundred paces.

Lara drank water after Leonor dropped the cup back in the bucket, then passed it to another man, eyes greedy and staring.

"Are you going back now, Barca?" Leonor asked.

"No. I'm staying here." He grinned again. "If those lizards want to eat me, they'll have to fight for the bite."

"You're not armed," Lara pointed out.

"There are plenty of muskets lying unused out here."

"Do you know how to use one?"

Barca sat up straighter behind a barrel. "Yes."

Leonor wasn't surprised. The young man had the air of more than a servant. "What're you doing here?" she asked.

Barca looked at her and blinked. "Bringing water and cartridges, and preparing to fight."

"No, I mean why were you here in the first place?"

Barca nodded back toward the rough fort. "I belong to Colonel De Russy."

Leonor was surprised. "He's from Pennsylvania, ain't he? I thought there weren't any slaves there."

"Some say that," Barca hedged, then shrugged. "We're not in Pennsylvania now." He lowered his voice. "The Colonel . . . bought me in New Orleans before we came here. He says I'm free." His eyes flicked back and forth. "*Some* in this army may not respect that, and as far as they know, I remain the colonel's property. But I *chose* to serve him and follow him, for my own reasons," he added with a strongly stressed defiance that implied there was a great deal more to his story.

"In Mexico—if we *are* in Mexico," Lara inserted uncomfortably, "there is no slavery."

Leonor glared at him again. "No, the poor live *so* much better here, while the rich and the Church lord it over 'em," she retorted sarcastically. "Sayin' there ain't a *kind* of slavery in Mexico is the most hypocritical thing I ever heard!"

"I didn't mean to start a fight," Barca objected softly.

"You didn't start anything," Leonor hissed, eyes blazing. "Me an' Alferez Lara were already fightin'. We're at war, in fact." She sighed and looked back at Barca. "But it ain't *your* battle."

Barca frowned, then gestured over the barricade. "*This* one is, I think," he said darkly.

Curious, Leonor turned over and despite the pain in her arms and shoulder and stiffening muscles, raised up to peer toward the tree line. It was light enough now to see hundreds of bodies lying on the beach. All were their attackers. Quite a few Americans had been caught in the open when the attack began, and others were pulled over the barricade and killed, like Leonor nearly was. She'd seen some carried straight away, lizards already tearing flesh from their bodies. It sickened her and left no doubt what their eventual fate would be. But Leonor saw few if any dead Americans beyond their defenses. Now, just at the tree line, about two hundred yards distant, scores of their heads had been staked out in the darkness like another long, macabre palisade, with every dead, bloody face staring back at them.

Leonor was no stranger to atrocity. Too many times her father's Rangers had happened upon charred, smoky cabins and seen the grisly work of marauding Comanches. The constant cross-border warfare between Texas and Mexico got pretty ugly too. And sometimes she was horrified to see what her own people did to Indians they caught. She thought she'd grown immune. Now, if there'd been anything in her stomach besides a single slurp of water, it would've come back up.

"We saw them putting that up from back behind," Barca explained, voice hushed. "Saw it for a while. But only the riflemen would've had a chance to stop them and with hardly a glimmer to see by, they would've missed as often as not. They were busy fighting anyway, so there was no sense drawing their attention from the business in front of them."

A heavy-shafted arrow lofted up and came down to stick in the sand not far behind her, and Leonor realized someone was shooting at her. She kept watching the mass of shadows she'd seen moving in the trees for a moment longer. "You better fetch that musket now, Barca, if you mean to stay."

"They're coming again?" Lara asked.

"I expect so."

A roaring rumble erupted in the trees—the voices of hundreds of lizard warriors—punctuated by the yipping and yelping of Indian archers. Drums thundered behind the one-sided timber fort, calling the exhausted men back to action. Few actually stood, however. Most were too wise to the arrows and waited tensely behind their barricade, knapping flakes off dull gunflints, picking the clogged vents of their muskets, and seeing to the priming in the pans. Some had to stand, brave infantrymen clumsily and inexpertly aiming and shifting the four howitzers positioned on the line. (One remained outside where it had been overrun, and the other was still in the wreck.) A final screeching shout heralded the rise of another cloud of arrows, and the four big guns roared—too soon—spraying the trees with canister. Almost instantly, the gathered monsters burst from those trees and swept down on the weary defenders.

Leonor didn't know where her father was, and Sergeant Ulrich, the other man Leonor first met here, was calling commands for this part of the line. Too many junior officers had fallen early on, seeming to think they must expose themselves to inspire their men. That left men like Ulrich, and increasingly corporals and respected privates to lead.

The last of the arrows stood bristling in the sand, and Sergeant Ulrich roared, "Mark your targets an' commence firing!" Even though one hadn't been called for, a virtual volley crackled out from all around the perimeter, and dozens of the lizards tumbled screeching in the sand. Leonor and those around her waited a moment longer, taking careful aim, and also fired at near the same instant. Leonor saw her target spin and fall. Barca fired as she hunkered down to reload—the lizards would be on them in an instant, and she had no bayonet—and she saw with satisfaction that De Russy's servant hit his mark as well. He immediately, coolly, reloaded as quickly as she did and raised his weapon again.

Leonor couldn't help wondering how Barca gained such proficiency. If De Russy had "bought" him, he'd likely been born and raised a slave regardless of his current status. It wasn't unknown for trusted slaves on the frontier to be allowed hunting rifles to put meat on their masters' tables, but New Orleans wasn't a frontier, and the loading process for a hunting rifle was different from a military musket. Barca's technique looked straight out of *Scott's Militia Tactics*. Leonor shook her head. This wasn't the time to contemplate that.

Sergeant Ulrich bellowed no more commands, but joined the terse, clipped, soldier talk Leonor had learned was common in combat, nearly everyone snapping or shouting things like:

"Get that one, Bill, I ain't loaded yet!"

"Pour it in, ye bastards!"

"Me goddamn flint broke! Someone gi' me another!"

"Mal, you fool, you jus' shot yer damn rammer at 'em!"

"Bleedin' Jesus, what *are* them things?"

"It's enough that *they* bleed, idn't it? Pay no mind ta the looks o' 'em!"

"Steady, lads, they're almost on us. You'll not forget to pull your stickers out hard an' fast if you want to keep yer musket. Pokin' the bastards is the easy part."

Pouring a measure of gunpowder into her cupped left hand—Leonor never poured straight down a barrel from a flask—she dumped the charge in before spitting one of several lead balls she'd popped in her mouth down after it. She wouldn't take time to patch the ball for accuracy, and didn't even ram it down. Without the patch, the ball was loose enough to seat just by thumping the butt in the sand a couple of times. As quickly as that went, she wouldn't trust that enough powder had trickled through the vent to the pan, but before she could prime it from the little horn dangling from her shooting pouch, the lizard monsters struck.

The shooting around her quickly diminished as the ravening, roaring horde slammed into the breastworks with a terrible, clattering smash, jabbing past the bristling bayonets with long, obsidian-pointed spears. Screams of all sorts joined the crash of battle. Some of the beasts carried on, using the backs of their comrades as springboards to leap over and behind the defenders. Leonor finished priming her rifle and shot one of these before it caught its balance, blowing its throat and much of its neckbone out in a fountain of bloody bone chips. Twisting around, she slammed the butt of her rifle into the head of another, feeling the now-familiar crunch of the skull.

The line was giving way, physically *heaved* back from the breastworks amid frantic cries for support. Barca was plying his bayonet desperately, if less expertly than those around him. Leonor drew her revolver, hoping it hadn't stiffened back up, and quickly shot two monsters trying to beat their way past Lara and Sergeant Ulrich. Another flung Lara to the ground, snarling as it poised its spear to nail him to the sand, and Leonor shot it in the eye. Lara rolled the corpse aside and sent her a grateful glance, perhaps aware of the same irony as she, but now she only had one bullet left and the enemy had sensed weakness here. Momentarily pushed back from the middle by a devastating blast of canister, they were massing at this teetering point.

Leonor was feverishly loading her rifle again when she felt three gentle pats on the small of her back. Despite the dire circumstances, she almost melted with relief because only one person in all the world would dare comfort her so, and the *way* the pats came were as familiar and reassuring as a voice. "Father," she murmured around the mouthful of rifle balls, her voice cracking.

"Take your time, do it right," encouraged Captain Giles Anson, speaking the beloved phrase he always used to drive away frustration or fear. Stepping past her, her father was absolutely washed in blood. She prayed it wasn't all his. Then she knew it wasn't, because, though his rifle was slung diagonally across his back once more, he held a dragoon's or rifleman's saber that was so thickly, disgustingly covered with drying, blackening blood, even the underlying shape of the blade was hard to discern. Taking the saber in his left hand, he drew one of the massive Walker Colts from where he'd stuffed them both in his belt. Still walking forward, he blasted lizards down with every shot, the ear-shattering pressure of each report making men flinch, but also sending unhurt lizard warriors reeling back to the breastworks. Just like the Indians with the strange "Yellows," these creatures obviously knew about guns or they'd never have pressed so costly an attack, but pistols that fired more than once, particularly with the awesome power of her father's, apparently struck them as unnervingly magical. They didn't flee in terror—none of them had all night—but they gave ground, and the imminent breakthrough was contained.

The hammer on Anson's Colt snapped on an empty chamber. He stuffed the big pistol in his belt and retrieved the other one, waving it menacingly at the enemy even as the infantry resumed their killing. A pair of tediously loaded howitzers belched cloud banks of white smoke and seething swarms of canister, point-blank, into the mass of lizards to the left. "These are my last loads," her father advised Leonor when she joined him, rifle ready. "A few other officers may have Patersons, but I won't have any more forty-four-caliber bullets until I cast 'em with my mold." He snorted at the rising sun through the haze of gunsmoke, already standing clear of the horizon. "I doubt I'll get the time," he continued dryly. "This attack's bigger an' it's lasted longer than others. I think it's startin' to taper off as they've done before, but we won't get a rest this time. Every damned lizard in the world must've joined 'em in the night, an' I expect they'll hit us with new arrivals as soon as the front's clear."

He sighed wearily. "I say all that like it makes sense—an' none of it does at all." He chuckled bitterly. "Me, predictin' what unknown Indians combined with *hellish lizard warriors* will do! But I'm too tired to ponder the meanin' of any of this anymore. Thank God the men are just as philosophical—or exhausted an' afraid—or we'd all be dead." He studied the infantrymen, firing again as the lizards did indeed start pulling back, leaving a gap for them to load. "We've lost near half our number. Most to wounds that'd heal, given time," he allowed, "but I don't think they'll get it either. Still, they've fought damn well—even Lara and his Mexicans," he grudged. "I'm proud to have fought with 'em."

"You sound like you're givin' up," Leonor accused, shocked.

Anson smiled at his daughter before stooping to stab his saber in the sand, raking it around and trying to abrade the dry blood away. It didn't help. "I'll have to step down to the sea an' wash it," he murmured before looking at Leonor. "You know me better than that. I'll never give up, an' I *refuse* to die until I know what's happened to us, how we got in this mess in the first place!" He grimaced. "But I won't spew false enthusiasm either. Look," he quickly added, "we better get under cover."

The lizards had only pulled about halfway back to the trees. There they stood, hissing, shrieking, brandishing weapons, and making odd gestures with clawed hands even while the howitzers flailed them with canister and rifles and muskets kept peeling them away. But arrows lofted once again, and another, larger mass of warriors was flowing out of the woods behind them, using the very bodies of the withdrawn assault to shield them as they deployed.

"Goddamn!" wailed a man at the breastworks as the arrows rained down. None hit anybody. "Won't they just *quit*?"

"They quit when we kill 'em," Sergeant Ulrich shouted gamely. "Stop wastin' your breath an' get ready for the bastards!"

"You don't think *we* might get reinforcements? Captain Cayce said they'd come for us if we didn't return," Leonor asked her father as they crouched by Lara. Most of his men were around him, now armed with American muskets and bayonets.

"He will too," Anson replied with certainty, "but he gave us until this evenin'. He won't come until tomorrow mornin', an' if we're . . . no longer occupyin' the enemy, they'll just turn on him and chop his column apart."

"He'll know there's a fight here," Leonor said with certainty. "Booger-bear an' Sal would've seen it as they went, if nothin' else. They'll bring him today."

"If *they* got through," Anson cautioned his daughter.

The lizard warriors on the beach never pulled back to the trees. Responding to harsh-voiced commands, they just came on again, whipped into a frenzy but walking slowly, straight into the withering fire.

"They're bringin' the next assault to us fresh," murmured someone in disbelief. His voice rose to near hysteria. "They're dyin' to block 'em from our fire so the ones behind can hit us without breakin' a sweat, by God!"

"Shut up, you, or I'll have *you* sweatin' when this is done," Sergeant Ulrich threatened, but his heart wasn't in it anymore.

"Your men are finished," Alferez Lara whispered at Anson. "This attack will break them."

"So?" Anson whispered back. "What do you propose?"

"We leave," Lara urged. "We go to the horses and ride out due west. Past the Indian pickets, there should now be few warriors."

"Like hell," Leonor hissed. "Run away? You're just a damn coward."

"No, he's right," Anson said, and Leonor gaped at him. The firing was intensifying, the men using their last measure of energy and hope to kill these terrible things before they came to grips again. Few could doubt it would be the last time, and there was no talking except for the growing, panicked calls for more ammunition. "Somebody has to break out an' warn Captain Cayce so he *isn't* caught out on the march," Anson insisted. "That's you," he told his daughter, "along with Lara and his men, our dragoons, an' however many mounted riflemen Major Reed'll let me send with you. More riflemen came ashore from *Isidra* with the regular infantry while we were gone yesterday." They were no longer whispering. The firing and roaring tumult of the terrible enemy had them shouting now, yet only Leonor, Anson, Lara, and, slightly to Leonor's father's apparent surprise, Barca had moved close enough to hear.

"You'll ask Major Reed?" Lara spoke carefully. "He might stop us."

"No. He'll agree to the necessity. I've no idea if Colonel De Russy would." Anson regarded Barca. "What do you think? You know him best."

"Colonel De Russy's a good man," Barca temporized, "but he's . . . strongly focused on *here*, right now."

Leonor was furious. She knew her father was right about warning Captain Cayce, but he was the better choice to lead a breakout. He clearly meant to stay, and sending her was another blatant attempt to protect her. No, she'd remain by him as she always had, no matter what. "The dragoons can lead. They know the way. I won't go," she said stubbornly.

"You *will*," Anson almost roared over the mounting thunder of battle. "For most of your life I've spoiled you badly, lettin' you do as you wanted. Even to the point of takin' you to *war*! That's on my head. I couldn't bear to be away from you after all we both lost an' thought only I could protect you—even from the danger I took you to. I considered it less . . . evil than what you might face—*had* faced—alone." He gestured at the advancing wall of monsters. "But this . . . ! This time, *for once*, you'll do as I say!"

Leonor had looked away as he spoke, he probably thought in anger or shame, but now she held up a hand.

"I'll accept no argu . . ." Anson began hotly, but Leonor cried out, "Listen!"

At first they only heard fighting. It had swelled to all-encompassing proportions, the men struggling to load and fire their balky, filthy muskets as fast as they could to kill just a few more terrifying monsters before they had to rely on their blood-crusty bayonets once more. That contest would be a short one, this time. The shielding rank of lizards were *throwing* their spears, taking a toll, and the defense was much weakened by casualties, exhaustion, and finally the mounting certainty of doom. But above the din, off to the east, there was a different, wholly unexpected sound.

"A bugle," Lara said excitedly. The infantrymen here, volunteers and regulars, had only used fifes and drums to signal. "Who has bugles?"

Captain Lewis Cayce had led a hundred and eighty men and all the horses (to pull his four-gun battery and mount a handful of dragoons) on a night-long march through a tighter, more difficult tract of the tangled forest. Using minimal light—just three one-side lanterns spaced along the length of the column and making eerie shadows that frightened the men—it was a grueling, nerve-racking ordeal. Warmaster Varaa's human Ocelomeh led and screened the blundering column to warn of large monsters and chase smaller ones away, but apparently the enigmatic cat-person had been right about big, noisy groups being relatively safe. And she wasn't much worried about discovery by the enemy, at least until they reached the promised road. The going got easier then, and the weary little army made better time, drawing inexorably closer to the sound of battle.

Briskly walking near the head of the column, just behind their squad of Rangers and dragoons, with Ocelomeh scouts ahead, Lewis and Holland kept pestering Varaa for information. She seemed willing enough to give them dreaded, half-suspected answers to most of their questions and even revealed that her species, Mi-Anakka, wasn't native to this land, though the willingness of their people here to follow and revere her kind implied there'd been other visitors in the past. She offered no other information along those lines. Through the combined efforts of Koaar and Boogerbear, who dropped back on his horse to help with Father Orno's strange Spanish, however, they learned more about the priest and his "True Christians." Some of Captain Holland's sailors, forming a protective guard around the officers, were actually Indians from another Yucatán—for Varaa-Choon confirmed that was indeed essentially where they were—and they recognized some of the Mayan words and phrases mixed in. As best Lewis could tell, Father Orno was no more an actual "papist" than he was, and his people's version of Christianity didn't significantly (to Lewis) differ from that of most of the men under his command, from Roman Catholic to Presbyterian. It had, in fact, bridged most of the outstanding differences by focusing more on the actions and teachings of Jesus himself rather than strict adherence to any particular dogma. If anything, it was only rigid in its nondenominationalism.

And that was the root of his people's problem.

The only "Pope" Father Orno knew was "His Supreme Holiness," the religious and secular ruler of the "Holy Dominion," which had, over time, apparently combined the somewhat militant Christianity brought to this world by a Spanish Manila-Acapulco galleon perhaps two centuries before with the barbaric and bloody rituals of "indigenous" peoples they encountered. Stubborn adherents to "true" beliefs, both Christian and native, were increasingly marginalized and persecuted, and ultimately forced to flee beyond the reach of the growing Dominion Empire. This attack by the always troublesome but previously religiously indifferent Holcanos and their Grik allies was merely the mask on the face of the Dominion, the sword in its hand, wielded to wipe out the "heretics" opposed to Dominion expansion. Lewis understood that well. The French and English had often used the Indians of North America—*his* North America—as proxies and auxiliaries. But though there'd been elements of religious bigotry (Protestant versus Catholic) involved in those conflicts—many still lingering among Lewis's own men—it seemed faith was the principal source of contention here. Lewis disliked religious disputes even more than political, especially when they were combined. But he hated tyranny in any form and found he rather liked Father Orno and immediately sympathized with his people. And even with only the most rudimentary understanding of the Dominion as yet, the mere fact its allies were attacking shipwrecked Americans was enough to dispose him against it.

"My Ocelomeh are here," Koaar said suddenly, as a couple dozen ghostly figures materialized alongside the column from the gloom. One leather-clad figure trotted up and whispered in Koaar's ear almost before Lewis knew they were there. He was disconcerted that they'd just appeared that way, without warning, but then it had been their own people screening the Americans who'd let them through. *They could've wiped us out,* he realized with an uncomfortable squirming sensation in his gut. *Final proof we really are on the same side, I suppose.*

Koaar spoke to Varaa-Choon in a completely unrecognizable language, presumably their own, and they began to step away. "I must leave you now," Varaa said. They'd only vaguely planned their attack, hopefully employing their respective strengths, but Lewis still wished they could've prepared better. They just didn't *know* each other well enough, so they had to keep it simple. "The road is clear, and you should come up on the side of the enemy attack by midmorning at the latest. Move more carefully the closer you get," she warned. "I don't know how you'll use your men or great guns, but you must attack at once if you mean to save your people. Things are going hard for them. We go now to position ourselves behind the enemy, and your attack will be our signal to strike." Varaa-Choon blinked rapidly, and Lewis got the impression she was just as worried about whether she could trust *him.* "Make haste," she urged. "I'll leave the scouts in front of you, and do keep Father Orno safe."

"Are you sure you don't need any of my men?" Lewis asked. "The dragoons, at least?"

Varaa hesitated. "Your riders would be welcome in an open ground fight, but we must move quickly and quietly through the forest. Horses can't do both." She grinned, displaying canines that gleamed in the darkness. "For this fight, at least, we'll each do what we're used to, until we learn from one another." With that, she was gone, and so were the rest of her warriors, as if they'd melted into the trees.

"Spooky," Captain Holland said. The sailor had insisted on coming, to lead his "company" of sailors. Lewis was glad. Holland had already proven his steadiness, and the way he walked with a brand-new 1835 Springfield cradled in his arm, he was at least as comfortable with a musket as his men. "They just come and go, like a puff o' smoke."

Lewis nodded. "Yes. I hope the enemy finds them equally surprising." He paused. "I won't even suggest that you keep your men back, since we may need every musket. I would, however, be obliged if you'd see to the safety of Father Orno." He raised his voice. "You as well, Corporal Beeryman. You and Private Hernandez can not only converse with him better than most, but can carry him to safety if necessary."

Sal and Boogerbear both pulled up their horses and waited for Lewis,

Holland, and Father Orno to join them. "We're here to fight," Sal said simply. "Our captain and his . . . son are fighting now. We'll help."

Boogerbear glanced at his companion, then looked back at Lewis. "Sal's right, sir, but so are you. Tell you what: we'll take turns watchin' over the padre. Why, he can hop up behind me now an' save wear on his dogs. I wouldn't mind polishin' my Mex'kin, an' maybe I can pick up some o' his other lingo?"

Lewis was impressed by the giant, hairy Ranger. Before they set out, Lewis very roughly explained to all the men that the bizarre, terrible storm they'd endured had somehow swept them much farther than they'd imagined possible. It likely wasn't purgatory (he'd said that with a laugh he hoped was convincing), but it certainly wasn't hell or any other unholy or supernatural place. It was only unknown, very strange, and obviously dangerous due to the abundance of undiscovered creatures they'd encountered. Helpless, bookish naturalists became famous every day because of odd little places and beetles they stumbled across, so just think of the stories they'd be able to tell! He'd then motivated them for this endeavor by reminding them they were American soldiers who could overcome any obstacle if they stuck together, and rescuing their comrades trapped at the shore would increase their numbers and chances.

He'd revealed as much of what Varaa-Choon confirmed as he thought he could, as promised, but couldn't bear to lay the full weight upon them just yet: that they were indeed on an entirely different world. Especially since he himself didn't understand how, as Varaa-Choon tried to explain, this different world was still the same, only . . . altered in some way. All cultures had different legends explaining how that could be, how people from the world they knew—perhaps even *others*—were drawn here from time to time, but Varaa-Choon predictably dismissed all but her own belief that the "Maker of All Things" had made *many* worlds, as alike and as different as a handful of musket balls. He could do whatever he wanted with them, even taking from one to put on another.

Absolutely worst of all, as far as Varaa-Choon knew, no one had ever found a way back where they came from.

Lewis decided it was better to ease the men into that, as they likely came to suspect it for themselves. Obviously, Boogerbear already did, his sudden willingness to learn a local language making it clear he expected to be here a long time. But as far as Lewis knew, Boogerbear was like him and had no family. He couldn't imagine how hard it would be for men who did when the full truth was known.

For the present, however, they'd soon have a fight on their hands. For the very first time since he rode with Major Ringgold and his battery out on the hot, muggy, cordgrass plain of Palo Alto, he found he wasn't afraid of what the battle would "do" to him and actually relished the prospect. Compared to what they'd been through and the dread of what was to come, battle was straightforward and easy to understand.

He smiled at Father Orno, now grinning sincerely back. "By all means, ask him if he'd like a ride, though he seems fit enough to walk us all into the ground."

The distant battle flared again, the sound deadened by the wind and surf churning the shore close at hand, but they were getting closer. The sky didn't seem as dark either, and Lewis knew the long night was coming to an end. Lieutenant Olayne trotted up beside him, and they both chuckled at the irony: the "flying artilleryman" on foot, and the young foot artillery-man mounted on one of their few horses. "How are they holding up, Lieutenant?" Lewis asked.

"Tired, sir," Olayne replied, face turning grave.

"Any stragglers?"

"None." Olayne snorted. "The men on foot would rather march themselves to death than fall back and be eaten, but I fear for their strength in the fight. Even the men riding horses pulling the guns and caissons, or sitting on the limbers . . . One went to sleep and fell off a limber. He was nearly crushed to death by the gun hitched behind." He shuddered at the thought of the narrow, wrought-iron tires bearing the full weight of a gun and carriage rolling over a man. It would practically cut him in half.

"Lucky," Lewis said. "Was he seriously injured?"

"No. And I doubt he'll fall asleep again."

"He'll have nightmares when he does," Lewis predicted.

Olayne nodded ahead. "Still fighting. Can't we give the men a short rest?"

Lewis sighed. "No. Our . . . allies are sure the enemy will mount their strongest attack shortly after dawn. If we stop even for a moment, as tired as everyone is, we'll never get half of them moving again."

Olayne nodded grimly.

They pressed on like that, slogging along, far past exhaustion, as the sun rose up and the heat bore down. Sweat-gushing men were encouraged to drink their fill since they'd brought some of the water they'd saved from the wreck in casks secured to caissons. Varaa-Choon assured they'd have all the water they needed after the battle, and Lewis was uncomfortably aware he had to trust the Mi-Anakka in this as well. Lack of water could destroy his force just as surely as the battle, or any other form of treachery at this point. He feared he'd been too trusting, but what choice did he have? He'd been swayed by the testimony of Privates Hudgens and Meder—both riding to the fight on a limber in spite of their injuries—the Infantry Lieutenant Manley, now commanding the foot artillery armed with muskets, and the two Rangers, of course. Ultimately, he'd gone with his gut. If they couldn't trust Varaa-Choon, they were all dead anyway.

Lieutenant Burton came galloping back, an Ocelomeh warrior clinging on behind. Reining up, he pushed a cloud of dust before him as the gasping horse dug in its hooves. "Just ahead, sir!" he declared. "This fellow has been watching."

The man jabbered excitedly at Father Orno, who spoke with equal passion to Boogerbear and Sal Hernandez.

"They've brought up all their lizardy reserves an' are fixin' to make a big push. Our boys are hard up, weak, an' wore out. They won't make it through."

The firing, much closer now, had been continuous but desultory for some time. Now they heard it rapidly quicken, growing more frenzied.

"How far?" Lewis demanded.

"Barely a quarter mile, sir," Burton said. "Just around the bend in the road. It curves in on the other side of that spur of trees."

Lewis's head jerked back and forth as he took things in and made quick decisions. "Lieutenant Olayne, take all the guns down on the beach through this cut and advance them abreast at the run. Pray the sand is harder than it looks, but you'll lash the horses to death if you must. Lieutenant Burton, all the dragoons will take up more of your fellows who are afoot and deploy between the guns when they unlimber. Lieutenant Manley?"

"Sir?"

"Bring your men up behind at the double time, but send a detachment to secure that area where the forest protrudes on the beach. That'll be our flank, understood? Bugler, I need your horse—no, stay atop her, just slide back. I need you as well."

As quickly as that, the specific battle plan Lewis longed to make earlier but couldn't was formed on the fly. Mounting in front of the bugler, he dashed down on the beach ahead of the dragoons, followed by limbered guns behind only four horses apiece. Lieutenant Manley was pushing the rest of the men straight through the trees, and the ragged column they formed practically sprinted ahead through the brilliant white sand.

"The colors, if you please," Lewis called to one of the dragoons behind him. The dragoons, artillerymen, and riflemen had all been going to join existing units, so they had no colors of their own, but the dragoon quickly uncased a national flag, and the Stars and Stripes whipped around him on its short staff as he galloped forward. It was a stirring moment, but Lewis was entirely unprepared for the scene awaiting him when he led his ragged, gasping force around the point of the clump of trees and saw the raging mass of lizard monsters, only described to him before, surging forward against the pitiful barricade and desperate men behind it. The shock gave him pause, but only for an instant, and he urged the bugler's horse forward to a point barely a hundred and fifty yards from the exposed enemy flank. Pulling back the reins, he cried, "Here, Lieutenant Olayne! Unlimber *here*, and load with double canister! Bugler, sound 'Column into Line,' then 'Battery, Action Front!' Over and over, do you hear?" He pointed at the beleaguered defenders. "You're doing it for *them*, not us!"

Fear of what lay before them must've gripped every man as they saw it, but they were too exhausted to flee even if they wanted to. Stopping to fight, even something so terrifying, actually came as a relief. Shock, fatigue, and inexperience combined to make Olayne's scratch cannon crews take three times as long to unlimber, load, and aim their pieces as Lewis was accustomed to seeing, but the process was still complete in less than a minute. Some of the lizards were edging toward them, and arrows started coming from the trees, but a flurry of rifle and carbine fire discouraged that as Sergeant Hayne led dragoons and riflemen in clearing the little wooded peninsula. The rest of the dragoons dismounted and took a knee between the guns as their horses were led to the rear. Gasping, coughing artillerymen serving as infantry piled in behind them in little fifteen-yard-wide clumps, three ranks deep. This was all accomplished by the time all four 6pdrs were double-loaded with canister and the gunners raised their fists to signify their readiness. It was a small force, but it was lethal, and it came as a complete surprise.

"Bugler, enough! I think they heard you," shouted Lewis. "Now let them hear *this*! Battery, on my command . . . fire!"

"Down, girl!" Captain Anson shouted, forgetting to maintain the fiction of her gender and throwing his daughter to the sand. "Everybody down, behind the barricade!" he roared, dropping low himself. Not knowing why he'd order such a thing even if they heard him, few of the desperate defenders complied. But they hadn't seen what he had. Hearing the bugle and braving the storm of spears arcing in, he'd quickly stepped up on an upright cask and gazed to the east—to see four beautiful, gleaming guns lined up from the trees to the water, with armed men hastily filling the spaces between them. Captain Cayce hadn't waited—he wondered why he was surprised—but he knew exactly what the man would do now. One after another, great, fiery yellow-white clouds of smoke blossomed in front of the guns, followed by the thunderous roars and hundreds of quarter-pound balls screaming into the surging horde. Anson had been concerned because he knew, at this range, the giant shotgun blasts might disperse enough to overlap the breastworks—and so they did, killing or wounding several men. But the vast majority of the swarm of projectiles churned their way through the tightly packed lizards, down the length of the assault, completely unexpected. Each ball smashed through two, sometimes three warriors, sending a flurry of bone and shattered weapon fragments all around, killing or flaying others with secondary projectiles. The howitzers De Russy's men had pulled from the wreck had done good service, but their crews were even greener than Cayce's, and they'd never had a flank to savage. More to the point, they were just too *slow* at loading and firing, and the men around them couldn't leave a gap for the crews to do their work. The sand made things worse. The howitzers could be loaded behind the line, but with the enemy so close, the infantrymen couldn't afford to make a gap long enough to help heave them into battery, so they'd played almost no role in what all expected would be this final defense. The effect of Captain Cayce's understrength battery of 6pdrs was utterly devastating, however, even before his men armed with muskets, rifles, and fast-shooting Hall carbines joined the slaughter.

Leonor struggled to her feet as the attack immediately ground to a halt all along the line because even those shrieking, bewildered lizards thus far unaffected were trying to determine what happened, which *direction* to attack.

"Have at 'em, damn you!" her father roared, even as the long-suffering infantry instinctively seized their opportunity and poured out a terrible fire. One of Lara's men screamed and fell, an arrow through his upper chest, and more arrows rained down, hitting men and lizards alike.

"They'll focus on Cayce's men, now," Anson shouted at her, shoving his last empty pistol in his belt and unslinging his rifle. "His men are even more exposed, poor devils." And that's what Leonor thought was happening when the arrows suddenly stopped, but then she heard an entirely new sound, a different clamor of shouting and shrieking and high-pitched yipping in the trees, and for the first time that day she saw Indians run out on the beach.

"They are joining the attack!" Lara called in dismay.

"No," she replied in growing wonder, "they're runnin' *from* somethin'!"

It was true. Hundreds of red-painted men of every band she'd seen—and others—with black, white, now yellow and pink swirling highlights, surged into the open before *they* started taking heavy-shafted arrows through their bodies!

"What in blazes . . . ?" Anson murmured, but it didn't stop him shooting a lizard that turned with a cawing wail as if to flee down the beach to the west. Four more thunderclaps shook the air, from the left, and more canister, better aimed this time, swept through the center of the teetering, bleeding horde. It broke. As if one mind controlled them all, the terrible lizards turned to sprint for the west, ignoring the flashing muskets and hot lead still savaging them as they swept past the breastworks, survivors not paying it the slightest heed.

Even before the front had cleared, however, it was plain another battle had commenced. Yelling and screeching, other Indians, unpainted and wearing leather tunics and leggings, were falling upon the painted men on the beach, trading arrowshots from mere yards and battling with flint-studded clubs and spears.

"*More* Injuns!" bawled an exhausted soldier with a tone of desolation, raising his musket to aim at one of the newcomers.

"Put that down!" snapped Sergeant Ulrich, voice raspy and raw. "Can't you see they're killin' the ones that was helpin' the bloody lizards? That puts 'em on our side, by my lights!"

But the man Ulrich stopped wasn't the only one still shooting. Spurred on by the sergeant's obvious statement, Leonor prodded her father because he seemed almost mesmerized. He quickly shook it off and nodded. "Cease firing!" he shouted as loud as he could, dry throat turning the words to a croak. "Cease firing, damn you!" he managed a bit louder.

Then sand was flying around galloping horses and Captain Lewis Cayce charged into view, saber raised, followed by Boogerbear, his color bearer, and a dozen dragoons. Several fired at the painted men while the bugler riding double with Lewis sounded "Cease Firing" at the corpse-covered barricade.

Lewis is putting himself between us and whoever these new Indians are! Leonor realized with astonishment, even though the fight wasn't over. His men were doing it too. At least a hundred sky-blue-clad soldiers with bright yellow trim on their jackets pounded through the sand in a mob to join their leader, hoarsely yelling and pouring fire into their enemies as they arrived. The bugle went silent, and Lewis was having trouble controlling his horse as it squealed and danced among the corpses, an arrow in its left hindquarter.

"In, boys, in!" came a strained cry Leonor recognized as Major Reed's. She hadn't seen him since the battle started, but he looked absolutely awful, waving his sword with his left hand, right arm in a bloody sling. "Back in the fight, my boys! That officer is my particular friend, and he just saved all our lives. You wouldn't have him lose his, would you? Get after those painted devils before they escape! The painted ones *only*, mind. Leave the others alone! Use the bayonet!"

A ragged cheer arose, venting fear, relief, and a thirst for revenge. Clumsily, bone-weary men heaved human and lizard bodies aside to crawl over the barricade and join comrades who'd so unexpectedly rescued them. *Most can barely stand,* Leonor thought, *and they won't be of any use. But maybe just the fact they're coming will help.* Her father grabbed his blood-caked saber, still standing in the sand, where he thrust it earlier, and joined the rush—such as it was. He was headed toward Lewis, now sitting still on his injured, frightened mount while arrows whipped past him. Leonor went the other way, followed by Barca, toward the arrow-bristling, one-sided fort. The scene behind was nightmarish, with scores of wounded lying on damp, salty sand. Each lapping wave was pink with blood as it drained back out to sea.

"What's happening? Have we lost?" asked a young woman, looking up from where she knelt by a groaning soldier. Her tense voice carried a strong, upper-class British accent, and Leonor thought she might even be very pretty if her dark blonde hair, face, and expensive beige gown weren't so covered with blood and her green eyes so sunken with worry and fatigue. Leonor barely recognized Dr. Newlin and Reverend Harkin, both equally drenched and drained. Her estimation of the fat preacher rose a notch. Only a few others were standing, mostly walking wounded helping as best they could, but a dark-haired woman stood utterly motionless behind the camp stool on which Colonel De Russy sat. She didn't look as bad as the busy one, but her face was ashen, eyes unseeing. Leonor wondered if she was actually dead on her feet. De Russy's expression was much the same as he stared down at the bright sword laid across his lap. Still bearing his musket, Barca went to the colonel.

Leonor looked back at the Englishwoman as she strode toward the picketed horses. "We ain't lost," she said, untying Arete and Colonel Fannin (both were still saddled, she noted with shame and annoyance), then spoke back over her shoulder, "Don't know if we won, though either." Without another word, she climbed on Colonel Fannin's back and led the other horse out.

CHAPTER 10

T he fighting was ending—slowly. Their lizard allies were abandoning the garishly painted Holcanos, and they were being assailed from the east, south, and now north as well, as their would-be victims boiled out of their works. They'd seen certain victory turn to crushing defeat so quickly that many fled with the lizards. But a couple hundred had been enveloped as three or four hundred Ocelomeh blocked their retreat. Fighting furiously, even maniacally, they killed attackers on all sides with their lethal bows. Lewis made a fine target and drew more than his share of rushed arrows, but he wasn't pressing forward anymore and there were more immediate threats. It tore at him to see a fearful number of Ocelomeh and his own men fall in those last, frenzied moments. But the trapped Holcanos were outnumbered and already low on arrows. Many were just as quickly shot down by muskets and bows, and the dragoons' Hall carbines finally came into their own, maintaining a rapid, murderous fire.

Probably hoping to break through to the woods, the Holcanos rushed the Ocelomeh, and the air was filled with high-pitched, bloodcurdling cries as the bitter enemies battled hand to hand. Still only briefly, however. These Indians, on both sides, fought as savagely as any Lewis ever heard of, but they were equally realistic. As soon as the Holcanos knew escape was impossible, they started tossing their weapons and dropping submissively into the sand. This didn't save them all. Many were ruthlessly butchered as they sat waiting, expecting it, and Lewis was horrified to see some of his own men, particularly the vengeful infantrymen, join the brutal slaughter with their bayonets.

"Enough!" he bellowed. "Bugler, sound 'Cease Firing' and 'Fall In.' Keep those men back, Sergeant McNabb," he ordered before the foot artillery-men could join the growing massacre. "Lieutenant Manley, take charge of those infantry. I want them in formation at once!" He glanced distastefully at the carnage. To his further dismay, the Ocelomeh—whom he'd imagined to be at least vaguely civilized—were enthusiastically hacking the heads off their victims.

"Don't you *dare* try to stop 'em, Lewis," came the wheezing voice of Captain Anson, now standing beside Boogerbear's horse. Lewis was sur-prised how glad he was to find the torn and blood-spattered Ranger alive.

"Of course not," Lewis grumbled reluctantly, finally slamming his un-bloodied saber back in its scabbard, "but our men will have no part in it."

"Some already have," Anson pointed out. A few men reluctantly joining the growing, panting line that Manley, McNabb, and now Lieutenant Bur-ton were shoving together had tucked bleeding scalps into their white leather belts. Lewis felt his hackles rise. Apparently reading his mind, Boogerbear leaned over to him. "Not yet, sir, if you don't mind a word of advice."

Lewis nodded. The big man was right. Still, it horrified him to see the scalps, as well as the Ocelomeh happily slaughtering helpless men and dancing with their grisly, dripping trophies.

"It's what they do, Lewis," Anson said, still trying to catch his breath. "The others have been doing it—an' worse—to *us*," he added grimly.

At that moment, Sal Hernandez pounded up alongside Justinian Olayne, who'd secured his guns and left them under the protection of their crews, Hayne's men, and Holland's sailors. Holland had stayed back as well. Father Orno was behind Hernandez and leaped off the horse before it completely stopped, already angrily haranguing the Ocelomeh in his curious Spanish. Some went on with what they were doing, but most stopped their capering at once, looking down, dropping heads in the sand.

"A priest?!" Anson exclaimed, astonished, understanding much of what Orno was saying. "I'm surprised enough by the warlike friends you brought, but where'd you find that fiery little fella?"

Before Lewis could reply, shocked and fearful muttering erupted in the ragged line of Americans that Manley and his helpers were shaping, and there was no telling what might've happened if it hadn't been mixed with men who came with Lewis. For it was then that Warmaster Varaa-Choon and Koaar-Taak pushed through their warriors, shouting just as angrily as Father Orno. Large eyes glaring, fur frizzed, teeth bared, and long tails held erect behind them, their outlandish nature couldn't have been displayed to more jarring effect. Though heads continued to be taken, Ocelomeh abruptly started roughly tying prisoners and herding them together instead of killing them. Captain Anson gaped, but Boogerbear raised his voice over those swelling in the ranks. "We know these fellas, so y'all just simmer down!"

Lewis nodded his thanks and exhaled a long breath. "It's quite a story, Captain Anson, and they're only part of it—as I'm sure you know already. Now at least we can compare what we've learned separately so we're better prepared for what comes next." His eye caught Leonor riding up, leading his horse. His relief to see Arete was a given and he'd wished he had her many times through the night, but he'd also been more concerned about the girl than he'd allowed himself to realize. She looked terrible, of course: battered, bruised, and bloody, yet erect and defiant in the saddle. She was certainly not beaten. He found himself drawn to her strength, particularly when he noted how quickly her surprised glance at the Mi-Anakka, still talking to their human warriors, turned to keen interest. She then met Lewis's gaze squarely as she slid off Colonel Fannin and handed the reins to Anson. "Your horse, Father," she said. "The day's just started an' I know you won't rest, so get up on him before you drop." Turning back to Lewis, she advanced with Arete's reins. "I'm obliged for the loan of your fine animal, sir. I apologize for takin' her into danger, though I reckon she got me out of it. As did you."

Lewis stepped down himself, flustered and unsure what to say. Looking up at the bugler, he told him, "Your horse needs attention. See she gets it." Turning back to Leonor, he took the reins she offered. "Thank you. I'm glad we could both be of service."

Anson was looking at his daughter, his expression similar to when he first saw Varaa and Koaar. "You berate me, then give Lewis the handsomest speech I ever heard out o' your mouth." He shook his head.

Lewis was looking around, really seeing many things for the first time.

He noted that the helpless British ship was still out there and wondered if it rendered any aid with its few guns. *Probably not,* he decided. *The wind wouldn't have let her bring many to bear, and she would've had to shoot right over the defenders. Without proper gun's crews aboard, that could've been disastrous.* Then he realized the steamer *Isidra* was gone. *Could she have developed an unstoppable leak and sunk?* "Who's in command here now?" he asked.

"Good question," Anson replied bitterly. "Isidra *left*, with Colonel Wicklow, his toadies, an' most of *Tiger's* passengers."

"Wicklow left?" Lewis asked, incredulously.

"For Vera Cruz," Anson confirmed.

"I doubt he'll find what he's looking for," Lewis murmured, dark and cryptic. "Who does that leave?"

"Colonel De Russy of the Third Pennsylvania." Anson lowered his voice and added delicately, "Who seems pretty flexible about delegatin' authority. There's also a Major Reed, who deserted Wicklow to stay with the regular infantry that came ashore to make room in *Isidra* for the civilians. Says he knows you. He led well enough, an' there's no doubtin' his courage, but he's hurt pretty bad. So . . ." Anson shrugged.

Lewis removed his wheel hat and mopped sweat on his brow, gazing at the awful aftermath of the fighting around the barricade. "Well, for the present . . ." He paused and took a small sip from his canteen before noticing the greedy stares of the others. Murmuring an apology, he passed the canteen to Leonor. "We brought a little water. Our . . . allies promised more." He looked at Anson. "Your, ah, son is right. Just when what we need most is rest, we have more to do. We have to see to our defenses, of course, and this is a terrible place for that. And there's the wounded. We already had more than we could care for at *Mary Riggs.* Now this!"

"At least there's a doctor here, an' helpers," Leonor said, remembering Newlin and the Englishwoman.

"That's good," Lewis said, "but just as important, we have to get everything out of *Commissary's* wreck, down to the last candle stub or musket ball that might've rolled into a crack."

Anson was looking questioningly at him. "Come," Lewis said. "Now that they seem to have finished their . . . victory celebration, you need to meet our new friends." He frowned. "I don't know that we *are* friends, exactly, since they only helped us to ensure our weapons didn't fall into their enemy's hands. But we're going to need them, as you'll see, so we'd best make sure they don't come to view us as a nuisance."

Before they could proceed, Varaa-Choon, Koaar-Taak, Father Orno, and several older Ocelomeh strode over to them. Varaa was grinning widely and immediately addressed the fear Lewis confessed as she clasped his arm behind the hand he'd extended under the assumption she meant to shake it. Lewis clasped her arm in return, near the elbow, and felt strong muscles under the fur.

"Captain Cayce! Father Orno has proclaimed you saviors of his people! This was the greatest victory ever achieved over the debased Holcanos and vile Dominion, and your people—like the Ocelomeh have long been—are now the brothers and protectors of the Uxmalos!" She made that *kakking* chuckle. "We fought so well together one might almost think we had a plan beyond 'you go that way, I'll go this way'! When King Har-Kaaska hears of this, I'm sure he'll be pleased to name you friends and brothers to the Ocelomeh as well!"

Lewis smiled with relief, glancing at Anson, Leonor, and Lieutenant Olayne, who'd joined them. "We're honored." He proceeded to introduce those closest and saw Varaa's large eyes appraising Leonor. Coughing slightly, he nodded behind Varaa at the trees where Ocelomeh wounded were being carried and tended. "I see you have wounded. We do as well— quite a few. We need to see to them all."

"Of course," Varaa agreed, more somber. "Our healers will do all they can to help yours." She caught his look of concern. "I understand better than you know how . . . awkward it might be while brothers learn one another. As I told you, my birth people have long experience with that." She gazed at the line of soldiers, now silent, straining to hear, and raised her voice. "Besides, suffering is a common language, and we've suffered together as we fought together! Few things bind brothers more firmly than that." She spoke to Lewis again. "Still, we'll go slow. For now, let's secure this area as best we can. We never linger on battlefields because the smell of blood draws so many monsters, but there's never been a battle on such a scale in such a small place, and there's no help for it in this case. Perhaps your great guns can discourage the bigger beasts, and my warriors who weren't engaged will keep pushing the broken enemy. They already found a number of horses the Holcanos stole!"

She looked at Father Orno. "But more Ocelomeh and Uxmalos should already be on the way. They'll come over the next several days, and we'll begin moving your people and supplies to Uxmal itself."

Filling with a growing relief, Lewis still couldn't help glancing back at the wreck and the wallowing British ship. Varaa guessed his concern. "We'll leave nothing for the Holcanos when they come sneaking back. I know the loss of your ships was tragic for you, but the salvage—just in iron!—is more valuable than you can imagine." She gazed almost longingly out at HMS *Tiger*. "And *that* ship, of course . . . The Dominion navy is small, but more than sufficient to sink or capture it as it is. We can't allow that. We'll help repair it well enough to sail to Uxmal harbor before word gets back to the Doms, never fear." Varaa looked around before clapping her hands together. "As you say, there's much to do. Take us to meet the rest of your people so they can get over their first shock"—she blinked and *kakked* again—"and we'll see what we can do to help."

Anson rushed to interject, "There's a preacher named Harkin over there, a, ah, 'priest' with strict beliefs similar to those of a lot of our people," he warned with a glance at Father Orno, who certainly looked and acted like a Jesuit. He looked back at Varaa. "And I've no idea what he'll make of *you*," he blurted. "There might be trouble."

Lewis frowned. There could be indeed. There were plenty of Catholics in the army, mostly Irish, but this "preacher" was doubtless Protestant. He'd have no love for what he might only see as a Catholic priest, and probably a nativist Jesuit.

"Is he intelligent?" Varaa asked simply.

Anson glanced at Lewis, then back at Varaa. "I guess. I don't really know him."

"Does his faith require abject submission to its worldly representatives? Does it condone torture? Murder? Demand the ritualistic disfigurement and sacrifice of younglings?" Varaa demanded flatly, coldly.

Taken aback, Anson angrily shook his head. "Of course not!"

"Does yours?" Leonor interjected sharply, waving at the rough treatment of prisoners and ongoing beheadings.

Varaa frowned. "A good point," she conceded. "No one's at their best after a battle, and all the Indios of this region take captives and trophies, but even if I understand their motivation—you know too little of our circumstances to judge—I've already chastised my Ocelomeh for their excess. And no, such things aren't part of their faith. Particularly not of the Uxmalos."

Varaa looked back at Anson. "So if your 'priest' is capable of reason, he'll recognize that any differences he has with Father Orno's faith, that of the Ocelomeh, or even mine, for that matter, are insignificant compared to what the Doms would force on the world. Father Orno is *very* intelligent," Varaa assured, "and if he can occasionally peel the misguided away from the Doms, he can gain the tolerance of any sensible, well-meaning man."

Anson arched his eyebrows at Lewis and pursed his lips.

LEWIS BEGAN PASSING quiet orders to dazed-looking officers and NCOs as soon as they crossed the barricade. Meeting Major Andrew Reed, whom he did know very well, he briefly explained the situation to the pain- and surprise-addled officer, who was completely content to let Lewis take the lead for the present. Captain Holland came up with the caissons, water was distributed, and Reed echoed Lewis's order that fatigue parties join the Ocelomeh in burying the Allied dead and moving everyone and everything up to the forest peninsula. There they'd cut trees, in and around it, to form a new defensive position. It was slightly elevated, there was shade, and most important, it would get them away from the enemy dead, which were simply too numerous to deal with. "Let the monsters have them and perhaps they'll leave us alone," Varaa-Choon had said, before suggesting they gather wood for fires as well.

Dead tired as everyone was, the work commenced rapidly. These men had lost too many already injured friends in the first attack and were anxious to protect the rest, as well as themselves. More to the point, with the noisy fighting over, flocks of lizardbirds began returning to the copious carrion, and those who'd come with Lewis quickly assured the rest that lizardbirds were nothing compared to other things. More quickly than Lewis would've imagined, with American soldiers and Ocelomeh toiling together in somewhat uneasy harmony, the dead were buried (and in some cases even reunited with their proper heads), the new position was completed, and Captain Holland and his sailors, along with Olayne and some artillerymen, hauled loads of those too hurt to walk over to the peninsula on limbers and caissons. The guns had all been posted inside the new "fort." Throughout all this, eyes were frequently drawn to HMS *Tiger*. They had a single, damaged boat, one of *Commissary's* smaller ones that might be repaired, and Captain Holland had a couple of his men start on it, but *Tiger* wouldn't send another despite frequent signals asking her to. Men were working on her, though not very many, and they seemed to be trying to jury-rig a bowsprit so she might hoist a headsail. It didn't make sense. No one could really blame them for being too afraid to come ashore during the battle—no doubt they'd seen the nature of the enemy through their telescopes—but with the battle over, why stay away?

As it turned out, Captain Anson was right to worry about how Reverend Harkin would react to the appearance of otherworldly beings in their midst. But he'd already seen the evil kind, so he was willing to reserve judgment on the Mi-Anakka who'd helped them. And as for Father Orno . . . Harkin had prepared himself for this expedition by acquiring a smattering of Spanish, so Father Orno, with the aid of Sal Hernandez, was able to convince him to do the same in all respects until he knew more. Besides, despite his admittedly pompous ways, Harkin was a dedicated servant of God who believed the requirements of the injured came before his own need to correct heathens, and he was simply too exhausted from his own attempts to help Dr. Newlin to press objections to any aid too strongly. Especially when it quickly became apparent the Ocelomeh healers not only really wanted to help, but Dr. Newlin himself was impressed by their skill. For the present, he'd accept that aid in the spirit it seemed to be meant while he rested and refortified himself for the theological battle to come.

Now, as the shadows of late afternoon began to lengthen and Dr. Newlin supervised the placement of the last of his patients on a caisson drawn by Lieutenant Olayne and three other riders, Lewis watched Harkin as Newlin's other equally tired and bloodstained helper (Reed told him her name was Samantha Wilde, daughter of the British vice-consul at Vera Cruz, of all things!) helped him remove a gore-stained apron. Both quickly washed themselves as best they could before joining the rest of the surviving officers and Ocelomeh leaders finally gathered around Colonel De Russy, the armed and bloody Barca, and the outwardly catatonic woman named Angelique Mercure, who hadn't moved from behind them. She stirred at the sight of the Mi-Anakka, dead eyes coming to light with terror, but that was her only reaction.

De Russy finally stirred as well, glancing up and around. His eyes also lit on Varaa-Choon and Koaar, but showed no surprise as he cleared his throat. "I must apologize," he said dismally. "Apologize to you all. It distresses me profoundly to confess that I found myself personally . . . ill equipped to do anything about the events that have transpired. That doesn't mean I've been *unaware* of them," he hastily added, "I just simply never imagined . . ." He sighed, looking up at Lewis. "You're Captain Cayce, are you not? Major Reed informed me that you and . . . our strange new friends are most responsible for our physical salvation. The initiative you took in consenting to an alliance with an unknown power"—he glanced at Varaa—"may have been unorthodox, but I see no basis for rebuke under the circumstances since that and your immediate forced march here with those same allies undoubtedly preserved our small force from a terrible extinction." He looked at Anson. The Ranger had worked as hard as anyone, largely from his horse as Lewis had, but had found a moment to wash himself and his shirt in the surf. "And you, Captain Anson. In addition to the courage you displayed scouting the enemy camp and fighting back through his forces and leading an element of the defense, without the men you supplied to discover the enemy preparations for attack, as well as make contact with Warmaster Varaa-Choon's Ocelomeh, Captain Lewis could never have known of our predicament in the first place. I commend you, sir."

"Thank you, Colonel," Anson said sincerely, realizing what De Russy was going through. He was passing honest accolades in spite of finding himself lacking. Anson had to do the same. "I have to bring Alferez Lara an' his men to your attention as well, sir," he said. "We wouldn't've made it back without 'em, an' they fought alongside us throughout the action. I strongly recommend we invite 'em to join us indefinitely, with no requirement for surrender or parole."

"Of course," De Russy agreed, peering at the youth in the Mexican uniform standing self-consciously beside Lieutenant Burton. "Do you still wish to join us, Alferez?" De Russy asked.

"I believe it's even more crucial to our mutual survival now than I did," Lara said.

"Very well." De Russy looked at Reverend Harkin, then turned his gaze to Varaa-Choon. "I know nothing about you," he said uncomfortably, "but I do know we'd all be dead without you and your warriors. Perhaps this truly is purgatory—a common sentiment just now, I understand—but I suppose even there it's important to have friends." He stood with a groan and sheathed his sword. "So, until I receive orders from a superior officer to the contrary, it's my order that we *be* friends and you may rely on us to be of equal service to you as you were to us in our need."

"I'm glad to hear it, Colonel De Russy," Varaa-Choon said. Angelique Mercure jolted and made a little squeak at the sound of Varaa's voice. Samantha Wilde went to her, possibly for the first time since the battle started, and the dark-haired girl almost melted against her.

De Russy reluctantly turned back to face Lewis and spoke in a tone of brittle dignity. "I have one final order to give. In light of my current . . . inadequacies, and Major Reed's dangerous wound—Dr. Newlin fears he may lose his arm and faces a lengthy incapacity at best—and in view of your own amply demonstrated leadership qualities, I hereby order *you* to assume military command of this combined American force upon these strange and unknown shores."

Lewis was staggered. He'd had enough of "overall" command, just of those forces stranded with *Mary Riggs*. He'd expected to assume more authority in their current situation, over all the artillery at least, and was prepared for that. But he'd been looking forward to dumping the rest back in someone else's lap. On the other hand, De Russy was right. Lewis admired his integrity, but he was clearly unready for something like this. *Reed should be . . . But no, Dr. Newlin's already evacuated him to the new fort. I didn't realize he was hurt that bad—but I didn't stop doing what needed to be done long enough to check on him either,* he realized with a touch of shame.

That and his uncertainty must've shown on his bearded face, because De Russy's expression turned sympathetic. "I'm a good politician, but was never a soldier before now. Turns out I'm *not* very good at that." He straightened. "Not yet. I intend to learn at your side, Captain. Perhaps one day I can relieve you of the burden I've thrust upon you. Until then, our relations with the Ocelomeh and these other people—Uxmalos, was it?—will require the efforts of a diplomat—a politician, if you will—and I'll focus my attention there while you do your best for our men. I promise not to interfere in any way, and yours will be the final say. Are we agreed?"

Lewis caught Anson watching him, nodding almost imperceptibly, while Captain Holland was nodding outright with somewhat embarrassing enthusiasm. Then he saw Leonor's expression, and it seemed as if she was pleading with him. *Yes? No?* He wondered which she meant.

"Very well, sir. If you think it's best, then I agree," he told De Russy.

"Agree?" De Russy growled indignantly. "Of course you do. It was an *order*, after all, and I only asked you out of courtesy." He sighed. "Now that command has been changed, what are *your* orders?"

Lewis looked over the top of the one-sided fort and saw frightening shapes already moving among the enemy corpses. Only the caisson, a handful of dragoons, and a squad of infantry and Ocelomeh in equal numbers remained with them. Everyone else, American and Ocelomeh, had already gathered in the new fort up in the trees. Lights were there: lanterns and growing fires. Out to sea, HMS *Tiger* still wallowed, and Lewis wished he knew what was what with her. Holland, along with Lieutenant Burton, Private Buisine, and several sailors, would be putting off in the repaired boat after dark. *Tiger* was acting so strange, there was no telling how she'd receive visitors. Holland preferred to approach her as if she was hostile. That was risky, of course, but it was his show. *Mine too, now,* Lewis realized. *From this point on, I'm responsible for everything and everyone.* "It's time to go," he said at last. "What are your intentions, Captain Holland?"

"We'll shove off an' lie in *Commissary*'s shadow until full dark, away from the feastin' beasties an' outa sight." He shrugged. "Then we'll head out an' have a look."

"Be very careful," Lewis warned, encompassing Burton and the others who'd go with his gaze. "We can't spare you. Can't spare anyone. Make for the lights of the new fort when you return."

Holland laughed. "Have no fear. I can't spare me neither."

CHAPTER 11

"W on't they hear us?" asked Coryon Burton as the sailors rowed the small boat across the choppy waves. Besides Captain Holland in the stern at the tiller, Burton and Private Buisine were the only ones not heaving an oar, and the noise they made, along with the slapping water, sounded terribly loud to him.

"The wind an' surf'll cover us," Holland replied, talking almost normally. "The moon's another hour away, an' dark as it's got, they won't see us neither. That's why we steered away before turnin' back to 'em, so the campfires an' lanterns onshore won't backlight us."

Burton looked down at the Hall carbine in his hands, then glanced at Buisine's identical weapon. "I don't know why we're sneaking up on them. Why not simply announce ourselves?"

"We've been tryin' that all day," Holland said with a frustrated snort; then he sat glumly a moment while they drew closer to the dark ship. There was a feeble glow in the windows at the stern and only a single lantern on deck. No movement could be seen. "Just seemed the thing to do, strange as they're behavin'," Holland continued with a sigh. "Maybe it's right, maybe not. I've always known what to do when my only concern was the sea. An' believe me, she's tricky an' inscrutable as any foe. But after the last couple of days . . . my wits're all adrift an' I ain't as bold as I was." A hand brushed his craggy, stubbly cheeks. "Gettin' old," he murmured. "Too old for the choices Captain Cayce'll face, an' I don't envy him," he added cryptically. The ship was much closer, and he nodded ahead, warning his sailors, "Ease up on them oars, you pack o' fishwives," before addressing Burton in a lower voice. "Brits are odd folk. I fought 'em, you know. No people on earth as genteel an' vicious at the very same time! Their man-o'-war's men an' soldiers're terrible brave, as brave as any. Arrogant too, 'cause they think they own the world. That's cost 'em from time to time. But because o' that, an' *bein'* genteel, they'll usually join a fight like we had today regardless that we don't like each other. Women ashore should'a capped it. But genteel alone can be kin to shyness, an' that makes me think there *ain't* no man-o'-war's men on that ship, nor soldiers neither. If there is, they ain't been *let* to help by somebody who's fit to shit with fear. Fear's too unpredictable an' I don't ever trust it. So that begs the question: do we go gallopin' an' hallooin' up to a ship full o' fraidycats that likely have every gun stuffed to the muzzle with harmful objects, or do we put the sneak on 'em?"

They were under the guns now in any event, closing beneath the looming dark fo'c'sle.

"I suppose a case might be made either way," Coryon whispered uncertainly—and was suddenly nearly pitched into the sea when something hit the boat. A large, pebbly-skinned creature rolled, flapping a webbed flipper as long as he was tall. Coryon saw a huge luminescent red eye behind long, tooth-studded jaws just before the thing sank from view.

"God save us!" Private Buisine cried out too loud. "There's devils in the water as well!"

"Aye, by Jaysus!" shouted a sailor, slashing at the water where the thing went down with his oar. A musket flashed and cracked above them, launching a geyser of spray alongside.

"Belay that shootin', above an' below!" Holland roared as Coryon aimed at a smoky silhouette leaning over the fo'c'sle rail by the starboard cathead. "We're from shore, come to check on your welfare, you gawpy looby!"

"Lord above!" came the excited response. "Beg pardon down there! Reckoned you was all dead, we did. Dead an' ate up! I took you for another sea monster, primin' to climb the side!"

"Well, we ain't sea monsters, or all dead either, so stow that musket an' throw down a line."

The man above hesitated. "Mr. Semmes said we was to alert 'im for anythin' unusual."

"Then I'm sure he's had a busy time," Holland groused. The boat heaved again, and its crew cried out in alarm. "Hook on, Barry," Holland told one of his sailors. "Throw down a line or we *will* be ate, an' what use'll we be to you then?" Holland shouted up.

Without another word exchanged, a Jacob's ladder tumbled down the side of the ship and the men started up. They were met on the fo'c'sle by a roughly equal number of sailors, quickly gathering. All were armed and very nervous.

"I'm Semmes, first lieutenant of *Tiger*," greeted a young-sounding man in shirtsleeves and weskit, holding a newly lighted lantern. He was taller than the rest and practically gaunt, but the light revealed large, intent eyes in a bony but boyish face. "Your presence would indicate there were survivors ashore."

"Aye," Holland returned bitterly, "no thanks to you. Despite my past differences with the Royal Navy, I'd expected better from a King's ship!"

Semmes looked stricken. "Sir, I beg you . . . there was nothing we could do!" He gestured around at the perhaps dozen men now gathered. "We're all there are, left merely as caretakers for the hulk until Captain Peese arranges a tow to fetch us."

"Your captain *left* you?" Holland asked, unbelieving.

"Captain and owner," Semmes corrected sourly. "*Tiger* is no King's ship, sir. Captain Peese's company bought her at auction when she was sold out of service." He waved at the sailors again. "And you wrong these men. This crew was barely strong enough to sail her even before she was damaged, so many being dissatisfied with their treatment by Captain Peese that they jumped ship at Vera Cruz before we took on passengers and cargo."

"You might have taken a hand with some of her guns," Coryon Burton accused. Two cannon stood on either side of the fo'c'sle, securely lashed.

Semmes gaped at the young dragoon officer and actually laughed. "Aye, though her heavier guns are gone, she still bears twenty 12pdrs on the upper gun deck, and ten 6pdrs on the quarterdeck and fo'c'sle. But they haven't been exercised since she left the service, and few of these men would know how to use them." He glanced at Holland and shrugged. "Captain Peese only kept them, aye, and ensured the men kept them polished and painted, to make his passengers feel safe from pirates and savages. Your people on-shore seemed burdened enough without us dropping a few roundshot among them!"

Holland nodded, finally mollified. "Aye," he agreed, "that might've done 'em in. It was very close."

"But all is now well?" Semmes persisted. Holland frowned, looking at *Tiger*'s anxious sailors, then his own men, eyes lingering on Burton.

"Didn't you see us signaling you?" Burton demanded.

Semmes looked down. "We did, but we couldn't be quite certain *who* was signaling, could we?"

Holland pursed his weathered lips. "Perhaps not, from here," he grudgingly allowed. "Well, with the help o' . . . some locals, we won on the beach. But I reckon you saw the nature of our enemy? An' you've seen the monster fish in the water. I'd be lyin' if I told you 'all's well.' An' I wouldn't count on your captain hirin' a tow if I were you, or even him—or anyone in *Isidra*—returnin'. Small loss as far as Captain Peese goes, I say, an' a few others as well," he added with disgust. "But from what I learned from Father Orno—one o' those locals I talked with durin' the fightin'—what we call Vera Cruz is in the hands of the enemy. Even if *Isidra* tried to come back, without her sails, she ain't got the coal to do it."

"Unfortunate for you if the Mexicans expelled the Americans from their city," Semmes agreed with false sympathy, "but it should make no difference to us."

Holland blinked, then understood. "Oh, you're wrong about that." He pointed at the glittering little fires in the woods near the dark, distant beach. "We, they, are the only friends you got in the world. There are no 'Mexicans' in Vera Cruz. It's controlled by the same people who stirred up the Indians and monsters we fought. Aye, they'll come for you in time, an' likely tow you away, but you'll find it makes *quite* a difference when they do." Forging ahead through the growing dismay, Holland waved at the beach again. "We'll help you get sail on this ship, us an' some of our new friends, an' we'll get you to a safe harbor. You'll know more by then an' can decide for yourselves what to do."

―――――

Lewis clutched his aching side and grimaced, but the move was unnoticed in the darkness as he stood with Lieutenant Olayne, Varaa-Choon, and one of the older Ocelomeh warriors—a dark, brooding man named Ixtla. Captain Marvin Beck, senior infantry officer after Andrew Reed, was there as well. Together, near one of the 12pdr howitzers, its muzzle jutting past a fallen tree, they watched the shore below them seethe with indistinct shapes gorging on dead Grik and humans, or fighting for choice morsels. The sight, which left much to the imagination, thank God, was bad enough, but the rough tearing sounds and squishy *slap* of entrails being torn out, along with the chilling *crunch* of bones, was utterly revolting. Lewis had ordered everyone not on watch to sleep, but few could. Not yet.

Instead, and in spite of the horror all around them and the presence of a large number of very strange Indians, the forest peninsula seemed populated by ordinary soldiers going about quite ordinary tasks. Combined with the water salvaged from *Commissary* and more brought from *Mary Riggs*, there was plenty to last a few days, at least, and many had enjoyed their first hot meal since they were stranded. Lewis still worried about water. For such a green land, it seemed very dry. But Koaar assured him water would come soon. He assumed that meant the Uxmalos would bring it. So, soldiers and Ocelomeh, still a bit wary of each other but happy to be friends, ate and smoked each other's pipes (the Ocelomeh had their own tobacco, harsh and strong but cut with herbs), and tried to learn to communicate. Other men, overtired and too keyed up to sleep, lounged around fires and smoked or chewed tobacco by themselves, thoughtfully cleaning their filthy weapons.

Musket flints were gently knapped until dull edges flaked away, leaving them sharp and ready to strike sparks again. More water was used to wash black fouling from bores grown so tight they'd become difficult to load. The usual hilarity ensued when a man used a tight wad of tow on his ramrod to compress the sludgy black water pooled in the breech of his gun to make it "piss" at an unsuspecting comrade by directing the vent and squirting a long jet of muck on his victim. Anyone who saw it exploded in laughter. It was a prank as old as firearms, and NCOs would normally jump on the men for doing it. There was always leniency for such things after a battle, however, and Lewis had instructed there be even more tonight. Let the men laugh if they could.

"Dr. Newlin," he said as the spare man in spectacles approached, accompanied by someone else. "And Mistress Samantha," he added, remembering the name of the woman who'd helped the doctor so heroically. She wore the same damaged gown as before, but the firelight revealed that her wet blonde hair and milky-white face and arms were clean. "We owe you both a huge debt."

"It is we who are indebted to you, sir," Samantha said with the slightest curtsey. Despite her appearance and fatigue, she managed to infuse the gesture with grace. "As Colonel De Russy said, without you and the *fascinating* Warmaster Varaa-Choon"—she beamed at the Mi-Anakka—"none of us would have survived."

Lewis felt the same discomfort that always came over him around attractive women. He understood soldiers, but women had always mystified him. Worse, the few he'd courted and one he'd actually fallen for all ultimately proved to be vacuous, entitled, capricious creatures, more interested in an attachment to the Cayce name and land than to him. His father had wholeheartedly approved of them. Lewis knew not all women were like that and genuinely admired the wives of some of his friends—Major Reed's, for example—but he'd tired of searching for one and devoted all his attention to the army. This Samantha Wilde was a different sort—as was Leonor, he quickly reminded himself. Both were brave, and . . . unselfishly useful and helpful (he couldn't think of a better way to put it), while shunning convention to the extreme. That didn't make him *understand* them, but he certainly respected them.

Before Lewis could compose a response to honor the Englishwoman's contributions while making light of his own, Varaa jubilantly remarked, "Very true! The Ocelomeh and Captain Cayce saved you all, and we whipped the Holcano, Grik, and creeping Doms in the greatest fight in the memory of this continent." Varaa gazed at Captain Beck. "I only regret we missed the first part."

"So do I," Beck wryly agreed. Of all the American officers, the dark-haired and relatively short but physically powerful Marvin Beck seemed to take the Ocelomeh, even the Mi-Anakka, most in stride. Lewis wondered if that was due to a childhood familiarity with peaceful Indians in the Wisconsin Territory, a generally friendly personality, or simple exhaustion. The latter, combined with relief, was probably the primary reason most of the men were so accepting, for now.

Lewis cleared his throat. "I'm sorry for all you've endured, ah . . ."

"'Mistress Samantha' will do nicely."

"Thank you. Is there anything I can do for you?"

"A change of clothes would do very well, but I don't suppose that's possible. Mistress Angelique and I came ashore with nothing but what we were wearing. It never remotely occurred to us we'd be left behind."

"Of course not," said Olayne, anger in his voice. "But perhaps Captain Holland will secure your baggage," he encouraged.

"Is Mistress Angelique quite well?" Lewis pressed.

Samantha pursed her lips. "She's sleeping now, poor thing, but I believe she will recover. I never should've allowed her ashore with me. She's French, you know, but our fathers are very close and involved in business together. Angelique and I have known each other since we were infants." She stood straighter. "But I'm a soldier's daughter. *Tiger* was dismasted but little hurt otherwise, and when I learned of the suffering ashore I *had* to offer my help—as I did after the Battle of Punniar, when Father helped defeat the Marathas," she added proudly. "Poor Angelique had no such experience but refused to be left behind. That was before the other . . . unpleasantness began, of course," she added darkly.

"I hope she feels better," Lewis told her sincerely, then turned his attention to Dr. Newlin. "The wounded are comfortable?"

"Tolerably," Newlin replied. "There are *very* many, and the army surgeons were murdered with the rest of the wounded we foolishly left so exposed." Newlin sighed, then belatedly bowed his head to Varaa. "Father Orno and the healers you loaned me are wonderfully accomplished, and their remedies appear at least as efficacious as any I know. Particularly in terms of pain relief." His puffy red eyes turned back to Lewis. "Your large, hairy Ranger friend told me Father Orno practically insisted I get some sleep." He smiled. "My confidence in him and my meager stamina compel me to obey." He cast an accusing glance at Samantha. "*Very* soon. My few remaining assistants should do the same. You really must rest, my dear."

"I shall," she assured, "but I couldn't relax before expressing my gratitude to our rescuers—and possibly, finally, learning more about our predicament. Speculation is rampant, but the only details that agree came with the men Captain Cayce brought." She turned her head to Varaa. "I assume you provided them?"

Varaa's big eyes looked at Lewis, who frowned. A moment later, he shrugged. "Tell them. I didn't tell the men everything, and only a few know all we're capable of understanding: myself, Captain Holland, and now Captain Anson." He shook his head, wincing at the pain in his side once again.

"But that's not enough. I need more people to know because I'll need their help. Besides, it might almost be better if word came out slowly, in bits and pieces." He took a deep breath, stretching the wound in his side. "So, if you promise to be discreet, informing only those who are responsible, I'd be grateful if Varaa-Choon would do her best to explain once more." He looked at Newlin, Olayne, and Captain Beck. "To all of you. I warn you, though, the truth is likely even more frightening than you expect."

"Oh dear," Newlin said worriedly. "Very well. Lance the boil, I say." Samantha said nothing, but looked at the Mi-Anakka expectantly. So did Lieutenant Olayne. Captain Beck merely nodded, sure he could cope. He was right, but only barely. "Dear God," he murmured when Varaa finished. "Preposterous!" sputtered Dr. Newlin. Olayne seemed downcast but unsurprised. "Amazing," said Samantha, excited but clearly troubled. "You say we can't go back—from wherever we are?"

"No way is known," Varaa confirmed.

Samantha looked at Lewis and almost reached for him. Dropping her hand, she looked down instead. "Poor Father," she murmured. "He'll think I'm lost."

"We *are* lost!" Beck exclaimed, almost loud enough to carry to the nearby artillerymen.

"Get hold of yourself, Captain!" Lewis hissed. "Yes, we're lost to the world we knew, and for that reason we bear a heavier responsibility to our men than we ever have." He was growing angry. "Why do you think I hesitated to take command, damn you? I already *knew*! But the only hope our people have is that *we'll* stay strong, keep them together, *keep them soldiers*, and set an example of courage and confidence. Do you understand?"

Slowly, Captain Beck nodded.

"That will only work so long," Newlin realized aloud. "The regulars will stay in line for a while. At least most will, as long as you keep them fed. But the volunteers . . . ? They signed up 'for the duration,' but *their* war is suddenly over. How will you 'keep them soldiers' without a legal right to do so, and without resorting to tyranny—which would only scatter them anyway?"

"That's simple enough," said Leonor, abruptly striding in among them. Lewis wondered how long she'd been listening but realized it didn't matter. Her father would've told her if she, like Boogerbear, hadn't already figured it out for herself. She stopped in front of Samantha, looking her up and down. "Fancy outfit," she grudgingly told her. "Not very practical, though.

I'd hate to try to fight in a getup like that." Before Samantha could respond, Leonor turned to Lewis. "Simple," she repeated. "First thing, we get everybody safe to that Uxmal place. Get set up an' start everybody healin'. Keep 'em an army the whole time, though. Flags, drums, everything. Keep 'em *proud* an' no lapse in discipline." She looked at Captain Beck. "But break any junior officers an' NCOs who live to lord it over fellas, an' keep the discipline *fair*, with punishment fittin' a crime for a change."

Singling Beck out for such criticism might've been unwarranted—Lewis barely knew him—but army discipline was notoriously capricious. Looking back at Lewis, Leonor continued, "Rumors'll fly the whole time, o' course, but when we get settled, you lay it all out. Tell 'em the *whole* truth." She chuckled. "By then, it probably won't be as bad as they think it is."

"But how do we keep them together? Keep them Americans?" Dr. Newlin insisted.

Lewis already knew. Gazing at Leonor with even greater respect for her intellect, he spoke softly. "Our men will never *stop* being Americans, Doctor. Even immigrants new to the States already loved the *idea* of America, and many could already quote much of our Constitution by heart." As if changing the subject, he looked at Varaa. "You say we're 'brothers' and 'protectors' to the Uxmalos now. That implies the battle we fought isn't an isolated incident and they need ongoing security."

"That's true," said the human warrior named Ixtla, surprising them all with his command of English. Lewis supposed he must've learned it from Varaa or Koaar, though he couldn't imagine why. From what he'd gathered, there were few Mi-Anakka in this land—and English wasn't *their* first language either. "The Ocelomeh have long provided that protection," Ixtla continued, adding simply, "We are a warrior tribe. Defending those who cannot defend themselves is our purpose." He said that so plainly, so sincerely, Lewis not only believed him at once but was struck with admiration for the apparent purity of his people's philosophy. Particularly since it rather mirrored his own. Though it had never really come to him quite so distinctly before, he realized now he'd always considered the small, prewar regular army of the United States a "tribe" unto itself as well, performing the very same duty.

Varaa nodded and twitched her rounded ears out at the beach of death. "That may become more difficult now. Those *things*, the Holcanos and Grik, are nothing compared to what the Doms could bring against us. They're merely the foul breath of the distant beast. You don't yet know how vast and powerful the Holy Dominion is. We in this Yucatán have remained isolated from it, and its attention has long been elsewhere." She sighed. "But its power is built on terror and unthinking obedience to its twisted faith. It won't suffer dissent to exist, and we won't be safe forever. Already they push us harder every year through their Grik and Holcano pets. In all honesty, I doubt we could've stopped them this time if they hadn't been drawn here, and were already savaged so severely," she concluded glumly.

Ixtla regarded Leonor. "I talked to Alferez Lara—interesting that some of your enemies would be among you, fighting at your side! And he speaks a language similar to mine." He waved that away. "But he told me when he joined you and Captain Anson in scouting the Holcano camp to the west, you saw Amarillos—'Yellows'—there."

This was the first Lewis heard of that.

"Yes," Leonor said, then described them for the others' benefit. "Those were these 'Dom' fellas you been talkin' about?"

"Dominion soldiers," Ixtla pronounced grimly. "We have called them 'Doms' since even before the Mi-Anakka came to us," he added dismissively. "You killed or injured some of them?" he pressed.

"We did," Leonor confirmed. "They didn't leave us much choice."

Ixtla looked at Varaa, who blinked and frowned. "The Doms care nothing for their so-called allies, or even the lives of their own people. They spend them wastefully enough," she added bitterly. "But the scope of our victory over those they support will trouble them. And that 'heretics' not only dared to harm uniformed Dominion solders but were actually *able* to will embarrass them and undermine the aura of invincibility they strive to project. It may inspire them to contemplate a more direct approach against us."

"What does that mean?" asked Olayne.

Varaa hesitated. "If they send a Dominion army into our land, a *real* army with professional soldiers"—she glanced at the 12pdr howitzer nearby—"with many great guns like yours, the time of harassment by surrogates will be over. They won't stop until this land is fully theirs and all its people slaughtered or enslaved. The Verdadero Cristianos will be gone forever." Her huge eyes narrowed at Ixtla. "We'll resist, and bleed them badly. They can't fight in the forest as we do." She shook her head. "But we're too few and can't fight as *they* do in the open, near our friends' villages and cities. Only another real army could face them like that."

Ixtla blew out a breath. "Perhaps they won't come," he said hopefully. "Why should they? What is the Yucatán to them?"

Samantha spoke up somewhat hesitantly, with a worried look at Lewis. "I still know very little, but I should think they might view it as a symbol to be crushed as an example to others."

"She's right," Varaa admitted, blinking a sad smile at Ixtla. "It takes a female to get to the heart of such things." She looked away. "So perhaps the best course of action is to leave. Lead our people and friends away."

"Where?" Ixtla demanded. "How? Yucatán is like this little fort, only cut off on one side by the Doms and all others by the sea. We'd have to go *through* the enemy to escape and then we could only go south. Who knows how far the Doms have spread in that direction? I don't. And what lies beyond them?" He shook his head. "To fight our way farther than we can imagine through lands we don't know, carrying old and young along . . . It's impossible."

Lewis cleared his throat. "It sounds like the Uxmalos and others you protect need an army of their own," he said thoughtfully, with a slight smile for Leonor and a significant look at Dr. Newlin. "If they're willing, *we* can help them build a 'real' one." He gestured at the tired soldiers, many finally sleeping. "You've seen how these men fight, even when they're hurt and confused, frightened, all mixed-up or spread out—and without proper organization. Think what they could do, what they could *teach others*, after we put them back together."

"How on earth will you do that?" Dr. Newlin persisted, then yawned tremendously.

"We'll elect new officers and NCOs. We need them, and that's the *volunteer* way. We'll give them stability in a time of uncertainty and 'keep them proud,' as you said," he told Leonor. "Finally, the army they'll all help build will be an *American* army, governed by principles they had every right to expect from the one they originally joined; that the Articles of War go both ways and their service will earn them honor and respect. All the things they taught me at the military academy, but tried to *punish* into private soldiers. The men will teach those things to the soldiers they train, and it'll be a better army for it." He gazed challengingly around. "And it's only appropriate that it *be* an 'American' army"—he paused and managed a slight smile—"because Yucatán was part of the Americas where we came from, after all."

Ixtla was frowning. "Where *you* came from," he stressed. "There are many tribes here, all proud, all independent, and none are 'Amer-i-cans.'" He snorted. "Some don't even like each other, and the only thing they have in common is their reliance on the Ocelomeh."

"Which can't save them alone," Varaa reminded him.

Surprisingly, it was the British Samantha who supported Lewis by saying, "Americans aren't any one tribe, they are a collection of them, of 'states' as diverse as yours, I suspect. They don't all like each other either," she added ironically, "but the ideals of America unite them for their common defense and prosperity in spite of their differences"—she actually chuckled—"and make them so irritating to their adversaries."

Ixtla sighed and looked at Lewis. "I'll have to learn more about these 'ideals' before I support your proposition."

"Just as we have much to learn about your people, the conditions here . . . and the Doms," Lewis agreed. Looking back at Newlin, however, he suddenly felt much better, more energized, the pain in his side nearly gone. "But taken together, all the challenges we face, combined with the threat Warmaster Varaa and . . . Mr. Ixtla described, our people will have the one thing that'll keep them together through anything."

"Really? Do tell. It sounds like idealistic enthusiasm, to me," Newlin grouched skeptically.

Lewis nodded solemnly. "Perhaps. But what could build a stronger bond between them"—he turned to face the others—"and all the people of this land, than a *cause* they can believe in?"

A thunderous roar came from the beach and the dim, rising moon outlined a monstrous shape, much like the dragon that got Lieutenant Swain, only considerably larger.

"Stand ready, lads," Olayne called to the artillerymen as he paced quickly past them to a 6pdr's crew who'd loaded their weapon with round-shot. "Stand fast," he told them. "Don't draw its attention, but be prepared."

Silently, they watched the thing, stalking back and forth on the beach, snatching up whole corpses and gnashing them down its gullet. Occasionally, it whirled and snapped at smaller things darting past its legs.

"Damned if there *ain't* real dragons hereabouts," one of the men by the 12pdr hissed in wonder. "I thought them fellas that brought the other guns was jus' tryin' to scare us."

"You scared?" came another voice.

"Not now," the first man replied after a pause. "Not after today. I *been* scared, an' now . . . I'm too damn tired. Besides, it's goin' away."

He was right. Taking up another ragged body in its jaws, the monster turned, its long tail lashing behind it as it paced southwest toward the trees.

Lewis was relieved, not only that the monster was leaving, but by the attitude of the men. They'd been through enough that even giant carnivorous monsters no longer had the power to break them.

"A '*dragon mayor*,' a 'greater dragon,' only middling size," Varaa-Choon observed.

"Middling." Newlin snorted, looking at Lewis, red-rimmed eyes wide open. "I take back all my cynicism, sir. With things like that prowling about, I've no doubt the men will remain united, if only in their own interests!"

"That's a good reason," Lewis confessed. "But they'll do it for more than that," he added with growing confidence.

"I hope you're right," Newlin said around another yawn. "Remarkable," he added, nodding in the direction the terrible beast had vanished. "Despite our respective professions, I'm not the natural philosopher Reverend Harkin is. But the creatures here do arouse a measure of fascination within me. Some recent controversial propositions by respected comparative anatomists spring to mind. . . ." He yawned once more. "Forgive me. Come, Mistress Samantha, I'll escort you to the tent where your friend is sleeping. Good night, all, and may tomorrow be a better day."

Lewis yawned also as the doctor and Englishwoman moved away. Olayne had to catch him as he swayed. *Fatigue, and perhaps a touch of fever,* he supposed.

"You *must* sleep as well, sir," Olayne insisted worriedly. "You've hardly done so since you regained consciousness after the wreck—and what will we do without you?"

"You'll manage," Lewis assured. "Besides, I slept a little last night—the night before last," he corrected, pressing his hand to his side.

"You wounded?" Leonor demanded.

Lewis shook his head. "Just an old ache." He sighed. "Maybe I will rest awhile."

"We brought few tents, and they're occupied by the wounded and the ladies," Olayne told him, "but Private Willis rigged a fly from a gun tarp and arranged a bed beneath it."

"Very well." Lewis looked at Olayne and Beck. "I trust the Ocelomeh to ensure we're not surprised, but at least one of you must remain alert at all times. Until Captain Anson stirs—or Captain Holland returns. Call me at once when he does. I want to know what he discovered on *Tiger.*"

"Yes sir."

Touching the brim of his hat to Varaa and Ixtla, Lewis turned to find his bed—and almost immediately staggered again.

"Oh, for God's sake," Leonor snapped at the young officers, going to Lewis's side to support him.

"I'm fine . . ." he objected.

"No you're not," Leonor scolded. "None of us are. An' we won't 'manage' at all if you go down. You know it too, so don't be a fool."

CHAPTER 12

"This is *your* fault, Capitan Arevalo!" groaned the big, red-painted warrior with a bleeding head and shattered leg as he was lifted and placed beside the wounded Dominion officer. Now they both lay on the bed of a boxy cart hitched to a large, indifferent, and extremely flatulent beast called an "armabuey." It was, in fact, one of the "giant armadillos" Anson had seen in the Holcano village, and the description wasn't inappropriate. There were a number of differences besides size, of course, and they came in various sizes, types of armor, and dispositions, but all were called armabueys and they were ubiquitous beasts of heavy burden throughout the Yucatán and the Dominion.

"And how is that, El Apestoso?" Arevalo hissed mockingly through his own pain. The warrior chief of the combined Holcanos preferred to be called "Kisin," after the god of earthquakes and death, who ruled the underworld. He even wore a Death Collar strung with dried, shrunken eyes. Arevalo was in no mood for him, however, and "El Apestoso" was another name for the same god, meaning "Stinking One." It was somewhat interchangeable with "the Devil" to those adhering to the "True Faith," and even the heretical Christian faith lingering in the Yucatán. Kisin despised it.

"You didn't give us guns, as promised!" he sulked.

"I promised you'd have guns when you'd *earned* them," Arevalo snapped. "And you could've earned all you needed by taking them from the blue heretics on the shore!"

"How could we get guns *without guns*? They *slaughtered* the Concha Band of Blood Lizards, and their survivors have abandoned us, limping away in hopes the Bosque Band will take them in. The Conchas are *extinct*! And those cursed Ocelomeh scattered my cousin's band of Holcanos—my strongest supporters on the coast—and my cousin himself was slain! Without his power, all the Holcano villages in this entire area will have to flee." Kisin almost shrieked when an old, filthy, bare-breasted woman—a healer, it seemed—began padding his leg as best she could in preparation for the rough motion of the cart. A younger healer, entirely nude and just as filthy, sat with Arevalo's head in her lap. Occasionally, he gasped in pain when she leaned over to suck on the small bullet wound in his upper chest and spit blood over the side of the cart. Arevalo knew the idea was to draw out the poisoned blood (and malevolent magic, he assumed) but doubted she could draw out the ball.

Medicine in the Holy Dominion wasn't much more advanced, since it relied more on the whim of a generally uninterested God than any real treatment beyond cleaning and binding a wound. But a Dominion surgeon would at least probe for the ball and any debris it carried in, removing as much as he could before consigning him to God's indifferent care. Perhaps he had singular value? If so, he'd heal fairly quickly. If not, he might suffer enough to earn God's casual esteem. At that point he'd either die in grace or live to be judged by a Blood Cardinal. *He* would decide if he'd suffered enough to *earn* singular value—or should entertain God with more suffering.

Either way, Arevalo expected he was as doomed as this little village astride the sweet stream west of where the calamitous battle occurred. The place had no name, nor would it, since the surviving Holcanos who'd been there just a few months were rapidly abandoning it. Most were already gone, streaming south, then southeast toward Nautla. Nobody lived there, but they'd shelter in the ruins until Capitan Arevalo either died or recovered enough for the much longer journey to Campeche. From there, he'd take ship if he was lucky, or travel up the Camino Militar to the Great Valley of Mexico and the Holy City. There he'd report the disaster of the day. Messengers would precede him so the setback in the Dominion's long, long plan to destabilize the region by proxy would surprise no one. He'd had no *part* in the disaster, of course, and even tried to restrain Kisin from mounting his impetuous attack on the apparently helpless but also obviously very *rich* new pilgrims from another world. Better to carry out the original plan against the Uxmalos—that Arevalo *had* helped him with—then observe the newcomers for a while. But it would be *his* disaster by the time he reached the Holy City. He'd only be surprised if he lived that long, and was allowed to live longer.

The cart finally lurched forward, and Kisin grunted in pain and grimaced, dry paint cracking and scattering in fragments on his face. "Who do you think they were . . . are?" he finally asked the Dominion captain.

Arevalo frowned, assuming he meant the shipwrecked strangers. With his coat and shirt removed, he felt the chill of the evening on his sweaty torso. "Others," he said dismissively. "Others who came here as my ancestors did. As yours did." He sent a scathing glare at Kisin. "Though we both missed the battle, I think we can safely say they're very *dangerous* 'others.' Armed much like the Holy Dominion in most respects, it seems." He reached vaguely toward the small wound in his chest. "But I'm certain some of their pistols fired more often than they should. I've seen double-barrel pistols, even some with *three* revolving barrels, but the one that shot me had only one, yet it fired many times. And they have cannon, of course. We heard them."

"And they're already allied with the contemptible Ocelomeh," Kisin spat. "They'll be in league with the Uxmalos next."

"'Contemptible' heretics they may be, but the Ocelomeh crushed *you* easily enough—"

"I . . . was not at the battle either," Kisin interrupted. "It would've been different if I were."

"Really? Still, the Ocelomeh seized their opportunity to combine with the 'others' with admirable eagerness when your precipitous attack drove the blue heretics into their arms. And I've no doubt they'll combine with the Uxmalos. Probably more city-states on the peninsula. *Very* dangerous 'others' indeed," he added gloomily, closing his eyes.

The cart shuddered, and he looked to see the terrifying shape of a gara-ache hovering over him, long, tooth-lined jaws slightly parted, big orange eyes regarding him, clawed hands digging into the cart's sides to support its precarious perch.

"T'ir?" it seemed to ask Kisin, then went on at some length in atrocious

Spanya—the more-or-less common language of the region. Like all creatures of its kind, it couldn't form words requiring lips.

"*Quién sabe,*" Kisin replied, then looked at Arevalo. "General Soor is concerned about you. Only he and a few dozen of his Concha Band of Blood Lizards have remained with us—for now—believing only a partnership with the Dominion can preserve his race."

Arevalo knew the Dominion wanted nothing to do with Holcanos, in the long term, and certainly not talking animals with pretensions to sentience. All such creatures were abominations, likely touched by demons. The Dominion would use them, of course, but certainly never "preserve" them when their usefulness was at an end. "How kind," he managed.

"He also wants to know if he can eat you if you're about to die—while your blood still runs," Kisin went on, matter-of-factly. "We have no time to gather much food to take, and this time of year the road to Nautla gets hungry. Especially if other villages join us on the road. And there's little food *in* Nautla, for that matter, besides the wild young of his own race."

"I'm . . . quite sure His Supreme Holiness would take it badly if I was eaten by one of our allies," Arevalo carefully replied. General Soor jerked a saliva-slinging diagonal nod and jumped from the cart.

"He'll eat you anyway, you know," Kisin said lowly. "We'll both be eaten by everyone if we die. Whatever it's like where you're from, that's the way of things here."

Arevalo knew. He also suspected that Kisin, for all his Death Collars, body paint, and other barbarous ways, would be shocked by the "wastefulness" of the ritualistic bloody-mindedness that was increasingly required by Arevalo's God. "If I live, I'll likely face a far less pleasant fate than being eaten," Arevalo murmured.

"What will they do to you?" Kisin asked, intrigued.

Arevalo didn't reply.

"I will go with you, if you don't die," Kisin suddenly blurted. "All the way to the Holy City of Mexico."

"Why?"

"I'll tell them this was not *my* fault," Kisin insisted. "Not *your* fault. It was those lazy, cowardly garaaches!"

Arevalo understood little of General Soor's . . . creatures, but knew they weren't "lazy" or "cowardly."

"Maybe I'll get guns from *your* war leaders," Kisin continued, more animated. "And if they kill you, I want to see what they do," he confessed.

Arevalo snorted. "I don't think it will be necessary—or wise—for you *ever* to go to the Holy City," he said with a wince when the cart hit a bump. "If we make it to Campeche, I do think you should take your remaining warriors to meet as many more as you can summon at Cayal. There you can prepare to push north against Puebla Arboras and Itzincab. After my report, I imagine the Dominion itself will march an army up the Camino Militar, and eventually on Uxmal itself."

"You think this will begin the final thrust?" Kisin asked anxiously.

"I believe it must, once my superiors understand the stakes. Whether I'm alive to join it or not," he added glumly.

"And I will rule *all* this land of the Yucatán?" Kisin demanded.

"Under the authority of His Supreme Holiness, of course," Arevalo assured evasively then gasped again when the young healer sucked his wound and spat.

CHAPTER 13

Lewis was disoriented when he woke under sun-brightened canvas billowing in the breeze. He was still in the trees, of course, and the shadows of leaves and limbs on the white gun tarp cast bizarre, shifting shadows. But that was ordinary, expected, even comforting. So was the smell of cook fires and muted sounds of an army camp. But it was broad daylight, and he realized he must've slept longer than intended—much longer than he should've. He sat up with a groan, every joint and muscle aching from all he'd demanded of them over the last few days and nights, and the apparent fact he'd hardly twitched in his sleep. Blinking gummy eyes, he looked around.

Leonor was sitting nearby, knees drawn up and chin resting on arms crossed on top of them. She'd been gazing west, past the beach where they fought the day before. Hearing him rise, she stood and kicked a snoring form on a mound of leaves and branches. "Get up, you lazy bastard," she hissed. "Captain Lewis is awake."

"I didn't do it! Lemme be!" cried Private Willis, leaping to his feet as if to run, but falling face-first in the sandy soil. Jumping back up, he looked blearily around. "What the hell? Oh." His face fell, and he glowered at Leonor. "I was havin' such a good dream. . . ."

"We could tell," Lewis said, voice raspy.

"Move yourself!" Leonor snapped at Willis. "Bring food an' coffee."

"Strikes me . . ." Willis began snidely, but Leonor took a step toward him. "*I'll* 'strike' you."

Muttering to himself, Willis shuffled away. Leonor was muttering too. "Of all the men you could've picked . . . I guess he ain't good for nothin' else." She crouched back beside Lewis and handed him her canteen. "Water's holdin' out," she assured before he could ask.

Gratefully, he took a long drink and cleared his throat. Instead of asking why she was there and how long she had been—the first questions that popped into his mind—he decided the answer was obvious. For some reason, she'd appointed herself his guardian while he'd slept and was probably responsible for making sure he'd done so as long as needed. He stifled a stab of irritation. In spite of his various aches, he really did feel better. He'd desperately *needed* sleep and wasn't as sure as he'd said that others would manage in his place—not that he felt particularly confident he could either. His notions of the night before might've been exactly what Dr. Newlin denounced them as—idealistic enthusiasm. But he couldn't see another way.

"What were you looking at?" he asked instead, voice closer to normal. Leonor pointed, and Lewis shifted to see around the popping fly. "Good Lord!" he exclaimed when he realized how clean the beach in front of the breastworks had been picked. There wasn't a complete body anywhere, and only thousands of scattered, red-black bones remained. Even some of these were still being fought over by mobs of flapping and cavorting lizardbirds, shrill cries blending in a constant, high-pitched counterpoint to the roaring wind and surf.

"Varaa says we can start salvagin' more casks an' crates this evenin,' an' the Uxmalos'll be able to start tearin' into the wreck itself by the time they get here." Leonor nodded toward the tree line. Just short of it, where De Russy had begun to bury his dead before the attack occurred, was a wide, blackened area covered with blowing ash and smoldering ships' timbers pulled from the breastworks. "Varaa an' some o' her warriors, along with Captain Beck an' some of our boys, dug a bigger grave for all our dead an' built a big fire on top just at dawn," she added grimly. "Varaa said it'll keep critters from diggin' 'em up from the soft sand." She hesitated. "Reverend Harkin an' Father Orno figure to hold a service there before we leave."

Preventing Lewis from dwelling on that, she pointed far beyond the beach at a distant plume of gray smoke slanting away to the south. "Koaar took a hundred warriors against the Holcano village. Most on foot, o' course, though they have *some* horses in these parts." She frowned. "Kinda weird ones: shorter faces, tan with dark stripes . . . I seen a couple that Koaar's messengers showed up on. Not like ours, or them Dom horses we seen." She waved that away. "But woods Injuns don't fight on horses, so Koaar went on foot while Sal Hernandez an' Sergeant Hayne led a handful o' dragoons with Alferez Lara an' his Mexicans as scouts. Made sense. They ain't sneakin' around anymore, an' the whole point is to put a scare in the Holcanos, keep 'em from concentratin' again. Father—I mean Captain Anson—told 'em not to harm women and children," she hastened to add, "but don't leave 'em a place to stay either. I think Koaar wants to raid a couple more villages before they head back." She shook her head and blinked. "You know, it's mighty strange rootin' for Mexicans an' Ins."

"Everything's changed," Lewis somberly agreed. Rising to his feet, he buttoned his sweat-crusty vest and shook the sand off his dark blue, red-trimmed jacket. Finally, he buckled his saber belt around his waist and plopped his hat on his head. Oddly, he didn't remember removing any of them the night before. "Has there been any word from Captain Holland?" he asked, stepping toward where he last remembered being the night before. The beach and British ship were both visible from there. Leonor followed. Lewis was immediately taken aback by how many men stood from where they were resting to salute him as he passed. All looked weary and haggard, and many wore bloody bandages, but instead of pretending they didn't notice him, nearly all seemed to make a deliberate point of rendering him this simple honor. Even a few Ocelomeh sitting with the men jumped up and imitated their new friends. Normally, Lewis would've suspected sarcasm. It wasn't unusual for soldiers to show contempt for martinets or officers prone to administering harsh punishments in this way, but he saw no disrespect, no insincerity. He returned all their salutes.

"Captain Holland came ashore this morning," Leonor told him.

Frowning, Lewis said, "I left specific orders . . ."

"An' Dr. Newlin countermanded 'em," Leonor rebutted with a note of challenge. "All's as well as can be in *Tiger.*" She went on to describe how the ship's crew had no captain, were virtually abandoned as well, and had barely enough men to work her, much less fight her. "Holland's already gone back out with his sailors and some soldier volunteers used to sailin' an' woodwork to help get her in some kinda shape. A few Ocelomeh with experience in fishin' boats—an' this coast, o' course—went too. He figures with the extra manpower he can get topmasts an' topsails on her pretty quick an' *Tiger* can carry our worst wounded to Uxmal faster an' gentler than a overland trip."

Lewis again refrained from commenting that he should've been consulted because Holland was absolutely right. *Maybe they can manage better without me than I thought,* he told himself, returning more salutes from artillerymen around the field howitzer and 6pdr, and then Olayne's and Burton's as well.

"Good morning, gentlemen." He smiled. "Nearer afternoon." He looked at Burton. "I'm glad you're safe."

"Thank you, sir. I'm glad to be back on land!" He shook his head. "There really *are* sea monsters out there!" he blurted.

"You may have noticed a few monsters on land," Olayne reminded.

"Yes." Burton shuddered. "But you can *see* them."

Lewis looked at Olayne. "Varaa-Choon said there's a Dom naval threat. I intend to offer Captain Holland some artillerymen for *Tiger*'s guns. Ask for volunteers."

"He was hoping you would," Burton informed him. "And maybe a couple of blacksmiths or farriers. There's another forge wagon, as well as limbers, two caissons, and a battery wagon for the twelve pounders still in *Commissary*'s wreck, but *Tiger*'s got the blacksmith's tools. She just needs men with know-how."

Lewis glanced at Olayne. "Volunteers for that as well, but no more than two. We'll need their skills. Skills of all sorts," he added lowly. "We must be extra careful who we risk with what in the future."

"I couldn't agree more, sir," said Olayne.

"Nor could I," approved a booming voice, used to projecting itself. Lewis watched several men, Ocelomeh, and Mistress Samantha approach. The voice was the obese Reverend Harkin's, restored to his dark-suited splendor. To Lewis's surprise, he was paced by the diminutive Father Orno. There couldn't have been a more unlikely, contrasting pair. Captain Anson, Varaa-Choon, a surprisingly restored Colonel De Russy, and Barca all attended Samantha, who wore a sensible, light blue day dress. Those around her, even Varaa, seemed pleased with themselves.

"We brought the lady some of her things," Burton whispered to Lewis. No one saw Leonor stiffen in the presence of the woman, who'd transformed herself into a slim, crisp, fresh-faced beauty.

Private Willis chose that moment to appear with a steaming mug and tinned plate covered with glistening slop. "Coffee's burnt," he hissed, "an' I reckon the cask the salt pork came from was condemned a decade ago. . . ."

"Thanks for the coffee," Lewis told him quickly, taking the dented mug. "I'll eat something later."

Willis looked dolefully at the plate. "What am I s'posed to do with it? *I* ain't eatin' it!"

"Git!" Leonor snapped at him.

Willis backed away, mumbling, "Go to all the goddamn trouble . . ."

Colonel De Russy pretended not to hear and said, "My dear Captain Lewis, Warmaster Varaa-Choon and Dr. Newlin described the scheme you hatched last night, and while I concur wholeheartedly with your aims— they seem our only recourse—the first obstacles to forming the . . ." He paused thoughtfully. "It really *must* be a Union of all the cities, mustn't it? But while you so deservedly slept"—he gestured at Harkin and Father Orno—"*they* immediately engaged over the momentous religious differences dwarfing such meager trivialities as the struggle between life and death."

Harkin glared at him, but De Russy held up his hand. "Fortunately, as I said, I'm a better diplomat than a soldier. Between Varaa-Choon and I, and Captain Anson as well, we've constructed a firm—if temporary—truce between the principal belligerents."

Anson chuckled. "First thing, Varaa had to convince Reverend Harkin she ain't a demon, nor are the . . . Grik critters we fought."

"I remain unconvinced of *that*," Harkin objected, furrowing his brows, "at least in regard to the Grik." He looked unapologetically at Varaa. "I've no idea what to think of her and those like her, however. Having spoken with her and Consul Koaar at length, I can't consider them 'animals,' but how can they be 'men'? *Races* of man differ, sometimes quite distinctly. Some are darker, some lighter, some even much hairier and with . . . surprising facial features. Why, even among my congregation back home there was a woman so profoundly . . ." He shuddered slightly and cleared his throat. "But all are still at least vaguely made in the image of God." He paused uncomfortably. "Yet until now, I would've been certain the presence of a *tail* most emphatically crosses the line between 'man' and 'animal.' I can't imagine God has a tail!" He seemed to wilt a little. "On the other hand, my hobby of comparative anatomy informs me even man possesses bony structures below the pelvis, contiguous with the spine, that might be viewed as a tail of sorts. So . . ." He lifted his chin. "I can detect no evil purpose in Warmaster Varaa-Choon and will contemplate further whether Mi-Anakka are 'man' or not."

"I'm honored," Varaa said, with just the right mixture of sarcasm and appreciation, Lewis thought with amusement. He personally believed the "image" of God was spiritual, not physical, and the only aspect of Varaa's appearance that had troubled him was how the men would take it. Now, since they were getting used to it and Harkin seemed disinclined to make it an issue, Lewis was much relieved.

"Indeed," Harkin murmured suspiciously, then raised his voice again. "But it's abundantly clear we have in fact found ourselves in a different . . . manifestation of the world we knew." He glanced at Orno. "As papists and even some of the more unenlightened Protestants have long assumed purgatory to be." He sighed. "And my own eyes and fears made me wonder at first. But the mysterious presence of otherworldly creatures and beings, not to mention the existence of"—he arched an eyebrow at Orno—"a dubious and misguided sect of Christianity—which would only be required if the inhabitants of this place might still be brought to the Lord"—he frowned—"however imperfectly—do not scripturally or even *scientifically* support any Wesleyan notion of purgatory. On the contrary. I've . . . long been troubled by growing evidence that fossil remains in various places around the world might indeed be those of creatures now extinct. But how can that be? The very idea that any of God's creations are subject to extinction implies they're imperfect in some way. I've wrestled with that to no end," he confessed, "but at last we may have an answer!" He suddenly beamed, waiting for everyone to grasp his meaning. When they didn't, he rolled his eyes. "They're *not* 'extinct,' you see? They're *here*! I shouldn't wonder if we don't eventually discover all manner of things we've despaired of locating where we came from! Wooly mammoths! Iguanodons! Even Dr. Lund's dagger-toothed cats—whose bones he found with those of humans, I might add!" His eyes darted to Varaa. "Doubtless there are others as yet unknown to science." He glanced again at Orno. "We may even find the Lost Tribes of Israel!"

Suddenly noting his excitement seemed to be generating more relief and amusement than wonder, Harkin frowned again and clamped his puffy jaws.

"You amaze me, sir," De Russy soothed. "But ultimately, since there are few New Testament differences between Reverend Harkin and Father Orno, they've agreed to focus on ministering to their separate flocks and refrain from active poaching upon each other's while they explore the implications of these theories together."

"But we must *survive* to do so!" Reverend Harkin exclaimed, looking at Lewis. "We'll need those blacksmiths, woodworkers . . . men of every conceivable experience. If this *is* a 'purgatory' of some kind, I believe God deliberately sent us to purge our ignorance of Him and grow in His understanding!"

Lewis scratched his beard. "I'm glad you think so. Maybe—when they're ready—you can preach that to the men and it'll give them comfort. It may be difficult to sell to most." Then he brightened as well. "But I'm glad you and Father Orno are getting along"—he looked at Varaa—"as our soldiers and warriors seem to be. It's a good start."

"As I told you," Varaa said, "they've fought and bled together. They *won* together. There's nothing to pull them apart as yet, since their priests will not. We have the people—at least the Uxmalos and other city dwellers do if they'll cooperate—and you have the tools and knowledge to build the army you spoke of. Consul Koaar and Ixtla were most enthusiastic about a union, and I'll support it also. I see no reason why King Har-Kaaska will object. His support will sway every band of Ocelomeh and many of the cities as well." Varaa-Choon blinked, something Lewis was beginning to think implied anxiety. "But it won't be easy. Nothing will be easy."

AS PROMISED, WATER finally came later that day—in the form of a torrential rain Ixtla gave them plenty of warning for. Dark clouds quickly stacked up in the east and all the sails and tents salvaged from the wreck were quickly erected among the trees to create the most bizarre assemblage of shelter Lewis ever saw. But there was room for everyone underneath, and empty casks were positioned under creases by the time the sky turned black and the heavy rain came down. Fortunately for the fragile shelter and still-helpless *Tiger*, the wind and sea didn't rise appreciably, though Ixtla warned violent storms would grow more frequent in months to come. As it was, Captain Holland had his sailors drop all three of the ship's anchors (he was concerned by how well they'd hold the sandy bottom), and she rode the mild but soaking blow with ease. The soldiers and Ocelomeh huddled together (growing even closer and more familiar) during another night of rest from battle. The following morning, the rest was over.

Three hundred Uxmalos in colorful, finely woven tunics, lace-up moccasins, and wide-brimmed straw hats came gaggling down the road at dawn, armed with a few long-barreled muskets, but primarily spears, bows, and farm implements. They hadn't come to fight, however, since runners had informed them of the victory. They came rejoicing, and to work. They held a short but festive ceremony right on the beach east of the little fort while Varaa-Choon and her Ocelomeh were cheered by the townsfolk and Father Orno introduced the Americans to the portly, beaming Ikan Periz, *alcalde* and war leader of Uxmal.

Only Periz and his retinue were mounted, on the strange, striped horses, and Periz himself looked more like a dark, smooth-faced version of De Russy than a warrior. The two quickly took to one another while Father Orno, Varaa-Choon, Ixtla, Captain Anson, Boogerbear, and even Reverend Harkin did their best to translate all around. Alcalde Periz and his attendants came under the copious shade of the fort now that the steamy sun was beating down again, where Periz marveled at the cannon and other weapons he was shown. Meanwhile, all his people—along with the captive Holcanos who'd perform more dangerous chores—went to work clearing every last thing of value out of *Commissary*'s wreck and started tearing the stranded ship apart. Large carts pulled by the giant armadillo-like armabueys arrived, and the beasts heaved on stout cables to pull large sections of wreckage up on the beach. There, all the now-mangled copper sheathing was wrenched from the hull, along with every fastener, bolt, spike, and strap. Most of the shattered wood was dragged over to be burned atop the common grave again, but knees and other framing timbers in good condition were saved.

Still standing in the shade with the rest of the leaders, Captain Anson cleared his throat. "I understand other parties have already gone to the wrecks of *Xenophon* an' *Mary Riggs* to break 'em up the same way," he told Lewis.

Lewis nodded at Alcalde Periz. "Between you and the others, please inform him that's fine. The wrecks and anything they salvage from them are theirs to keep. But anything *in* or *around* them—weapons, powder, shot, supplies, even personal belongings—are *ours*." He paused while this was conveyed, watching Alcalde Periz's eyes begin to narrow. "That stance may change or be . . . modified as we get to know one another, but for now I must insist on it, and that the graves of our people near those ships be given the same treatment as those buried here." He motioned down where flames were leaping once again, pushing up a new cloud of steamy gray smoke. Periz made a short reply.

Anson snorted. "He asks—in a friendly way, he assures me—how we mean to retrieve things they find abandoned and unguarded." Anson's voice held a trace of amusement.

"Nothing at *Mary Riggs* was 'abandoned' or 'unguarded,'" Lewis reminded, "and I better not hear any of our people were abused in any way. Damn it, I want to *help* his people—and we need his help to do it—but we can't do anything for his or ours if we're pillaged." His expression turned hard. "And I won't see any difference between him and the Holcanos if he allows it."

"Captain Cayce!" De Russy objected.

"You promised you wouldn't interfere in military affairs," Lewis reminded.

"But surely this is a diplomatic matter," De Russy sputtered.

"No. Nothing that threatens the well-being of our soldiers and impairs their ability to fight, to not only survive but have *value* here, is a 'diplomatic matter.'"

Varaa-Choon's eyes had grown wide at this exchange, and she spoke very rapidly to the *alcalde*, blinking fiercely, tail lashing. Occasionally, she gestured out where the battle was fought, sometimes motioning at a cannon. Periz listened carefully, alternately smiling and frowning, but his expression changed first to one of disappointment, then fear, then something that looked like hope. It may not have made any difference, but the scouting and raiding party that left the day before and spent the night in the rainy forest chose that moment to return. The Ocelomeh appeared from the woods, encircling at least an equal number of captives and quite a few more armabueys. The dragoons and Mexican horsemen came last, as if herding the whole bunch in. Alcalde Periz's face brightened at once, and he jabbered in apparent happiness.

Varaa sighed and blinked her huge blue eyes at Lewis, ears and tail now only twitching. "That was close, as you say. These people, Uxmalos, Holcanos, even Ocelomeh"—she only rarely differentiated herself from her Jaguar Warriors—"behave so much like younglings around loot. Probably no different from anyone, I suppose," she qualified, "but it's difficult to make them take a longer view." She flicked her ears at De Russy. "We've already hinted at the army, and even a possible union, and Periz is agreeable to discussing it. But as you know, little remains to be seen of the aftermath of the battle, and it's hard for him to imagine we actually *broke* the Holcanos and Grik, and they'll find it difficult to trouble us for a considerable time. Much less that a union might provide real security for his people, even against the Doms. I described the . . . numbers involved, and now that he sees even more captives, I think he begins to understand." She *kakked* a laugh. "Besides, not only could your scheme benefit him, you might already be as strong as any force the Doms could quickly send—and you're here already. I strongly counseled him not to make you angry," she ended with a touch of irony.

Alcalde Periz spoke again, eyes gleaming at De Russy, then Lewis.

Varaa nodded politely. "He says all your equipment will be returned— as long as you teach his people how to use it and how to make more."

Lewis nodded with relief. "That was the idea from the start."

CHAPTER 14

E ven more colorfully dressed Uxmalos came over the next three days, loading and hauling off salvage. Soon, there was no sign *Commissary* had ever fallen on this shore, or even that a battle had been fought. Most of the bones not already gnawed to splinters had been tossed up into the forest, where they eventually would be. Only the blackened sand and blowing ash over the mass grave remained. Captain Holland used the time to complete sufficient repairs for *Tiger* to get under way, and the most seriously wounded Americans and Ocelomeh Dr. Newlin feared would have trouble reaching Uxmal overland (roughly ninety miles west-northwest) were ferried out to her. Lewis spent the time ensuring his men remained soldiers, working personally with the artillerymen on their flying artillery tactics. Unfortunately, at present, he had to share horses with the dragoons and mounted riflemen so Captain Anson could get them used to working together with his Rangers and Alferez Lara's men. Anson told Lewis he'd try to work out new tactics to maximize their diverse strengths. Captain Beck drilled all the infantry and unoccupied artillerymen together by battalions, combining companies of regulars and volunteers. Lewis cautioned him against implying their units' identities would be compromised. That might prematurely confirm the fear too many already felt: that they were stuck here indefinitely.

Varaa-Choon's Ocelomeh were warriors, not laborers. Unlike the American soldiers who Lewis insisted must at least help the Uxmalos load their carts, especially with their own critical supplies, the Ocelomeh were content to sit and watch. They did participate in the various military drills, however, falling in with gun's crews or joining a line of infantry practicing close-order drills in the sand. This induced considerable hilarity from time to time, but Lewis was adamant that their allies never be discouraged from learning. He even persuaded Alcalde Periz to allow his Uxmalos to pitch in and get a feel for it when they weren't otherwise employed.

"You have to start somewhere," Samantha Wilde told him and Varaa as she urged Anson's Colonel Fannin to join them where they watched the training from the road above the beach. *It was here,* Lewis remembered, *where I led my men out to their first real battle . . . on this world.* He was sitting atop Arete, of course, and Varaa had accepted the short loan of one of the dragoons' horses. She'd learned to ride "in her youth" but still refused to reveal the slightest hint where she spent it. Lewis noted with interest that Samantha rode confidently as well, even sitting sidesaddle.

"Yes," he agreed, awkward as ever around her, diverting his gaze from her pretty, smiling face, back to where artillerymen and dragoons were trading horses again. Drill had actually become a welcome relief from fatigue parties helping the Uxmalos. The Ocelomeh training with them simply changed from one military branch to another, or sauntered back to the shade to listen to music made by all the combined drummers and fifers practicing together. Lewis patted Arete's neck. "We'll need recruits," he said as if she didn't already know. "I've no idea how many men we'll eventually have fit for duty, of course. Some are still at *Mary Riggs* and are supposed to meet us on the march to Uxmal. And Varaa has reports that more of our men were found hiding in the vicinity of *Xenophon*'s wreck. But some of the wounded may never return to duty, and . . . even some of the healthy may not be fit for it for it once they understand the enormity of our situation." He sighed. "I doubt we'll have more than seven hundred when all is said and done"—his voice turned bitter—"out of over *fifteen hundred* from all the ships that came here!"

He banished his frown and waved down at the troops. "But we'll have arms for many more, so recruiting is important." He patted Arete again. "Actually, our most pressing shortage is horses. We can't even pull all our guns and mount the horsemen we already have."

"*They* seem to be trying to cope," Samantha suggested, referring to a

group of artillerymen under Sergeant McNabb, working with some Uxmalos to fashion a kind of harness to hitch a gun and limber to a bored-
looking armabuey. McNabb's cursing was audible even here:

"The limber's got a *single* goddamn pole out front, for hitchin' between
pairs o' animals!" he ranted. "You wanna just tie it tae that fat bugger's *tail*?
He'll snap it the first time he gets happy an' wags it!"

Samantha concealed a chuckle behind her hand.

"We'll get you as many horses as we can," Varaa promised. "The indigenous sort aren't exactly scarce—they run wild in herds. They're quite different from what you're used to, however. They haven't been domesticated
long, and few people raise and train them. The wild ones are *very* difficult
to catch and train. That makes them somewhat scarce in practice. The
Doms raise horses from another world, as . . . Mi-Anakka do, and have all
they need to mount their lancers." She blinked confusion. "But Doms pull
their great guns with armabueys. Why won't they serve for you?" She
pressed on over Lewis's growing frown. "A simple modification to your ammunition vehicles would suffice. Armabueys may be slow, but they're tire-
less, fearless, and can eat almost anything. It takes only one to pull larger
guns than yours, and they're not spooked by monsters or battle."

"They sound almost perfect, don't they?" Lewis appeared to concede.
"Easy to understand why the Doms use them. And they *would* be perfect—
for siege guns or heavy supply trains in friendly territory. But the greatest
advantage our guns have enjoyed over . . . previous enemies is that they're
light and easy to move quickly, both to and around the battlefield." He
glanced at Varaa. "As you said, armabueys are slow, and armies relying on
them must keep the same pace." He sat silent a moment, then continued,
"We were badly outnumbered in the battle here and whatever enemy we
face in the future—Doms or whoever—will likely have a numerical advantage. We'll assume so." He smiled tightly. "As long as we always balance
caution and boldness and make allowances for the worst that can happen . . .
our surprises may not always be pleasant, but they shouldn't be debilitating." He nodded at the soldiers on the beach. "I can't say the leaders of the
United States' little armies have always done that, but I've learned the keys
to beating larger, more ponderous armies are superior training and leadership, and better-disciplined, more confident troops. Just as important is the
ability to quickly maneuver in the face of an enemy whose size and power
makes him too arrogant to prepare for 'the worst.'"

Varaa and Samantha were both looking at him intently. "You seem to know what you're about," Varaa said at last. "Very well. You may have to pull your beautiful guns with lowly armabueys for now, but we'll get your horses." Swishing her tail (the high brass-bound cantle of the Grimsley must've been uncomfortable) and cutting her huge eyes between Lewis and Samantha, she cleared her throat. "I believe I'll go talk to Alcalde Periz. He's listening to that charming if somewhat squeaky music with Colonel De Russy." She grinned. "They've grown quite comfortable, and I'm not sure either is ready to dismantle that monstrous shady contraption we've been enjoying, or begin the long march to Uxmal in the morning."

Lewis nodded out at *Tiger* where she lay with new yards crossed. "At least she'll carry all but the marching tents. And Captain Holland's ready and anxious to sail."

Varaa nodded, then urged her borrowed horse into a gallop that took her pounding across the white sand "parade ground," through the drilling men, and up to the tree- and canvas-shrouded fort.

"An interesting creature," Samantha said brightly when they were alone. Lewis looked at her. *"Person,"* he stressed.

"Of course," Samantha assured. "I didn't mean it like that. It was just a figure of speech."

Lewis gazed at her a moment, then nodded. "I'm sure. I guess I'm a little touchy. Considering all the sectional, cultural, racial, even political differences my troops already had and brought here with them—not even counting the friction between various branches, regulars, and volunteers . . ." He snorted. "Somehow, relations have remained surprisingly good between our people and . . . all these others. We have to keep it that way to survive, and it won't last if we start thinking of them as less than we are."

Samantha bit her lower lip. "I know it doesn't matter now, but I get the impression you weren't entirely enthusiastic about your country's war with Mexico."

Lewis hesitated, then shrugged. "As you say, it doesn't matter, but I honestly never gave it much thought," he confessed. "The annexation of Texas might've sparked it—and I believe Texas had the right to join the Union if it chose—but that was only the spark. The tinder for the fire had been gathering a long time and the United States and Mexico both went to war with their eyes wide open. Like overproud, mutually aggrieved gentlemen meeting for a duel, both expecting to win." He smiled faintly at Samantha's expression. "Regardless of the fact most of the world is—was—betting so firmly on Mexico. Understandable because, ever since Palo Alto and Resaca de la Palma, the president of Mexico has been on the defense, on his own soil, with contracting lines of supply. His armies have always been larger and—one would think—better motivated. That hasn't proven to be the case, largely because they've been so poorly led. You remember what I said about arrogance crippling the larger, apparently more powerful force?"

He looked away. "I abhor the bloodshed of war, but must admit I'm proud of how well our troops have performed in battle. So in the end I'm just a soldier," he stated simply. "I fight who I'm ordered to, and believe in the founding principles of the government that sent me to do it." He frowned. "And though I'm no convert to the rousing notion of 'manifest destiny' that seems so suddenly popular, I'm sympathetic to people and places who're oppressed by their own governments and would embrace the principles of mine.

"On the other hand, I dislike how divisive the war was becoming back home among civilians and politicians: the 'slave state' versus 'free state' factions. Being opposed to slavery myself, you might find it ironic that I consider many 'free state' politicians the most hypocritical. I believe the one, *single* flaw in the American Constitution is that it abandoned the notion laid down to your king in our Declaration of Independence, that *all* men are created equal. Perhaps I'm an idealist, but that should've been settled from the start. Yet instead of pressing for the universal abolition they claim to seek, many 'free state' politicians think only of political advantage, to the extent, in some instances, of subverting support for troops in the field, already at war!"

Lewis's tone had turned quite bitter, and he was surprised he'd revealed so much to this woman he hardly knew. She moved her borrowed horse closer to his. "It sounds as if you've given this more thought than you realized," she observed.

"Perhaps," he admitted guardedly.

"It also explains your quest for a cause. Yours, it seems, has always been your army. Fortunate for me"—she smiled—"and for the rest that you're the sort of soldier who can command obedience and trust even under the . . . strangest circumstances. But armies require more than mutual affection to remain effective and stay together. Your soldiers aren't all as devoted to the army as you and must have a reason to stay in it."

"I know. That's exactly why the army needs a cause beyond itself."

She tilted her head toward the training men, specifically the Uxmalos and Ocelomeh. "Do you think protecting *them* will be enough? *They* use slaves, you know."

"Yes," he acknowledged, "though we don't yet know to what extent. As to the ones they took in battle . . ." He suddenly remembered a similar talk he'd had with Captain Holland. "I suppose it would've been worse to slaughter them." He looked back at her. "But whether they're *worth* protecting or not, we'll soon find out. If they are, all the better, and we can focus on the cause of building a union to protect. If not . . ." He hesitated. "We must make them so." He snorted wryly. "And that takes us back to the beginning of this delightful conversation. We can't let bigotry form and fester in the ranks. It'll be hard enough to stamp out what's already there. Our people must embrace the Uxmalos and whoever joins them as their own, but they must embrace us as well." He smiled. "That means unguarded references to 'creatures' should be avoided. At least until we find out whether we share a similar sense of humor."

They both laughed at that, which was good for them. "Speaking of 'creatures' in the manner you meant," Lewis continued, "and a fairly delicate one, it seems, how is your friend Mistress Angelique?"

"Much better," Samantha said warmly. "I'm so relieved. She even mustered the strength to help Dr. Newlin shift the wounded to the ship." She pursed her lips. "She's careful to keep away from the Indians, however. I don't know how she'll react when she learns she'll have to remain among them forever. She's really very sweet," she defended, "but easily frightened."

"Unlike you."

Samantha allowed a most unladylike snort. "Not unlike me at all, I assure you!"

"Nor I," Lewis agreed easily. They laughed together again.

LEONOR WAS WITH her father, both on borrowed horses, while Boogerbear and Alferez Lara coached the mounted troops on how to deliver the hardest blow in a charge. Boogerbear had helped smash bands of Comanches like that, and as Leonor now knew, Lara had been a lancer. The dragoons pretended boredom when Boogerbear spoke, but Leonor could tell they were keenly interested. Dragoons and mounted riflemen were trained to fight from horseback, but both—riflemen in particular—were best at riding to the fight and then dismounting to engage. Lancers never dismounted, and their nine-foot lances were their primary weapons. Whether they admitted it or not, Americans respected and feared Mexican lancers. They'd never faced such weapons, dropping in unison and charging home, unintimidated.

"Enough," Anson said. "Lieutenant Burton, dismiss the battalion. Time to take the horses to the water casks and cool 'em down. Give 'em a good brushin'," he reminded. "We think *we're* startin' a long march in the mornin', but most of the horses'll have to drag those damned heavy guns." He looked at the Indians among his listeners. "We've done what we set out to, for now."

Burton and the men started leading horses to shade. Leonor caught the sound of distant laughter and looked across the beach to where Lewis and Samantha were in the shade overhanging the road. A flash of some unpleasant emotion lit her chest, and she was taken aback by it. She couldn't deny feeling a kind of . . . proprietary protectiveness toward Lewis, especially after all he'd done for them—and watching him sleep so exhausted and helpless when he finally nearly collapsed. *I got no call to be jealous, though, or mad,* she told herself. *It ain't like he's mine.* She frowned. *But he don't belong to that fine lady, neither,* she told herself a little triumphantly.

The funny thing was, despite not expecting to—she'd never been around anyone like her—Leonor actually liked Samantha and didn't know why her growing friendship with Lewis bothered her. *She's got no better chance with him than . . . well, than I have right now,* she told herself. *Lewis is set on his course, an' from what I've seen, even a fine English lady can't pull him off it till it's done!*

She turned to tell her father they should take their horses to shade as well and caught him watching the pair with a strange expression. *Seems he's a little bothered too,* she realized with a start. "C'mon, Father," she said. When he looked at her with a blank expression, she added, "The horses," and he finally nodded and smiled. "Of course."

TWO HOURS BEFORE dawn, the final tents were struck, breakfast served, fires put out, and the grand procession of four hundred Ocelomeh, nearly eleven hundred Uxmalos, their remaining sixty armabueys burdened with carts, the battery of 12pdrs, two sections of 6pdrs, and all the other American vehicles, three hundred and eleven Holcano captives, and six hundred and eighty-eight American soldiers set out on the long road to Uxmal. Shortly after the sun came up and the horsemen at the rear of the serpentine column were finally beginning to move, *Tiger* made sail, weighed her anchors, and beat out away from the shore. Exactly one week after their arrival on this different Earth, a week full of desperate fear and confusion, battle and hard toil, the little army Lewis had taken to calling the "Detached Expeditionary Force" unfurled its banners and marched into the new destiny he hoped it would make for itself.

The Ocelomeh had pride of place in the lead—just as well, since there might still be clots of enemies, and they needed scouts familiar with the territory—but the remaining men of the 3rd Pennsylvania came next, followed by the artillery and most of its members still marching as infantry. The dismounted dragoons and riflemen were interspersed among all the units, and—today—the 1st US Infantry brought up the rear. Behind them came all the armabueys and their burdens and the gaggle of Uxmalos and captives. Captain Anson and the mounted men acted as a rear guard for the whole disorderly thing.

As Lewis predicted, they were slowed to match the pace of the giant, lumbering armabueys, but it didn't slow the infantry much. In fact, it was probably a godsend since they weren't yet hardened to long marches. Besides, they were in no hurry. Uxmal was expecting them, and Alcalde Periz said they could take their time. Lewis only hoped the Uxmalos knew *what* they were expecting. But it was a leisurely march, and the men's high spirits, lifted by moving again, doing something, slowly began to flag. None straggled or became unruly, but it was easy to see their excitement waning.

Riding Arete at the head of the 3rd alongside De Russy, with Captain Beck and Lieutenant Manley walking behind, Lewis suddenly called out to some young drummers and fifers striding along, listlessly tapping out time on large drums with eagles painted on them. "Let's hear the 'Old 1812'!" That particular piece was always a favorite and one they hadn't played for Alcalde Periz and Varaa-Choon. With considerably more enthusiasm than before, the drummers tapped louder, waiting for the fifers to retrieve and poise their instruments. At a slight nod, the drums thundered a flourish and the fifes joined in. Soon, so did musicians all along the column, and it seemed every man stepped a little brisker. Lewis smiled as Varaa-Choon came trotting back to join him, staring in wonder at the troops, listening to the music, seeing the effect it had.

"By the Maker," she cried, "that tune makes me *want* to go out and fight! I didn't know you used music like this, on the march!"

Lewis was surprised. Of course they did. Everybody did—he thought. "Don't the Doms?"

"They use music," Varaa said, nodding, "great loud horns. But not to entertain or inspire their people, only to intimidate others." She turned to watch the marching men. "You must do this when you reach Uxmal," she said as the tune finally came to an end.

"We will," Lewis assured. "But if you liked that, listen to this." He raised his voice. "Who's the best singer in the Third Pennsylvania?"

"Sergeant Ulrich has a fine voice," De Russy said.

"Sergeant Ulrich!"

"Sir?" the infantryman called from behind the musicians.

"Can you lead the men in something they know?"

"Yes sir. Patriotic or popular?"

"Why don't we save the patriotic airs for later?"

"Yes sir." Ulrich raised his voice. "'Blue Juniata,' boys!"

And so they sang, two, three, eventually as many as five hundred voices thundering together to perform the jaunty, popular song about the Indian maiden Alfarata singing about her warrior lover as she canoed down the Juniata River. The men were happy, and Varaa-Choon was enthralled. So were the Ocelomeh, as Ixtla and Koaar rapidly, delightedly translated words that might've described their very own people. The Americans were perfectly willing to sing it again, and this time many Jaguar Warriors tried to join in.

The road gradually veered from the coast as the scenic beach gave way to a swampy, mangrove-choked estuary they had to go around. There was a crossing point for the first of several small streams contributing to the marshy region, and the men, still in good spirits and not overtired, erected their first marching camp late that afternoon as the lowering sun sent gleaming streamers through the clouds. The forest had opened onto a broad, grassy, coastal plain only dotted with trees, but also holding clumps of bizarre, elephant-size beasts of several different kinds. Some were utterly massive, with long, whip-thin necks and tails. Others were comparatively squat, with protruding horns and bony frills covering their necks and shoulders. All seemed generally indifferent to their arrival, only moving a discreet distance away as the column slowly coiled in on itself and the men set up tents and threw up field fortifications that Lewis insisted upon.

Higher spirits or not, no one complained or argued against the wisdom of that. Still, as their wonder at least briefly overcame their fear, the men seemed more adventurously interested in the giant creatures than Lewis was comfortable with. Worried they were more likely to go out and pester them than the other way around, he passed orders that only designated scouts and pickets should stray from camp, and they should always be accompanied by some of Varaa's Jaguar Warriors until the threats around them were better understood.

One of these pickets was Private Felix Meder, still sore from his wicked wounds, but feeling better than he would've expected. Obviously, judging by scars on many of the Ocelomeh, they were accustomed to dealing with such hurts, and the crusty old medicine man Father Orno turned him and Private Hudgens over to had fixed them up well enough to astonish Dr. Newlin. At present, Meder and another rifleman named Bill Todd were with a small squad of the 1st Infantry under a young lieutenant named Sime, going to inspect the brown, nearly stagnant water of the crossing the army would use the next day. The crossing looked straightforward, with a tended cut in the bristly mangrove-like trees along the bank where the rutted road dove under the water and out the other side, but the opaque water was very dark, and the air around it full of mosquitoes and a truly stupendous thunder of toads.

Meder was . . . uncomfortable. They were only a couple hundred yards from the bustling, growing camp, but Lieutenant Sime led his party out without waiting for the Ocelomeh he was supposed to bring. Now he walked with his sword blade on his shoulder, occasionally swiping at flowers protruding from the grass.

"Orders were to have a local with us," one of Sime's men reminded.

"Captain Cayce's acting like an old woman." Sime scoffed. "Of course, he *is* only an artilleryman," he allowed condescendingly. "We can get *ourselves* out of anything we get into"—he gestured around with his sword—"and it's quite clear enough to see anything dangerous approaching. The trees along the water aren't very thick at all, and otherwise there's just this tall grass. We can see for miles." His tone hardened, and he ended haughtily, "Besides, we don't need those ridiculous savages leading us about by the hand."

Meder didn't speak, but he disagreed. True, the woods weren't as thick ahead, even beside the stream, but they were twisty mangroves, not tall trees. The gnarled roots provided sufficient hiding places for all sorts of frightening things. And the "grass" the lieutenant so casually dismissed stood as high as a man's waist in places—more than adequate for predators to conceal themselves. Bill Todd had fought Seminoles in similar terrain and appeared to be thinking the same. Meder wouldn't forget that when he and Elijah Hudgens were on their own, they nearly wound up eaten. If it hadn't been for Varaa's Ocelomeh, they would have, and he respected and appreciated the friendly native warriors. As for Captain Cayce, Meder's estimation of his judgment was running fairly high. "Only an artilleryman" or not, Cayce had a better grasp of their situation than anyone else, especially this self-important little lieutenant, probably younger than everyone with him, Meder included. And *Cayce* respected and appreciated the Ocelomeh as well.

"I think we ought to go back, sir," he told Lieutenant Sime, turning in the grass with his rifle up, halfway to his shoulder. Bill Todd was doing the same. Other infantrymen, perhaps remembering fighting in Florida as well, had caught their caution, unslinging muskets and looking around.

"Nonsense." Sime scoffed. "We're there. I want to see how deep the crossing is." He smirked. "Wouldn't want to sink any of Captain Cayce's precious cannon!"

"No sir," murmured a burly corporal with dry blood from the monsters they'd fought still darkening the wool of his jacket. One thing about wool: even bloodstains would fade as they dried and flaked out like dust. "Them cannon saved our arse, they did," he added.

Sime scowled. "We did well enough without them before Major Reed got so banged about. Now he's off on that loathsome British ship! And why didn't Captain Beck take command? Whoever heard of *artillery* officers commanding infantry? Outrageous!"

Breaking out of the grass onto the rocky dirt road again, Sime led his men down the gentle slope to the water. Standing at its edge amid the booming, gronking shrieks of amphibians, he peered intently at the dark, creeping surface, half-covered with floating leaves, twigs, and what looked like rough, greenish-brown spheres the size of bodark apples. He wrinkled his nose. "It smells, and I can't see the bottom at all," he said loud enough to be heard over the roaring creatures. "These blasted frogs!" he complained, looking around to spot one.

"I b'leve they're toads," the corporal corrected, just as loud. "Sound like toads."

Sime stared at him. "You amaze me. Toads, frogs, what possible difference could it make?"

"Frogs can be ate," the corporal said. "If they was frogs, these sound big
enough to make a meal on one!"

Several men chuckled, but Sime frowned with distaste. "How revolting.
I wouldn't eat either of them. I wish I had a stick," he said louder. "Someone
find a stick to test the depth, or I'll choose one of you to wade across." He
paused, leaning closer to the water, inspecting the knobby, floating balls
more closely. "Good heavens!" he blurted. "It's looking at me!"

The water exploded all over him, and something about six feet long,
glistening pink and shaped like a long feather, whipped up and slapped him
in the face. He screamed in pain and terror as it jerked him forward, head-
first, toward a gaping set of dripping jaws rimmed with sharklike teeth rising from the stream beneath a pair of greenish-brown spheres that revealed
huge, liquid yellow eyes concealed behind their lids. The corporal had
snatched the lieutenant before the thing, easily as big as a flat, pebble-
skinned calf, could pull him into those terrible jaws, and the young man
screamed even louder. Another tongue—it *had* to be a tongue—shot out of
the water to the right of the first and struck the corporal's arm. He yelled as
hundreds, maybe thousands of tiny barbs ripped his sleeve and slashed the
flesh beneath, but didn't let go of his officer.

"It's tearing my face off!" sobbed Sime in terrible agony.

Felix fired his rifle down the first monster's open mouth and the jaws
clamped shut, spraying blood from its own tongue, which the jagged teeth
nearly severed. Todd shot the other creature and then the infantrymen
were firing as well. The first one—it *did* look like a giant toad—abruptly
disappeared under the water, but its blood-streaked tongue was still pulling
Sime. Snatching the officer's sword (he'd dropped it when he was attacked),
Meder hacked at the thing, each blow punctuated by another screech as
barbs tugged at the young man's cheek and jaw, both now flowing with
blood. The tongue finally parted and the corporal and lieutenant fell back
from the stream, dragging themselves up and away. Another tongue darted
out, striking an infantryman's musket and gouging grooves in the fore
stock and barrel band. The man cursed and recovered his aim before firing.
Dark water geysered with blood.

"Get back!" Meder shouted at the others, helping drag the lieutenant
farther up the road. The men had no targets but were reluctant to retreat,

rapidly reloading and shooting at bubbles if nothing else. Plumes of reeking water rocketed up with every stabbing jet of fire. "Back away!" Meder roared, turning his attention to the sobbing lieutenant. The corporal had already pulled the bloody end of the tongue off his face and was dabbing at the free-flowing blood with the officer's own neck cloth. The flesh beneath was beginning to blacken and swell and looked like it had taken a blast from a fouling piece.

"Cease firing, you fools!" came a cry from behind as horses galloped up the road. Meder saw Captain Cayce leading several men and Ocelomeh, while other riders spread out in the grass on their flanks. Varaa jumped down from a horse she'd been riding behind the young Ranger Meder thought looked too much like a girl and trotted up to examine the moaning lieutenant.

"Bad," Varaa said. "Very bad. An ugly wound for one so young and dangerous as well." She cut her big eyes up at Lewis, still mounted. "They call them 'sapos cortantes,' 'slash toads,' and they're very bad." She looked at the writhing infantry officer, then the corporal now holding his arm. "They're also poisonous."

"Poison, hell!" shouted the corporal. "I'm gonna die from gettin' licked by a *toad*?"

Varaa flicked her tail. "No. The poison makes you sleep. It weakens the victim as it struggles. You didn't get much and will recover." She looked at Sime, now lying still, but his eyes were wide and frightened. "We'll have to see about him," she said.

"Get him on my horse," Leonor said in her man voice.

Lewis was looking down at the bloody, muddy squad of men, and Meder in particular, for some reason. "You don't even have to tell me, I know," he said. "You thought, 'It's only a little way off. We don't need any help.'" He frowned. "But you *do*. We all do." He nodded at Varaa. "And they need ours. But for now we have to let them guide our behavior. We don't know enough about what's lurking out here, in the woods, the grass, or the water. Until we do, *no one* ventures out without someone to advise them. Is that *perfectly* understood? We can't lose people to ignorance!"

Meder and Todd both nodded. So did the infantrymen.

"Ah . . . begging your pardon, sir, but . . ." Meder tilted his head back toward the stream. "How do we avoid things like that, hiding in the water, just waiting to snatch a fellow down?" He looked helplessly around. "And not just 'slash toads,' but . . . anything."

"We learn, Private," Lewis replied. "We'll all learn to be woodsmen here. Just as the Uxmalos and others will learn to be soldiers."

Varaa was blinking rapidly, angrily, it seemed. "Many things you avoid by not letting them notice you, but most you just . . . scare away." She pointed at the crossing. "When we come down here with wagons and arm-abueys crashing through the water, the slash toads will go. They're . . . scareder of us than we are of them—unless you come creeping up like a fearful food beast."

Private Todd was nodding. "I guess we did. We weren't afraid of the water—didn't know nothin' was in it—but I reckon we prob'ly acted like it."

Leonor was already heading back, holding Lieutenant Sime on her horse behind her.

"And we would've known how to act if the lieutenant waited for someone to tell us," Meder said.

"That's right, Private Meder. You understand at last," Lewis snapped, then paused. "I'd have thought *you* already would after your ordeal. Gather these men and return to camp at once." Wheeling his horse about, Lewis pulled Varaa up behind him and broke into a trot.

"I *did* understand," Meder told the men—and the single Ocelomeh warrior who'd stayed behind—as he watched their rescuers move away. "But I never expected Captain Cayce would remember my name!"

"Not always a good thing, lad," the infantry corporal glowered.

Meder shook his head. "I think it is, when he does it."

CHAPTER 15

They began the crossing just after dawn, the 1st US Infantry in the lead this time, but following a tumultuous passage of armabuey-drawn carts as Varaa had directed. The men were understandably nervous, wading through water up to their waists, and all were told to stop and check for leeches by squads as they proceeded on, making room for the men behind them. Aside from the occasional discovery of a leech, however, there were no injuries to horses or men. They managed two more swampy streams that day, also without incident, and an important lesson had been learned by the time they camped at the edge of the plain in the shadow of the forest once more, assured they were finished with creek crossings. To Alferez Lara's surprise (he remembered no large rivers in the Yucatán), they were told to expect a wide, sluggish, seasonal river called the Cipactli when they neared Uxmal, but even if it rained heavily before they reached it, there was a fine bridge.

And so they went uneventfully on, back in the dense forest for the most part, but finding good campsites every night. And the nights were fairly restful, the goodwill between the troops and their strange Indian friends enduring. There was free association, music, and song. The Uxmalos had drums and flutes of their own and endeavored to join the Americans when they played. They were particularly fond of guitar, banjo, and fiddle music since they had no string instruments. Men who could play those became instant celebrities.

To Lewis Cayce, it seemed an idyllic time in many ways. The weather was hot and humid, and the mosquitoes remained a dreadful nuisance—particularly in the mornings and evenings—but the nights were cool and breezy, there was no sign of the enemy, and though they saw increasing numbers of bizarre creatures, some quite large and intimidating, none attacked the weapon-bristling column or hampered its movements. The army was holding together, *growing* together in important ways during the easy marches as former strangers became fast friends and the trauma of their arrival and the terrible battle gradually faded. The pleasant evenings of entertainment and fellowship (with the pretty, friendly Mistress Samantha Wilde and Mistress Angeligue Mercure often in attendance) put many of the men's fears away for the time. Lewis knew they were still there and could easily explode into the open, but as he confirmed the election of new NCOs, he took the steadier ones into his confidence.

"It seems your policy of letting the truth—that we're stuck here—filter out in a calm, controlled manner has been for the best," Colonel De Russy remarked one evening. As had become their custom, he and all of Lewis's senior officers, as well as unofficial advisors, had gathered to eat and discuss the day's events at the "command tent" shortly after dark. Now, regardless of what De Russy said, all were increasingly on edge. Not only would the army reach Uxmal in a couple of days; they'd soon have to "officially" reveal its new cause and purpose.

"I hope so," Lewis replied, leaning to the side on his camp stool to accept a cigar from Captain Anson. He wondered how many the man had left and what he'd do when they were gone. *Take up the more jarring native variety of tobacco, no doubt,* he thought. Many already had. Lieutenants Olayne, Burton, Manley, and Wagley; Captain Beck and Dr. Newlin; even Reverend Harkin were smoking pipes filled with the local mix of tobacco and herbs, just like many of the men were already doing. Others chewed the stuff, mixed with their store of molasses from *Commissary.* Lewis understood there'd be other sugars available here when the time came. Still, it was important. Depriving men of tobacco when he needed their nerves rock steady might've prompted disaster.

De Russy's servant, Barca, leaned in and lit Lewis's cigar with a small burning stick from the fire. Lewis eyed him in the flickering firelight, still struck by his presence as the apparent "property" of the officer from Pennsylvania. It bothered him, and he intended to inquire about it when things were more settled. He'd heard from Leonor, Lara, even Captain Anson, that Barca had performed as well as anyone in the battle, and the thought of him sharing the same status, if not circumstances, as the Holcanos they'd taken captive spiked Lewis's temper. He forced himself to puff his cigar to settle his mood.

"Alcalde Periz was certainly in a rush to leave us, all of a sudden," Samantha Wilde observed with a discreet little cough.

"Yes," agreed Varaa-Choon, refilling her own pipe and blinking at Samantha with apparent amusement as the woman tried to avoid the gray cloud the others were making. Periz had taken a hundred Uxmalos and a guard of fifty Ocelomeh under Consul Koaar on ahead after the army made camp for the night. "He has to prepare for our arrival, and the city will be full. Messengers have already gone to summon the important *alcaldes* of the closest cities," Varaa continued. "Some act as *his* advisors." She blinked thoughtfully. "The idea of a strong, united union has grown on him over the past few days and during our little consultations." She waved around, then looked directly at Lewis. "He was especially impressed by my interpretation of your readings from the 'Constitution' governing your people"—she nodded at Alferez Lara—"so very much like the one that once governed yours as well. We'll have to discover why it binds some, while driving others apart." Lara nodded and pursed his lips. He'd been a strong supporter of the Mexican Constitution of 1824, but now wasn't the time to describe all the reasons it hadn't flourished. "In any event," Varaa went on, "Alcalde Periz wanted to speak to several other *alcaldes* before this 'great army'"—she grinned— "makes its appearance below the walls of Uxmal. Especially since some of those *alcaldes* may actively oppose closer cooperation. He—*we*—strongly suspect the *alcalde* of Puebla Arboras—far too often in Uxmal already, in my view, and doubtless there now—will be one."

"Why? Who is he?" Reverend Harkin asked.

Varaa nodded to Father Orno, who haltingly took up the explanation. Despite theological differences they didn't even know the depth of yet, he and Reverend Harkin had been practically inseparable, first working tirelessly to assist Dr. Newlin and the Ocelomeh healers, then because they'd discovered they shared a passion for natural philosophy and the study of God's creation. Harkin knew he had a long way to go to catch up with his new friend in this place. They prattled together incessantly, and Father Orno's growing grasp of English was amazing to them all.

"He calls himself 'Don Discipo,'" Orno said with distaste, "and Puebla Arboras lies on the fringe of . . . La Tierra de Sangre—the contested 'Land of Blood.' I *say* it is contested," he added grimly, "but it's thoroughly under the control of the Holcanos and Grik, who strongly hold the ancient city of Cayal south of Puebla Arboras." One of his eyebrows twitched upward. "Some find it strange that even though Don Discipo's city has long been most exposed to Holcano aggression, it remains . . . *sin molestado.*"

"Unmolested," Lara clarified for some of the others.

Varaa nodded and took over the explanation, tone dark. "Many believe it's because he's allowed Dom Sacerdotes de Sangre—Blood Priests—to reside among his people as missionaries and has grown too close to them."

"What precisely are these 'Blood Priests'?" De Russy asked. "I've heard them mentioned unflatteringly in association with the Doms. . . ."

Harkin glowered and glanced at Orno. "I won't preach a sermon, only explain," he assured before clearing his throat. "Apparently, they *are* the Doms in the sense that it's their horribly warped version of the faith— which Father Orno and I share the *true* fundamentals of—that increasingly defines the so-called Holy Dominion and guides its people." His expression clouded. "We, nearly all of us here, I should hope"—he glanced questioningly at Varaa-Choon before continuing—"firmly believe that, through the blood of our Lord and savior Jesus Christ, we who surrender ourselves into God's divine hands are bathed in His grace. It abides in us, helping us achieve the tasks He calls us to perform for the benefit of others and His glory." Harkin slightly shrugged his large shoulders. "Some are called to be ministers, to spread the word. Others are sailors, whalers, wheelwrights, blacksmiths, farmers"—he glanced at his friend De Russy—"even politicians, I suppose." He peered over at Lewis, the firelight glinting off his small eyes. "Even righteous soldiers do a service for their fellow man that is not displeasing to the Lord—if they perform their duty guided by the grace of God in their hearts. God's grace, given freely and wholly undeserved to those who accept it and endeavor to *deserve* it through good works and rejection of sin," he added meaningfully, "will carry us to salvation, if we let it."

His face contorted with a mixture of horror and fury. "Blood Priests also teach that 'grace' is the pathway to salvation—of a sort. Theirs is not so attractive to most, since their notion of 'paradise' is one of degrees. The exalted among them remain so, only more, and their servants still serve. The only difference for them is that they do so without want for a change. I suppose that might be a *kind* of paradise to some. . . .

"But the most hideous and perverted difference is that instead of earning the right to *keep* the grace freely given by a loving God, a grace that sustains us in our toil and suffering, they must earn . . . *their* god's grace (I can't call him 'ours') through pain and suffering. Over the years, the bloody pagan rituals the Spanish found in this land twisted and subverted the Christianity they brought to such a shocking degree that even the meaning of our Lord and Savior's crucifixion has been perverted. Instead of dying for *our* sins, to ensure *our* salvation, the brutal scourging and execution of Jesus has been turned to an example of what's *required by all* to gain the grace required for salvation!" He shuddered.

"What are you saying?" Samantha almost whispered, horrified.

Varaa answered. "Doms believe they must be 'cleansed' by pain to earn the 'grace' of a bloodthirsty Maker who glories in their sacrifice to him. The more painful it is, the more notice he takes!"

"That's . . . ghastly!" Lieutenant Olayne objected.

"Yes," Father Orno agreed, eyes blazing.

"Just as bad," Reverend Harkin went on, "they've integrated many . . . pagan practices into their faith. Human sacrifice is one. Ostensibly, it serves as an example of the 'purification' they must endure—and the victim is consoled with the assurance his or her soul will fly straight to their 'heavenly underworld'—but it's primarily a means of delighting and gaining the favor of their god for various reasons." He glanced at Orno. "I understand it occurs quite frequently."

Reverend Harkin sat up straighter, proud belly straining against his waistcoat, but his expression was wreathed in gloom. "In any event, to answer your question, Colonel De Russy, Blood Priests are members of a newer, more aggressive sect of messengers and harbingers of that way of thinking now gaining power over"—he snorted—"their more 'moderate' bretheren. That power struggle within their 'church' makes little difference to us or our friends, however, since 'moderate' in this case seems only a question of relative enthusiasm for the effusion of blood rather than any meaningful doctrinal dispute." He drew on his pipe and blew a frustrated gust of smoke. "One wouldn't imagine such a depraved faith would attract many followers, but the Dominion has grown vast and powerful as much through the *fear* of conquest as the actual fact of it because those who resist . . ." He shook his head, perhaps still unbelieving.

Varaa resumed again. "All their leaders of any consequence, including *every single* family member, is publicly impaled—along with two in ten of the *entire population* of the region they absorb. At least half of the rest are taken into slavery, and many of *those* die in an orgy of sacrifices to delight their Maker. The rest are still slaves, left to work the land or mines or perform whatever occupation makes the conquest beneficial to the Dominion." Varaa looked around at each face, large blue eyes flaring with the flickering flames.

"*This* is the ultimate enemy I hope you'll help us resist." She sighed. "As I've told some of you, I and the few others like me came to this land long ago. We came as explorers, perhaps traders, and never meant to stay, but were wrecked and cast on this shore the same as you—in some ways." She blinked and swished her tail, then *kakked* a humorless chuckle. "We were nearly as isolated from our home as well, since ours are a cautious people not given much to exploration. We get strangers enough at home, I assure you," she said cryptically, "and generally see no need to discover more. Unlike you, however, with the help of our 'pagan' Ocelomeh"—she sent a genuine grin at Harkin and Orno—"we could've built a ship and sailed back where we came from." She waved her pipe in a circle in front of her face. "But the Jaguar Warriors embraced us, practically *worshipped* us for a time, since we do somewhat resemble ancient deities of theirs shaped like creatures that don't even exist on this world. Their beliefs have slowly changed, gently leaning more toward those of Father Orno in interesting ways, but they've remained content to let us lead them—and help them protect the Uxmalos and other peoples who sustain them like their collective army. King Har-Kaaska, Ko-aar, myself—a few others—all came to realize we *loved* these people and were needed here more than we ever were at home. So we stayed," she ended simply.

"*You* don't have the option of staying voluntarily," she resumed. "You *can't* go home. You *have* no home besides what you might build here. I'd think that would make it easier for you to convince your soldiers to help the only people who'll help you do it, but I won't take that as a given. Especially as they learn more about the Doms. I only hope they learn to love the people here as I have and come to see them as their own."

Reverend Harkin stirred and actually patted Father Orno on the shoulder. "I'll help with that. I've learned a great deal from you, Varaa-Choon, and my little friend here." He patted Orno again. "I'm Presbyterian, of course, but there are many denominations in my flock: Methodists, Lutherans, Congregationalists, Baptists, Anglicans, and I shall not scorn papists either. Why, I think there's even a Mohammadan or two and various pagans among Captain Holland's sailors. All will be part of my flock if they choose because what you told Captain Cayce was right: the differences between all those faiths, and what I've come to know about the Uxmalos— even Ocelomeh!—pale to insignificance compared to the abomination of the Doms." He looked earnestly at Lewis. "As God is my witness, we *will* build a union, and I'll daily preach on the glory of Godly unity—and the wickedness of the Doms!"

The gathering began to dissolve shortly after, as usual, since Harkin and De Russy always retired early and the hard-pressed junior officers—no new ones had yet been selected—had to see to the needs of the men. Eventually, also as usual, only Lewis, Captain Anson, Varaa and Ixtla, Dr. Newlin, Alferez Lara, and Samantha and Leonor remained. Whether she knew it or not, everyone there had either guessed or learned Leonor's secret. Samantha and Varaa had never been in doubt from the moment they saw her, and Lara had his suspicions confirmed when her own father called her "girl" in the battle. Newlin was a doctor, and Ixtla was accustomed to female warriors among the Ocelomeh. He and Varaa might wonder *why* it was a secret, but decided it wasn't their place to ask. And without discussing it among themselves, all at least suspected the others already knew. Still, it was never spoken of, each believing Leonor had earned sufficient respect and appreciation in the fight to keep her secret if she wished. Samantha, on the other hand, never brought Angelique to these meetings. Lewis suspected she didn't think her fragile friend was ready to hear the bigger secret yet.

Now Samantha broke the silence with a sigh and looked at Varaa. "Grotesque as your description of the Doms has struck me, I confess Reverend Harkin's growing flexibility has lifted a weight from my heart," she proclaimed. "I'm *terrified* of the Doms, but they don't yet seem real." She turned her gaze to Lewis. "The damaging confusion I feared might erupt after a break between Reverend Harkin and Father Orno concerned me more."

"The good reverend has risen higher to the challenge than I expected,"

Newlin agreed. "As must we all," he added with a glance at Leonor, still sitting as far from Alferez Lara as she could. The young Mexican officer was obviously aware of her reserve but never remarked on it. Lewis thought he'd guessed its source. On the other hand, he was relieved that Leonor's father—the most implacable hunter of Mexican soldiers Lewis had ever known—was at least professionally courteous to the young man who'd voluntarily placed himself and his troopers under the Ranger's command.

"Coffee, anybody?" grumbled the always-ill-tempered Private Willis, approaching with a blackened copper pot. "Won't be hardly fit to drink tomorrow, even heated. Shame to waste it, what with us prob'ly never gettin' any more," he whined. Days before, Willis overheard enough of one of their discussions to be conscripted into the "inner circle" and threatened with a return to the ranks if he spilled more information than allowed. Not only had he readily agreed, he'd actually become a more conscientious orderly. He remained abrasive and disagreeable, but must've realized he did have it easy compared to those who had to fight monsters, whatever the "Doms" were, and any other manner of thing.

Lewis, Newlin, and Varaa held out their cups.

"There's no 'coffee' here," Varaa said sadly, "but there are other stimulating beverages I think you'll like." She peered at Samantha. "The Doms are quite real, I assure you, and I fear it's inevitable they'll come." She blinked for emphasis. "We should have time to prepare, however. They have many soldiers, but they're widely scattered. There are also rumors many are preparing to embark on an expedition to the northwest." She paused. "Other humans who came to this world about a century ago have made an empire of islands across the great sea to the west. I'll tell you more of them sometime. But they've traded with the Doms, mostly for female slaves, I understand, which doesn't recommend them to me as potential allies. Neither likes the other, and the intensity of their rivalry gives me the sense it has a hereditary, even prehistoric foundation, but the great sea has always kept them from coming to meaningful blows." She snorted. "Now those other people, 'Imperials,' have established colonies on *this* continent, in the far northwest. Again, rumor has it that though the Doms have no more use for that vast territory now than they do the Yucatán, they mean to push them out."

She blinked reflectively. "So, as I said, we may have time to prepare before the Doms come for us in earnest." She flicked her tail and warned,

"That doesn't mean we won't be opposed *reflexively* from the start. Even before news of the battle reaches their leaders, there'll be obstruction, spying, political disruption, even assassinations. They have people in our cities who'll do what they *know* their leaders would want."

"Blood Priests from Puebla Arboras?" Anson growled.

"At least in the background," Varaa confirmed, looking at Lewis. "They'll want to study you and make their reports, perhaps even try to sway you to join them. They've done it before," she added bitterly.

"That'll never happen," Anson said definitively.

"You say that now," Varaa murmured, "but you haven't seen . . ." She shook her head. "Joining them will save nothing. They'd wring you dry of information—then blood—and discard your dead husk. It's what they do."

Lewis pursed his lips. "Will these 'Blood Priests' be with Don Discipo at Uxmal?"

"They're not supposed to be," Varaa told him. "Alcalde Periz and most of the people in the city hate them as much as I and my Ocelomeh." She blinked thoughtfully. "With Periz away, however, they may have come to join Discipo. I fear he's only their puppet."

"How much sway do they have over other *alcaldes*?" Dr. Newlin asked.

Varaa bowed her head at him and gazed around at the others. "A most pertinent question indeed—and I can't answer it. Nor can Alcalde Periz. That's why he left—to get a feel for things. We must accept the fact that our victory over the Holcanos and Grik will cause great excitement, even joy, but there'll also be fear. Don Discipo and the Blood Priests will try to exploit it." She looked back at Lewis. "Whether our union can be built or not depends a great deal on what Alcalde Periz discovers when he gets home, how well he convinces the other *alcaldes*, and honestly, how impressive your soldiers look when we reach Uxmal." She broke the gloom she saw deepening around her with a sudden snort of humor. "Fear not. All your men have to do is march as smartly as I've seen them drill—and sing, of course." She laughed. "By all means, have them sing!"

CHAPTER 16

Two days later, under a cloudy, breezy, late-morning sky, the Detached Expeditionary Force finally emerged from the forest into a broad coastal vale surrounded by low, rolling, tree-cluttered hills. The gentle slopes and plain down by the last river they'd have to cross (the very first real one) were intensively irrigated and cultivated into a checkerboard of multicolored crops, mostly green, amber, and yellow, with something almost the red-purple of sorghum here and there. Outlying dwellings, interspersed among the fields, were generally modest in size but built of stone and covered with thatched roofs. Farmers and laborers wore the same rough—if still somewhat colorful—homespun smocks as the Uxmalos who'd joined the Americans at the beach, along with supple moccasin boots laced up to their knees and wide-brimmed straw hats differing only in age and condition. And many used the same massive armabueys as draft animals, though there were also perfectly ordinary oxen and burrows. All seemed to stop what they were doing to stare as the Ocelomeh first appeared.

The locals must've thought it strange to see Jaguar Warriors marching in column four abreast, and even in step to a degree, instead of just sauntering out of the woods in a pack as they usually did. Especially since they were accompanied by the rattle of unfamiliar-sounding drums and something like flutes in the dense trees behind. Then, to their astonishment—and possibly fear—a dozen dark- and light-blue-clad horsemen appeared on the track in a perfect column of twos, beneath a pair of festive-looking, odd-shaped flags held sharply aloft by a pair of riders. One was smaller, red above white, resembling two pointed pennants attached where they touched. Some who could read (a few Uxmalos could) recognized the numbers and letters painted on the fabric. The other flag was larger and a comparative riot of color, its red and white stripes and blue field full of white stars edged all around in gold.

More flags preceded a tightly packed procession of foot soldiers: hundreds of men dressed all alike in sky-blue uniforms, dark blue hats, and white cross belts. Some wore different-colored trim, but all carried muskets on their shoulders, many with wicked lance-point things on the ends of their barrels. This column was broken at intervals by teams of horses carrying men and pulling strangely shaped vehicles with more men on top. And behind each of these trailed a monstrous great gun—something Uxmalos also recognized and feared.

Most of these first spectators were essentially peasants. Everyone had heard of the strange people coming, who'd joined their Ocelomeh friends to defeat the Holcanos and Grik, but no one really expected *this*. There were *hundreds* of them and many great guns, all moving relentlessly forward like a gigantic centipede. The more learned might imagine a Dom army moving something like this, but they'd never seen that either, so they had no basis for comparison. The sight was thrilling, chilling, fascinating, and horrifying all at once. And the noise! Drums thundered all along the line, as did the strange, high-pitched instruments, but the men were loudly singing as well, roaring alien words to an equally unfamiliar—if not unpleasant—melody. It was the strangest thing most of the increasingly stunned spectators ever saw.

Lewis Cayce, riding at the head of the dragoons with De Russy, Anson, Reverend Harkin, and Mistress Samantha, was equally mesmerized by the city of Uxmal lying just across a long stone bridge, spanning what could clearly become a mighty river when it ran. Probably only knee-deep and a few dozen yards across at present, the Cipactli River's eroded banks extended a great distance to either side of the lazy, silty stream. And almost reaching the base of high stone walls like some massive moat, it described an arc around the city to drain in a well-sheltered bay full of fishing boats.

The gray, white-capping sea could just be glimpsed in the distance beyond a pair of breaking shoals. Lewis was surprised not to find *Tiger* already anchored in the bay, but the thought was pushed aside as the city reabsorbed his attention.

"My word!" cried Reverend Harkin over the music. "How much like the *real* Uxmal it appears!" The others looked at him questioningly. "I mean the one . . . where we came from, of course," he clarified. "I've never been there myself, but a New York traveler and explorer named Stephens, serving as 'special ambassador' to this . . ." He shook his head in frustration. "*That* region a few years back, rather rediscovered an ancient city. He and an English artist named Catherwood documented the ruins in a pair of popular books." He nodded ahead. "Those structures, minus the high wall, of course, remind me of Catherwood's lithographs." He squinted. "Though these don't seem as ornate, or festooned with dire pagan images."

The wall was eighteen to twenty feet high and, except for some geometric sculpture around a massive gate beyond the bridge, wore no adornments at all. It was a simple, straightforward, pragmatic defense against the monsters roaming this world. Still descending into the river valley, they could see buildings beyond it, and they were quite impressive indeed. There were a lot of dwellings and many people in Uxmal, and the principal building materials were stone for walls and thatch for roofs throughout, but larger buildings of various shapes looked almost classical: long, high rectangular structures with flat roofs built of skillfully shaped stone. Others were bigger up high than down low, which looked odd, but one in particular resembled a small, round-edged Egyptian pyramid with steps up one side and a small house on top. "That looks like Stephens's 'Governor's Palace,'" Harkin said with growing enthusiasm as he pointed, "and *that* one resembles what he described as 'The Nunnery,' though I can't imagine why. And that, of course, appears to be a version of his 'Pyramid of the Dwarf Magician.'" He frowned. "That sounds very strange. Perhaps I misremember. In any event, except for 'The Nunnery' they're all smaller than Catherwood rendered them and somewhat mixed about." His customary gloomy expression returned. "I'm driven to speculate that whoever originally built this place, however long ago, must've come here the same way we did and rebuilt what they remembered."

"Have you considered it might've been the other way around, Reverend Harkin?" Samantha asked innocently.

Harkin glowered at her. "Indeed I have, Mistress. I find myself considering a *great many* unexpected things." He paused. "Perhaps Father Orno may enlighten us." He looked around. "Where *is* the little fellow?"

Captain Anson snorted. "First time you've let him out of your sight in days and you've lost him."

"He went ahead into the city with Varaa-Choon," said Lewis. "Consul Koaar-Taak is leading the Ocelomeh. They're mostly his, remember."

They all grew silent for a while, enjoying the pageantry of their "triumphant" arrival. Lewis had taken Varaa's advice to heart, determined to make an impression, and they'd camped early the day before in a broad, pleasant, parklike clearing with rising, rippling terrain someone had dubbed the "washboard glade" less than seven miles from the city so the troops could prepare themselves and their equipment. Varaa said there was only one other good place to camp before they reached Uxmal, and if they went that far, they might as well go all the way. But the soldiers needed to clean themselves and their weapons, brush wool uniforms and polish brass buttons, belt and cartridge box plates. Steel musket barrels and bayonets were brightened, and the bronze gunmetal cannon tubes were rubbed with fine sand to remove battle tarnish and buffed to a glittering, red-gold sheen. Dragoons, artillerymen, and mounted riflemen brushed the overworked horses late into the night and fed them much of their hoarded grain. The Uxmalos with them, and even some Ocelomeh at Ixtla's direction, got into the spirit as well, cleaning carts full of salvage and even fetching water from a swampy pond to bathe the filth off their uncaring armabueys.

Lewis scratched his neck. Most of the men had even shaved or trimmed their hair, but not only had he been very busy, he didn't trust Private Willis with a razor against his throat. His neck whiskers itched. His beard was going a little wild as well, and he needed to get it under control. He must set an example, after all. Anson's beard remained perfectly groomed, as did Harkin's and De Russy's side whiskers. He'd have to inquire how they managed. But all the tiring activity that distracted him from his own appearance was paying off handsomely now. The little army marching down to Uxmal not only acted like the consolidated force it was growing into, it looked like a proper army as well—whether any of the locals had ever seen such a thing or not.

Townsfolk were gathering as the Ocelomeh neared the bridge. Many had probably been coming and going from the city on their daily affairs, but more were streaming out the great gate. The apparently well-to-do didn't dress much different from anyone else they'd seen, though they wore a lot of gold and silver jewelry adorned with gems. And the quality of their clothing was much finer, of course. They still seemed to delight in color, and that was more varied among them as well.

Then, for the first time, the men saw Uxmalo women. Even dressed much like the men except for an absence of belts, smaller, triangular brimmed hats atop straight black hair, and more formfitting clothing on the younger ones, Lewis was taken aback by how heart-stoppingly beautiful many of them were. Even the older, broader women with silver-white hair were quite handsome. Their presence created a predictable sensation, making men forget the words to their song or fall out of step. The caustic and near-instantaneous verbal thrashing of NCOs quickly returned them to their duty.

All began to gather around the marching men and animals in evident delight, pacing them, yet somewhat to Lewis's surprise, none tried to gaggle in amongst them. They appeared very pleased, but respectful—until they cried out jubilantly up ahead when Varaa-Choon and Father Orno galloped out the gate, quickly followed by Alcalde Periz, attended by more men on dark-striped horses. Most outdid Periz in their finery, wearing more riches by far, and several sat saddles so heavy with gold that their horses must've been hard-pressed. *At least Periz—or Orno? Both?—is liked by his people,* Lewis thought.

The Ocelomeh ground to a stop and Lewis called his own column to halt. For the first time since they left the trees, his men were silent, and they heard the growing uproar around them and from the city ahead. Lewis turned in his saddle to see hardened soldiers stiffen with pride and grins appear on unexpected faces. One even flashed across Private Willis's face before the scruffy little man caught him looking. He turned back at the sound of hoofbeats and saw Alcalde Periz's party pull up in the gap between the Americans and Ocelomeh. Forewarned, Lewis and his officers saluted Periz. The man bowed deeply in his saddle in response. He was smiling hugely in genuine pleasure, but his dark eyes moved a little nervously, expressing a measure of warning.

"We were right," Varaa said lightly, grinning, her own eyes cutting toward the man by Periz. "That's Alcalde Don Discipo. And his damned Blood Priest *is* in the city. Periz was not amused. Still, I suppose you'd better salute him and those others as well. The next in line is Ortiz, from Pidra Blanca—up the coast. Past him is Truro, from Itzincab. They're good fellows. More are coming, but this is all who's here." She nodded at Lewis's growing frown. "Don't worry. None of them speak English. Just salute them and we'll move along." Varaa straightened. "My Ocelomeh fought with you and had the honor of leading you here, but now the honor shifts to you—for a variety of reasons." Only then did Lewis realize Varaa's Jaguar Warriors were moving aside, making way for the Americans to pass. "The *alcaldes* and their deputies will join your procession through the city while my people go around." Varaa grinned again. "They'll guard your supplies—and our captives and the booty in the armabuey carts—where space has been provided for your camp on the east side of the city, astride the Pidra Blanca road. Perhaps you'd send a few men with Koaar to help him lay it all out. I know how you like things just so."

"But you're coming with us?" Samantha pressed.

Varaa nodded. "Of course. Father Orno's English is progressing, but he's not ready to lead you through *that*." Varaa tilted her head at the gate.

"Very well," Lewis agreed. "Lieutenant Burton, detail a party to accompany our friends around the city and lay out company streets"—he paused—"and field fortifications as well, of course."

Burton blinked at him. "Field . . . ? Yes sir."

Lewis smiled and saluted the dignitaries. "Why do I suddenly feel like I was safer in the woods with the monsters, Varaa?"

Varaa blinked something (Lewis was increasingly convinced blinking conveyed meaning or emotions beyond a grin or a frown that her otherwise relatively unexpressive face couldn't convey) and said, "Maybe you were, personally. I as well. Your men will be safe enough, even outside the wall. Large monsters rarely come close to the city. But the battle, your very presence, has thrown fuel on the fears I predicted, and Discipo's Blood Priest has been doing his best to ignite them. Some, even besides him, might think you and I are problems more easily disposed of than the warriors we lead."

Lewis controlled another frown. "Then let's get this over with." He raised his voice. "Forward, Captain Beck! Let's give them the 'Old 1812,' boys!" he called behind. Marvin Beck gave the preparatory order to advance while drums tapped and exploded into the tune along with a dozen fifes when the men stepped off. The crowd roared with delight as the troops tramped over the bridge and through the gate, flags high, drums stuttering, fifes skirling loudly, every man marching in step with his glittering weapon high on his shoulder. Hundreds more people were just inside the gate, happily waving bright little pennants of every imaginable color and giving way to line the sides of a broad thoroughfare leading toward the four- or five-story pyramid situated near the center of the city. More men and women and scampering youngsters constantly gathered until there must've been thousands choking the open-air markets under thatch or bright fabric awnings, filling the patios of stone-columned buildings, and even cheering down from balconies and rooftops. The noise confined within the city's walls nearly drowned the martial music. Lewis saw Alcalde Periz stiffen in his saddle, absorbing his share of the adulation with a broad smile on his beefy bronze face.

"It's as if we've already won a war for them, not just survived a small battle," De Russy shouted in Lewis's ear, almost incredulous.

"Small by your reckoning, perhaps," Varaa yelled, "but larger than anything in *their* experience. And I fear Colonel De Russy is right. Many of these people will think the Holcanos and Grik are broken forever, and the Dominion menace is past—at least less pressing."

"You don't think so?" Captain Anson asked, but there wasn't a question in his tone.

"I'm sure it's not," Varaa told him. "The Holcanos and Grik have been firmly chastised and would probably, by themselves, leave these people be for a time. But it can't be much longer before word of their defeat reaches His Supreme Holiness—the Dom 'Pope,'" she reminded, "at his capital in the Great Valley of Mexico."

Lewis was still struck by the profound irony that their current ultimate enemy's capital was in roughly the same place as the one they'd originally come to fight. But he'd been consoled to a degree that the seat of Dominion power was 350 leagues, or more than 1,200 miles, away.

Varaa nodded ahead as the avenue opened on a vast, grassy plaza surrounding the conical central structure. "That's the Temple of the Lord Jesucristo, the pulpit where Father Orno preaches. It once had . . . a darker purpose," she growled, glancing aside at Alcalde Discipo, then nodding at a group of men and women at the foot of the single long stairway leading up to the boxy structure on top of the pyramid. Most were dressed like Father Orno, in dark, simple garments buttoned up the front rather than being pulled over the head, and the only difference between men and women again seemed to be their head wear. The men wore wide-brimmed straw hats, painted brown or black, while the women's hat brims were brilliant white triangles. All had long wooden staffs upraised with simple wooden crosses on top.

Others stood slightly apart from the rest. One was an apparently frail, stoop-shouldered old man, covered by a roughly woven bloodred cloak, hood thrown back to reveal long gray hair, a large nose, and tiny, beady black eyes like a ferret's. He held a wooden staff as well, but its cross was a jagged, lightning-bolt-like thing, cast in gleaming gold. He was flanked by two hulking brutes in ordinary dress, except their knee-length tunics were also bloodred, with jagged yellow crosses stitched on their chests. They held spears with golden points.

"Discipo's Blood Priest and his beasts," Varaa snapped. "They'd happily return this temple to its former blood-drenched use and will be the eyes, ears, and perhaps daggers in the night for the Dom Pope until he stirs." Her tail whipped behind her. "Or Father Orno gets them to declare themselves," she added cryptically with something like hopeful anticipation. Lewis looked at De Russy and Anson, and they all merely shrugged.

The crowd noise respectfully diminished to almost nothing as the column entered the plaza and Father Orno galloped ahead to join the other clergy. He didn't dismount, only turned his horse to face them, holding both hands high. Lewis respected the ease and familiarity with which the little priest exercised his calming, spiritual influence over so many people. He also noted that even as Orno had nodded and waved to each of his colleagues, he pointedly ignored the Blood Priest and his henchmen. Alcalde Periz's fixed grin had turned to a grimace of anger.

"As I told you," Varaa hissed at the American officers, "Blood Priests are all but banned from the city. They should be. Then again, just as they spy on us and foment dissension, it's useful to keep a watch on them as well. But to find one standing *here* in this sacred place . . . It's a calculated insult to Alcalde Periz. The captain of the city guard should've never allowed it." Oddly, Lewis thought Varaa sounded almost gleeful.

"Then why is he there?" Samantha asked.

"To insult, as I said," Varaa told them, then indicated the mass of people. "And to intimidate, of course."

"Ah," De Russy murmured with an arched-brow glance at Lewis, "then perhaps **his presence** will help."

To Lewis's confusion, Varaa nodded.

De Russy smiled and tried to flatten the bulge his sword belt pushed the front of his coat up into. "I'm a politician, you know, and I recognize others when I see them. I've just decided Alcalde Periz may be one of the best." He nodded respect when Periz threw him a sudden, secret smile and continued, "We already know one of our most difficult tasks will be to remind people here, and throughout this region, that the war *isn't* over, the threat of the Doms *not* past." He tilted his head at the Blood Priest. "He'll do it for us." He snorted. "And though I'm sure our dear Alcalde Periz truly does detest his presence here, I'm equally sure he *ordered* his guards to allow it!"

"So all this—" Captain Anson began, but Periz himself interrupted in broken English.

"The union. We . . . build, begin today."

Father Orno was already addressing the gathered throng, voice carrying through a large bell-mouthed speaking trumpet one of the other priests had handed him. Varaa, now joined by Ixtla, quickly translated as Orno first told of their discovery of the impending Holcano and Grik attack. Everyone would've known of that, of course, but then Orno got uncomfortably flowery for Lewis's taste, describing how God Himself sent the "Americanos" from the very heavens to intervene on their behalf. Lewis heard Dr. Newlin snort derisively, but Reverend Harkin smiled and nodded.

Cheers erupted when Orno related how the combined American and Ocelomeh forces utterly routed the enemy, securing many captives and much plunder before coming to join the Uxmalos and teach them new ways that would forever secure their safety and prosperity.

The cheering was deafening then, and Lewis turned in his saddle to see many of his men joining in, some waving their wheel hats over their heads. He caught Captain Beck's questioning look and shook his head. *Let them celebrate. It's good to be appreciated,* he thought. *I hope it lasts—and helps them get over what I'll have to tell them.*

Captain Anson reached over and patted his arm, redirecting his attention to the gathered priests. The rodent-faced Blood Priest seemed about to explode. Suddenly, taking even his guards by surprise, he strode out beside Father Orno's horse and rudely tugged on his arm, gesturing at the speaking trumpet. With a graceful bow, Orno handed it over.

"Here it comes, I bet," Anson said. He was right.

"*Deja de animar!*" the Blood Priest screeched through the trumpet, and now Alferez Lara, who'd also drifted forward to join the command group, quickly told them what he said. "Stop cheering!" he repeated. "I am Father Tranquilo, Blood Priest to His Supreme Holiness, the Messiah of Mexico, who reigns by the Grace of God as Emperor of the World! All who cheer these diabolical heretics will be *damned* in his eyes!" Remarkably, that did the trick, but Lewis doubted the silence came from obedience as much as shocked fury that a *Blood Priest* would dare command them here. Either way, Father Tranquilo—*What a name!* Lewis thought—seemed satisfied and proceeded to rant, "Your heathen Ocelomeh are not *heroes*, selflessly protecting you! And these savage foreigners"—he waved at the Americans—"were *not* sent by God! How utterly absurd! Only His Supreme Holiness acts directly for God in this world!" The man's beady little eyes seemed to smolder. "And only the Devil floods it with his minions. The *truth* is that a peaceful village of Holcanos had invited some Godless garaaches among them to *minister* to them and show them their proper place as animals among men!" The little eyes stabbed at Varaa. "Even animals may serve in paradise if they earn sufficient grace. But the heathen Ocelomeh and their . . . Amigos del Diablo fell upon them without warning and mercilessly murdered them while they engaged in pious worship!" Incredulous shouts began to rise, and Alcalde Periz bellowed, "Lies, of course, but even if not, how could you know if you weren't there—or spies from our enemies didn't tell you?"

"*God* told me!" Father Tranquilo cried.

"Directly?!" Periz exclaimed in mock wonder. "I think not. God would only tell you and your kind to open their veins, perhaps in his mercy letting you *think* you were going to him as you die."

Father Tranquilo stabbed a bony finger at Periz. "He will have no mercy on *you*." He glowered at the crowd. "Worst of all, there were peaceful Dominion traders among the Holcanos when they were attacked, and some of *them* were slain by the devils in blue!" He glared straight at Lewis. "You know what that means, and I warn you now: the Dominion will never rest until the perpetrators of this heinous crime, the Ocelomeh and these . . . *demonios extranjeros* are disarmed and surrendered for *cleansing*!"

"Is that a threat?" Father Orno yelled. In spite of his volume, his voice seemed amazingly mild. "Do you, a *Blood Priest*, here only at our reluctant sufferance, *dare* to threaten the peaceful people of this land in the name of the Dominion, for the *crime* of protecting ourselves against the monsters your masters employ?" He looked around at the sea of suddenly hostile faces. "I just want to be clear."

"Yes!" Tranquilo seethed, spittle flying from the hissing word. "I threaten *all* the people of this squalid land with eternal damnation! So helplessly, willfully ignorant of God and His ways, you celebrate these heretics when you *should* be falling upon them to tear out their beating hearts with your teeth!"

In spite of the angry shouts now rising around him, he turned his accusing finger on the people.

"If *you* won't punish them, or give them over to the Holy Dominion, every degenerate man, infested woman, and verminous brat on this entire profane peninsula will be deemed as guilty as they. *Every last one of you* will be burned on the impaling stake, enduring agony without grace and death without life!"

Alcalde Periz exploded forward, galloping right up to the suddenly cringing Blood Priest and showering him with grassy clods of earth as he wrenched his striped horse to a stop. Tranquilo's guards advanced with their weapons and, without thinking, Lewis spurred Arete and whipped out his saber, yelling, "Captain Anson, if you will. Everyone else, stand fast!"

Tranquilo's guards hesitated as Lewis and Anson stopped by Periz, then dropped their spears when Anson pointed one of his huge revolvers at them and shouted, *"Tiran tus armas!"* Lewis suspected he'd used that phrase fairly often.

Periz hardly seemed to notice their presence but Lewis saw the corner of his mouth quirk upward. This was *exactly* what he'd hoped—probably expected—would happen. "Go!" Periz roared at the Blood Priest in his odd Spanish. "Get out of my sight! Slither back to your master in the Great Valley and tell him we're *ready* if he comes! We'll crush him like the Holcanos and Grik, and his survivors can slither home as well!"

A thunderous, raging roar swept through the plaza, and Tranquilo's protectors pulled the sputtering Blood Priest back and away, ushering him out of sight around the temple.

"That's actually . . . a bit more than I expected," Captain Anson drawled at Lewis after he told him what Periz said as they returned to their place at the head of the American column.

"Periz and Orno, both pitched it in red hot!" De Russy exclaimed. "And look around you! These people, few of them warriors, are now *anxious* to fight! By God, I only *thought* I was a politician," he confessed in admiration.

"They want to fight *now*," Samantha corrected him. "How will they feel when it comes to it?" She looked directly at Lewis. "After weeks, perhaps months of training, marching their legs off, long after this moment of enthusiasm fades and fear begins to mount?" She added a touch of sarcasm. "What will they do when they finally meet the enemy and experience the 'exquisite thrills' of battle they've been content to let their Ocelomeh protectors enjoy in their place so long? *Can* you make an army of them, sir?"

Lewis looked at De Russy, Anson, Reverend Harkin, and Hernandez, then glanced behind him again. "If we can keep the army we've got together a little longer, I think we just might." He took a deep breath and blew it out. "And it's time we got that settled." He gestured around at the still-jubilant crowd with his head. "As soon as we finish this parade and make camp to our satisfaction, we'll assemble the men and lay it all out. *Everything* we know."

"But, sir," Captain Beck began to protest, "maybe just a few more—"

"No, it's time," Lewis said decisively. "I only regret we didn't do it sooner. They *deserve* to know. But when the whole story of the exchange we just witnessed gets around and the men realize how much all these extremely welcoming people need them . . ." He smiled sadly. "Let's move out. And Captain Beck?"

"Sir?"

"I'd like to hear that 'Blue Juniata' again, I believe."

A LARGE NUMBER of Uxmalos followed the army out the east gate, still cheering and watching as details were dismissed to erect tents or form fatigue parties to prepare yet another field fortification to protect the camp. "They're getting better at that," Lewis said grudgingly while he, Anson, and Samantha rode around the shaping perimeter. He and Anson were looking to their defenses, watching stakes they'd gathered along the way be driven into the ground and spadefuls of soil arch out of a shallow trench to land among them. Samantha was gazing at the watching Uxmalos. "Of course, they've had a lot of practice, now," Lewis continued, "and just the hazards they already know have limited complaints about the extra work."

"They'd *still* gripe after a long, hard march," Anson predicted, then grinned. "But like you said, they see the sense in it. An' look. Even some Uxmalo drovers an' a few Ocelomeh are pitchin' in." He nodded in satisfaction. "It's like they already feel like part of your army. They'll build forts like this as good as the Romans, before long."

Samantha turned her head to gape at him.

"What? You think Captain Cayce's the only one of us provincials to read a book or two?"

Samantha pursed her lips, then nodded. "I suppose I did. Unforgivable, of course."

Anson shrugged and smiled. "Not 'unforgivable' at all, an' almost right, I bet. Fact is, I've always been a reader. Good thing too. Next to bloody, hard-won experience—which you don't always live through earnin'—readin' history teaches you a lot about leadin' men. If you really take it in," he qualified, "you can pick up a lot of examples of what *not* to do!" He gestured around. "First thing you learn is to use the ground. An' if you can't get ground you want, you make what you've got into what you need."

"He's right," Lewis agreed, "and the ground commands armies as much as generals because men will almost always take the path of least resistance. If you catch your enemy doing that, you can tear him apart."

Anson arched both eyebrows. "Doesn't always work that way chasin' Comanches, I'll tell you. They'll lead you places a coyote couldn't go." He nodded. "But like anybody else, they come at you the easy way when they can."

"Something to remember," Lewis said lowly, then decided to change the subject as Leonor, Boogerbear, and Varaa-Choon trotted their horses up to join them. As he often did of late, Lewis wondered how he'd never realized Leonor was a woman during the campaign in Northern Mexico, culminating—for him—at Monterrey. He'd only seen what he expected, subconsciously defining what he now saw as a very pretty face as only boy-ishly handsome. Of course, the intense, even severe expression she almost always wore went a long way to support that delusion. It still disconcerted him. "You were looking at the locals, Mistress Samantha," he prompted. "What's your opinion of them?"

Samantha was grimacing at a procession of captives, still wearing weathered remnants of the grisly paint they'd fought in, being led away by armed Uxmalos and Ocelomeh, but her gaze settled back on the brightly garbed townsfolk still observing the newcomers. Some had gone boldly into the camp, likely to greet returning family members, but most remained respectfully, almost fearfully out of the way, making no effort to cross the defensive perimeter under construction. "They're a good-looking people," Samantha acknowledged. "Some of what must be the 'quality,' as they deem such things, seem rather soft and puffy"—she smiled—"but that's probably universal. Otherwise, a large percentage seem strong and hardy, well suited to life on this dreadful, perpetual frontier." Her eyes flicked mischievously at Lewis. "And don't tell me *you* haven't noticed that their women are quite beautiful—even if their wardrobe does them no justice."

Lewis felt his face heat. He *had* noticed that, of course, as had every man under his command, no doubt. He even somewhat shamefully hoped that might help soften the blow of truth he must reveal.

Samantha continued, "Still, all I can base an informed opinion on are the ones who joined us at the battle site, and upon the march."

Lewis knew she and Angelique, along with Reverend Harkin, had spent quite a lot of time amongst those men.

"They strike me as an honest, friendly lot, no different from your soldiers." She frowned slightly. "Aside from a generally shorter stature and darker skin, of course. Somewhat to my surprise, such dissimilarities have passed almost unnoticed thus far. I hope that indifference continues."

Varaa spoke up. "I've learned a lot about the culture most of your people spring from, and it isn't so different, deep down, from the Uxmalos. They too have a 'democracy' of sorts, with those who support the government through taxes on property or revenue eligible to select their *alcaldes*." She grinned. "They can *unselect* them too." Then she blinked something else and glanced sharply at Lewis. "And they have what you'd call 'slave labor,' though there's no *racial* element to it, as seems to be the case where you came from. Only enemies are used so." She shrugged. "Even then, I can only defend the practice by saying it's been the way of these people since before they ever came to this world, hundreds of years ago, and I suppose it's slightly less barbarous than slaughtering their foes to the last woman and child—as you just heard their enemies threaten to do to them." She looked over at the encampment. "Nor have I seen much friction arise, attributable to Mistress Samantha's 'dissimilarities.' Perhaps, as I've said before, it's because we've already fought together. One who is pressed sorely in battle cares little about the appearance of whoever—or whatever—comes to his aid." Her grin widened. "And after that initial shock—admit it, Captain Lewis, it was amusing!—your people have been amazingly accepting of *me*. If they can look past *my* dissimilarities, they can hardly notice those of the Uxmalos!"

Lewis was nodding. "I hope you're right," he said.

Samantha waved at the watchers. "Back to my point, these city folk appear little different from the Uxmalos we've already met." She became more animated. "And I was *extremely* impressed by Alcalde Periz and Father Orno! My God, how they stirred their people, and led that detestable Tranquilo into the snare they set for him!"

"Colonel De Russy acknowledged that was masterfully done," Lewis agreed. "Periz has certainly prepared his people to embrace the *idea* of what we've proposed, if only out of dire necessity." He gazed into the camp, the tents and company streets already almost completely established, and saw what looked like a disturbance erupting near where the command tents and colors had been placed. Even as he watched, more men were drawn from what they were doing to see what was happening.

"Damn," he muttered, whipping his horse around. "Periz has done his part. I only hope we don't disintegrate before we do ours!" Jabbing Arete with his blunted spurs, he dashed into the camp, the others close behind.

CHAPTER 17

Private Felix Meder of the US Mounted Rifles and Private Elijah Hudgens, R Company, 1st Artillery, were as different as two men can be, yet their shared experience on that first day had made them friends. They even shared a tent. The forty surviving riflemen fit for duty, from both *Mary Riggs* and *Isidra*, no longer had an officer, and only their election of a sergeant and two corporals had been confirmed. They were learning their jobs, directing details, and reporting their men's fitness as best they could, but the Rifles had lost their distinct identity and remained somewhat at loose ends. They had no horses of their own yet and had been used primarily as pickets and security forces, most often for the two artillery batteries on the march. Naturally, they'd more or less attached themselves to those batteries for mess and billeting, and their sergeant looked to Lieutenant Olayne, the acting artillery battalion commander, for guidance.

With half the guns now positioned around the perimeter of the camp and half held in a central reserve, Meder and Hudgens, and a few others still on light duty, were released to gather firewood for the battery cook. Passing through what was becoming a modest parade ground in front of the command and hospital tents where troops of the 1st US Infantry were rigging large awnings, Hudgens hesitated and started easing wide enough around that they had to duck under ropes and dodge men pounding stakes on the other side of the open area.

"What's the matter?" Meder asked.

"That big bugger there, you see 'im?" He nodded at a tall, black-bearded mountain of a man wearing the three white stripes of an infantry sergeant on his sleeves.

"Sergeant Hahessy, right? Big fellow," Meder conceded.

"Aye, an' 'e hates me guts."

"Why? For what?"

"No reason." Hudgens shrugged. "Partly because I'm British an' he's Irish. Mainly though, he's a cruel, heartless bastard, an' we've . . . met before."

Mystified, Meder asked no more. It seemed to him that even such long-standing ethnic tensions had eased of late as everyone grappled together to come to grips with their new circumstances. Particularly after the battle on the beach. But he trusted Hudgens's instincts. They'd almost made it past and would've soon blended with other men, busy erecting more shelters or digging fire pits, when Meder glanced back and saw Hahessy slap his own back, grasping for something under the sky-blue shell jacket.

"Goddamn it!" Hahessy shouted, "I've popped a button off me braces!" Turning to peer at the ground, he pointed triumphantly at a spot under the short green stubble of grass. "*There's* the little bugger! Fetch it for me, some-body. I'll be poppin' the other if I stoop." When no one rushed to seize the little pewter button, Hahessy's face clouded and he glared around. His gaze paused on Barca, supervising some cheerful Uxmalos in their effort to ar-range De Russy's things in his tent, but must've realized—black or not—pestering the colonel's servant was a bad idea. His gaze settled on Hudgens who'd turned to watch with Meder, but something he saw in Hudgens's eyes, and the way he stiffened and clenched his fists, must've made him decide a button wasn't worth a real fight right now, especially with so many watching. *Maybe later,* his eyes seemed to promise as they moved on. They stopped on the skinny, towheaded Private Cox of the 3rd Pennsylvania, carrying two sloshing buckets from a large public water well just outside the east gate. "You there, *Hanny* Cox," he growled sarcastically. "Yer a 'vol-unteer' so-jer. Volunteer to take up me button, why don't you?" He grinned wickedly. "An' sew it back fer me too!"

Cox flinched but ignored the big man, whose face went purple with rage. "I'm talkin' to ye, Private Cox! Insubordination, is it? I'll have ye flogged!"

"He'd flog a man over a *button*?" Meder hissed. Hudgens nodded grimly. Meder realized now, though everyone had been getting along amazingly well, that amity might've been artificial and more fragile than it seemed. The relief of being near civilization—of whatever sort—made them feel safer, and the veneer of shared purpose and goodwill might already be cracking under the strain of an ill-defined but ever-present pressure.

Shaking with fear and fury, Cox set his buckets down and turned to face the now gleefully belligerent infantry sergeant. "M-my name's Hannibal. Only my f-friends call me 'Hanny,'" he stuttered defiantly.

"Aye, ye've destroyed me now, young Hanny, not to number me amongst yer snivelin' 'volunteer' friends! Now I'll *hear* ye volunteer to get me damn button an' sew it on me backside!" He slapped his back above his rump, where the threads had parted. A few men laughed uneasily, but most, even many of the infantry in Hahessy's detail, stood stone-faced.

"I will not," Cox almost whispered, voice cracking.

Hahessy rushed him and seized his shoulders, shaking him violently. "Refuse a direct order? I *will* see ye flogged, by God!"

Without thinking, Meder burst through the circle quickly forming around the two, plucked up the button, and tried to hand it to the big sergeant. "Here," he shouted. "Here's your damn button!"

Hahessy sneered. "I don't want it from *you*. All ye damn riflemen, so high an' mighty 'cause ye can strike a man down from afar, while us *proper* so-jers has to get close enough to smell their breakfasts on their nasty breaths an' poke a bayonet in their guts." He shook Cox again. "No, *this* is the one I want, a pansy volunteer—not even a *real* so-jer a'tall—who defied me order!"

Hudgens was there now. "That's a damned black lie! He refused no order; he just wouldn't volunteer to do somethin' no *real man* would stoop to, you filthy, villainous bastard!"

Hahessy's eyes flared, and he nodded brusquely. "He wouldn't be here if he didn't volunteer—as bloody volunteers so often remind me to prove their temporary courage. I'll do what I will with him now that he is. An' I'll be floggin' *you* for insubordination as well, Private Hudgens!"

"And me?" Meder demanded, flinging the button on the ground and grinding it in the grass and dirt with his heel.

"Aye!"

Meder was a regular and had seen his share of capricious discipline, but this was beyond the pale: utterly pointless, mere meanness and wanton cruelty. Something inside him snapped, and without even thinking he whipped his rifle off his shoulder and swung it back to drive the buttplate straight into Hahessy's leering face. Before he could, someone snatched the weapon from him, almost pulling him over backward. Another man—not as young or large as Hahessy, but with a presence just as powerful, handed the rifle to someone else and shoved his way between Hahessy and Cox.

"Why, Sergeant McNabb!" Hahessy crooned at the craggy face staring up at him. "Is it yer intention to interfere in me business, then?"

"Aye. I watched yer heartless, bloody-minded tyranny over yer helpless lads for much of a year at Pensacola an' New Orleans. There was never any purpose to it then, an' now there's even less. Ye'll finally start tendin' yer duties like the 'proper soldier' ye claim to be, or I'll break yer jaw for ye. At least I'll shut yer flappin' mouth!"

The mood of the men quickly changed. Before, even the infantrymen were sympathetic to Hahessy's victims, but now an *artilleryman* was threatening one of their own.

Hahessy saw, and realized he had some support. He grinned. "You all heard," he shouted, then smirked at the smaller man. "Yer soul to the Devil, Sergeant McNabb. Strike me, will ye?" He laughed. "I think n—" His statement ended with a loud *crack* when McNabb's scarred, powerful fist slammed upward under the point of his jaw and sent blood and broken teeth spraying in the air. Hahessy's head whipped back, and he fell like a poleaxed ox.

"That's it, then," roared some of Hahessy's soldiers as they rushed at McNabb. Meder and Hudgens squared off beside him, and Cox picked up one of the buckets and threw the water at the oncoming men before swinging the bucket and shattering the light wooden staves against the side of a man's head. Meder and Hudgens joined McNabb in punching and kicking as more men came shouting and surging. Most of the newcomers didn't even know what started everything, but long-standing rivalries combined with pent-up frustration and fear were enough to ensure that sides were taken without thought. The only confusion stemmed from the unlikely alliance between regular artillery, riflemen, and volunteers. Still, the melee quickly spread. Uxmalos watched in wide-eyed horror as men they'd been among so peacefully suddenly smashed together in battle against themselves, roaring and swinging fists.

There came the thunder of more running feet and horse hooves as well, then another *crack* as a shot sounded out. As if by magic, most of the men simply froze in place, some still grappled together, and all looked to see Lewis Cayce furiously whipping his smoking pistol over his head while Arete stomped in a circle, hot gusts blasting from flared nostrils as if the horse was as angry as her master. Captain Anson and Leonor were there, revolvers also raised, and Boogerbear, joined by Sal Hernandez and Alferez Lara, was just behind, as if shielding Varaa and Samantha from the sight of such a scene.

"Get these men under control, damn you," Lewis shouted at Lieutenants Olayne and Burton and Captain Beck as they came panting and shouldering their way to the front, followed by NCOs and a handful of troops. "God in heaven!" Lewis roared. "Haven't we enough troubles without nonsense like this? I'll *instantly* know what started this outrageous behavior . . . under the very walls and eyes of the city that welcomed us so handsomely such a short while ago!"

"It was I, Cap'n Lewis," growled Sergeant McNabb, nodding at the groggy Hahessy, trying to rise. "I struck the first blow, right enough."

"With *cause*, sir!" Meder blurted at Lewis, to the murmured assent of more than could've seen.

"No cause was worth this, lad," McNabb whispered gently at the rifleman from between bloody lips. Then he stood at attention and called out loudly, "Cap'n Lewis, beg to report a dispute between regulars an' volunteers. The usual aggravations, but I take full responsibility for not containin' it."

Hudgens hissed, "But you were *defendin'* the bloody volunteers, Sergeant!"

"Shut yer mouth," McNabb snapped.

LEWIS HAD WATCHED the exchange, simmering. All this time he'd agonized over how and when to break his news with the least amount of trauma. Now it all seemed so simple. Seeing Private Willis just standing there, he tossed him the empty pistol. "Clean that and reload it," he said harshly, then called out to the officers, "Assemble the men. All of them. Right here, at once." He turned in his saddle. "Private . . . Leon, fetch Reverend Harkin and—oh, I see Colonel De Russy and Dr. Newlin are already coming. But do bring Reverend Harkin, if you please."

Beck had been on the other side of the camp when the disturbance erupted and still hadn't caught his breath. "Drummers," he croaked, "beat assembly! Lieutenant Burton, you have buglers. Have them sound assembly as well."

A bugle, quickly repeated by a couple more, blew the general assembly call while an increasing number of drums rattled out the same command. At present there was only one place where such an order might call the men together so all who were able to move, along with many of the Ocelomeh and Uxmalos, rapidly crowded onto the parade ground in front of the headquarters area and among the half-erected tents. Varaa-Choon and Samantha moved to join Lewis and Anson, while Boogerbear, Sal, and Lara spread out a bit among the troops. They were the only ones mounted until Leonor pushed through with a puffing Reverend Harkin perched on her horse's rump, clinging almost comically to the saddle cantle to avoid laying hands on her. He looked profoundly uncomfortable for more than the obvious reasons, but Leonor must've described the situation, because he seemed as furious as Lewis.

"Should I form the men?" Beck asked.

Lewis shook his head. "No. I want them all to hear what I have to say, so let them come as close as they need to." He waited while men shuffled nearer, some looking merely curious, others ashamed. A few seemed filled with dread. Almost none were talking now, and NCOs swiftly silenced those who were. Finally, gazing out at the small sea of upturned faces reflecting the hot glare of the midday sun, only their eyes in shadow under the small, pointed brims of their wheel hats, Lewis took a deep breath and began to speak. His voice was still angry, but under complete control.

"I heard Private Meder say there was 'cause' for what happened here. 'Cause' for what nearly became a riot, with all of us fighting one another." He shook his head disgustedly. "The same stupid animosities and rivalries between regulars and volunteers, but it just so happens there's now a much *greater* 'cause' at stake, and if we don't face it together, we're lost."

There was some murmuring, but Lewis pressed relentlessly on. "On its face, our new purpose is simple: we must seamlessly work together—and with our new Ocelomeh and Uxmalo friends—just to stay alive. You all must know or guess by now that we're *not* where we were supposed to be." As he'd hoped, there was nervous chuckling when he uttered such an understatement, but he licked his lips and continued in the same heavy tone, "I think you'll agree it's equally clear we aren't simply—somehow—somewhere else on our known world. Captain Holland assures me the moon and stars are all where they belong, but even here—a hundred miles from where we were wrecked—we *should* be swimming instead of standing on an undiscovered land full of unknown creatures and people. All these things you know, but evidence amassed by the officers of this . . . Detached Expeditionary Force, and more presented by our new friends and allies"—he jerked a nod toward Varaa-Choon and Ixtla, who'd stepped up beside her horse—"convinces me our unexplainable presence here and isolation from all we've known is in fact"—he paused—"the result of some . . . unimaginable transportation from our own world to another one entirely."

Lewis had steeled himself for an eruption of frightened and angry voices, full of denial, but to his astonishment, other than a few cries of "What of my wife? My children?" there was only a brief, urgent murmur of something almost like morbid satisfaction. *They already know,* he realized.

Reverend Harkin spoke up, still sitting behind Leonor, and his anger had drained away. "Apparently, this has all been better guessed or communicated by the men's association with our new friends than we expected, Captain Cayce." He raised his own voice. "This *is* a different world," he told the American soldiers, "but also the same in many ways." He smiled. "It seems the Lord God was busier than we ever imagined, making *many* 'Earths' in his firmament, upon which to plant countless seeds." He bowed at Varaa-Choon, the somewhat customary glower on his heavy visage now shining with an inner light. "To borrow an example the Ocelomeh warmaster gave Captain Cayce, imagine if you will a handful of musket balls, all similar at a glance, but each slightly different. Some will be bright, others a bit blue or wrinkled or frosty looking, depending on the heat of the metal that made them. Some will turn gray with age, or go chalky white with corrosion. And every one will carry different dents and scratches from the way they've been handled, regardless of the fact they *all* came from the exact same mold, poured by the very same hand!" He waved around. "*God* has molded these many Earths and must have had a reason to take us from one to another. How else could it occur? Never doubt we have a purpose here. *His* purpose! And just because we're not where we were, don't suppose for an instant God has sent us from *Him!*"

"Thank you, Reverend," Lewis said with a slight smile for the portly preacher. He'd watched the change coming over the man, seen the dour, self-centered preacher growing in benevolence, piety, and purpose. He hoped Harkin was right, that they *were* here for a reason. It was some consolation for the men to cling to, at least. "Regardless of why or how, here we are. And coincidentally or not, we've been handed a worthy cause beyond our simple survival—and it's a cause our survival depends on. There are monsters aplenty on this world; we've all seen them. And though they're certainly 'monsters' of a smaller sort as well, I'm reliably assured the 'Grik' you fought are merely a ferocious, hostile tribe, not the 'demons' some of you think." He grunted. "You've killed enough of them that I expect you'll agree with that.

"But there *is* a great evil in this land, and the Grik and Holcanos are only its weakest fingers. There's a fist and mighty sword behind them. You saw the confrontation at the temple, and if you haven't learned what was said, you will. I think anyone could tell that Blood Priest was just a mask for the great evil that threatens the people here." Lewis pointed at Harkin. "And the Reverend believes *that's* what we were brought here to face. I may not be as spiritually certain as he, but I'm just as morally convinced we've been given a better . . . *purer* 'cause' than the cloudy, political, even somewhat divisive one we left behind. It's one we can fight for together, *sure* we're in the right!"

He paused a moment while this sank in and listened to the surf-like sound of voices, catching occasional snippets. Some were obviously doubtful, and quite a few seemed finally, belatedly struck by the confirmation they were truly stuck here. Most appeared only intently thoughtful, though Lewis saw some nodding their heads. When he resumed, he finally softened his voice somewhat, and the men went silent to hear him.

"I suppose I'm presenting you with a 'bright side,' of sorts, to a terrible situation. I also know many of you left families behind. You had *lives* to return to, farms, shops, loved ones who'll miss you. I can't do anything about that, but Reverend Harkin stands ready to counsel you." He shrugged. "I honestly can't say I even know how you feel. I left no loved ones behind at all." He patted Arete's neck. "The closest I had was this fine horse, and she's here." His expression hardened again. "But I did leave a home and family of sorts, just as dear to me in some ways as yours were to you. My home was all the United States of America, which I've devoted my life to defending, and my guiding 'father,' after God, was the Constitution I swore to uphold." He took a breath. "And my 'family' has been the army. I hope I still have part of it with me as well."

His tone became abrupt, and his eyes flashed steel. "*You* are my family, as you must become for each other. Our new cause is just, and in any event, we have no choice but to take it up. As I said, our survival depends on it, and we must remain soldiers until it's won." He almost smiled. "Still, I want only *real* and *true* soldiers in my army. I already see some of you thinking about the terms of your enlistments, how much time you had left—or what does your enlistment for the 'duration' mean now? I'll tell you. *Anyone* who wants his discharge may go, right now, this very day—and you'll be free to make your own way in this wild, dangerous world. I warn you, though, you can't stay here. We'll feed no apathetic mouths. I'm sorry, but that's the way it must be. We may soon be making soldiers of every able-bodied man for hundreds of miles, and no shirkers can be tolerated. Even local farmers and craftsmen will likely train to fight while they keep doing what they do, as will the upper classes of Uxmal if I have *my* way, with no exemptions or substitutes." He shook his head. "Otherwise, for those who choose to stay, 'the duration' must now apply to the fulfillment of the cause of survival."

"What of our oaths?" a man demanded. "We won't be swearin' no oath to no *foreigner!*"

"No," Lewis said forcefully. "The oaths you already swore remain in effect, to the same flag and Constitution, and you'll be bound by the same Articles of War. That nation *still exists*," he emphasized, "and the ideals enshrined in the Constitution and Bill of Rights are universal." He glanced at De Russy. "And we hope to ensure they're recognized *here* before long."

"What about pay? I got *two months* comin'!" someone else cried amid a brief gabble of agreement.

"Colonel De Russy? Will you address that?"

"Certainly." De Russy had laboriously climbed on the ammunition chest atop a limber and now held his hands out. "Many . . . details about our alliance with the Uxmalos, Ocelomeh, and others, we hope, remain to be formalized. During our discussions with Alcalde Periz, he agreed to much in principle, but he's only had the last few days to begin sorting it out with his people and the *alcaldes* of other cities. I'm confident all we tell you now—and more—will be part of the, um, 'Treaty of Alliance' we'll agree to with our new friends." He looked in the direction from which the question had come and smiled. "We'll try to do something about 'back pay,' if we can. There were pay chests in the wrecks. But we'll see to the welfare of the army first, and paper dollars are no use. People here can't be expected to trade in them. Silver, gold, copper, even zinc and iron, have value, however, and I advise you to take care how you spend what coins you have until we know what they're worth. But you'll be paid," he stressed, then paused. "Let me be clear. We are and will remain United States soldiers, not mercenaries. We'll only have a different paymaster for a time. We'll dress, act, and fight like Americans, and only for the overall 'cause' Reverend Harkin believes God chose us to pursue. We *won't* get involved in petty disputes between the city-states of this region." He gave Varaa a look, expecting his words to travel. "Nor will we make unreasonable demands in regards to pay. But Captain Cayce and I concur that if our new paymaster attempts to exert unacceptable influence, he'll regret it."

"Sir," began De Russy's Lieutenant Wagley a little hesitantly, "will the regulars and volunteers get the *same* pay?"

De Russy glanced at Lewis, as if asking if he'd like to answer that.

Lewis nodded. "I haven't made myself clear. From this day on, there'll be no such distinctions between us. We all have pride in our respective regiments, of course, but all who stay and serve will by definition be *both* 'regulars' and 'volunteers.' There'll be no more foolishness like we had here today."

The justice of that caused an upwelling of excitement and satisfaction, though still not exactly enthusiasm. Lewis hadn't expected to flood his people with happiness, but that they seemed willing to stay together and give this a try without falling to pieces was more than he'd really dared hope. Perhaps true commitment to their cause would come in time.

"Finally," Lewis continued sternly, though he didn't particularly mean to be now. Speaking so loudly in this heat had left him dry and hoarse, and maybe he'd waved his pistol too vigorously? He seemed to have aggravated the pain in his side. "I know you never signed up for this—none of us did. That's why Colonel De Russy *will* issue your discharge when this assembly is dismissed." He frowned. "If you take it, I'll have to insist you turn in your weapons and leave this camp before morning reveille." He sighed. "I know it's not fair, but our old world wasn't either, and not only will we need all the weapons we can get, we have to start consolidating around known numbers and capabilities even before we begin training the locals." He shrugged almost helplessly. He really was sorry. "Perhaps you can find work as farmers, teamsters, or put other skills you have to use, but I warn you: the time may come when Alcalde Periz calls you up for *his* army."

He forced a smile. "We're all in 'uncharted territory,' in more ways than one, and for those who volunteer to become regulars in this Detached Expeditionary Force, a few things will be different. The Articles of War will remain strictly in effect, as I said, but we'll proceed with the election of officers who'll be required to remember you're *all* 'volunteers' and keep you better informed of things that affect your daily lives. This army will *never* be a democracy. Mere favoritism can't be allowed to rule those elections, and they'll be subject to confirmation, as senior officers will be selected from those you elect. But we'll continue to make sure you're better treated than you might've grown accustomed to. Petty tyrants *won't* be tolerated in ranks!" He said that as much in warning as assurance.

Reverend Harkin cleared his throat and whispered to Leonor, who edged her mount slightly forward. "If I may, Captain Cayce," Harkin said, "now that you've laid things out—and likely begloomed everyone—I feel compelled to add a word about the greater purpose God has set us to."

Lewis frowned, but nodded. It couldn't hurt and might help. "By all means."

A little self-consciously, Leonor slid down from the horse and handed the reins to Harkin as the fat preacher heaved himself over the cantle and into the saddle. Once there, he had everyone's attention. "I'll say only this," he began in his booming pulpit voice. "I've learned a great deal about our 'bigger enemy' on this world from Father Orno." He waved a hand. "Dismiss him as a mere papist as I once did if you will, but he *is* a dedicated man of God and has many parts—as you saw today. Through him I've come to the conviction that we *were* all carried here by the hand of God."

"Not all that bloody gentle about it, was 'e?" grumbled a voice from the crowd.

"No," Harkin agreed, "he couldn't protect us all from the storm any more than He can shield us from the tempest of battle—but the manner of our arrival has *prepared* us, has it not? For the arena in which He placed us, where He expects us to act!" He spread his arms wide. "Most of you followed the drum to Mexico for national pride or loyalty to the Constitution Captain Cayce so rightly reveres. Some even went because of a popular notion that America has a 'Manifest Destiny' to expand from sea to sea and spread its ideals across a continent. To those I say we now have an opportunity to spread them across an entire new world!" He beamed.

"To the rest of you, I won't attempt to beguile you with the heady prospect of a holy crusade that moves me, but I'll appeal to your national pride and the loyalty you owe the officers who led you against the hellish Grik and Holcanos, the friends you've made among the Ocelomeh you fought beside, and the Uxmalos who welcomed you here with shelter and sustenance in this terrible land. It has *become* our duty, our 'Manifest Destiny,' to protect *them*—and their women and children—from a despotic cult washed in bloody pagan sacrifice and a tyrant sinister and depraved enough to make Santa Anna's odious antics seem like those of a childish bully in comparison! The evil Dominion he leads will sweep all before it if it's not stopped, and only we can do it. That's the task I believe God has set us to."

He frowned. "But now I'll appeal to what I hope is a trifling minority, with no ideals or purpose beyond self-interest and survival. As Captain Cayce so succinctly put it, embracing this new cause and winning is the only way you'll live."

"THAT WENT WELL, I think," Varaa-Choon said, blinking something like amusement as she, Lewis, Anson, Leonor, and Reverend Harkin, now on Sal Hernandez's horse, rode out of the crowd and positioned themselves watchfully near a half-fortified gun astride the road leading northeast, toward Pidra Blanca. Harkin had seemed content to stay and launch a lengthier sermon, but Lewis judged his pitch had been powerful enough. Not only must the men complete the camp; they needed time to think or talk among themselves.

"I wonder how many takers De Russy'll have?" Anson glowered.

"Not too many, Father," Leonor said with a strange expression. "Not with Mistress Samantha so cheerfully offerin' to stay an' write out each discharge for De Russy's signature."

Reverend Harkin nodded enthusiastically. "A remarkable woman. If she shares the prejudice of her nation—and class!—against Americans, she certainly conceals it well. And quite beautiful!" He chuckled. "So much so that

I feared some of our men may abandon us just to get close to her. But she's as shrewd as she is attractive and seems to have taken up our new cause with surprising enthusiasm." He directed an uncomfortable, somewhat embarrassed smile at Leonor. Even with her so often in his company and that of their top commanders, it took Harkin longer than most to discover Leonor's secret on his own. Far longer than it apparently took most of their troops to accept a growing awareness of their plight. Father Orno had been incredulous. "I thought you were interested in 'comparative anatomy.'" He'd scoffed. Harkin was less sure what to *think* of Leonor, but he'd grown enough over recent weeks to treat her as she clearly preferred, as he always had. "And you're entirely right, my d— I mean, Private Anson. What man could step boldly up to *any* young lady and proclaim himself a coward?"

Lewis scratched his itchy neck again. "I don't think it's a question of cowardice. . . ." He shook his head. "I wish we could've given the men a *real* choice. They deserve it."

"You want 'em to live?" Leonor asked sharply, then answered her own question. "Sure you do. An' you know they'll have to fight to do it. You did the right thing."

"I hope so," Lewis murmured, absently rubbing his side. "I hope we all are."

"Your wound's been botherin' you, I can tell," Captain Anson accused. Several people knew about it, but only Anson had seen how ghastly it had been. "You need to let Dr. Newlin have a look. He strikes me better than the butchers who tended you after Monterrey."

Lewis quickly dropped his hand. "It's nothing. And Newlin still has plenty to occupy him."

Varaa's tail was swishing behind her, and she blinked at Lewis with something he thought might indicate impatience. "As I've told you, your Dr. Newlin is very good at dealing with large numbers of battle wounds. Better than my healers, or those of the Uxmalos. But ours may be better at other things, especially pain relief—and septicity. Not to mention prevention and treatment of local maladies your men may be more vulnerable to."

"I understood the exchange of medical knowledge was already well under way," Lewis said, then attempted to change the subject. "How soon can I give our people leave to enter the city—in small groups, of course, at first. They need a break, and they need to get to know the people they're defending."

"That'll doubtless be decided when we attend the *alcalde*'s reception this evening," Varaa said, but pressed on. "You should see one of my healers first. Your welcome will be friendly for the most part, and that vile Tranquilo won't be there—if he even remains in the city—but Alcalde Discipo could be present and may attempt to provoke you. I've noticed your patience with fools . . . is shorter when you ache." She flicked her big eyes at his side and smiled, revealing sharp canines. "It might be best for us all if you govern your temper. My healers can relieve your pain."

"Dose me with something like laudanum, you mean?" Lewis snapped. "I can control my temper. And I'll need my wits intact." No one knew how dangerously close he'd come to opium addiction while convalescing and how much he feared how attractive its oblivion sometimes was to him now.

"Yes, we have things like your laudanum," Varaa retorted, "and you'll be glad of it when Dr. Newlin's stock is exhausted. But we also have milder things that don't dull the senses."

"Perhaps another time," Lewis said definitively, shifting his gaze from the nearly complete and—for the moment—perfectly normal and quiescent camp, out to the surprisingly still waters of the bay to the north. There were even more small craft on the bay than before, darting to and fro in the light, tree-sheltered airs, and he wondered what they were doing. *Perhaps Captain Holland would know,* he told himself with a spike of concern for the grizzled old sailor, the ship, and all their wounded aboard.

"They fish," Varaa explained, guessing his curiosity. "The fish on this world are as terrible as the creatures ashore, even more so, yet they're a necessary part of the local food supply." She pointed. "Fishermen go beyond the mouth of the bay for their morning catch, then bait the bay with their offal. You see the first boat of each pair throwing it over the side, while the second drags its net? Most efficient."

"And terrifying!" Harkin exclaimed with wide eyes. "What happens if someone falls overboard?"

"Fishermen here are *very* careful," Varaa said, then shrugged. "They understand, practically from birth, they can survive only seconds in the water." She glared at Lewis. "No matter how stubborn they are." She relented. "But I too am worried about your great ship. Some of my injured are aboard her as well."

"I'm no sailor," Anson said, "but Captain Holland's a good one. He'll take care of his cargo, an' I reckon there's a reason he's not here. Maybe one of his jury-rigged masts carried away, or somethin'. He'll fix it."

They heard hoofbeats and turned to see Alferez Lara galloping toward them. He reined up and grinned.

Lewis couldn't help grinning back, even as he again noted the tension sweep across Leonor's face, and to a lesser degree, her father's. Lewis believed Anson's was on behalf of his daughter because the Ranger seemed to have accepted Lara and his handful of Mexicans easily enough. Not Leonor, even now, though she showed no discomfort around Ocelomeh or Ux-malos, who *looked* as much like most of Lara's men as anybody could. He hoped he'd begun stamping out prejudice and factionalism in his army to-day, but knew it would be harder for some than for others. And Leonor's bias was very personal and deep. He hoped it, like others lurking among his men, would fade with time.

"You seem pleased, Alferez Lara," he observed.

"How many did we lose?" Harkin asked anxiously. "That's what you came to tell us, is it not?"

Lara nodded and held up three fingers.

"*Three*, by God!" Harkin exclaimed. "That's all?"

"*Sí*. And they were all older men. Very apologetic. They didn't see them-selves as drill sergeants—which many of us will essentially be for a time, I suppose—nor did they consider themselves fit enough to set an example. All, however, are willing to fight when called." Lara looked at Lewis, hold-ing out a crinkled page. "Colonel De Russy proposed a . . . reserve status for men currently unfit due to age or injuries, but who have other skills to teach our friends. That way they can remain in uniform, keep their weapons, and still be 'one of us.' He also reminds you there'll be more of the same when our badly wounded arrive, so we should 'sort this out' now." He hesitated, nodding at the page. "He also suggests we consider an expansion of that 'reserve' as more is learned about the background of each man. The unfit aren't the only ones with essential skills we must preserve and share. He means to detail a Mr. Finlay, Captain Holland's purser, the task of ques-tioning every man and compiling a list of what they know and what they can do."

Anson slapped his forehead. "Finlay! I saw him rejoin with the rest from *Mary Riggs*, but almost forgot about him! He was already startin' a list like that back at the wreck, I think. Holland told him to."

Lewis was nodding. "Very good." He glanced apologetically around. "I should've thought of this."

"You can't think of everything," Harkin objected.

"And you've had plenty of other stuff to worry about," Anson agreed.

"More will be added tonight," Varaa said, "but it *is* a good idea." She laughed at Lewis's expression. "Politicians have their place, you know. You and I think alike: we plan for battle, even plan how to plan for battle. Colonel De Russy put you in charge of such things because he can't think like that. I can't think like King Har-Kaaska or Alcalde Periz. De Russy can, and you should be glad."

She clapped her hands. "Now the sun begins to fall. Did I not tell you Alcalde Periz's reception will be a formal affair? We have just enough time to clean the battle and long march off of us at last, put on our finest things"— she grinned—"and arrive just a *little* late."

CHAPTER 18

ather Tranquilo was still smoldering with rage when he reached the well-guarded camp a few miles southeast of Uxmal. One of his huge assistants—a reaper monk named Brother Arana—planted his cere-monial spear and crouched so a groaning Tranquilo could stand from the light wicker *silla* seat he'd been riding, strapped to the big man's back. "Wine!" he demanded as Brother Escorpion bawled at ordinary-size ser-vants scampering from within the airy marquee standing among smaller tents in the trees. Two naked girls, filthy beyond recognition, brought a crystal decanter and three glasses, quickly pouring for Tranquilo and the two larger men.

"You're angry with us, Father?" asked Brother Arana.

Tranquilo swished wine in his mouth and spat, clearing the dust. "Not at *you*, dear Arana. I know you did your best to soften the tedious trek." His ferret eyes flared. "I'm angry at the heretics, of course . . . and my own lack of control. Only that *thrice-damned* Orno can enrage me so, and instead of the days I'd hoped to use observing this new army of heretics, gently per-suading, sowing dissension, perhaps arranging a shocking accident or two . . . my passion for God got the better of me and I utterly destroyed our position here. Don Discipo's also, no doubt, due to our association. He's leaving the city as well." He gulped the rest of his wine and held the glass out for a refill. "All the same," he mulled, "I doubt our continued presence would've answered for long, and I already learned a great deal about the . . . 'Americanos' from Don Discipo. Periz couldn't very well exclude him from their peninsular scheming sessions." He barked a bitter laugh. "They would *now*, I'm sure, and likely in confinement. I expect Discipo and his escort here before long, hoping to travel in company down the Cipactli River road back to Puebla Arboras. Discipo is a great coward," Tranquilo lamented. "But even if he could've lingered, I doubt it would've helped. The Americanos are already much attached to those barbarous Ocelomeh, and Alcalde Periz is besotted with them and their meager power." He paused to reflect. "They're ridiculously few in number and could barely defeat the Holcanos and their demon pets, but they *do* have modern weapons. Their puny victory poses a threat to the Dominion by its example, and the influence it has given them over the local heretics."

Gulping his wine again, he fished a sheaf of folded parchments from his pouch. They were a report of all he and his spies had gathered about the strangers and their battle, confidently carried on his very person. Father Orno might've tried to have them stolen from the rooms he'd taken in the city, but no one would dare take anything directly from him—before today, of course. "That influence might prove tedious in time," he continued, "and must be cleansed away. Since it will be difficult to assemble sufficient forces to do so in this remote wasteland, we must begin at once. A dispatch case!" he called loudly, and a novice in a plain red tunic raced to the marquee and returned with a leather tube. Tranquilo handed him the parchments to roll and stuff inside. "Come, Brother Arana, Brother Escorpion, the very first thing we must do is send these off. I suspect His Supreme Holiness will already know more than I by the time they arrive, but the *means* of communicating them is as important as the information—and we must utterly *erase* this camp before the Ocelomeh find it."

"We won't wait for Don Discipo?" Escorpion asked.

"No. He must make his own way to Puebla Arboras. You and I, and a sufficient guard, will strike out due south through the terrible forest directly for Nautla. Where's that loathsome Holcano guide? Eating worms? Painting himself with feces?"

"As always, he lurks out of sight as instructed, Father," the young novice with the leather tube spoke shrilly. He'd been gelded just as his voice was beginning to break, and Tranquilo wondered if he'd always sound that way.

"Just so," Tranquilo acceded. "Ocelomeh scouts would know him at once and feel justified in slaughtering everyone in sight whether I was here or not. It's of no consequence now. Call him in and instruct him to prepare."

Half a dozen guards with muskets, Dom soldiers dressed like Don Discipo's Arboranos, converged on them as they strode a short distance into the dense forest. More guards were there, surrounding a small clearing where a colorful creature vaguely resembling one of the Holcanos' reptilian allies was secured to a tree by a heavy chain attached to a harness on its back. It looked at them as they approached, tongue darting between jagged teeth in anticipation, doubtless hoping they'd feed it. All around were the shattered bones of previous meals, the most recent being Uxmalo captives taken while cutting wood in the forest. Such men were usually already captives, so their disappearance would inspire small concern and no search.

"Secure the dispatch and show the dragon where it must go," Tranquilo commanded. A soldier went to a line of cages, each confining a few of the vicious little flying reptiles. Most such creatures wore a variety of colors, but these were all either predominantly green, red, blue, yellow, or even black, and separated accordingly. The soldier seized a specimen with bright yellow plumage, and it squawked piteously, snapping at his gloved hands and pathetically flapping short wing stumps as he stepped as close to the larger beast as he dared and tossed the squealing snack. The "dragon" caught it in the air. A cloud of downy feathers erupted as it chewed voraciously, and the novice sprang forward to secure the tube to the harness on its back (where it couldn't chew it off) and strike off the chain that held it. Backing quickly away, since the "route morsel" didn't always fully distract imperfectly trained or inexperienced beasts, the novice sighed with relief when it paid him no mind. The tidbit gone, it quickly sniffed around for any fragments, leveled its gaze on Tranquilo for an instant, then unfolded its arms—actually disproportionately long, light, and incredibly strong wings—and leaped directly into the sky.

The powerful leap only took it so high, and the clearing was barely large enough for it to beat its way above the trees, but once it was clear it disappeared at once, already aiming west-southwest.

"Interesting creatures," Tranquilo observed, "and quite difficult and time consuming to train."

"How do they do it?" Brother Arana respectfully asked.

"I'm not entirely sure," Tranquilo admitted a little uncomfortably. "They're a 'new thing,' and God doesn't encourage such, as you know. As I understand it, their ability to associate colors with places and then go there on command was only recently discovered—quite accidentally—in one of His Supreme Holiness's mountain menageries. I'm told their handlers must begin with the very egg, and there are still so few of them that I was surprised to have one sent to us. No doubt it was so we could report on the outcome of the Holcano effort to crush the Uxmalos and others at last," he added bitterly.

Arana hesitated. "It seemed . . . The look it gave you almost seemed . . . aware."

Tranquilo snorted. "Nonsense! I confess to being astonished such a malevolent creature can be trained to do *anything*, as a horse or armabuey might, but its only 'awareness' is of punishment and reward. Like any animal." He frowned deeply. "True awareness in animals doesn't exist. They can't talk or think or feel—unless a demon does it for them. *Through* them. Take that vile 'Warmaster Varaa-Choon,' for example! No, grotesque and unnerving as dragons are, they're stupid, innocent beasts." He actually smiled. "And doing God's holy work, as they surely do, how could a demon reside within them?"

"But what of the Blood Lizard tribes, allied to the Holcanos? They're aware to a degree, and don't *they* do God's work, aiding us?"

"You think so?" Tranquilo asked blithely. "You've seen them fight. Do you perceive any *reason* behind their mindless ferocity? Granted, their determination might serve as an inspiration to men, but it comes only through obsession for their reward and they're too stupid to comprehend punishment."

"They talk," Arana pressed.

"Do they? Or do only a very few, owned by demons, stir the rest to their ends? *Not* ours, not even the Holcanos'." He pondered that. "The Blood Cardinal Don Frutos, a deeply devout servant of God and champion of our reformed doctrine"—he meant that of the Blood Priests over the traditional, slightly more restrained servants of His Supreme Holiness—"has wondered aloud whether they're actually *people*, descended from pagan serpent worshippers whom God changed to a kind of serpent themselves when they came to this world. The Ocelomeh fashion themselves after a pagan deity from another world as well, after all, though they remain 'human' enough to be heretics." He shrugged. "*I* think they're only animals. Either way, they'll be destroyed when their usefulness ends."

Tranquilo's tone abruptly changed as he began barking commands to those around him. "Strike the camp. Wipe away any sign it was ever here." He gestured at the cages. "Slaughter those for the table, but bury their skins, their cages, and all the bones scattered about. We'll have to travel hard through the night and the next few days to gain as much distance from Uxmal as possible." Brother Arana started to help with that, but Tranquilo stopped him. "A moment. You recall that I said the 'first' thing we must do?"

"Yes, Father. There's more?"

"Oh yes. More for *you*, my son, and a number of others. You know the man Tukli, in the city?"

Brother Arana frowned. "A prominent man of business—and a heretic."

"Of course, but also a greedy and fearful man. Knowing my time in Uxmal may be short, I tossed together a little scheme of my own," he said modestly, but shook his head. "It may accomplish nothing"—he looked intently at Arana—"or a very great deal indeed, depending on how it's executed. And by whom." He smiled as benevolently as his gnarled visage allowed and produced another parchment from his pouch. "Here are your instructions. Commit them to memory on your way back to the city, then destroy them. Once there, go to Tukli. He knows nothing of what you'll do, but will provide the means and make certain arrangements." His smile turned almost sad. "I doubt we'll meet in this life again, Brother Arana."

Arana dropped to his knees, face glowing with joy.

"Yes," Tranquilo said softly. "Rejoice! You'll very likely be in paradise this very night, and I'm anxious to have you serve me again when I join you there at last!"

CHAPTER 19

The Uxmalos and Ocelomeh salvaging *Xenophon* hadn't yet arrived, but Lewis had collected another uniform and his few personal things when the rest of his people, the other two 6pdrs, and everything recovered from *Mary Riggs* joined them on the march. Unfortunately, even before it got soaked and mildewed, his extra uniform was no better than the one he wore. Colonel De Russy had several new frock coats of the best lightweight blue broadcloth, however, and insisted Lewis and Anson each accept one. He then immediately set Barca to work taking them in, transferring Lewis's shoulder boards, and stitching a spare set from his dead quartermaster's stores to the coat Anson would wear. De Russy himself was carefully brushing and putting on his magnificent full-dress uniform, complete with tails and gold braid on black velvet collar, cuffs, and tail pockets. He took particular care with his feather-plumed cocked hat. But Barca was hard-pressed to make the alterations in time, and Private Willis only stared in horror when Lieutenant Olayne asked if he could sew. He was sent to help De Russy instead. Several fellows volunteered—nearly anyone could sew on a button—but Samantha swept in with Mistress Angelique and set to work with professional confidence. Angelique actually seemed pleasantly excited for the very first time. And astonishingly, by the time they took over, both ladies had already bathed in their tent with lightly heated water from the well and bedecked themselves in ball gowns of the highest quality and fashion. Now, as the sun began to set and their operation neared its conclusion, they took turns working on each other's hair.

After sponging off, Lewis and Anson had stood dutifully and somewhat abashedly in their cleanest shirtsleeves and brushed wool trousers while the coats, tailored to fit the somewhat wider Colonel De Russy, were fitted. Leonor was watching, and Lewis could see she'd also bathed, but then put on the same rugged mix of civilian clothing and uniform parts she'd always worn. And the way she stared at the other women merrily chattering in French with a vague frown on her pink-scrubbed face wasn't lost on him. He thought she disapproved of their frivolous conversation, but Samantha occasionally shot him strange looks and cocked her head at Leonor. That's when he realized the tough female Ranger might be a bit envious, at least in a subconscious, lost-girlhood sort of way. And Anson saw it too: lips set in a thin, hard line, eyes reflecting an inner sadness.

Varaa, Koaar, and Ixtla rejoined them in fresh bright tunics and highly polished silver scale armor, riding beautifully groomed and appointed local horses provided by Alcalde Periz. A caisson would carry the ladies, Dr. Newlin, and Reverend Harkin like a carriage. To Private Meder's and Private Hudgens's complete surprise, particularly after the fracas that day, Sergeant McNabb had told them to "clean yer filthy selves," and ride the lead horses on the left side of the four-up team. Lewis and Anson, self-consciously resplendent in new coats and crimson sashes under freshly whitened saber belts, mounted their own horses. So did Alferez Lara, who'd made his own uniform as presentable as possible. The pool provided animals for De Russy, Leonor, and Hernandez, along with half a dozen dragoons led by Lieutenants Olayne and Burton.

That was it, for now. Captain Beck, Lieutenants Wagley and Manley, and Boogerbear (who'd achieved an officer's respect among the men, regardless of his rank) remained in charge of the camp. And they might have their hands full, since no one had been neglected by Alcalde Periz. Hundreds of festively dressed men and women descended on the camp with musical instruments and carts full of fresh local fare. They'd been asked to limit the drink they brought to a kind of dark amber-colored beer made from quite ordinary-looking maize. Beer should be sufficient to help the men cut loose a bit, and doing it in camp, under control and supervision, would test the responsible officers and new NCOs. It had to be better than just turning the men loose in Uxmal before they knew what was what.

Moving through the outward flood of friendly, smiling faces, Lewis's party passed through the torch-lit east gate behind Varaa, Koaar, and Ixtla, who led them through the city to the grassy plaza surrounding the pyramidal temple. Across from it was Harkin's "Nunnery," a long, rectangular stone building erected on a kind of terraced mound Varaa now told them was the *alcalde*'s Audience Hall. Several sets of steps led to the elevated "ground" floor, and the plaza in front of a brazier-lit stairway, wider than the others, was crowded with people going inside, leaving finely fashioned carriages of a simple, solid-wheel, but ornate design, mostly hitched to teams of burros. Burros certainly predominated, but there were quite a few of the oddly shaped and colored horses too. *More gathered here, just standing around, than we have for our artillery and dragoons combined,* Lewis reflected.

Men in gray tunics—"Trusted captives," Varaa whispered to him— dashed forward to take charge of their animals. Lewis smiled at them as he dismounted Arete and moved to help the ladies down from the caisson, but said, "Lieutenant Olayne, you'll remain here with the dragoons and the rest of our horses for now. Perhaps you can all come inside at some point, or at least a few at a time. Either way, you and Lieutenant Burton can change places before long."

"Yes sir," Olayne said with what sounded like relief. "What about them?" he asked, nodding at Meder and Hudgens.

Lewis scratched his beard.

"Oh, let them come, Captain Cayce," Samantha said. "Don't you think your enlisted ranks should be represented?"

"I recognize those men!" De Russy exclaimed. "They were *intimately* involved in the trouble we had earlier today!"

Lewis nodded, controlling a smile. "I know. But from what I already knew of them, and what I heard today, they're the same kind of 'troublemakers' we are, Colonel." He looked at Meder and Hudgens intently, then decided. "Follow us."

Reverend Harkin exclaimed again that the building looked *much* larger than its apparent old-world inspiration. The central columned open area inside was easily forty yards across and fifty wide, leaving space for other rooms on either end behind sculpted plaster walls. That same bright, relief-carved plaster covered the other walls and high ceiling, reflecting the flickering fires in intricate brass braziers well enough to provide plenty of light. Only in the smooth-polished floor could the underlying stone be seen. At first glance, standing in the main entrance before those inside reacted to the Americans' arrival, Lewis was reluctant to enter. There were so many people, and combined with the braziers, he expected it to be unbearably hot and stuffy. But there were as many entrances as stairways outside, and he detected the movement of cool air. Samantha Wilde suddenly snaked her arm around his elbow, and Angelique did the same to De Russy. The two men blinked at each other, belatedly realizing they should've offered their arms.

"Provincials." Samantha scoffed with a chuckle.

"Forgive me, my dear. I'm aghast at myself," De Russy told Angelique as he gently patted her tiny hand with his white-gloved paw. She laughed and said something in French.

"My apologies as well," Lewis told Samantha. "I'm just . . ."

"Thinking about more important things?" she asked with a smile.

A horn sounded, deafeningly loud, and Alcalde Periz stepped through the throng with the same men—including Father Orno but minus Don Discipo for some reason—who'd accompanied him that morning. They were dressed like before, only in fiery long tunics of an even finer weave, almost like silk, fringed with gold or silver thread embroidery. And each—significantly, Lewis was sure—wore lightweight scale armor like Varaa's, only theirs must be gold. Beaming, they strode quickly forward and grasped their guests' arms, hand to elbow, while their ladies, all very beautiful in even longer, formfitting tunics that somehow became dresses on them while practically dripping exquisitely fashioned jewelry, did the same to Samantha and Angelique. And while the European women might've been stunned by the sheer weight of gold and precious gems the Uxmalo ladies negligently wore, the Uxmalos were equally enraptured by their visitors' gowns. Samantha's was bottle green, accented in white, while Angelique's was a flouncy, dusky almond, offset by black lace. Both were perfect for the women's hair and complexion and plunged only slightly, revealing no cleavage, but the modest exposure was still wider and deeper than the V-cut local style. And the expertly fitted bodices and short, puffy sleeves, in addition to crinoline skirts and petticoats, accentuated Samantha's and Angelique's narrow waists. Neither really needed a corset, and combined with the lingering heat of the day and the realization "society" here would be oblivious to their discomfort, they omitted them and various other layers they would've otherwise felt compelled to wear.

In any event, they made a sensation. Despite their own modest jewelry (compared to the locals), Samantha's and Angelique's gowns served as settings for the genuine jewels both women were in their own right. This was not lost on the Uxmalos. Varaa whispered something to Ixtla, and the gruff human Ocelomeh grimaced. "Must I?" he pleaded in English.

"What?" Lewis asked.

Vaara laughed. "I just 'detailed' him, as you say, to translate for the ladies after our welcome is complete. And judging by the looks"—Varaa's ears flicked around the room, where many Uxmalo women intently watched them—"I expect he'll be very busy!"

Alcalde Periz raised his voice and announced his visitors by name and title, somehow equating De Russy with Koaar as "consul," over the Americans, Lewis to Varaa as "warmaster," and surprisingly, putting Reverend Harkin on equal footing with his own Father Orno, whose official title was "Padre Alto." Harkin seemed taken aback and a little conflicted, but managed to smile all around as people called out and applauded at the end of Periz's introduction. The *alcalde* then presented the wives. Most looked very fine, though the older Truro's had a matronly air, but Periz's diminutive wife, Sira, outshone them all. Lewis was struck by her dark beauty, proud bearing, and frankly appraising stare. He was equally intrigued to learn that she, and all the *alcaldes'* wives, held the title of *"segunda alcaldesa"* and were required to assume their husbands' duties when they were absent, or if they died. Lewis suspected Sira, at least, was Periz's equal partner on a daily basis.

There was music then, of a strange but no longer unfamiliar sort, since they'd been given samples on the march. It was performed by muted drums and flutes, and while still somewhat alien it had a certain appeal. Men and women began pairing off, finding open spaces to perform intricate steps without touching. "Good heavens!" Harkin exclaimed. "They look like courting birds!"

"As do those engaged in fashionable dances where we came from, do they not?" observed Samantha with a twinkle in her eye.

"I suppose," Harkin agreed dourly, "but those events don't necessarily lead to the, ah, consummation of the courtship." He glared at Father Orno. "I hope that's *not* the case here!"

Orno laughed. "Not *always*."

Harkin harrumphed and Samantha coughed. "Tell me, Warmaster Varaa, with the introductions complete, why does everyone remain away from us?"

"We're still in the presence of the *alcaldes*, for official purposes. No one will interfere with that." Varaa grinned. "Uxmalos, indeed all the civilized people of the Yucatán, are quite polite. The 'official presence,' even for *alcaldes*, is broken when we disperse."

Samantha glanced at Angelique, focused intently on the growing dance as if memorizing the steps. "So we must detach ourselves with the *alcaldesas* and go to them?"

"Yes, Mistress."

Samantha smiled. "Very well. Come along, Angelique." She chuckled. "And *you*, Mr. Ixtla!" She darted a glance at Lewis and Anson. "Perhaps you'll join us in a dance when you're finished with business?"

"Delighted," Anson said. Lewis cleared his throat and jerked a nod, but turned to Meder and Hudgens. "Stay with Mr. Ixtla and the ladies until they're *entirely* comfortable." His expression darkened. "And behave yourselves for a change! I've developed a generally good opinion of you both, but it's neither fully formed nor without reservations, is that understood?"

"Yes sir," they chorused.

"I'll stay with 'em too," Leonor said, somewhat to the surprise of Lewis and Anson.

Periz spoke, and Varaa told them he wanted them alone for a time, for a more private meeting with the other *alcaldes* before rejoining the reception in earnest. Periz bade his wife, Sira, and those of his other native guests to join Samantha and Angelique as they mingled, then led the way to a heavily carved wooden door in one of the sculpted plaster end walls. A servant opened it, and they filed into another surprisingly large room. Here, the stone and framing timbers of the impressive structure were exposed, but in a tastefully rustic, not skeletal way. It was cooler too, with only candles and lamps for light and air ingeniously vented from above. Other servants brought painted ceramic jugs and mugs and placed them on a long wooden table dominating the center of the room before departing. Once the great door closed behind them, the noise of the crowded reception hall dwindled to a humming murmur. Even before, however, the visitors' attention had fastened on a huge woven tapestry suspended on the far wall. The craftsmanship and artistry was stunning, but it wasn't just decorative. It was in fact a map of the region; the first they'd seen that was more detailed than scratchings in the dirt.

Momentarily oblivious to all else around them, Lewis and Anson stepped to what was essentially a modeled atlas of the world these people knew. The central landmass was obviously a distorted, somewhat bloated Mexico, extending from a little north of what had to be the Rio Grande, all the way south to where Guatemala and Honduras ought to be. Lewis was amazed by the embroidered detail—different weaves and colors meticulously differentiating terrain to the extent that plains and forest, streams and stony mountains were as sharply distinct as they'd be to a high-flying bird. Boldly stitched roads laced across the landscape connecting cities, and more subtly sewn traceries represented lesser tracks or trails between smaller, more remote towns. Lewis almost touched a point marked by a fish bone and ribbon, realizing it was where they'd fought their battle and *Commissary*, *Mary Riggs*, and *Xenophon* were wrecked. He followed the threads of a coastal road to the tiny, intricately detailed city where they now stood.

"Amazing," he breathed, gesturing at the oversize mass of this Yucatán. "Everything seems so exactingly rendered. . . . The shoreline's accurate?"

"Yes," Varaa replied softly. "I'm . . . personally less sure about the *western* shore of the continent, but the nearer coast surrounding the Great Gulf is quite precise. The map incorporates some of my own observations," she added proudly. "We—the people from whom I sprang—though not ardent explorers, have a tradition of carefully marking what we find"—she paused—"or what's reported to us." She waved at the great map. "Our leaders have been compiling a painted atlas such as this for generations, to the extent that perhaps a quarter of the coastlines depicted on maps of 'new arrivals' has been adjusted to reflect them as they actually are on this world." She nodded at the Yucatán Peninsula, where they stood. "There's more dry land on this world than on anyone else's who's come here, as far as I know. Yours as well, I assume, since your ships fell upon it. How far offshore do you believe you were when . . ." She paused and flipped her tail.

Lewis looked at Anson. "Ten or twelve miles, I suppose. *Tiger* should've been farther."

De Russy nodded solemnly.

"There's more ice in the north and south," Varaa informed them, "and some have proposed that the ice *eats* the water." She shrugged. "I don't know." She nodded at Yucatán. "But this land is bigger than can be accounted for, even with the ice, I should think."

Alcalde Periz had been quietly talking with Ortiz from Pidra Blanca and Truro from Itzincab. Thanks to the atlas, Lewis now knew Pidra Blanca was about a hundred miles up the coast to the northeast and clearly relied on Uxmal as a buffer against their common enemies. Itzincab was almost two hundred miles inland, east-southeast, and uncomfortably close to Don Discipo's Puebla Arboras, in territory the Holcanos and Grik had infiltrated for the Dominion. Simply by looking at a map, Lewis immediately understood why Truro and Ortiz were Periz's firmest friends.

Periz now spoke through Varaa, addressing Lewis, Anson, De Russy, Dr. Newlin, Reverend Harkin, Lieutenant Burton, and Alferez Lara, each by name. "It's good that you recognize you've been given the greatest gift any warmaster can receive: an image of the ground you'll fight on."

"Doms don't make maps?" Anson snapped derisively, not believing it.

"Of course," Koaar retorted. "They may even have one just like this in their unholy lair in the Great Valley, but it won't show the detail, here, that this one does. And their troops on campaign do little more than scribble lines on parchment to show roads from one place to the next."

"I wouldn't be so sure theirs'll *stay* less exact," Dr. Newlin warned. His eyes arched in surprise. "Don't tell me Don Discipo's never been in this room." The *alcaldes* exchanged worried frowns. "As I thought. His bloody Tranquilo—or servants he may've suborned—could've copied this at their leisure."

Alferez Lara acknowledged the doctor's point but said, "Why go to that effort when they've got Holcanos and Grik to scout for them? Perhaps . . . even your sense of security based on superior local knowledge is misplaced?"

"He's right," Varaa assured the *alcaldes*. "The attack we broke, originally aimed at *all* the free cities, was carefully planned."

When this was relayed to the *alcaldes*, their confidence seemed to shatter and Lewis was struck by what now seemed a rather poignant air of vulnerability among them. "I'm afraid you may have undermined what they thought was their greatest advantage," Lewis whispered to Lara.

The young Mexican soldier frowned. "My people were much the same.

Relying too much on local knowledge and the advantage of defense. Always assuming the enemy—you—would do what we expected." He shook his head.

De Russy cleared his throat and spoke delicately. "I do hope this admittedly wondrous map isn't the only thing your people plan to contribute to our alliance."

Periz shook his head, both in denial and to throw off his gloom. "No. We'll provide for the army of . . . Americanos as well as the Ocelomeh, while both of them help us build our own armies, as we discussed," he promised.

"That's not *exactly* what we talked about," Lewis interjected. "If the Doms come, they'll have *one* army united under a single command. We have to do the same."

Periz was nodding slowly as Varaa translated. "I did speak to my friends and fellow *alcaldes* of this union." He glanced at those others and sighed. "We've long known we must join together—in some fashion—against our common foe," he confessed, "but our cities and peoples are so different. *How* do we bring them together in a way that will benefit all, while protecting those differences we enjoy? As Father Orno has described your 'Constitution' to me, and now the other *alcaldes* here, particularly its 'Bill of Rights' and the protections it guarantees to the various 'states' . . . This is a framework we might use, might build upon. Something that might even work." He looked straight at Lewis. "Your 'states' have apparently managed it well enough to assemble your great army, so perhaps we can do the same." He waved his hand at Ortiz and Truro. "They have agreed to try."

"It won't be easy," De Russy cautioned. "Even after half a century, we're still pulling up some of the stumps." He waited while Varaa and Lara tried to translate that. "And after our Union was established and won a war against its oppressor, *keeping* it together requires constant effort and compromise." He frowned. "Honestly, some of those compromises have left enduring bitterness, and I occasionally wonder if our Union will endure." He shrugged. "But it has so far. God willing, it will continue—as long as men of good faith continue to compromise for the good of all."

"All our people share fundamental principles," Alcalde Truro said hotly through Varaa. "We can 'compromise' on the little things, to oppose the Dominion—which will compromise on nothing."

"Sometimes it's the 'little things' that loom largest in the long run," De

Russy almost whispered, and Lewis suddenly wondered if he was trying to talk them out of it. "But even in the short term, there'll be disputes over who can provide the most to the army, who'll bear the greatest burden manning it, feeding it, equipping it with weapons—and how will we do that?" he asked as if of himself. "Ultimately, you'll almost certainly argue over where the army goes, what approaches it defends, even how it does so. I'm not the soldier Captain Cayce is, but even I know that sort of contention will ruin us."

"We will all contribute equally," Alcalde Ortiz pronounced, "and decide together where to fight."

"No," Varaa now said emphatically, in both languages. "You've never told King Har-Kaaska or I how to defend your people, and we couldn't do it if you did. Captain Cayce must lead our *combined* army and have the same free hand to fight where he thinks best."

"And who'll determine what's 'equal'?" De Russy challenged. "Do you all have an equal number of men? Equal resources in food and raw materials?" He groped for a cigar in a pocket of his splendid dress coat and grimaced when he couldn't find one. "You must decide this *now*, before we even attempt to do more." Anson handed him one of his last cigars, and De Russy took it with thanks, but didn't light it. "And once you decide, you must swear—*swear* before Father Orno—you'll abide by your oaths until the Dominion's driven back or destroyed." He smiled mirthlessly. "Just as our men did today, you must 'sign on' for the 'duration' of the conflict to come." He shook his head. "I'm not saying you can't make changes from time to time, to deal with new things as they come along, but they must be agreed to by everyone, for the benefit of all."

Periz stepped closer to De Russy. Like his fellow *alcaldes*, his expression had turned chagrined as Varaa told him what the colonel said, but now it was firming with resolution. "Something like this, to build this Union and cooperate as you describe, might be impossible. In normal times it might take years to argue over." He shook his head sadly. "But we are desperate," he confessed. "In my hubris, I provoked Tranquilo and through him the Dominion." He waved the denials of the others away and continued. "At worst, I only slightly accelerated the inevitable march of doom because we *won't* abandon our faith and submit to the cruel tyranny of those such as Tranquilo, who'd be our masters if we let them." He smiled sadly even as his strong face hardened. "So we don't have years—perhaps not even months."

He turned his gaze to Lewis. "We *will* prepare to fight, and I beg you'll show us how. I only pray we have time to gather sufficient men and resources to do it." He turned back to De Russy. "Truro, Ortiz, and I—hopefully others—will remain *alcaldes* of our city-states, but will rely on you to advise us on how to coordinate our efforts. We have no choice but to *trust* you, and King Har-Kaaska, Varaa-Choon, Father Orno, and Reverend Harkin, to help us decide what's fair, what's equal, because it will be hard to do by ourselves." He waved his hands a little nervously. "We've never done it before."

"Nonsense," De Russy said with a smile. "The people you lead, from Uxmal, Pidra Blanca, Itzincab—they do *like* one another, I assume? They know and trade with one another. You can all bring different things to your alliance, the Union, and you can trade in those. I think you'll find it's not as difficult as you fear."

Harkin cleared his throat. "What of Don Discipo? I didn't see him here. Will you tell him what you've decided?"

Now Alcalde Ortiz almost wrung his hands. "We must, I suppose, as we have to tell all the *alcaldes* of the Yucatán. Our decision to fight will affect everyone, and they must decide for themselves," he added earnestly.

"Well," Periz said abruptly, "even if Don Discipo has arrived by now, I see no need to tell him tonight. He'll only object, and tonight's a night for celebration, not angry debate!"

Despite the profound change, upheaval, even genuine trauma of the conversation behind the ornately carved door (everyone, possibly De Russy in particular, felt like they'd been swept up by another terrible tempest), they rejoined the reception in a somewhat buoyant mood. Momentous things had been set in motion, but as is so often the case, everyone now felt an urgent determination to get on with it, no matter how fearful they were. Of the *alcaldes*, Ortiz still seemed a bit overwhelmed, but Periz and Truro immediately sought their wives and enthusiastically joined a boisterous dance. De Russy looked a little stunned, but pleased, and stayed back from the merriment with Father Orno and Reverend Harkin, huddled so intently no one dared approach. Lewis and Anson said nothing as they drifted back into the crowd with Lieutenant Burton and Alferez Lara close at hand. Leonor noticed them first, hanging around the periphery of women (and men) gathered around Samantha and Angelique. They were tirelessly answering questions about all sorts of things, from European high society to what people ate where they came from. When she saw the meeting break up, she made a beeline toward Meder and Hudgens. Lieutenant Burton intercepted her, however, as he strode toward the grand entrance.

The two privates had been effectively cut out and hauled away from their charges by what were probably equally highborn women by local standards. Felix Meder was profoundly uncomfortable. Women, *beautiful* women, kept . . . touching him in shocking ways, practically caressing him like no one ever had, and he was blushing beet red. Hudgens seemed happy as could be, immersing himself in the attention and snagging brightly painted mugs of the strange beer whenever someone passed with a sloshing crate of them.

"What's the matter with you?!" Meder hissed loudly at his friend. "What was the last thing Captain Cayce told us?"

"Bee-hayve!" Hudgens belted out.

"Yes, and stay with Mistress Samantha and Mistress Angelique!"

"Only until they was comfterble," Hudgens countered, waving back where they came from. "Which they were an' still are, best I can tell. Now we're stayin' close to *other* ladies!" He beamed happily at a lithe, dark-eyed beauty who seemed fascinated by the eagles and A's embossed on his brass jacket buttons. She giggled when he showed her his equally shiny US beltplate. Meder gently pushed small, probing hands away from his own beltplate and twisted before the girl could grab it again. That only showed her the engraved eagle on the pommel of the short sword in the scabbard on Hudgens's belt, and she gurgled with glee. "You call this behaving?" Meder almost roared. "We're just private soldiers, consorting—much too close— with high-class ladies!"

"We're officers, far as these girls're concerned. Why else would we be here?"

"They'll *find out* what we are," Meder insisted. "Look, I bet Captain Cayce brought us here to see if he wanted to nominate us for corporals. You'll ruin it!"

Hudgens belched loudly, provoking a chorus of laughter. "Why the bloody *hell* would we want to be corporals?" he asked, genuinely amazed.

"Damn, you're drunk too."

"Gettin' there, mate."

Meder felt someone grab his arm and pull. He figured it was another young woman and tried to shake the grip, but it only tightened, hard. He turned to see the tall young Ranger who looked like a girl, and, grabbing

Hudgens's arm, helped pull the artilleryman out of the protesting press as well. Hudgens was sputtering, but the Ranger jerked a nod toward the large entrance where Lieutenant Burton was waiting.

"He wants you two," the Ranger said, and Meder did a double take. The voice didn't sound as deep as he remembered. "You sound . . ."

"She's a girl too, you goose wit." Hudgens grinned. "Din't you know? I s'pect *ever-body* does but you by now." Hudgens laughed. "Girls ever-where! Different world er no, I'm in heaven!"

"I'll *send* you to heaven, you brainless Brit," Leonor seethed. "C'mon."

Together they joined Lieutenant Burton, lit against the dark night outside. His eyes lingered on the swaying Hudgens, and he frowned. "How are you armed?" he asked quietly.

That sharpened Meder's attention and even seemed to steady Hudgens. "We have no firearms, sir. We left them with the horses." He shrugged. "I have my saber, and Private Hudgens his short sword."

"And I have only my saber as well," Burton murmured.

"I have my pistols," Leonor reported.

"Fine. Excellent."

"What's the matter, Lieutenant?" Meder asked.

Burton glanced at him. "Probably nothing. I just . . . It's very dark out there. I was going to relieve Lieutenant Olayne and thought you fellows had enjoyed yourself enough to let a few dragoons have some fun. . . . Anyway, standing here, I noticed the torches outside have been extinguished and I don't see any of the horse holders anymore. You remember, the men in gray tunics."

Leonor nodded, squinting. "Right. I don't see anything movin' at all. It looks like some of the carriage drivers are still out there, and I *think* I see Lieutenant Olayne an' the dragoons standin' together as before, horses tied to the caisson. . . ." She shook her head. "But it's so damn dark, it could be anybody." She started to turn. "I better report to my fath—I mean, Captain Anson."

Burton stopped her. "Not yet." He paused. "It's probably nothing, and I don't want to raise alarm for no reason, but listen to me carefully. If something *is* wrong, I don't think it's treachery on the part of our hosts." He grimaced, and his voice turned deadly serious. "So be *very* careful who you kill. The meeting I attended"—he waved behind—"well . . . just trust me when I say it can't be anything official. But the people here have terrible enemies, and I wouldn't put it past them to try something." A thought seemed to strike him. "I didn't expect to see that revolting Tranquilo fellow here, but I detected surprise that Don Discipo was absent as well." He drove a fist into his palm and looked at Leonor. "I've changed my mind. Please *discreetly* report to Captain Anson at once and discover what he wants to do. I'll remain here with Private Hudgens and Private Meder and join them in a smoke." He shrugged. "Hopefully, Lieutenant Olayne will just step up here and join us and we'll find all this was for nothing. Go!"

Samantha had finally captured Lewis and forced him to join her for a dance that looked more bizarre and humiliating than anything he'd ever attempted, but Anson and Leonor appeared beside him before the music began. "Trouble?" he asked, almost hopefully.

"Maybe."

"Really, Captain Anson!" Samantha protested with a smile. "You two are like a pair of turtles! The lengths to which you'll go to support each other's social isolation . . ." She paused, realizing he was serious.

"Stay here," Lewis told her, looking around. "No, find Mistress Angelique and join Colonel De Russy and Reverend Harkin by the doorway we went through earlier. If . . . something happens, duck inside and bar the entrance until we come for you.

"What is it?" he asked Anson as they weaved through startled dancers, collecting Alferez Lara and Varaa, before heading for Alcalde Periz. He and Koaar were engaged in a cheerful discussion with prominent local citizens.

"Maybe nothin'," Anson unconsciously parroted Burton, "but Leonor has a bad feelin' I've learned to trust. Lieutenant Burton thinks things are too dark an' quiet outside."

Varaa's big eyes narrowed to slits. "There are people whose only purpose tonight was to ensure there was sufficient light for anyone to walk home or reach their carriages. Even to leave the city if they wish. It should never be 'too dark and quiet.'"

Together, they maneuvered Periz and Koaar away from their companions before Lewis asked lowly through Varaa, "Where are your guards? You *do* have guards here, don't you?"

"Of course," Periz replied a little hotly, looking around as if to point them out. Uxmal had a small defense force to secure and police the city, but the enormity of the task before them had left him extra sensitive to the fact his people had always relied so much on the Ocelomeh. He blinked with surprise. "There should be several here. I can't imagine where they've gone."

Lewis looked significantly at Anson. "Sir," he said, "I recommend you gather the other *alcaldes* and your wives and join Colonel De Russy and Father Orno. Something's up."

"I'll come with you!" Periz said forcefully.

Lewis spoke once more through Varaa. "Let me be plain, sir. I smell Tranquilo in this. If something happens to me, others can take my place and train our army. If *you* fall . . . I doubt your arrangement with the other cities will hold. There'll *be* no army, certainly not larger than I and the Ocelomeh, and perhaps Uxmal itself can field. All your people will die," he ended bluntly. At the same time, Varaa was quickly telling Koaar to assemble the few Ocelomeh present and protect the *alcaldes*. Lewis turned to Leonor. "Tell Lieutenant Burton and the others to remain where they are, as casual as possible. Try to stop anyone attempting to leave. Strike up conversations, whatever you must do."

"I stay with Burton?" Leonor asked unhappily.

"If you please. You and Captain Anson are the only ones with pistols." Anson didn't have his huge Walker Colts, but like his daughter, always carried his smaller Patersons in twin holsters at his side.

"What do you have in mind?" Anson asked. If he was uncomfortable being separated from his daughter, he gave no sign. Lewis suspected his confidence in her far outweighed his concern.

"You, Varaa, Lara, and myself will go out one of the opposite entrances and work our way around."

Lara frowned, resting his hand on his own saber hilt. "Enemies may be watching everywhere."

"True, but if there're enough for that, we're already finished, whatever we do. Let's go."

Leonor darted away while they made for the narrow, high-arched opening closest to the chamber they'd been in, but on the opposite side of the building. Some partygoers seemed distressed as they pushed brusquely past, but more by disappointment that the strangers were ignoring their attempts to get their attention than any kind of fear. Just short of the archway, Anson drew one of his long-barreled pistols and stepped in front of Lewis. "The torches're still lit on this side," he murmured in surprise, glancing through the opening. "I'll go first an' hop to the left. Follow quick, if there's no response!"

There wasn't one, and Lewis's steel heel plates and Lara's hobnails clacked on the stone patio as they jogged after the Ranger, sabers in hands. Varaa had drawn her basket-hilt rapier, but her feet made no sound. Pulling up at the corner of the building behind a massive column, they hesitated a moment. It was darker here, and their eyes needed to adjust.

"Wait, what the devil?" Lewis growled, pointing east. The city inside the walls was already slightly elevated above the river valley surrounding it, and the mound under the foundation of the *alcalde*'s Audience Hall allowed a view over the wall surrounding the city, particularly to the north toward the bay, but also to the east, where the Detached Expeditionary Force was camped. A great column of orange-tinged smoke was rising above it, more than all the campfires could've made, and Lewis had heard the sound of bugles and rolling drums, along with the occasional *thump* of a musket.

CHAPTER 20

M y God, what a mess!" Captain Marvin Beck exclaimed miserably, gazing out at the camp. The well-meaning locals had brought
a wonderful feast and a tasty beer he'd even sampled himself,
but some had also brought a powerful spirit called "octli." That took Beck
by surprise, though he supposed it shouldn't have, and it spread faster than
he could stop. He couldn't blame the men for taking the stuff; it was freely
given in abundance, and the homesick soldiers had good reason to forget
things for awhile. But with a few clearly innocent exceptions, most of the
locals who so quickly doled out the milky-looking fluid just as quickly vanished. Beck had experience with unscrupulous sutlers descending on army
camps, selling things the men wanted or needed (including forbidden
booze) at exorbitant prices, but these charged nothing before they disappeared. That gave Beck an uncomfortable feeling. It was as if they *knew*
they were doing wrong and were deliberately trying to disrupt the camp
and incapacitate as many men as they could with drink. Worse, now that so
many of the big painted jugs of octli were on the loose, even the big Ranger
named "Boogerbear" doubted they could do much but "ride it out." Shut-
ting it down "in the middle," as it were, might only breed fierce resentment
and make it harder to rebuild discipline after the outburst of inebriation
passed. "Besides," Boogerbear had told him philosophically, "they had a

hell of a day. This is better than 'em dwellin' on their loss—on *bein' lost*—not to mention what they got to look forward to; they may be in the army *forever*, fightin' the god damned Doms." That last part made sense. Tranquilo's threats had circulated, and the Dominion sounded like an unimaginably barbarous enemy, liable to "make the Comanches sick to their stomachs," as Boogerbear had put it.

Still, if the revelry was hard to watch, it was even harder to control. Men whirled squealing women around in dances they didn't know, accompanied by the scrape of fiddles and laughing and roaring in all directions. Tents collapsed and cook pots clattered when drunken soldiers crashed into them. Beck was reminded of an account he'd read of the wild fur trade fairs in the far Rocky Mountains. He didn't remember who'd said it, but the description of "maleness gone berserk" had amused him at the time. It didn't now.

"The very idea of a . . . party like this in a military camp was absurd in the first place!" he added to Lieutenant Manley and Lieutenant Sime. Manley was doing his best to keep things under control and ensure some of their people remained sober, but Sime was no use at all, practically drunk all the time himself from the laudanum he consumed to excess to deaden the pain from the terrible wound to his face.

"We've got some good NCOs, at least," Manley consoled, "and not just those we brought with us. Some of the new ones are keeping hold of enough men to respond to emergencies."

"I hope so," Beck groused, looking around. "Where did that damned Ranger go? I want you and him to gather larger details to intervene if any fights break out."

"Yes sir," Manley said. "I think that's what he went to do. Some men"—he blinked—"and Ocelomeh, for that matter, chose to hold a, um, 'spiritual service' rather than debauch themselves, over on the other side of the medical tents. I expect the Ranger's there."

Private Hannibal "Hanny" Cox had made a new friend on the way to Uxmal; a short, dark (compared to Hanny, anyway), and very black-haired young fellow about his own age named Apo Tuin. Neither knew much about the other because, even though they'd been working very hard to learn each other's languages, they could barely communicate. But Hanny was a little bashful and didn't have many friends in the 3rd Pennsylvania, and Apo, a grinning, gregarious sort, had seemed to sense that and quickly latched onto him as if determined to pull him out of his shell. He'd marched alongside him during the days, cheerfully pointing at trees and brush, rocks and small creatures, rattling on about them as much to the interest of the men around Hanny as to the gangly farm boy from Bucks County himself. Apo was impossible not to like and was essentially adopted by Hanny's whole squad—which, by association, finally started to get to know Hanny better as well.

Apo hadn't been there when Hanny confronted Hahessy, having run to see his mother and sister in the city, but was clearly angry when he returned and learned about it. He was mad at Hanny's comrades too, for not standing by him better, even giving their senior platoon sergeant named Visser a bitter tongue-lashing in his own language. Sergeant Visser, already armed with some Spanish, had picked up more of the local lingo than most and assured young Apo they'd all jumped in as fast as they could before the fracas was stopped. That appeased the fiery Uxmalo to a degree, but like Hanny, he hadn't been interested in joining the debauchery that seemed to be escalating in the camp. Instead, the two of them went to a "service of thanksgiving" near the medical tents, where a number of the more pious soldiers from all branches had declared their intention to speak to anyone who wanted to listen.

One of these was an otherwise dour young Scot from their own platoon called "Preacher Mac" McDonough. A staunch Calvinist, even he begrudgingly supported Reverend Harkin's interpretation of their place and purpose in this world, concluding: "A better explanation for our situation isnae in the scriptures, but the same can be said o' much we cannae be expected tae ken."

"Worlds, plural, are mentioned in Corinthians and the book of Hebrews," someone argued.

"It isnae the same," McDonough objected impatiently. "What that means . . ." He sighed and shrugged, for once unwilling to quarrel. "One thing *only* is certain: it *is* the will o' God that we've come wherever we are. How else could we be here an' why? All we can do is have faith in His design an' do our duty."

Another man stood to speak and Apo tugged Hanny's sleeve. "Let's eat," he said, a simple enough phrase he'd learned right off. Hanny nodded and turned to walk with his friend. It was too hot by the fire illuminating the gathering in any event, and Hanny was hungry too. Tired as well. He hoped he could sleep through the growing ruckus in camp. Eyes adjusting slowly and moving carefully through the tents so he wouldn't trip on stakes and ropes, Hanny suddenly saw three distinct shapes of men in the gloom, one hulking over the others, and heard a rough voice that chilled the marrow in his bones.

"Faith, it's young Hanny again, me lads! Look there, with his pet darkie Injin! Thought he'd got off without sewin' me button, he did. Reckon it's time to sort that out."

Fear lanced through Hanny as the shapes moved closer and resolved themselves into Sergeant Hahessy, of course, and what he now recognized as his chief minions. One, named Cole, wasn't really much shorter than Hahessy, but he was skinny as a rail and always wore a malevolent sneer. The other was short and burly, but Hanny didn't know his name. Both carried large, open jugs, and were grinning with a kind of wicked glee Hanny had never seen.

He wanted to run but couldn't. The fear almost paralyzed him, but that wasn't why. Apo probably didn't understand all that was said, but clearly understood what was happening, and *he* didn't run. More than that, the... *injustice* of their predicament, that three drunken men, all larger than they were, could feel so casually free to terrorize them left him shaking more with fury than fear. Despite the terrible odds, running just wasn't in him.

"Got a floggin' comin' to him too, I recall," the burly man with a jug reminded.

"Aye, as it happens, he does," Hahessy agreed in a mock-thoughtful tone, now towering right in front of Hanny.

"I'll flog 'em both!" said the tall Private Cole, bursting out laughing.

"Now, now, none o' that," Hahessy said, gently scolding, staring hard at Hanny. "Ye heard Cap'n Cayce about the Articles. Ye'll get yerself thrown outa the army, an' this ain't the time fer that. If the bugger just does as he's told, I'll still let it go with only"—he paused and grinned harshly—"we'll call it 'administrative punishment.'"

Hanny balled his fists at his side and cleared his throat so his voice would be clear. "Never, Sergeant. You can go to the Devil. I *know* you, and I'll *report* you if you don't step aside—and apologize for what you called Apo."

Hahessy's eyes, reflecting the light of the meeting fire where those gathered were reacting loudly to something the latest speaker said, went wide with surprise, fury, and hate, all mixed together. "The only report'll be the findin' of ye both dead as stones in the marnin'," he hissed.

The next instant was so full of motion, Hanny hardly caught it. Hahessy's huge right hand left the white belt it was resting on and lashed out as quick as lightning, backhanding him hard enough to knock him off his feet and cause an explosion of sparks in his eyes. Apo crouched, ready to spring, a long, shiny dagger—maybe bronze—suddenly gleaming in his hand. Private Cole dropped his jug and yanked a bayonet from its sheath at his side. "Enough o' this," he hissed. "We was gonna stick 'em anyway."

Suddenly, Hahessy himself was on his back, slammed down from behind, breath knocked out, gasping for air. A man almost as big as he was loomed over him, boot on his chest and a long-barreled pistol aimed steady at his eye.

"Easy there, son," came a low, rumbling voice directed at Apo, and the Uxmalo slowly uncoiled as the two drunken henchmen tripped over tent ropes and scurried away on the ground. "You still alive, Private Cox?"

Hanny's spinning vision finally focused, and he recognized the big Ranger called "Boogerbear." "Yes sir. I think so."

"I ain't no 'sir.' Just a corp'ral."

"Then get yer damned bloody boot off me or I'll have ye on a charge!" Sergeant Hahessy managed to wheeze.

Boogerbear slowly shook his head. "Don't think so. If ever-body don't already know what kicked off that fuss earlier today, I do, an' I got a idea what you was fixin' to do here." He pressed down harder on Hahessy's chest. "I know your sort an' I won't have it, hear? Never did hold with fellas th'owin' their weight around just 'cause they was big, an' you didn't even have the guts to do it alone. You ever want some exercise with a fella yer own size, I'll be tickled to oblige. In the meantime, you leave these boys be."

"It's none o' yer concern. It's a matter o' discipline, an' I'll do as I see fit!" Hahessy hissed.

"It *is* my concern, an' if any harm comes to these fellas—outside the line o' duty—I'll kill you," Boogerbear replied so calmly, so matter-of-fact, that it sent a chill through Hanny. "Killin' raunchier critters than you has been my trade an' pleasure fer years," he added with the slightest shrug.

The side of Boogerbear's bearded face was lit up by a lurid, orange light that quickly brightened, and he looked up and peered off, away from the camp meeting fire. Giving Hahessy a final, brutal stomp, he said, "Git yerself out'a my sight. Cox, you an' yer amigo run over there an' fetch as many o' them religious fellas as you can." He paused. "Arm yerselves an' meet me at the command tent."

"Fire!" somebody shouted drunkenly. "Tent fire!"

Sergeant James McNabb looked back at his six-man detail. "Get a move on, lads," he cried. They'd already seen the darting, twisting flames shooting up at the sky and snatched sloshing water buckets from where they'd been filled and placed by casks, scattered about just in case of this sort of thing. Most of the wedge-shaped canvas tents the army used were just that: plain, untreated canvas. They leaked in the rain until the fibers swelled, and *then* they'd keep sodden soldiers and their things from getting any wetter. Some men treated their tents with a mix of linseed oil and mineral spirits. That made them heavier and kept them a little tacky, but made them practically waterproof. They'd also burn like coal oil if they took a light. It didn't much matter. Untreated canvas was almost as bad when it was dry. As tightly as the tents were pitched, one might ignite dozens when it burned.

"Hurry, lads!" McNabb urged again. "There it is! There's *two* afire, now! Get yer water on 'em!"

Only one was really burning; the first had already been consumed, leaving only smoldering fragments of canvas around lightly charred, fallen poles. Two men tossed water on these, and the other closest tent, while the rest doused the one now involved. A naked man and woman squirted out the smoke-boiling flap and disappeared in the darkness.

"You forgot your musket, you useless bastard!" One of McNabb's artillerymen yelled, then knocked the tent over to help smother the flames and make it easier to stomp them out. "Oughta piss on it," he grumbled.

"Aye"—McNabb laughed—"we should!"

"I'll do it," came a voice by the firepit, a man they hadn't seen, who'd apparently just sat and watched. "Don't like that bastard anyway. He stole the girl that went off with me!"

"Who's that?" McNabb roared, then recognition came. "Damn ye, *Private Willis,* what're ye thinkin'? What'll Captain Cayce think? Did ye burn these tents?"

"Nah," Willis grumped, swaying where he sat on the ground by a large painted jug. "Didn't hardly notice till you showed up—though I reckon it *did* get brighter all of a sudden." He shook his head. "I's jus' watchin' this here pig cook. Me an' Barca's gonna eat eem all ourselfs!" He waved grandly at a darkened, skewered carcass, slung low over the coals in the fire pit. McNabb doubted it was really a pig, not with clawed toes on its feet, but it did otherwise look and smell like a roasting shoat. "Work harder'n anybody, we do," Willis muttered darkly, "an' nobody gives a damn! It's all 'Willis do this, Willis fetch that,' an' 'Willis, make me a goddamn *dress coat* outa that there shredded napkin, if you please!'" He frowned. "Barca's better at that sort o' thing, but I do my best, by God—an' next thing ya know, there's these damn foreign *wimmin* swoopin' in an' stitchin' and cuttin' on *my* goddamn napkin! Cap'n Cayce'll throw me back in a gun detachment where I'm bound to be killed er maimed by some big ole' boundin' round-shot. I dreamed it once!" He stared owlishly at McNabb. "He'll prob'ly give me back to *you*, you damned, bloody-minded tyrant! I ain't fit for such labor. Danger neither. I got a delicate compostituency!" He belched and poked the scorched meat with his finger.

McNabb rolled his eyes. "Willis, Barca ain't just a better orderly, he's a better *soldier*, I hear. Why do ye think I gave ye to Captain Cayce? I didn't know him then, an' wanted rid o' ye. I'm ashamed o' meself now. But knowin' 'im better, I reckon he'll treat ye as well as ye treat him—an' you're no use under heaven to anyone else! So sober up, clean up, an' get back to the headquarters tent where ye belong."

Willis poked the smoking, fat-spitting carcass again. "But what about my pig? It was near all me an' Barca could get off them heathens for ourselves—after we laid in some other things for the derned officers." He looked indignant. "Them damned infantry fellas thought we was back for more for *us* an' near crushed us down in their rush fer the booze!" He grimaced. "Talked a girl away from them local sutlers too, though Barca said I oughtn't. Didn't last," he added mournfully, nodding at the second burned tent. "Never lasts. She thought Private McIlveen was purtier than me." He giggled, probably thinking about what happened to them and how much trouble McIlveen would be in.

"We'll get ye an' yer bloody pig back—if ye share 'im with us," McNabb told him. "We been a bit busy to see to ourselves as well."

Willis nodded reluctantly and let one of McNabb's men stand him up. He looked around. "You ain't seen Barca, have you? He went for somethin'. Salt, maybe." He yelled out, "Where you at, Barca? We're takin' the pig!"

Even over the rumble of revelry, one of the men thought he heard a groan nearby. "Have a look," McNabb said. A moment later, a pair of artillery- men came dragging the young black man back near the fire pit. Barca was shaking his head and trying to walk.

"An' you tole *me* not to drink that octli juice!" Willis accused. "I been waitin' all this time, an' you're laid out drunk a dozen paces off!"

Barca managed to stand on his own and shrugged off the hands holding him. "I'm not drunk," he retorted hotly. "I saw people trying to fire one of the tents, and someone struck me from behind!"

"Knocked on the head, sure enough," another man said, holding up a lantern and seeing matted blood in Barca's hair.

"*Who* fired the tents?" McNabb demanded.

Barca looked at him. "Locals, Sergeant."

McNabb frowned. "But why?" He shook his head. "Never mind. They were likely drunk as well—or McIlveen had one o' their sisters. Let's get these two back." He grinned. "An' don't forget the pig!"

The blood and sweat on Barca's dark face suddenly glowed, and they turned to see several more tents burst into flames at once.

"Goddamn it," McNabb shouted. "*Leave* the pig. Grab yer buckets an' follow me. There's another water butt this way."

The fire had spread to half a dozen more tents by the time they got there, with Barca and even Willis staggering behind. They all threw water on the fires, but it made little difference. Worse, nearly everyone on this end of camp must've been elsewhere, and there was no one to pitch in and help. "Get more water, fast as ye can. I'll get some attention," McNabb bellowed, unslinging the musket from his shoulder. Cocking the weapon, he pointed it up and pulled the trigger. It flashed and cracked. In the bright flare of the vent jet and muzzle flash, something on the ground drew his notice, and he took a few steps and stooped. Barca and Willis joined him to look at two dead infantrymen, their high collars and sky-blue jackets under their chins black and slick with blood. "Poor bastards. Somebody's cut their throats for 'em," McNabb muttered, standing and looking around. Without conscious thought, he pulled a paper cartridge from the black leather box at his side and tore off the end with his teeth. Priming the pan of his musket, he clapped the frizzen back in place and poured the rest of the gunpowder down the barrel before shoving the wadded-up paper, still wrapping the ball, into the muzzle. Even as he drew his rammer, he turned to Barca and Willis and asked, "Can the two o' ye make it back to the command tent?"

"I can," Barca said.

"Then go, run, tell Captain Beck we're under attack an' we'll need to stand this drunken mob to."

Even as his eyes swept around the rest of the camp, another clump of tents went up, flames rolling and licking high in the night. Then came the screams, and several shots.

"Agh!" cried one of the men returning with a bucket as he was thrown to the ground by one of the big, heavy-shafted arrows they'd already seen too many of. The man never made another sound, other than the noise of his feet drumming in the grass. The arrow had slammed straight through his heart.

"Bloody hell!" shouted one of the other soldiers as they all dropped their buckets and took muskets off their shoulders. One fired at a flitting shadow.

"Watch what yer shootin' at, damn ye!" McNabb roared. "This ain't the Uxmalos we been amongst for a week, nor them that fed ye! This is *their* enemy too!" There were more screams of terrified women, drunken cries of alarm or outrage, then came the drums, calling the men to action. "Stay with us, an' fetch that man's weapon," McNabb told Barca. "The alarm's already out."

"What about me?" Willis almost squealed.

"Ye'd be no use with a weapon even if ye'd thought to bring one. Fetch yer damn pig if ye like," McNabb snapped, then relented. "Get McIlveen's musket. It won't be hurt, an' he ain't usin' it."

"The camp's under attack!" Lara exclaimed, advancing beyond the corner of the long building for a better look.

"It's certainly burning," Lewis agreed. "Now get back before someone sees you."

They were distracted by more unexpected fire when a ripple of startlingly bright flashes stabbed out in long, horizontal tongues of orange flame far out in the bay. Moments later came a rumbling, booming sound, like heavy, distant thunder. "Those are *cannon*, by God!" Lewis said. He'd know as well as anyone, but he also knew these had to be mounted on a ship. *Could the Doms be here already?* he wondered frantically. But the jets of flame were still far away, not directed at the city. It made no sense—until there were *more* flashes, stabbing back at the first.

"That's Captain Holland an' *Tiger*," Anson declared. "An' somebody's chased him here!"

Lewis looked at Varaa, who was blinking her luminous blue eyes. "That, or the other way around," she confirmed. "An encounter with Doms at sea would explain his tardy arrival." She shook her head. "I doubt, however, that beyond their inspiration, Captain Holland's difficulties are related to our own. He must fend for himself. As must we." She gestured at a low stone wall separating the grounds of the Audience Hall from a cross street fronted by shops. Most had been lit when they entered the city, but all were now ominously dark. "We can use that wall to get to the front and perhaps see what awaits us." Simply assuming agreement, she darted lightly across the opening, tail high behind her. Anson quickly followed, as did Lewis and Lara.

Gasping slightly from his sprint and jump, Lewis nodded Varaa on. He'd learned Mi-Anakka had better night vision than humans and it made sense for her to lead. Scrunching along as low and quiet as possible, they moved fairly quickly as their eyes searched for movement and they listened to the booming on the bay and the growing stutter of shots from the camp. Lewis risked a glance over the wall and saw they were even with the caisson and their horses. Some of the local carriage drivers appeared to be looking around in concern, but some were just gone. Up at the main entrance, it looked like people inside were starting to panic, trying to get out, and Burton, Meder, Hudgens, Leonor, and now some Ocelomeh, were pushing them back.

"Those *are* your men over there," Varaa hissed, flicking her ears at the dragoons, who'd moved to surround their animals. Crouching down, they had their Hall carbines pointed all around. A slim figure in an officer's frock coat was jogging toward the entrance.

"That's Olayne," Anson stated definitively. "Maybe all our concerns, here at least, have been for nothing."

"No," Varaa hissed. "There are men with bows near some of the coaches and quite a few more gathering to join them from the direction of the temple!" She hesitated. "Most are dressed in gray tunics."

"'Trusted captives.'" Lara snorted sarcastically.

"Indeed," Varaa said. "They'll be Holcanos. Tranquilo or Don Discipo must've armed them and set them against us"—she glanced at Lewis—
"promising freedom, no doubt, for the murder of our leaders." She added
ironically, "You were right, Captain Cayce. We *were* safer in the forest with
the inhuman monsters. I see their plan now, however. The disturbance in
your camp was designed to draw us out of the Audience Hall, where we'd
be well-illuminated targets for the archers. But the warning Lieutenant
Burton raised alerted us before they were ready."

"Makes sense," Anson agreed. "But what's *our* plan?"

Varaa grinned. "Come now, Captain Anson. Yours, mine, Captain
Cayce's—all our plans are the same, are they not? We kill them." Her eyes
shifted to Lewis. "We have the advantage. Our enemies already in position don't know we're here. We take them from the side and fight our way
to your dragoons, then attack the larger force by the temple before it's
ready, yes?"

"Damn. That *is* what I was thinking," Lewis admitted with a smile, removing his saber belt and scabbard and laying them quietly on the ground.
The bright steel scabbard might make a noise or trip him in a fight like this.
"And our firing away from the Audience Hall will send people back inside,
or at least out the back, where it's safer."

"Good plan," Anson agreed, raising his pistol, "but I'll go to the right
an' start that firin' as the others come. That'll discourage 'em, an' distract
the ones you have to go through."

"Fine," Lewis agreed. "Go with him, Alferez Lara—if you please." Lewis
still felt uncomfortable giving orders to a former enemy officer, but—even
more ironic—the man already seemed much attached to the Ranger.

"I was going to ask if I may," Lara whispered a little defensively.

Varaa pointed where she saw former Holcano captives/servants using
carriages for cover—there were six, at least, on the near side of the clump of
dragoons—and showed Captain Anson where he and Lara could go to get
in front of the larger force starting across the broad plaza from the temple.
It's a good thing we have her along, Lewis thought. To him, the figures were
all but invisible. Anson and Lara scuttled away behind the wall while Lewis
and Varaa hopped over and spread out, each aiming for three specific adversaries. It wasn't until then that Lewis realized, for the next few moments
at least, he'd be alone. He was no stranger to fierce combat, and the excellent artillery saber in his sweating hand was an old and trusted friend, but

all his fighting had been in the midst of battle, a group effort, so to speak. Regardless of the same very personal risks, his opponents had always been *impersonal*, almost faceless members of their own groups. This was the first time he'd ever set out to kill other men, other individuals, on his own. Yet he was doing it for the "group," for his people and their new friends, and strange as it might feel, he didn't hesitate.

The commotion in the entry arch where partygoers tried to get past Coryon Burton's detail was growing shriller, more determined, as the thunder on the bay intensified. The first Holcano Lewis neared was raising his big, powerful bow, anticipating the break sure to come, readying himself to shoot leaders as they appeared. Lewis crept silently closer, heel plates on his boots making no sound on the grassy soil, but "city" clothing or not, the Holcano was an Indian who'd spent most of his life honing survival instincts in a forest wilderness more lethal than any Lewis could imagine "back home." Either he actually heard Lewis or some inner voice told him he'd gone too long without checking his surroundings. Arrow still nocked, he suddenly glanced around, eyes fastening on Lewis.

"Aii!" he cried, spinning as fast as a striking snake to bring his weapon up. Lewis leaped inside the long, heavy head of the arrow and crashed into the man at the same instant the point of his saber passed through ribs high in the Holcano's chest and crunched out his back through his shoulder blade. The man tried to scream or shout a warning, but only hot dark blood flooded from his mouth, spraying Lewis full in the face and drenching the right side of his beautiful new coat. Lewis savagely wrenched his saber in a circle, to widen the wound and free the blade, then pulled it out and let the man drop. Gasping with adrenaline and effort, he paused to look at the next carriage Varaa assigned him.

They were out of time. Festively dressed people were breaking past Burton's American and Ocelomeh guards and Lieutenant Olayne, now standing at the bottom of the steps. Burton must've called out what they were doing, and Olayne was trying to urge people back. For an instant, it seemed to be working. An impatient Holcano must've thought so as well, and Olayne might be the only "leader" he'd get. An arrow slashed across his upraised arm and deflected straight into the chest of a plump-looking woman charging down the steps. Olayne staggered aside, clutching his bicep, but the woman screamed and fell. Then everyone screamed and more arrows flew.

Lewis dashed toward the next archer just as he released his arrow and his sweeping blade cracked into the heavy bow stave the man used to block it. The Holcano lunged, and Lewis jumped back, instinctively aware that any man who could draw such a bow and hurl such heavy arrows could probably crush the life out of him. One of Captain Anson's pistols barked sharply, farther than Lewis expected, but it drew the big Holcano's gaze, and Lewis darted forward, bringing his heavy blade slashing down between his opponent's neck and shoulder. More blood fountained in the darkness, and the man staggered back and fell.

An arrow tugged at the coat at his side, and Lewis sprinted toward "his" third carriage. "Keep those people back, Lieutenant Olayne!" he roared, uncertain he'd be heard over the tumult and Anson's continued shooting. To his dismay, he also heard the heavy *boom* of muskets. "Lieutenant Burton, to your dragoons! There are more enemies coming!"

The Holcano in front of him launched another arrow at him, but all it did was tear off his left shoulder board. At only ten yards, he was sure it would've killed him if these men hadn't been without weapons so long. Or maybe his commands, bellowed so fiercely in an unknown language, unnerved the man? He'd never know. Just as the Holcano turned to flee from his upraised saber, he ran directly onto Varaa-Choon's rapier and screamed in agony and terror. Lewis well understood the man's dying fear. Even if he'd seen Mi-Anakka before, with Varaa's luminous blue eyes peering from a face with fur as thick with blood as Lewis's beard, she looked every inch a demon.

"You finished your three?" Lewis gasped at her as she withdrew her blade and they ran for the dragoons. "And one of yours," she confirmed lightly, "though you would've had him." Lewis got the impression she was surprised he'd done as well as he had. So was he. "Don't shoot!" he called ahead, where dragoons were aiming carbines in their direction. "It's Captain Cayce and Varaa-Choon! Form a skirmish line, face to the west and take a knee. But hold your fire! Captain Anson and Alferez Lara are out there!"

Burton, Meder, Hudgens, and Leonor all ran up, even as more arrows whipped past from the left, reminding Lewis they'd only dealt with half the closer assassins. "Koaar and Lieutenant Olayne have assembled all the Ocelomeh who were here, sir," Burton reported. "The people are returning to shelter, but I fear a dozen or more fell to arrows," he added bleakly.

"Yes, thank you, Lieutenant. You did your best." Lewis retrieved his pistols from the pommel holsters in front of Arete's saddle. Without his saber belt, he had to tightly knot his sash and push them in it. He saw Leonor already taking her father's pommel holsters with his big revolvers from his horse, Colonel Fannin. "Everyone, get your weapons. You have your rifle now, Private Meder?"

"Yes sir."

"Good. Take cover behind the caisson and shoot anyone you see to our left. You'll stay with him with your musket, Private Hudgens, in case anyone rushes him while he's reloading."

"Sir!"

Lewis nodded toward the flare of one of Anson's pistols and the answering flashes of several muskets. More arrows still came but they were less accurate and falling from high trajectories. The nearest Holcanos must be falling back. "The rest of us will join Captain Anson against those other"—he paused—"rebels, I suppose."

"On foot?" Leonor asked. "Some'll get away."

Lewis managed to smile at her, though he doubted she saw it.

"I admire your confidence and priorities," he said, "but as much as I'd love to send a force galloping around behind the enemy, we're not sure where 'behind' them *is*, and there aren't enough of us. Certainly not enough to split in a city the enemy knows better than we do. As you've probably seen, there's more going on than our fight. There's a sea battle in the bay and an attack of some kind on our camp. We'll destroy as many attackers as we can, but must be content with just stopping them, for now."

"Then let's just mount up and charge 'em!" Leonor persisted.

Lewis had never questioned orders in battle and wasn't used to explaining his own. This was a different situation, of course, and he'd probably have to learn to do that as they built their new army, but at the moment they were wasting time and he was losing patience. "We won't fire until we join Captain Anson," he said flatly. "Hopefully, the enemy won't realize we're there until we do, and that alone will break them. They *will* see us sooner, charging on horseback, and that'll increase the risk to ourselves and our animals." Meder's rifle flashed and cracked behind them, and a man screamed off to their left.

"Take that, you sneakin' bugger," Hudgens muttered, patting Meder on the back as his friend began to reload.

"Well done, Private," Lewis told him, shifting his gaze to Coryon Burton. "Advance your men in skirmish order, Lieutenant, but keep them low." He looked around. "We'll all stay low. Varaa, tell me what you see as we go." They started moving in the direction they last saw Anson shoot. An enemy musket flashed and boomed and a ball whizzed past.

"Anson and Lara are in those decorative shrubs that serve as a boundary between the plaza around the temple and the one around the Audience Hall," Varaa said. "You may remember from earlier. The shrubs provide little protection, but should already conceal our movement, and Captain Anson has been moving between shots."

"And the enemy?" Lewis asked.

"Still in the open in front of the temple. They've halted and seem to be bunching up." Varaa chuckled quietly. "In light of the failure of the first part of their plan and Anson's continued harassment, I suspect they're debating whether to press their attack. Remember," she added, "these are *not* Doms. They hate us and will work for Doms for their aid, but few would fight to the death for them."

"Then let's end their debate and make up their minds," Lewis muttered. "Where's Captain Anson?"

"He and Lara are just ahead, to the right." Without a word, she scampered forward, lithe as an otter, and hissed at Anson that they were coming just as Lewis made the man out. "Spread out along here," he told the dragoons, "down behind this brush." Dropping to earth beside Varaa and the Ranger, immediately joined by Leonor, Lewis winced at the perpetual ache in his side, resigned to the probability he'd aggravated it further with all his exertion, and peered through the tangled limbs. Now he could see perhaps thirty men of the "main" force starkly silhouetted against the whitewashed backdrop of the pyramid. Apparently unaware how visible their position made them, they did indeed appear to be arguing among themselves.

"Took you long enough," Anson growled. "Alferez Lara an' I had about decided you'd forgotten us."

"Never, Father," Leonor said, pushing the pommel holsters up beside him.

"Bless you," he said. "My Patersons're almost empty an', silly me, dressed for a ball, I didn't bring reloads. I'll never do that again," he swore darkly. "What are your intentions, Captain Cayce?"

"You can speak to them?" he asked Varaa.

"Of course. Their language is virtually the same as my Ocelomeh."

"Then call for their surrender. I want prisoners, and you said they won't fight to the last for Doms."

Varaa hesitated, then whispered back, "Not for Doms. But don't forget, many are Holcano warriors who've already been captives. Whether they fight or run, they won't meekly surrender back into captivity. Especially the harsher variety that'll await them now."

"Harsher?"

"Farming farther from the city where predators are bolder—if they're lucky. More likely, the mines."

"Nevertheless," Lewis insisted, handing one of his pistols to Alferez Lara. "Press yourselves down as flat as you can, lads," he called around.

Varaa raised her voice very loud, calling on the enemy to lay down their arms if they wanted to live. Most of that was in straightforward Spanish that Lewis understood. Varaa immediately hugged the ground—just as a fusillade of arrows and a half dozen muskets fired in their direction. "I told you," she said through the grass in front of her face.

Fortunately, there'd been no screams from his people, and Lewis called, "Third dragoons. Take aim!" He heard hammers cocking back as he pointed his pistol at the clump of men about fifty or sixty yards away. That was a near-impossible range for him, though he might hit someone in the press, but this would all be about volume of fire. Burton had retrieved his Hall as well, and his dragoons could fire their odd breechloaders very quickly. Lewis saw Anson, Leonor, and Lara aim pistols. "Fire!" he roared, and a stuttering volley slashed out.

His otherwise excellent-quality Johnson contract M1836 smoothbore pistol might be limited in power and accuracy at this distance, but it was point-blank for Hall carbines. They could easily hit a man, and sometimes another behind the first at this range. People weren't nearly as tough as the monster that got Lieutenant Swain. More men tumbled screaming to the ground than shots had been fired and a few poorly aimed arrows whipped through the shrubs in a shower of clipped leaves. "Reload," Lewis shouted, aware most had already begun. He couldn't reload either of his pistols, but Anson slapped a Paterson in his hand, and another in Lara's, before pulling one of his big Walker Colts from its holster. "There's only two shots left in each of those," he cautioned them.

Lewis gazed at the ingenious long-barreled revolver, surprised to see no trigger until he cocked the centrally located hammer. He almost chuckled when the trigger popped down out of the frame. "I've never fired one of these," he confessed.

"Neither have I!" said Lara.

"It's easy," said Anson. "Just cock it and pull the trigger. Pretty accurate too, even from here, but probably not lethal unless you hit 'em in the eye!"

"Or up the nose," Leonor murmured, and they both snorted at some secret joke.

"Ready, sir!" Burton said.

"Take aim!" Lewis called. "Fire!"

Sparky orange jets of flame stabbed out at the huddled mass of men, and another large number melted to the ground. Quite a few were starting to run, bolting into the gloom around the corner of the temple where they'd come from.

"That's it," Lewis cried, shifting the smoking Paterson to his left hand and taking up the saber in his right. "At them!"

"Charge!" Burton bellowed, young voice suddenly deep and fierce.

Few arrows came as all eleven of them, including the dragoons, leaped over the low shrubs. Most enemies still standing seemed too stunned to do anything but stare, and Lewis believed—as he'd hoped—even as puny as his volleys had been, they'd crushed the spirit of those whose bodies they'd spared. Few Ocelomeh possessed firearms (Lewis had forgotten to ask where Varaa and Koaar had gotten theirs), and for some reason even fewer Uxmalos had them. He wondered why. They knew about guns, and judging by their fine jewelry, their artisans had the skill to make them. For whatever reason they couldn't or wouldn't before, that would have to change, Lewis resolved.

But at the moment, his plan of attack was based on the fact none of *these* Holcanos had been at the battle on the beach and had almost certainly never received a concentrated volley of fire—however small—in their lives. He'd counted on panicking them, but even he was surprised by how thoroughly it did. Of the fifteen or twenty still standing when the Americans came for them, few even tried to fight. There were a pair of wild musket shots and a few more panicky arrows—one taking a dragoon in the leg—but most who could simply bolted. A couple were hacked down from behind by dragoon sabers as they ran, and all the dragoons and Alferez Lara gave chase, loudly shouting at one another. Varaa was beset by two men with empty muskets, trying to bash her, but nimbly avoided every blow, darting past with the tip of her rapier, poking and slashing them almost as if in sport. Anson shot one, then stopped and stood, almost casually shooting anyone who seemed inclined to make a stand. Leonor was beside him, reloading one of her pistols. She'd carried a small flask of powder, as well as percussion caps and pistol balls tucked in her vest pockets.

Lewis felt strangely feverish but dismissed it to the excitement and his pounding heart. He was about to shout for everyone to cease firing and bring any prisoners back to the sprawling mound of dead and loudly wounded men when a giant stood in front of him. His bearded face was covered with blood pouring from a bullet crease across his forehead, yet even in the dark Lewis instantly recognized one of the guards standing by the Blood Priest Tranquilo in this very place, that very morning. He'd replaced the vestments of his twisted church with the coarsely woven gray tunic of his comrades, but still held the gold-tipped spear. Most troubling of all was the maniacal, blood-drenched fury on his face, and—no longer viewed from atop Arete—how truly huge he was.

With a roar, Tranquilo's guard swept his spear in a wide arc, bashing Lieutenant Burton down. Stepping forward, he drew the spear back to pin the young officer to the ground. Lewis shot him right in the chest with the Paterson, but all it did was draw his attention. He tried to fire again, but the hammer only snapped on an empty chamber. The giant grinned as Lewis backed away, bringing his saber up to deflect the spear already lunging for him. The giant was so strong that Lewis barely managed to shift the glistening point at all, and it sliced into his coat and grazed his ribs near the old, aching wound. He gasped, staggering backward.

"*Shoot* him, Father!" Leonor screamed, frantically reassembling her pistol.

"Damn thing's jammed on a burst cap!" Anson shouted, pulling back on the big revolver's hammer while trying to turn the cylinder with his other hand. Leonor dropped the pieces of her Paterson and snatched the pommel holster off her father's shoulder. Varaa had finished with her other opponent and rushed up to drive her rapier deep in the giant's back. He roared in pain and spun, tossing Varaa aside like a doll, and she crashed down next to Burton. Dizzy now, Lewis charged forward and drove his saber into the huge man's belly. The giant roared again and, finally dropping his spear, wrapped huge arms around Lewis and picked him up, crushing him against his chest. Lewis groaned as all the air gushed from his lungs, his back popped, and it felt like ribs were snapping like dry sticks. He was already dizzy, now unable to breathe, and a sparkling blackness swirled in his eyes.

He was barely aware of a booming *crack* nearby, an agonized grunt, and then a sense of falling. His impact with the ground jarred him to his senses, however. Scrambling drunkenly, painfully, to his feet, he saw Leonor standing by him, her pretty face no longer merely severe but contorted by rage as she held her father's other big pistol in both hands, pointed at the giant's face. He was on one knee now, spitting bloody hate at the woman with his eyes, but also still grinning in triumph. His other knee, both hands clasped over it, was a shattered ruin.

"She was afraid to shoot him without hittin' you, so she knocked a stilt from under him," Anson said with a mix of relief and pride. Without a word, Leonor cocked the big Walker Colt again and took deliberate aim.

"No," Lewis whispered.

Lara and the dragoons were coming back now, prodding a few prisoners before them. One of the dragoons trotted over to their only seriously wounded man, but everyone stopped in their tracks when they saw the unexpected tableau.

Varaa and Burton were both sitting up, as if supporting each other, and Varaa said, "Finish him. You're giving him what he wants."

Lewis's mind reeled. "What he *wants*?" he asked dumbly.

"You've forgotten already," Varaa lamented, standing slowly and helping Burton to his feet. "They *earn* 'grace' through pain, and the worse it is, the better. The more 'exalted' they'll be in their perverted afterlife."

"Lord," Burton murmured.

"I understand," Varaa consoled. "It *is* hard to grasp. But here you see it before you." She waved around. "He led these Holcanos against us, at Tranquilo's command no doubt, utterly indifferent to their fates or even his own—beyond what's happening now. The failure of the plan and all the suffering it caused is unimportant beside the grace *we're giving him* as we speak!"

"That's madness," Anson said, deeply troubled.

"*Of course it is!*" Varaa actually yelled in frustration. "Yet that's what we're fighting, at its heart. A cultural and spiritual madness that promotes evil beyond anything I know on this world!" She glared at Leonor. "Kill him! Put him out of *our* misery!"

"Wait," Lewis insisted, mind still reeling from what he'd heard and seen as well as the flaring dizziness and pain in his side. He wondered if it was mostly his new wound or the old. "Perhaps we can at least get him to confirm it was Tranquilo who put him up to this."

"Between your sword and mine, he's finished." Varaa kicked the gold-bladed spear on the ground. "And that's proof enough. You think you can induce him to tell us more? He'll never live long enough for kindness to work, even if it could, and torture is useless. Blood Priests *make* men like him with pain!"

Suddenly nauseous, Lewis almost fell. Leonor grabbed him and held him upright, expression finally changing to concern. *Maybe something else?* Lewis wondered. Then he shook his head and gently pushed away, determined to spare this woman another painful memory, another callus on her soul. He was aware of how quiet it now was, the cannon thunder in the bay having ended, and the drums and bugles and musket fire in the camp outside the walls now silent. Did all that mean the crisis was past or only just beginning? He also vaguely became aware they were surrounded by many more people now: luminaries he'd met in the Audience Hall, more Ocelomeh, and there were Colonel De Russy and Dr. Newlin, watching him somberly alongside Alcalde Periz and Alcalde Truro. He was surprised to see Periz with a naked sword somewhat like Varaa's, his expression tense and angry.

"Very well," Lewis said, nodding at the dragoons and wounded Holcanos lying about. "Varaa says this spear will tie this man to Tranquilo. We have other prisoners. Perhaps they can link him to Don Discipo. I pray we've put an end to it for now, but regardless how close this effort may have come to succeeding, it strikes me as hastily and ill conceived. A move of desperation." He looked straight at Periz and Truro. "It's like Tranquilo knows how dangerous our cooperation and a united Yucatán will be and attempted to nip it in the bud." He sighed and shivered despite the warm night air, and the pain in his side was as bad as when he was shot at Monterrey. "We won't let that happen," he ground out. "Instead, we'll make sure this attack, on all of us," he stressed, "only binds us tighter and helps us destroy the Doms when they come."

Teetering forward, he quickly reached down and whipped his saber out of the giant's belly before the man could react. Blood spurted from the wound **and spat**tered the ground at his feet. "Even bleeding so freely, it might take you minutes to die, my friend," he mumbled at the giant, then raised his voice. "Like the twisted empire you serve, I think your 'grace period' has lasted long enough." With that, he lifted the bloody saber over his head and brought it down as hard as he could, slicing through the knotted muscle between the man's neck and shoulder and deep into his chest. Wrenching the saber free with a grunt, he turned to look at Periz—but the man's face was spinning, his expression of satisfaction turning to concern, and Lewis felt himself falling. He never seemed to reach the ground, but even as his vision went completely dark, he heard Leonor's—and even Samantha Wilde's—cries of alarm, and then Dr. Newlin shouting over the others who'd joined them: "My God, the man's on fire with fever! Bring the caisson up at once, though a carriage would be better!"

"You can't take him to your camp," Varaa declared. "We don't even know what's happening there!"

"The room of the *gran mapa*!" Periz said firmly. "It is the place . . . most secure, and . . . *conveniente para nuestros curanderos*. Close to our healers," he clarified.

"By God, whatever help they can offer'll get no argument from *me*," Newlin declared.

After that, for Lewis, except for the odd feeling someone was holding his hand, there was nothing.

CHAPTER 21

L ewis knew he was hurt and even out of his head, but wasn't sure exactly where he was, or even *when*. Sometimes he was sure he was still
in the grimy field hospital outside Monterrey and everything that
happened since had been wild, delirious dreams stacked up on one another
and even comingled. Then he'd catch hazy glimpses of his surroundings—
stone walls and heavy beams overhead—and believe with alarm he was
back in the even more squalid and stifling hospital set up in the city, where
the air was thick with the stench of disease, death, screams of pain, and
harsh shouts of drunk or exhausted surgeons and insensitive orderlies.

But that wasn't right either. Fevered or not, his mind still worked well
enough to reason on some level, and besides the fact all he smelled was the
pleasant odor of charcoal smoke, mixed with something like . . . almost
minty sage, he often heard other voices, genuinely concerned, that he knew
were more recent and real. His present beckoned him at times like that, and
he came to understand there *was* a present he must return to. And even as
his hot, restless mind recoiled from the frightening nightmare-like *sense* of
his urgent present, he knew he belonged—and was needed—there more
than anywhere he'd ever been.

Fresher memories and newer faces returned to his dreams as he finally
slept more normally, more peacefully, and the full reality of his present re-

turned. That's how he knew with complete certainty he was dreaming of the past when he found himself sitting in the old white wicker rocker on the porch of his childhood home. His father, beard and wild hair streaked deeply with gray, was leaning forward in his own rocker, waving a smoldering pipe.

"I would've thought as a soldier—an officer now!—you'd have finally discarded such silly notions that the idealistic, hypocritical rantings of the 'Constitutional framers' were anything more than that." He fumed. "*Practical* 'equality for all men' has never existed, nor can it!" the old man insisted in a voice even raspier than when Lewis left for the military academy. "I served my time under arms," he reminded—as he so often did—"and there's no purer example of the necessity for the separation between leader and led than the army!"

Lewis remembered this conversation well, further proof he was dreaming, but had to try to reason with the man once more, just as he had at that final meeting. "No matter how imperfect the men who wrote it might've been, I swore to *defend* that Constitution, Father, and that includes all the 'ideals' in it. *Good* ideals," he stressed emphatically, but then tried another tack. "You were in the militia, called up against the Creeks." He held up his hands. "I mean no disrespect. You *did* your duty. But you returned home when you were released, as did those who commanded you, and you were all 'equal' once more." He shook his head. "I could resign my commission today and instantly be the legal 'equal' of any officer placed over me. I wouldn't do it, but I could." He glanced at the field east of the modest house where three black slaves in wide straw hats stooped under the hot June sun to twist yellow squash from their stems and drop them in baskets hanging from straps over their shoulders. "Do you 'lead' those men, Father? Will they be 'released' when their task is done? Will they be your equal then?"

"Of course not!"

"Why?"

"Because they're *mine*," the old man stated flatly, anger rising as it always did.

"Why?" Lewis persisted.

"Because I *paid* for them, boy, damn you!" He jabbed at Lewis with his pipe. "You sit there in a fine uniform, an *officer* in the army—against my wishes, I'll remind you once more—because of the upbringing I gave you. An upbringing financed by the labor of slaves. We don't have old money, hoarded and tarnished with age, or a sprawling plantation with rents as well as crops to live off when times are hard. We have a small farm, a *good* farm, which your mother and I—God rest her—hacked out of the wilderness with our own bleeding hands. We did the *hard* work, boy, harder than any slave we scratched up enough to buy has ever done since." His face turned stormy. "And what choice did I have after your mother died trying to give me another son? I had a daughter and *one* dream-addled boy, neither willing to do the hard work it takes to keep this farm alive! Now all you ask is *Why, why, why?* like some half-wit infant pointing at the moon—or a starry-eyed lieutenant with his head filled with flighty, musty philosophy, pondering the meaning of life! The only answer to 'why'—anything!—is 'because that's the way it is'!"

"I would've stayed here and worked *with* you, Father," Lewis softly told the old man. "I never shirked a task and worked right alongside your slaves." He paused. "But that's how I learned there's no difference between us, in God's eyes—or yours. Is that why you sold the ones I befriended? Would you have sold *me* if you could?"

"Yes!" the old man snapped furiously. "If I could've replaced you as easily, I *would* have. So help me God!"

LEWIS JERKED HIS eyes open and tried to sit up. Gentle hands restrained him.

"Look at you!" boomed Captain Eric Holland, stooping to peer in his eyes, "wide awake at last, an' alert as well! Call Dr. Newlin," he said aside. "Man's mortified enough that these 'primitive witch doctors' did more to save the good captain than he. He'll swoop in an' claim the cure!"

Only then did Lewis fully realize he was in the map chamber inside the Audience Hall. He was also quite naked beneath a stuffed, silklike comforter, and not only were two young women gently holding him in place, but Samantha Wilde stood from a chair to peer at him with a relieved expression. "You gave us all a scare, Captain Cayce," she said.

"I was a little concerned myself, from time to time," Lewis admitted hoarsely, remembering more, as Samantha poured something that looked like red wine from a big ceramic pitcher and held a mug to his lips. It tasted like wine too. Sweet but very bitter. At the moment, the fact it was wet was enough. "Thank you," he said self-consciously, pulling the comforter up over his bare chest. That's when he felt the soft bandage wrapped around his torso and was amazed to find that, though it hurt to the touch, the constant, deep burning ache he'd grown used to was gone.

Coryon Burton was the first to appear through the sturdy doorway, eyes bright with relief. Dr. Newlin pushed him aside and stepped purposefully toward the rigid but comfortable cot Lewis was lying on. He immediately plopped himself on a bench and seized Lewis's wrist. "Show me your tongue, if you please," he commanded. Varaa-Choon followed him in, huge blue eyes alight and a grin on her furry face.

"I apologize in advance for the cliché," Lewis murmured, "but what happened?"

"The spear point that grazed your side was poisoned," Newlin brusquely explained. "Not particularly deadly, but fast acting. Like the toxin in the tongue of the monstrous toad that wounded Lieutenant Sime. A deeper cut would've incapacitated you sooner." He paused seriously. "The fever was more serious and already mounting, however. It was due to a combination of the climate, I fear—a number of the men are affected—and the old wound you wouldn't let me see." He frowned and peered scoldingly over his spectacles. "I'm *tempted* to tell you all the unpleasantness you've endured over the last several days only serves you right, but I won't. Still, your stubbornness and the carelessness or incompetence of whoever first treated that ghastly hole very nearly ended you!"

"Really, Doctor," Samantha said, rolling her eyes. "I applaud your restraint!"

"In any event," Newlin went on, "with the, er, assistance of some of the extraordinarily knowledgeable locals, I decided it was past time to explore your long-festering wound." He nodded graciously to the young women. Lewis now saw one was an Uxmalo and the other Ocelomeh, each wearing a silver gorget around her neck like he'd seen on respected, senior healers after the battle on the beach. He'd since learned it symbolized a quarter moon, radiating light and holding life and knowledge. Newlin blinked. "Not only did we find a small curl of lead from the ball that struck you; we removed a splinter of rib and some fragments of the uniform you wore that day!" He shook his head in disgust. "But the infection was severe, and I honestly held out little hope for you." He cleared his throat and added more gently, "Or us, for that matter, if you were lost." He leaned back and regarded Varaa. "*She's* the one who ultimately saved you, providing a small measure of some curative paste that arrested the infection at once! I've no idea what it is or why it works, and I must have more of it!"

"There *is* no more," Varaa said regretfully. "Or at least as close to none as makes no difference. It's called 'polta paste' and is made from a fruit that grows only in . . . the part of the world I originally came from. In the years we've been here, we've used up almost all we had. Fortunately for us—and you, Captain Cayce—the paste may be reconstituted with its curative properties intact long after it has dried and turned to dust."

"We must have more!" Newlin repeated, insistent. "All the wounded I must treat . . . Captain Holland brought them in," he reminded darkly, "and when the war starts, as it surely must . . ." He could only sigh.

"I *can't* get you more, Dr. Newlin!" Varaa said, exasperated. Obviously, this argument had been ongoing. "But the people here have their own natural remedies that work just as well. They don't always work as quickly or comprehensively," she cautioned, nodding at the woman beside Lewis, "but she and others will gladly acquaint you with them, as well as remedies for the fever afflicting some of your men. It's *not* wholly due to the climate," she added sternly, obviously returning to another argument. "I strongly suggest you listen to her, as she and others must learn *your* methods."

Resignedly, Newlin nodded. "Of course. We have much to teach each other to prepare for the time to come." He stood. "Now, Captain Cayce, you seem well enough. Better than most who came with Captain Holland. I'll leave you to the myriad reports you doubtless crave, but caution you not to exert yourself."

To Lewis's growing consternation, Captain Anson came in with Alcaldes Periz and Truro as Dr. Newlin left. Both *alcaldes* seemed pleased to see him recovering and very relieved as well. Anson glanced quizzically at Samantha but grinned at Lewis. "Must be strange waking up to a room full of people, but it hasn't been like this the whole time. Mostly, it's just been the lady healers an' Dr. Newlin." A frown flicked across his face. "An' Mistress Samantha. Leonor sat with you a little each day as well." He shook his head. "Somethin' about you has stirred a maternalism I've never seen in that girl. Don't know what to think about it," he added flatly. Lewis glanced at Burton. Judging by the lack of surprise on the dragoon officer's young face, even he must be in on Leonor's secret now—if it remained a secret at all. He also briefly wondered if Anson was more annoyed by the attention paid him by Leonor or Samantha Wilde.

"I apologize . . ." Lewis began a little helplessly, but Periz rushed closer, holding out his big, strong hands.

"You . . . no apologize!" he stated adamantly. "Is us . . . apologize . . . you! You already save Uxmal . . . two times now. Us almost let you destroyed!"

Wide-eyed, Lewis looked at Anson.

"He's learning English fast. They *all* are!" Anson said with a hint of wonder. "Varaa told 'em there's not even Uxmalo words for a lot of what we have to teach 'em, an' our troops can't learn their language an' train 'em to fight at the same time."

"That's . . . unfair to them, and very gracious, but probably for the best," Lewis admitted, then chuckled. "With all their different accents, half our men can barely understand one another. Imagine how they'd butcher the local version of Spanish, or whatever it is. . . ."

"They call it 'Spanya,'" Anson supplied. "A mix o' Spanish an' old Mayan, like we figured."

"Makes sense, I suppose," Lewis said, then nodded at Periz. "But what's he talking about?" He glared at Holland, who'd kept silent since his first greeting. "I'll ask again, what happened?"

They all started talking at once, but seeing Lewis's pained expression, they silently agreed to take turns. Periz and Varaa first told him that his suspicions were confirmed; Tranquilo had apparently panicked after he saw the might and professionalism of the army that marched into Uxmal, and then got slapped down so hard and humiliatingly at the temple. He and Discipo (neither to be found) quickly plotted to sow confusion in the American camp (which worked too well) and murder all the leaders at the reception when they responded to the disturbance. As Lewis knew, that attempt badly failed. Still, seventeen Americans were murdered in the camp, and almost forty Uxmalos died. Twenty-eight were killed in the camp by soldiers (probably more than were actually traitors, sadly), but all were deemed Tranquilo's victims. So all the Blood Priest managed to do was inflame the city against his vile order and the Dominion, while further cementing the new alliance.

As Lewis expected, Holland's story was stranger. Under her jury-rigged masts, *Tiger's* scratch crew had beaten away from the shore for the run-up to Uxmal Bay. Even in the shape the ship was in, it should've only taken a couple of days. With the hazy coast still in sight, however, she'd encountered a Dom ship. Holland described her as a galleon, like something right out of the seventeenth century, likely built on the same lines as the ship that brought the first Spaniards to this land two centuries before. Holland admitted he was tempted to fight, figuring his old ship's 12pdrs and quarterdeck and fo'c'sle 6pdrs were a match for the galleon's equal number of bigger, if cruder guns. But *Tiger* was no longer a warship with a man-o'-war's crew, and she was packed with wounded. Quickly discovering that, with *Tiger*'s relatively clean copper bottom and sleeker shape, even her reduced sails could keep her at arm's length from the more awkward Dom, Holland ran north into the gulf, away from Uxmal. The chase lasted two whole days, all while the enemy closed or fell behind as Holland's crew strengthened and improved repairs to the masts, bent on new canvas, and exercised the guns. And regardless of her flag, *Tiger* and her crew now belonged to Captain Holland, even in the mind of First Lieutenant Semmes. He was the one who suggested shifting a pair of guns aft to the taffrail and rigging the necessary tackles to use them there. Allowing the Doms to creep within range of their own forward guns, Holland unleashed his new stern chasers. All it took was half a dozen shots before they shattered the enemy's fore-topmast and split her forecourse into flapping rags. By dusk of that evening, the wounded Dom was low on the horizon and Holland turned back for Uxmal at dark.

That's where the Doms found *Tiger* again, sweeping down behind her in another gathering twilight as if they'd known where she'd go all along. Holland wouldn't fool them again—if he ever had—and knew he had to fight. Fortunately, though a sad number of the wounded had passed beyond care, the Ocelomeh healers had helped many recover enough to at least use a musket. Even Major Reed, arm now safe from amputation, was sufficiently fit to insist they stop the Dom ship. So it was that once in the bay— well-known to some of the Uxmalos who'd joined the crew—*Tiger* turned on those who'd had her by the tail.

That was the source of the crashing cannon fire Lewis saw on the bay, just as devastating to the pursuing Doms as it was unexpected. Their ship rounded the point and sailed directly into carefully aimed, concentrated raking fire from the hove-to *Tiger* that sent all their masts crashing down around them and their battered ship wallowing downwind toward the coral heads on the west side of the bay. Their return fire was ill directed and relatively ineffective. There in the darkness of the choppy sea just inside the bay, the Dom ship struck. Jagged coral bashed in her hull, and she heeled on her side, an utter wreck.

"Well done, Captain Holland," Lewis said. "How many prisoners? We might learn a great deal from her officers—such as *why* they were so sure you'd come here."

Holland pursed his weather-worn lips, and Anson exchanged looks with Varaa and Alcalde Periz.

"There *were* no prisoners, Cap'n Cayce," Holland said uncomfortably. "No survivors a'tall, in fact."

"What?" Lewis exclaimed. "Good Lord. Did she break up before you could get boats to her?"

Holland shook his head. "It wasn't that, an' she didn't break up. She's ruined, o' course, but still lyin' out there while the Uxmalos strip her."

"Then . . ."

Varaa spoke up. "Captain Cayce," she said slowly, "you've . . . begun to see the evil the Dominion does to others, but they're equally evil to their own. The worldview of Blood Priests and the man you killed in front of the temple isn't yet universal among them, but it's no aberration. The common Dom sailor or soldier may not be as committed to their faith as Tranquilo's guard, but they're increasingly subject to those who are." She hesitated. "With defeat and capture certain, every single man aboard the Dom ship that Captain Holland so gallantly bested was either . . . slaughtered by their more fanatical shipmates and officers, or like those who murdered them, cast themselves into the sea." She paused, blinking, searching the horror reflected on Lewis's face. "I see you remember what I told you about the predators in the water on this world."

"My God."

Periz spoke rapidly through Varaa, unwilling to rely on his new English. "You should also see more clearly why we must oppose the Dominion," Varaa translated. "If they do that to their own, imagine how they'll treat *my* people when they conquer us."

Periz drew himself up. "Alcalde Ortiz has returned to Pidra Blanca to prepare his people"—he nodded at Alcalde Truro from Itzincab—"but we're all of one mind. The formation of a true Union will take longer to bring about than we hoped—Colonel De Russy raised a number of issues that must be addressed—but we'll take his counsel. At the same time, however, all three of our cities—at least—are fully united in opposing the Doms and will do all we can to support your efforts to support us. In all things to do with defense, we'll follow your direction."

"Right," Lewis said, unsurprised that the *alcaldes*, upon reflection, had drawn back from the bigger commitment of joining their city-states into one nation. The notion simply remained too alien for them to leap directly into it without testing the waters first. Hopefully, they'd have time to recognize the advantages for themselves. *We'll have to* make *them that time*, Lewis realized with a sigh. He tried to rise again. "My God, we have so much to do!"

Anson snorted a laugh and nodded at Lewis's bare chest. "I guess we can wait for you to put some clothes on."

With a reddening glance at Samantha, Lewis lay back again.

"Tomorrow is soon enough," Samantha said firmly. "They cleaned and repaired the fine coat Colonel De Russy gave you amazingly well. The things these people can do with cloth! But I suspect you'll want your everyday things?" She stood. "I'll have that hopeless orderly of yours, Private Willis, bring them in the morning." She turned to the other visitors and said, "Now shoo! All of you. Let Captain Cayce rest!"

When everyone but the Ocelomeh healer had filed through the door, Lewis asked Samantha to stay a moment. The painful memory of the bitter dream/final meeting with his father was still lingering heavy in his mind, and Samantha's mention of De Russy made him realize it was past time for him to sort something out. "I've a somewhat . . . delicate request to make. Pass the word for young Barca to bring my things now, if you please. I'd like to have a word with him in private."

"Indeed?" Samantha asked, but her expression told Lewis she might've been expecting something like this.

"Yes," he said simply.

Waiting for Barca, Lewis was more anxious than he'd expected to be. *Probably more lingering effects of the dream,* he thought. He liked and respected De Russy, but his ill-defined, perhaps even hypocritical connection to Barca troubled him deeply. Now his own failure to confront him about it sooner suddenly left *him* feeling hypocritical. The problem was, there might be a perfectly sensible, even innocent explanation for the association—he'd never seen De Russy treat Barca with anything but respect and appreciation—but he *needed* an answer to the awkward question that couldn't be taken back once asked, and regardless of the answer, the question itself might be deeply resented. A rift between him and De Russy now could be disastrous. Getting the truth from Barca first might help him determine whether a dangerous confrontation was even necessary.

"Good morning, Captain Cayce," Barca said a short while later after knocking on the door and stepping inside, carrying folded clothes. He had a clean bandage wrapped around his head but was otherwise dressed as usual, as an infantryman, except there was no branch trim on his jacket. Lewis wasn't surprised to see the new M1835 Springfield slung across his back. On this world, no one had made an issue over arming black men since that very first day. Lewis doubted anyone would, after the attack on the camp.

"Is it morning? I didn't even think to ask anyone."

Barca nodded. "Yes sir. For a little while yet." He smiled. "There aren't any windows in here, and I expect sleeping so long can warp your sense of time."

Lewis nodded back and then gestured at a little table when he caught the young man looking for a place to set his burden. He considered asking him to have a seat where the Uxmalo healer had been, but decided too much informality was out of place and might even come across as condescension. "So does activity," he said when Barca stood straight again. "We've been very busy. Still, that's no excuse for letting things go that should've been attended to sooner." He looked at the Ocelomeh healer and asked her to give them a minute, but she didn't even look up from the fine embroidery she was working on. "I suppose that means she either doesn't understand English or she's Varaa's spy," he mused aloud. "Doesn't matter." He looked back at Barca. "I've been meaning to have a word with you and Colonel De Russy, but decided I'd rather hear from you before I talk to him." He shifted uncomfortably, and Barca leaned to help him to a better position, but Lewis held up a hand. "First, I'd like to say I appreciate how you've attended to your duties so quietly and competently, even managing that villainous Private Willis. Doing much of his work for me, no doubt. I also want you to know . . . Private Anson told me you fought very well during the battle on the beach, but"—he frowned—"now I've heard from others that you 'belong' to Colonel De Russy. I thought that might be the case, though, considering where he's from, it surprised me. And it surprises me more the better I get to know him."

Barca seemed ready to protest, but Lewis said, "Please, I'd like to get this out. It's bothered me for a while." He waved vaguely around. "Involuntary servitude is the way of things in this world, just as it's been throughout history on ours. At least here it seems only captured enemies are forced to labor, with the only alternative being killing them so they don't rejoin the fight. That doesn't make it sit better with me, or keep me from hoping we can change it.

"On the other hand," he continued more bleakly, "as I told the men when we got here, I wouldn't be surprised if Periz and the other *alcaldes* eventually resort to conscription. That's 'involuntary servitude' of a sort itself, but if the Doms are as bad as they say—and I've no reason to doubt it—I don't even disapprove. Better that than what will happen to their families if the enemy wins. And even in the army, conscripts are still free men, *fighting* for freedom. I . . ." He hesitated, looking at Barca, who was now watching him with a strange expression. "I just wanted to say, to speak to you before I talk to the colonel . . . I'll insist you have the same right as anyone to be a free man in this army, to *choose* whether to stay in his service or transfer to a combat unit of any branch." He glanced at the dark-skinned Ocelomeh healer and tilted his head to the side with a slight smile. "If our time here has taught our people nothing else, they seem to have begun to grasp that white men—or black—are now a distinct minority, and skin color"— he thought of Varaa and actually chuckled—"or appearance in general, is no basis to judge the quality of an individual." Lewis snorted. "Background either, since even some of our most . . . belligerently insular troops originally from England and Ireland have lately been heard to use the words 'we' and 'us' collectively. My point is, between that and your fighting reputation, you'd be welcome in any branch you chose."

Barca looked down for a long time as if considering how to reply. Finally, he looked back at Lewis. "Thank you, sir. I appreciate the offer and may even accept when the time is right. But with respect, perhaps I should clarify something. Colonel De Russy did 'purchase' me from a family of long acquaintance to his in New Orleans. They were business associates, even related by marriage, and my relationship to their children—and the young De Russys when they visited—was more as a companion than slave. But then Mr. Mounier's shipping interests and health began to fail. He affected to take great public offense at the words of a creditor and met him under the Oaks in City Park." Barca sighed. "The duel was with pistols, at which Mr. Mounier excelled, but he was shot dead. Some suspected it was a 'suicide duel' from the start, to provide insurance money for his family, and that was the sentiment that ultimately prevailed in court, denying Mrs. Mounier any money. She was obliged to sell nearly everything of value to meet Mr. Mounier's debts." Barca's voice turned bitter. "That's when I first fully appreciated the distinction between 'family' and 'property.' What it really meant to be a slave," he added bleakly. "My mother had known all along and was terrified we'd all be split up—her, myself, my brother and two sisters—going to God only knew what fate, never to see each other again." Barca's expression changed, almost to one of wonder. "But the De Russys bought us all, immediately filing our freedom papers in the deeds office at Philadelphia. Colonel De Russy's lawyer, a Mr. Emerson, escorted my family to Pennsylvania himself to protect them from the slave catchers that are so active there."

He took a long, relieved breath. "For my part, I felt a strong obligation to the De Russys for what they'd done. Knowing the colonel would soon be in New Orleans with his volunteer regiment, I *voluntarily* remained to serve him in whatever capacity he required when he arrived." He shook his head. "He doesn't own *me*, but he owns my loyalty. Of course I 'belong' to him, in a way, after what he and his family did for me and mine." He looked away, jaw set. "And after the upbringing I had, the learning and *sense* of freedom and independence I felt—if never the real thing at all . . ." he added caustically, the betrayal he'd felt quite clear in his tone. Touching the musket sling, he continued, "Even the amateur martial training Mr. Mounier gave me alongside his sons—he'd been a militiaman in the battle there, in 1814, you see—just imagine what would've become of me if I'd been sold to virtually *anyone* else. I'm sure I would've done murder and been hanged."

Lewis was nodding slowly. "I suspect you would have, at that," he said softly.

Barca looked at Lewis again. "So, sir, though I do appreciate your intentions, I beg you'll leave things as they are. Even mentioning my sense of obligation to the colonel might only embarrass and distress him." He bit his lower lip. "He may not be . . . a professional soldier, but he is a staunch advocate for freedom and equality and an honorable man."

Lewis nodded slowly. "Very well. If it's as you say, I understand completely and apologize for intruding, nearly causing the very distress you'd like to avoid. I'm only glad I spoke to you about it first."

CHAPTER 22

The long, grueling trek to Campeche had been a nightmare of painful shaking, rattling, fever-racked delirium, biting flies and other insects, and the constant, nauseating stench of the armabuey's gaseous bowels. Capitan Arevalo lost all track of time, even who he was, and suffering and misery became the norm. He couldn't remember life without it. In more lucid moments he tried to console himself that this was *good* and he was surely accumulating sufficient grace to enter paradise in the underworld when life finally fled him, but he couldn't entirely abandon an impious yearning for the torment to end, no matter where his soul went. And very slowly, by degrees, he did begin to feel better, becoming aware of the continuing ministrations of the Holcano healer—she still sucked on his wound, but now only to remove the maggots she applied from time to time.

She gave him water then, from a reeking distended bladder, but he drank it with thanks. He was then allowed some dried fish to chew. By the end of that day he was sufficiently aware of his surroundings to note that the warrior chief Kisin was in about the same shape as he: weak and miserable, but alive and recovering. They began to talk, and it wasn't long before he heard what sounded like a disappointed snort and saw the terrifying visage of General Soor peering in at them. He said something guttural to Kisin, probably in his own language, and the warrior grunted.

"What?" Arevalo asked, voice scratchy.

Kisin accepted water as well, cleared his throat, and said, "You may remember I predicted a hungry march. General Soor had been given to understand we'd both reached the point of recovery or death and was disappointed not to get at least one of us. I expect he and his few warriors will have to eat one of their own now."

Arevalo shuddered, and Kisin regarded him, eyes still bright with a touch of fever. His leg stank, but not from mortification, only the rotting blood in the filthy bandage around it. "It's their way. Ours too as a last resort, but the Blood Lizards need to eat more than we do and can't go as long without. *Won't* go as long." He gestured forward with his head. "But it shouldn't *be* long now, since we'll be in Campeche by morning."

"Not Nautla?" Arevalo asked, astonished. He'd obviously been delirious longer than he knew, and they'd come almost two hundred and fifty miles. At least twenty days, probably more. He tried to reconcile that, looking at himself, and saw how wretchedly wasted he was. Still, the healers must have fed him something. . . . He almost retched again at the mental image of a filthy bosom thrust in his face.

"There was nothing in Nautla," Kisin replied. "I was awake when we passed through. Even the wild garaaches were gone—either already eaten by refugees or fled." He sighed and lay back. "Of course, we may rejoin the rest of my people only to find them starving in Campeche as well. The city has been abandoned these many, many years."

"Sacked by marauders from the sea, was it not?" Arevalo murmured.

"So some legends tell."

The next day found Kisin's dreary column of Holcanos and Concha Blood Lizards plodding out of the forest into the bleak landscape around the ancient city of Campeche. The road was bordered by rotting tree stumps and bramble-clotted fields once planted with crops. The city itself looked much like Uxmal, even Nautla, only considerably larger than both. Yet it was like a moldering, weed-choked corpse compared to Uxmal, worse even than Nautla, which the Holcanos themselves had ravaged more recently. There was life there, however, and more activity than Arevalo expected. They were in fact met by a squadron of Dominion lancers almost at once, its officer brusquely ordering the Holcanos and their "demons" to a dejected camp established for them south of the old city walls until Arevalo managed to rise from the box of the cart.

"I am Capitan Arevalo, envoy and advisor to Chief Kisin, war leader of all the Holcanos—who lies wounded here beside me," he gasped. "Take us to your *commandante* at once, see to our medical needs, and"—he paused—"feed all those with us, even the demons."

The lancer commander, only a *subteniente*, gaped at the filthy, bloody-bandaged Arevalo, wearing no uniform, but coming from within this mass of heretics and animals, his voice had to be genuine. "I . . . Of course, Capitan. Please follow me. Sergento!" he called behind. "Race ahead and inform General Agon we're coming." He looked at the Holcanos with distaste—he pretended not to even see General Soor and his warriors. "And make sure rations are prepared and the surgeon is called."

LYING ON CLEAN sheets on a cot in a hospital tent, Capitan Arevalo believed he was as close to paradise as he'd ever be, especially with the terrible filth washed off him, his thirst quenched, a small meal in his shrunken belly, and his wound properly cleaned and bandaged. He'd also just completed his report to the squat, powerfully built, and surprisingly solicitous General Agon, who'd begun by expressing his admiration for Arevalo's father, whom he'd served under as a junior officer, and went on to assure him no disgrace for the Holcano and demon defeat could touch him. He'd had no command and wasn't even at the battle, had actually been wounded protecting the leader of one of His Supreme Holiness's allies. All that and the fact he'd survived his ordeal was perfect proof he had "singular value." What made Arevalo happiest of all was that he needn't go on to the Holy City, where His Supreme Holiness might question that value, because all he could report—and much more—was already known well enough that decisive steps were being taken.

Sitting on a stool by Arevalo's bed, General Agon stoked a reed-stemmed clay pipe and lit it from a candle flame. "My Eastern Brigada of the Army of God is garrisoned in Mazumiapan, as you know. Its usual complement of four thousand men was almost up to strength, preparing to march west through the Holy City and join the Gran Cruzada against the Imperial invaders in Las Californias." He snapped his fingers. "Just like that, I was ordered northeast and told to strip every garrison along the way to Campeche, which I was to occupy and prepare for the arrival of *more* troops coming with Blood Cardinal Don Frutos himself."

Arevalo blinked. "I know these—you called them 'Americanos'? Obviously, I know they're dangerous, but I never dreamed they'd excite such concern. Has the Gran Cruzada been delayed?"

General Agon shook his head. "No, no, nothing like that. There are a hundred and forty thousand men at Tepic, preparing to move on to join those already gathered at Culican." Culican was the northwesternmost outpost of "civilization" in the Holy Dominion. Agon frowned. "Many will die crossing the terrible desert before they ever meet the enemy, so more men are always wanted, but my *brigada* and whatever Don Frutos brings will make little difference." He puffed his pipe. "And that difference can be made up elsewhere. In any event, from what I've learned about these Americanos, we're wise to deal with them before their half a thousand is joined by more heretic rebels."

"If I may ask, *how* did you learn so much about them?"

Agon looked evasive for the first time. "Dispatches directly from the Holy City, at first. I assume spies somehow reported. And one of the Blood Priests lurking in the region, in a teetering city called Puebla Arboras, arrived here even before I did." He frowned. "His name is Tranquilo, and he claims to have *seen* these Americanos, coming straight from Uxmal itself." He shrugged. "And Puebla Arboras—Cayal first—is where your Holcano friends must go." He said that whimsically so Arevalo wouldn't be offended, but his expression grew troubled. "Don Frutos specifically sent that he wants all the Holcanos prepared for a simultaneous campaign against the eastern heretic cities as we march up the coast and wants no heretics, pagans—or beasts, of course—with his army when it moves."

"Kisin and his band would be useful scouts," Arevalo said guardedly.

"Yes," Agon said simply before going on. "Don Frutos has never been in the wilderness and doesn't understand the importance of local guides. I believe he most fears the enemy will infiltrate spies among them. Ridiculous, of course. Holcanos and Ocelomeh can practically *smell* each other, but there it is." He raised a brow at Arevalo. "One reason *you'll* be so useful to me. You've been where we're going."

A sick attendant came in to check Arevalo, and General Agon stood. "One last thing. God clearly values you as a soldier or you wouldn't be alive. And aside from your being the son of a prominent Dominion officer I held in the highest regard, I do value your experience. But stay clear of Don Frutos if you can. He's a great favorite of the Blood Priests, who gain ever more influence." He frowned. "Their methods grow more erratic and unpredictable. I suppose they think, combined with their power, that makes them more fearsome—and it does—but they value examples above all else . . . even making them of soldiers from prominent families."

CHAPTER 23

Well never make 'em proper soldiers," groused the newly minted Second Lieutenant Elijah Hudgens to the equally "new" Second Lieutenant Felix Meder, glaring at excited young men in the 1st Uxmal who'd stacked their muskets after morning infantry drill on the "parade ground" where the Americans had camped on the east side of Uxmal two months before. These particular fellows were actually from Pidra Blanca—they called themselves "Los Pidros"—and would hopefully form the foundation for a regiment of their own someday. But watching them undergo their first day of training on a section of two 6pdrs from Hudgens's C Battery wasn't very encouraging.

Captain Cayce still required every soldier in the army they were building to have at least some proficiency with every weapon on the battlefield, being particularly insistent that infantrymen also be artillerymen and vice versa. Even mounted troops had to be familiarized, though the requirement was slightly relaxed for them. The dragoons, mounted riflemen, and Rangers—all six hundred so far—had their own horses now, as did a growing number of lancers Alferez, now Teniente, Lara was recruiting. Alcaldes Periz, Truro, and Ortiz were still purchasing or impressing as many of the strangely built, actually rather handsomely colored native animals as they could, but the problem remained that even though wild ones weren't uncommon in more open country, there was no real "horse culture" in the Yucatán. The animals were difficult to domesticate and keep in a land where their training and confinement made them vulnerable to myriad relentless predators, sadly affecting their ability to thrive and multiply in rural captivity. That made them precious, and the army's insatiable greed for them caused the first real friction with affluent locals until the *alcalde*'s representatives emphasized the stark choice between inconvenience or impalement by the Doms.

So just teaching recruits to ride and training (or retraining) horses took a great deal of the mounted troopers' time, and the material they had to work with varied. Some horses had been the spirited mounts of the rich, but most had never been ridden at all, taught only to pull elaborate carriages and treated like pets. The latter took readily to artillery traces, though teaming them and actually making them *work* to pull heavy guns was difficult—as was the continued transformation of the foot artillery into a more mobile force. Fortunately, most artillerymen only had to know how to stay on a horse, or hold on to the handles of ammunition limber chests. They'd have to get better eventually, learning to direct the lead horses of the teams, but they could absorb that knowledge from those who already knew how at the same rate as the animals.

In any event, considering everything the American soldiers had been through, all the work there was, and that few had much more real experience than the animals and men they'd been tasked with training, it had been a stressful and exhausting time. Barracks had been built inside the walls of the city after the half-burned camp was abandoned and men with special skills in civilian life were recruited from the ranks and teamed with local businesspeople and craftsmen to create a logistical infrastructure. Others went out to the various mines, frontier croplands, and timber-cutting missions (all considered hazardous undertakings and largely performed by captive or convict labor) to see things for themselves and report what resources they could draw upon. Some with mercantile or industrial backgrounds coordinated with their local counterparts to discover the depth of supply the "Three Cities Alliance"—as some called it now—could realistically provide, and what they could do to broaden and increase it. All that seemed to be going fairly well, if slower than most would prefer, but slowest of all, and somewhat surprisingly under the circumstances, was the growth of the army.

Second Lieutenant Felix Meder (who'd hoped he and his friend were being groomed as corporals, only to be elected officers by the men and quickly
confirmed by Cayce and De Russy) was now in charge of *all* their two hundred riflemen. Still attached to Olayne's artillery for the present, they'd recovered enough rifles from the dead and the wrecks to eventually double
Felix's force. The same was true in respect to infantry muskets. The 1st Artillery and 1st and 3rd Infantry had lost more than half their men in the . . .
event that brought them here and the battle that followed, but most of their
weapons were serviceable or repairable. They could theoretically double
their numbers with those alone. But *Mary Riggs*, *Xenophon*, and particularly *Commissary* carried more than a thousand new, unissued muskets
combined, so just with what they already had, they should be able to field
almost 3,500 well-armed troops. The artillery was in similar shape. There'd
been the batteries of 6pdrs in *Mary Riggs*, 12pdr howitzers in *Commissary*,
and another mixed battery of four 6pdrs and two heavy 12pdr field guns in
Xenophon's overturned hulk. The *potential* force was impressive. Unfortunately, much of the ammunition in the wrecked ships had been ruined, and
they were only now getting real numbers of recruits from the Allied cities.
At present, counting those they'd already trained—primarily Ocelomeh
and a few Uxmalos—they *might* put a thousand men in the field, with
enough ammunition for several hard fights.

Felix was sitting on his very own horse beside Elijah Hudgens and felt
compelled to respond to his friend. "They're coming along," he defended
half-heartedly. "It's their first day on your guns, for God's sake. The Uxmalos who were with us on the march have settled in well enough," he encouraged, then added, to lighten his friend's mood, "Besides, it takes longer
to make good artillery than infantry."

"But they ain't even good *infantry* yet, are they?" Elijah Hudgens countered with growing anger. "What're them dumb oxen teachin' 'em before
sendin' 'em to us? Button whizzin'? Hunt the slipper?" The Pidros were jab-
bering like children, practically crawling on the guns, while red-faced Corporals Dodd and Petty roared at them to take the positions they'd been
shown or rejoin their formations.

Felix chuckled at his friend, but when he spoke his voice was serious. "I
feel like I'm not really one to talk, but compared to the Ocelomeh, they really are like a bunch of kids when it comes to war." He gestured toward the
rowdy recruits. "These people work hard in an unforgiving land with more

dangers than we ever could've imagined before we came, but they know those dangers well enough to avoid them pretty well." He shrugged. "There's strikingly little disease, and people live well, especially in the cities. But war is foreign to them, like a lark. Like it was for me when I enlisted," Felix confessed. "The Ocelomeh have seen to that, and they've good reason to be proud of their efforts. But protecting these people from their enemies so well for so long has left them unprepared for what they must do now."

"Aye," Elijah Hudgens agreed, a little self-consciously. "I reckon yer right. Doesn't help that we're all learnin' as we go along as well, an' many o' the new NCOs're barely proficient at what they're tryin' ta teach. They ain't got the confidence experience gives 'em ta spew the kind o' authority other men see without thinkin', without even fully *understandin'* what they're sayin'."

Felix knew what Elijah meant and hoped that elusive spark would ignite in him one day, but officers and NCOs like that were rare. *We're lucky to have a few,* he thought, *but we need more.* Fortunately, a mere moment later, one such man approached.

"What in *blazes* is goin' on here?" demanded a thunderous voice, and Felix saw Sergeant McNabb's stocky shape stalking over from another, much more organized-looking section of guns and crews nearby. "If they weren't so much better behaved, I'd think they'd loosed a pack o' bloody goats on the field an' lured 'em on these beautiful guns by hidin' flowers down the bores." He glared at a young man with short black hair, little more than a boy, holding the spokes at the top of one of the fifty-seven-inch wheels just under the fellow, standing on the hub and bouncing up and down. "P'raps I'm mistaken. Are ye a goat, boy?"

"*No . . . no se, Sar-jant.*"

McNabb snatched the kid off the wheel and effortlessly flung him sprawling in the tall, lush grass. "Well, I *do* say, an' don't be talkin' back to *me!*" He scowled, looking around while a longer-serving Uxmalo translated for him and the Pidros quickly fell back from the guns and formed a line at stiff attention. *So they do know how to act, to a degree,* Felix thought. He also saw McNabb's eyes linger longest on the two corporals. "Yer all disgraces to the glorious uniforms ye wear," he went on. "Uniforms Captain Cayce *insisted* yer people provide ye, knowin' ye gotta *look* like soldiers if ye hope ta be one." He shook his head, looking at the fine, lightweight, sky-blue copies of the uniform he wore. The only apparent differences, for now, were the wide-brimmed straw hats and heavy moccasins instead of boots or shoes. "Wasted effort by Captain Cayce, not tae mention them that wove an' cut that cloth, then sewed it up fer ye," McNabb pronounced. "Ye might *look* a bit like soldiers, but ye act no more like 'em than a bunch o' bleedin' blue birdies!"

He didn't have a musket today but drew his short sword from its scabbard. Instead of menacing anyone with it, he merely laid the gleaming blade on his shoulder and touched it with his chin.

"Like as not, some of ye'll get a sticker like this. God knows we've got 'em ta spare, fer men on the guns. They're good for pokin' yer enemy in the belly if things get close an' bloody. I'll even teach ye how if yer chosen for a gun crew—though that'll be wasted effort on me own part." He sighed. Suddenly whipping the blade off his shoulder, he pointed it at one of the 6pdrs and his voice rose again. "*That's* the weapon ye *really* need ta learn, instead o' caperin' on it like flies. *That's* what wins battles an'll kill bloody Doms farther than their muskets can hurt ye. Learn that, an' ye'll only ever need one o' these"—he waved the short sword—"ta clear brush an' cut firewood." He lowered his voice and looked at the blade, glittering under the hot, bright sun. "Comes ta turnin' these red, they won't save ye anyway, 'cause it'll mean yer tryin' ta save yer guns—or ye've already lost 'em." He slammed the sword in its scabbard. "If it's the latter an' we lose the fight, lose the *war*, the Doms'll have yer families on spikes an' ye better hope *they* get ye before I do."

He glared at everyone, even the instructors. "So what am I gettin' at? What's the 'moral' to me story?" He pointed at the gun again. "Ye fight with *that* as hard as ye can an' don't ever leave it. Ye protect it as ye would yer families, since it's the best protection for *them*!" With wide-eyed Pidros wordlessly gulping and swaying, McNabb turned to the corporals and snapped, "Get on with it, then. If ye waste more time—waste these *men*— I'll have a handspike so far up yer arse, it'll squirt yer meager brains out yer ears!"

With a new enthusiasm mixed with fear, the corporals started grabbing contrite recruits and physically placing them in various positions around the guns. Corporal Dodd pushed a tall young Pidro up even with the right wheel hub on the left-side gun and handed him a rammer staff. "You're a 'Number One' man," he said tightly. "Number *One*," he stressed as the interpreter explained. "You'll sponge the bore and ram the charge." Stepping back to the line of men, Dodd fetched another and positioned him a pace behind the first, a long pace to the right of the shiny round cascabel on the breech of the gun tube. Handing him a brass priming wire or "prick" and padded leather "thumbstall" with ties to go around his wrist and hold it on his hand, Dodd said, "Number *Three*. You'll clear the vent—that hole in the back of the barrel—and tend it. Cover it with your thumb and press down *hard* while the piece is sponged or loaded. You'll also move to the back of the gun to help the gunner aim, shifting it from side to side with the hand-spike as the gunner commands. Got that?" The Pidro nodded uncertainly when the interpreter finished. "Finally, you'll prick the charge and prime the gun, so this job's *damned* important," Dodd stressed. He and the other corporal filled the rest of the positions required to fire both weapons: Twos, Fours, Fives, Sixes, and Sevens—gunners (the corporals themselves) didn't have a number—and told the men what their duties were.

Felix watched Sergeant McNabb finally start to nod to himself before he called for attention and boomed, "Each o' ye devils'll learn *every one* o' these positions—what they do an' why, an' in what order—even how to take on two or three at once in case yer friends're knocked on the head. Ye'll learn the drill till ye do it like a bloody *dance* an' can do it in yer sleep! Then, *if* yer chosen fer a crew, we'll let ye shoot the big buggers an' start learnin' ta *slaughter* the goddamn Doms!"

That actually raised a hesitant cheer, and Sergeant McNabb sent Felix and Elijah a covert wink before turning and stalking toward another section training under Emmel Dukane.

"Hard to believe you outrank him now," Felix said dryly.

"Aye. But as long as we have men like him, we might make soldiers of the rest after all." Elijah paused and smiled. "Me too. How are your rifle recruits?"

Meder frowned, then brightened. "Not quite so bad. Like Captain Anson's Rangers and dragoons, I'll never get as many as the line infantry, or even your artillery. And most came from the Ocelomeh before we ever reached Uxmal, as you'll recall." He paused. "Subject to the approval of their King Har-Kaaska, of course, which Varaa-Choon expects. I understand he's been southeast, toward Don Discipo's Puebla Arboras, keeping an eye on things. But he's finally coming here, and I'll admit I'm curious to meet him. In any event, hunters and woodsmen make better riflemen, and Rangers as well. Now I get to choose the best of those who've completed basic infantry and artillery training!" His frown returned. "I only wish I had more powder and shot." He waved at a gleaming 6pdr. "Just as a gunner needs live fire to get good with one of those, a rifleman needs practice as well—or he may just as well stay in the infantry with a musket!"

Elijah was nodding. "We can build an army, given time," he agreed, "but we can't bloody miracle it—an' its ammunition—from the thin air!"

"Ammunition manufacture must be our utmost priority," Colonel De Russy insisted again. He, Lewis, Captain Anson, and now Major Reed, were riding around the parade ground, where soldiers and recruits were hard at drill, accompanied by Alcalde Periz, Varaa-Choon, and Ixtla. Reverend Harkin and Father Orno shared a carriage with Captain Holland's "villainous" purser, Mr. Finlay, who, along with a man named Samarez, the "Procurador" of Uxmal, was attempting to construct an "Allied Quartermaster's Corps." Building an army was hard enough, but supplying it, as Lewis had feared, was posing even greater difficulties and causing the most friction between the Allied cities.

Periz glared at De Russy. "I thought horses and uniforms for recruits were the first things you wanted." After only two months, Periz was as fluent in English as Teniente Lara had been. He now swept an arm to his side, encompassing the parade ground. "I confess I considered the latter rather ridiculous at the time, but now I see the importance. It was something all three cities could immediately contribute together—along with *feeding* the army, of course. And not only, as you said, do uniforms make men feel like soldiers; it makes them feel like soldiers in the same army, no matter which city they're from. That helps build the unity you've insisted"—he held up a hand—"and I agree we must have." He shook his head. "But other things tear at that unity." Periz glared at the carriage where Samarez brooded and Finlay still managed to look like a weasel in spite of the new uniform he also wore. "On one hand, as you know, though there's iron ore in this land, we got by well enough with softer metals and never developed iron production. That makes iron as precious as gold. Yet you want us to hoard all the iron we took from your wrecked ships to make weapons. That annoys the Itzincabos, who want to make tools to extract copper and tin and lead from their mines—which you *also* want for ammunition, and perhaps even more great guns!"

"We must have lead for rifle and musket balls," De Russy stated flatly, as he'd done before, "and you wouldn't have us make roundshot out of that iron when copper will serve, would you? As it is, we can add what we have to the iron hoard and replace it with copper—if there's time. And we can ultimately cast more 'great guns' from those other metals as well."

"But how do the Itzincabos get those metals in the . . . preposterous quantites you demand without better tools? Especially if *we* give you all the blasting powder we make for their use in their mines as well!"

Lewis had been pleased if not wholly surprised to discover the Uxmalos made crude gunpowder for mining and blasting out the stones they used for construction. It wasn't properly combined or corned, and they'd have to build a powder mill to make it usable, but they wouldn't have to start from scratch. Still, Lewis had finally found out why firearms were so little used around here. The few who had them, like Varaa, some of her Ocelomeh, and various wealthy Uxmalos, got their gunpowder from some of Father Orno's brother priests (almost considered magicians), who ran a tiny mill upriver and made decent stuff in small batches. Examining the guns and ammunition Tranquilo smuggled in for his assassination attempt, they'd seen what sort of arms the Doms had. Some were old matchlock "trade guns" of a sort Doms once provided their Indian allies, but they didn't do that anymore, and the rest were newer weapons: robust, if somewhat crudely shaped and bored, flintlocks of the Spanish miquelet style. Varaa believed they were current Dom issue. There was no provision for a socket bayonet—Varaa said they used the "plug" type, inserted in the muzzle—and they couldn't be as accurate as American muskets for a number of reasons, but they were probably just as reliable. Equally daunting, though the powder they recovered seemed rather weak, it was properly and uniformly made. Lewis and Father Orno had sent people to the "powder monks" to discuss how to make the various granulations required and increase their capacity to a scale they never could've imagined.

"You'll have to increase your own production," Lewis told Periz. "Make enough to use in the mines *and* feed our cannon."

"And how do we do *that* as more of those who leech the *sal-petrae*—the 'saltpeter'—char the wood, not to mention quarry and transport the . . . sulphurus from La Tierra del Sangre—the very land of our Holcano enemies—are taken into your army?" Samarez demanded through Finlay. He, like Captain Holland, had already had Spanish and a smattering of Mayan and had combined them into the local Spanya as well as anyone.

Lewis frowned angrily. "It's *our* army, sir," he retorted sharply, "and the sooner you get that in your head and heart, the better! But as we've also gone over before, aside from the necessary training all must eventually receive, *your people* will generally, also necessarily, continue their lives much as they have. They'll drill once a week so they don't forget what they've learned, but will only be called up when needed." He looked at Varaa. "The people I brought here, the Ocelomeh as always, and a *small percentage* of townsfolk, will serve as the 'standing army' for the Allied cities, able to handle the Holcanos and Grik if they harass us again." His expression turned hard. "Unlike before, however, if the Dominion sends a major force, we can't fight them alone." He shifted his gaze to Periz. "*Everyone* must be ready to fight, and we need ammunition. Not only to fight, but to *train* to fight!

"Much of our gunpowder was ruined, and Mr. Finlay has calculated that we used almost seven hundred pounds—a *third* of what we had left—in our tiny fight on the beach! And that was fixed ammunition. We have to replace that as well. We have molds for small arms projectiles and can cast those out of lead, but we need paper to wrap cartridges." Uxmalos made a kind of rough wood-fiber paper but preferred parchment. Lewis wasn't sure that would do. He shook his head without pausing. "And we need thousands of cloth powder bags for cannon charges. Not to mention wooden sabots, strapping, tin cylinders for canister, something to use for slow match when our cannon primers are exhausted . . ." He shook his head, not even trying to explain what percussion caps were. Only the dragoons needed large numbers of them for their Hall carbines, and they had enough, for now, carefully shipped in waterproof tins. They'd eventually need more, of course. . . . He sighed at Finlay and Samarez. "There's more to do than I can even think of at present, but *you* two and your assistants must think of it all. And ways to get or make what we need. *Not* how to get by without it," he finished with another glance at Periz.

The *alcalde* of Uxmal snorted and pasted a pained smile on his dark, square face. "War with flaked arrowheads and spear points seems so much easier."

Varaa laughed. "You think so? You think it's easy to make such weapons— or use them? They may be cheaper in materials, but they're *much* harder to make than you think. I cast my own musket balls, as Captain Cayce says, and when the lead is flowing I can make a hundred in an hour. It takes *many* hours to knap a single hunting point for an arrow and a lifetime to learn to shoot it well." She shook her head. "And all my warriors against an equal number of Doms with modern weapons would be slaughtered." She glared at Periz. "So as hard as it sounds, it'll be easier on us all in the end—in every respect—to get Captain Cayce what he needs!"

Anson slapped his forehead. "Jesus!"

"What?" Lewis asked.

"Gunflints! We have a lot in barrels, but what about when they're gone? The stuff the Ocelomeh use for their points is more glass than flint. It'll spark like the devil in a flintlock *once*—as it shatters into a thousand pieces." He looked at Finlay, already resignedly scratching on a cluttered slate with a piece of chalk.

"I'll look into a source for honest flint," Finlay said in his dejected, reedy voice, glancing at Varaa. "Gunflints must be easier to make than spear points, and folk here should know how, once we show them the necessary dimensions." He took a long, mournful breath. "I didn't know Captain Holland hated me so, punishing me with this appointment!"

They all laughed at that, and it lightened everyone's mood but Finlay's. He still looked quite serious.

"Speaking of the good captain," Reverend Harkin remarked, nodding to the northeast, "he seems quite taken with his fine new ship!"

Everyone looked out to sea beyond the wide bay to watch *Tiger* sweeping past the point where the last remnants of the broken Dom galleon still jutted from the surf. *Tiger* was far from "new," of course, being almost sixty years old, but in her refitted, repainted glory, and without the weight of her long-gone lower-tier guns, she was quite a sight, flying along under a pyramid of taut canvas braced almost fore and aft.

"He's been putting her through her paces," Lewis agreed, nodding appreciatively at Alcalde Periz. "Used to such large ships or not, your boatbuilders were a big help with her repairs." He smiled. "Holland has no complaints about the seamanship of the Uxmalo fishermen who've joined his crew either. On the other hand, I know he's getting fidgety, just cruising off the mouth of the bay. He wants to stretch the ship's legs."

"The Doms lost a ship here," Alcalde Periz reminded, with a glance up at the walls of the city. Twenty-eight large-bore but light-for-caliber banded iron cannons—mostly 16pdrs, but about a third 9pdrs—had been recovered from the wreck, along with a large quantity of stone shot. Lewis was appalled by their crudity, and Holland refused to take any aboard *Tiger*. Periz was glad to have them, however, and stonemasons were piercing the high wall for gun embrasures all around the city. Lewis supposed they could be replaced with bronze guns after the Allied cities started making them and their iron could be used for other things. Until then . . . surely they were strong enough for the light stone shot they fired, and once mounted they'd give invaders a hard time in the bay. "They may send another ship to investigate," Periz continued. "It comforts me to have *Tiger* protecting us from the sea."

"Holland understands that," Lewis assured, "but he might protect us better with a more *forward* defense. Lightly armed or not, his ship can outsail anything the Doms have—that we know of," he qualified. They had no idea what became of *Isidra*—and all those aboard—after the ship steamed away and left them. That bothered Lewis a great deal. If *Isidra* was taken by the Doms on her way to a far different Vera Cruz than she expected, and Lewis feared that was likely, they may wind up with few surprises for the enemy. "I'd be inclined to let him scout about—once we're more secure here," he quickly added with his own glance at one of the embrasures being opened in the wall.

Varaa blinked thoughtfully. "It might even be to our advantage if she was seen doing so. In the short term, until their spies report her"—no one believed Tranquilo and Discipo were the only Dom assets in the Yucatán—"they won't know she's from here unless they *discover* her here"— she pointed out gently—"and might send much of their fleet to search her out." She looked at Lewis. "The Doms are very aggressive at sea, always hoping to pounce on peoples from other places or worlds. Not only to learn what they can from them but to prevent"—she shrugged—"what you and your soldiers are doing now. I once told you my own small ship was wrecked in a storm, but that was only because we were pressed onto a lee shore by two Dom galleons." She blinked bitterly. "We already knew of them, you see, and knew what they'd do to us. We drove our ship aground and burned her, taking our chances in the surf and the frightful forest. Many of us died," she said, matter-of-factly, then suddenly grinned. "But it hasn't been such a terrible life for the rest of us."

"*Divina providencia* brought you to us," Father Orno said with quiet certainty before looking at Reverend Harkin, then Lewis. "The same that brought you, I believe."

Harkin nodded seriously.

Lewis cleared his throat. "Be that as it may, our time could be running out. We're *not* prepared to face a real army of any size and never will be if we don't get our logistics, recruitment, and training issues resolved." He looked at Alcalde Periz. "You need to sort that out with the other *alcaldes.* You chose a 'looser' Union than originally envisioned, and that's your affair, but you *must* tighten it in respect to your mutual security."

"Indeed," De Russy grumbled. "If I may make a suggestion?" Periz nodded and De Russy went on. "I think *you* should start wearing a uniform." He grinned. "A colonel's, I believe, like mine! And start training a bit as well. It's . . . different where we come from, but I understand *alcaldes* are also the traditional war leaders of their cities. Not only would wearing a uniform serve as an example for your people; it'll show them and your allies you're ready to lead the defense of your land." He paused while Periz considered that. "I also think you and I"—he waved at Finlay and Samarez—"and them as well, in addition to Consul Koaar of the Ocelomeh and a modest escort of course, should *go* to Pidra Blanca and Itzincab, and perhaps other reluctant cities. Thus far, we've expected them all to come here." He shook his head. "Not the best way to win them over."

"I won't *beg* for their help!" Periz stated adamantly.

"I'm not saying you should. But nothing's wrong with begging for their understanding"—he nodded at the amateur logisticians—"and *explaining* why the things we need are so important"—he smiled faintly—"and how all things, all contributions from true friends to a common cause, tend to even out in the end."

"It would be easier to get their cooperation if the Doms were already upon us," Periz muttered darkly.

"Of course," De Russy agreed, "but then it would be too late." He looked at Lewis and Varaa in turn. "I agree it's time to 'scout about' a bit, and not just at sea. Deeper than the Ocelomeh ordinarily go, and closer to known concentrations of the enemy. Captain Cayce's right. We *don't* know how long we have, and we need a better feel for that." He nodded toward a line of mounted Ocelomeh "Rangers" and a squad of Lara's new lancers working their way along a distant tree line near where the Pidra Blanca road disappeared into it. "There are sufficient scouts now, I believe."

Lewis frowned. All the mounted men, even "professional" American dragoons and riflemen, were green, but with men like Boogerbear and

Lara, Hernandez and Ixtla, even Anson and Varaa to lead them—though Lewis couldn't spare the latter two—it probably was time to set them loose. *In any other wilderness, I already would have,* he realized. *But with monsters like the one that killed Lieutenant Swain, and the Grik horde on the beach . . .* He pursed his lips. *That's the whole point of scouting, though, isn't it? To learn* whatever *is out there. And with all the Ocelomeh in the Rangers and lancers, they should avoid most* inhuman *threats . . .* "Yes," he said aloud. "Captain Anson, please detail at least two scouting missions. Use whatever mix of Rangers, dragoons, Rifles, and lancers you deem appropriate. If Alcalde Periz accepts De Russy's suggestion to go to Itzincab, one scouting party will accompany them, then press on to Puebla Arboras and beyond. The other, bigger party will take the road back the way we came and continue on into the disputed territory between—what was it, Nautla? Yes. Between Nautla and Campeche. That's the farthest extent of the Doms' Camino Militar on the great map in the Audience Hall. If the Doms are massing against us, we'll see the first evidence there."

They were distracted by a lone Ocelomeh horseman galloping out of the east gate of the city. He paused a moment to gaze at the activity on the parade ground, then, apparently seeing them, urged his mount in their direction.

"That's Klashi!" Varaa exclaimed as the horseman drew closer. "He's one of King Har-Kaaska's personal, ah, 'aides,' I think you'd call him!"

"*Ave,* Warmaster Varaa-Choon!" the man called, somewhat shrilly, as his lathered horse slid to a stop in the tall grass. "*Ave,* Alcalde Periz!"

"*Ave,* Klashi!" Varaa replied with a glance at Lewis.

"Isn't that a *Latin* greeting?" Reverend Harkin murmured aside to Orno.

"I believe so," Orno whispered back. "The Mi-Anakka used it among themselves, and it spread to the Ocelomeh for formal use."

"Indeed?"

"Greetings, Klashi," Periz said in English. "I assume your presence implies your king isn't far behind?"

"The great King Har-Kaaska nears the west gate as we speak," Klashi confirmed. "He'll wait for you to receive him, but bears urgent news. Perhaps it would be more convenient to dispense with formalities and meet at the great temple in the center of your city?"

Periz glanced at Father Orno and his other companions. "Of course. We are coming."

Klashi wheeled his horse and galloped back toward the gate.

"We should all go, and be quick about it," Varaa said. "Klashi seems excited, and King Har-Kaaska will likely reach the temple before us!" She looked over at Lewis. "*He* will know things! Perhaps your scouts won't be needed after all."

Lewis doubted that, but maybe Har-Kaaska could give Anson a better idea where to focus them. He nudged Arete alongside Alcalde Periz's beautiful new black mare. She was booty from the battle on the beach and had likely belonged to one of the Dom "Yellows." "After you, sir," he said respectfully.

CHAPTER 24

V araa had been right. Har-Kaaska and a fairly large entourage of mounted human Ocelomeh and a couple more Mi-Anakka were waiting near the front entrance to the temple when they arrived. They'd been slowed somewhat by the carriage bearing Reverend Harkin, Father Orno, and the increasingly uncomfortable heads of their new logistics department. Samarez was more used to the presence of high officials than Finlay, but neither seemed pleased by the responsibilities heaped on them, or even how casually their momentous new roles were accepted. For his part, Lewis's daily association with Varaa and Koaar made him think he was inured to the sight of Mi-Anakka—their fur, wide eyes, even tails no longer shocking—but Har-Kaaska brought all those differences back to mind at once, striking him as even more outlandish.

He was bigger, for one thing, almost as tall as Lewis, it seemed, and alone among his party was mounted on a bizarre bipedal creature as similar to a giant lizard as a fat duck, complete with a broad bill protruding from its face in front of small, questing, almost thoughtful black eyes. And like the *alcaldes* at the disrupted reception, Har-Kaaska wore gold scale armor in sharp contrast to his black-and-brownish-gray brindled pelt, each scale as small as that of a fish and individually engraved. Engraved gold greaves covered his shins from moccasins to knees, and to literally top it all, he wore a high-combed Morion-style helmet—also gold washed—with holes cut in the sides for his ears.

The big Mi-Anakka urged his strange mount forward, sitting near the same height as the *alcalde* of Uxmal, and fondly clasped his forearm. Then he regarded De Russy, Lewis, and Anson with eyes as bright yellow as the gold he wore and held his right hand up, palm out.

"In case you're wondering, *that's* King Har-Kaaska," Varaa hissed. "Return the gesture, if you please. It's a traditional greeting among warriors unknown to one another where he and I come from. It's called 'the sign of the empty hand,' but since no one's hand is truly empty in this land"—she snorted ironically—"consider it equivalent to your salutes. You need not bow," she hastened to add.

It had never occurred to Lewis to bow, but he'd certainly render a salute. He and De Russy did so now, fingers almost touching the down-pointed brims of their wheel hats.

"*Ave*, great warriors from another land and world," Har-Kaaska said, grinning. "Greetings," he added. "I've not used this tongue in . . . many years. Forgive me if I stumble."

Lewis wondered once again why *any* Mi-Anakka spoke English.

"Greetings, King Har-Kaaska," De Russy replied. "We're at your service."

Har-Kaaska glanced at Varaa, then Periz. "As I understand it, we are at *your* service now. Perhaps my warmaster hasn't fully explained. I'm no Caesar, or even *alcalde* like Periz. Nor do I rule any permanent 'city-state.'" He *kakked* a Mi-Anakka chuckle. "I'm called 'king' because I lead all the Ocelomeh on this peninsula—I suppose they must call me something, but I exercise no control over Periz and his fellow *alcaldes*." He gestured vaguely around. "My domain may be larger than theirs, but it includes only the forest and wildlands, not the cities. We protect their people and they provide for us."

"So you're mercenaries," Reverend Harkin said lowly.

Har-Kaaska blinked at him. "I suppose, in a sense, but what does that make you?"

Lewis sent Harkin a sharp stare and eased Arete between them, holding up a hand. "Like you, *as I understand it*, the protection of these people from the greater evil is our primary concern, beyond any reward for ourselves aside from sustenance and support. But I don't understand what you mean by being at our service."

Har-Kaaska laughed. "You must be Captain Cayce, the 'hardened yet

idealistic warrior, motivated by honor, who thinks as sharply as he fights.'"
He looked at De Russy. "And you're the 'statesman, organizer, diplomat in
uniform, sensible enough to know you're *not* a warrior, but ready to use
your other skills.'" He glanced finally at Anson. "And you're the '*pure* warrior, who fights for a vengeance he'll never find—and perhaps other things
more like Captain Cayce than he knows.'" He laughed again. "Do any of
you disagree with those assessments? You see, though we've never met, I
know you already. My warmaster has very diligently sent her reports."

They all looked at Varaa, who shrugged. "I told King Har-Kaaska your
way of war was closer to the Dominion's than ours and you could raise an
army to face it on more equal terms. You'll note I'm equally objective in assessing my people as I am yours. Regardless, King Har-Kaaska had to know
you, know who he was dealing with, before letting even more of his people
join under your leadership."

"And?" Lewis asked.

It was Har-Kaaska's turn to shrug. "I'm here, am I not? I've left scouts in
place, of course, and must return to direct them. Varaa-Choon will stay
with you, to learn your ways of war," he added definitively before Varaa
could suggest they exchange duties. He puffed himself up and gave her a
canine-tipped smile. "I'm a king! Too old and too . . . *set* to learn to fight all
over again. And there'll still be need for the old ways." He looked back at
Lewis and De Russy. "But many of my people will be joining you for training. How the bulk will be used then . . . I *will* retain some say," he warned.
"The Holcanos and Grik are still out there, and one threat doesn't simply
vanish when another draws near. Often it's quite the opposite."

"How will we *feed* them all?" Samarez almost moaned.

Alcalde Periz cleared his throat. "Does . . . Does this mean *my* people
need no longer participate in the trainings? They can resume their lives as
they were, now that those better suited for war can relieve them?"

Lewis started to protest, to demand what he meant by "better suited,"
but Har-Kaaska's stern gaze beat him to it. "No. It means you must train
harder and faster." His eyes settled back on Lewis. "Word of your battle has
flown as far as the Great Valley and City of Mexico. Troops, *Dominion*
troops, are moving toward Campeche from all over the empire. Holcanos
and Grik gather east of there, at Cayal. They may raid past Puebla Arboras
toward Itzincab, at least."

Lewis looked at Anson and raised an eyebrow. Just as they'd expected.

"You'll be going back soon?" he asked Har-Kaaska. "We were going to send scouts of our own. Maybe some can come with you."

"Interestin' fella," Captain Anson said as Lewis rode with him back through the east gate and out on the busy parade ground. There'd be another reception at the Audience Hall that night, and Lewis and Varaa would post sufficient troops to ensure no recurrence of the previous unpleasantness. De Russy, the "logistics division," and the two clergymen had stayed with Periz to help arrange things.

"Very interesting," Lewis agreed. "Mi-Anakka look so very strange," he suddenly blurted, "but they're just people like us, after all."

Anson looked at him oddly. "People, sure," he agreed, "but I doubt even Reverend Harkin's ready to allow they're 'like us' just yet." He frowned. "An' they ain't, you know. Not with tails an' fur all over 'em." He looked thoughtful. "But all the 'His image' stuff in the Good Book aside, they're like us where it counts." He patted his chest and the heart underneath. "Has to be hard for Har-Kaaska just to turn his people over to us."

"With reservations," Lewis reminded.

"Sure. But not that we'd treat 'em bad or teach 'em stuff too strange for 'em, even try to take 'em away from him. He only 'reserved' the right to call 'em back under his command if the need arises."

"A 'need' defined as whatever he wants," Lewis objected.

"I guess." Anson said nothing as they rode along the wall to the north, toward the bay. A couple of 6pdrs boomed in the distance, firing at a rotten old fishing boat anchored several hundred yards from shore. With suitable copper roundshot already being cast, they had enough for a little live-fire practice. And artillery trainees formed at least part of the crew whenever a big gun was fired. It was good for them to be around it, feel the roar and overpressure and observe the basics of what they could do. They were too short on exploding case shot to practice with it, however, and no one had figured out how to make more. Lewis had some ideas, but it would take time just to make the things to make things. In the meantime, exploding case would be hoarded for battle, and any inexperienced gunners would have to rely on the tables of fire to set fuses. At present, the water around the boat amply demonstrated what kind of accuracy to expect from solid shot, and how to achieve it. A round from the first gun splashed down long, sending a plume of spray in the air. The second gun sent its shot skating along the top of the water, shattering wave crests, before slamming through the rotten wooden planks.

"Shows it's better to shoot short and skate it in than miss completely," Anson murmured, pulling Colonel Fannin to a stop.

A third gun roared, probably laid by Olayne himself, and the ball flew true and smashed right through the boat near the waterline, spraying jagged splinters in all directions.

"*Best* to hit what you're shooting at," Lewis quipped, "but you're right." He sighed. "We've got to increase ammunition flow so the men can practice more. We don't have *nearly* enough to make professional artillerymen! And the infantry has it just as bad."

"There's lead to make musket balls," Anson pointed out.

"But we're still stuck with the gunpowder we brought until the very *process* for making more is improved," Lewis retorted. "And what will the men use for paper cartridges then? Riflemen can load from flasks, since they're not supposed to get close." He pursed his lips at what he'd just said. "Supposed to" often fell victim to "had to" in battle, and he wanted their gunsmiths and blacksmiths (wildly important people now) to modify enough bayonets to fit their M1817 rifles if "had to" occurred. "But infantry on the firing line relies on volume of fire to survive," he continued. "Fast loading and shooting with *paper* cartridges." He snorted. "I never thought good paper would be as important as powder—and probably as hard to make. God knows how much the Uxmalos who salvaged the wrecks, even our people with them, destroyed when they burned the ships' skeletons. I should've had them save every old newspaper, logbook, and journal, even outdated daily reports."

Anson scratched his beard. "Well, there's at least a few hundred pocket Bibles amongst the men. . . ."

Lewis shook his head. "No. Those little books are all some fellows have to cling to. I won't take them away. Even if we did, it wouldn't make much difference. I hope Mr. Finlay comes up with something." He looked thoughtful. "Maybe wood or leather tubes with stoppers, like we found with those Dom muskets?" He shook his head. "Too bulky."

"It's always the little stuff you have to worry about," Anson conceded, then grinned. "On top of the big stuff." He grunted. "Varaa sure nailed you down, tellin' Har-Kaaska you're 'idealistic.'"

Lewis urged Arete onward, speaking over his shoulder. "You think so?

Then that means she was right about your vengeance—and maybe you're a little idealistic too."

Anson caught up as they turned to follow the lapping waves on the shoreline, working their way around huge nets stretched between tripods to dry in the sun. Soon, they drew even with the 3rd Pennsylvania, performing close order drill with Uxmalos in its ranks, raising its number (so far) to almost five hundred. The 3rd looked a shambles at a glance, poorly executing the most basic maneuvers. And when Lieutenant (now elected Captain) Wagley called for them to deploy from column into line, the whole force disintegrated into chaos amid indignant shrieks and bellows of harried NCOs.

Lewis was intrigued by the different training methods used by the 3rd and 1st, but had given Wagley and Captain Beck their heads. Major Reed, commanding all the infantry now, seemed to agree. The Pennsylvanians were using "total immersion" to train their new men, the old hands guiding the recruits at their side. The whole regiment would suffer for a time, but Wagley believed the new men would catch on quicker by example.

Beck was more traditional, forming companies of recruits who knew nothing at first while keeping other companies intact and ready. There were good reasons for both approaches, and Lewis wondered which would be best.

"Maybe you've rubbed off on me. I never imagined myself an idealist," Anson confessed at last. "An' maybe I've let vengeance consume me too long," he added lowly. "I've spent a *decade* burnin' to get even for my family . . . for Leonor. But you never 'get even' for somethin' like that. No way in hell to find the ones *really* responsible." He sighed and looked out to sea, where *Tiger* was beating back east past the point, a little farther out. "An' you can't kill your way out of *tryin',*" he murmured. "You only kill your soul, piece by piece." He blew out a breath. "Then this war started"— he waved his hand helplessly—"the one back home, where we met. I was after revenge again. For *her,*" he added significantly. "For Leonor. For what a few shabby, undisciplined Mexican soldiers did. I never hated Mexicans *as* Mexicans, even after the Alamo an' Goliad, an' when I fought 'em at San Jacinto. There were Mexicans on our side too. Still are. Sal Hernandez's been ate up for revenge—for *both* our families—as long as me."

He squinted at Lewis. "Maybe we hated ourselves the most, for not bein' there to protect 'em like we should, but fightin' an' hatin' was all we had after . . . what happened. Worse, I still had my Leonor, but she was . . . broken inside in a way I couldn't get at to fix. She couldn't or wouldn't go back to bein' a child, an' I couldn't leave her *again* . . . So, Sal and I, an' Booger-bear, finished raisin' her together, spendin' more time chasin' Comanches an' Mexican bandits than we did at home. After a while, Leonor wasn't a 'girl' at all, anymore. She was a 'pure warrior,' like Varaa called me. When our Ranger company joined General Scott to kill Mexican soldiers again"—he looked away—"Leonor made me take her, swore she'd go however she could if I didn't. I couldn't have her makin' her own way where I wouldn't be close . . . the next time. So, God help me, I brought her." He paused, and looked searchingly at Lewis. "What kind o' father takes his little girl to war?" he demanded in a tone of self-disgust.

"The kind who loves her more than anything, I think," Lewis said softly, suddenly realizing that somewhere along the line, he and this fierce Ranger he'd never really liked had become friends.

"The crazy thing is," Anson continued, "I don't even hate Mexican *soldiers* anymore. I didn't know it at the time, but I figure the proof is Teniente Lara. I actually like the kid!" He waved toward the city walls. "An' the people here could all be Mexicans, the way they look, an' all I want is to help 'em. Feels strange. I guess that's the 'idealistic' part Varaa saw. But lookin' back, even when we were with General Taylor"—Anson's lip quirked upward—"an' you thought I was a murderous bastard, I wasn't killin' in hate anymore. It was war, an' I was just doin' my job. I'm better at fightin' than anything else," he confessed, then frowned. "But so's Leonor now, an' she still hates." He hesitated. "You know she fought by Lara at the beach. I think she *wants* to like him. Might even learn to if he'd shed that Mexican uniform—but he's got the Uxmalos makin' *more* of 'em for his lancers!" He shook his head. "Leonor just can't get over . . ."

He shut his mouth as Leonor herself came galloping up on the smallish striped horse she'd chosen for her own. She'd named him "Sparky" for the way his energy seemed to flare and die. He was very fast and would work hard until he got tired. After that, she couldn't get him to do much at all. Anson disapproved of her choice, but Leonor liked the animal. At the moment, she was distantly followed by Samantha Wilde and Angelique Mercure sharing another horse. Both still rode sidesaddle, and the image struck Lewis as one of the strangest things he'd ever seen—aside from Har-Kaaska's giant duck-lizard. . . . He grinned. *And just about everything else over the last couple of months!* Leonor stopped and nodded at Lewis and her father while Samantha and Angelique drew near. Lewis noted Leonor's pretty but hard-edged face bore an expression he'd never seen. She looked angry, like almost always, but he would've sworn she also looked slightly embarrassed.

"There you are!" Samantha cried. "We've been looking everywhere." She glared at Lewis. "Your ridiculous Private Willis swore you were still in the city, only you weren't, of course. We went down to see Father Orno at the temple and discovered preparations for another reception already under way at the Audience Hall! Not only were you not there either; you sent no warning to *us* to get ready!"

Lewis and Anson exchanged looks. There was no excuse. They owed Samantha and Angelique a lot for all they'd done, assisting Dr. Newlin and adding their own insights from time to time. And of course, their very presence and generally bright natures helped maintain the men's morale. Perhaps most important, they'd become excellent cultural ambassadors between the Americans and Uxmalos, making friends with highly placed local ladies and (ironically, considering neither was a citizen of the United States) demonstrating that—despite frequent appearances to the contrary now that the men were housed in barracks in the city and enjoyed regular leave to mingle with the civilians—Americans weren't all just a bunch of smelly, uncouth barbarians. They'd even started a revolution in ladies' fashion, and Angelique in particular was in much demand for her dress drawings. Finally, receptions like this weren't just opportunities for social intercourse; the ladies obviously enjoyed them and deserved a chance to have fun.

"I apologize," Lewis said sincerely. "I'm afraid Captain Anson and I have a lot on our minds and are very bad company."

"Apology accepted, M'sieu," Angelique said in her quickly improving English. "Colonel De Russy has already sent a note requesting the honor of escorting me," she almost twittered, "but *this* time the two of you will dance with me as well."

Anson bowed in his saddle. "Of course, Mistress." He glanced at Samantha. "An' who'll escort you?"

Samantha laughed. "Captain Cayce endured that 'honor' last time and was badly wounded. And I imagine he had enough of my company while he was ill, whether he remembers it or not. I think it is *your* turn, Captain Anson."

The Ranger bowed again. "Delighted."

"I want to go," Leonor blurted defiantly.

Anson looked at her in surprise. She'd attended the last reception and been in the fight as well. He had no objection to her going again, but didn't understand her tone. "Well . . . sure. Why not?"

Leonor clenched her teeth. "I want to go as a *girl*, Father. Mistress Samantha's offered to loan me a gown," she went on rapidly. "She's more"—she cut her eyes at Samantha—"girl-shaped than me, but we're about the same height. . . ."

"And I can quickly alter a *very* suitable dress," Samantha stated forcefully, daring either man to defy her. Anson looked helplessly at Lewis, but there was hope in his eyes as well. Perhaps there was a chance his daughter might become more than a hate-filled warrior after all.

Lewis was silent a moment, staring at the young women, then out across the parade ground, where men were preparing for war. Finally, he shrugged and smiled. "I've no objection. If anyone here hasn't figured out Leonor is . . . a young lady by now, we should probably know who they are. They don't have the brains to be trusted with deadly weapons." His expression hardened. "Nor should that knowledge make any difference how she's treated when it comes to her chosen profession. She's proven how capable she is, and our strongest military ally and advisor, Varaa-Choon, is also female. Anyone who objects to *whatever* she wants to do—for the benefit of us all—will have me to answer to."

Leonor actually grinned, and the effect was striking. Gone were the sharp, severe angles and hard intensity in her eyes. It was as if five hard years suddenly fell from her face. Anson cleared his throat. "Um, in light of this development, Mistress Samantha, perhaps you'll release me from my obligation so I can escort my daughter?"

Samantha blinked astonishment. "I will not! As I said before, it's *your* turn!" She shifted her gaze to Lewis and arched an eyebrow. "Leonor is not a child, nor does she require the protection of her father in all things any longer. She might even be better prepared to protect *him* in various circumstances than the reverse," she pronounced, "and that's something *both* of them might profit from learning!"

"But . . ." Anson balked.

Lewis licked his lips and said, "I'll be honored to escort your daughter, Captain Anson. If she's willing, and you have no objection."

CHAPTER 25

Leonor had never felt like this in her life. She knew Mistress Samantha and Mistress Angelique had been working on her for some time, but the final decision to become a "lady," even if only briefly, had been momentous. And it came so suddenly, like the instantaneous choice to draw her revolvers and charge an enemy. There'd been the same flash of anger and anxiety, crowned by determination, but also a . . . sense of vulnerability she'd never even tasted in battle. Perhaps the strongest impulse was rebelliousness, however. Not against Captain Cayce or her father or the military conventions she'd flaunted; no one *made* her do that. But something inside her decided it was time to rebel against the dark part of her soul that had worked so long to construct the persona she'd assumed. There was another part, small and lonely, that still vaguely remembered a strong, happy mother who'd tolerated a willful little girl's preference for the company of her father on the hunt or in the field over more feminine pursuits. And that hazy, barely remembered woman never begrudged her daughter doing "boy things," because she knew her husband enjoyed the company. Leonor loved her mother even more for that, and had suddenly realized her bitter rejection of all things "girl" over the years had been like a rejection of her mother's hopes for her as well. It was much more complicated than that, of course, and she couldn't simply wall off everything that happened and all she'd become with the blue silk gown Mistress Samantha loaned her, but she and Mistress Angelique, barely older than she, if at all, had awakened those misty memories of a time when she *had* been a happy girl—along with everything else.

The gown was beautiful, but it felt so strange, so . . . *useless* when she put it on. And the shoes Samantha provided were uncomfortable and equally impractical. She'd groused half-heartedly, "How on earth can you ride in these? An' you'd cripple yourself if you had to run. Can't I just wear my boots?"

"You may not," Angelique told her firmly.

Then came the makeup, something Leonor never even saw her mother use, and she sneezed when the light dusting of powder went up her nose. "You need little of this," Angelique said with satisfaction, then added sardonically, "when you are clean." Samantha tried to do something with her straight black hair but had little success. It was too short. She settled for combing it back and curling it lightly inward at the bottom with an iron before—triumphantly, Leonor thought—tightly gathering the spray of hair that resulted at the back of her head in a slick blue ribbon that matched the dress perfectly—and according to local custom, proclaimed her to be "available." When Samantha was finished, she produced a wavy, wood-framed mirror, and Leonor regarded the image with fascination. "That ain't me!" she exclaimed.

"Indeed it is, my dear," Samantha assured, but Leonor shook her head in amazement. "I'm . . . I'm kinda pretty, huh? But damn, I look so . . . *silly*!" The ladies laughed and she hastily added, "No offense! Y'all look fine all the time, but I'm like a painted lizard." She lifted the wide, pleated skirt. "Is there room for my pistol belt under here? I feel helpless as a painted lizard too."

Samantha looked sympathetic. She'd gathered a great deal about what Leonor had been through, but Angelique shook her head. "This one night you will go unarmed and rely on the gentlemen to defend you—as is your right."

Leonor was dubious and a little frightened.

The journey from the quarters the two European women shared, adjacent to Reverend Harkin's and his "protection," took them through the middle of the tiny parade ground on the bay side of the city, surrounded by all the new barracks for the soldiers. A few locals had begun to move in—

Periz had been generous, and space remained plentiful—but even the local "regulars" were allowed to stay in their homes if they had them, as long as they reported promptly for duty, day or night. That left Leonor's "debut" exposed mostly to men who recognized her. There was shock, even confusion, on quite a few faces, and all the talking and noise of the troops preparing for a night on the town, or others just now marching dustily in from the drill field, was abruptly swallowed by a surrealistic silence. Men simply froze, staring at her, mesmerized, dumbstruck. A few pipes dropped from open mouths, spilling their smoldering contents, and Leonor was torn between upwelling fury and a cringing impulse to run and hide.

Sal Hernandez had appointed himself the "armed escort" for the ladies, Reverend Harkin, and Dr. Newlin. Now he glared challengingly around, one hand dropping to rest on a Paterson Colt at his side, the other absently twisting one corner of his monstrous black mustache. Combined with the look in his eyes, it was difficult to say which gesture was more intimidating. But Captain Cayce had been right. Most who watched her grim march in company with the others to the six-burro-drawn coach Father Orno had sent only grinned and nodded knowingly, quite a few with satisfaction. They *had* known, for a while at least, either from guessing or hearing rumors. And who knew how long and strong the speculation had run rampant? Leonor even reflected that, given their situation, she probably hadn't maintained her persona as diligently as she had in the past.

A new confidence suddenly filled her, and she straightened as she walked, still clumsy in the uncomfortable shoes. The most important thing to her was that whether the expressions she'd glimpsed seemed surprised or not, she didn't sense any hostility or outrage. That meant the men had accepted her as a steady fighter, no matter what else she was, and that was all that mattered.

The badly scarred (and finally sober) Lieutenant Sime was waiting to assist them into the coach. Clearly less observant or perceptive than most, he seemed utterly astonished at the sight of her. "M-my word," he stuttered. "My word."

"Don't just stand there gawping, young man," Dr. Newlin snapped. "Give the ladies a hand up."

Sime complied mechanically, but continued muttering, "My word."

Captain Cayce, Captain Anson, and Colonel De Russy were waiting on the steps of the Audience Hall when they arrived, nodding and smiling at extravagantly decorated Uxmalos passing into the great building. Leonor's father gave a big smile when he saw Samantha Wilde, but looked confused when Leonor stepped down beside her. Then recognition came, and his eyes nearly popped out of his head. Major Reed was there as well, arm still supported by a dark blue sling matching his uniform, and Justinian Olayne stood beside him. Both were distracted at the moment. Leonor noted the different shoulder boards Olayne wore at once and quickly looked at Lewis's coat. In addition to having been perfectly repaired, it now bore the rank of major. Samantha also noticed, smiling at Olayne as she advanced and touched a faded, gilded rectangle on his shoulder. "*Major* Cayce's old ones, no doubt?"

Olayne reddened and jerked his eyes away from Leonor. He didn't seem as surprised she was a woman as he was suddenly captivated by how she looked. "Uh . . . yes, Mistress. I'm proud to wear them."

"Necessary promotions, my dear," De Russy said. "It may have confused Major Reed's men to have him taking orders from a mere captain."

Reed bowed to all the ladies, with a special, gallant smile for Leonor, before holding up his good hand. "Not me. Even if I gave a damn about seniority, I've been helpless while you all did so much. And I don't have Major Cayce's combat experience." He shook his head and grinned. "I'm content to lead the infantry and leave decisions how to use it in someone else's hands!"

"It's not that simple, as you well know," De Russy said a little impatiently. "I'm doing my best to learn to lead while I perform my other duties," he continued with a glance at Reed's sling and a touch of embarrassment, "but you've at least fought, and you must be Major Cayce's second in command."

"Of course, Colonel," Reed assured. "I'll advise and assist him any way I can."

De Russy nodded, glad that was settled, then brightened as his gaze settled on Olayne. "And may I present *Captain* Olayne. Duly elected to lead his battery, we've put him in charge of all three. Despite his still-insufficient rank, I give you the commander of Batteries A, B, and C of the First US Regiment of Artillery!" He blinked. "On *this* world, of course. The local regiments are still being consolidated, but meager as it is, with Captain Anson's leadership of all other mounted elements, the um, Detached Expeditionary Force and Army of the Allied Cities finally have an *official* coherent chain of command."

He looked at Lewis. "All under *your* overall authority. God grant that they prosper and grow." Then, with a hesitant smile at Angelique Mercure, De Russy crooked an elbow out to his side. "Shall we, my dear?"

With a lingering look at Leonor, Anson offered his arm to Samantha. Leonor glared at Lewis, expecting the same reaction as her father's, but if her transformation surprised him, he'd already hidden it well. He only smiled gently and said, "You're beautiful, and I'm the luckiest man here tonight, to have you on my arm." When he offered it, she felt the most amazing flaming chill inside as she thrust her hand through the waiting gap and ascended the stairs at his side.

Dancing was another entirely new experience, or *attempted* experience. She was so incredibly clumsy! But Lewis only laughed at himself, *not* her, and apologized that he'd never been any good at it. She felt that same freezing fire in her chest. She'd been this close to men before. Her father, Sal, Boogerbear, other Rangers or soldiers she barely knew who'd thought her just "one of the fellows" and made no effort to keep their distance when fighting or performing tasks. That very familiarity and informality probably did more to keep her from violently recoiling from *any* man after that one terrible time. Even Teniente Lara had been this close during the fight on the beach, and she hadn't mentally drawn away from *him* as much as his uniform. But this was the first time she'd ever been so close to any man in a social setting, let alone allowed herself to be *held*—even as loosely as Lewis did it.

All washing and brushing aside, Lewis certainly *smelled* like a man. The scent of Arete was strong on him, as was the sweaty leather of his sword belt and boots. And whoever had fixed his coat couldn't completely remove the aroma of sweaty wool. But those weren't *bad* smells. They'd been in her nose all her life, worse often coming from her. She realized with a shock she *liked* him to hold her and was suddenly glad there were no pistol grips distorting her figure below her slim waist, bumping his right hand where he lightly laid it. She wondered briefly what he would've thought if there had been, then realized he wouldn't have cared. That's when she finally admitted to herself that she'd always admired him as more than a competent soldier. His broad shoulders and rough good looks seemed so intriguingly at odds with his disciplined, thoughtful manner. He was about ten years older than her but looked much younger this close—less tired and worn, as if he was actually enjoying himself.

The strange music stopped and so did they, both only then noticing they'd abandoned their efforts to follow the steps and finished by simply swaying back and forth—much closer together than they started. Lewis cleared his throat and gently urged her back in the direction of her father, who'd just finished dancing with Samantha. Leonor saw her father's expression, still wide-eyed and torn between satisfaction for her, no doubt, and something between worry and outrage directed at Lewis at the sight of her flushing face and how the dance ended for them.

Lewis cleared his throat again. "Perhaps you'd like the next dance with your daughter?" he asked Anson a little awkwardly.

"Damn right," the older man growled, then relented a little. "I've never had the pleasure before." He glanced between Lewis and Samantha. "I've the two of you to thank for it now."

———

No attack by snooping Dom ships or treachery by Blood Priests and their servants marred the reception for King Har-Kaaska. And it was as much for the Americans again as him, since that first event was so tragically interrupted. More important, all the people in the grand Audience Hall knew each other better now, and knew—with various degrees of commitment—they were in this together. Whatever "this" turned out to be. Building the army was a nuisance, of course, but so were the Holcanos and Grik. And making an army, supplying it, and sending enough sons to fill its ranks was less a nuisance than the Dominion would be if it came to Uxmal unopposed. Most people accepted that, intellectually, especially since the fighting that would constitute that "opposition" remained an abstract concept to peaceful people who couldn't imagine the ghastly nature of the modern war their new American friends were preparing to wage.

King Haar-Kaaska knew. Mi-Anakka and other species (mostly descendants of other transplanted humans), who'd built a civilization in the land he and his companions originally came from, had reached near military parity with what he saw of the Americans. They'd fought bloody wars of unification, then fallen into a terrible civil war that consumed vast armies across his homeland and slaughtered a generation. Since then, they'd fought to keep what he considered "real" Grik at arm's length, and he could trace almost every tactical and technological innovation leading to how the Americans were equipped and trained by remembering his own history and how others who came to this world influenced his people. Unless there'd been another "crossover" there while he was here, he thought the Americans might be less than half a century "ahead" of what he knew. But what they'd *done* with those few decades!

Now standing back from the press with Varaa beside him and a mug of wine in his hand, he watched the American "warmaster" Lewis Cayce awkwardly, even laughingly attempt to dance with a young woman in a sweeping blue gown amidst a swirl of others (quite a few wearing new dresses patterned after the foreign ladies), and the locally beloved music Har-Kaaska always found jarring. Varaa had told him the woman with Cayce was also a warrior, and she seemed oddly pleased by the pairing. "Both need to enjoy themselves very badly," she'd said. It was clear to Har-Kaaska that Varaa liked them, and he wondered how objective she'd remain.

"I suppose our human countrymen would find her beautiful, though she seems quite unconscious of it. But a warrior?" Har-Kaaska snorted. "Her appalling inability to master the few simple steps of the dance doesn't recommend her agility in battle."

"She didn't grow up in Caesar's court as you did, my king," Varaa admonished, "and this is the first time she's ever tried to dance, or even worn a dress. I understand that she moves quite well in battle."

Har-Kaaska changed the subject. "Her *dress* wouldn't be out of place at court," he granted, "which is to be expected, I suppose." One of the most recent "crossovers" to his land had been British sailors and passengers off a topsail schooner driven ashore in the terrible storm that swept her to this world in 1811. The ship brought people, yet another language, better weapons, technology, and a lovely design for fine, swift ships—as well as clothing styles still considered the height of fashion when Har-Kaaska and his Mi-Anakka companions last saw their homeland. It also brought news of Americans, who largely sprang from but weren't British anymore. Caesar added this information to the rest he and his predecessors had gleaned across the ages, trying as always to make sense of the mishmash of other histories touching his land. "And there are other similarities between their home and ours," Har-Kaaska continued. "Their infantry still relies on flintlocks, for example, though their newer weapons fired by 'percussion caps' are interesting."

"If they can create the facilities to make them here, they represent a real improvement," Varaa agreed. "They lend themselves well to repeating weapons, like revolving pistols, and work in virtually any weather."

"A formidable advantage," Har-Kaaska murmured in his own tongue when one of Alcalde Periz's servants brought a large ceramic jug to replenish the visitors' mugs, "and yet another thing we can't allow to fall into the hands of the Doms. Still, I'm even more troubled by the steam-powered ship *Isidra* you described, though not for the same reasons as Captain Cayce. He worries only about her people, but must be made to fear that the ship may be in the possession of the enemy even more."

Har-Kaaska's people knew the might and utility of steam and great engines were used to power cranes and other industrial and agricultural machines. No engine they'd ever made to move a vehicle had been as efficient as a large draft animal, however, and how could anything move a ship faster than the wind? But the advantage of a steamship became obvious to Har-Kaaska at once after Varaa told him she'd steamed away after losing her masts.

"If the Doms have her, they'll copy her," he pressed. "Eventually, they'll cross the sea and threaten our homeland." He glanced at Varaa. "Encourage Captain Cayce to discover what happened to her. If the Doms have her, he must destroy her or get her back." He blinked intensity. "Never forget, as much as I share your passion for our Ocelomeh and helping the people here against the Doms, my main purpose in staying here, probably forever, is to keep the Doms from *our* home. You and I accomplish this by remaining a thorn in their side, but Captain Cayce has brought us a spear."

"I was wondering why you decided to give the Americans so much support, essentially putting nearly all our Ocelomeh under Cayce's command."

"*Nearly* all—over time," Har-Kaaska reminded.

"Either way, you must think he'll beat the Doms."

Har-Kaaska looked at Varaa, wondering how honest he should be. Finally, he blinked resignation and sighed. "You forget that I was a prisoner of the Doms?" Varaa shook her head, but Har-Kaaska continued, displaying his fingers where nail-claws once were. "The Blood Priests hadn't even risen yet, making them even worse, but their ordinary priests didn't even attempt to torture me into 'converting' to their twisted faith because I was merely an animal." He wiggled his fingers. "They only did this—and other things— to make me safer to handle, to display in a cage. And because they enjoyed it," he added. "But I saw the Dominion as far as the Great Valley of Mexico before I escaped, and *even before the Blood Priests*," he stressed, "I realized we could kill nine in ten of the 'faithful,' but the one who remained would spring back to preach their vile celebration of suffering—citing the very suffering we inflicted on them as *proof* of their perverted dogma!"

The music had ended, and he watched Captain Cayce escort the young woman from the area set aside for dancers and noted the girl's face was flushed bright red. *Not from fatigue, if Varaa's right about her. Perhaps embarrassment?* he wondered. "No," he continued, "I *don't* think Captain Cayce—any of us—will win. No one we know of on this continent can, any more than our people could ever truly defeat the *real* Grik infesting most of Africaa." His tail whipped aggressively behind him. "But he and his people have quality weapons and a strong core of military competence to build around. Most important, as you reported, they're idealistic and determined and have found a cause they believe in. With that combination"—he blinked deep sadness—"I think they—and we—will fight very hard and come closer to destroying the Doms than I ever imagined possible." He sighed. "But there are simply too many of them, and their beliefs spread like a disease. As many as we kill, they'll only make more. We'll *convulse* the Dominion and bleed it half to death," he said with unusual savagery, "and from what you told me of these American officers, the battle on the beach, and what little I've already observed of Captain Cayce, the Doms will face a war like they never imagined . . . but I expect we'll lose in the end." He blinked determination. "Not before we set them back a *very* long time, however, and that's 'cause' enough for me!"

─────────

A different, livelier tune erupted, performed by some of De Russy's Pennsylvanians and a fiddler from the 1st Artillery. There were exclamations of appreciation as the locals tried to adapt their own steps to the unfamiliar rhythm.

Leonor held back when Anson tried to drag her into it. "I can't dance to *that!*" she exclaimed.

"Why not? You did fine before," Anson grumped, then relented with a grin. "Besides, nobody else here knows how to do it either!"

Lewis stood watching with Samantha Wilde. Strangely, he wasn't uncomfortable around her anymore and hadn't been for some time. Not only was he grateful for her attention while he was sick; her other aid to Dr. Newlin and the strong, positive influence she'd cultivated with the Uxmalo citizenry and especially Alcaldesa Periz had solidified his admiration. Being so busy with the army, he hadn't even considered courting her, but despite an occasional air of flightiness too much like other women he'd known—he now understood she affected for her own amusement—he liked her quite a lot. Now, he was suddenly surprised to feel her hand on his arm.

"You're a good man, Captain"—she smiled—"I mean *Major* Cayce."

"My father—sister too—who both aspired to our version of aristocracy—*your* level of society, I suppose," he bantered lightly, "would've disagreed."

"For all the wrong reasons, no doubt," Samantha assured. "But there's no 'level' between us. Certainly not here. My father was—*is*—a soldier, just as you are." She smiled. "As Captain Anson is."

"Perhaps." Lewis looked at her and quirked his lips upward. "I take it you're growing fond of our daring Ranger? It's obvious he's fond of you." He grinned. "Surely you've noticed the occasional . . . keen expression on his wooly face. Ever since we met you on the beach."

Samantha laughed. "Somewhat surprisingly, considering the frequent contentiousness between our two countries, I've grown very fond of all your officers." She looked at him intently. "You as well." She opened a bone-framed oriental fan and waved it briskly. Another of her affectations, though somewhat appropriate in the warmth of the Audience Hall. "Quite amazing, is it not? Just as well, because under the circumstances Mistress Angelique and I may have no choice but to attach ourselves to one of you. We're not fighters, you see, and we need protection. There's no great rush, but that's the way it is." She pointed with her fan. "I believe dear Angelique has already ensnared Colonel De Russy, poor fellow. He had a wife back home, but seems to have quite forgotten her."

Lewis shifted uncomfortably, pondering that. De Russy and his wife hadn't been parted by death, so any formal match between him and Angelique would certainly constitute bigamy. But Varaa was adamant none of them would ever see "home" again and De Russy's wife would be informed her husband had been lost at sea. He'd be "dead" to her, eventually even declared so legally, so what was De Russy to do? Some of the men had taken that aspect of their stranding worse than others, and there'd even been a couple of suicides. Most seemed to approach their situation more philosophically, however. Like De Russy. Lewis decided not to worry about it now, though he doubted the young Frenchwoman would consent to any "informal" match. And De Russy would know that would set a bad example when it came to relations between their troops and the locals.

Lewis condensed all that thought into a noncommittal "Hmm," then asked lightly, "And you? Who have you decided to 'ensnare'? You'll have quite a wide selection, you know."

Samantha arched her eyebrows in amused surprise. "Really, how could you ask such a thing?" She grinned. "I'll confess I had set my heart on either you or Captain Anson from the start. With all respect to Colonel De Russy, he was quite helpless during the fight on the beach. So was dear Angelique, for that matter. Both are adapting quickly and doing rather well, but action doesn't come naturally to either of them. They're well suited for each other. I, on the other hand, like a man with more fire in his belly." She snapped her fan closed. "I shall have to settle for the good Ranger—though I shouldn't call it 'settling.' His years and rough, 'wooly' shell aside, he'd be quite a catch anywhere."

Lewis nodded with mock disappointment, still not sure how seriously to take all this. "May I ask what took me out of consideration?"

Samantha looked at him, astonished. "Good heavens, don't you know?" She pointed her fan at Leonor, now laughing like a girl with her father. Something about the scene almost broke Lewis's composure. "*Her* heart is set on *you*, sir. Just look what *one dance* with you has done!" Samantha shook her head. "And unlike me, she *is* a fighter. A very lethal one! No, Major Cayce, you may be a fine man and a 'good catch' as well, but I won't fight *her* for you. I told you before, Angelique and I must find husbands for security. Opposing that girl would make it all pointless, don't you agree?"

Lewis was thunderstruck, unable to reply. Fortunately, he didn't have to. He saw Lieutenant Felix Meder purposefully working his way through the crowd in his direction and, after excusing himself, stepped to meet him. De Russy was near, and he turned as well. "What is it?" Lewis demanded.

"Trouble, sir. Bad. At one of the cantinas the off-duty men were given leave to visit."

Lewis nodded. He'd actually expected it sooner—just as he'd prepared himself to come down so hard there'd never be "bad" trouble again. He'd promised that capricious punishment would cease, but consequences for serious breaches of the Articles of War would be swift and terrible. "Very well," he said.

"What're you doing?" De Russy asked loudly over the music. Lewis explained and said he was going with Felix.

De Russy shook his head. "Lieutenant Meder, do you see Major Reed over there? He's standing with Alcalde Periz and his wife, and that large woman in the purple . . . whatever it is."

"Yes sir."

"Inform him what's happened. He'll take care of it."

Felix looked at Lewis, surprised. "*You're* not coming, sir?"

Lewis glanced back at Leonor as the exuberant dance ended. The girl and her father were both breathing hard, eyes alight. The transformation in both was astounding. Then he saw Teniente Lara tentatively approach Leonor and begin to speak. After a moment, to Lewis's amazement, Leonor gave a reluctant nod, and the pair waited patiently—at a wary distance—for the next piece of music. "I'll be damned," he murmured.

"He is not," De Russy said, turning his gaze on Lewis, who was looking at him again. "I may never be qualified to lead men in battle," he said matter-of-factly, "but I understand things like this. Reed is your executive officer, and you must rely on him as more than just your commander of infantry. Get that in *both* your heads right away." He turned back to Felix. "You'll recall that Major Cayce's evening was interrupted the last time he was here." He smiled. "I believe it's Major Reed's turn. Have him inform Major Cayce if he can't handle whatever has occurred, but I don't expect that'll be the case."

CHAPTER 26

Bathed, hair combed, uniforms brushed, and buttons and beltplates polished, Hanny Cox, Apo Tuin, "Preacher Mac" McDonough, and several other members of the 3rd Pennsylvania, Americans and Uxmalos, were sitting on benches by a long table at one of the "approved" open-air cantinas in the city. Hanny didn't know the name of the place, if it even had one, but it was festively lit by colored overhead lamps, very busy, loud with local music, and the food—beans, rice, dark-colored squash, and something that tasted like chicken—was pretty good and not too expensive. There was no telling the American and local "regular" troops apart from a distance now, since wheel hats had been made and provided to all—much to the disappointment of those who already had them and would've preferred the more practical, wide-brimmed local headgear themselves.

In any event, and especially after the attack on their camp, the American leadership had realized they couldn't keep the men bottled up forever. It was dangerous, and it wasn't right. But they couldn't just unleash them all on the city at once, for disciplinary and security reasons. They settled on a rotating liberty schedule allowing two hundred or so out at a time, and this worked fairly well. The men accepted it, and the locals generally welcomed it. The approved cantinas hosted dances, or *bailes*, every night, and everyone, even the locals, seemed to enjoy them immensely. Plenty of pretty, young señoritas attended, and the men were well pleased by that. Despite being a port city, Uxmal had little commerce with others and got only a trickle of visitors by sea or land. It did offer some of the same . . . entertainments the men would've expected at ports back home, but in a different, more civilized, perhaps less worldly way, and the small supply of "professional ladies" had suddenly been swamped by high demand. Most of the young ladies at the *bailes* came innocently for the dancing and music, however, perhaps even hoping to catch a soldier's eye for more traditional reasons. There was almost no rivalry between them and the professionals, since, in their minds, they weren't after the same men. The subtle, long-established means of telling the difference between the ladies was deemed sufficient to avoid confusion and embarrassment, once the Americans knew what it was.

Never a beer drinker before, Hanny didn't like the foamy, dark-colored stuff Apo called "chicha" and had chosen a tart-tasting fruit drink instead. He was sipping it now, helplessly staring at Apo's sister, Izel. She was easily the most beautiful thing he'd ever seen: small, wasp-waisted, in a bright-red, unusually tight-fitting Uxmalo "dress." Enormous dark eyes peered back from a cheerful face framed by blue-black hair. It was bound behind her head in a tight red bow before cascading onto her shoulders like a spray of midnight. Hanny had met her the first time Apo took him to his widowed mother's house just inside the city wall for dinner. He'd been besotted on sight. He couldn't help it. Now he went "home" with his friend every chance he got, in spite of the mother's obvious and growing disapproval. He thought—hoped—that might be because Izel liked him too, but in spite of his improving Spanya, he was too shy to ask her. Now he just sat and stared, smiling stupidly, trying to summon the courage to ask her to dance. He got the impression she was actually getting impatient with him, and that made it even worse. He had no idea how to dance to the weird local music and was sure he'd make a fool of himself.

Also apparently impatient, and keen to be seen with a beautiful girl on his arm in his dashing new uniform (wheel hat and all), Apo finally took his sister into the swirl of soldiers and young ladies himself. Watching them go, McDonough shook his head at Hanny and sighed. "I may not go in fer drunkenness, gluttony, er loose behavior like dancin' meself, but ye're a shoogly eejit."

"What's that?" Hanny asked glumly as the other men with them, even the Uxmalos, exploded in laughter. The latter still barely understood English, and the Scotsman's version remained even more elusive, but his tone was clear, and Hanny glared at them. "I was *about* to ask her when Apo ran off with her!" he objected.

The drum and flute music droned on, annoyingly repetitive and far too long in Hanny's view, but the boisterous, sweating dancers didn't seem to mind. Part of the point of the dance seemed to be to purge and exhaust the participants' passions, in fact. Good and bad. *Probably not a bad idea,* Hanny reflected. The music and dancing had reached a rousing tempo, like "Turkey in the Straw" often did before it ended, and the dancers were clearly exhausted and breathing hard. Then, somewhere near the middle of it all, a disturbance began and couples started spinning out of control, crashing into one another and falling down away from it amid confused laughter and angry curses. At first, Hanny assumed that was how the dance was supposed to end, but the Uxmalo troops in his squad were standing angrily, poised to jump into whatever had caused the disruption. A woman screamed in earnest, and shouts grew louder as the dance disintegrated entirely and the music screeched and rumbled to a halt.

Hanny and McDonough jumped to their feet as well, and it was then they saw the towering form of Sergeant Hahessy at the center of the commotion, luridly lit under the hanging lanterns. He was clearly badly drunk from the octli jug he held, chin jutting forward, hat tilted over his face so only slitted eyes could be seen under the brim. As always, he was attended by the usual characters: the skinny, grinning form of Private Cole and the other, beefier man Hanny didn't know. That one had a struggling, crying woman by the arm, her face contorted by pain and fury. At first, in a panic, Hanny thought it was Izel, because Apo was holding her other arm. Then he realized the girl's dress was yellow, not red. He was only *seeing* red as he and McDonough and the rest of their comrades pushed forward through the jumbled crowd. "Get the corporal of the guard—get an officer!" he shouted to anyone who could understand him. Several men, not all in uniform, rushed to Apo's aid, but Hahessy actually seemed to be protecting the girl's abuser, because he effortlessly batted the first ones away before lifting one up in the air and bowling more down with his body. They knocked over more of the crowd, and Hahessy roared with laughter.

"What're ye at, ye villainous bastard?" roared Sergeant McNabb, trying to push through from the other side. Hanny was relieved to see him, but between people trying to get away from the maniacs in their midst and others trying to help, he wasn't making much better progress than Hanny and his friends suddenly were.

"Startin' a fight, ye lickarse amadan. Ain't that what the fine Reverend Harkin tells us we're *here* for, then?"

"He don't want us fightin' with our friends!"

"*These* little brown buggers are no friends o' mine." Hahessy scoffed sharply, then roared, "I've no friends a'tall, 'ave I, Sergeant McNabb? May as well fight one an' all!"

To Hanny's surprise, he thought he detected a trace of self-pity in the big man's rage.

"Ye want a fight, I'll oblige ye meself, but loose that poor lass at once!" McNabb thundered.

Hahessy blinked. "The hoor? What for? Me fella's already tossed 'er a coin!"

"She's no hoor!" McNabb shouted over the growing outrage, fighting even harder to get through the press.

"Course she is—they *all* are, throwin' themselves at their soldier saviors. Some're just more honest than most. Look around yerself, will ye? An' her hair was up!"

Those who'd been baffled by the professional/nonprofessional status of ladies at the *bailes* had been taught that gathered hair in a social setting was a sign of availability, but only those with hair tied with *white* ribbons had services for sale. This girl wore a yellow bow, matching her dress, but with alcohol stoking their cynical, coarse natures, Hahessy and his companions seemed inclined to disregard such distinctions.

Swatting Apo unconscious with the same brutal backhand he'd given Hanny before, Hahessy grabbed the shrieking girl up and plopped her on his shoulder despite blows and kicks she rained on him. Reaching up the the V-neck of her dress, he pulled briskly downward, ripping the fabric, scattering her necklace, and exposing her small, young breasts. "Ye see?" Hahessy bawled lewdly, "Looks like a hoor ta me!"

For an instant, even the girl was too stunned to react to such an outrage, but then she turned into an absolute wildcat, knocking off Hahessy's wheel hat and kicking, hitting, even biting, so savagely that the big man finally hurled her away with a yell. The crowd reacted much the same and swept in to tear the three men apart. Hanny caught the slightest glimpse of Hahessy's face as the giant seemed to realize his "bawdy fun" had turned deadly. In the next instant, he was fighting for his life, swinging his great fists like clubs and battering rams, bashing people down and back. Nearly everyone was focused on him, of course, but this time his companions couldn't run. What's more, they'd probably just been along for the laugh of watching Hahessy cow everyone, as usual, or kick off a big fight between Americans and Uxmalos. They hadn't expected to provoke *this* kind of fight, in which everyone wanted their blood. A shrill scream of pain and horror came from around them, followed by another, and people started falling back just as Hanny and McDonough burst through. Half expecting to find Cole and the other man dead on the ground, they were totally unprepared for what they saw. Both men still stood, crouching low and grasping long, triangular-bladed bayonets, held by the socket rings, gleaming wickedly in the lamplight. Ruby drops fell from needlelike points onto several men they'd already stabbed. Apo had grasped the one named Cole by the leg, and the tall soldier, wide-eyed, inverted the bayonet to strike downward.

Hanny rushed him, head low and to the side, driving him back with his shoulder until he smashed into Sergeant McNabb, who'd also emerged behind him. Slammed hard between them, Cole's breath gusted away and he vomited on Hanny's back. McNabb brought his fists together, pounding both sides of Cole's head, and he dropped the bayonet, out cold.

"Behind ye, Hanny!" McDonough shouted, grabbing the burly soldier before he could stab Hanny in the back. With a snarl, the man spun out of the young Scotsman's grasp and stabbed him instead, the ill-directed blow piercing the muscle between McDonough's neck and shoulder. Drawing the blade out, but before he could strike again, Hahessy himself grabbed him by the throat and wrenched him back.

"Oh, Jesus, Mary, an' Joseph, jus' lookit what ye've done!" Hahessy lamented in the sudden, shocked near silence that fell. "Turned a bit o' play to bloody murder, ye have!" Wrapping his huge hands around the back of the man's head like he was caressing a beloved horse, he crooned, "Put the sticker down, now, there's a good lad. They're much too serious about such things here."

"But . . . they'll jump me if I do!"

"Nay, I'll stop 'em, but I'll push me thumbs through yer murderin' eyes an' mash yer wee brain if ye don't," Hahessy warned softly.

Eyes wide and without the slightest doubt Hahessy would do what he said, the man dropped his weapon.

Before the crowd could decide what to do next, Lieutenant Sime was pushing his way through, backed by Sergeant Visser and a squad from the 1st US that had the duty. "Back away, now. Stand clear, if you please," Sime was calling loudly.

Hanny left Cole with Sergeant McNabb and other willing hands to hold him, moving to check on McDonough and Apo. The young Uxmalo had managed to stand, and his sister had joined him, holding him steady. The girl in the yellow dress was gone, but what had happened to her was still fresh in many watching eyes, and the mood was actually growing uglier by the moment. No one tried to grab Hahessy, still holding his henchman, but looking up at him, Hanny said, voice simultaneously horrified and amazed, "You're an unspeakable bastard."

"I am," Hahessy agreed.

Major Reed arrived in the new barracks area, red-faced and puffing, just in time to prevent a growing horde of angry locals from swarming through and taking the three men Lieutenant Sime brought in. He did it by quickly assembling two armed companies, one of infantry, one of artillerymen, and physically standing against them while pleading with the leaders to disperse before there was more violence, swearing the accused would face justice. The crowd was equally irate to meet armed resistance in their own city, but finally backed away. Reed had "handled" it for the moment.

When Lewis, De Russy, and Captain Anson finally escorted the ladies (including a glowing Leonor) back to their quarters after the reception, they noticed the tension of the guards. They were also immediately met by a very worried Major Reed, just as a furious-looking Alcalde Periz, Varaa-Choon, and King Har-Kaaska galloped up with two dozen armed Ocelomeh running alongside their horses. The corporal of the guard sounded the alarm, but Anson immediately ran to stand the guards down and push the few already gathering out of the way. The local leaders surged into the little parade ground and dropped from their mounts by the American officers while the Ocelomeh practically surrounded them. That's when Lewis first suspected how much work it might take to save the new alliance and suddenly fragile friendship between the Americans and their Uxmalo hosts.

"I just heard!" Periz blared loudly. "I want those vermin handed to me at once!"

"A moment, sir, if you please," Lewis said, despite the warning blinking Varaa sent. Har-Kaaska revealed nothing, his furry face opaque. Even his tail was still. But Lewis hadn't imagined Periz could be this angry. "We've only just arrived ourselves. Let's get to the bottom of this together." He saw Leonor, Samantha, and Angelique come back out of their quarters, quickly joined by Reverend Harkin, still pulling a shirt over his momentous belly. Leonor started to come over but actually stopped when Samantha held her back. Lewis was grateful. More men were coming out of their stone-walled barracks buildings to stare, however, and Lewis called out to Sergeant McNabb. "Get those men back to bed. We'll start just as early tomorrow. Private Willis," he added, seeing his orderly in the doorway of the senior officers' quarters, "something to drink for our guests."

"We're not here as *guests*," Periz seethed lower, glaring at Major Reed. "We're here for the 'justice' he promised!"

"And you'll have it, sir, as soon as we define it!" Lewis snapped irritably back. "Listen to me," he added, lower as well, "we don't even know what's happened yet. *We* didn't storm your city seeking the accomplices—which must exist—to the attack on our camp, so you'll extend us the same courtesy. If we can't work together as equals and friends, our cause is lost from the start."

Still fuming, Periz pursed his lips, but Lewis saw a slight nod from Varaa. Willis rushed forward with a pitcher of wine, and Barca was carrying a deep tray full of mugs.

"I've had enough wine already," Periz snapped.

"So have we all, sir," De Russy agreed. "Perhaps *too* much. But let's have a sip for companionship's sake while we sort this out with cool heads."

Periz reluctantly nodded and accepted a mug from Barca, who gave Lewis a worried look. "You may send your guards back beyond the perimeter set aside for our allies, King Har-Kaaska," Periz said at last. "I don't think they'll be needed."

"I never thought they would," Har-Kaaska agreed, motioning his warriors back the way they came. The barracks doors were closing.

Once they were all served and the atmosphere calmed, Lewis hoped they were standing together as friends once more. He turned to Reed. "What exactly happened?"

Reed rubbed his eyes. "By all accounts—and there were quite a few—Sergeant Hahessy, Private Cole, and Private Nagler, all of the First US Infantry—*my men*," he inserted bitterly, "raised a shameful ruckus at one of the cantinas. A young lady was . . . unforgivably dishonored and terrified. During the understandably outraged reaction, three men were murdered and three more were seriously wounded. Others were hurt." He paused and glanced at Periz. "The casualties were spread about evenly between his men and ours." He flicked his eyes at Periz again and cleared his throat. "I haven't had an opportunity to interview the young lady, but again, given the number of witnesses, I believe we can spare her that." He bit his lower lip before continuing, "Those same witnesses all agree on who was responsible for starting it all and the abuse of the girl, as well as who the murderers are. Lieutenant Sime, Sergeant McNabb, and Sergeant Visser have all reported that Privates Cole and Nagler had bayonets tucked in their trousers, despite standing orders that no one go armed to the cantinas." He held his good arm out at his side. "A sad but common enough tragedy back home, when soldiers descend on a town—"

"Not all soldiers," Lewis stated flatly.

"Perhaps, but among the gutter sweepings we're given in the regular infantry—"

Lewis interrupted him again. "We called upon *all* our men to rise to this cause above what they were before. Even that percentage once fitting your description. Their origins won't defend them—or damn them. Am I understood? *All* will be held to the same standard." He took a breath. "Is there any doubt at all about their guilt?"

"We'll have to have a trial," De Russy spoke up worriedly. "A public one," he added with a nod to Periz, "and it must be quickly done. We have too much to do to let this hang over us." He seemed at a loss. "I suppose I must preside. I've been trained at civilian law, but I've never done anything like this." He looked at Lewis. "Whatever happens, you need to stay out of it. Above it. You have to lead these men in battle, and they mustn't resent—"

It was Anson's turn to interrupt as he stepped back to join them. "An' he has to lead by example. *Make* an example of those who don't follow"—he grunted—"gutter sweepin's or not."

Lewis heard the exchange with gritted teeth. "*I asked Major Reed* if there is any doubt concerning the guilt of these men."

Reed sighed, somewhat bitterly. "Actually, yes, in regard to degree. The two murderers, Cole and Nagler, have no defense. *Dozens* saw what they did. Hahessy, on the other hand"—he almost spat the name—"who actually started everything and dishonored the young lady himself, not only had nothing to do with the killings, but saved a man's life and apprehended one of the murderers. He was very drunk, but unarmed."

"'Degree,' indeed," Lewis smoldered. "I know this Hahessy, and I'd wager none of this would've happened without him, nor does he need to be armed to kill."

"The man's a beast," Reed agreed.

Lewis sighed. "But not a murderer."

"Not that anyone saw," Reed said.

Lewis looked at Periz, Varaa, and Har-Kaaska, then back at Colonel De Russy. "There'll be no public trial. We—all of us here—will listen to what the accused have to say for themselves in the morning and render summary judgment."

"But—" De Russy began.

Lewis cut him off, this time. "That *is* in accordance with the Articles of War in extraordinary circumstances, in case that was the objection you were about to make. If you don't think our situation is 'extraordinary,' I shudder to imagine your definition. As you say, Colonel, we have no time for this, nor can we let it divide us." He faced Periz once more. "And we have to make sure neither of our peoples preys on the other again." He paused, considering. "How do you conduct executions?"

Periz blinked, surprised. "We don't. Those who can't live peacefully among us aren't allowed to." He frowned. "Sometimes a mob rises up and kills them, as perhaps nearly happened tonight," he said with the first trace of apology in his tone, "but usually they're whipped and sent into the terrible wild for God to decide their fate. To do otherwise would make us like the Doms." He gestured at Varaa and Har-Kaaska. "We came here tonight to ensure your bad men would be whipped and banished. Not to kill them."

Lewis shook his head. "You came to *demand* of us, but now I'll demand of you. The two murderers, at least, will have to die, Alcalde Periz. Hanged by a rope around their necks. And not only for what they did, but to show *your* people what'll happen if they run from battle. We hang deserters too. Going forward, *you* will hang deserters, enemy spies, murderers, and rapists as well. We must be of one mind on this—we can't have different laws for my people and yours—and until you join with the other cities and build your own country with equal laws for everyone, we'll have to make do with the Articles of War. It's the only way." He was tired and took a tired breath. "That doesn't make us anything like the Doms. We don't kill people on a whim, for pleasure, or for any twisted notion that it's God's will. We do it to protect others from them, period. Releasing murderers and rapists into the wild . . . If the beasts don't get them, they can only continue to prey on trav- elers and those living farthest from aid. That won't do anymore, Alcalde Periz, not for any of us." He saw Varaa nodding slightly, but Har-Kaaska was still inscrutable. Lewis took off his hat and ran fingers through sweaty hair. "Now that we know God has more than one world to watch over, I fi- nally understand why His attention is so often elsewhere and we have to do the hard things ourselves from time to time."

UNDER A SUDDENLY dreary gray sky the following morning, in front of most of the city and all the troops gathered in the temple square—the only place capable of accommodating so many—Sergeant Hahessy was stripped of his rank by Major Reed and given forty lashes by the city punisher—a man at least as large and strong as Hahessy himself. The locals seemed pleased by that. Word of what happened had spread like the wind, and the familiar punishment seemed appropriate. Some might've been disap- pointed that Hahessy took it without a whimper, even outraged when he was led away by an Uxmalo healer instead of shoved bleeding through the city gate to fend for himself in the wild, but the two grisly hangings imme- diately after silenced any protest they might've made. No gallows was rigged, there hadn't been time, but the executions were quickly, efficiently, even humanely performed under tall tripods; the platforms on which the guilty were placed were simply jerked out from under them so they could drop the specified distance. Both died quickly, necks cleanly broken, in vivid contrast to executions performed by the Doms.

The hangings doubtless disturbed a populace unused to *seeing* con- demned criminals die, but also seemed to strike them as appropriate. What's more, the fact that *all* their leaders, Uxmalo, Ocelomeh, and Amer- ican, along with Father Orno and Reverend Harkin, had gathered together to proclaim their guilt, pass the sentence, and see it carried out, probably did more than just heal the rift the crime nearly caused. And though ini- tially met with hushed apprehension, Periz's proclamation that in this time of emergency, this new punishment would be meted out to *all* convicted of heinous crimes, no matter who they were, the justice and certainty of shared rules and consequences brought the troops and locals closer as well. All had been nervous about what would happen next, but the promise of better behavior the hangings gave the people, and the equally strong assurance that the Americans wouldn't abandon them came as a tremendous relief.

"Odd," Reverend Harkin said to Orno in the strangely comforted aftermath while people dispersed and the troops marched out the east gate for their daily training.

"Odd how, my friend?" Orno asked.

Harkin shrugged. "That suffering and death should *relieve* people so."

Orno put his hand on Harkin's dark coat sleeve. "All else aside, my people are very afraid. They hate and fear the Dominion and its creatures, the Grik and Holcanos, but fear just as much how unprepared they are to face them. And even as they rely on your Americans for help, they believe your very presence made that long-dreaded confrontation inevitable. Combined with the disruption your arrival has brought to their generally peaceful little lives, they can't help but be fearful, resentful, and grateful all at once!" Orno shook his head. "But after what happened last night, they awakened today with an even greater fear that you'd *all* be cast out. Or angered by everything else that's occurred—the attack on your camp, the near riot last night. Major Cayce might simply choose to leave.

"Your people might've feared those things as well," Orno continued, "and *everyone's* ashamed of things. Now? It's like the battle at the beach, in a way. Your people and the Ocelomeh grew close after fighting and suffering together. Now your people and the Uxmalos have suffered from mutual shame, which might be even worse. With as much suffering as we'll all likely share in the future . . ." The little priest shrugged. "This day's dreadful events might've been for the best."

Harkin felt big, heavy raindrops start pattering the wide brim of his hat. "Blast," he murmured, then brightened. "My apologies. As dry as this land seems, a good rain is just the thing to settle the dust."

Orno was looking at the sky, more rain splashing his face. "It will do more than settle the dust. Today, tomorrow—perhaps Ixtla knows—the rains will come in earnest. Crops will thrive, the Cipactli River will rise, and preparations will become more difficult."

"Well," Harkin said. "If I understand correctly, that means we have a couple of months before the Doms begin to move the forces King Har-Kaaska suggests are building near Campeche and Cayal. Time for Major Cayce to continue to train his army. He'll adapt, I assure you."

"I never doubted it. But many of the things he so desperately needs—more gunpowder, for example, which can only be made when it's dry, I believe—will have to wait. Even the mines for the copper shot he wants will flood and close. So yes, perhaps two months before the Doms march, but just as long before it's dry enough to properly continue making ready for them." They saw Lewis, Periz, Varaa, and Anson now, as the rain picked up and started falling in sheets. They were facing Har-Kaaska, Boogerbear, Lieutenant Burton, and Teniente Lara. Behind were drawn up Har-Kaaska's warriors, as well as the Rangers, lancers, and dragoons that would both accompany Har-Kaaska and strike out on their own.

"*Septiembre*, I believe," Orno said, tugging Harkin's coat and motioning toward the shelter of the temple. "In September we will know what's coming, and what we have to stand against it."

CHAPTER 27

"Rain and mud are everywhere, with every step we sink,
Our uniforms are rotting off, and in our bunks we stink."

Private Hanny Cox's little rhyme was met by tired, half-hearted chuckles that turned to groans as he and the men around him heaved with all their might on a bogged-down 6pdr, half-sunk in the slurry of a rutted forest path several miles south of Uxmal. His battalion of the 3rd Pennsylvania, a battalion of the 1st Uxmal, and Hudgens's C Battery of the 1st US Artillery (along with a flanking battalion of Ocelomeh to discourage the forest monsters) had been on field manuevers for the last three days (and nights), and it hadn't stopped raining the entire time. Everyone was exhausted and miserable, and a lot of the troops complained because the enemy wasn't expected until the dry season. But Hanny knew they couldn't count on that and it actually *might* rain even then. Besides, he figured if they learned to move troops and guns swiftly in these conditions, it almost couldn't get harder. He, for one, welcomed the tough training for all their sakes. Just because he was more philosophical about it than most didn't mean he enjoyed it, however, and he'd been diverting himself and his comrades by coming up with little ditties, usually changing the words of famous works he'd read to fit their circumstances. He himself was pushing on a slippery spoke of the stranded gun, trying to get a purchase with sodden, mud-caked shoes that seemed to weigh ten pounds apiece while the four-up team of horses hitched to the limber strained in their traces, the gun's crew dismounted and pushing and pulling as well.

"What was that, Private?" Lieutenant Elijah Hudgens called down from his horse, squelching to and fro beside them. He was the one who'd "stolen" Hanny's squad from the passing infantry to "muck aboot" in the mud, as McDonough put it, in the first place. Lieutenant Hudgens wasn't covered all over in the stuff like Hanny and his comrades, but his oilcloth cape was saturated, and he was just as soaking wet under the rain as anyone.

"Nothing, sir," Hanny wheezed.

"I ain't exactly educated," snorted Elijah Hudgens, "but even I know the source o' that'un. P'raps we could hang one o' those offensive little lizard-birds 'round your neck ta inspire your wit further. Are you a *educated* man, Private Cox?"

Hanny was surprised the lieutenant remembered his name. He'd been just another private the day they stood against Hahessy together. "I've read a lot," he confessed self-consciously, voice strained as he put his shoulder to the spoke.

"Educated an' imaginative too. Have you any notion what a dangerous mix that is for an infantryman? Bloody hell, why didn't you get pinched for the artillery when you had your training? I remember now. You were pretty good. 'Specially as a gunner. You hit your mark, first try."

"Yes sir," Hanny admitted, looking around at his squad-mates now. "I chose to stay with the infantry."

"In God's name, why?" Elijah demanded in humorous horror, and the artillerymen on the mud-spattered piece laughed weakly.

The truth was, Hanny had friends in the squad, friends for the first time in his life, and one of them was Apo Tuin, who had a sister he was crazy about. He couldn't admit that, of course. "Well, sir," he said instead, "the fact of the matter is, I may be tall, but I'm not very strong. Can't even carry a musket. They had to make me color-bearer so they could pretend I was useful for something, even in the infantry." He shook his head. "No sir, *everything* in the artillery is heavy, and I'm just not cut out for heaving cannons out of mudholes."

Everybody laughed at that, even Hudgens, but as he kicked his horse forward into the drizzling gloom he called back, "Everyone knows why they picked you for color-bearer, Private Cox, an' it ain't because you're weak."

"He a nice officer," Apo grunted, his English much improved. "He say nice thing to you. I tell Izel."

"Why should she care? Your mother won't even let me come over anymore."

Apo's eyes flashed with humor, visible even in the darkness. "*Mi . . .* mother *y hermana* don't always care about same things."

"What's that woman got against you, anyhow?" asked another of the fellows. Most of them had Uxmalo sweethearts by now, and Hanny's crush was common knowledge. "You get too grabby or something?"

"No!" Hanny snapped indignantly.

Apo laughed. "She say Hanny *es . . . demasiado blanco . . .* too white, yes? She say he look sick. Make sick babies!"

There was a little more laughter, but several of the men seemed more thoughtful than amused.

"Aye, weel, they'd be skinny enow," Preacher Mac finally said.

More horses were splashing and plapping up behind them, and Hanny recognized Captain Anson and Teniente Lara leading a soggy, mixed squadron of Rangers and lancers. Most rumbled and splattered past without a glance, geysering globs of mud as they went, but he heard someone near the rear call out, "Hey, hold up there. Let's give these fellas a hand." Half a dozen riders pulled up, then fell back to join two already stopped. Hanny was surprised to see Leonor Anson, as rough and scruffy and lethal looking as always once more, but was even more startled to see Colonel De Russy's servant Barca mounted beside her. "You don't mind the delay?" Leonor asked him.

"I'm in no hurry, Lieutenant," Barca said with a smile. "I'm just along to 'observe' for the colonel."

"Fine. C'mon, fellas, let's go up in front of the team an' tie on to the traces."

Barca made a face and slid down from his horse. "I'll help out here, I think. I can barely stay on a horse when all it's doing is trying to carry me."

"You're gonna get muddy"—Leonor laughed—"but suit yourself."

"I'm sure I'll wash off fairly quickly," Barca responded wryly, tying his horse to a tree and stepping over near Hanny. They all had a moment to rest then, while Leonor directed the addition of her men's horses to the tired team.

"You're Private Hannibal Cox, aren't you?" Barca asked.

Hanny was startled again to find himself so well-known. "Uh, yes . . ." Then he was at a loss for how to address De Russy's servant. Should he call him "sir" or what? He was *practically* an officer, wasn't he? And Hanny'd watched him fight like the very devil on the beach. But before joining the army and leaving his rural home for the first time, Hanny had never seen a black person in his life. He knew about them, and slavery of course, and had seen it for himself both in New Orleans and here, where Holcano captives—more like prisoners of war, he figured—were set to labor, but he still wasn't sure exactly how it worked back home. The notion that one person could *own* another, like a horse, was too hard to get his head around. He knew it was true and had been for ages. Rome was built by slaves. But unlike Holcano captives, not all black people back home were slaves. Some even owned slaves themselves! (He'd seen that in New Orleans too, which confused him even more.) One thing was sure, here, now: word had quietly but firmly gone around that Barca wasn't *anybody's* slave and De Russy, Cayce, Anson—all their senior officers—expected him to be treated with respect.

"Yes sir," Hanny finished, deciding he'd have said the same to anybody he didn't know.

"Just Barca," the young man said with a flash of teeth.

"An' I'm Apo," the young Uxmalo pronounced, taking a quick gulp from the tinned American canteen he wore before nodding at his friend. "We call him 'Hanny.'"

"I've heard that," Barca agreed. "A pleasure to meet you, Apo." He looked back at Hanny. "We're both named after the same man."

"Aye!" affirmed Preacher Mac. "Hannibal Barca!"

"Who's he?" asked one of the artillerymen resting against the other wheel of the gun.

"He *was* a great Carthaginian general. Nearly brought Rome down," Hanny said with a smile. "What's your last name?"

Barca's own smile vanished. "It used to be Mounier, I suppose. I don't . . . choose to have one now."

Hanny didn't know what that meant or what to say.

"Ready back there?" Leonor called.

Barca's smile returned as he nodded at the gun and grasped a spoke himself. "'I will either find a way or make one!'" he quoted, and Hanny grinned.

"All together now . . . heave!" roared Corporal Petty. With a squealing groan from the horses and a late panting surge by the men, the limber wheels finally jounced out of their hole, and the combined ton-and-a-half weight of the limber and gun splashed and slithered forward, dumping many of those pushing into the mucky pit they left.

Hanny rose dripping out of the ooze, slinging it off, and saw Apo, McDonough, and several other men, even Barca, had fallen in as well and were just as covered as he. They all burst out laughing. What else could they do?

"'Many things which nature makes difficult become easy to the man who uses his brains,'" Hanny grumbled sarcastically, and the laughter grew. Probably only Barca and maybe McDonough realized he was quoting Hannibal too.

"Get outa there, you buncha mud ducks," snapped Corporal Petty. "We gotta get movin'. You infantry, get yer muskets an' run along. Sergeant Visser only borryed you to me."

Leonor had cast off the rope she'd looped around her big saddle horn and come back to collect Barca. Now she sat grinning. "Whenever you're ready," she said with mock impatience as Barca dragged himself out of the hole and stopped to stare at himself. "Well, it's still raining. I suppose I *will* wash off." He turned back to Hanny and the others. "Good luck, fellows. I expect you'll be heading back to Uxmal tomorrow." Untying his horse, he climbed back up and, together with the Rangers and lancers who'd helped free the gun, trotted on ahead.

"Another nice officer," Apo said, helping the others out of the mud.

"I . . . don't think he is one," Hanny told him, heading toward where they'd stacked their soaked muskets by threes. There was no point bringing the colors out in this and he had a musket too. Now he inspected it sadly. The stock was swollen and the bright steel was rusting. It would take a lot of effort to polish it up again. If it had been loaded, it never would've fired.

"Nay," Preacher Mac said with a thoughtful expression on his face, "but I ken he'd make a good 'un if he ever had a chance."

Hanny tossed him his musket and cartridge box, then did the same for

Apo while the other men retrieved their weapons from another tripod. "I bet he would too," he said. "Maybe now, here, he'll get that chance."

―――――――

SOUTH OF ITZINCAB

Corporal Bandy "Boogerbear" Beeryman was riding a little to the right of a huge Ocelomeh warrior as they eased through the dripping forest, their horses' hooves making hardly a sound on the wet carpet of leafy needles as they ranged ahead of the main party on its way to Don Discipo's Puebla Arboras. Discipo was an outlaw in Boogerbear's book, pure and simple. A man to be hanged if caught and therefore the sort to lay an ambush. Especially after how long King Har-Kaaska and his party were delayed at the city of Itzincab, bolstering its defenses (and the courage of its somewhat timid Alcalde Truro). Boogerbear sympathized with Truro. Situated near the very headwaters of the Cipactli River, his was the most remote and exposed of the three firmly Allied cities, and some of their most important mines were there. Still, despite worsening weather and almost daily rains, Boogerbear was glad to get moving and approved of the way his companions disdained known tracks and trails, yet still made decent time. He was also impressed. The trees all looked alike to him, and the ground rose so gently, it was almost impossible to tell. He wondered how they did it. He suspected he could've done it himself, not even being a "forest critter," as long as he knew where they were going and could see the sky. But even if he could catch a glimpse through the trees above, *this* sky wouldn't tell him anything.

It didn't seem to matter and they kept unerringly on, without hesitation, never even consulting a compass. Boogerbear knew their course remained steady because he *did* have a compass. *Let it go,* he told himself. *They're better at this than me. Me an' Sal are only here in case o' fightin'.* His companions might be better at that as well, for all he knew, but he was pretty sure nobody was a *lot* better.

His mind wandered, even as his eyes swept the dim surroundings, missing nothing. He was surprised the Ocelomeh took to horses so well, considering they had so few and most seemed to walk everywhere. *Prob'ly like Major Cayce, they want their fighters able to do most anything,* he supposed. *They got messenger horses in all their villages, I hear, so maybe they pass 'em around for ridin' lessons for the kiddies? An' what about that big duck-faced booger King Har-Kaaska rides? How come they don't use more o' them?* The creature seemed to behave itself and didn't slow their pace, though it did eat an awful lot. *That's probably why,* he decided. *An' maybe breakin' 'em is a particular chore for Injins that prefer goin' on foot anyway.* He figured the Ocelomeh were as good at being "woods Injins" as any he'd heard of. He doubted, even on horseback—*especially* on horseback—they'd match any "plains Injins" he knew. *An' Comanches'd rip 'em to shreds in the open,* he suspected.

Then he reconsidered. King Har-Kaaska was the biggest "Cat" he'd seen (he thought of all Mi-Anakka as "cat-people," even though he liked Varaa and she was obviously smarter than him), but even Har-Kaaska didn't have the arms and shoulders of the Ocelomeh he led and couldn't launch one of their massive arrows with anything like their power. Boogerbear had met five Cats now, counting the two with Har-Kaaska. All, like Varaa, carried one of those British-looking muskets. *I bet even Comanches'd respect Ocelomeh bows. 'Specially for stickin' buffalo.*

It struck him as ironic that, even as he was contemplating those big, heavy arrows with long obsidian points and fletching as big as turkey feathers, one should whip by his face from the left, inches from his nose.

He jerked back on the reins, stopping and whipping his horse's head to the side, just as another arrow hissed past where his chest would've been an instant later. Snatching the double-barrel shotgun from the saddle boot, he wrenched his horse around and charged directly where the arrows came from, noting that the big Ocelomeh to his left was already down, an arrow through his throat. *Silly bastard,* he reflected philosophically. *Guess I should'a been lookin' his way too.*

A black-painted Holcano leaped up from where he'd been lying on his back by the base of a tree, bow across his body. Even as he reached for another arrow, Boogerbear pulled the front trigger of his shotgun. The right barrel fired almost two ounces of swan shot, blowing off the Holcano's jaw and ripping out most of his throat in a geysering arc of blood and teeth. An arrow stung his horse's flank, and Boogerbear forced the frightened animal in the direction that one came from. This Holcano was painted red, and Boogerbear shot him in the back of the head as he ran, exploding it like a ruptured gourd. Taking the empty shotgun by the muzzle with his left hand, ready to use it like a mace, he drew one of his revolvers.

Mingled with shouts and high-pitched yipping shrieks, muskets boomed in the forest behind, and he whirled and charged that way. "Goddamn trees," he grumbled aloud. Even then his deep voice was deceptively mild.

The main party was engulfed in a melee, most everyone off their horses, the struggling forms making it hard to discern friend from foe in the gloom. Har-Kaaska's strange mount was mooing piteously with a pair of heavy shafts in its side, even as it stomped a man to paste under the claws of its big, three-toed foot. But Har-Kaaska wasn't on the rampaging animal, and Booger-bear saw that two Holcanos had him down, trying to stab him with spears used as knives. Boogerbear shot them both in the back, not much concerned the little .36 caliber bullets would punch through and harm the king. They didn't, but the carefully placed bullets shattered the attackers' spines, and Har-Kaaska flung the screeching, helpless men away with a grunt. Then his yellow eyes went wide and he leaped for his musket. Boogerbear spun and saw another pair of Holcanos drawing bows. He shot them both in their foreheads without aiming. One loosed his arrow high in the limbs, but the men dropped like sacks of beans. *These little Colts ain't much,* Boogerbear thought with a certain fondness for his tools, *not like them big new ones like Cap'n Anson's, but they point pretty well.* With one shot left in his first Paterson, he gently dropped the shotgun and drew his second.

Kurk-bang! roared Har-Kaaska's musket, dropping another shadowy figure, just as a thunder of hooves approached through the wet, drifting smoke. It was Sal and the rear guard, coming up. Boogerbear watched with admiration as something attracted Sal's attention and he almost casually shot a Holcano with as little apparent effort as swatting a fly. Men were still grappling on the ground, and the giant duck thing curled a toe around a red-painted man, pulling him off a Cat before stomping him with a squealing *crunch.* Har-Kaaska battered another with his musket butt, bashing in his skull, before reaching down and hauling the Mi-Anakka to his feet. An arrow whickered in from nowhere—it was impossible to see through the standing smoke—and slammed into the chest of the grinning Cat Har-Kaaska just raised up.

"Non!" Har-Kaaska almost wailed as the grin turned to a grimace of agony.

"Stay here, Sal," Boogerbear rumbled softly, dashing through the smoke in the direction the fletching pointed. There was something dark on the ground ahead, a stump maybe—that instantly transformed into a Holcano who jumped up and tried to stab Boogerbear's horse in the chest with a long, wicked spear. The horse sidestepped the thrust without a touch from the big Ranger, and he shot the man in the top of the head, right alongside the stiffened, bristly crest of his hair. Boogerbear patted his huffing horse on its broad, striped neck. "You're gettin' good at this, girl. Hafta give you a name." He'd been reluctant to do that. He'd had his pick of "local" horses and chosen a good one, he thought, but it seemed indecent to take a new one "for keeps" so soon after losing his old companion in the wreck. And naming a horse made it yours. "How 'bout 'Dodger'? You dodged that spear well enough."

It started raining hard again, washing the smoke from the air. Boogerbear put his poncho on and took Dodger on a circuit of the little battlefield but found no more lurking enemies. Returning to where Har-Kaaska and another bloody Mi-Anakka were kneeling on the ground by their friend, Boogerbear looked around. He figured they'd lost four, counting the dying Cat. There were eleven or twelve dead Holcanos. An Ocelomeh had drawn the heavy arrow shafts out of the duck thing and was soothing it as best he could. Its wounds were bleeding freely, but it didn't seem much hurt. Sal and another pair of Ocelomeh had caught all the horses, but one was blowing blood with an arrow high in its chest behind the shoulder. Seeing Boogerbear's sad gesture, Sal quickly stepped in to cut the suffering animal's throat. A moment later, it was thrashing on the ground while Sal gently patted its head, saying, "*Lo siento, mi amigo.*"

Not long after, the Cat-man died.

"Twenty years," Har-Kaaska whispered, then stood and roared, "*Twenty years* he's been with me!" He glared at Boogerbear, frizzed-out tail whipping behind him. "*You* can't go home, but *we* might've done. Instead, we stayed and toiled and suffered to lead the Ocelomeh and protect others of this land—and *avenge ourselves* upon the Doms! Now . . ." He waved helplessly at the dead Mi-Anakka. "There were almost thirty of us once. Now there are six. *Six!*"

Boogerbear cleared his throat. "Beggin' your pardon, sir, but there won't be but four if we don't get a move on. I don't reckon we killed every Injin that came at us, so they know where we are an'll likely bring more. Might be a little mad at us too."

Har-Kaaska took a long breath, blinking rapidly. "You're right, of course. We must go." He paused. "But how did they find us? We were on no road, no known trail. Even if someone betrayed us, they could never tell the enemy *exactly* where to wait!" He looked up searchingly. "Nor could they have been guided by eyes in the sky!"

Boogerbear had no idea what Har-Kaaska meant by that, but knew where he was heading otherwise. "They didn't know where we'd be, so they set theirselves up to bushwhack us all along a line. Must'a took every Holcano there is, maybe lizard-man too. An' a fair number might'a heard our little fight."

Har-Kaaska was nodding grimly.

"There's little point going on, then, is there?" Sal asked angrily. "That many of the enemy between us and Puebla Arboras . . . How else could they stay here as long as this might take if they didn't hold the city already?"

"Or are *guests* there," growled the Mi-Anakka with the bloody fur beside Har-Kaaska.

Boogerbear couldn't pronounce his name, so he never tried to remember it. He shrugged. "Go on or go back, but whichever it is, we better get at it."

"We'll return to Itzincab," Har-Kaaska decided. "Alcalde Truro must know of this . . . and that *his* city is now on the frontier with the enemy!"

NORTH OF CAMPECHE

Unlike Boogerbear's small joint scout with King Har-Kaaska, Lieutenant Coryon Burton's probe down the coast, roughly following the rutted, overgrown coastal track toward Campeche, had started more like a reconnaissance in force. He had his own eighty-man J Company of the 3rd Dragoons (fleshed out by more than twenty Ocelomeh recruits), and the almost entirely Uxmalo fifty-man B Company of the 1st Yucatán Lancers under former sergeant, now Alferez, Espinoza. They were accompanied by another fifty Ocelomeh under Ixtla. None of the latter was mounted, but could run alongside a trotting horse longer than the horse could keep the pace. In any event, it was a respectable force that swept down through the coastal town of Nautla, long in the hands of the Holcanos, and liberated it without a fight. Not that there was anything to liberate. The only sign of previous inhabitants were long-abandoned cook-fire pits where they'd been eaten by their occupiers. Otherwise the place was a ghost town with nothing living there but garaaches—"wild" young Grik that had turned the once-cheerful little stone-and-adobe dwellings into warrens of filth.

They'd sent their report and pressed on into the disputed Tierra del

Lagarto de Sangre, or "Blood Lizard," as Coryon's Sergeant Hayne called it, about the time the rains became constant and they'd slowed to a crawl, carefully plodding through its terrible forests and avoiding even more terrible monsters whenever the Ocelomeh gave enough warning. The monsters seemed to thrive in the endless rain and oppressive wet heat, but Coryon's party, even the Ocelomeh hardened to it, grew increasingly miserable. Clothing and everything leather began to rot, and tents turned black with mildew and started to disintegrate. Weapons were impossible to keep dry, as big a problem for the Ocelomeh's bows as the dragoons' carbines. Even the men's skin and the hooves of their horses started to deteriorate. There were only the great Cipactli and distant Usuma Rivers on the whole peninsula, as far as anyone knew, but swamps and marshes were resurrected everywhere. Long-dry gullies became roaring rivers in their own right, cutting directly across their path, and they had to be crossed.

All these things took a toll in sickness, injury, and death, but monsters of all shapes and sizes remained the most terrifying hazard. Ixtla said the weather emboldened them, since they could move with greater stealth. It also revived the more amphibious sorts dependent on this short time of year not only to mate, but to eat enough to sustain them in buried torpor through the drier months. These were the ones that cost them the most on the march, exploding from the swamps they attempted to skirt like long-legged, catfish-skinned crocodiles, snatching men and horses in apparent disdain to fusillades of bullets and arrows. Other men simply disappeared at night, sometimes without even a scream. Those on guard had it worst. Torn between terror and a reluctance to allow their imaginations to disturb exhausted comrades, at least one a week was snagged by savage teeth or claws and dragged shrieking into the wet darkness by things they never really saw. Searches never found the victims alive, and more men were occasionally lost.

Despite Coryon's determination to press on and complete his first independent mission, he started to doubt they'd ever reach Campeche. "I thought a force as large as ours would intimidate the monsters more," he'd confided to Ixtla one day, remembering the army's relatively pleasant march from the beach to Uxmal.

The Ocelomeh had only shrugged. "Large, noisy groups *do* scare some of the monsters," Ixtla had replied. "Even ours would normally do so, less large and noisy by design. But during the rains, along this low path?" He'd shaken his head. "A *thousand* men would lose just as many, probably more—though they wouldn't be as sorely missed."

"I'd thought the Doms would wait for the rains to end because it'll be easier to move their men, guns, and supplies. Now I know different!"

"Do you?" Ixtla had asked harshly. "I think not. The Doms care nothing for the lives of their men. They'd still come through this if they could, and the suffering of the men they lost to sickness or monsters would be *celebrated*." He'd paused then, considering. "No, if they were ready and could move their guns and supplies, we would've already met the scouts ahead of their vanguard." He'd looked at Coryon, rain dripping from the wide-brimmed Uxmalo hat he wore. "It speaks well for you that you think of your people first, but pray your Major Cayce never forgets the Doms do not. He can't expect them to act as he might under *any* circumstances in which the welfare of his troops is foremost in his mind."

They finally reached the vicinity of Campeche with less than three-quarters of the men they started with, never once meeting enemy scouts, not even Holcanos. Coryon couldn't help but hope that might mean the Holcanos and their Grik allies were still reeling from their defeat on the beach, and maybe, just *maybe*, the Doms weren't really mustering a huge army to come for them after all. The next day they'd view the city itself and know for sure. In the drizzly, predawn darkness, Coryon, Ixtla, and Alferez Espinoza took a small mixed company to some low-lying wooded hills east of the city that a grizzled old Ocelomeh crept ahead to find. There they waited for the dawn of another dreary, sopping day. When it came, it brought a surprise: for the first time in weeks, rain wasn't pouring from leaden clouds. It also brought disappointment, to Coryon Burton at least. The Doms were in Campeche, and they were there in force.

Various legends had described Campeche as a bustling coastal city carved from the dense woodland, much like Uxmal. It was obviously older, larger, and—once—significantly more populous; its stone buildings even more refined and ambitious in size and complex architecture. As the light gathered, Coryon saw the great central pyramidal temple was taller and more impressive than the one at Uxmal too, with entryways to unknown interiors on each stepped level, but it—like the rest of the once-thriving city—was a dead ruin. Much had been shattered into rubble in the distant past, though it was impossible to tell if age or artillery had done the work. And there were no homes, unless one counted the seemingly endless expanse of tents and canvas shelters radiating outward from numerous large marquees erected under the sodden red flags of the Holy Dominion.

A haze of wood smoke lay low on the encampment, and few men were about as yet. Most were either fetching wood or tending vast herds of horses and armabueys on the desolate, briar-choked plain, but every person they saw wore the bright yellow coats and breeches with black facings, cuffs, boots, and tricorn hats of Dominion soldiers.

"Yellows," Burton hissed. It was the first time he'd seen them, but the name had stuck in his mind. He took a small telescope from a leather pouch and extended it. "Damn," he muttered, wiping the foggy lens with his fingers. It didn't help. Finally, he sighed and returned the instrument to its pouch. "Not another single soul," he told his companions. "No civilians, no Holcanos or Grik. Just Doms."

"How many?" asked Alferez Espinoza. Like Teniente Lara, his English was nearly perfect after four months of constant practice.

"How should I know?" Coryon snapped bitterly. "A lot." He looked at Ixtla. "How many troops to one of those tents? Maybe we can figure out that way."

Ixtla gaped, then closely echoed him. "How should *I* know that? I've only ever seen a handful of Doms. I don't know anyone, besides King Har-Kaaska, Varaa-Choon, and Koaar-Taak, who've seen an *army* of them and lived!" He looked at the camp. "We'll just have to count them," he added simply. "There may have been no residents here for years, and now we know why we met no Holcano scouts." He frowned. "The Doms use them but won't *stay* with them. Won't allow them to linger near. Even as vile as Holcanos are, and as close to the Doms as they hope to be, they're still heretics."

Coryon nodded at the camp as well. More men were appearing, going about ordinary tasks. Like ordinary men. It seemed strange to be so afraid of them. "They don't act worried. Why should they? We're two hundred miles from Uxmal, in a straight line. Closer to three hundred by the path we took."

"And who'd be mad enough to make such a trek during the rains?" asked Ixtla with a grin. "Distance, numbers, their very Dom arrogance, won't let them imagine they're under threat here."

"They're not, from us," Alferez Espinoza pointed out wryly.

"No," Ixtla agreed. "Not directly. But as soon as we report, our leaders will *know* they're here and they *are* coming. *That* will hurt them," he said with conviction.

Coryon looked thoughtful. "So where do you think all the Holcanos and Grik went?"

"Cayal," Ixtla replied at once, "or even Puebla Arboras, if Don Discipo has given himself to Tranquilo. King Har-Kaaska and your 'Boogerbear' will know by now."

"If they weren't all eaten on the way," groused Alferez Espinoza.

Ixtla grinned at them. "They took a 'higher' path with fewer swamps and gullies. Fewer predators to be revived by the rain. Besides, with Har-Kaaska's skill and Boogerbear's size—and matching lethality, I suspect—they won't have been eaten. Just as important, they'll know what to do." He looked at Coryon and raised his eyebrows. "You command here. What shall *we* do?"

"We're not supposed to engage unless they start it," Espinoza reminded, thinking Coryon might be contemplating a raid.

Coryon had been thinking exactly that, scratching the sparse whiskers on his chin. His side whiskers had exploded, but he'd never have a full beard, he feared. He doubted he looked very dashing in his scruffy whiskers and rotting uniform. Unfortunately, trying to shave a face that never fully dried struck him as a good way to disfigure himself for life. So did getting caught by the Doms—very briefly, if what he heard was true—and what would it achieve? "We'll send a report, of course," he said reflectively, "but after all we went through to get here, I won't just turn back now. Some of us, at least, have to watch and wait until they move. Give an exact report of that—and how many there are by then."

EASTERN ARMY OF GOD ENCAMPMENT
CAMPECHE

"*Un día hermosa!*" exclaimed the Blood Cardinal Don Frutos del Gran Vale in "High Spanish" as he stepped out of an archway onto a platform adjacent to the center level of Campeche's ancient pyramid. The stones where he stood were smooth and rounded where they joined by ages of weathering and still dark with moisture. That would change as the brilliant rising sun steamed them dry. Raising his arms at his sides, spreading his gold-embroidered, dark red robe like the wings of a bird about to take flight, Don Frutos seemed to be absorbing the sun's rays into his gaunt, pale, and otherwise naked form. Turning to General Agon, short and stocky, dressed in his finest yellow-and-black uniform adorned with dripping gold lace, he blinked large black eyes and cracked narrow lips into something like a smile. The long, dark, pointed beard on his narrow face made his eyes seem unnaturally huge at times. "The sun again, Mi General. How I have longed to feel it."

"Enjoy it, Your Holiness," Agon replied. "The rainy season is not yet over."

"Soon, though," Don Frutos declared eagerly, gesturing out at the vast sea of tents and stirring troops infiltrating the ruins around them and even lapping against the base of the pyramid below. "While the Gran Cruzada continues to labor endlessly just to *begin* to lurch ponderously northwest to confront the heretical 'New Britain Isles' Imperials in the Californias, *I* will march this magnificent host to smash the heretics of the Yucatán forever. *I* will secure the largest territory brought wholly under Dominion rule in generations! All for the glory of God and His Supreme Holiness, of course," he quickly added.

"Of course, Your Holiness," Agon agreed, also looking out on the army. Even then, in the disorganized morning bustle, it *was* a glorious sight. He could only imagine what the Gran Cruzada must look like by now in its *hundreds of thousands*, but the Eastern Army of God was bigger than anything he'd ever seen, and he wondered what it would look like from higher. He determined to use this one pretty day to climb to the top of the pyramid. Glancing back at Don Frutos, he knew his lord would've preferred to be installed in a higher level himself, but the floors above were considered unsound and had even collapsed in places. At least the quarters prepared for him here were dry and cleaned and aired of timeless filth, even decorated enough to be livable, if not presentable to his peers. *But what can one expect, even a Blood Cardinal to His Supreme Holiness, when one is on campaign?* General Agon wondered irreverently.

It was more than Don Frutos's insistence on "High Spanish" that bothered General Agon. Most high-ranking military officers used it because it had been the Spanish who'd brought so many military words and phrases to this world. Blood Cardinals had to know it to read ancient texts, but used it more as an affectation—he believed—since the True Faith was best preached in Spanya for the widest understanding. But since the Blood Cardinals spoke it all the time, a growing number of Blood Priests had started as well, angling for legitimacy in spite of their claim they were "closer to the common faithful and their stricter understanding of God's will" than humbler, more traditional priests.

No matter that such "stricter understanding" is bloodily enforced by the Blood Priests themselves, Agon thought glumly. Like most soldiers, Agon was a traditionalist, even if his commander, Don Frutos, wasn't. That bothered him even more. The majority of Blood Cardinals were *opposed* to the rise of the Blood Priests and viewed them as a threat. Don Frutos rarely demonstrated anything like what Agon would define as the . . . excessive piety of Blood Priests—except when it came to punishing those who displeased him—or really much authentic piety at all. He wasn't impressed by Don Frutos's strategic sense, apparently limited to simply marching his army against the enemy. Presumably, he expected his opponents to either surrender themselves to his "mercy" or be trod underfoot as the army marched on. He spoke enthusiastically of a "real battle" and seemed to desperately want one, but appeared disinterested in discussing what to do if they got it.

Most of all, perhaps, General Agon despised the self-important Blood Priests Don Frutos surrounded himself with—particularly the arrogant, grasping Father Tranquilo—to the exclusion of other priests the troops themselves favored, and Agon was tired of being caught between the Blood Priests and the Obispos (whom they sought to supplant). Since the very dawn of the True Faith on this world, Blood Cardinals could only be chosen from Obispos *related by blood* to that holy event that brought the spark of the True Faith here. Agon himself could claim a Filipino (whatever that was) crew member of that ancient Acapulco/Manila galleon as an indirect ancestor and might've aspired to become an Obispo himself. Priests without that blood connection never could, and only Obispos ever became Blood Cardinals. It was from the very small number of these, the virtual spiritual rulers of various provinces in the Holy Dominion, that His Supreme Holiness Himself was chosen to ascend. Blood Priests were a relatively new sect that styled themselves after the Blood Cardinals yet sought to achieve sufficient grace in God's eyes to be elevated chiefly by the "grace" they spread around—in the form of actual blood and suffering. Agon was inured to that, since it was nothing new, but the extremes to which the Blood Priests went was bothersome to the traditionalists and, as far as he knew, all the properly ordained Blood Cardinals *except* Don Frutos.

Trying to keep the Blood Priests and Obispos from tearing out one another's throats—or sacrificing half the army to bored Blood Priests sitting
around without sufficient victims to cover themselves with grace—while
simultaneously preparing the army to march was all so very tiresome. *As
much as I wish we had them for scouts, it's just as well I sent all the Holcanos
to Cayal or there wouldn't be any left by now,* Agon mused.

With Cayal already on his mind, he was surprised a moment later when
Don Frutos finally closed his robe and led him back into his chamber. Young
female servants, all naked as well and painted in gold, scattered from the
entrance, where they'd been waiting in case Don Frutos requested anything.
He ignored them and said, a little evasively, "I, ah, have news from Cayal.
Through Father Tranquilo. He reports that Don Discipo has openly declared
himself for us at last and has opened Puebla Arboras to the Holcanos. A
great number of them are moving there and will advance on the heretic city
of Itzincab as closely coordinated with our own advance as possible."

Agon blinked, stunned. "Indeed? How old is this news?"

Don Frutos waved the question away. "Quite recent. Astonishingly so,"
he hedged. "Father Tranquilo has quite surprising resources when it comes
to information."

Agon bowed. "I readily acknowledge that. His was the first explanation
I had regarding why I was so suddenly and mysteriously ordered to march
my Eastern Brigada of the Army of God to this place from Mazumiapan
and prepare for more troops to arrive. Capitan Arevalo brought me the first
details of the fighting, even if most were secondhand, but Tranquilo had a
lot of very basic information, even some names and numbers, and knew
about the Americano steamship even before you came to assume overall
command and told me you'd been in Vera Cruz when it arrived." He
paused. "Nothing compared to the information I got directly from the captive you brought with you, however."

"That's certainly true!" Don Frutos actually gloated.

Agon grimaced slightly, thinking of that captive and imagining how
Don Frutos had made him so pliable. Agon might be a true believer, but
didn't revel in the suffering of others like Blood Priests did. There were still
a number of survivors in *Isidra*, of course; people of "singular value" who'd
be preserved for a time. Others had been disposed of in the usual ways—
perhaps some still lived?—but Agon himself had only seen that one single
person who arrived on this world in that remarkable ship.

"Still," Agon murmured, "your information was best, but Tranquilo's was quickest by far. How does he do it? How can we possibly hope to coordinate our movements with the Holcanos, a hundred and thirty–odd *leguas* away, when we can't yet know for certain when it will be dry enough for *us* to move?"

Don Frutos waved airily. "Tranquilo cultivates heretic spies all over, no doubt."

Agon said no more, but didn't believe "spies" could possibly move information as quickly as Don Frutos implied.

Don Frutos cleared his throat to change the subject, then commanded, "Tell me again, General. Leave out all the trivial details about sick and injured, the condition of our animals, and state of supplies. Another battalion of infantry came ashore from transports this last week, along with another pair of the great wall-smashing siege guns! How many troops will we have when we march? How many guns? I can't wait to use them!"

CHAPTER 28

As predicted, almost to the day, the constant rains came to an end near the first of September. It was phenomenal. One day the rain was sheeting down as it had nearly every day for the last two months, but the next dawned bright and hot and incredibly muggy. Everyone said it would rain no more than one day in four for the next few weeks, then they'd be lucky if it rained once a month. De Russy and Periz had returned from their embassy to Pidra Blanca, Itzincab, and the hesitant city of Techon. After a meeting with Alcalde Truro and King Har-Kaaska (who'd confirmed their fears that Puebla Arboras was in open league with the Holcanos), they'd asked for no recruits from Itzincab. It might need all its people for defense. They did bring several hundred more volunteers from Pidra Blanca, as well as a few hundred men and a firm commitment to the alliance from Techon.

And even through the rains, much had been accomplished at Uxmal. The "powder monks" had abandoned their meager facility upriver and helped erect a new gunpowder mill near the city, harnessing the fervent flow of the Cipactli. Armabueys could carry on the work after the river slowed to a crawl. There'd been disagreement between the powder monks and some lads from Pennsylvania about the best kind of wood to use for gunpowder charcoal, even the best way to make it, but the Pennsylvania boys were stumped when the monks demanded to see a willow tree. They were forced to admit the grain of the wood the monks preferred looked as good as it could, and their primitive method of cooking it down would have to suffice for now. As they'd worked in large powder mills before, however, their experience was invaluable when it came to scaling up the operation. As soon as things dried out enough, they started making gunpowder in earnest.

Cottage industries for all sorts of things had sprung up. Aside from Anson and his Rangers with bullet molds for their own unique weapons, thirty more molds had been brought by soldiers or retrieved from armorers' stores in the wrecks. That was actually more than anyone hoped, but less than half were .69 caliber for the musket balls they'd need the most, both for the infantry and hundreds of rounds of canister shells Lewis wanted for the cannon. The most numerous belonged to the riflemen, many of whom carried a .525 mold for their more precise .54 caliber weapons. These could also make projectiles for the dragoons' Hall carbines and close-range canister rounds in a pinch. In any event, once they got started, none of the molds ever got cold, and Uxmalos—children, mostly—spent long days in front of hot furnaces casting lead balls as fast as they could. A couple of American blacksmiths forged and filed cherries to make "gang" molds to cast dozens of balls at a time, but without any rotary power, or even vices beyond those in the forge wagons, gang molds—any new molds—required a lot of time and effort.

One thing going better than expected was the sand casting of copper round shot at the smelters near the mines. Men couldn't go in the flooded mines until they were pumped out or drained so they poured roundshot after roundshot of surprisingly high quality that rarely needed more than a little attention from a file. Fortunately, files were known and used in Uxmal, though good ones were properly hardened almost by accident. At least the American armorers and blacksmiths didn't have to wear their good ones out for such things. Wooden sabots required for best accuracy were something else, however, and were waiting on the completion of rotary tools as well. Lathes were under construction down by the river, to be powered by the same water (or armabueys) as the powder mill, but if the Doms came before they were ready and they used up all their fixed shot, they'd have to stuff wadding down the barrels of their cannon, navy fashion, and lose a lot of the accuracy they took for granted and relied on.

Uniforms were made from fine Uxmalo fabrics, of course, but leather accoutrements, saddles, and shoes had to be fashioned as well, as did buttons, tents, buckets, barrels, haversacks, blankets, and countless other things. A lot of that had been salvaged from the shipwrecks, but only a little more than the men who brought it needed. Nowhere near enough to equip even the modest force they absolutely had to have. And with all the new additions and Ocelomeh Har-Kaaska had sent, that "modest force" now numbered nearly nine thousand men. Less than half had undergone daily training to become proper soldiers, and little more than half of *them* carried firearms. There were still a few unissued muskets, but spares must remain in reserve to replace those damaged by experienced men.

In respect to arms, despite the hard work of the few Uxmalo gunsmiths, only a handful of new ones had been made. Facilities simply weren't up to the task, and locals were accustomed to taking a year or more to complete a single fine piece. Worse, even rolled barrels had to be bored true, and rotary tools were the hang-up—again—because local gunmakers took all their barrels to a single man with a hand-turned cutting and lapping machine, not even a proper lathe, for final reaming and polishing. The American gunsmiths were deeply frustrated, insisting that in another month or two they could *make* all the tools they needed. The problem was, they might not have a month. They might not have a *week*. Lewis instructed them to focus on keeping the weapons they had in repair. The unspoken expectation was that captured Dom weapons would soon be issued—if any of them lived to see that day.

In the meantime, Major Reed had followed Lewis's example of making sure everyone knew how to use a musket, whether he had one or not. And he'd given special attention to bayonet practice, since rough-hewn musket-shaped pikes with forged iron blades could be used the very same way. In any event, by the time the rains stopped and De Russy, Periz, and Consul Koaar returned with Sal Hernandez and Boogerbear (Finlay and Samarez came straight back from Pidra Blanca), the Detached Expeditionary Force and Army of the Allied Cities could field five thousand men beyond the walls of Uxmal, retaining four thousand less well-trained "reserves" or

"Home Guards" for defense. With all the guns from the wrecked Dom galleon properly mounted, any attacker would find the city a bloody proposition.

THE COMBINED ARMY would stand under a variety of flags (the blue saltire
on white for Uxmal, a stylized beast of some sort on a red saltire in bright
green for Pidra Blanca, now the red, white, and gold pennant of Techon
beside the Stars and Stripes, not to mention all the regimental banners—
and, somewhat ironically to some, a green, white, and red guidon over
Lara's lancers), but all the troops except a large contingent of Ocelomeh
under Koaar, still armed with bows and spears, wore the very same uniform. There were variations, of course: different-color branch trim, for
example—white for infantry (and Mounted Rifles), yellow for dragoons,
red for artillery, and all the foot soldiers wore sky-blue and mounted troops
had dark blue jackets. Even the uniforms of Lara's lancers were hardly dis-
tinguishable aside from the coats, using the exact same trousers and wheel
hats as everyone. Coats were medium blue, with tails and scarlet cuffs and
collars.

"They look absolutely splendid. You've done wonderful work," De Russy
said aside to Lewis and Anson as the combined force paraded around the
great temple square to the cheering of thousands under a bright morning
sky. They were with Major Reed, Varaa-Choon, the newly commissioned
Lieutenants Leonor and Boogerbear (Lieutenant Sal Hernandez was in the
parade), as well as Dr. Newlin. Even Captain Holland and Mr. Semmes, his
first lieutenant, stood by since *Tiger* was in port to take on supplies.

"It rained a lot," Lewis replied wryly. "The troops got wet but didn't have
much else to do but drill and practice manuevering and moving in line
formation." He snorted. "Went for a few soggy hikes as well. God knows
how many old ladies and children spent the whole rainy season cooped up
sewing, cutting leather, and stitching it together or burning themselves with
hot lead."

Drums and fifes thundered and squealed for the Americans (and the
locals mixed among them), while flutes and different-sounding drums did
the same for purely local troops. Four regimental blocks of roughly seven
hundred infantry followed Lieutenant Hans Joffrion's L Company of the

3rd Dragoons and Teniente Lara's A Company of the 1st Yucatán Lancers, marching purposefully past the reviewing stand, erected on the very spot Lewis hanged two men. First came the 1st US, led by Captain Beck on a fine local horse. Olayne followed at the head of his A Battery, composed of six beautifully polished 6pdrs and all their attendant vehicles. The clatter of harness and *creak* and *pop* of wheels were audible despite the music. Next came the 3rd Pennsylvania under the newly elected Captain Wagley. His men carried the Stars and Stripes as well, but also the distinctive blue flag of their state despite being heavily outnumbered by locals. Lieutenant Emmel Dukane's B Battery with the six 12pdr howitzers recovered from *Commissary* followed close behind. Then came the 1st Uxmal, commanded by Captain James Manley. It was the best local regiment of "regulars," and all carried muskets salvaged from the shipwrecks, their dark, young, beardless faces looking grimly determined beneath their city flag and forest of bright weapons on their shoulders. Lieutenant Hudgens's C Battery of four 6pdrs and two 12pdr guns were followed by Koaar's 1st Ocelomeh Infantry, still in their own "uniform" of leather and bright-colored breechcloths. The 1st Ocelomeh carried no flag. The rest of the horse soldiers, including Felix Meder's Mounted Rifles, brought up the rear.

"I hope the sight of them makes the Doms think twice," De Russy added with satisfaction in his voice.

The praise made Lewis feel odd despite the beautiful day and magnitude of the accomplishment. "It wasn't just us," Lewis replied, waving at those around him. "It certainly wasn't just *me*. Captain Anson and I spent most of our time begging, buying, even stealing horses before Anson and Varaa vanished for longer than I liked, mapping every path and game trail all the way back to where we were wrecked while I went on pounding 'mobility, mobility, mobility' into everyone's heads. Olayne's had individual gun's crews and sections practicing mounted artillery tactics since we got to this world, but they needed the full treatment: battery- and even battalion-level maneuvers—in conjunction with infantry and other mounted troops."

"Damned hard work in the rain every day," Major Reed grumbled. "But we had to learn to work together. Most of us—and not just the locals—had never done that on the scale required. And don't sell yourself short, Lewis. Of the few of us who've ever seen a major action, you and Captain Anson"— Reed frowned slightly—"and Teniente Lara, oddly enough, were among the even fewer who could actually *show* us how it's done, how to get the most out of every element of our force while still supporting one another!"

Holland cleared his throat, and they noted Alcalde Periz glancing strangely at them from where he stood a little apart with Father Orno, Reverend Harkin, and a number of Periz's priests and advisors. Sira Periz, Samantha Wilde, and Angelique Mercure—all in stunning new gowns and attended by Barca—were with them as well. *Maybe that's the way it should be,* Lewis thought. *With the exception of Dr. Newlin, we've formed a small clot of military men—and females,* he added, thinking of Leonor and Varaa. *Maybe we should set the example of keeping a little apart from civilians.* He frowned. *But Dr. Newlin's in uniform—and so is Alcalde Periz, now.* His eyes narrowed. *As is Father Orno, in a way. He wears no rank, but his black frock coat looks as "military" as mine.* He sighed. *That was De Russy's idea. Was it a good one?*

He didn't really know how he felt. Perhaps . . . cheated a bit. He and his officers, all the soldiers, old and new, had worked miracles getting themselves and these townsfolk ready for the Doms. But that was just part of the "cause" he'd set himself, that he'd put before the men he commanded. Yet it increasingly seemed as if the notion of a true Union had practically been forgotten.

"We'll see," Anson said noncommittally, as De Russy eased away to stand by Alcalde Periz—and the ladies, of course. "We got good soldiers out there, but most are still untested. Sure," he continued, "they won the fight on the beach, an' that was rough. More for some than others. But almost *none* of those fellas ever fought a *real* battle."

"True," Varaa agreed, "but neither have the Doms." She *kakked* an ironic chuckle and blinked something like derision. "Everyone's afraid of them, and rightly so. Not only are they vile, terrible creatures; they're the most numerous, best equipped, most fanatically *disciplined* power in this hemisphere—that I know of," she hastened to qualify, tail whipping behind her. "But that's why—again, as far as I know—they've never fought a 'real' battle either. Why should they? Who could stand against them before now?" She shook her head. "So just as you should never underestimate an enemy, don't be seduced into *overestimating* him either." She lowered her voice and flicked her eyes at Alcalde Periz. "Just as you should never assume your rear is secure. Alcalde Periz—all these people . . . I *must* believe they're *good*, or King Har-Kaaska wouldn't defend them." She nodded at the marching troops. "But Periz is unquestionably the principal *alcalde* in the Alliance of Cities and may be tempted to view this power you've brought him more as *his* than *ours*."

"What's that supposed to mean?" Leonor demanded.

Varaa blinked at her. "Nothing. I grow cynical in my old age. I'm almost forty!" She looked at Lewis. "But have a care. And when the enemy's finally arrayed before you, look to the rear as well."

Lewis was more troubled by that than he could allow himself to show. He'd trusted Periz and Father Orno implicitly, believing their greater ambition remained the same as his in the long run. It might *seem* "forgotten" for now, but *only* for now. Varaa's offhand comment undermined all that and reinforced his sense of disappointment in them—and himself—because he wasn't sure what to do or say. He frowned as the familiar anger his father always inspired suddenly surged to the surface again. He'd suppressed it for half his life before realizing it was directed more at himself than the old man, because he'd waited so long to confront him. And the reason now was almost the same: fear of an irreconcilable break. But the consequences for revealing his displeasure, forcing a confrontation, would affect more than him this time. He *couldn't* risk a rupture when everyone's very survival had to be his chief concern, his foremost "cause."

He frowned more deeply, studying Periz. *I can't imagine what he might do there, but I'll make sure I don't have to "look to the rear" to see him.*

His expression must've been dark enough to make Leonor look at him with concern. He managed a smile for her. Samantha had been right, at least in certain respects. Her now-obvious machinations to soften Leonor's brooding, hostile persona into something a bit lighter had succeeded amazingly. The astonishing, almost blooming transformation at the reception had been fleeting, but hadn't entirely faded. One could never say Leonor was a different person now, but she was less intense and standoffish. Even with Teniente Lara. That was good for her and the army, as was her unprecedented (and surprisingly unopposed) commissioning.

She and her father's other "original" Rangers might command Ranger companies or act as "unattached scout leaders," empowered to requisition squads of men from all their mounted forces at need. Her acceptance in that role gave her a new confidence to get along better with others. Lewis saw no evidence for Samantha's assertion that Leonor had her heart set on him, but ever since their dances at the reception, she'd been easier and more open around him and acted more like a friend than a wounded, belligerent wildcat. He smiled more broadly at her, and she returned a nod as if she'd been reading his thoughts.

The Pennsylvania boys had struck up a new local favorite as they marched past the reviewing stand again. This one was based—like so many popular songs they knew—on the melody of "Lucy Neal." It started with Sergeant Ulrich, as usual, but quickly swelled to include every regiment.

"I fear no haughty blood-soaked Doms,
They make me feel no dread,
Their yellow suits'll all be red,
When we shoot 'em dead!

For Uxmal will be free, my boys,
Uxmal will be free!
An' when we chase the Doms away,
How happy we will be!"

Suddenly, even over the singing and other music of the troops, Lewis felt as much as heard the thudding pressure of a cannon shot. He looked at Anson, who nodded back. He'd recognized it too, as had quite a few others, because the singing began to falter. "That was the warning gun above the main west gate," Varaa said without inflection. Everyone was already staring in that direction, watching a rising white cloud of smoke in the distance, drifting away to the north.

Lewis strode to Alcalde Periz. "I hate to interrupt the festivities," he began.

"Of course," Periz interrupted. "The great gun wouldn't fire without cause. See to it, if you please."

Lewis controlled another frown. Periz's tone was almost imperious, but there was nervousness as well. He turned to Major Reed, who'd followed him over with a dragoon bugler. "Stand the men to and call the Home Guards to their stations." The guards hadn't been on parade today.

Reed gestured at the regiments, now halted and silent. "Should I send the rest to their assigned defensive posts as well?"

Lewis shook his head. "We don't know anything. Just hold them here, but be prepared to draw ammunition and post them at once." He was watching Sal Hernandez, Lieutenant Meder, and a squad of Mounted Rifles approach with horses enough for nearly everyone on the reviewing stand. "Reassure your people, Alcalde Periz," Lewis said, tilting his head toward the many spectators growing increasingly alarmed. "Then perhaps you should come with us."

THE ALARM HAD been caused by the approach of horsemen erupting from the distant woods and urging their exhausted, foaming animals down the road through the fields beyond the river as fast as they could. Lewis, Anson, Leonor, and Felix Meder mounted the new parapet above the gate first, followed quickly by Periz, De Russy, and Father Orno. Captain Holland practically shoved Periz's followers up the steps, but was joined by Samantha Wilde and Sira Periz, who'd apparently ridden together. Lewis had already pressed in among the Uxmalo gunners who'd fired the big, hoop-reinforced wrought-iron piece to watch the horsemen through his small pocket telescope.

"They're Burton's dragoons," he announced flatly. They'd almost reached the bridge by now, and everyone already knew. "Only about forty or so of the eighty he took," he went on, "carrying about thirty of Ixtla's Ocelomeh, riding double. They look like hell," he added grimly, collapsing the telescope, "and I don't see Coryon or Ixtla, or any of Espinoza's lancers." He didn't need to call down to open the gate—it had never been closed—but he shouted for healers and water as he burst through those still arriving and plunged back down the steps. "Ah, there you are, Doctor," he said, meeting Newlin and Reverend Harkin as they trotted up on a shared horse. "Hurt men coming in, and there may be business for you both."

Sergeant Hayne was first through the gate and slid off his staggering mount to give Lewis the best salute he could. "Beg to report, sir," he said through dry, cracking lips.

"Drink first," Lewis commanded as a woman raced up with a sloshing copper bucket straight from the well. Other men were coming in, some collapsing to the ground when they left the saddle. "More water!" Lewis shouted. Hayne drank greedily, pouring as much on his ragged, rotten uniform as he did down his throat, then passed the bucket to other anxious hands. Leonor was taking horses from riders and handing them off to more gathering locals to lead to the troughs.

"God," Hayne gasped, "I needed that. Thankee, sir." He swayed, but Newlin steadied him as he peered at all the sores and bumps on the sergeant's skin over the top of his spectacles.

"This man needs attention," Newlin snapped. "They all do, I'm sure. I see more serious wounds!" he added and scurried away.

"The only attention I need is someone to *listen* to me," Hayne called after the doctor.

"Tell me," Lewis pressed, expecting the worst. He got it.

"The Doms're comin', sure as can be. Thousands of the buggers—beggin' yer pardon, ma'am," he added, noting the approach of Samantha ahead of the rest.

"How many?" Periz demanded.

"How far?" asked De Russy.

"Where's Ixtla—and the others?" pressed Varaa.

"Give the man a chance!" Anson snapped at them all.

Sergeant Hayne nodded his appreciation at the Ranger. "We sent word when we confirmed they were gatherin' at Campeche. Did those fellas get through?"

"Yes," Lewis assured. Four of the eight had finally made it, losing half their number to "swamp monsters," and then only to confirm what Har-Kaaska already suspected. There'd been no word since.

"We watched 'em assemble through the tail end o' the damn rains. More of 'em all the time. Lieutenant Burton wanted to keep count an' report when they moved." He blinked. "After a week with the road dryin' fast, we figured there was twenty thousand or so. About four thousand lancers like Lara's, but in helmets an' armor. An' thirty big guns. Ten *really* big ones, pulled by them armored beasties that don't seem to notice." He sobered. "That's when we lit out, soon as their lancers got frisky an' we saw 'em start drivin' the beasties in to hitch up their guns an' vehicles." He looked away. "Lieutenant Burton wanted to report, but keep shadowin' 'em, like. Trouble was, once them Dom lancers get goin', they move *fast*. Lieutenant Burton got concerned we'd all get cut off, so he sent us on. Only kept ten dragoons, eight mounted Jag-wire Indians, an' all Espinoza's lancers." He shrugged miserably, glancing at Varaa. "An' we had to carry the Indians without horses, so that slowed us some." He looked back at Lewis. "He also made us take all the Hall carbines. Said such weapons couldn't be taken by Doms."

"Good thinking, that," Varaa mused, but Hayne glared at her. "Maybe so, but that left his fellas with nothin' but sabers an' pistols, an Espinoza's lancers to try to break through."

"Break through?" Anson demanded.

"Aye. Bastards got between us somehow. They didn't have any Holcanos with 'em, but maybe they know the woods better than we thought. Even better than the Jag-wire-istas, eh?" he accused, then sighed. "Or maybe they took some lancers up the coast on barges an' put 'em ashore. Either way, on top o' the damn boogers—which're still springin' about but didn't get any more of us, thank God—there's been two or three hundred of the devils doggin' us the last week an' more. We ambushed 'em twice an' bloodied their noses for 'em, but lost ten good men. They just kept comin'." He shrugged and waved around. "We done all we could with our horses so worn down. We were lucky to get here."

"Well done," Lewis said. "Now see to your men and animals." He paused. "How far behind do you think the enemy lancers are?"

"Half a day, maybe. Probably less," Hayne replied, then glanced at Varaa again and added more respectfully, "Ran into some more o' your Ocelomeh in the dark. Said they'd keep lookout on the road."

Varaa nodded. "That's one of the reasons they're there."

"And the main enemy force at the pace you last saw them?"

"A week or ten days. No more."

Lewis nodded, then looked intently at Anson before turning to Lieutenant Meder. He saw Joffrion's bugler too. "I want every mounted man we have, each carrying one of Captain Wagley's infantrymen and all prepared to fight on foot. A section of Dukane's B Battery howitzers as well. Canister only." He spun to Captain Holland. "How soon can *Tiger* be ready for sea?"

Holland looked surprised. "As soon as I get out to her," he said. "The wind an' tide are right."

"Set sail, then, and cruise down the coast. If our cutoff people see you, they may attempt a signal. Pick them up if you can, but don't confront any Dom ships, no matter how sure you are of them. We can't risk damage to *Tiger.*"

Holland nodded with a scowl, convinced his ship could tackle anything the Doms might have. "Just lead 'em away again?"

"No point," Lewis said. "They know where we are. They're sending an army, after all."

"What will you do, Major?" Periz asked anxiously.

Lewis eyed him closely. There was no imperiousness in the *alcalde's* manner now. "Go and set up *another* ambush, sir. Big enough to annihilate the Doms chasing Sergeant Hayne."

Periz looked hesitant. "But what purpose will that serve? You'd leave us without any mounted troops?"

"Teniente Lara won't like it, but I'll leave him here. I don't mean to charge anyone and break their formation, I just want to kill them. As for what it'll accomplish . . . first, I hope to save Coryon Burton's men. Just as important," he added darkly, "when the main enemy force arrives, I want it to find everyone they sent ahead lying dead on the road as they pass!"

"Critters won't leave much," Leonor said mildly, speaking for the first time.

Lewis glared at her and answered hotly, even as he was struck by the apparent reversal of their ordinary tones, "Even better if all they find is gnawed armor and bones, and shreds of yellow uniforms."

Things were starting to happen, and Periz looked about to say or ask something else. Anson stepped forward and steered him and his attendants away, his daughter and now Samantha watching. "Major Cayce comes off all mild and friendly, but I've seen him like this before. He'll get cold an' calm when the fight starts, but when men's lives he feels responsible for are on the line, he gets *crazy* to get on the move to do somethin' for 'em. That's one of the best things about him, in a way, 'cause he'd feel the same for me or you. But if I *were* you, I'd stay out of his way right now. Especially if you're fixin' to try an' stop him."

Periz was blinking, much like Varaa would, but there was no meaning to it. "But the Doms!" he said at last. "They're practically here!"

"As we knew they would be, eventually," Varaa said, stepping up beside Anson, tail whipping behind her.

"But . . . they're actually almost *here*! I somehow thought . . ."

"They'd never really come?" Varaa asked severely. "That our preparations would simply scare them away? No, Alcalde Periz, the Doms are coming, and we'll fight them. And as Lewis Cayce said, we'll kill them. Make your peace with that, because there'll be no more peace of any sort until we win—or die."

CHAPTER 29

Somehow, the same grizzled old Ocelomeh warrior who found the vantage point where Lieutenant Burton watched the Dom buildup at Campeche was not only still alive but had managed to return from another dangerous scout up the road toward Uxmal. He found Coryon, Ixtla, and Espinoza, along with their six surviving dragoons, thirty-three lancers, and two of Ixtla's six remaining mounted Ocelomeh (the others keeping watch behind), concealed in the sultry woods near the washboard glade, where the Americans made their last camp on their way to Uxmal.

"They still don't know we're behind them?" Coryon asked when the man dropped from his horse and squatted in the leafy needles in front of him. He was referring to the Dominion lancers between them and Hayne's detachment. "Those devils screening the main Dom army certainly know we're here," he added grimly. There'd been a few vicious scrapes on both sides of the dead city of Nautla, first when Coryon's small force was caught from behind, and again when it was driven away from watching what the enemy did when they arrived there in force.

Ixtla translated the question and reply. "So intent on pursuing Sergeant Hayne, they seem to have no notion of us. They don't even *watch* behind them," Ixtla added significantly. "It appears our efforts to prevent communication have been successful." They'd caught and killed eight couriers. "I would expect them to start, however," he continued sourly. "Even if only because they've had no contact with the army behind them. They'll leave watchers to report its approach."

Espinoza grimaced. "If we don't smash through the Doms ahead of us, we'll be squeezed to death or forced aside into the woods, unable to report what we saw to our friends."

"Forty-odd of us against two hundred?" Coryon asked with a small, grim smile.

"He says closer to three hundred," Ixtla said with a glance at the scout.

Espinoza tilted his head at the almost disinterested-looking man, now gnawing a strip of jerky. "Some of us should live to carry word."

Coryon reluctantly nodded. They'd lingered near Nautla long enough to watch the enemy begin to deploy as if for an attack and start practicing with their artillery against the city's ruins. By Lewis Cayce's standards, even those of the foot and coastal artillerymen he'd brought to this world, Dom gunnery was slow and inaccurate, their weapons of an older, heavy-for-caliber style, mounted on cumbersome, solid-wheel, split-trail carriages. But even Coryon could tell their field artillery was much more modern than the crude cannons they'd salvaged from the galleon. They also fired metal roundshot instead of stone. He didn't know if it was iron or copper, but that didn't matter, since their monstrous siege guns in particular had utterly shattered portions of the standing ruins of Nautla. They'd make equally short work of the walls around Uxmal from a distance even Lewis's best guns couldn't reply. "Some of us have to get through," Coryon finally agreed aloud. "I don't know Cayce well enough to say for sure, but he doesn't strike me as the static defense sort. Why work so hard to make flying artillery out of foot artillery? I doubt he means to meet the Doms behind the walls of the city. But what if he has no choice? What if . . . others"—he glanced fleetingly at Ixtla—"feel so secure behind their walls they won't *let* him go beyond them? He has to be told that can't work."

Coryon caught the expectant expressions on the tired faces gathered around. "Mount up," he said, then looked at the old Ocelomeh. "Lead us back to the enemy, if you please."

CHAPTER 30

L ewis's rapidly assembled force, moving quickly, was nearing a rare, bald, grassy mound in the midst of a small clearing about three miles from the city. They'd thought of camping their refugee army there on its way to Uxmal, instead of at the more distant washboard glade, but it wasn't as open, and the sinister trees would've been too close to the tents. It was perfect for what Lewis had in mind now. He and Anson, Varaa, and Leonor were riding at the head of the column, and Captain Wagley and Lieutenant Joffrion galloped forward to join them when Lewis called a halt. It had been oppressively humid in the dense woods, but when they left cover, the midafternoon sun beat brutally down. The place was like a narrow, grassy lake in the forest, barely two hundred yards wide but several hundred yards long, dominated by a rounded hump with large, weathered stones exposed at its summit. The short, browning blades of grass they remembered were now tall and green, drawing large beasts that munched contentedly in small herds differentiated by their bizarre shapes. A cloud of lizardbirds hovered over the trees to the south, joined by larger things that looked like flying Grik and acted like monstrous vultures. *Those are the things that "flew off" when the boys went to inspect the dead pile the morning after Lieutenant Swain was killed,* Lewis now knew. *Some great predator*

must've made a kill over there. This many "prey" animals must surely attract them. He pursed his lips. *Like the Uxmalos draw the Doms.*

A cloud of fine dust was rising beyond the rise. Moments later, six riders appeared, pounding toward them, dun-and-black-striped ponies laboring mightily. Two were obviously Boogerbear and Sergeant Buisine of the 3rd Dragoons, who'd accompanied a pair of Varaa's Ocelomeh scouts. They'd been joined by more Jaguar Warriors, possibly those Sergeant Hayne met.

Buisine saluted when the group drew up. "They're coming, sir, maybe three hundred lancers. No guns or infantry, but they're barely a mile and a half behind us." He gestured to the strange Ocelomeh. "These fellas seen 'em. Others are screening their flanks. If they leave the road, we'll know."

"They're coming right at us?"

"Yes sir."

Lewis turned to look behind. Between Dukane's section of two howitzers and their crews, Lieutenant Joffrion's dragoons, and Lieutenant Felix Meder's mounted riflemen—many riding double with some saddle-sore and resentful members of the 3rd Pennsylvania—Lewis had about four hundred men. An advantage in numbers, but they weren't prepared for this. *He* wasn't particularly prepared for the reception he had to conjure on the fly, but the position gave him his plan. "Captain Wagley, how many infantry do you have?"

"About ninety, sir."

"Very well. Have them dismount and form a line at the top of that rise, refusing the road, flags flying. I'll join you presently." He looked at Joffrion and Felix as Wagley shouted commands, taken up by NCOs, and men slid gingerly down from the horses. "The dragoons and riflemen will dismount as well, horse holders to the rear, and take positions at the edge of these woods. *No* flags, and stay out of sight. Dukane," he called to B Battery's commander.

"Sir?"

"I hate to split your section in its first action, but we must." He pointed vaguely northwest and southeast. "I want a gun on either side of the road, all the riflemen and dragoons between you." He grinned. "You'll be in position to rake the enemy without mercy after they 'rout' our infantry, do you understand?" Dawning comprehension came, and Lieutenant Dukane nodded with grim satisfaction. "We'll lay 'em in fast and hot, sir."

"I know." Turning to his other officers, already shouting commands, he raised his voice. "I'll be with the infantry. Captain Anson will command here." Anson started to protest, but Lewis shook his head. "When the enemy pushes the infantry back, and they will, I don't know how close behind us they'll be. We must make it convincing, mustn't we, boys?" he called out to the foot soldiers already stepping off. A chorus of surprisingly good-natured jibes replied, and Lewis smiled before turning back to the dragoons and riflemen. "You men may have to be careful of your targets, and that's why you're back here: accurate rifles and rapid-fire carbines. If any of the enemy escapes, I don't want them learning of those." His voice turned grim. "That said, I don't *want* them to escape. Once you break their charge, you'll mount and give chase." Some of the men actually cheered at that, and after a meaningful nod at Anson, Lewis turned Arete to follow the infantry. He wasn't surprised when Varaa joined him, but he was to see Leonor urge her horse up on his other side. He'd assumed she'd stay with her father—would've preferred it—but sending her back might undermine the respect she'd earned from the men. Inwardly, he sighed.

"How exciting, Major Cayce!" Varaa said. "I fully approve of your dispositions, by the way. I only wish more of my Ocelomeh were here to see what may be the very first battle ever fought by two modern armies on this continent!"

"I don't anticipate much of a 'battle,' if all goes well."

"But things so rarely do, do they?" Varra observed lightly, then her tone grew more serious. "I heard you say you expect the Doms to 'break'?"

"What of it?" Leonor asked, unable to keep her silence.

Varaa blinked rapidly, and her tail flicked behind her. "I thought you understood. To the truly committed Dom, and their lancers are required to be such creatures, agonizing death is the very key to paradise. I doubt they'll 'break,' as you imagine, and you may be proud to call this a 'battle' by the time it's done."

They rode up beside Wagley, still on his horse, and took position behind his men as they went from column into line, forming two forty-three-man ranks directly astride the road. Lewis saw Sergeant Visser and a newly elected corporal he didn't know striding behind the line as file closers. Visser's musket was slung, but he had two iron ramrods in his hand. One had a worm screwed on the threaded end, a flower of fuzzy tow already twisted into it. If anyone's musket got too fouled to load, he'd wet the tow and let the man swab his barrel. The other rammer had a screw for pulling the ball a nervous man might load without powder. That unlucky soldier would likely take a few blows from the rod as well. Lewis doubted they'd stand here long enough to need either implement, but Visser was prepared. He was mainly there to keep men from running and close the gaps when they fell.

It was hot as hell, and sweat soaked the blue shell jacket Private Willis had quickly exchanged Lewis for his good coat. Looking around, the view struck him as surreal. The sky was an almost perfect, cloudless blue, the grass and trees the deepest green he'd ever seen. But there were huge, dangerous-looking beasts grazing disconcertingly close without any apparent concern. If anything, the occasional glares they sent from giant, cow-like eyes seemed almost contemptuous. *As well they might be,* Lewis realized. *A 6pdr might lay one out, but a concentrated volley from all ninety of these men would probably only enrage it.* He looked more carefully at one of the closer animals with two great horns protruding from its bony head like those of a rhinoceros. *Thick, rough skin, bigger than elephants if not as tall,* he decided, *though there are taller things by the far trees, tiny heads on great long necks stripping leaves higher than any giraffe.* He snorted to himself. *And here we stand among them, almost as oblivious to them as they to us: a tiny clot of men in blue on this brilliant green rise, waiting for other men to come and fight.* "It seems particularly ridiculous when you think about it like that," he murmured absently aloud.

"I hardly believe it's happenin'," Leonor said, as if her thoughts mirrored his. She confirmed his suspicion when Varaa asked her, "The battle? The Doms come at last?"

"No," she replied and gestured helplessly around. "Only that we're fightin' 'em here."

Varaa blinked. "The sun may soon prove a problem if the Doms delay until late afternoon, but I think Major Cayce has chosen a good place," she assured.

"That's not what she means, Warmaster Varaa," Lewis said lowly. "Not what I mean."

"Oh. Indeed." Varaa looked around and *kakked.* "You get used to it, you know."

"I'm still not 'used' to *you!*" Leonor retorted.

Lewis turned to gaze behind them, the leather of his Ringgold saddle creaking loudly. Nearly all the men had disappeared back in the woods, leaving only Anson, Felix Meder, Hans Joffrion, and Emmel Dukane in the open, about a hundred yards back. They'd be invisible to the approaching enemy but could still see Lewis.

"There they are," hissed Leonor, voice now focused and flat.

Lewis looked back to the front. About four hundred yards to the west, two men had loped out of the forest track gloom aboard beautiful but entirely ordinary-looking black horses. The yellow and black of their uniforms looked a bit tattered and stained, but they also wore highly polished brass breastplates and helmets with long red plumes spilling from the top. Lances slightly longer than those of Lara's men were held upright beside them, burnished tips glinting above flowing red ribbons.

They saw the Americans at once and stopped, perfectly still and staring.

"I wish we had some of Meder's riflemen now," Wagley said wistfully, nervously. Lewis had to remind himself this was the first time any of them (aside from Leonor and Varaa of course) ever laid eyes on the dreaded Doms. A shout echoed down in the woods, and the two men spurred forward. A moment later, the vanguard of the Dom column appeared. A few more shouts were all that were needed to send men flowing out to the sides of the road, advancing slowly until the first rank achieved a breadth of about a hundred yards. But the Doms kept coming, forming more lines behind the first until there were no fewer than five. And still they came on at a slow walk to within three hundred yards, unfurling a huge red flag with a crooked gold cross upon it.

"Goddamn their souls," Wagley said bitterly, voice cracking as he pulled on a chain around his neck and fingered a cross of his own. "What'll happen now?" he asked. Lewis heard the nervous mutters of other men in the ranks, a few crossing themselves. He wasn't nearly as confident as Reverend Harkin in respect to *why* they'd been brought to this world, but he too had a visceral reaction to the twisted flag of the enemy and all it represented. "Will they have a word with us first?" Wagley pressed.

"I think not," Varaa replied.

"Uncase your colors," Lewis said.

"Uncase the colors!" Wagley cried. Only then did Lewis notice the color-bearer for the Stars and Stripes was the young, towheaded Private "Hanny" Cox, who'd stood up to the brutal Hahessy—twice now, if the rumors were true—and he'd doubtless saved some lives at the cantina. His comrades must've wanted to honor his courage. Another young man unrolled the blue banner of Pennsylvania, and both flags stood out just enough in the light, humid air to challenge the jagged Dom cross. The challenge was accepted with the blare of a horn, an anonymous shout that carried across the field, and the long lances of the leading line of horsemen came down with an admirable, intimidating unity, polished points unwaveringly aimed at the small clot of men on the rise.

"It appears they've said all they intend to," observed Lewis. In his mind, by lowering their lances, the Doms might as well have fired a volley.

"Load!" Wagley shouted, confident he could dispense with twelve-count commands, even with all his new recruits, who practiced loading often enough they could probably do it in their sleep. Extracting cartridges from leather boxes at their sides, they bit the ends off, primed their muskets, and upended the paper tubes at the muzzles. Flashing steel ramrods seated lead balls still tied in the ends of the tubes before being returned to grooves in the stocks under the barrels. Lewis was impressed by the new men, and it seemed their "immersion training" had paid off.

"Fix bayonets!" Wagley cried when the lancers were about two hundred and thirty yards distant. There was another rippling flash of polished steel in the sun as long, triangular blades were drawn and locked in place.

"Those will come as an unpleasant surprise to the enemy," Varaa observed beside Lewis.

Leonor looked at her questioningly.

"You've seen their weapons. Not unlike yours in their basic form, if not so finely made, but they think of musketry only as the music before the dance, and the bayonet's their primary weapon. Your men can keep loading and shooting with bayonets in place. Theirs are like the short swords your artillerymen carry for various purposes, but when its tapered handle is inserted *into* their barrels instead of slipping so ingeniously over the outside, they can shoot no more." Varaa flicked her tail and nodded at the lancers. "They'll be coming on faster soon."

"I'm sure your men can hit something the size of a man and horse at two hundred yards if they aim a bit high," Lewis prodded Wagley.

The man gulped. "Front rank, make ready!"

Forty-three men raised their weapons up in front of their faces, locks on the outside, and thumbed the cocks grasping lead-padded flints back to the second notch with an audible chorus of *clicks*.

"At the tops of the riders' heads, take aim!" Wagley shouted. The sun glinted off polished steel once more as long muskets and bayonets came down in a ripple and steadied on a horizontal plane for an instant before starting to bobble as each man endeavored to keep the little brass blade on his front barrel band centered near the rounded top of the back of his barrel while still pointing it where he'd been told. Their weapons had no rear sights, and most of these men were actually shorter than their weapons, with bayonets fixed, and couldn't hold them like that for long, but Wagley hesitated, glancing at Lewis, as if afraid to utter the fateful word that would plunge them into war with a still-mysterious power known largely only for its relentless malignancy.

Lewis understood how he felt. Yet despite some new nagging reservations about Alcalde Periz, perhaps even King Har-Kaaska, he was sure of Varaa. She'd left him no doubt the Doms were evil, the *true* demons in this land, and his own experience with the smallest of their "fingers," Tranquilo, Discipo, the Holcanos and Grik, only confirmed what she said. "Fire!" he shouted, and with a flashing, smoky roar, the first volley boomed out with gratifying precision.

They *heard* the big musket balls slam into human and animal flesh, thumping and smacking or clanking through armor. Men and horses screamed and squealed as they crashed to the ground or into one another.

"Reload! Rear rank, take aim . . . fire!" The second volley was more ragged than the first but even more effective. Two hundred yards was a very great distance for any smoothbore musket, even the fine American examples, but the enemy was so closely spaced, few shots could fail to hit something. More horses screeched and rolled, crushing riders and throwing the front rank of lancers into confusion. But even as the survivors fought to control their animals, another horn sounded, and the following ranks charged through at a gallop. Lewis knew they had half a minute before the enemy was on them and those lances would tear them apart. "Pour it in, lads! Another two rounds each, as fast as you can, then we'll run for the woods and take new positions!" He caught Wagley's guilty stare and gave an encouraging smile. "My apologies, Captain. I got a little excited."

Wagley jerked a nod and shouted, "Independent, fire at will! A gallon of Uxmalo corn beer to the man who fires *three* shots before we retire!"

"Cuttin' it mighty close," Leonor said over the crackle of muskets and growing thunder of hooves. She was inspecting the revolver she'd drawn, not looking at him.

"If we retreat too quickly, they may suspect our trap," Varaa told her before Lewis could. She'd taken the British-style musket from where she kept it slung diagonally across her back and was inspecting the priming, testing the sharpness of the flint with her thumb.

"You said we can't 'break' 'em, an' they're already takin' more punishment than other lancers I've seen. They'll smash us like a sack of eggs."

"I meant you won't chase them away," Varaa corrected. "They'll fight you to the death"—she bowed her head at the woods and all the men and guns concealed there—"but the forest will break their *charge* and you may kill them at your leisure."

Lewis had his saber in his right hand and had withdrawn one of his M1836 pistols from its pommel holster with his left. "Just a few moments more, I think," he said, eyes flitting back and forth between the woods and the dashing, bleeding Doms. The first crushing volleys had been replaced by continuous fire, and nearly every ball found its mark as the range wound down and the Doms were increasingly desperate to smash this lethal little obstacle. Their precise alignment had combined into a heaving, rushing horde, bristling with lances, leaping or falling over men and horses still being chopped from the front.

Our men are feeling it now, Lewis judged, watching some waver, glancing behind as well. *How could they not? Determined lancers are always intimidating, and no matter how many these inexperienced troops take down, there are still more of the enemy than of them.* A young local in the rear rank, really just a boy, dropped his musket and tried to run. Sergeant Visser blocked him, whacking him brutally with one of his rammers, roaring, "Back in ranks, you gutless bastard, or I'll see your backbone at the whipping post!"

"We'll overlook it just this once if he retrieves his weapon, Sergeant," Lewis shouted over the din, catching a glimpse of wide, terrified eyes before the youngster scrambled back for his musket on all fours. Large, low-velocity balls whined and warbled past as some of the lancers, losing their primary weapons in the crush, fired musketoons. "Captain Wagley, dismiss your men to the rear. Run for it, lads! Make it look good. Pretend to be afraid!"

He knew there'd be no pretending, but they could say so later. Sometimes that was all that mattered.

It was as if the men had been panicking horses secured to a picket line and someone cut their leads. A few stood firm for a final shot, but almost as one the rest surged back, then turned and sprinted downslope for the trees. Varaa's horse was giving her trouble, and she took a moment to settle it before raising her musket and firing at the yellow-and-black tide barely fifty yards distant. Lewis was sure she'd lingered deliberately, braving a thickening hail of musket and pistol balls just so the enemy would see her. And by the way the lancers whipped their horses bloody, it was apparent nothing enraged them like the very existence of her kind. Now she bolted, and quite a few Doms made as if to chase her alone. Arete sidestepped, and a lance head swept past Lewis's shoulder. Without thinking, he whipped his saber across the Dom's throat before he had a chance to recover. He tottered from his horse, clutching the spraying wound.

"Go!" Leonor roared at Lewis, firing her revolver over the head of the man with the Pennsylvania colors as he tried to reach her horse. He was too slow. A lance head and a shower of blood exploded from his chest and he went down hard on his face. Lewis shot his killer with his pistol and then let it drop. "Let's *all* go, shall we?" he shouted, seeing Wagley haul Hanny Cox and his flag up on the saddle in front of him. They were right at the head of the storm, with lances questing for them as they urged their horses into a sprint after Varaa. Leonor emptied her pistol at some of the men around them, and Lewis hacked another with his saber. Arete flinched when a lance head pricked her flank and sped even faster. Lewis risked a glimpse behind and saw all the Doms crest the rise, churning down upon them. It was lucky he did, because he was just able to deflect a lance aimed at his back with his saber. The Dom was going to thrust again, however, and already twisted so far around, Lewis couldn't avoid the wicked blade again.

Then the Dom dropped his lance and clutched his face with a scream. More Doms inexplicably tumbled from their saddles, and a black horse crashed down, throwing its broken rider. Lewis looked to his front and saw dozens of pearly-white smoke flowers blooming in the brush at the base of the trees. And there was Captain Anson, fully exposed and swathed in smoke atop his horse, Colonel Fannin, a huge revolver in each hand.

"Kill them!" Anson roared. "Shoot the bastards down! Well done, riflemen! Let your dragoons give 'em a taste, Lieutenant Joffrion!" Carbines boomed rapidly, and more Dom lancers fell, the ones behind brought up short by surprise and the tumbling, rolling, screeching mounts. Lewis and Leonor wheeled in behind Anson as Varaa and Captain Wagley came up on the other side. Hanny Cox had jumped to the ground and now stood waving the big national flag over his head. *Poom!* went the 12pdr howitzer on the southeast end of the line, spewing its load of canister—forty-eight one-

inch iron balls—into the milling Doms. *Poom!* went the other gun, shredding more men and animals. Both screamed so shrilly, it was impossible to
tell which was which. *Poom! Poom!* went the guns, again and again, at intervals of twenty seconds or less, combined with a relentless storm of rifle,
carbine, and now musket balls again.

A rational foe would've fled. The Doms had started with almost three
hundred men, and not only had they quickly lost half that number; they were
in a sack. Shock, the forest, the mass of dead and withering storm of lead had
stalled their charge completely. Even given a cultural or psychological inability to withdraw, an enterprising leader might've rallied and shifted his survivors one way or another, perhaps overruning one of the guns that kept
pounding, mulching them down. There was no commander of any sort by
then, however, and the Dom lancers could only keep trying to do what they'd
last been told. Wounded men urged bleeding horses at the clump of apparent
officers gathered near that demonic *thing*, trying to get their shattered animals to climb over others if they must. All cried out in fury and despair as
they were blown or shot to the ground. Some tried even then, dragging their
mangled bodies, screaming in agony—but agony was good!

"My God!" gasped Captain Wagley, face white with horror. "This is
worse than those Grik things!"

"Far worse," Varaa agreed darkly, "because most would define these
creatures as 'people,' yet their behavior is even more . . . mindlessly animalistic."

Even Captain Anson looked disturbed, staring out at the carnage, particularly when he saw a man with shattered legs, eyes glazed with shock,
pain, and loss of blood, but still lit with determined hate, dragging himself
toward them with a musketoon in his hands. He shot him.

Poom! Poom!

"My God!" repeated Wagley. "Can't we cease firing now?"

"Yes," Lewis said, voice as dark as Varaa's as he gazed at what was left of
the once-proud column of lancers. A lot of horses had bolted when their
riders fell, much more sensible than their masters, and less than a score
were still standing before them, perhaps half with men still in the saddle.
The way they just sat there, Lewis suspected they were dead. "Cease firing!"
he shouted aloud. Many had already done so, and a sudden almost silence
descended, broken only by the sounds of pain. There was no cheering.
"Lieutenant Joffrion, mount your dragoons and take them back down the

track. Ensure that none of the enemy escaped. Lieutenant Meder, mount your men as well and seize the enemy horses. Be so kind as to end the misery of any that are badly hurt."

"What about them?" Wagley demanded, waving at the bloody field under the afternoon sun. "What about the enemy wounded?"

"They won't surrender," Varaa sighed. "It would be a kindness to them and safer for you to 'end their misery' as well."

"I won't do it, damn you!" Wagley practically seethed. Lewis put a hand on his arm.

"Of course not," he said gently, "but have your men *secure* the enemy wounded before attempting to help them. Is that understood?"

The dragoons had accepted their horses from the holders and now pounded off up the road. Felix Meder was looking around with a haunted expression while his own men mounted as well. Careful infantrymen were starting to pick through the dead and wounded while Wagley remained with Lewis, Anson, Leonor, and Varaa. Lewis noted that Hanny Cox had stopped waving the flag and stood as if stunned, now joined by a couple of friends. One was a short Uxmalo. All were breathing hard.

"By the way, Captain Wagley," Lewis said at last, "my compliments to you and your men for the way they stood today. This victory, such as it is, is theirs." He paused. "How many did you lose?"

"Eleven killed, sir. Only eleven," Wagley answered wanly, as if hardly believing it himself. His voice firmed. "And six slightly hurt. Seems they got off awfully light, or died."

"We lost four in the woods," Anson said. "Carbine fire," he added by way of explanation. "We got off *mighty* light . . . considerin'."

"Yes, considerin' how many there were, an' they're a pack o' maniacs," Leonor almost spat. She looked around, expression softening slightly. "Look," she said, "all the big critters are gone."

"Even they must be in awe of the violence they saw today," Varaa said, "as I confess to being." Her tail whipped. "I *do* understand how you must feel, but to my certain knowledge, this 'battle'—as it surely was—will be remembered as the greatest victory ever achieved over regular Dominion forces. You can be proud of that, at least. It will give the Uxmalos hope. It will give *everyone* hope." She paused. "But don't expect all your victories to be so one-sided. You're better soldiers than they; I knew it at once. But there are a great many of them, and you haven't faced their infantry yet"—she glanced at Lewis—"or their artillery."

"Is this truly the face of things to come?" Wagley softly asked, gazing at where some of his men had been forced to bayonet a wounded Dom who'd probably tried to kill them for helping him. "*This* is the kind of war we fight? Without mercy? Without honor?"

Varaa hesitated. "Essentially, yes. The common Dominion soldier isn't as . . . fanatical as their lancers. Most are conscripts, after all." She blinked at Lewis. "I know what you're thinking. You might break *them*. But their commanders are true believers, as bad as Tranquilo's guard, and even their rank and file will treat you just as these men would have if they won. They'd have slaughtered us all, or perhaps tortured a few survivors for entertainment." She looked at Wagley. "But there'll be 'honor' enough, never fear. Ask Father Orno or Reverend Harkin. What could be more honorable than opposing evil for the benefit of others?"

Boogerbear had drifted over by Leonor, massaging her shoulder and tousling her hair like an annoying older brother. She punched him hard in the arm. "I don't care about heapin' honor on myself," Boogerbear said, then added, offhand, voice as steady as ever, shading his eyes, "We got riders comin'."

Lewis started to call an alarm, wondering why no one else had, but realized the silhouettes topping the rise were their own people. They paused a moment, gazing down at the scene before them, then urged their animals on. It was only when Lewis saw the battered, rotten uniforms and sadly hungry look on tired, weatherworn faces that he knew these weren't Joffrion's men. "Lieutenant Burton, Ixtla, Alferez Espinoza!" he exclaimed, returning their awkward salutes. "I'm very glad to see you." He squinted at the few men behind them. "Glad to see you all! Sergeant Hayne believed you might still be a few days out. We even sent Captain Holland and *Tiger* looking for you."

Burton licked cracked lips. "We have information, sir. Didn't think it could wait." He gestured somewhat helplessly around. "We'd planned to catch up to these fellows and try to break through to reach you, but"—he managed a tight smile—"I guess we don't have to now. I didn't really think we could."

"You see?" Varaa told Wagley. "Honor enough for all."

CHAPTER 31

The map room in the Audience Hall was filled to capacity with all of Alcalde Periz and Father Orno's closest advisors and influential locals involved in supporting their preparations. Varaa, Ixtla, and Consul Koaar represented the Ocelomeh, and virtually all of Lewis's senior officers, including Captain Holland—just returned—were present. The place was packed, and benches had been crowded around the great wooden table dominating the center of the room. Other benches had been added until the entire space was filled with their close-packed ranks. To Lewis's surprise, there were quite a few females (aside from Varaa, of course, and Leonor, who simply wouldn't leave her father's side). *Or mine, it seems,* Lewis considered, remembering how she'd nearly been overrun with the rest of them on the rise. *It's as if she feels compelled to serve as aide and protector to us both now.*

And Samantha Wilde sat at the main table with Sira Periz, the *alcalde*'s beautiful wife and *segunda alcaldesa*. Lewis had been so busy building the army that De Russy, Samantha, Angelique, Reverend Harkin, and to a lesser extent, Dr. Newlin, had been obliged to represent the Americans at the near-nightly social functions. To many, De Russy had become the "American face" of the alliance, and Lewis hadn't paid as much attention to local society as he should. He was therefore surprised to discover that in addition to owning property and various businesses, many other women were just as influential as Sira Periz, financing much of Uxmal's industrial expansion with their own fortunes. Samantha had finally explained it to him. Though not allowed to fight like some Ocelomeh women and still somewhat constrained by conservative propriety, the ladies of Uxmal were theoretically equal to any man in every other way and were often Uxmal's staunchest patriots. "They have the most to lose if they're conquered by the Doms, after all," Samantha had told him. "You men will likely only die, but besides the fact that women are mere property to the enemy, less valuable even than slaves for labor, they'll lose their men, their sons, even their pride—which *you* can at least preserve on the battlefield."

And battle was the subject of this meeting. Word of the annihilation of the advance force of lancers had swept through the city, reinforced by glimpses of the few badly wounded prisoners brought in. News of a vast Dom army, just a week away, spread just as quickly. The reaction combined giddy celebration with abject terror. Lewis felt the sense of it even now, in this room, silently watching Periz stand and call them to order before giving a brief, glowing account of the action as Lewis and others reported it. Then he called Varaa to speak, and she stood.

"I've just received word from King Har-Kaaska that Itzincab is besieged by Holcanos, Grik, and even some warriors from Puebla Arboras under Don Discipo. All their mines, crops—everything—is under enemy control, and the people surrounding Itzincab have been forced into the city."

There were murmurs of alarm, but Varaa raised a hand. "We knew Don Discipo couldn't be trusted to resist the enemy and they'd use him thus. That's why Alcalde Truro's been so nervous and King Har-Kaaska remained in his city." She smiled slightly and blinked encouragement, adding, "Itzincab won't fall. Aside from the regiment already formed *here*, most of the Ocelomeh everyone thought were coming to join us are in fact already *there*— as are many of the pike-trained troops from Pidra Blanca. Itzincab was presented as a ripe fruit to be plucked and pillaged, irresistible to the enemy's irregular allies, but it's a *trap* to hold them with sufficient warriors and supplies to resist them indefinitely." She grinned more fiercely. "Har-Kaaska already repulsed a major attack—the Holcanos and Grik have no artillery at all—and virtually destroyed the Grik, at least. They constituted the bulk of the assault force, as usual. So severe were their losses, there's word they may even abandon their allies at last, to preserve their very race!"

The "Grik" as a species were as numberless as flies, but their small, fractious, territorial tribes rarely banded together. The current "confederation" joining so many under a single leader for so long, proclaiming itself a separate, superior "race" from the rest, had been a fragile anomaly. Attempts had been made to approach its leader over the years, to make peace, but the Grik shared too many traits with the Holcanos to prefer friendship with more settled peoples they considered their natural prey, and emissaries never returned. Now . . .

"In any event," Varaa ended triumphantly, "the Doms coming here will have no local support, no eyes in the forest but ours."

There were exclamations of delight as Varaa sank down on her bench, blinking satisfaction at Lewis. He smiled back. *Warmaster indeed,* he told himself. He'd known most of what she planned from the start—and it had been *her* plan to ensure all his army had to deal with were Doms—but he was frankly amazed it had worked.

"Wonderful," came the ironic voice of a man named Tukli, who aside from owning many of the fishing boats supplying food to the city, was known to be skeptical of their efforts to resist the Dominion. He was a sinewy little fellow with a broad, sweaty forehead he often wiped with a blue cloth matching his finely embroidered tunic. "That leaves only—what was it? *Twenty thousand* Doms coming here! What are we to do about them?"

Lewis stood and nodded all around before staring straight at Tukli. "We fight them, sir."

"How?" came several voices at once. Lewis looked at Alcalde Periz, nodding nervously back. Even among these men—no one suspected any of the women—there might be spies for the Doms. Or at least a few who were willing to pass information for better treatment if all was lost.

Lewis took a step back and pointed at a place on the great map near where *Commissary* was wrecked and the battle on the beach occurred. "Varaa's scouts and Captain Anson's Rangers place the enemy vanguard *here*. We can't really meet them anywhere between here and there because of the forest and treacherous crossings—and by 'treacherous,' I mean there'll be more of them when the floods subside. We'd be too far from our base of supply, and they could get around us." He shook his head. "Really, if you consider the terrain, there isn't anyplace to fight them on anything like equal terms on the other side of the Cipactli River, and it presents problems of its own. First, it would prevent retreat to the city if we're defeated, and second"—he shrugged—"the same is true for it as the other crossings. All the Doms have to do is *avoid* battle until the river runs low, then cross at any point upstream between here and Itzincab—possibly joining with the Holcanos when they do."

"But . . ." someone said.

Sira Periz narrowed her eyes. "Are you proposing we follow Itzincab's example and fight them from the city?" she demanded. She looked at Coryon Burton. He was still haggard from his long ordeal but had been bathed, shaved, and given a new uniform. "Let me get this clear," Sira continued sharply. "You're saying that despite the fact that our new powder mill lies *outside* the city, and the great guns Lieutenant Burton observed, all we can do is defend the walls of Uxmal?"

"I'm afraid so," Lewis conceded dismally. "It's the terrain, you see, and the fact there's only the one meager road. What isn't too thickly forested to move our troops through is just too damned flat. There isn't any other place, and it's our only hope."

There were a variety of reactions to this announcement, ranging from horror on the faces of the locals to disbelief among Lewis's officers. Only Anson, Holland, Leonor, and, oddly, Varaa and Samantha seemed unsurprised. Colonel De Russy bit his lip and whispered aside to Samantha Wilde. "I should've thought even I could come up with something better than that."

There was an insistent banging on the door to the grand audience chamber. Private Willis and Barca were closest to it and opened it a crack when Periz nodded to them. Willis listened to urgent whispering, then closed the door and turned, bemused, back to the expectant faces in the map room. Looking at Lewis, he saw him nod.

"Which it was one o' Boogerbear's—I mean Lieutenant Beeryman's Rangers. They glommed onto a pack o' Doms with that damn Tranquilo bastard—'scuse me, ladies—comin' to the city under a white goddamn flag. 'Scuse me. Boogerbear blindfolded 'em, trussed 'em up, an' brought 'em in." He paused. "Seems their high priest general witch doctor wants a palaver to discuss 'terms'—he says. They already know about their lancers and'll 'honor' us by meetin' where we licked 'em. They swear to their prickly God there won't be no troops but a honor guard of a hundred men within a mile o' the place, an' whoever comes from our side can bring the same."

Periz looked flabbergasted. "A truce? With Doms?" He looked at Lewis and Varaa, unsure.

Varaa blinked something that looked like delight while her tail whipped behind her and Lewis nodded slightly. "Might as well hear what they have to say before the fighting starts." He arched his eyebrows. "*More* fighting."

Periz stood, frowning at Father Orno and Reverend Harkin. "I suppose we must meet with Tranquilo to make further arrangements. All of you, please leave us. We'll reconvene when we know more."

The room slowly emptied with a great deal of shuffling and shifting, eventually leaving only those seated at the big table. Nearly everyone who didn't know his mind was glaring at Lewis, including Sira Periz.

"Is a meeting so irregular?" Reverend Harkin asked.

"Most irregular," Father Orno murmured. "Doms *never* 'negotiate.' They impose their will and destroy anyone who stands in their way."

"Maybe the corpses of three hundred lancers changed their minds," Leonor said.

"No," Orno denied. "Not by themselves. There must be more to this than we know." He looked around. "The very *idea* of talking to us would never enter their heads," he insisted.

"Unless someone gave it to them," Lewis said darkly, remembering USS *Isidra* again. He'd considered having Holland search for her, perhaps even looking into Vera Cruz, but had a horror of losing *Tiger* and all her people. Besides, she'd be their only warning if the Doms came from the sea.

"So we go? We talk to . . . whoever represents them?" Periz asked with a slight quaver. He was afraid, and Lewis couldn't blame him.

"I say yeah," Anson growled. "See who we're up against, at least. Maybe get an idea how their leader thinks. How he'll react."

Sira frowned at Lewis, looking between him and Anson. "Reacts to us crouching behind our walls and waiting for them to batter them down around us?" She paused when she saw Samantha's smile and the near smirk on Leonor's face. "Wait . . ." she said.

De Russy regarded Lewis with dawning comprehension. "You've no intention of doing that, do you?"

Lewis shrugged at Sira Periz, then grinned at De Russy. "Of course not. I thought you knew me better." He glanced at the door where Private Willis still stood with a look of satisfaction pinching his narrow face. Barca seemed confused but relieved. "Most of those people who were here don't know me at all," he added. "And if even one lets our 'defensive strategy' slip

to the Doms—which I'm sure Tranquilo will be aware of before he leaves…"
He took a long breath and regarded his friends with a serious gaze, eyes finally resting on Periz and his wife. "The enemy will be even less prepared for something a few of us have been planning, almost since Har-Kaaska told us the Doms might be massing at Campeche." He smiled apologetically. "Forgive me, but considering how quickly Tranquilo threw his attack together *the very first day we were here*, there *must* still be enemy spies in the city. We had to hold our true plans close."

"You couldn't even tell *me*?" De Russy asked, looking hurt.

"*Especially* you, my dear," Samantha said, patting his hand on the table. "You've been very public and have no talent for evasion or deceit. If anyone *suspected* you were withholding some grand secret, they might've drugged you—or worse—to get it, or even targeted poor Angelique, hoping you'd confided in her." De Russy and Angelique Mercure were practically betrothed.

"I see," he said stiffly.

Lewis pressed on. "Now we have this … parley that Tranquilo proposes. We must attend," he said firmly. "Not only to measure our enemy, as Captain Anson says, but it may provide the perfect opportunity to set our plan in motion." He paused. "If you trust me, *truly* trust me as I trust all those in this room—and you're prepared not to breathe a word of it beyond that door—I'll tell you what we're *really* going to do."

THE ARRANGEMENTS WERE made, and the meeting was set for the evening of three days after next. The Doms insisted they needed time to prepare facilities for a "suitable reception," and that might even be true. Nobody knew what they meant by "suitable," but they didn't halt their army either. Nor did anyone in Uxmal waste time. A certain percentage of the Home Guards drilled incessantly or helped farmers bring in all the nearby crops a little early. People moved into the city from all over the countryside, herding goats; burros; swarms of fat, short-winged lizardbirds the locals called *gallinas*; and armabueys of every size from that of a dog to larger than an ox. These pulled carts heaped with fruit and squashes of every imaginable shape, long-eared corn and bean pods of countless colors. Uxmal began to bulge. Great batches of gunpowder were being combined into a paste from its various components and set out to dry. Flat, black, tile-shaped cakes were ground on the huge new ball mill by the river before being screened, sorted, filled into casks, and taken into the city. Some of those casks went to the scattered munitions manufactories, while more were trundled deep underground for storage in bunkers built during the rainy months. To any observer it looked exactly like Uxmal was preparing for a long, bitter siege.

The Detached Expeditionary Force and Army of the Allied Cities drilled even more than ever, it seemed, noisily firing its first taste of "new" powder and copper shot from the cannons so their gunners could learn the different points of aim. The infantry did the same with their muskets (some new recruits for the very first time). Muskets were least affected, ballistically, and old hands even complimented the new powder as cleaner burning and more robust, if slightly more prone to absorb moisture from the humid air. And every evening, as they had for weeks, guns and troops moved again, creaking, clopping, and tramping in time on dark paving-stone streets, going on "night maneuvers" to get accustomed to marching and sleeping in this wild, dangerous land. The large, deliberate movements of so many men made predators less sure of themselves and prone to keep their distance. The locals generally approved of that. What most didn't notice—hopefully no one did—was not all the guns and troops came back. And after the last two nights in particular, Home Guards marched out to meet them and escort them to strangely quiet barracks in a curiously disorganized way.

It was midmorning on the day of the conference (no one knew quite what to call it) when Alcalde Periz—dressed in his showy, if not very practical, gold scale armor—awkwardly kissed his wife and joined Father Orno, Reverend Harkin, and Colonel De Russy in his ornate carriage, cheered somewhat hopefully by those nearby as they set off at a leisurely pace. Lewis, Anson, Varaa, and Leonor, of course, rode on either side of the carriage, speaking with the passengers through the open sides. Tranquilo had transparently hinted they should bring two carriages, one for servants—numbered as part of the honor guard, of course, but Lewis wanted as few "helpless" men in their party as possible and detailed Barca and Private Willis to "wait on the gentlemen, if necessary." They rode with the escort. Barca had expected to go, even planned to, invited or not, but Willis hadn't been happy, muttering about joining the "goddamn dragoons if I wanted a horse under my arse all day." A block of twenty lancers under Alferez Espinoza led the way, followed by Coryon Burton and twenty dragoons. Twenty more dragoons under Sergeant Hayne followed the carriage and Lieutenant Hernandez's Ocelomeh Rangers brought up the rear. They were only eighty or so instead of the hundred allowed, but all were fighters and more might be difficult to extricate if the need arose. *Besides,* Lewis thought, *everyone else I'd like to have with us has other things to do.*

And it wasn't as if they were alone. Waiting just a bit to assure any onlookers they weren't really part of the delegation, Lieutenant Felix Meder set off with the entire mounted A Company of his riflemen, followed by the rest of Burton's dragoons and Lieutenant Hudgens's two sections of four 6pdrs and their caissons. Three hundred more heavily armed men poised at the one-mile mark from the meeting place. *The Doms'll expect to see* something *there,* Lewis told himself. *They'd be suspicious if there wasn't.*

A careful observer in Uxmal might've been extremely suspicious already because there weren't even many of the Home Guards in evidence this morning and Captain Olayne's 6pdrs and the 1st US Infantry never returned from their night march. And none of the Pennsylvanians with their curious blue flag seemed to be about, for that matter. In fact—such an observer might note with growing alarm—*Tiger* had put to sea before sunrise, and of all the cannon the Americans brought, only the two big 12pdr guns—not the lighter howitzers—were in evidence at all.

There was nothing such a person could do about that now. Just as the great western gate swung closed behind the final caisson in Hudgens's Battery, Segunda Alcaldesa Sira Periz and Samantha Wilde mounted the new battlement above the gate. Drums thundered and people gathered, more than Sira had ever seen in the city before. Finally, taking a speaking trumpet from one of Father Orno's priests, she addressed the throng.

"Despite what many of you may have heard or hoped, there can be no accommodation with the Dominion. This talk they've invited is a ruse to weaken our resolve and put us off our guard. Still," she said after a pained sigh, "my brave husband *will* speak to them. He'll do anything other than surrender us and our allies and our liberty to avoid war with the Dominion." She shook her head sadly. "I don't think he'll succeed." She gestured beyond the gate. "But one way or another, great things will happen out there over the next few days, and *no one* here will influence them." She turned and placed her small hand on the arm of one of Felix Meder's rifle-men who'd stayed behind. "This man and others like him can hit a mark at three hundred paces with their fabulous . . . rifles. They'll watch with me until my husband returns." Her tone grew harsh. "*No one* will pass outside the gates until then, and anyone dropping over the walls must be assumed to be in league with the enemy and will be shot."

CHAPTER 32

E ven with everyone mounted or riding in Periz's carriage—or on limbers and caissons, in the case of some of Hudgens's artillerymen—
the procession to meet the Doms set a leisurely pace. The time had
been set for the "cool of the evening," and there was no hurry to reach the
clearing where they'd crushed the Dom lancers a few days before. Not this
time. And it was just as well, because the humid heat of the day quickly
spiked as they crossed the bridge over the briskly running Cipactli River,
trudged up the gently sloping road flanked by harvested fields and abandoned farmhouses, finally threading their way into the great forest to the
east. It was sweltering by then, and as before, the dense cover of trees relieved a little of the misery the bright sun inflicted. All the mounted forces
were proud of their dark blue jackets, the only difference between the
branches—Rifles, artillery, and dragoons—being the color of trim on their
collars and shoulder straps, but they secretly envied the infantry's sky-blue
jackets on days like this. Spirits revived in the shade, and men who'd begun
feeling oppressed started chatting again, as soldiers do.

The men in the carriage had never stopped, nor had Lewis and Varaa for
a time, joining their conversation, but everything they could do was already set in motion, and the discussion turned to anxious speculation
about how the Doms would react if this or that happened, or what the

meeting would be like. Lewis had planned for various contingencies, but couldn't control everything and eventually tired of making assurances. Leonor and Anson had long since moved forward to talk with Alferez Espinoza and Coryon Burton, both now admiring the holsters Anson had commissioned in Uxmal. They were large and somewhat awkward looking, but beautifully tooled. Most important, they allowed him to carry both his Walker Colts at his sides, suspended from a waist belt held up by braces that put their weight on his shoulders. His Patersons were tucked in smaller, matching holsters under his arms. He'd also obtained a dragoon saber or still had the one he'd used on the beach fastened to his saddle. Always lethal, Anson looked downright piratical now.

As if by mutual agreement, Lewis and Varaa drifted back from beside the carriage and the tedious exchange inside. There they found young Barca now riding alone. Willis was close, a little farther back, apparently amusing himself by grousing at Sergeant Hayne, who'd provided Willis's horse.

"Good morning, Mr. Barca. How do you do today?" Varaa said, cheerfully flicking her tail.

Barca smiled. "Good morning, Warmaster." He bowed his head to Lewis. "Major Cayce. Quite well, actually." He looked down at his own horse. "My riding skills are much improved—and it's not raining." He raised his eyes to gaze down the forest path. "And I'm ... strangely relieved by the prospect of this meeting, whatever the outcome may be," he confessed.

"Waiting, preparing, and imagining the worst, always preys on the mind," Lewis agreed, "especially when you're never quite certain *exactly* what you're preparing for"—he paused, thinking back—"and you're never prepared for the fact that the 'worst' can be more terrible than you ever imagined," he added grimly.

"Was that how it was for you, sir? After your first real battle?" Barca asked.

Lewis nodded. "Even when we won."

"I've seen battle before," Barca reminded.

"Yes, and you did very well," Lewis acknowledged, "but as traumatic as it was, that one just ... fell on you, as it were. There was no time to contemplate it in advance. You obviously feel the difference now, or you wouldn't be so anxious to get on with it."

Barca thought about that for a moment, then nodded. "Yes sir."

Varaa-Choon coughed. "Major Cayce has described the . . . peculiar nature of servitude that prevails in parts of your country," she said, somewhat
delicately for her, "but assured me that such wouldn't apply to you. Certainly not here. He's also said he gave you a choice of serving the army in
whatever capacity you chose. After spending so much time with it, observing for Colonel De Russy, have you given that any more thought?"

Barca looked oddly at Varaa, remembering a gun stuck in the mud and
the brief sense of camaraderie he'd experienced. And that hadn't been the
only time. It *did* seem—with a few exceptions—many of the prejudices the
"Americans" (regardless of regional, even national origins) had brought
with them here, whether racial, cultural, even religious, had been so overwhelmed by the unfathomably strange nature of this world that such differences hardly mattered anymore. Particularly in the face of their infinitely
more pressing, even existential "us versus them" disagreement with their
terrible new enemies. He almost chuckled at the irony of having been taken
so little notice of during his comings and goings on behalf of Colonel De
Russy.

"I have," Barca confirmed, gently patting the neck of the animal he
rode. "And I've become a *much* better horseman as well," he added dryly
before turning quite serious. "I honestly didn't believe Major Cayce at the
time he made the offer, but I do think I'd be welcome almost anywhere in
the army, horse or foot"—he frowned—"with the exception of . . . a certain
company in the First US Infantry."

Lewis frowned as well. "Private Hahessy's company," he said. "We
should've hung him with the others."

Barca shook his head. "He saved a man's life."

"After initiating the circumstances that threatened it," Lewis reminded
angrily. "And I wouldn't put it past him to *murder* Private Cox if he ever
gets the chance."

Varaa *kakked* a laugh. "If what I hear is true, Booger—I mean, Lieutenant Beeryman—has sworn to murder *Hahessy* if anything happens to Cox.
That probably includes being killed in action or struck by lightning. Hahessy's a bully. It'll do him good to live in fear."

"It has been my experience that most bullies are cowards already," Barca
said lowly.

"That's probably true," Lewis agreed, "but I don't think that's the case
with Hahessy. There's just something wrong with him." He shook his head.

"I'm not as great a believer in redemption as Reverend Harkin, and I'm not sure if Hahessy is redeemable or not." He cleared his throat, looking back at Barca. "Now, you said you've reconsidered my offer?"

"*Am* reconsidering," Barca stressed. "But for the present, I feel I still belong at the colonel's side, and will as long as he needs me."

They rode quietly, companionably for several moments before Lewis spoke again. "I honor your loyalty." He snorted. "I've always honored loyalty above all things, I suppose. But I'm confident that Colonel De Russy will learn to cope without you someday. And *especially* if he doesn't, I suspect the army will need you more than he does.

"Just goes to show," Lewis murmured as he and Varaa moved forward a little again.

"What?" Varaa asked.

Lewis took a long breath, gaze now settled on Leonor up ahead, and said somewhat absently, "Just how many different sides there can be to various things, and how rarely they are as they seem."

"A lesson we'll soon teach the Doms, I hope, with them convinced we're all quaking behind the walls of Uxmal," said Varaa.

Lewis nodded. "Let's just hope we don't only see what *we* expect to see as well."

IT SEEMED THEY weren't, so far. Scouts galloped up the forest track on blown and gasping horses all afternoon, relaying observations of other scouts a surprising distance away. The last few days had seen more than just the covert deployment of nearly the entire Detached Expeditionary Force, 1st Uxmal, and 1st Ocelomeh down murky, parallel tracks in the forest long known only to the Jaguar Warriors before Varaa and Anson mapped them. A few Holcanos probably knew them too, but fully engaged at Itzincab with their entire villages shifted to support them, no Holcanos—or Grik—had been seen. And the Ocelomeh would know if they were about, having also completed a series of watch posts, high in the trees, within visual signaling range of one another. None of the ships wrecked on the Yucatán carried parts for the amazing new electrical telegraphy apparatus Lewis had been hearing about, but semaphore telegraph towers had been in use for decades. Weeks before, De Russy suggested they come up with something similar, but Varaa told him her people had used polished silver discs to reflect sunlight for the same purpose longer than anyone knew. They even sent signals at night with shaded lamps. All the Ocelomeh had to do was establish such observation posts where they needed them to watch and report on the approaching Doms.

This was undertaken even as the Allied troops rushed to the one place Lewis believed the Doms could gather their entire force: the washboard glade where the Americans themselves made their last camp before pushing on to Uxmal, only four miles beyond where they'd savaged the lancers and the Dom emissaries now waited. The place was ideal for *them* in many respects, with more convoluted terrain than usual. Lewis couldn't *know* that's where the Doms would stop. With all the low places and so soon after the rains, it might be too boggy. But the road they'd followed was actually in view of the sea at that point, nearly touching it in fact, and boats could land supplies and troops through light surf on the sandy shore. The Doms would likely secure the area for that reason alone. Finally, the next closest place to concentrate out from under the trees was the Americans' *previous* camp, eleven miles farther back, and its only access to the sea was through a dangerous, tangled marsh. Lewis was betting everything that whoever Tranquilo brought to treat with them would want his army closer than that, to intimidate them, and have it ready to march on Uxmal at once.

The reports from the "tree signals" were encouraging. The leading Dom elements were already encamped at the washboard glade, the great command marquees Burton described already erected, and more troops had been flooding in all day, setting up tents. Lewis was astounded to hear they weren't throwing up breastworks or even scouting the nearby woods.

"They're amazingly arrogant, after all," Varaa reassured him. "But with their numbers, they can be."

Lewis frowned, unconvinced. He remembered this stretch of forest well; the trees were particularly old and tall, untouched by wildfires for centuries, and there was almost no undergrowth at all. He hadn't seen one, but he'd heard of the strange "horned turtles" that seemed to be happy to keep the deadfall clear and give certain parts of the forest an almost parklike impression. He hadn't really appreciated it the last time he passed through, but they'd been moving much quicker then. He marveled at it now despite the fact there was much more at stake this time. Much, much more.

A short while later, he and Varaa left their places by the carriage and went forward to join Anson and Leonor at the head of the column with

Espinoza and Burton so they'd be there when they reached their destina-tion. Scouts trotted back and guardedly reported no apparent traps, but they were clearly disconcerted. Lewis and his companions soon discovered why. The trees fell away and the afternoon sun beat down on them when they emerged from the forest onto the familiar ground where they'd fought their little battle—only nothing but the lay of the land was recogniz-able now.

The Doms had spent the days they were given to "prepare a suitable reception" to macabre effect. A great long rectangle of the tall grass repre-senting the boundaries of the battlefield had been very precisely scorched to the ground, leaving only blackened stubble and dusty ash clouding around the horses as Espinoza's lancers and Burton's dragoons deployed on each side of the track. And the boundary had been fenced, after a fashion, by a flimsy stockade of limbs and brush reinforced with scavenger-gnawed bones of the lancers that died there. Worse, the grisly avenue leading up the slope to a huge marquee erected where Wagley's infantry stood was lined with two hundred new, red-painted lances (those of the fallen had been re-covered by the victors), and on each was mounted an equally gnawed skull of the fallen, complete with polished brass helmets and flowing plumes. It was like the dead still defended this place, empty eye sockets glaring down.

"They do exult in death, do they not?" Reverend Harkin said from within the carriage as it pulled into view.

"They wallow in it. They *worship* it," Father Orno was heard to reply.

Lewis was looking at the marquee while the rest of the escort emerged from the woods, dragoons forming together in a line, Ocelomeh behind them. *Some of the Ocelomeh,* Lewis reminded himself. A few would already be probing to the sides in the woods. Living Dom lancers were positioned around the scallop-edged tent, its two inner support poles piercing the top and soaring high in the air so the jagged gold cross on bloodred flags could stream away in the wind. There were only about a dozen lancers in view, however. The rest must've stayed another hundred yards back, as promised. Staring around at the clearing, Lewis was surprised not to see a single one of the massive herbivores that browsed so disdainfully there before.

"Perhaps the stench of the Doms drives them away," Varaa told him qui-etly, noticing the same. "They'd all be downwind, after all, and nothing enjoys the company of predators and carrion eaters."

Colonel De Russy opened the door and stepped down from the carriage.

Frowning all around, he stretched. "Barca, be so good as to bring us some-thing cool to drink, will you?" A jug of beer wrapped in coarse cloth that Private Willis was supposed to be keeping wet was tucked in a cupboard on the back of the carriage. "What'll happen now?" he asked with a nervous glance up at the marquee and the silent, unmoving lancers.

Anson pulled a watch from his vest pocket. "We're early, damn it," he growled.

"I wanted to be," Lewis said, nodding. "No point having them wonder-ing about us. Now their attention is fixed." He dismounted and stood on aching legs as he rubbed Arete's cheek, looking at De Russy, Orno, and Harkin, then into the carriage where Periz was fanning himself. "Now we wait."

The afternoon passed and the sun set quickly, as always at that latitude. As soon as it disappeared, torches were lit and placed in iron brackets all around the marquee. Lights were kindled inside as well, and the red-trimmed white canvas glowed orange. Still they waited.

"It's time now, ain't it?" Leonor asked her father.

"Yes," Lewis answered for him, "but we'll wait a bit longer." He smiled in the twilight, teeth bright in his beard. "We've come to them, now they have to invite us in. If they take too long, we'll start preparing to leave. See what they do."

"Shouldn't that be Alcalde Periz's decision?" Father Orno asked.

Lewis looked at the dark shape of the *alcalde*, who hadn't said anything since they arrived. He'd merely sat there, staring out at skulls on lances. "It can be if he wants," he said, "but I was given command of the Allied armies, and even this is a military maneuver, of sorts." He paused. "Unless he hopes for something besides posturing and intimidation from the enemy?"

Anson looked at his daughter and shrugged.

A crescent moon was already up when the sunlight failed entirely, so it was still bright enough to see to move when Lewis remounted Arete and gave the order to prepare to return to the city. As if the Doms had been waiting for this (more probably a nervous approach by the Uxmalos), the east-facing sides of the marquee were taken down, revealing the illumi-nated interior. There were people in there—that's all they could tell from this distance—and they seemed to be seated, waiting.

"That's probably as close to an invitation as we'll get," Anson said.

"I wonder," replied Lewis, but shook his head. "With the *alcalde*'s permission, we'll proceed as agreed. Horses for the gentlemen," he called to Barca and Private Willis, already holding the mounts. Reverend Harkin was an indifferent horseman at best, but Lewis refused to let the carriage make the final approach. Harkin would ride if he wanted to go. He did. "Alferez Espinoza, Lieutenant Burton, assemble our escort." He looked meaningfully at Lieutenant Sal Hernandez and Sergeant Hayne. "Keep a firm hold on the men staying here. Accept no provocation. But if things go badly, you know what to do."

Pulling Arete around, he waited until Burton and Espinoza took their place at the head of six dragoons and six lancers, then fell into line by Alcalde Periz. Anson was beside Father Orno, Varaa next to Colonel De Russy, and Leonor by Reverend Harkin. Barca and a grumbling Private Willis brought up the rear. Though allowed a guard of a hundred, only a dozen were to accompany the "principals" and their servants, not to number more than a dozen themselves. Lewis fudged the first number a little, Burton and Espinoza making fourteen guards while it seemed the Doms had stuck to twelve, but counting Barca and Willis there were only ten more of them while there must be twenty Doms under the open-sided marquee. *It doesn't much matter,* Lewis decided. *Everyone in our party is a fighter, with the probable exception of Orno and Harkin, and I'm not so sure of Orno.* And strangely enough, not even the Doms had demanded they meet unarmed. Lewis would've refused, of course, but wondered about that. *Maybe it never occurred to them since they don't do this sort of thing,* he thought, observing the long, upright lances as well as sabers and musketoons the mounted enemy troopers bore as the procession moved closer. *Or maybe they really are that arrogant. I hope it's not because they're sure.*

"You . . . stop there," called a slightly quavering voice in strangely accented English. "The guards and animals you leave. There will be no harm." Lewis had only ever seen one Blood Priest, and the scrawny speaker might've been Tranquilo at a glance, draped in the same coarse scarlet cloak. He seemed just as frail and stoop-shouldered as well. The torchlight revealed a different face, however, covered by a reddish-blond beard. The eyes were less like a ferret's too, though just as predatory in their way.

Lewis nodded at Periz and the embassy dismounted, relinquishing their horses to dragoons and Espinoza's lancers. They'd stay in the saddle as long as the enemy guards did so.

"I could hold Arete for you, personal like, Major," Willis hissed hopefully. Lewis ignored him, and Willis reluctantly trailed past beribboned ropes and under the scalloped edge of the great enemy tent.

Lewis's first good view of the interior took him aback. It was like an audience room in a canvas-sided palace, richly carpeted in pure, unlikely white. Gold was everywhere—lamps, braziers, even the frames of well-padded chairs flanking a tall-backed throne on the other side of a long, low table right in the center of the space. Twisted Dom crosses were everywhere, the closer to the throne, the more barbarously warped and entwined with what looked like spiky vines. Even the canvas walls were covered with Dom flags and beautifully woven tapestries, each seeming to tell a story of some kind, possibly the history of the Doms on this world? Lewis suspected Harkin was intrigued, greedily trying to decipher the scenes, but all his attention was focused on two of the seated enemy.

The first was a short, solid, dark-faced soldier, dressed in a yellow-and-black uniform adorned with more gold lace than it seemed it could bear. Large black eyes under heavy brows returned Lewis's scrutiny. The second was a tall, almost gangly man somewhat reclined on the throne. He wore a red robe like those around him, but the material was finer than all but those sitting closest. The cuffs and facings were heavily embroidered in gold thread reminiscent of the vines on the crosses and a wide-brimmed galero as white as the rug except for red tassels hanging from the brim like dripping blood topped a sharp, narrow face, made even longer and more severe by a lengthy, pointed beard. The eyes behind the tassels looked as big and black and remorseless as a shark's.

The English-speaking Blood Priest's eyes went wide at the sight of Varaa. "The animals you *leave!*" he snarled.

Lewis stopped, putting a hand on Periz. "Warmaster Varaa-Choon's forces are part of our army. If you want to speak to us, you'll speak to her as well. Without perfect understanding by us all, this meeting is a farce, and we'll only meet again on the battlefield."

"Hold you tongue!" the Blood Priest practically squeaked in outrage. "You is in the presence of His Holiness, Don Frutos del Gran Vale, Blood Cardinal to His Supreme Holiness, Messiah of Mexico and Emperor of the World! Only *he* will speak. You obey!"

Captain Anson actually laughed, and all the seated figures—except Don Frutos and the soldier—lunged to their feet in fury. Don Frutos's expression was just as harsh, but he affected calm. "Father Solicito!" he called in a deep, kindly voice, wholly at odds with his seething glare. "You're a fine linguist—in many languages, of necessity—but you're rude! I've learned enough of this English speech—perhaps even better than you—to conduct this . . . conversation perfectly well." He sent a mocking glance at Alcalde Periz. "You'll concede we must, since it's the language of your protectors?" Periz seemed to smolder and wilt simultaneously while Don Frutos regarded Father Solicito once more. "Join Father Tranquilo outside, where he prepares for the service I hope to hold." He glared back at Lewis and Periz. "To seal our 'understanding' when we reach it. In the meantime, tell me who you are."

Periz did the introductions, and Don Frutos seemed keenly interested in Lewis and De Russy, vaguely so in Father Orno, and not at all in Harkin or Leonor. He bestowed an appraising stare on Captain Anson, but as for Varaa, he merely waved a hand at the myriad flying bugs swarming around the lamps and immolating themselves in the braziers. "If we can ignore these annoying insects, the animal's presence shouldn't distract us."

An attendant clapped his hands and servants, *naked young girls, painted gold*, erupted from behind the throne, each carrying a small, compact chair. There were exclamations of outrage, even from Willis, but everyone stood fast. Especially when Varaa hissed, "They don't do it to shock. It's just what they do." Somehow knowing Barca and Willis were their counterparts, the girls brought the chairs for them to arrange.

"Which there ain't but six of 'em, sir," Willis murmured uncertainly with an uncomfortable glance after the golden children, who disappeared back behind the throne. There must have been an annex attached to the marquee they hadn't seen from the east. Lewis wondered what else lurked there.

"Animals don't need chairs," Varaa quietly told Lewis, "and most women aren't 'people' either, as you've just seen. They're servants and ornaments," she added, flicking her ears at Leonor. "I suppose they've decided to 'ignore' her too."

"Just as well," Lewis whispered back. "They'll wish they hadn't." Raising his voice he said, "Thank you, but we'll stand. We've been sitting all day."

Don Frutos casually tilted his head as if it was no concern of his. "Very well, but it may make taking refreshment awkward. I understand you expect to be treated with civility and entertained during ceremonies such as these?"

Lewis wondered who told him that but was afraid he knew. He also saw that Periz, nervous and introspective all day, seemed about to burst beside him. Taking a step forward, the *alcalde* of Uxmal finally spoke, voice almost shaking with fear and rage: "We didn't come to be entertained or refreshed and didn't 'expect' or seek this meeting." His lip twisted. "You've set your bloodthirsty surrogates against us for decades and now march aggressively into our land. Tranquilo informed us you desired to make a proposal. In the interests of avoiding further bloodshed, we've come to hear it. That's the *only* reason we're here. But if you don't withdraw and leave us in peace, we'll destroy you as we did your spying lancers!"

The priests—or whatever they were—surrounding Don Frutos explosively objected once more but the Blood Cardinal remained perfectly still, only clasping his hands in front of his face and assessing Periz once more. "Bravo," he said. "Such a bold little speech! I'm sure you will remember it with pride while you writhe on an impaling pole." Periz's expression remained defiant, but his dark face managed to pale. Don Frutos's gaze shifted to Lewis. "Quite bold indeed, and enlightening. I confess I was intrigued when I learned of this 'getting to know your enemy' custom. Sharing thoughts with men—even the most abominable heretics—who'll soon be gone forever obscurely appealed to me. No matter how misguided, their viewpoints should be preserved in memory, don't you think?" He looked back at the *alcalde* of Uxmal. "My dear Periz, believe me when I say I understand *perfectly* how you must feel! I'd feel the same if heretic invaders came to my sacred land and threatened it with extinction."

He shook his head with apparent sadness, then pointed a long finger at Lewis. "But that's what *they* have done!" He leaned back in his throne-like chair. "God will have this land someday, Alcalde Periz. It's preordained. He'll have the whole world! But the Dominion is patient and besides being . . . interested elsewhere at present, was content to play the same long game—watching you and the Holcanos and your animals tear at one another as you have for generations. When you do so long enough, you'll *beg* the Dominion to succor and heal you and take you to its bosom." He sneered at Father Orno. "You and I *know* the same God, but you don't *understand* Him. He's only kind and loving to those who please Him—and nothing pleases Him like the effusion of heretic blood or the re-creation of the cleansing pain his son endured to show us the way to Him! Once you and the Holcanos have bathed in enough blood to cleanse yourselves, spilled all the heresy from your veins, you'll willingly join us, and we're happy to wait."

He frowned at Lewis again. "But these . . . Americans have tilted the happy bloody balance between you and the Holcanos and reinforced your heresy. How long would it be before you brought it to the Dominion like a dagger in the back?" He shook his head. "It cannot be permitted."

"An' how do you expect to stop it, skinny?" Leonor demanded. She'd remained silent till now, oblivious to the slight to herself and Varaa, but understandably fuming ever since the girls came in. It was plain on her face that she'd love nothing more than to kill every Dom in sight.

Surprisingly, Don Frutos replied, tone deceptively mild. "Females have no voice among men, but as you ask their question for them, I'll answer." He sighed. "I'd so hoped this would go differently. More 'civilized,' I believe was the term. But I suppose we should get to it." He looked intently at Periz. "I won't stop it, *you* will."

Periz blinked confusion, much like Varaa would. "How? Why?"

"Simple," Don Frutos said, shifting his gaze to Lewis. "You'll break with *him*. Withdraw your support of his forces and leave the Americans entirely to me. In turn, I'll . . . deal with them and simply march away, leaving you to return to your bickering with the Holcanos. You'll have to surrender any modern weapons they've given you, of course," he added as if as an afterthought.

"Madness!" Reverend Harkin exclaimed, unable to contain himself. "Don't you see? He's the very Devil! He'll split us apart and shred us separately! God would . . ."

"Silence, priest!" Periz snapped, looking at Father Orno. "What of the other cities in our alliance? What of our faith?"

Don Frutos practically rolled his eyes. "Alone, all your cities together are no threat to the Dominion, and your feeble, isolated heresy will eventually die of its own accord as it has in Don Discipo's Puebla Arboras. I see no need to hasten its end. Its existence actually helps maintain the equally deteriorating balance the Dominion desires, don't you see?"

Periz shook his head as though stunned.

"It may be the only way to save our people," Father Orno conceded quietly.

"You too!" Harkin practically shrieked. Anson said nothing, but his expression was dangerous. Leonor looked like she'd start spitting fire.

"And how do you intend to 'deal' with me, Don Frutos?" Lewis ground out. "Even without the Uxmalos, I'll tear your army apart."

"The Army of God will suffer," Don Frutos conceded, "but its soldiers *yearn* to suffer and die in battle, harvesting heretic souls as the playthings of God! What do *your* people want, Major Cayce? More than anything."

Lewis seemed to contemplate that, glancing from Don Frutos to Alcalde Periz. "I expect they'd like to go home, if you know the way," he said almost lightly.

"Sadly, I do not." Don Frutos regarded him carefully. "But I might offer *another* home in exchange for certain . . . cooperations. Father Felicidad! Do show our guest in."

One of the flags behind the throne-like chair moved a little, and another Blood Priest appeared. In contrast to the others, this one was somewhat obese. Trailing hesitantly behind, tugged by a rope around his waist, was a much taller man, practically cadaverous. His cheeks were gaunt, eyes sunken, and though his chin was freshly shaved, his hair and side whiskers were like wiry bramble patches. Draped on his skeletal frame was an immaculately cleaned and pressed uniform of an American colonel.

"My God," Lewis muttered, his worst fears confirmed.

The fat priest pushed his charge to the table beside the Dominion officer, who pursed his lips. It was the first sign of emotion Lewis had seen in the man, though he couldn't tell if it betrayed pity or disgust.

"Colonel Wicklow?" De Russy whispered in horror, speaking for the first time since they entered the tent.

"Rube?" asked the man, looking around, voice surprisingly firm. "Ruberdeau De Russy? My God, is that really you? I . . . I don't see very well, I'm afraid."

"What have they done to you?" De Russy demanded, hand going to the sword at his side. Lewis had never seen De Russy so ready for violence and stopped him before he could draw his blade.

"Oh," Wicklow said absently, "no more than I deserve, I suppose. Is Captain Cayce with you?"

"*Major* Cayce," De Russy corrected distractedly. "I brevetted him."

"Well deserved, I'm sure." Wicklow looked in Lewis's general direction. "I'd heard of you before we sailed. Capital behavior at Monterrey. Capital behavior since, as I understand it. But see here, what you're attempting now . . . It will never do. The Dominion will crush you if you resist. I *know* . . . " His voice almost broke. "It's perfect cooperation or you're off to see their God in the most horrible imaginable way."

"You were taken. In *Isidra*," Lewis stated.

"Yes. Easy as could be for them. I'm very sorry we left you, by the way. Sorrier than you can know," he added bitterly, "but I thought I had a responsibility to get to Vera Cruz, then to aid the passengers we'd rescued from *Tiger*. Things were . . . confused, as you'll recall, but I never suspected, never dreamed . . ." He had to stop and collect himself before continuing. "In any event, we weren't expecting trouble. Had no idea where we were—what kind of world this is. There was fog as we neared Vera Cruz, and we found ourselves surrounded by strange-looking ships that suddenly came aboard us. *Isidra*'s no warship, and with her decks so crammed with frightened civilians we could mount no real defense." His milky eyes—Lewis wondered what had happened to them—flicked toward where he must've heard Don Frutos's voice, and he huskily added, "Still, I suspect even the women and children would've fought like terrors if they'd known what was to come."

"What happened to them?" De Russy asked.

Wicklow stiffened, and tears spilled down his hollow cheeks. "I can't say for certain in every case. Some were sold as slaves, but others were . . . sacrificed in the most horrific fashion. I was forced to witness some of those dreadful events: women stripped naked—*gentlewomen*—and carried shrieking up the blood-washed steps of a high, conical structure surrounded by countless gleeful spectators. At the top was a Blood Cardinal, like Don Frutos, who harangued the crowd for a while before tearing the beating heart from the victim laid out before him and tasting its final spurt of blood." He shuddered at the memory before continuing in a whisper, "The victim was then beheaded and the . . . remains hurled down the steps to the crowd. I don't know what became of them after that, thank God"—he hesitated and sent another blind, nervous glance toward Don Frutos—"but perhaps most bizarre of all, the . . . principal performer, if you will, was aided and surrounded by red-robed priests, all piously genuflecting like a pack of papists—though I don't imagine even papists ever behaved in such a . . . singular fashion. No, not even in the darkest days of the Inquisition."

"The likeness to Father Orno's faith is a feeble thing on your world as well," Don Frutos stated complacently. "Do continue, Colonel Wicklow. I'm sure our guests are anxious to hear the rest."

Wicklow nodded, gulping. "Almost all the men were . . . tormented to death in various ways—resisting," he quickly added with an imprecise bow toward Don Frutos, as if to assure him he understood it was necessary. "I was still attempting to resist myself," he mumbled miserably, "until they chained me down with all my officers arranged around me, opened their bellies, and poured glowing coals inside. . . . The screams . . ." He gulped again, repeatedly, controlling an urge to retch. "That was the last thing I shall ever see." He flicked a hand toward his eyes. "Cooked by heated irons, held quite close."

Now Anson had to restrain Leonor, who'd reached for one of her revolvers. Her pretty face had turned to a cold, expressionless mask. Wicklow saw none of this, of course, and eventually completed his dismal summary. "A few of *Isidra*'s sailors have been preserved, like me, to tell them all we know."

"Enough reminiscing!" Don Frutos pleasantly exclaimed. "Now you know who taught me your tongue so well. And despite that initial reluctance— which he regrets extremely—Colonel Wicklow has been most accommodating. That's why you see him now, so safe and well, a valuable and trusted advisor! He's told me *everything* about your capabilities and tactics, very similar to ours in fact, and in spite of my real fear for the fate of his soul— I've grown quite fond of him, you know—we've treated him very gently, and he hasn't been subject to the full and *proper* cleansing. That would've made him a different, better person, but also put him on another . . . level of consciousness. You might not have recognized him as he was or taken his advice." He looked Lewis in the eye. "Rather than destroying you, I'll offer you and your people the same indulgence so long as you lay down your arms and willingly teach us any useful technologies you've brought to this world."

Lewis looked at the apparently blind, starved, possibly insane Colonel Wicklow. "You'd treat us like him?" he asked.

"Madness," Harkin seethed, scowling.

"Somewhat better," Don Frutos encouraged. "I must be at least as benevolent to you as the Uxmalos. And your resistance—up to this point—has been founded on ignorance. In that light it's understandable, even admirable to a degree, but now you *know* and have a proper choice; you may be embraced as cherished friends to the bosom of the Holy Dominion"—he glanced aside at the soldier, and his tone turned stark—"or General Agon will destroy you. There will be no mercy, no surrender, and any survivors will be impaled on heated spikes and burned alive." He glared at Periz. "As will every man, woman, and child in Uxmal, if you continue your ridiculous resistance."

Reverend Harkin was looking back and forth between Periz and Orno, incredulous that they didn't simply turn and go. "You can't seriously be considering—"

"Fight them!" Varaa urged Lewis, almost shouting, pointing at the blinded colonel. "Would you become like him? Lead your *men* to that? You *must* fight them." She glared at Periz. "And the Ocelomeh will stand with you even if the Uxmalos don't!"

"Oh yes," said Don Frutos, "there is that final condition. Ordinarily, I can't hear the demon speech of animals, of course. Only heretics are susceptible to the vile lies they spew. But this modest tent has been consecrated by sacrificial blood, and here I discern the faintest echoes of the thing behind the animal mask! Amazing, is it not?" He leaned forward in his chair. "The proviso is this, Major Cayce: as the Uxmalos must break with you to prolong their miserable lives as they know them, you'll break with the Ocelomeh if you wish to be friends of the Holy Dominion."

"Reconcile yourself to this, Major Cayce," Colonel Wicklow pleaded loudly. "Tell him, Rube! You can't win. The Army of God is vast and ponderous, suffused with the inflexibly relentless discipline of ants. And the battlefield tactics it employs are almost indistinguishable from those of General Arista at Palo Alto—and you know how that turned out!"

Lewis was stunned to silence for a moment, and glancing at Anson he saw the surprised, arched eyebrows. Everyone with him would've heard, even those outside. What's more, Periz and Orno both knew what *really* happened at Palo Alto. Mad or not, Wicklow was on their side. Lewis cleared his throat. "Don Frutos," he said, "if you . . ."

"You'll address me as 'Your Holiness,'" Don Frutos snapped.

Lewis merely bowed his head slightly. "As I was saying, we'll have to discuss this among ourselves. Whatever we decide, we're still allies—until we're not. I'll do what I think is right for my people, as I'm sure will they, but honor demands that if I'm going to break an alliance, I do it to their faces. I expect the same from them."

Don Frutos seemed to consider that, ignoring Reverend Harkin's sputtering. "Very well." He motioned to an acolyte several seats to his right, who placed an hourglass on the table. "You may step a short distance away, but don't join your guards or leave the torchlight. If you do, I'll assume you've declined my gracious offer. Hostilities will commence at once, and General Agon will advance the Army of God with the dawn. You have until the turn of the glass to give me your decision." He smiled with a strange benevolence. "In the meanwhile, hoping you'll see reason, Father Tranquilo and Father Solicito will complete arrangements for the service I spoke of. It's quite late, and I grow hungry and weary—this has taken longer than I expected—but I trust we'll have even more reason to celebrate the service with a companionable meal among friends!" He frowned. "Don't bring the animal back in the tent, however. My patience is not without limit, and I won't eat with animals."

Lewis and his friends filed outside, staying away from the dragoons and lancers but moving as far as they thought they'd get away with. No one said a word as they walked, but Harkin was clearly beside himself with fury, his bulbous form almost rippling as he shuddered with horror and rage.

"Let it out, Reverend," Lewis said, almost flippantly.

"By God I will! This is monstrous! Monstrous! You *can't* accept these terms, none of you. Father Orno, I beg you! I thought we understood each other perfectly! You *all* know that beast is lying. Every putrid word—lies! Forsake your honor, your alliance, and your cause, and you also forsake the God who brought us together to *oppose* the evil lurking in that tent, not appease it!"

Harkin went on like that for several minutes while the others watched, nodding or shaking their heads, surreptitiously glancing inside the tent from time to time, watching Colonel Wicklow and Don Frutos talk, probably discussing the reverend's unrestrained diatribe. When Harkin finally paused to take a breath, after repeatedly damning them all to hell, Father Orno stepped to him and put a hand on his arm.

"It weren't me, Reverend. Honest," Private Willis piously proclaimed. Barca yanked him away and whispered furiously in his ear.

"Well done, Reverend, you've convinced us," Lewis said, very low.

Harkin gaped, then blinked. "What the devil do you mean?"

"We knew the only possible purpose the Doms—that 'Don Frutos'— could have for this parley was to try to divide us," De Russy told him gently, "so we pretended to let him think he has. Aside from meeting our enemy, we're only here to focus, delay, and confuse him, after all. And reinforce his arrogance, of course. We couldn't make it look too easy to split us, however, so we didn't tell you of our plan. We *needed* a sincere voice to rise in opposition, in genuine righteous indignation, and decided yours would serve us best."

"They didn't tell me either," Leonor growled resentfully. "I was fixin' to shoot somebody." She looked at Lewis. "I would've shot *you* if it was true."

"You . . . you infernal *bastards!*" Harkin puffed, apparently shocked by his own use of such a word. "You frightened me out of my mind. Why me? Why not let Father Orno do it?"

"Orno had to seem to be counseling Periz for peace. We couldn't have both our clerical fellows on the same side, could we?" De Russy explained, and that's what he believed. Lewis hadn't told him that Orno actually came to him, afraid the *alcalde* might accept terms of some sort if they seemed at all reasonable. He couldn't look in his face and gauge his reactions if he was as exercised as Harkin had been. But even Periz couldn't find Frutos's terms acceptable, could he? He *had* to know they'd leave him utterly at the mercy of the Doms. Now Lewis hoped for some signal from Orno, one way or another, but perhaps he still didn't know.

"One interestin' thing," Anson said, looking curiously back at the activity in the tent: "Colonel Wicklow's still inside that shell of a man, an' *he* doesn't want us to quit."

"No," De Russy agreed. "Poor man. I was confused at first, thinking his wits had gone, but 'ponderous' and 'inflexible,' as well as his reference to Arista, conveyed his meaning perfectly. It was a wonderful bit of intelligence regarding Dom tactics—considering we've never seen them before."

"I was confused by that as well," Alcalde Periz finally said, speaking for the first time since they exited the tent. He looked at Lewis. "I understood that Palo Alto was a great victory for your army and this 'Arista' was on the other side. You were there."

"That's true," Lewis said. "So was Captain Anson and Leonor. A few others too. So was Teniente Lara, I hear. I guess it wasn't very big as modern battles go, but it was 'great' in the sense that it was a decisive victory against a larger force." He looked at Anson and Leonor, then back at Periz. "And none of us have forgotten what we learned there—and later."

"You were outnumbered," Periz almost whispered, "but not by nearly so many, I think."

Lewis took a deep breath. "It's been a pain and a rush, Alcalde Periz, especially over the last few days. Two months ago I would've said we'd never do it." He smiled in the darkness. "But we're *ready* for this fight. My people, yours"—he nodded at Varaa—"hers . . ." He shook his head almost angrily. "*Our* people are ready, and the Doms only think they are. Even if you just want to break it down to numbers, that's three-quarters of any fight right there."

Anson was nodding back at the tent. "Wicklow's gone. Weird stuff goin' on in there, an' they're gettin' antsy. I think our time's up."

"Varaa," Lewis said, "you and Leonor join Burton and Espinoza when we go back inside. Tell them to be ready."

"Don Frutos said the *war* would start if we rejoin our guards," Periz objected.

"The war's already on, sir," Leonor told him coldly, "an' they don't want neither of us in there anyway. Damned if we'll just stand out here by ourselves."

"She's right," said Orno firmly, pushing his friend and secular leader ahead of him toward the lurid marquee. "The war has been 'on' since long before the Americans ever came, and I for one will be glad to have the end of it start."

Varaa *kakked* quietly as she and Leonor started for the dragoons and lancers. Leonor snorted. "We ain't gonna end it *tonight*, priest. Or tomorrow neither."

"No," Orno agreed. "But a thing must be *properly* begun before it can ever be finished."

"Anybody tries to stop you gettin' over there, we'll 'start the end' right here an' now," Anson whispered loudly after the Mi-Anakka and his daughter, eyeing the enemy lancers still holding their positions. None moved. Stepping over to walk by Lewis as they went to confront Don Frutos, Anson muttered, "We still want to drag this out as long as possible?"

"Yes. Our people are still getting in position, moving through monster-infested forests in the dark!"

"An' they can't so much as fire a shot to defend themselves," Anson unhappily agreed, though if something the size of the dragon that got Lieutenant Swain appeared, a hundred shots might not make a difference.

"Ocelomeh escorts with those big bows should help," Lewis murmured, unconvinced, as they reached the scalloped edge of the tent. "The curtain rises again," he quipped, then, "Jesus. What're they doing now?"

CHAPTER 33

All the chairs had been moved to one side of the marquee, and everyone was standing, waiting, expectant, gathered around the long, low table, leaving a gap barely wide enough for Lewis, Anson, De Russy, and Father Orno. It was clear they were expected to fill it, and they reluctantly did so. As before, Barca and Willis hung back, but now so did Reverend Harkin. Colonel Wicklow was still absent.

"I'm glad you returned to us!" Don Frutos exclaimed with what looked like a genuine smile. He regarded Alcalde Periz. "I presume you know that can only mean one thing?"

Periz jerked a nod, flicked a glance at Lewis, and cleared his throat. "The cooperative association between Uxmal, Pidra Blanca, and Itzincab must remain intact to oppose the Holcanos, but as that alliance's only representative present, I release the Americans—the Detached Expeditionary Force— from their commitment to it." He looked squarely at Lewis. "I do in fact *insist* they leave the defensive positions they've erected behind the walls of Uxmal just as soon as they can."

General Agon respectfully whispered something to Don Frutos, who said, "You have two days to accomplish this, Major Cayce, or the Army of God will descend upon Uxmal regardless, bringing all the consequences I already described. For everyone concerned."

Lewis clenched his jaw, never looking at Periz, suddenly even more unsure of the *alcalde*'s real intentions. At least he'd implied all the Americans were still in his city. "What would you have us do?" he asked.

"Disavow the Ocelomeh at once, of course," Don Frutos told him, "then march out of the city and stack your arms and all your gear."

"My men will be treated well?" Lewis asked.

"As promised. As long as they cooperate in every way and don't resist conversion to the True Faith."

Lewis imagined how such an order would go over with his men. *They'd string me up,* he thought with dark amusement. Virtually every man in his command was devout to some degree, adhering to diverse Protestant denominations and even the real Pope in the Rome on the world they left behind. A few now followed Father Orno's version of Christianity. Surely Wicklow had warned Don Frutos how few would willingly convert to a faith they considered abhorrent? *Don Frutos won't care,* Lewis knew. *He'll do whatever he wants with us after we're helpless.*

"I don't think it'll take two days to vacate Uxmal," Lewis said lowly, almost cryptically.

"Nevertheless, you shall have them," Don Frutos said pleasantly, as if granting a favor.

Which confirms it'll take that long to bring his whole army up from the washboard glade, Lewis decided, *at which time he'll attack us, arrayed helplessly in the open, then fall on Uxmal itself. He thinks. No wonder he looks so cheerful.*

"Very well," Lewis said. "I hereby denounce the Ocelomeh and divorce my forces from theirs. I also accept . . . His Holiness's generous offer to take myself and my troops into the service of the Holy Dominion." Just saying those words made his stomach rebel, but he kept the disgust off his face.

"Excellent!" Don Frutos exclaimed and turned to another heavy priest in a finer robe who'd been very near him earlier. "Obispo Estupendo, proceed with the consecration!"

The fat priest nodded gravely. Staring at the ground and extending his arms to his sides, he began to chant in what sounded like a mix of Latin and the Spanya that seemed universal on this continent. More braziers were lit as if by magic, and pungent smoke filled the tent with a fog that bleared the eyes . . . and possibly other senses. Lewis immediately felt a spike of alarm as he grew light-headed, but as the effect increased, so did his apathy and willingness to accept it. Long wooden flutes retrieved from within the priest's robes made a sharp, plaintive, monotonous sound, probably annoyingly audible all across the clearing around the tent. Other voices joined the chant, though Don Frutos made no sound, only gazing benevolently about. Suddenly, the tapestry behind the throne stirred again, and two figures were ushered out between the weaselly Tranquilo and portly Felicidad. Both were naked, bound, and apparently drugged, and through the rising haze in the tent—and in Lewis's mind—it took him a moment to realize the first figure was one of the gold-painted girls, but the other was Colonel Wicklow. He looked at Don Frutos and caught him watching him. "One of mine and one of yours," he almost shouted over the din of flutes. "Of no further use to either of us. Besides, I told you I've grown fond of the colonel, and it's time he was rewarded for his service. He will go to heaven, Major Cayce! Accompanied by that wretched child as his everlasting servant!"

Whatever was in the smoke kept this from fully registering for a moment. Longer still before Lewis began to piece together a response or plan of action. In that time he dimly heard shots outside and fighting, as well as insistent cries of alarm. As if he was watching a dream, he saw the girl flung down on the table as the chanting increased in urgency and volume and willing hands, probably accustomed to whatever was affecting Lewis's mind, cut the girl's bonds and held her arms and legs while Father Felicidad took his place at the head of the table, drawing a long, green obsidian blade, its serrated edges and faceted sides reflecting the flames of the closest brazier like a malevolent jewel. Lewis felt the grip of his saber in his hand but couldn't seem to draw it. Looking desperately at Orno and Periz, he saw the horror on their faces made more intense, like his, by their inability to do anything but watch as Felicidad cried out and raised the wicked blade above the bare breast of the unresisting child.

Just as he began the fatal thrust, Father Felicidad's triumphant expression bulged to the side and exploded all over the anxiously expectant Doms on the other side of the table amid an earsplitting *crash* and roiling ball of smoke. Lewis felt someone grab him from behind, dragging him back, while Captain Anson leaped on the table with one of his huge revolvers in hand, swaying drunkenly, reaching to lift the golden child.

"Kill him, you fools!" Don Frutos roared, backing behind his throne-like chair. "He's already fired his shot!" Lewis distinctly saw an idiot grin spread across the Ranger's face as a priest produced a sword from beneath his robe.

Anson shot him too. "This pistol's magical, made by a fiendish demon named Sam Colt. It'll shoot a *hundred* bullets at a throw, an' I can do this all damn night!" he bellowed, snapping off another shot that blew a hole in the throne as Don Frutos and General Agon ducked out of sight—and men in yellow-and-black uniforms swarmed in from the hidden annex. They fired quickly, frantically, trying to protect their masters, killing a couple of red-robed figures in their haste. Lewis finally freed his saber from its scabbard, but whoever had him kept him from tottering to the Ranger's aid.

"Shake it off, Major!" shouted Private Willis in his ear. "Take deep breaths an' blow that nasty shit out. Barca smoked the smoke right off, if you get me, an' said they was up to somethin'. Sure enough! Them squeaky flutes must'a signaled their hunnerd-yard guards to come creepin' up. Here's your horse, sir. Up you git!"

Lewis's head was already clearing as he climbed in the saddle and saw the result of the fighting he'd vaguely heard. Men lay dead all around, mostly Dom lancers, but a dragoon and a couple of Espinoza's lancers as well. Balls fired by Dom muskets were whirring past as the hundred—more—Dom infantry continued to advance, lighting the night with their sparkly muzzle flashes very close.

"That gal Leonor killed *half* these buggers," Willis said admiringly, using a dead lancer as a step to his stirrup, "then covered us while we went for you." Lewis now saw that despite his bulk, Reverend Harkin had practically carried Father Orno and Alcalde Periz back to their horses while Barca half dragged a nearly insensible Colonel De Russy. Varaa, Burton, Anson, and Leonor were still shooting at Doms in the marquee, forted behind the heavy, overturned table. Dragoons and lancers were shooting carbines at the other advancing Doms while the rest of their "hundred" dragoons, lancers, and Ocelomeh Rangers galloped up to join them from behind. It looked like there'd soon be another battle here—not that Lewis hadn't half expected it from the start—but, shaking his head and blinking his eyes to clear the intoxicating smoke, he saw that Don Frutos had cheated again. There were at least three or four hundred Doms coming up the rise. "Let's go, Captain Anson! We've more company coming than we can entertain."

"I just wanna get that slimy Frutos bastard," Leonor raged.

"You think he just stayed behind that chair?" Lewis shouted. The marquee was starting to burn, ignited by an overturned brazier or torch. A lancer's horse squealed and went down, but the rider hopped off in time to avoid being crushed. "He and the rest are out the back and down behind the infantry by now. Let's go!"

Reluctantly, Anson called the others away, still carrying the drugged girl when he climbed in the saddle. Lewis looked around. Leonor was mounted, and so was Varaa. Barca was behind De Russy, holding him up. Father Orno seemed to be doing the same for Alcalde Periz. "Take them down to the trees, Lieutenant Burton," Lewis ordered, waving his sword at the Doms. "We'll meet them the same way as before."

Seeing them start to pull back at last, the Doms broke ranks and charged, swarming up and around the marquee. That's when Lewis saw the emaciated, naked form of Colonel Wicklow walking in circles in front of the big burning tent, hands still bound. "Jesus," he hissed, turning Arete back and preparing to touch her with his spurs. "I can't leave him to them. God knows what they'll do to him now." The roaring overpressure of Captain Anson's Walker Colt buffeted his right ear, and forty yards away, silhouetted by the growing flames, Colonel Wicklow dropped like a stone. Lewis turned to glare at Anson and was surprised by the fury he saw.

"What do you reckon they'd do to *you*, Lewis?" Anson snapped. "An' what would we do without you?"

"He did Wicklow a mercy, Major," Varaa shouted over the swelling musket fire, "and probably saved your life. You can fight later. Now we fight Doms. To the trees!"

Lewis had no business faulting Don Frutos for cheating—though the drugged smoke was a bit much—because Lewis had "cheated" as well. All of Felix Meder's mounted riflemen and Hudgens's two sections of artillery had moved up the forest track to the edge of the trees under cover of darkness. Much like the Doms must've done. And they'd deployed the same way they'd met the Dom lancers by the time the enemy infantry swept down. The result was much the same as well. Silhouetted against the burning tent, the enemy made a perfect target for massed rifle and carbine fire as well as the thundering, whistling canister belching from four well-plied 6pdrs. In moments, it seemed, the slope descending toward the trees was covered with steaming, mewling carrion once more.

"Now we move," Lewis cried, Leonor beside him as he urged Arete toward the carriage Father Orno and Reverend Harkin had packed Alcalde Periz and Colonel De Russy back into. "Lieutenant Burton, pass the word for Lieutenant Hudgens to replace the canister he expended from his caissons and have the rest of the men replenish ammunition as well. Wounded to the rear, and prepare to advance. Messengers!"

Two pairs of mounted Ocelomeh joined him as he rode. In these woods, at night, no single rider could be relied on to carry word of this importance. "Other couriers down the line have heard the fighting, no doubt, so Major Reed will probably know what to do before you even get there. If not, however, he must be told to 'execute his movement as planned.'" Even these runners wouldn't know exactly what the 'movement' was, in case they were taken, though its general purpose must be obvious. The Ocelomeh Rangers galloped away as Lewis and Captain Anson dismounted by the carriage, finding Varaa and a cluster of her healers there. "Has the *alcalde* recovered his senses yet?" Lewis asked, but Varaa clutched his arm.

"Yes," she said lowly, "but he was hit by a Dom ball as Reverend Harkin and Father Orno were getting him on his horse."

Lewis's racing thoughts and plans blanked for a moment as he pushed his way through to the carriage. Orno was in there, supporting his friend, and De Russy was hovering over him, hat gone and wispy, blood-spiked hair astray. He looked slightly deranged when he met Lewis's gaze. Ominously, the healers had withdrawn. "If Dr. Newlin was here . . ." De Russy began.

"He could do nothing," gasped Alcalde Periz.

Lewis knew it was true at once. The gold scale armor had done little to slow the ball that slammed into Periz's chest. If anything, it only flattened it into a wider missile that made a bigger wound, joined by the golden scales themselves. It hadn't hit anything immediately vital, but there'd be no stopping the blood from such a gaping hole. De Russy was trying to slow it at least, pressing the stuffed pillow-like top of his hat hard against it.

"Don't try to talk, my friend," Orno admonished, but Periz only snorted at him. "Would you have me die with things unsaid? *Necessary* things?" He looked at Lewis. "I know you feared I'd abandon you and accept Don Frutos's terms." He squeezed Father Orno's arm. "As did you—and you weren't wrong." He looked back at Lewis. "If we could've built the Union you sought from the start, I would've been more confident. I loved the idea of it but feared it as well. More than I believed the Doms would really come. I thought Uxmal would diminish within it." He gave a gurgling sigh. "Actually, Sira feared that more than I, but even as I encouraged the other *alcaldes* to preserve a looser alliance, Sira came around to my original thinking.

By then it was too late, and though our alliance grew stronger than I ever dreamed—making me think the Union would've succeeded after all—I held no hope it could prevail against the might of the Dominion." He pursed his bloody lips. "So yes, if I could've been certain things would go back to the way they were before you came, even with the unending strife against Holcanos and Grik, I would've betrayed you to preserve that." He shook his head. "These last weeks, and particularly these final days, knowing what was coming—what it would mean for my people—I prepared for treachery and war at the same time." He looked away, gasping from the effort of speaking. "But after actually meeting the Doms and hearing Don Frutos, *seeing what I saw*, I know peace was never possible." He reached for Lewis's hand and clasped it weakly. "War is here, and I'm resigned to it. I only wish I could fight it with you, but you'll find a steadier, more reliable ally and friend to your Union in my beloved Sira than you did in me. I only beg you to remember I *didn't* betray you in the end, and that you'll build your Union and protect it—and my Sira—as if they were your own."

Lewis squeezed the weakening hand. "I suspected you were tempted," he confirmed. "Who wouldn't be, under the circumstances? But I never believed you would. I don't believe it now." He smiled. "And even if you had, I still would've protected your people as best I could since I already think of them as mine. Rest easy, Alcalde Periz. All will be well. Rest easy, my friend."

Stepping back from the carriage, he heard Father Orno praying aloud, possibly conferring his version of the last rites. Lewis pushed a couple of healers back toward the door, saying, "Stay with him. You too, Colonel De Russy, if you please. Sira may need you no matter what occurs. Do you need Barca? Good. I'd like to keep him." He called sharply to the driver who'd resumed his post. "Get him back to Uxmal as quick as you can. Lieutenant Hernandez, detail a dozen escorts, but the rest of us are pressing on before the enemy gathers their wits."

"What about me, Major Cayce?" Reverend Harkin asked.

Lewis considered, watching the dragoons and riflemen finish re-forming their column and the guns pull in near the front. Anson had already remounted and galloped forward to lead with the Ocelomeh Rangers and Espinoza's lancers. Leonor was still mounted, waiting for him, and now Willis and Barca joined her. *What a strange staff I've assembled,* he thought. "Return in the carriage or ride with us, Reverend," Lewis finally answered. "Wherever you feel called to be."

"Then I'll stay with you," Harkin replied, hauling his bulk up on an un-happy local horse. "Alcalde Periz has Orno to pray for him. All of Uxmal will be blanketed in prayer. But who will pray for you?"

Lewis smiled. "Who indeed?"

Harkin grinned back, then called out loudly in his far-carrying pulpit voice, "Be strong in the Lord, lads, and in His mighty power! Our struggle is not against flesh and blood alone, but the very spiritual forces of Evil in this dark, unholy world. Tonight, tomorrow, and forevermore, we stand against the Devil himself!"

There was a ragged chorus of "Amen!" and Lewis called for the small force to advance.

"That wasn't straight from Ephesians," Leonor accused as the column set out.

"True," Harkin serenely agreed, "I may have edited it just a bit, but the sentiment remains intact. All the best prayers and sermons are reinforced by the *meaning* of scripture as it applies to the moment, if not the actual word for word."

"Ain't that what the Doms have done?"

Even in the darkness, more complete now that the marquee had burned away, Lewis knew Harkin was struggling for control, especially when Varaa *kakked* behind him. "Not at all, my dear," Harkin said at last, voice the same as before. "I've never seen a Dom Bible. I don't know if it exists. If so, I imagine a vile, vomitous manifesto, entirely fabricated to justify their evil ways. But even if it were the same as ours and they validate their hideous acts with words taken directly from it—which I suppose they could, select-ing a phrase or sentence out of context here and there—it's still the holy sentiment, the *essence* of the words they've perverted to their barbarous ends. I'd *never* do that." He paused reflectively. "Though God alone knows how much blood's been spilled on the world we came from because two people read the exact same words and came to different understandings!"

They'd crested the corpse-strewn rise, and Anson and some of his Rangers—visible as dark, mounted shapes under the three-quarter moon that turned the long grass around them almost silver—abruptly disap-peared in the gloom of the far tree line. There was no shooting. All the Doms there must've raced into action or fallen back with Don Frutos.

"Let's pick up the pace, Lieutenant Burton!" Lewis called, and the col-umn broke into a canter, the only sounds the rumble of hooves, the creak and pop of cannon carriages amid the rattle and jangle of traces, and the crackle of fluttering guidons as they plunged down into the forbidding forest on the enemy leader's heels.

Lewis had less than four hundred men under his direct command. They were good men, some of his best, and they'd drive forward as far and strong as they could. But there were bound to be enemies along the track, now ready and waiting, and at the washboard glade just four miles away was an army of twenty thousand. Numbers wouldn't count for as much as speed, determination, and firepower on the confined forest track, but they'd matter a great deal in the open when they were deployed and arrayed to face him. Still, now that the thing was set in motion, Lewis was content, almost cheerful. After long months of training, waiting, and preparation for what they'd expected to happen, they'd quickly, professionally improvised for what they hadn't as best they could. The results of the bizarre meeting with the enemy would lay to rest any lingering political reluctance or opposition among the people of this land, and its army would know the stakes and consequences of failure. Suddenly all was clear at last—or would be once Father Orno got Alcalde Periz back to Uxmal, and messengers went to Lewis's other forces. Necessity would turn support for the cause, perhaps the Union, universal. There'd be no more doubts or equivocation, no more thought of appeasement, and all the people would recognize the simple choices between good and evil, fight or die. The "cause" would become as stark and unencumbered as battle itself.

Lewis had seen his share of war and battle and hated the horror of it, particularly the tragic loss or maiming of young men with such promise, but as complex as battles often were—and their hasty deployments would make this one more complex than usual—they were often simplicity itself compared to the political maneuvers that set them in motion. The Doms seemed too arrogant to realize it, but Lewis hoped and believed the perversity, cruelty, and treachery they'd exhibited at the parley, designed to divide and intimidate, would have the opposite effect. The clear-cut choices represented by the cause would reach his whole army before it fought. Any lingering doubts his men might've carried, old hands and new, would be cast away. They'd be afraid. *He* was afraid. But they'd fight even harder than they would've before the parley was held.

Now Lewis could go into battle without cares of that sort on his mind, and he was *glad* for this battle. It would give substance and meaning and hope to the cause, no matter how terrible it might be, because just as his Americans had an affinity for the Ocelomeh they'd already fought beside, nearly everyone in the Alliance of Cities was represented here. All their people, and the army, would become one at last—he prayed. *First we have to win, of course,* he told himself with a rueful grin.

Leonor was riding beside him and noted his expression in the growing moonlight. "Looks like you're actually enjoyin' yourself."

Lewis laughed at her. "I've never seen anyone appear to enjoy a fight more than you, except perhaps your father," he retorted, "so considering the source, that's a strange accusation."

"No accusation. Observation." They were nearing the trees. "Do you think there's a chance this half-baked plan'll work?"

Lewis nodded at Reverend Harkin, bouncing back and forth in his saddle. "I think in one respect, after what I saw tonight, I have to agree with the good reverend's theory. Surely the Doms—their leaders, at least—represent pure evil in this land. They may even be the strongest manifestation of it on this entire world, for all we know. So I *do* believe God's primary purpose in putting us here must be to oppose them—and He's on our side."

"Why not just smite 'em, then, like he did them Gomorrans an' nasty Sodomites?"

Lewis chuckled. "He could, I'm sure, but what good would it do the people here? How long would their faith in Him—and their liberty—endure if they weren't called to defend it? There are still the Holcanos and Grik."

"It might save a bunch from gettin' killed."

"But they wouldn't have *earned* it, would they?" Harkin asked, voice jouncing with his bulbous body.

"I didn't know you were in the 'God helps them who help theirselves' camp," Leonor countered. "Father says that's Greek, an' ain't in the Bible at all!" She paused. "He does seem to live by it, though."

"Thessalonians 3:10 says, 'The one who is unwilling to work shall not eat,'" Harkin went on pedantically.

"It ain't the same."

"Is it not?"

"No," Leonor insisted. "An' what about us? Why did God pick *us* to fight the Doms?"

Lewis cleared his throat to reply as they finally cantered down into the forest. The track was wide and clear, better than it would be later on, and for the first time he noticed the bark on the north sides of the trees emitted a faint phosphorescence and the dense woods glowed with just enough light that they'd have no trouble keeping the road. He'd heard of the phenomenon and counted on it, but they'd used lanterns the only time *he'd* ever moved troops here at night and he hadn't seen it himself.

"We were at hand, and it fell to us," Barca suddenly said behind them. "'To whomever much is given, of him will much be required; and to whom much was entrusted, of him more will be asked.' I think the Lord put us here because he trusted us to do the right thing," he added a little self-consciously.

"There you are!" Reverend Harkin declared triumphantly.

"Thank you, Barca," Lewis said. "I believe so too, and I hope you're right."

"I won't argue that," said Leonor.

CHAPTER 34

B oogerbear returned to the roughly established command post on the southeast side of the washboard accompanied by four of Consul Koaar's 1st Ocelomeh mounted messengers after leading the Rangers and lancers out on the extreme left of the line on the south end of the big clearing. Boogerbear would go back as soon as he could, but Major Reed had called all commanders to make a report on their dispositions and state of preparations. Boogerbear liked Major Reed and respected his desire to look his subordinates in the eye and make sure there were no misunderstandings before the festivities began. He was able to do so since the 1st Ocelomeh Infantry had erected a large animal-hide tent when it arrived almost two days before and a light could be shone inside without risk of detection.

It was hot and stuffy in the tent, and it smelled of the smoke that preserved it. The great hide must've been fairly fresh as well, since there remained a hint of putrefaction. No one seemed to mind. Boogerbear didn't. And large as it was, the tent was packed with only fifteen men and one Mi-Anakka (Consul Koaar) gathered around a small table and equally small map, hand-sketched in charcoal on the flesh side of a hide little bigger than a rabbit's. It depicted the general shape of the washboard glade resembling a wineglass with a broken stem about two miles across in most dimensions, toppling to the west. All around was forest except for the sea to the northwest. The artist had drawn the enemy camp as best he could and even attempted to represent terrain features: the slight little ridges and shallow gullies that, except for a larger central wash, sloped generally upward to their present position. Though they might provide some cover from fire in battle, none would really hide an approach on the enemy. Of course, up until now, the great forest had hidden their approach amazingly well.

Boogerbear never would've believed it. He'd heard stories of great armies of French and Indians moving through forests against the British (or vice versa), never to be seen until they attacked, but despite Koaar's assurances, he couldn't see how they'd accumulate almost six thousand men and two batteries of guns right on top of the enemy without being detected. They did it slowly, over several nights of long, dangerous marching, and the enemy hadn't been here in force, at first, but somehow, they did it. He'd written it off to Dom arrogance at first; no one would dare attack *them*, especially in such numbers. It never happened before. Incompetence played a role as well; the enemy was in unknown country without Holcano scouts, and their commander probably decided that in their bright-yellow uniforms, Dom scouts would only be seen before they noted any skulking spies in any case. Quite true, actually. They'd never catch a handful of scouts, which they had to be expecting, but they'd missed this massive buildup just as well.

Boogerbear and the Ocelomeh Rangers had come first, frightening away many of the local animals—capable of being frightened—before the infantry and artillery started trickling in. This so they wouldn't send animals fleeing onto the plain, compelling the Doms to inspect the surrounding forest more carefully as their army grew. In retrospect, Boogerbear wasn't sure even that had been necessary, nor had the terrible deaths of some of the following infantrymen, killed by monsters they couldn't chase away. Except for a cursory inspection of their environs when they first arrived, the Doms appeared content to await their next orders in camp, even dragging firewood up from directly behind them. That made sense, Boogerbear supposed, staying close to the road and even using it to reduce their burden, but he finally decided fear of the woods—not of any human enemy, but the monsters dwelling there—did as much to squelch the initiative of Dom scouts as arrogance or orders.

"Everyone knows what to do?" Major Reed asked earnestly after they went over their deployments once more. There were nods, but no comments or questions. Everyone was tense but determined. Word of what happened at the conference had already arrived, first blinkered from the treetops in the simple expected sequence reporting failure, but soon came exhausted messengers on half-dead horses bearing further details—including that Alcalde Periz had been desperately wounded. Now the commanders in the darkened tent were ready for this, even anxious. Reed looked at them all and sighed. "Very well. God be with you all."

The lamp was extinguished, and they filed out under the tree-filtered moon and phosphorescent bark. They were still inside the forest, all the army was, but they had a good view of the enemy camp down on the plain by the sea. There were hundreds of campfires guttering there, but it was late and most of the enemy slept.

"If it was up to me, I'd hit 'em now," Boogerbear said quietly once most of the others dispersed.

Reed managed to chuckle. "I'm sure you would. You Rangers have always been a murderous lot. Killing a man in his sleep would make no difference to you."

"Not a bit," Boogerbear replied. "Prob'ly even be a mercy for most."

"I'm with you entirely," Reed said, tone more somber. "I'd be for it myself if it weren't for the confusion such an assault would bring on ourselves. Deadly confusion, emerging from the forest and bordering brush and crossing the better part of a mile of broken ground. Men—whole regiments—losing alignment, lagging, moving ahead unsupported, falling down, weapons going off . . . some would load them despite the direst warnings. I doubt the enemy would sleep through our bumbling advance." He paused. "And this will be the very first action for most. For all of us as a combined army."

"*Your* first real action too, I reckon," Boogerbear observed evenly, noting Reed's contained anxiety.

Reed took a deep breath and sighed. "Well, yes. I was at the beach, of course"—he half raised the arm that would never recover completely—"and I'm not concerned I'll prove shy—some never know until they're in it—but I've never had this much responsibility. Even at the beach, with Colonel De Russy . . . indisposed, I had Captain Anson." He patted his pockets and then dropped his hand. "Oh, I do wish I could risk a cigar! It might even be worth returning to that reeking tent!"

Boogerbear withdrew a tobacco pouch from his haversack. "Have a chaw. I mixed some honey-like stuff—might be real honey; the bees look honest enough—with some local tobaccy. Chews pretty sweet an' mild."

Reed took the pouch and fished out a wad of sticky leaves, pushing them into his mouth. "Thank God," he murmured. "Thank *you*, Lieutenant Beeryman." He chewed a moment before saying, "Very good. Listen," he added awkwardly, "I didn't mean to sound so nervy. I'm really not, you know." He chuckled again. "And even if I was, I'm sure Major Cayce's plan has taken that into account as well. He's an extraordinary man and will make this as easy as possible on all of us. We'll know what to do when the time comes— if everything goes as he expects."

"Not easy on *him*, though," Boogerbear observed.

Reed frowned. "No. He seems to love this and hate it all at once, but he clearly has a talent. He also seems to put himself too much to the front for my liking. I'm glad we have him. I just hope we can *keep* him." He suddenly held up his hand. "What's that?"

Something like distant thunder rolled in through the trees from the northeast, but there was no lightning and the stars and moon still washed the glade in their silvery light.

"Cannon," Boogerbear declared. "Deep in the woods, about three miles?" He seemed uncertain. "Hard to tell in all these damn trees."

"He's coming, then," Reed said.

"Sure he's comin'," Boogerbear assured. "The questions are, will he make it, when'll he get here, an' what'll he have left when he does? Finally, even then, will the Doms do what he thinks?" He wadded some of the sticky leaves into his own cheek and nodded at his horse. "Reckon it's time for me an' ol' Dodger to get back where we belong. It'll take a while, an' with such a heavy day comin', I don't want him tired."

"God be with you, Lieutenant Beeryman."

"You too, Major Reed."

BY THE TIME Boogerbear was back with his Rangers on the far left, the sky was beginning to turn a hazy gray over the tall trees to the northeast. There hadn't been any more cannon fire for some time, but now he heard it again, actually seeing a brief pulse of light in the damp sky and a sharp flash in the trees beyond where the road pushed into them. Oddly, there were just a few

Doms gathered on the road, just milling about and talking, apparently discussing what was coming. Surely whoever was defending the road, attempting to slow Lewis's deliberate advance, had sent messengers back. Still, there'd been no evident alarm in the great camp—though quite a few men had come out of tents as the fighting came closer. Finally, as the gray sky started turning gold, horns sounded and the rest of the men began to stir, rushing from their tents to fall into company formations.

Boogerbear laughed and, reaching over, thumped Teniente Lara on the shoulder. "Look at that. I *told* you Major Cayce'd time his arrival to suck them devils into ranks before they got fed! Up an' about or not, I doubt many got any sleep, an' now they'll fight on empty bellies."

Lara yawned hugely. "I didn't sleep either," he reminded.

"So? You ate somethin', even if it was cold. An' you knew what was comin' today. None o' those poor bastards did." He sobered. "Good thing they didn't send reinforcements up the road. Might've stopped him, then."

Ixtla had joined them and shook his head. "Then they couldn't have their battle. And they desperately want a proper battle!"

Boogerbear looked at him in surprise. "Major Cayce knows this? An' what the hell's the rest o' that mean?"

Ixtla laughed. "Of course he knows. I'm sure a large percentage of his plan relies on it. As for why, well, as numerous and powerful as they are, the Doms have never fought a 'proper' battle any more than our troops have! They *yearn* to do so and will be quite certain our whole army has come up to join Major Cayce on that road. Why else would he keep pushing? If they stopped it up entirely, it couldn't come out and deploy where they can destroy it. And they *must* destroy it or its survivors can slow their advance on Uxmal to a crawl! The table is turned, as you say. See those officers down where the road runs into the forest?" He practically giggled. "They're planning how much room to give us as we so conveniently appear."

"Mighty considerate," Boogerbear groused, annoyed he hadn't been given Ixtli's little tidbit until now. "Is Major Reed in on it?"

"Of course. But other than him . . ." Ixtli counted on his fingers, then laughed at Boogerbear's expression. "Most of the Ocelomeh will have figured it out, I expect, but few will have been told. I doubt even Alcalde Periz was informed."

"I can believe that." Boogerbear nodded. "Damn spies creepin' all over Uxmal. Best to keep things to yourself."

It was brightening very quickly, and Boogerbear saw the officers Ixtli pointed out now mounting and galloping back to the camp where companies were forming into regimental columns five hundred long and four abreast. The huge siege guns were still where they'd been parked, but smaller guns with split trails were being hitched to clumsy-looking low-lying limbers already harnessed to big, brutish armabueys. These were being led forward or off to the sides in pairs, or sections.

"Twenty field guns," Lara counted.

"Slow, though," Boogerbear observed. "Damn slow-moving." He glanced at Lara. "You'll remember Arista's guns an' limbers weren't all that different, but he deployed 'em faster. Still, once they were set for the fight at Palo Alto, I don't believe they moved again until they got pulled out."

"I do remember," Lara sadly confirmed, then compressed his lips, "and I remember *very* well how devastating the mobility of your artillery proved that day."

"Made the difference." Boogerbear nodded.

"I hope it will again," Lara said softly.

LEWIS HAD BEEN reinforced shortly before dawn by almost a thousand Home Guard troops and Hudgens's section of heavy 12pdrs. De Russy—somewhat impulsively joined by Dr. Newlin—brought them up from Uxmal on a grueling forced march at Sira's insistence after her wounded husband was delivered. Lewis had been surprised and gratified to see them. Pulling the city's defenders hadn't been part of the plan. But tired as they were, Lewis was impressed by their determination, and he really did need them. The fighting on the track hadn't been fierce, the resistance fairly sparse and isolated, but they'd suffered some casualties, and his force had to look as impressive as possible when it emerged in the washboard glade just a couple hundred yards ahead. Few of the guards had firearms of any kind, and most carried only pikes, but they were *good* with those pikes and wore the same uniform as American infantry. Their footsore but well-drilled ranks would make Lewis's demonstration more convincing.

"How was Periz? And how did Sira behave?" he asked De Russy and Newlin, now riding with him, Varaa, Leonor, Barca, and Willis, just in front of Hudgens's fully reconstituted battery. Only the Rangers remained between them and the glade.

"Periz was dying. Nothing *I* could do for him, at any rate," Newlin reported gravely. After a short pause, he snorted angrily. "I've taught the Ocelomeh and Uxmalo healers all I know about battlefield medicine—something they were already acquainted with, of course, if not on the scale they'll face—but with a few exceptions, their fundamental medical skills are better than mine. Sometimes I'm the teacher but more often the student. I've actually been more focused on chemistry of late, experimenting with fulminate of mercury to supply your weapons that require percussion caps. Tricky, dangerous stuff," he murmured, then shook his head. "But today I'm just a surgeon again, and at least here with you I might be of use."

"Major Reed will have established the primary field hospital," Varaa said. "Perhaps after we deploy and things . . . begin in earnest, you can move to join him."

"Perhaps." Newlin looked at Lewis. "Sira behaved admirably under the circumstances, by the way." He waved behind, where the Home Guards were marching. "And quite decisively. Mistress Samantha has become her chief advisor in this crisis, and it was actually her idea to reinforce you. Sira Periz agreed at once. In spite of her understandable grief and worry, she's fully aware that if you lose, Uxmal cannot stand."

Captain Anson pounded back down the track and pulled back on his reins. Colonel Fannin danced to an agitated stop. Like Arete, Anson's horse could sense a battle brewing. "I had a look ahead," Anson informed them, "an' it's just like we predicted."

"*I* predicted." Varaa huffed slightly.

Anson rolled his eyes to the heavens. "Who cares, you self-absorbed 'possum? They're formin' up right in the center of the glade, about nine hundred yards, leavin' us plenty of room to place ourselves and clearly invitin' us to their battle."

Lewis nodded acceptance—and amusement at the Ranger's familiar jest at Varaa. Then again . . . There was no doubting Anson's steadiness in battle, but he had to wonder if the uncharacteristic remark was due to camaraderie and confidence or uneasy concern. "Very well, Captain Anson. Take the lancers and Rangers out as skirmishers, dragoons on the flanks. Lieutenant Hudgens," he called when Anson whirled his horse around and galloped out of the trees, "you'll unlimber your battery in three widely spaced sections, leaving room between them for Lieutenant Meder's riflemen, as well as the Rangers and dragoons when they fall back." He looked almost apologetically at De Russy. "I'll go out with them. You'll have to lead the Uxmalo Infantry."

De Russy looked unhappy. "I . . . I'm not sure I can. We *agreed* it would be better . . ."

"You can certainly deploy them as if on parade," Lewis told him gently, forging ahead. "Bring them out when we're in position and go from column into line. *Two* lines, not shoulder to shoulder, but at arm's length, and leave five paces between the lines when you bring them forward. Hopefully, the second rank will seem to fill the spaces in the front from behind while giving an impression of depth." He shrugged. "It's all I can think of to make us look like twice our number. From ground level, and from the distance Captain Anson described, it should serve."

"What's a 'possum?" Varaa asked.

Lewis raised an eyebrow at her, then, turning to the front, gently applied his spurs. "Let's go."

"But what's a 'possum!" Varaa demanded, racing after him. "Is it a good thing?"

The mounted men had already spilled out of the woods when Lewis and his companions trotted out under the rising morning sun. Anson was in the center, his Rangers, lancers, and dragoons still on their horses and presenting a sparse front about five hundred yards wide—roughly equal to the width of the two closest tightly packed Dom regiments so far away, the rising sun in their faces and yellow uniforms blazing gold. Ocelomeh observers in the tops of tall trees estimated each regiment was composed of around two thousand men and the enemy had stacked them two wide and three deep as they assembled, with more still falling in in the camp. Hudgens led his guns out next, spokes blurring as hooves rumbled and trace hooks jangled. He started placing them in pairs as Lewis told him—like Olayne, he was shaping into a fine artilleryman—with a hundred and fifty yards or so between each section. Men jumped down from horses and limbers, unhitching the guns, and the horses and limbers proceeded a short distance to the rear, where they turned to the front once more. Lieutenant Meder's riflemen came out at the double, thinly filling the gaps between the sections. De Russy appeared more ponderously, peeling men off to either side of the road just outside the trees, cajoling them into the unfamiliar formation where the enemy might not see them before he marched them forward. The left side of the line carried the flag of Uxmal—the blue saltire on white—but Hudgens had entrusted his battery's four-by-four-foot Stars and Stripes to the Uxmalos on the right to make it seem the American infantry was here as well. *I should've thought of that,* Lewis scolded himself. *Hudgens will do very well indeed.*

English-speaking NCOs shouted at the Uxmalos to keep their alignment as De Russy gave the word and the Home Guards pushed forward to the deeper sound of their native drums, pikes on their shoulders and bayonet-like blades glittering in the sun. Flags flapped in the offshore morning breeze, and the tramp of feet in time with the drum was very loud.

"We *look* fairly impressive, at least," Newlin stated critically.

"So do they," Reverend Harkin said lowly, glowering across the field at the Doms. They carried many more of the twisted-cross flags than the number of regiments accounted for, streaming above yellow-clad troops like a kind of bloody smoke. "Damn them," he muttered.

Anson fell back and trotted past, heading toward Lewis. "If you ain't gonna arm yourselves, I suggest you stay back behind the infantry, out of the way."

"And damn *you*, sir!" Harkin snapped. "Arm me and I'll fight! I can use a musket!"

Anson paused and gave him a curious look. "What can you do with a rifle, preacher? Felix Meder lost two men on the trail and has their weapons on one of the caissons."

"I'm better with a rifle than a musket. Why, I often shot squirrels for my dinner as a lad!"

Anson tilted his head at the Doms. "They ain't squirrels. But talk to Mr. Meder if you like." He pushed on to where Lewis sat on his horse with his unlikely staff. "Well, here we are. They let us come out an' everything. What's next? You think they expect us to attack *them*?"

"*Someone* will tell me what a 'possum is before this day is done," Varaa grumped, "but the Doms may expect exactly that. Remember, as confident as they are in their numbers, they're new at this too."

Lewis scratched the beard on his chin. "We have to make them attack us, and soon. The rest of our army can't hide forever. We might ask for another parley, I suppose. Try to insult them into coming." He frowned. "I don't think so. I don't want to talk to them anymore. But we need them closer, focused on us." He looked at Anson. "We'll give them a jab. Have your horsemen take their mounts to the rear—not too far, keep them handy—and rejoin the riflemen between the guns."

"Yes sir," he said. "Bugler!"

"Then?" Leonor asked, speaking for the first time in quite a while.

Lewis grinned at her. "Then we open the ball. I hope you like this one as much as I enjoyed our dances at the last. Lieutenant Hudgens," he shouted at the mounted officer behind the nearest section of guns. "Load and hold. Prepare to commence firing."

"Solid shot or case, sir?"

Lewis considered. Their exploding case shot was extremely limited, and they hadn't solved the problem of making more. Time fuses were difficult enough, but simply casting a hollow metal ball had defeated everyone involved in the project so far. In addition, Varaa had recently questioned the wisdom of "introducing" case shot to the Doms at all. They didn't have it, but might make their own if they saw it in use, perhaps even collecting unexploded examples. But Lewis might need it today, and he'd have to trust his people to solve the problem of replacing it. As for the Doms . . . *I must let the day decide,* he told himself. "Solid shot, for now. At least until they spread out a little. As deep as their ranks are at present, each shot might kill a dozen men. But you're free to load case at your discretion when they shift to a more open formation," he replied.

"If they do," Varaa said.

"Surely they will?"

Varaa pointed to the southwest, just a few hundred yards from where Boogerbear and Lara were reported to have their Rangers, lancers, and Ocelomeh. A large block of Dom lancers was gathered there, just south of their tents. "They learned not to send *them* straight against us," Varaa *kakked*, "and no doubt they mean to come thundering over to strike our flank at some point, but other than that little skirmish last night—that was *not* a 'battle,'" she stated definitively, "Dom infantry has never *received* cannon fire. They'll learn some new lessons today." She shook her head at Lewis, blinking irony and grinning. "Really, Major Cayce. I protest. You're educating the enemy far too freely."

Lewis grinned back. "Then let's see how high we can raise their tuition. Lieutenant Hudgens, you may commence firing."

The two heavy 12pdrs fired first, almost as one, flattening the tall grass in front of them with a great thundering, clanking *boom*. Twin jets of yellow fire leaped from muzzles dipping violently downward amid huge rolling clouds of smoke before breeches crashed loudly against elevation screws. The guns rolled back past their crews—about seven feet in all—while brake chains rattled and swayed and the shriek of their shot tore downrange like ripping sheets. Neither had fired an exploding shell, but there were a pair of bright red explosions among the Doms. Mere bodies can't stop such projectiles, not even a dozen of them, or even sap much of their energy. Whole files of men exploded like melons, shattered parts geysering up all around. Ribs, arm bones, shattered muskets, even buttons, slashed men standing near. Four 6pdr solid shot crashed into the Doms as well, doing similar if lesser execution. Amid the screams and wails of pain, the whole Dom army seemed to voice a collective groan.

The guns had barely stopped moving before men seized their spokes to roll them back into battery. Others were clearing and thumbing the vents and bringing fresh charges and shot from the limbers. Lewis watched the 12pdr crews race each other through the motions of his modified, standardized drill. The Number Two men on the left dashed their sponges in water buckets before swabbing hot barrels, then handing their implements to the Number Five men, took the ammunition brought in a pouch and thrust it in the muzzle. The Number One men to the right of the guns had been waiting, rammer heads poised. Now they leaned in, driving the fixed charges down to the breeches in single smooth strokes. Both gave them quick taps to make sure they were seated (or just for luck) before withdrawing their rammers and standing away. All this time—six entire seconds— the Number Three men had been pressing leather thumbstalls hard on the vents. Now they raced to the handspikes inserted in the trails of the carriages as the gunners stepped forward. Placing their sights, gunners aimed through the smoke, adjusting elevation with the screws and windage by hand signals to the Threes on the handspikes, who shifted the guns side to side. Taking their sights, the gunners stood clear and signaled they were satisfied. The Threes then returned to their places and stabbed brass picks in the vents they'd tended, piercing the woolen powder bags in front of the breech faces before securing the brass hammers on the Hidden's Patent locks. That's when the Fours primed the guns with the large, strange-looking percussion caps that this day might also see the end of, forcing them to revert to linstocks and slow match. But now the Fours stretched lanyards to the sides, ensured their crews were clear, then signaled their gun was ready to fire.

Both 12pdrs and most of the rest were ready in less than thirty seconds—very quick for inexperienced crews' first action together. And few things satisfied Lewis as much as watching well-run guns; men performing carefully coordinated tasks and steps in perfect sequence without a word reminded him of a ballet. He remembered what seemed like just a few weeks before when words were necessary to train them, of course, and they'd "loaded by detail" with a command for each step. They learned their trade just like the infantry did, but infantrymen were only responsible for their own weapons and didn't need to synchronize loading them with others once they knew how, except for show. Artillery required their crews to perform their intricate dance in silence—words were hard to hear in battle—to send each round downrange. Lewis had heard it called the "dance of death," and that was very apt, but preferred to think of it as an example of absolute cooperation among disparate men who might not even like each other. It gave him hope that all men might cooperate as well if the cause was dear enough.

"Fire!" bellowed Lieutenant Hudgens. *Poom! Poom! Pppooom! Poom!*

CHAPTER 35

H ammer your flints and clear your vents, lads," called Sergeant Visser of the 3rd Pennsylvania. All 760 men of the regiment were waiting, fully formed, inside the trees a few hundred yards south-southeast of where Major Cayce's little force had deployed in front of the whole Dom army.

"Hammered to a sparkless nub is mine, Sergeant dear," replied a nervous soldier.

"Then replace it while you can," Visser growled. "Our turn's coming." He looked at Hanny Cox and hissed, "Scared, son?"

"My God, the Major's tearing them up!" cried Captain Wagley, creeping back from the brushy edge of the woods, collapsing his telescope and mounting his horse. His tone had been gleeful but it held a hint of anxious overexcitement as he continued. "They've finally started their infantry moving—and there's a godawful lot of them, widening their front as regiments shift from column into line. Prettily done, I must say. Looks like a parade. But every gun in Hudgens's Battery is throwing the sweetest shot!" A muted cheer escaped the Americans and Uxmalos in the 3rd. They were conscious of the need to remain undetected, but the growing roar of artillery had made perfect silence superfluous. Besides, the Doms had indeed focused all their attention on Major Cayce's tiny force—just as he'd planned—and twenty or more big guns were pounding back at him. Not even Wagley had seen how effective they were, but the din was tremendous.

"No, Sergeant, I'm not afraid," Cox denied determinedly, with a glance aside at Apo and back at Preacher Mac. He was absently rolling the trailing staff of the cased Stars and Stripes in his hands.

"Liar," Visser whispered with a grin. "I'm scared to death!"

"You?"

"Of course I am, boy." Visser nodded out at the washboard glade, quickly becoming a battlefield. "We're next. You and I and some of the lads're the only ones who already faced this enemy." He glanced at Hanny's friend Apo, the new color-bearer for the cased Pennsylvania flag. They'd recovered it after all the lancers that overran them were killed. Hanny was glad to have Apo beside him, but was worried about him too. Visser raised his voice. "Any man unafraid to step out there and face those devils has lost his intellects. But fear don't make you a coward; it makes you a goddamn hero! It's how you use your fear that counts, how you overcome it and do what needs doin' in spite of it, hear?" He smiled back at Hanny. "Now tell me the truth."

"*I'm* terrified!" Apo admitted with a shaky grin.

Hanny nodded. "Well . . . I suppose I am a little afraid—and though I'm sensible to the honor, I'd prefer a musket to this flag staff. But the funny thing is, I wasn't afraid when we fought the lancers. Not like this. It must be because it all happened so fast. This . . ." He nodded at the smoky field. "Marching here in the dark with monsters all around us—I heard the Jaguar Warriors fighting a large one with their bows and was sure it—or another one—would get me. . . ." He shivered in spite of the heat. "But then we were here, making ready, and waiting so long with the enemy so close. . . . It's the *ponderousness* of it all that makes me so apprehensive."

"'Ponderous' means 'slow'?" Apo asked. Visser nodded, then patted his and Hanny's shoulders before gesturing out to the west. Though the Americans remained invisible under the trees, the long yellow-and-black lines of the Dom infantry pressing into the storm of Hudgens's shot under their bloodred flags could now be clearly seen.

"Well," Visser said, "while the enemy's certainly ponderous in his movements, we're about to step off quick. Not much of anything'll seem 'slow' after that."

—————

A man fell screaming, rammer staff twirling, as dark earth and grass rocketed in the air by one of Hudgens's 6pdrs, a Dom roundshot bounding up and away to crack into the trees behind them.

"They're getting better, sir," Hudgens shouted at Lewis. The enemy cannonade had been furious from the start but had very little effect—mostly striking short and skating over its target or splintering trees in the woods— and Lewis's artillery had largely ignored it, focusing on shredding densely packed men instead. He wouldn't be surprised if his few guns alone hadn't already killed or wounded hundreds of the enemy. But the Doms figured this out and began laboriously advancing their guns by hand with their infantry. One reason the infantry approach was so slow. Repositioned at five hundred yards, the enemy gunners were firing everything they had at their counterparts. This preserved Lewis's tiny force of infantry and dismounted troopers, but was starting to take a toll on his cannoneers. None of his precious weapons had been seriously damaged yet—a few shattered spokes on one—but more than a dozen of Hudgens's men had been killed or injured.

"Leave the twelve pounders in place and keep pouring in the solid shot. Switch to canister at three hundred yards," Lewis told him. "Get your six pounders moving from flank to flank to spoil the enemy's aim and target their guns." He hesitated. He'd hoped to save his exploding case for "later," but there might not be a "later" if he held back now. "They can use case to kill the crews."

A roundshot gouged the earth right between Arete's feet, spraying long grass blades around in a cloud. She merely walked in a circle and returned to her place and Lewis patted her neck affectionately. Leonor, Barca, and Willis, still on their horses as well, looked at him with mixed expressions.

"A fine, fine animal," Varaa observed, walking up. Nearly everyone else had dismounted, even Captain Anson up on the line, where he commanded the "skirmishers" and kept relaying Lieutenant Meder's request for permission to open fire with his riflemen. Lewis would let them momentarily, also at three hundred yards, and other things would begin to happen then as well. Observers in the trees and especially messengers from the south had reported the enemy was fully committed: six entire Dom regiments of roughly two thousand men apiece and all their guns except the monstrous siege pieces. Only three regiments and the lancers—about eight thousand total—were being kept as a distant reserve or to guard their camp. Considering the almost mile-long gap that had formed, only the lancers might still be an immediate additional concern.

"A fine animal," Varaa repeated, "certainly worth preserving. I might say the same for her rider and those around him," she added pointedly, flicking her ears at Leonor as if hoping she might persuade him. No help there. Leonor and Barca seemed utterly unfazed, faces set in determination to remain with Lewis no matter what. Willis alone looked profoundly unhappy, but Varaa had noted a change in him, especially since last night. She wasn't sure if he wanted away from his commander or just off the horse he hated. She sighed. "If you won't withdraw to safety and direct your battle like a rational being, at least step down and make yourselves less conspicuous!"

"Worried about me, Varaa?" Lewis asked with a grin as the first section of 6pdrs, secured and limbered within seconds of the command, thundered past behind them headed for the flank closest to the sea. Lewis watched them go, then raised his gaze to the sea itself.

"I'm worried about you all, of course," Varaa retorted. "*Us* all, if you fall."

Lewis shook his head. "I need to see."

"Then climb a tree!"

"Don't worry," Lewis said, "you could finish this battle without me, or Captain Anson or Major Reed could."

"You're too confident," Varaa scolded. "And what of the next battle? And the next? Even if we win, do you think this will be the end of it?"

"Of course not," Lewis denied, nodding toward the enemy as the other section of 6pdrs wheeled out to the right. The first pair of guns had already unlimbered, loaded, and belched their first sputtering case shot over the enemy. Ragged white puffs of smoke appeared in the sky, and musket balls and shards of hot iron slashed down on a Dom gun crew. "*They're* too confident—they always have been, and it's about to cost them. Commence firing your rifles, Lieutenant Meder!" he shouted, the command repeated. A rapid crackle immediately ensued when Felix's impatient troops opened

up with their excellent M1817s. Surprised, shrieking Doms started dropping from the advancing front rank from farther than they could effectively reply with muskets. Their examination of enemy weapons captured
the night before confirmed what they'd already seen: they were mechanically sound and reliable, but fired a .70 caliber ball from rolled and forge-
welded barrels with bore diameters ranging from .74 to .80 caliber. They
might be lethal at this range, but probably couldn't hit a specific target
much past forty yards. "Still, they'll reply soon, distance or not," Lewis
thought aloud. "And with their numbers, accuracy isn't as important."

"Put enough lead in the air, they're bound to hit somethin'," Leonor
agreed. "An' they'll charge us soon, I bet. Gotta be hard on 'em, just takin' it
this long."

"Exactly." Lewis nodded. "Private Willis, my respects to Colonel De
Russy, and ask if he'd be so good as to bring his infantry forward, just behind the skirmish line. We'll be needing their pikes."

"With pleasure, sir—if I can get off this savage beast when I deliver the
message," Willis said tightly.

"Of course. And stay with the colonel, since I have Barca with me."

"Oh, no sir, I'll be back directly," Willis hastily assured.

Barca pursed his lips. "I should go to the colonel, sir. I should've been
with him all along, and he might need me."

Lewis looked significantly at Varaa. "Certainly. He might need others as
well."

Varaa blinked an objection and whipped her tail but jumped up behind
Barca, and the trio galloped the short distance back to where the guards
nervously stood in their extended ranks. A few had been hit by enemy
shot—their first taste of such a thing and traumatic to those who saw it—
but hadn't sustained anything like the enemy casualties.

Though surrounded by their little force and the growing noise of battle,
for the moment, Lewis and Leonor were alone in a sense.

"It's shapin' into a rare fight, Major Cayce," Leonor said, almost shyly,
"but I enjoyed our earlier dance together even more. Just . . . had to say
that."

Lewis looked at her, astonished, suddenly snatched from the detached
sphere that had apparently formed around him. It was a different plane of
focus and concentration that seemed to enfold him at times like this, when,
though keenly aware of his surroundings, he was *living* the battle, *wading*

through it, even—God help him—loving it. Varaa had seen it, probably knew what it was like herself, but with the battle raging as much in his head as it was around him, the meaning behind her warning that as long as he paraded around on his horse, Leonor—not just other soldiers—would do the same, hadn't really penetrated. Only Leonor's utterly unexpected admission did that.

Not trusting himself to reply, he looked to the front. Sure enough, the Doms had stopped, and at nearly two hundred and fifty yards, the first and second ranks of three regiments—probably three thousand men—leveled their long muskets to aim.

"Section! Load canister!" Hudgens roared at the crews of his 12pdrs.

"Stand by the signal," Lewis told the bugler Lieutenant Burton left him, now belatedly, desperately, wanting the young woman beside him off her horse and lying on the ground. It would be pointless to order her. He'd have to throw her down, and there wasn't time. "Thank you," he told her, and the Dom muskets fired.

They survived the first volley, and the second, though they had to be the primary targets of an awful lot of men and the air around them literally screamed with the flight of balls. One of Lewis's reins was cut, as was his left sleeve from cuff to elbow. His hat whipped off his head and a shoulder board spiraled away while clippings of Arete's fur and mane drifted downwind like mown hay. Leonor and her horse were equally charmed because aside from some holes in her loose-fitting jacket, some blood trickling from a graze on her left ear, and one of her stirrups and a boot heel shot away, she seemed little the worse for it and actually laughed!

Both 12pdrs, some of their crewmen scattered or stumbling as others ran up from the limber to help or replace them, roared and leaped back, spewing great clouds of smoke touched by the yellowish tinge of canister, and great swathes of Doms went down, disappearing entirely in grass as tall as their knees. Smoldering chunks of sabots landed among them as well, and smoke started rising in several patches.

"Bugler!" Lewis shouted, "sound the signal!"

But the bugler was down, writhing on the ground. A lot of men were down, it seemed, but more were firing at the Doms, even the men with carbines. The guards were coming up resolutely, stepping in time with the thundering drums, expressions a study in contrasts between terror, determination, and fury. Lewis saw De Russy, naked sword blade resting on his shoulder, joined by Barca, marching beside the streaming flag of Uxmal. Varaa was exhorting the others bearing the Stars and Stripes forward as well. Willis was back, looking around in quick, jerky motions, eyes wide. "Let's step down and join your father," Lewis told Leonor. "Private Willis, take our horses to the rear, if you please."

"Which I will if I must, sir," he anxiously chirped, reaching for the reins they handed him. In an instant, he was gone, just as a third massive Dom volley sheeted through the defenders, sending more of them sprawling. A small number of the front rank of Uxmalo guards had their own firearms, and they'd double-timed forward to join the Rangers, dragoons, and musketoon-armed lancers, shooting as fast as they could. The gunsmoke was thick, but so was the darker smoke of little fires the sabots had ignited. Even as Lewis shouted for Hudgens's bugler, he wondered how grass so green could burn. *Probably some kind of resin in it,* he decided, *like the cordgrass at Palo Alto.*

The bleeding bugler was beside him now, eyes disoriented. "Do you know the signal for Captain Wagley?" he demanded.

"I do, sir," he managed strongly, sounding very Irish.

"Then sound it now!"

"We can't go yet; we ain't heard the signal!" one of the men in the 3rd Pennsylvania cried.

"They *must'a* sounded it. We just never heard it over all them goddamn guns. Look how close they are, goin' at it hammer an' tongs, an' the Doms so bloody ripe! Their right flank's there in front of us, swingin' in the breeze!"

Captain Wagley apparently agreed, and, his urgent request for permission from Major Reed now granted, he gave the order to advance.

"Forward, lads, through that tangly brush, then dress your ranks," the recently elected Lieutenant Ulrich cried, his fine singing voice projecting well. "Forward, *march!*"

No command was given for the men to shoulder their arms, and many were surprised by that, even though the brush at the edge of the woods was so thick. Then again, their newest officers came from the ranks and hadn't yet lost all practical understanding. No matter how well the Ocelomeh cleared these woods, no one could clear everything, and a surprising number of very strange creatures—many quite frightening, but more frightened of the noise and mass of men now pushing them—leaped from their brushy lairs and bolted into the clearing. Trailing their arms or carrying them at the ready even though NCOs had warned of brutal punishments if any were loaded, the troops at least had their fixed bayonets to probe hiding places as they went. This gave them confidence to advance in something like an orderly formation. And just as the whole 3rd Pennsylvania finally cleared the brush and quickly dressed its ranks, they *did* hear the tinny sound of a bugle, muted by the clatter of independent fire and the crash of volleys.

"Better early than late," quipped Sergeant Visser. "'Specially since I doubt the Doms've even noticed us."

It looked that way to Hanny Cox as he gazed at the panorama before him. They'd emerged less than two hundred yards upslope of the enemy right, not right on it, but at an oblique angle to its front, and the serried yellow-and-black ranks of the Doms made them appear almost numberless from here, stacked up in two rows of three, still converging on Major Cayce. Messengers—Dom lancers—galloped back and forth between the engaged formations and the surprisingly distant reserve still formed in front of the enemy camp. Cayce's position, now shrouded in the smoke of guns and a growing grass fire, appeared pitifully small in comparison. Looking around, so did the 3rd Pennsylvania, also alone for the moment, the men's sky-blue uniforms, white crossbelts, and glittering weapons shockingly conspicuous under the blazing bright sun on the vast green plain. But now Captain Olayne was wheeling his battery of beautifully polished bronze 6pdrs out on their left, and Hanny saw the flag of Captain Manley's 1st Uxmal a short distance beyond, its men hidden by one of the "washboard" features of the ground. Wagley, on his horse, must've seen it as well. "Uncase the colors!" he shouted, and Hanny and Apo released the ties on the blue silk tubes and pulled them off the flags, raising them up as they unrolled them. They were soon streaming over the field as well.

"Advance the regiment," Captain Wagley called.

"Third Pennsylvania! Shoulder—arms! Forward—march!"

———

"My God," Captain Anson shouted over the shooting, pouring sweat blowing from his lips as he rammed another ball down the fouling-choked barrel of his rifle, "don't they see them?"

In spite of the fury of the intermittent storm of musket balls, Lewis was wishing for Arete again, to be a little higher. Still, if *he* could see the 3rd Pennsylvania and 1st Uxmal—fifteen hundred men—sweeping inexorably down on the right flank of the enemy . . .

"The men about to die have," Lewis called back, smoke-dry throat cracking his voice. "They just don't know what to *do* about it because nobody's told them! I doubt their commanders know. This is what I was counting on. Who'd ever train to refuse a flank nobody's ever threatened before? Look!"

Olayne's Battery had just opened a murderous fire with solid shot, ranging down the length of the Dom regiments, shattering scores of men with every rapid blast. The grass fire was spreading almost protectively in front of Lewis's force, keeping the Doms from simply charging them, but its smoke wasn't so thick that he couldn't see the Pennsylvanians and Uxmalos abruptly halt, load, present their weapons, and fire. The effect of that first volley at less than one hundred yards was appalling. Doms fell away like bloody yellow dominoes, and the next volley hacked even deeper.

"Yes!" Lewis hissed, drifting back into that heightened state where the battle consumed his consciousness. His senses were as cold and sharp as could be, and he retained a concern, a defensiveness for his people, but pity, humanity, even self-preservation submerged beneath a quickening excitement, even lust to crush the enemy. Ironically, his critical mind understood even then that this was what he hated and feared most about war—and himself: what war did to him, what it turned him into, what it left him feeling like in its aftermath, when the fighting was done and he saw what he did. He'd felt it first at Palo Alto, but it was most profound after Monterrey. Even wounded, he'd seen what he'd done to an enemy he didn't hate—and the men who'd fought them with him. He'd never wanted to feel that way again. Now he did, but it was different, even stronger. His critical mind was only a spectator, a mere passenger at the moment, but it recognized the difference at once. He'd finally found a cause he could fully unleash himself for, and an enemy that deserved what he did to it.

Even if the fire had stopped their advance a little more than a hundred yards distant, the Doms in front of them were still shooting, still taking a toll—especially on the Uxmalo Home Guards who couldn't even fight back. But the enemy artillery was suddenly all but silent. It, at least, must be turning to engage the new threat. "Lieutenant Hudgens," Lewis shouted, hoarse and detached, "reconcentrate all your guns here, at intervals along the line. We haven't enough small arms to match the enemy, but rapid-fire canister can. Have you enough?"

"The twelve pounders are getting low, but more is coming from the caissons. The six pounders haven't used any yet."

"See to it."

Hudgens's wounded bugler called to the guns.

"Major Cayce," Barca cried, gasping as he ran up to join them. "Colonel De Russy's compliments, sir, and he asks, can the guards be withdrawn to the trees? They're getting slaughtered to no purpose."

"There *is* a purpose," Lewis replied hotly, mind resurfacing for a moment. "We have to keep the Doms where they are. We can't charge *them*— not yet," he inserted cryptically, "but if they see us pull back, they might charge after *us*, fire or not, and smash us from behind before we re-form. We couldn't hold them at the trees, or even on the forest road after that. No, Colonel De Russy and the guards must stand. With all this smoke, the enemy can't know they aren't firing back."

Barca nodded unhappy understanding. "I'll tell him," he said, then blurted, "He's doing quite well, by the way. He's only concerned for the men. He'll stand, and so will they."

"I'm sure of it," Lewis said with a lighter voice, "and hopefully they won't have to take it much longer." Barca hurried away.

The Doms were still firing in slow-timed volleys and the men on the skirmish line had taken to ducking them. That didn't always work, and a dragoon next to Anson took a large ball through his hat and the crown of his head as he lay on the ground. Lewis felt another sharp tug on his jacket. *At least Leonor is ducking down now,* he thought before he saw something else and plunged wholly into the battle again.

The enemy's withered right regiments were attempting to turn and face their tormenters at last, but there wasn't much left of them and the Dom Commander—was it General Agon?—was sending the regiments backing the two on his left, right in front of Lewis, to reinforce them. The confusion was terrible, made worse by the fact they were doing it under fire. Furthermore, Hudgens's 6pdrs had come rattling up and unlimbered right on the line, immediately coughing sprays of lethal canister and decimating the men left in place. This compelled their commander to compound the confusion by trying to split the reinforcements he was sending to the flank and pull some back. The movement collapsed into chaos as the fresh 1st US marched out of the trees in time with their fifes and drums, banners flowing, and took its place by the 1st Uxmal. And on its left, due south of Lewis, Dukane came out with his six 12pdr howitzers. All opened up together on the increasingly terrified, milling mass of the Holy Dominion's Army of God.

The men around Lewis all stood to fire now, the 6pdrs mulching the wavering line in front of them—only one man deep in places now—while Captain Anson capered with glee. "By God, it's like shootin' rats in a bucket. They don't know *what* to do!" It was true. The Doms were still dangerous, many still loading and shooting as their officers commanded, but their fire remained largely ineffectual. Especially since, rattled as they were, most pointed their weapons even more vaguely at the enemy than before when they jerked their triggers, sending bullets into the ground or even the sky, more often than not. And the wildly jumbled Doms attempting to refuse their right flank were hardly even capable of that, being hacked down by steady, accurate fire from superior American muskets at barely sixty yards. The howitzers moved forward by hand to that same distance and added to the carnage with canister. A few Dom artillery pieces were still in action, though quite a few had been stripped of their crews by Hudgens's well-aimed case shot, but one managed to strike the left cheek of Dukane's Number Three gun with an 8pdr ball. The howitzer barrel flipped in the air, smashing its Numbers One and Three men, while the shower of jagged splinters from the shattered carriage mowed down the gunner and half the crew of the Number Four gun beside it. More solid shot started crashing through the ranks of the 1st US and 1st Uxmal, shredding men just as horribly as only the Americans had accomplished so far.

Lewis saw none of this, nor did Leonor. Of all those fighting for their lives in the washboard glade, they were probably the only ones expectantly staring down where the trees behind them met the sea. Leonor, Varaa, and Anson were among the few who knew *every* aspect of Lewis's plan. Not only had they almost always been with him, suggesting big parts of it; they'd been there when he mentioned little things he'd added in his mind. Even Major Reed wasn't expecting what happened next, and though there'd been no way to time it perfectly, it came as if there had.

"There's her fore-topmast," Lewis said with satisfaction, and as swift and fluid as running mercury, HMS *Tiger* emerged completely in the open, barely a mile offshore. "Captain Holland won't be happy with this wind; he doesn't dare come any closer, but he's worked his crew up well and won't have any trouble tacking."

"He wouldn't have missed this if he had to run her ashore," Leonor said somberly.

Others had noticed *Tiger* too, and a great cheer swelled as a cloud of white smoke blossomed from her larboard bow. Then, one after another, all ten 12pdrs and five 6pdrs of her reduced larboard battery spat projectiles; not at the men fighting in front of Lewis, but at the distant, unengaged formations and the Dom camp itself. Something like a moan arose from the Doms, loud even over the shrieks and cries of the wounded and dying. Varaa had told Lewis that Doms wouldn't break, but she'd also said their semi-divine leader, "His Supreme Holiness" in the Great Valley of Mexico, was the next thing to God in this world to them. And the next thing to *Him* was his Blood Cardinals—like Don Frutos. There was no telling how an attack on him would affect his troops. Would it inspire them to protect him, or further inflame their rage? Unconcerned with keeping enemy infantry off her or dueling other guns (as long as the big siege guns remained undeployed and silent), *Tiger* was free to rain shot after shot into the rear area as fast as she could, and Holland's gun's crews went at it with a will. It was a calculated risk, but it might tip the scales. And as for whether regular Dom infantry (as opposed to their lancers) would break, even Varaa hadn't been sure. They might be "inhuman," as Lewis would define it, in their beliefs, culture, and depravity, but they had human minds and hearts, and those can only take so much.

A horse galloped up through the flying lead, squealing and falling just as it slowed. A muscular, older officer in a shot-torn frock coat hopped off the animal before it could roll over him and ran up to Lewis. "Lieutenant Ulrich, B Company, Third Pennsylvania, sir!" the former sergeant breathlessly proclaimed.

"He *knows* who you are," Leonor snapped impatiently while Lewis smiled.

"Yes sir," Ulrich acknowledged without thought, pale, sweaty cheeks reddening slightly. "Captain Wagley's respects, Major, and we've closed the gap between the Third and the guards." He nodded to the left. "Captain Olayne was forced to abandon his position as the grass fire burned toward him, and moved his guns around between us. That's weakened our connection with the First Uxmal, but all the other gaps between our forces have closed as the engaged regiments tighten around the enemy!" he added excitedly.

"As hoped and expected," Lewis replied, looking to the front. The fire between him and the enemy was still creeping restlessly out to the sides, slightly broadening its largely exhausted, blackened path, but no longer a real barrier. "Is the Third in good condition?"

"Pretty fair, sir," Ulrich hedged. "The enemy's in great confusion at present, and their volleys are slow and inaccurate." His eyebrows went up. "You've doubtless observed they simply won't fire without a command. There's no independent fire at all. But we're right on top of them, and our casualties are mounting."

Lewis scratched his beard, glancing at Anson's powder-blackened face. He'd finally stopped shooting long enough to pay attention to larger affairs. *The difference between us,* Lewis mused. *I get too wrapped up in the life of the whole battle, and he does the same with his own small part of it.*

"We've let 'em push us long enough," Anson said darkly.

"I agree. Let's push back and see how they like it. Has Private Willis returned? There you are. Run to Colonel De Russy and tell him to prepare to advance."

"Run here, run there," Willis mumbled dejectedly as he trotted away and Lewis looked at Ulrich. "Get another horse and return to Captain Wagley. Compliments, of course, and ask him to make ready as well. *He* must signal 'General Advance' so Major Reed and the others will hear," he stressed, "and we'll all step off together. The guns will advance in support of the infantry."

Lieutenant Ulrich ran to take a horse from a wounded rifleman holding a pair of them back by the guards and dashed off to the left. Only a moment later, it seemed, the high sharp sound of a bugle pierced the tumult of battle, repeating the call for a general advance over and over again. Lewis sent a reluctant Anson and his Rangers back for their horses when the drums began to stutter, but kept the dragoons and riflemen to support De Russy's guards. Anxious to return some of the punishment they'd taken, the guards lowered their pikes and went forward to flank the guns as their crews heaved them toward the enemy. The Doms, in response—and much too soon in Lewis's detached view—ceased firing entirely at the rapid, almost panicky, high-pitched commands to draw plug bayonets to insert in the muzzles of their weapons. Quite a few dropped them in their excitement—or was it panic?—and had to retrieve them. Soon, there were no Doms firing at all, and Lewis felt the first hint of pity for them. His force was inexperienced, badly outnumbered, and very unsure of itself. But although the Doms were just as inexperienced, far more so in reality because their leaders had no idea how to deal with the unexpected, they'd come to this fight with absolute confidence in their superiority. Now, after suffering more than they could've imagined, their confidence had shattered, and it had to unnerve them even more that so small a force would *attack* them on open ground like this.

Lewis's battered force, including the guards and touching the 3rd Pennsylvania, must be down to less than fifteen hundred effectives by now, and the combined 1st Uxmal and 1st US never had more than that to begin with. Canister from the guns effectively doubled the number of projectiles they fired, but even savaged, confused, and increasingly demoralized, the Doms in direct contact had a huge edge. Yet with bayonets fixed—inflexible doctrine when attacking in close quarters but never envisioned as a defensive measure—the six engaged regiments of Doms made no sound above the shrieking and crying of wounded while HMS *Tiger* mercilessly hammered their camp and their lord while Allied drums and fifes kept up a lively rumbling, piercing cadence as American and Uxmalo infantry advanced by crashing volleys and the artillery spewed thunderous sprays of canister.

Despite the iron discipline that kept them enduring the terrible slaughter no matter how much confusion their conflicting, ineffectual orders created, the men they were, Doms or not, couldn't take it anymore. Almost simultaneously, the various regimental commanders or their successors took it upon themselves to make decisions on their own. The partial and currently least-pressed regiments that had returned to bolster the one in front of Lewis abruptly turned about and marched to the rear, reforming with admirable precision. The shattered survivors of the three intermingled regiments facing the onslaught of the 3rd Pennsylvania and 1st Uxmal did the exact opposite and charged, en masse. And those longest engaged, right in front of Lewis, though clearly now faced chiefly with pikes, felt the sudden absence of the troops that abandoned them and started to back away.

"Charge them!" Lewis roared at Colonel De Russy. Varaa, just visible under the Stars and Stripes farther away down the line, held her musket up and used it to gesture forward. De Russy still had no hat, and his brushy side whiskers and wispy hair were plastered to his face and head with sweat, but red-rimmed eyes burned with determination when he raised his sword and nodded back at Lewis.

"Charge!" he bellowed, repeated by Barca and Varaa, whose voice rose even above the sudden yipping, screeching, almost animalistic chorus of the guards as they surged at the faltering Doms.

Lewis drew his saber, but Leonor grabbed his arm. He whipped around to face her, and she shouted, "I thought you wanted to watch the *whole* battle. Can't do that in there." She nodded at the backs of the guards as they slammed their pikes home into the enemy. Rifles and carbines spat another long flurry of shots before riflemen plied their own newly fitted bayonets and dragoons dropped their carbines to hang from their straps and turned to their sabers.

Captain Anson and his Rangers thundered up behind, leading Arete and Leonor's horse. "You still ain't told us where you want us," Anson pressed, nodding at Arete. "Hop up, have a look, an' show us."

Lewis nodded thoughtfully, realizing he was just as capable as Anson of getting too involved in his "own small part" of the battle. "You're right," he agreed with a last look at the guards. Pikes or not, their skill far surpassed that of the Doms, and they were killing them with a kind of wild abandon. He saw Varaa swinging and thrusting her sword, musket slung over her back. Lieutenant Meder and Barca—and there was Reverend Harkin with a rifle!—had pulled a strangely agitated De Russy from the press, and all but the colonel were still loading and firing. Lewis used his hat (Willis had returned it) to soak sweat off his forehead and looked around.

He couldn't see everything, the smoke was deep, but the retreating regiments—drawing men like iron filings to a magnet—were completely out of the fight. For whatever reason whoever led them turned away from the battle, he seemed intent on taking them back to Don Frutos intact. Then Lewis noted with alarm that the enemy lancers were moving at last, heading for the exposed and apparently unsupported left of Dukane's battery. "First smart thing they've done," he murmured, "and the most obvious." The clearest threat at present, however, was the countercharge of nearly three whole regiments smashing primarily into half of the 3rd Pennsylvania and its tenuous contact with the 1st Uxmal—while the other half of the 3rd had joined De Russy's charge. The 1st US and Dukane's battery were firing into the Doms on the far side, but the Uxmalos, Olayne's battery, and Wagley's remaining Pennsylvanians were reeling back.

"It's that damn gap made by the fire," Lewis cried. The fire had swept all the way to the trees, flaring again when it hit brush, scattering even more strange creatures. It had almost died away entirely on the plain, but the Uxmalos and Americans hadn't completely rejoined before the Doms hit them. "*Somebody* over there has a brain, damn him," Lewis growled. "That's where we need to be!"

"What about the lancers?" Anson asked.

"They'll be taken care of," Lewis replied with complete certainty. "We need to find Captain Wagley and Major Reed." Lightly kicking Arete, he surged ahead on the big mare, followed by Leonor, her father, and about thirty Rangers. An appalled and very saddle-sore Private Willis hesitated.

"I'm coming with you!" cried Reverend Harkin, puffing up with his rifle.

"Which you can have this fat sack o' fleas to yourself, Preacher," Willis offered, but Harkin was already clawing his way up behind. The horse groaned. "Nonsense," Harkin wheezed. "Such a fine animal—he could carry three more. Hurry along after the major!"

CHAPTER 36

Teniente Ramon Lara was sitting on his horse at the head of his lancers in a draw on the south end of the washboard glade. The "draw" was only a depression when viewed from the east or west, and his lancers were actually somewhat elevated and probably visible to anyone directly to the north. He could see the retreating Doms a mile and a half away, for example, and they might've seen his three hundred blue-clad men if they looked his way. Maybe they did, but they seemed more concerned with the battle behind them—and the three regiments of Dom infantry that had finally stirred, marching out from their camp to meet them. But a runner had just come from Boogerbear, telling him of the Dom lancers, not yet in view, and warning him to make ready. Lara's lancers, and indeed Boogerbear's mostly Ocelomeh Rangers, had been ready and in position for quite a while. Now Lara turned to look at the men under his command, many more than he'd ever had. Aside from Alferez Rini and two others from the old world—both NCOs now—nearly all were Uxmalos, with a sprinkling from Pidra Blanca and Techon. Ocelomeh didn't like being encumbered by the nine-foot weapons lancers had to carry and master. Lara was about to instruct Rini, sitting quietly beside him, to take his post when Boogerbear himself came tearing down from his vantage point atop the low ridge above the gully and pulled Dodger to a stop.

"Is it time?" Lara asked.

"Now or never." Boogerbear nodded, long black beard wagging up and down. "I reckon there's fifteen hundred o' the devils, already in line, fixin' to swoop down on Dukane an' the First US. Near eight hundred o' us, countin' my Rangers an' Joffrion's dragoons, an' we'll hit their flank a bit from behind as they swing past—if we hurry. Roll 'em up like a ball o' string," he added with satisfaction, then shook his head. "Silly bastards. We never could'a done *none* o' this if they had a half dozen decent scouts. Even bad scouts would'a told 'em that plain out yonder is a sack. Ain't complainin', mind"—he grinned—"an' I reckon we'll have educated a passel of 'em before the day's through, so let's make sure there ain't many left!" He paused as if listening, then bolted back toward his Rangers. "Good luck, Tenny-entay!" he called behind him.

"And to you, Lieutenant Beeryman," Lara answered lowly before raising his voice. "*Primeros Lanceros de Yucatán! Adelante en el galope!*" The 1st Yucatán swept forward in line abreast, closely followed by Boogerbear's Rangers, then Lieutenant Hans Joffrion's two companies of the 3rd Dragoons. Lara almost immediately saw what the big Ranger described and thought they might've cut it too late; the Doms were *right there*. But like Boogerbear said, coming in behind them, they'd have precious seconds before their presence was fully apprehended.

"*Lanzas!*" shouted Alferez Rini, and three hundred lances came down all together.

"*Cargar!*" whooped Lara, drawing his saber, kicking with his spurs. Exploding into a thundering sprint behind and on the right of their still-trotting prey, the 1st Yucatán smashed into the enemy before they even got up to speed, impaling men on bowing and splintering lances, throwing them from their mounts or sending horses tumbling and crashing into others. Lara hadn't seen it, but the effect was much like what the 1st Uxmal and 1st US did to the Dom infantry earlier, only this was on a larger, more intimate and savage scale, the screams of wounded and broken horses so much louder and more terrible than those of men. And Lara's lancers didn't stop. They'd struck right flank to right flank so those still slashing in after the first impact had fresh targets in front of them, spearing men in the back from behind. The catastrophe only spread from there, causing a ripple in the whole Dom line that became a convulsion of rearing animals and roaring men, trying to wheel and face the bewildering horror of complete and brutal surprise. Horses went out of control, dashing riders to the ground, where they were trampled or crushed, or smashing their legs between them. Some simply ran amok, riders helpless to stop them. The few men who gained control were either pinned by more lances or hacked down by sabers. And then the Rangers were among them, launching huge arrows from mere feet away or swinging the heavy flint-bladed clubs Ocelomeh liked so much.

Boogerbear was shooting his brace of revolvers as fast as he could cock them, and men screamed and slumped in their saddles or fell and rolled in the tall dusty grass. Some of his men had musketoons taken from the lancers destroyed at what would become the conference site, but they were all fired in the first moments of the fight. Boogerbear's pistols were empty almost as quickly, and so was his double-barrel shotgun. Yanking a dragoon saber from its scabbard he'd recently clipped to Dodger's saddle, he slashed at the enemy. He had no skill with a long blade—would've done as well with an axe—but what he lacked in practice and art was more than made up for in power and ferocity. A very few Doms managed to draw their own musketoons or sabers, but it did them little good. Some of their attackers were shot or cut, but the blows were invariably rewarded by a fusillade of long-bladed arrows.

And then came Joffrion's dragoons, and the rout became a massacre as they added their sabers or rapid-fire Hall carbines to the fight. True to form and as expected, the Dom lancers never broke. Even their horses were unusually committed, but they were perhaps somewhat smarter. The shocking, overwhelming nature of the attack was sufficient to undermine the scruples of the most dedicated animal, and dozens, then hundreds were streaming away, some with riders, most without. In mere moments, it seemed, all that remained was to spear or shoot dismounted Doms still trying to win their bloody passage to heaven. Lara's lancers, Joffrion's dragoons, and Boogerbear's Rangers were happy to send them on their way.

"Oh my God," Joffrion murmured, aghast. He'd just joined Boogerbear and was wiping sweat from his face with a blood-flecked pocket handkerchief. Now he used it to cover his mouth.

"Stop that shit!" Boogerbear roared, pointing his saber at a cluster of Ocelomeh Rangers who'd jumped off their horses to take enemy heads. "Any man I find with a damn head when this is done is gonna eat it *raw*, you hear? Teeth, hair, eyes an' all. Git back on your horses, we ain't done!" Heads arced in the air as men raced back to their mounts.

Leaning carefully out to the side, Joffrion politely vomited. "I beg your pardon," he murmured hoarsely, gently wiping his lips.

"What now, Lieutenant Beeryman?" Lara asked, breathing hard as he guided his horse around a cluster of corpses to join them. Lara was covered in blood, some likely his judging by the way his right arm hung slack, saber dangling by the knot around his wrist. His eyes were burning with an inner triumph, however, and Boogerbear suddenly remembered he'd been at Palo Alto and Resaca de la Palma as well—on the other side. This was his first taste of victory in a really big fight, doing what he'd trained for and taught others to do as well. *I hope his glad outlasts the sad—an' pain that'll come,* Boogerbear mused. He wasn't hurt, but probably looked just as bad. *Splashed myself up some,* he supposed.

"Git somebody to patch you up, sling that arm at least, an' I reckon your lancers an' Joffrion's dragoons oughta head over yonder." He waved his bloody saber toward where the Dom counterattack had pushed the 1st Uxmal, 1st US, and part of the 3rd Pennsylvania almost back to where the gun's caissons had stood shortly before.

"What about you and your Rangers?" Lara asked.

Boogerbear looked surprised. "Why, there's still the Dom camp to account for, ain't there?"

———

Private Hanny Cox had gotten his wish in a manner of speaking, exchanging the flag for a musket as "his" half of the 3rd Pennsylvania was battered relentlessly back. Still conscious of the honor of bearing the national colors in the firing line and feeling a little weak—but more like a fool as good men fell around him—he'd tied the flagstaff to the bullet-splintered spokes of a caisson and seized an M1816 Springfield musket and cartridge box from the body of a man with most of his face blown away. That occurred, and the splintered spokes too, because many of the enemy had taken things upon themselves as well, finally driving bayonets out of their barrels and firing independently as they surged against the thinning line. Firing was continuous, buffeting his ears, almost crushing his chest when one of Olayne's 6pdrs went off right beside him, sweeping men down.

"More canister!" cried Sergeant McNabb, serving as gunner on Olayne's Number One gun.

"Which there ain't none!" replied a panicky voice.

"Take it straight from the caisson, ye clatty bastard! They've already overrun the damned limber," McNabb bellowed back. The horses hitched to the limber had been shot down in their traces, and Number One's crew had pulled the gun back past it.

"*There ain't none in our caisson*, Sergeant! We shot it all up!"

"Bring case," McNabb shouted louder. "I'll cut the fuses for a muzzle burst. Then rob *another* caisson!"

Hanny wasn't watching this, too absorbed with loading and firing his inherited musket while Doms shot back less than twenty yards away. Fumbling in the leather box at his side, he handled another cartridge, tore the paper with his teeth, and spat out bitter, salty black grains. Dashing a sprinkle of powder in the brass pan on the side of the lock, he slapped the steel down over it and let the musket slide until the butt hit his shoe. Pouring the rest of the powder down the barrel, he wadded the paper under the ball and pushed it all in the muzzle with his thumb. Drawing his rammer with a metallic *shick*, he inverted it and seated the ball. Whipping the rammer out, he returned it to its place, cocking the weapon all the way as he brought it to his shoulder. The front sight drifted for an instant until it found its own target in the press: a dark-haired kid about his age looking right at him and feverishly loading as well. Hanny squeezed the trigger. The cock leaped forward, flint striking steel. It managed to scrape only a single, meager reddish spark that missed the priming powder completely, however. *Misfire!* Hanny screamed at himself, lowering his weapon with a sense of horror and betrayal. Glancing up, he saw the kid he'd tried to shoot finish loading and aim deliberately at him.

A vent jet sprayed his left cheek, and he flinched away from the blast.

"Hateful little bastard," Sergeant Visser declared and spit a stream of tobacco juice as the kid opposite Hanny folded and fell. "He was aiming for you in particular. What kind of scrub does that?" Visser had saved Hanny's life.

"I was aiming at *him*," Hanny confessed miserably, taking the little brass hammer on a small ring of tools Visser offered, striking a rounded knob off his flint before closing the steel and handing the tools back.

Visser had already reloaded and was raising his musket again. "Well," he said, considering. "Then maybe he had cause. But you wouldn't've killed him out of meanness, like *he* meant to do." His voice clouded with anger. "I told all you bastards to hammer your goddamn flints!"

"It isn't my musket, Sergeant."

"Oh? Yeah. Where's the flag?" he quickly demanded, and Hanny gestured behind them with his head.

"Just as well," Visser grunted after he fired again, nodding down to the right where the other half of the 3rd Pennsylvania, under the regimental flag, was still pushing alongside the pike-armed Home Guards, dismounted dragoons, and rifles. . . . The enemy had practically collapsed in front of them. "That Uxmalo boy Apo got knocked on the head. He'll be all right," he quickly added, knowing Hanny and Apo were friends, "but another local took up the regimental flag before Wagley sent everybody to the right of it to join De Russy. Damn flag's gone down twice more, that I've seen, and some other poor bastard always takes it up again and gets shot. Better to have a shot-up caisson hold it than a fighting man right now. We need all we have." A ball snatched the right side of his collar off, showering him with fuzzy blue and white fibers. He didn't seem to notice. "I think they're about to push us again."

The Number One gun fired with a double thunderclap, the case shot exploding just inches from the muzzle. Balls and shards of iron scythed through the enemy like canister, but not as effectively, and Doms pressed forward over their dead.

"Give 'em a cheer, boys, and *charge bayonets!*" cried Captain Wagley somewhere behind, voice loud but strained. Hanny and Sergeant Visser and what was left of their part of the 3rd—Hanny didn't know where Preacher Mac McDonough was—lowered their tight-clenched muskets and swept forward with a rasping, breathless *"Huzza!"* There was a terrific *crash* as men and weapons slammed together with a final *crackle* of musketry, but then there was only the screaming, heaving, roaring noise of desperate hand-to-hand fighting. It sounded like a ranting sea hurling a ship on a rocky shore, the splintering timbers and wails of the dying heralding the triumph of the elemental force. The only element here was a surging, frantic terror suffused with the rage and hatred it caused. Hanny bashed a Dom's musket aside and—for the very first time—speared a man with the wicked triangular bayonet affixed to the muzzle of his musket. The man's scream was lost in the din, but Hanny distinctly felt his life quiver out through the wood and steel in his hands before wrenching the weapon back. It appalled him, but he had no time to dwell on it because he instantly had to do it again or die. Sergeant Visser was an inspiration, bare headed and bloody, plying his bayonet with mechanical skill far beyond that of his opponents.

And this was when the Doms' earlier confusion, rigid tactics, and uninformed training combined with their current desperation to cost them most cruelly of all. Many who'd taken the previously unimaginable initiative to knock their bayonets back out and resume shooting—doing a lot of damage—had thoughtlessly flung the offending weapons away. Now they didn't have them. They tried to fight anyway, of course, using their muskets as clubs. Effectively done, their numbers alone should've still been enough to overwhelm the exhausted, beleaguered Pennsylvanians, but they'd never really trained for that either. Hanny, Visser, and their desperate, dwindling comrades stabbed and battered the Doms to a standstill, just as the decimated 1st Uxmal (defending their very homes and loved ones, they'd stood the onslaught as well as any veteran regiment) fired a final deliberate volley from mere paces away and charged as well, followed immediately by the 1st US, the strongest remaining cohesive block of Allied troops.

Hanny and the Doms in front of him, swinging muskets or jabbing with bayonets, couldn't know any of this. The point of contact was so intermingled, the noise so great, nothing mattered but the next gasping breath. And Hanny had nothing left. His hands were bashed and bloody claws, clinging to a battered musket slick with blood. Even Sergeant Visser was down, struck on the head and dazed. Hanny was sure he had only seconds to live before a Dom ball struck him, a musket butt smashed his face, or a bayonet pierced his body. But something was happening to the Doms even before more firing flared and crackled and the next crash came from his left. The enemy was bunching together, pushed from the *right*, and Hanny vaguely heard the rasping but familiar voice of Lieutenant Hudgens roar, "Make way lads! Stand back, damn you!" and was almost run down by the big left wheel of a smoke-blackened gun pushing past him. He staggered back, numbly wondering why Hudgens was here instead of Olayne. Blowing men, stripped to red shirtsleeves, dropped the trail of the gun with a clank and crouched away from the wheels.

"Fire!"

Canister screeched, and a score or more Doms tumbled into a shoal of mewling mush. A young Uxmalo with a pair of bulging gunner's haversacks over his shoulders actually *tossed* a heavy tin cylinder full of balls strapped to a wood sabot and powder bag *over* the gun. The wildly cursing Number One man caught it with one hand, holding a rammer staff in the other. Screaming "Thumb that vent, Goddamn you!" at the Three man already inside the right wheel, he stuffed the round in the muzzle. Smoke gushed around it as he slammed it to the breech, eyes clenched shut, before jerking the rammer out with an expression of surprise that a lingering ember hadn't lit the charge and blown his whole arm off. His happiness lasted only a second before a Dom musket ball exploded from his chest, dropping him like a sack over the axle.

"Fire!"

Poom-shhh!

More rapid firing came from the right, and suddenly there was Major Cayce himself, crashing through Doms on his big mare, slashing around with his saber. Captain Anson and Leonor were behind him, firing revolvers into faces, chests, backs . . . and there were more Rangers, even a few lancers, shooting carbines and pistols or savagely hacking through the recoiling press with their own heavy sabers.

"Have a care with that bayonet, young fellow!" boomed a big, rather fat man, clinging on the back of a horse behind a crouching Private Willis. Hanny was astonished to recognize Reverend Harkin. "Make way! See to that man on the ground, will you? His wits have gone astray." Sliding to the ground, Harkin paced forward with a rifle in his hands, apparently oblivious to Dom musket balls snatching holes in his big black coat as he called loudly, "Lord God! Lend your strength to those who repel the onslaught at the gate!" More guns, two of Olayne's under Sergeant McNabb this time, creaked and rumbled forward, shirtless men streaked with sweat and grime wheezing at the spokes.

Hanny looked around. The Doms were still fighting, and more were shooting again, but whatever pushed them on with such fury before had been beaten out of them by the trip-hammer blows of a reinvigorated 1st Uxmal, 1st US—and now Hanny saw Lara's lancers and Joffrion's dragoons charging down the gradual, convoluted slope from the southwest to meet the lighter but critical strike Major Cayce and some hastily gathered guns had made on the right. As he stood watching with other stunned and spent Pennsylvanians, the battle shifted away. Heavy smoke from furious firing was blowing in his face, but he saw individual Doms here and there finally, amazingly, start to turn and run. He dropped down by Sergeant Visser, sitting up now, holding his sleeve against his forehead. He was unspeakably relieved when a limping, bloody Preacher Mac and a dazed-looking Apo, each apparently supporting the other, collapsed in the grass beside them.

"My wits are fine, damn—blast him," Sergeant Visser growled.

"Mine aren't," Hanny said.

"Cease firing!" croaked Captain Olayne as Lara and Joffrion's charge went home and they entered the cone of fire in front of the battery he and Lieutenant Hudgens had combined to roll in the fight.

"Cease firing!" Hudgens repeated, then added, "Service your pieces, for God's sake, but load and hold!"

"They're running!" Leonor cried, voice filled with predatory glee as the lancers and dragoons almost literally peeled the enemy from in front of them. She started to spur her horse in pursuit.

"Hold up, Lieutenant," Lewis snapped as he would at anyone else. "We need to take this in."

Anson was using the unexpected pause to reload his revolvers and glanced up with approval. His face was almost as black as Barca's except for the sweat streaks. So was Leonor's and everyone else's. Lewis knew why the perfect white gunsmoke left everything black—the powder was black to begin with and the charred remnant of its ingredients was even more so when it settled out of the smoke. *Unless the air's very dry, then it's white,* he mused vaguely, always struck by that irony.

"Hear him, girl," Anson chimed in. "We can't go chasin' ever' which way like dogs after rabbits—an' these ain't rabbits. Load your pistols."

Lewis pointed. "Look." From their mounted vantage they could see the Doms in front of De Russy's Home Guards and half the 3rd Pennsylvania streaming after the regiments that retreated independently. De Russy or Varaa—whoever was really in charge—had actually pressed too far and could've been taken on the left flank in turn by the shattered regiments pulling back from here, but they'd had enough, giving De Russy's pike and bayonet bristling ranks a wide berth as they aimed to rejoin the organized portion of their army. And that portion was still a major threat, advancing from its camp three regiments abreast, even as Captain Holland maintained a murderous fire from the sea. The few Dom guns still in the fight had split their attention between *Tiger* and Dukane's diminished battery.

Both were moving targets, however—hard to hit. *Tiger* was sailing back and forth, tacking and wearing, and Dukane kept shifting his guns as well, raining explosive case on the enemy as rapidly as he could.

"What do you think?" Anson asked.

Instead of answering directly, Lewis called, "Messengers!" A shabby, exhausted clot of horsemen gathered around him, as did Olayne, Hudgens, and suddenly even Major Reed. Lewis swept his eyes across them. "Where's Captain Wagley?"

"Gravely wounded, I'm afraid," Reed reported mournfully, gesturing back toward the line of riddled limbers and caissons. "Shot through the body even before he gave his last command. Dr. Newlin holds out little hope."

Lewis caught a glimpse of the big, brutal, former sergeant Hahessy "helping" a lightly wounded 1st US comrade to the rear and wondered why the likes of him always seemed to be spared when promising young men like Wagley fell. He pursed his lips and jerked a nod before continuing. "First, we must get word to De Russy. Tell him to stop before he's gobbled up—and I want as many of Burton's dragoons and Meder's riflemen back to their horses and here with me as possible. I *hope* De Russy won't need them anymore, and I do," he added cryptically. "What of Captain Manley?"

"Up there," Reed said, pointing at the reedy, blond-haired officer, still mounted and waving his sword and trotting back and forth behind the battered but proud 1st Uxmal, plodding after the retreating enemy alongside the 1st US, Lara's lancers, and Joffrion's dragoons—now hanging on their left.

"Tell him to halt as well. *All* the infantry will stop their pursuit at once." Lewis's instinct would always be to press a beaten force, but this enemy wasn't *much* more beaten than his—and still had a lot more men. He glanced around at the milling or collapsed remnant of half the 3rd Pennsylvania. "The First US is in good hands. Re-form these men yourself, Major Reed, then find a suitable officer to take them to rejoin the rest of their comrades with De Russy."

Reed frowned doubtfully. "I don't know how much fight's left in them." He wiped his brow. "How much *any* of us have. And our ammunition's almost exhausted."

"Nevertheless," Lewis pressed relentlessly, "I want all our infantry in a continuous line, re-formed and reconsolidated and looking as sharp and ready as possible. Home Guards on the right, then the Third Pennsylvania. First US in the center, since they've suffered the least. To their left, I want the First Uxmal." He looked at Olayne. "Gather every gun that will move, and you can pull and form a grand battery on that highest ground where Dukane just unlimbered. Lara's and Joffrion's lancers and dragoons will help you, then deploy on your left."

"It's starting to sound like you won't be here," Reed noted suspiciously.

"I won't."

Reed sighed, unsurprised.

The messengers and artillerymen galloped away, and Anson swiveled his head from side to side, looking toward the sea, then back up where Dukane had resumed firing his remaining howitzers, envisioning what Lewis had in mind. "A very long line, an' a thin one."

"A display," Lewis said harshly, largely still talking to Reed. "All flags flying, and music too. We'll finally show the Doms *most* of what we have. Not as many as *them*, of course—if they can reorganize what we already handled, they must still have ten or twelve thousand—but more than we first stopped them with and many more than they thought we had." He paused to observe Reed's reaction. "And just enough 'fight' and 'ammunition' for you to stop them again, I think—if they choose to renew the action here." He looked around. "There you are, Private Willis! And Reverend Harkin, I'm pleased to see you well." Harkin had walked up to hear, and Willis had gingerly dismounted, now holding his horse. It looked as unhappy as he did.

"Tolerably well," Harkin said cheerfully, "though my coat has been badly abused." He hefted his rifle. "A fine weapon. I'm sure I hit three of the devils, down with the guards, and another when I came here. Spreading the Word and smiting the enemies of the Lord!"

Lewis smiled. "I'm sure we all appreciate your efforts so far, your prayers in particular, but one more rifle won't make a great difference. I'd be obliged if you'd coordinate with Dr. Newlin and his hospital corps." He looked at Reed. "I do hope he made it there?" Reed nodded. "Good, then assemble more fatigue parties from whatever lightly wounded are capable of helping others to the surgeons. I'd also like you to make it your personal mission to see that water is brought to the men, if that's not already in hand."

"Very well, Major Cayce," Harkin somberly replied. "Perhaps a more fitting task for me in any event—but I shall keep my rifle," he added defiantly.

"Of course. Private Willis?"

Willis took a deep breath and looked up. "You're gonna make me get back on this damned vicious nag, ain't you, sir?"

"With Reverend Harkin again, at first. He can find another horse at the hospital tents. Then I want you to ensure our reserves of ammunition are getting where they're needed. No hoarding, no malingering. Do that well and you'll be *Corporal* Willis."

Willis formed an aggrieved expression and shook his head. "Nobody'll vote *me* to a corporal."

"Battlefield promotions don't require a vote. Go."

Major Reed still looked troubled. "You said my First US has suffered the least, but where's the First Ocelomeh?" He glanced at Anson. "And the rest of the Rangers? I know the Rangers helped smash the enemy lancers, but what of Consul Koaar's troops? I haven't seen them all day." Reed's tone actually held something like accusation.

The roar of battle, so dreadfully intense short moments before, had dwindled to nearly nothing; a few musket shots still chased the retreating Doms and cannon still rumbled regularly over the washboard glade, but except for the cries of wounded, it was almost surreally quiet. The infantry was already responding to Lewis's orders, raggedly shaking themselves out, redressing their lines, and shifting where he'd sent them. Varaa was visible in the distance, back on her horse and galloping up from where the Home Guards had stopped at last, around the coalescing crescent of men. Lewis was glad she was alive and seemingly unhurt. She clearly meant to rejoin him for what she knew was coming. Smiling at Reed, he spoke. "The enemy hasn't seen the First Ocelomeh either, but they will."

Varaa arrived, horse blowing, both their tails high and swishing. Only at times like this, it seemed, did Lewis remember how truly strange she was. Especially when he saw how rapidly she was blinking. He'd picked up enough over time to recognize parts of what that blinking telegraphed in lieu of complex facial expressions—beyond a grin or frown—but sometimes it was too fast, or combined into meanings beyond his understanding. Like now.

"De Russy?" Leonor asked. Of them all, she probably grasped the blinking best of all.

"Alive," Varaa said, "but I was forced to relieve him." She held up a hand. "It wasn't like at the beach," she quickly assured. "Quite the opposite, in fact. He wouldn't be stopped and tried to keep pushing even after you ordered a halt. Said he outranked you and would do as he pleased. The enemy was on the run and he'd win the battle." She flicked her tail. "It was obvious, of course, how exposed we'd become, and . . ." She blinked. "He was seized by a kind of madness, the perfect reverse of what took him before. Young Mr. Barca tried to reason with him, and I believe hurtful things were said, but I ordered him relieved and—regrettably—restrained for a time. An unhappy business. Barca is still with him."

"Who's in command, with you over here?"

Varaa waved that away as if it was of no importance. "Oh, Alcalde Periz, of course. The Home Guards are Uxmalos, you know."

"He's alive? *Here?*" Leonor blurted.

Varaa blinked. "Ah. A sad misunderstanding, and I misspoke. A runner was sent to inform you, but perhaps he was killed. I'm sorry to tell you Alcalde Ikan Periz died within an hour of reaching the city. Sira Periz is the *alcaldesa* now. She immediately set all but a token force of Home Guards on the march to join us"—she glanced at the sun, now a little in the west—"though they'll never get here before dark. She raced ahead in her mate's bloodstained carriage with Father Orno, the Home Guard commander, and Mistress Samantha Wilde."

"*Samantha's* here too?" Anson demanded hotly. "What the hell does she think she's doing? A woman . . ." He stopped, looking blankly at his daughter, then Varaa. "Shit."

"She's perfectly safe, I assure you," Varaa said with a grin. "She and Barca are comforting Colonel De Russy." She looked back at Lewis. "And as to who I *really* left in command, why, the guard captain, of course. He's quite competent and rather good with a pike." She nodded back the way she'd come, and they saw a mixed force of about a hundred mounted men already pounding up behind the redeploying troops in their direction, briefly held up by a gun being pulled by a depleted team of two horses. "I would've left Lieutenants Burton and Meder—able young fellows—but you called them here."

Lewis watched for a moment while his battered army struggled to complete the great crescent of troops he'd envisioned, but it wasn't as great as he'd hoped. They'd lost a *lot* of men. Still, it would *look* intimidating to an enemy it already half defeated, particularly when every flag was set streaming over troops who appeared readier to renew the engagement than they were. And this was reinforced by music, each regiment attempting to play various airs together. The same rising wind forcing *Tiger* to stand off and on farther out, diminishing the effect of her fire, also badly confused the fifes and they became a sad jumble. The drummers redoubled their efforts, however, now dueling to play the loudest. The result was as good as Lewis could've hoped: an impression of light-heartedness and men cheerfully anxious to fight again.

The riflemen and dragoons arrived quickly, horses still fresh, and Lewis leaned over in his saddle to shake Reed's hand. "I must leave you, Andrew. Our infantry's suffered enough today, more than I'd hoped or planned for," he confessed. "It's my expectation they've fired their last shots, but"—he squeezed Reed's hand—"if you must fight again, you'll have plenty of time to prepare. And maybe the rest of the Home Guards will arrive before then. I know you'll do well."

"Good God!" cried Coryon Burton, standing in his stirrups to see more clearly even before his horse came to a stop. His outburst drew their attention back to the center of the field, where the three reserve enemy regiments had been advancing very slowly in spite of the galling barrages still coming from land and sea. The retreating forces, chivvied and wrangled into something like the formations they'd begun the day with, had seemed almost hesitant, marching slower as they approached their countrymen. The sight subconsciously stirred an odd sense of foreboding in Lewis, as well as a dreadful memory from his childhood: A scraggly stray dog started hanging around the house, and his father only fed it once that Lewis knew of (he'd done it after that), but the old man named it and it became utterly devoted to him. Unfortunately, rough play or mere instinct caused it to injure one of the old man's beloved guinea fowl, and he savagely beat the animal with a limb. When the yelping, terrified dog retreated, he called it back. To Lewis's dismay, it returned, head down, tail between its legs, uncertain and afraid but still devoted. His father proceeded to beat it to death.

He'd never admired his father—he'd had his share of senselessly brutal beatings too—but the sickness and horror of that particular act stuck with him more than almost anything else from his childhood. The hideous abuse of trust perhaps most of all. Now he saw it again on an unimaginable scale, out on the battlefield before him. What nobody expected, even Varaa, was that Don Frutos and the Holy Dominion wouldn't tolerate *any* degree of defeat. With less than thirty yards between them—Lewis had assumed

the newcomers would let the ravaged troops pass through to the rear—
there came the sound of bitter horns. Coryon Burton had reacted to the
sight of Dom muskets coming down, leveling, and firing a seething volley
into their own people.

It happened more than half a mile away, and they saw the smoke and
fire long before they heard the stuttering rumble of the volley and wailing
screams of pain. And no one else around them said a word, too shocked to
believe what they'd seen. Then there was another volley, and another, as
rank after rank was commanded to fire on troops whose only crime was
that a percentage—only a percentage—had endured too much for a while.
Most would've been ready and willing to go at it again after a rest and some
reorganization.

"My God," murmured Major Reed, then he exclaimed, "they're not even
shooting back! They're just taking it!"

A fourth volley came, and Lewis had no doubt there'd be a fifth, sixth,
however many it took. Even soldiers who'd desperately fought these victims
of mindless barbarity were starting to shout horrified protests, some even
yelling they should "save" them.

"They're executing them, aren't they?" Lewis demanded of Varaa. "Don
Frutos is *executing* them! Did you know this would happen?"

Eyes wide, Varaa shook her head. Usually so urbane, she seemed as affected as the rest. "I expected them to make examples—they crucify one in
ten in a company for the least infraction by a single soldier—but this! I've
never heard of anything like it!"

"Maybe they never had a commander like Don Frutos," Leonor growled.
"Think about it. He tried to trick us to death last night, then had to run for
his miserable life. Now, not only did we stop the Doms cold on their own
chosen ground; we surprised 'em an' made 'em retreat." She narrowed her
eyes at the one-sided "battle," perhaps most bewildering because it had
nothing to do with the greater issue at all. "After all his boastin' about puttin'
us all on sticks, we humiliated him. He's takin' it out on those poor fellas."

Lewis thought she might be right.

"We could attack, distract them from their murderous—" Major Reed
began, but Anson interrupted. "Are you *insane*? We should *die* defendin'
men who were tryin' to wipe us out half an hour ago? Men who'd probably
turn an' fight *us* while the rest keep shootin' 'em? *They're winnin' the battle
for us right now,* cuttin' their own damn throats!"

"Not quite," Lewis ground out. "Even if they kill them all, which it looks like they mean to do—my God—there'll still be more than we can attack in the shape we're in. Even if we 'won,' if that word could even apply, where would we be? Half our army gone and starting from scratch. . . ." He fumed as the atrocity continued. "No," he finally said, "we *are* going to win the day—would've done it without . . . what they're doing." He looked around at their surprised expressions. "Most important, they're going to know it. Stand fast, Major Reed, whatever occurs. Captain Olayne? Finish assembling your grand battery and continue firing as long as you have ammunition and targets present themselves. The rest of you"—he swept his gaze past Anson, Varaa, Meder, and Burton, as well as the tired but willing troopers they'd brought, then rested it on Leonor—"come with me."

CHAPTER 37

J esu Christo!" Sal Hernandez cried out as the last volley flashed out, striking down several hundred more men. Horns blared again, and the three "reserve" regiments stepped forward, bayonets flashing in the sun. "They're really gonna kill 'em all." His voice was full of horror mixed with wonder.

"Well, I guess that's up to them," Boogerbear said philosophically, "an' they *are* mighty preoccupied at the moment. Where's Koaar's signal? No sign he's riled anybody, an' he should'a been ready by now."

Beginning before daylight and then all through the battle, Consul Koaar's 1st Ocelomeh—eleven hundred men—had been creeping down through the dense forest upon the increasingly preoccupied and sparsely populated enemy camp. Boogerbear and his Rangers were ready, all two hundred, but couldn't make a move until they knew Koaar was ready as well. Everything depended on it. After the madness they'd just seen displayed, they realized more depended on it than they ever even imagined.

"We ain't just waitin' on Koaar," Sal reminded, still shaken. They'd seen the small mounted force detach itself from behind the defiant, stiffening crescent, riding hard to get around the "Grand Battery" of fifteen operational guns—they'd even pulled the two 12pdrs up to join Dukane—and disappear from view in one of the washed-out features of the convoluted terrain. It was clear they were coming to join Boogerbear's little force, probably led by Captain Anson or even Major Cayce himself.

"Yeah, we are, but the Cap'n wouldn't want us waitin' on him if the time was right. We'll go when it is, if he's here or not." He nodded back down at the massacre, morbidly fascinated. "Hard to see how fellas who ran from gettin' licked could just stand there an' get shot—an' now poked," Boogerbear finally conceded, revealing it bothered him too.

"They're Doms," Ixtla said, offhand, as if that explained everything.

"Doms or not, they're *not* men," Sal urgently insisted. "They truly are demons. I thought the savages—Holcanos and lizard men—were bad, but once we fought the Doms, a 'modern army,' we'd find honor and glory in this war." He spat. "It seems the more 'civilized' our enemies are on this world, the more savage and barbarous they are as well."

"I don't care about 'honor' an' 'glory,' amigo," Boogerbear said slowly, "I just kill who the Cap'n says. Comanches, Mex-kins, the weird Injins here, lizard fellas, now these damn Doms." He paused. "But I reckon you're right."

The small reinforcements coming to join them were visible again, cantering up the dry wash behind the two hundred Rangers, and Boogerbear saw he'd been right. The riflemen and dragoons were indeed led by Major Cayce, Anson, Varaa, and Leonor. He also recognized Coryon Burton and Felix Meder, whom he considered pretty solid soldiers, for young "professional" officers. *Course, Meder started out a private, an' I was a "volunteer" corporal. I ain't as young as them, but I guess we're all "professional" officers now,* he mulled.

"Well, Lieutenant Beeryman," Lewis said, stopping beside him, "are you ready for this?"

Boogerbear nodded. "Just waitin' on Koaar. Takin' his damn time." He looked meaningfully at the slaughter. "Sure you don't want us jumpin' on *them* instead?" The first two ranks of the reserve regiments were in complete disarray, now actually having to fight to finish the troops who'd embarrassed Don Frutos. (Lewis was sure Leonor was right about that.)

Anson rolled his eyes. "Temptin' as it is, I recommend we don't."

Leonor snorted. "They're half a mile away. Even if they only got their rear ranks sorted before we hit 'em, they'd smash our charge with one volley."

Boogerbear chuckled and half smiled at Lewis. "Just makin' sure I ain't fightin' with idiots, an' only poor Sal's brains has been rattled by all this craziness."

"*Tú eres el loco, hombre grande!*" Sal retorted.

"The signal!" Ixtla pointed. Reflected sunlight flashed rapidly from a polished silver disk high in the trees almost bordering the road on the west side of the washboard, right behind the enemy camp. Quick flashes instead of long, slow ones indicated the 1st Ocelomeh was in position but the signaler, at least, had been discovered. A smattering of musketry came from the trees, the only musket fire on the battlefield at the moment since the Doms killing their own were using bayonets, but the grand battery was now hurling exploding case in earnest at the remaining Dom guns and the reports of bursting shells ensured no one in the camp even noticed.

Lewis turned to Captain Anson. "You command the mounted troops."

Anson nodded and straightened in his saddle, shouting, "Rangers! Riflemen! Third Dragoons! *Destroy* that camp!"

LEONOR RACED FORWARD with the others, forming a loose knot in the center of the charging line as it vomited out of the wash and extended out to the sides, Burton and Meder near the flanks leading their own men. For the very first time going into a fight, she was torn. She'd always stuck close to her father, and they made a formidable team with their revolvers, firing forward or on opposite sides as necessary, watching out for each other while punishing the enemy. But her father had privately asked her to stay with Lewis today, either to spare her from his own deep involvement at the beginning, or, as he said, to protect the man commanding them. If the first was truly his intent, she doubted he'd been in more danger than she, sitting on a horse next to Lewis while they drew disproportionate fire. If the latter . . . she'd learned that Lewis was a fighter, and a pretty good one. She doubted he'd reloaded his pistols after he used them the first time, but he seemed better with his saber than any of the dragoons and, with his broad shoulders and strong arms, put terrible force behind his blows. Still, a saber is a very short-range weapon for an artilleryman used to fighting at a distance. He hadn't had much to do with the big guns today, but except for when he was right amongst the enemy, he'd still acted like he was far away, oblivious to the greedy musket balls. She'd decided he *needed* protecting and was surprised by how strongly she wanted to do it. But what about her father? Giles Anson got just as wrapped up in a fight as Lewis apparently did, in similar and different ways. She couldn't count how many times in the past she'd shot somebody drawing a bead on him. *Just have to look out for 'em both, I guess,* she told herself. *I hope they stay close together.*

She needn't have worried. Her father and Lewis Cayce once viewed each other as somewhat incompatible colleagues: very good in their respective fields, but not someone they'd choose as a friend. In spite of that—perhaps even because of it—they'd not only become close friends after all; they'd unconsciously developed their own complementary fighting styles practically on the fly when they slammed into the Doms in front of the 3rd Pennsylvania. It was ironic, of course, that in a melee, the artilleryman preferred to get closer than the Ranger who used his powerful revolvers to kill beyond the range of most other pistols. Mainly, however, both were naturally drawn where they were needed and intuitively steered the thundering line toward Doms that were running to assemble a defense on the south side of the camp. An officer quicker than most they'd seen even called for his men to load before they all gathered. He managed a rushed volley that emptied a few saddles and tumbled several horses before, shouting and shooting, Anson, with Lewis beside him, drove his charge home and crashed the brittle line. All Leonor had to do was keep up.

Horns blew panicky, strident notes while the Rangers and dragoons went among the enemy, shooting and slashing and sleeting big arrows about. The riflemen, also armed with sabers, slashed through as well, but dashed on toward the artillery park, where the great siege guns remained unused. Lieutenant Meder and his men had volunteered to secure them and defend them with their rifles. Not only might the things still crush the assault on the camp if brought to bear, spewing monstrous loads of canister or grape; Lewis wanted them intact. Just as important, it was believed Don Frutos must keep his headquarters there. The clearing around the guns held the biggest marquee in the camp.

Anson blasted men down with his big revolvers, and Lewis hacked them with his saber. Leonor caught herself watching for threats to them instead of herself when Boogerbear dashed past and shot a man in the face who'd been running at her with a fixed bayonet. *Glad* somebody's *lookin' out for* me, she thought glumly, before returning the favor and shooting a Dom aiming his musket at Boogerbear. The man fell, writhing and screaming, but his musket went off under his chin and blew off the front of his head.

There might've still been as many as two thousand Doms in the sprawling camp, but they were slow to respond. Scattered all over, they couldn't see what was happening or where to go because of the virtual sea of marquees and white canvas tents. Besides, many were support troops, even slaves, not real soldiers. Still, there were more than the three hundred–odd attackers, and the fighting got sharper and fiercer as even the slaves and cooks streamed to the sound of battle.

"I think we got their attention," Anson rasped, holstering his second Walker and drawing a Paterson from under his left arm. Lewis spurred Arete and let the big horse bash a man preparing to leap on the Ranger with a blade bayonet in his hand. His face looked positively rabid. Arete took it upon herself to stomp the man on the ground, just like she would a snake. Lewis heard his back snap. "Lieutenant Joffrion!" he shouted. "Your bugler!"

"Sir!" Joffrion yelled back from within a hastily drawn-up circle of dragoons shooting carbines in all directions. His bugler heard and didn't wait, nor was the call he sounded really necessary. Lewis himself saw the tents on the west side of camp erupt into flames, sparkling black fragments of scorched canvas rising in the terrible heat plume and smoke.

"Koaar and Ixtla are here already!" called Sal Hernandez triumphantly, whipping a shot off at a Dom officer trying to direct some men around him, mostly slaves dressed only in dingy yellow smocks who'd armed themselves with whatever they could grab. To Leonor's amazement, Sal seemed to miss—Sal never missed at this range—and she started to shoot the man herself. He suddenly seemed aware of a .36 caliber hole in his chest and clutched weakly at it as he fell on his face. "Kill the others!" Sal roared at the slaves. "*Matar a los demás!* We'll free you!"

They stared at him blankly for a moment but then saw Varaa bounding forward, sweeping around her with her sword. They ran. Nearly everyone started running then, from the advancing wall of flames if not the "demon" Varaa, and the fighting abruptly waned.

"Sal almost had 'em," Leonor scolded the Mi-Anakka warmaster, "until you scared 'em off."

"Best that I did," Varaa stated simply, taking a gulp from an army canteen. "'Had them' indeed. What possible use would they be? Even Dom slaves are steeped in their depravity, and those influenced by Blood Priests—as these have certainly been—are even worse. Barred from the 'traditional' Dom priesthood, Blood Priests will occasionally accept them in their order. Pray you're never taken prisoner and given to them so they can prove the fire of their faith!" She shook her head. "Pray you're never taken at all!"

A great *thump!* came from an exploding ammunition store as the leading edge of the fire the 1st Ocelomeh was spreading curved around on the seaward side of the camp and the wind began blowing it toward them.

"Onward or back?" Anson shouted.

"On to the artillery park to relieve Lieutenant Meder," Lewis said. "And the headquarters tent. I *want* Don Frutos!"

Anson and Joffrion quickly gathered their men. There'd been amazingly few casualties—only six dead and nine wounded too badly to go on. These were sent back the way they came. The rest pushed into the growing inferno, coughing on smoke and actually glad for the protection their wool uniforms gave them from the heat. Almost everyone else must've already abandoned the camp, fleeing back down the road past the 1st Ocelomeh, or streaming out to join the three regiments on the field. Lewis wondered what their commander thought of all this. He'd just murdered half his force and now had an army in front of him and a conflagration—consuming all his shelter and supplies—behind.

Cattle, goats, sheep, pigs—and piglike things with teeth and clawed feet—were running everywhere, as were the curious reptilian local chickens, but the dozens—scores—of massive armabueys rampaging through the camp draped in burning tents and spreading fire as they went were the greatest hazard by far. There was even a monster like the one that got poor Swain that first night. It must've been lurking at the edge of the trees hoping to pick off some Dom livestock when the Ocelomeh charge pushed it into the camp as well. It screeched frantically and raced away when it saw them. Nor did a single man remain willing to fight, and they finally emerged in the smoke-fogged clearing where the artillery park and command marquee stood.

All had been preserved from the flames by distance and a number of providentially placed water butts that Felix Meder's men were using to fill buckets to throw on the tents and guns. A couple hundred Ocelomeh arsonists had made it this far as well and were helping. Everyone was wearing dark red bandannas, wetted and tied around their faces, and Lewis supposed they'd cut them from the piles of Dom flags scattered on the ground.

Ixtla awkwardly saluted Lewis, and Consul Koaar rode over beside Varaa and embraced her.

"Well done, Lieutenant Meder," Lewis said, then raised his voice. "Well done, the First Ocelomeh!" Cheers were muted by soggy cloth. Everyone dismounted to get out of the thickest smoke. Hundreds of tents were burning directly upwind, and it was still very bad, but the wind was falling a little as it tended to in the late afternoon, and bandannas were sufficient to let them breathe. "Can we save this area or should we get out?" Lewis asked Felix, frowning at the great guns. They were utterly immense, probably 36pdrs, cast from good bronze with intricate geometric designs in relief. Their limbers were at hand, but without armabueys it would take all their horses to move them.

"I think we can keep it, sir," Felix replied hoarsely. "The fire's intense, and we're getting the worst of it now," he conceded, "but it's only tents. It can't last long." Another ammunition dump exploded loudly nearby, and the smoke now smelled of powder too, and other things. "We moved as much ammunition as we could find nearby into that tent"—he nodded at the marquee—"but couldn't get it all, of course. I think most has been cleared from around us."

"Did you have to fight hard for it?" Anson asked, looking around. Several men were covered with blankets, and quite a few Doms were scattered around, including some Blood Priests.

Felix looked at him. "Why, yes, at first. They seemed most determined to keep us back while they loaded an ornate coach. After it sped away, the fight just went out of them." He kicked a dead Blood Priest Lewis thought he recognized from the night before. "These devils all stabbed each other. The last one did for himself."

"But the coach?" Lewis pressed.

Felix looked down. "Some of the priests got in. One was taller, dressed better than the rest. I fear Don Frutos escaped. There's no one left alive in the tent."

"He escaped us as well," Koaar fumed, blinking rapidly, tail rigid. "The fiend couldn't have timed it better. We only sent a single company of firestarters to the sea side of the camp. There were fewer Doms there. Shortly after they started their work—we'd already advanced from the rear—about two hundred lancers bashed through the small force we left on the road, and that same coach burst through." Koaar gave a very human shrug. "We had no mounted men to chase it."

Leonor had been watching, growing impatient. "What does it really matter? Sure, it would've been nice to hang him, but he ain't a military genius, that's sure. Besides, if they shoot whole regiments for retreatin' in battle, what'll they do to his cowardly ass for leavin' a whole army behind?"

"What indeed?" murmured Varaa, then cleared her throat before putting on a damp bandanna Ixtla handed her. "And we still have that army to deal with," she reminded Lewis, who was staring at the leaping flames all around, but couldn't see what that army was doing now.

"We need to know what's happening," he told Anson.

"Lieutenant Beeryman," Anson called.

"Cap'n?"

"Take five men an' find your way out of this. . . ." He frowned. "I bet Reverend Harkin would be amused to hear we're surrounded by fire." He looked back at Boogerbear. "The way we came in might still be open. Whatever you have to do, go see what's happenin' an' report back." He glanced at Lewis. "An' send a man to tell Major Reed what we've done."

Lewis was nodding. "By all means."

Meder had been right. The camp burned furiously for another hour or so, but even before it was reduced entirely to blowing ash and smoldering tent poles and frames—even before Boogerbear could return (the way back in was blocked when the south side of the camp was consumed)—Leonor could see for herself through the lingering smoke and heat shimmer that the three murderous Dom regiments (somewhat swollen by refugees and no longer under artillery fire) remained almost exactly where they'd been. What's more, though it seemed they'd reduced their numbers by half, at least, they'd stopped killing their own people. *That prob'ly leaves 'em with eight or ten thousand fit to fight,* she calculated glumly, *an' I bet we ain't got half that many. But will they fight? Can they?* She couldn't imagine the ones so recently abused really would. *But what the hell do I know in this crazy place?*

Boogerbear finally returned, coming in from the west and trailing a cloud of swirling gray ash. He and his men, joined by Captain Beck, were dusty gray as well, red eyes streaming over moistened bandannas. Beck jumped down from his horse and saluted Lewis with evident pleasure. "The enemy's at a stand, sir. They don't know what to do! They've requested another parley—marching straight out under artillery fire and waiting until we stopped! In any event, Major Reed and Alcaldesa Periz are waiting for you and Varaa—very keen to hear your views."

"Remember the *last* 'parley.' They prob'ly just want to kill you," Leonor warned darkly, somewhat shocked at her own tone. She'd done her best to speak more pleasantly to Lewis—*Why?* she demanded of herself—but her voice sounded more like a croaking toad than the young woman she'd been trying to become.

Lewis nodded at her. "I won't forget." He looked around. All the people with him were just as covered in ash. Perhaps it would blow off as they rode. "Very well," he told Beck. "Consul Koaar, it seems about half your force has found its way here. The rest are probably nearby. Assemble them on the east side of the camp with Lieutenant Joffrion's dragoons, Lieutenant Meder's riflemen, and most of the Rangers under Lieutenant Hernandez. You're in command."

"We'll make the best show we can," Koaar said slowly, "but I doubt we can stop them with . . ." He paused, considering. "We might gather twelve or thirteen hundreds."

"It won't matter," Lewis went on brusquely. "Captain Anson, Lieutenant Anson, Warmaster Varaa-Choon, and I will accompany Captain Beck, Lieutenant Beeryman, and his remaining Rangers. We'll go to this parley and see what we see, but in the meantime you'll make it appear as if you mean to hold your position. You might even do so for a very short time if the Doms advance on you, but in that case your essential mission will be to spike these big guns and smash their carriages before withdrawing to the south. Is that understood?"

"Perfectly," agreed Koaar.

"Fine," Lewis said, moving to retrieve Arete from where he'd tied her to one of the guns in question. The others he'd named did the same. Mounting his horse, Lewis raised his voice so most could hear. "I don't know what'll happen. It might even be that Leonor—Lieutenant Anson—is right and this is just another attempt at treachery and the battle will resume without warning." He grinned. "It's not generally considered wise for commanders to acknowledge uncertainty to their troops, but I really *don't* know, and you must be ready for anything. I *do* know this: you've all fought magnificently and done all that was asked of you." He waved eastward across the field. "Everyone has. If nothing else, this disparate force we assembled has become a real army today, and I can promise you that whatever happens, we've already won this battle because we didn't *lose* it, and we've fatally crippled the Dom army that came against us. All we have to do now is survive. And build."

They cheered him as he left, cantering at the head of the small group accompanying him, and Leonor would've cheered him too if she weren't so worried. *How will we "build" if he doesn't "survive"?* she asked herself.

CHAPTER 38

I t took a while to ride all around the battlefield, stopping for a report at Olayne's grand battery, before rejoining Major Reed. He was already mounted and waiting with Alcaldesa Sira Periz. She looked very small but fiercely determined in her own gold scale armor similar to (and just as useless as) her dead husband's, sitting atop his horse. Lewis and his party had lost a lot of the ash that coated them, but the battle itself had left them quite bedraggled compared to her, and their lathered horses had had quite enough of all this running around. Father Orno and Reverend Harkin were mounted as well, looking adamant and resolute. Samantha Wilde, Barca, and Colonel De Russy were there as well, though Lewis noted with relief that none of them looked as if they expected to go. Lewis, Anson, and Beck bowed to Sira in their saddles, and Lewis spoke first. "Alcaldesa, please accept my most sincere condolences. Your husband was a good man, a brave man. I considered him a friend and hope he felt the same."

"That's neither here nor there at the moment," Sira replied sharply, but then her voice softened. "You served him well, as you've served our people." She looked at him intently. "*Your* people. He could be . . . confused at times, especially of late, and that was largely my fault," she confessed bitterly. "But he wasn't 'confused' at the end, nor am I now." She waved out over the field, and Lewis followed the gesture with his eyes. About ten thousand Doms left, he confirmed, drawn up for battle—*Though they look as hard used as we do. And some, probably survivors of their "execution," don't appear very firm.* Of particular interest was the cluster of horses and riders about halfway between the respective forces, just sitting there, patiently waiting. "And look what you—*we*—have wrought together!" Sira continued. "The terrible Doms, humbled at last, and the remnant of their army at our mercy!"

Leonor coughed. "Not exactly at our mercy, Alcaldesa," she said dryly.

Sira's eyes flashed, but Lewis shook his head. "She's right. They still outnumber us two to one, and even with the ammunition they carry—we've destroyed the rest—they could smash right through us with a determined, concentrated attack. We're low on ammunition as well, and our artillery is nearly spent. They don't know that, but they have to suspect. I'll tell you what I told the Ocelomeh: the best way to win this battle and a breathing space to prepare for the next one is not to *lose*. We *can* still lose if we don't handle this right."

"Hear him," said Colonel De Russy, voice subdued. He glanced repentantly at Lewis, and particularly Varaa. "I apologize for my earlier . . . indisposition. I fear I was trying to make up for something. I'm quite recovered now and fully reminded of my limitations."

"No, I should apologize to you," said Lewis with a sad smile. "We *did* have a deal, and I pushed you past your end of it. We'll keep things more straightforward in the future."

"I couldn't agree more," Varaa stated, staring hard at Sira with her large, blue eyes. "Which is why De Russy should be on that horse at this moment and you should not, Alcaldesa. This *is* his 'end' of it, as it were."

Sira bristled. "Are you saying I can't conduct the affairs of my city?"

"Not at all. But this is a battle, not a city. And though De Russy may be more suited to a city than a battle as well, he's been in both."

"Uxmal can't risk another leader today," De Russy agreed firmly. "I'm far more expendable than you, my dear." He looked down. "Proven conclusively once more."

Barca, standing by him, frowned deeply, and Samantha spoke up, "Really, Rube, don't be absurd." She looked at Reed, arching a brow. "And you can't go either."

"Mistress . . ." Reed objected with surprise.

"She's right," Lewis said, growing impatient. This was taking too long, and the Doms might interpret the delay as shyness. "I'm going, so you stay."

He bowed as respectfully as he could in the saddle to Sira Periz. "For the same reason you must. If they're planning treachery, we can't make them a gift of us all." He glanced down at the clot of waiting Doms. There were six of them, and even at a distance, Lewis thought he recognized the squat, powerful form of General Agon in his yellow-and-black coat, dripping lace. "I'll take Colonel De Russy, Varaa, and Captain Anson."

"And me," Leonor said dangerously. "My revolvers are reloaded."

Lewis sighed.

"Will you leave us as well?" Harkin demanded. "Shouldn't have even waited for him," he said aside to Father Orno.

"No. Come along if you like."

"But keep your mouths shut," Anson warned. "Battles are no place to argue scripture either."

They had to tread carefully for the first part of the way out to meet the enemy, guiding their horses through the maze of bloody bodies still lying where they fell after the Allied stroke that finally broke the Doms' furious but uncoordinated effort to smash through the 3rd Pennsylvania and 1st Uxmal. Even down here, Lewis saw the occasional American corpse. Their death was no more tragic than that of their indigenous allies, but Lewis felt especially responsible for them. They'd followed him into a war they had no stake in before he made it so and died in a land unimaginably distant from their homes. It made him very sad, but even more grimly angry as he approached the leaders of the invaders who killed them. The most extraordinary thing to him was that, absent the weird, surrealistic setting of the marquee full of gold and flags and Blood Priests—and then the debilitating smoke they'd conjured and sacrifices they'd prepared—the men before him were only men. All were soldiers, no Blood Priest was with them, and despite their grave, even hostile expressions, here beneath the late afternoon sun there was no palpable aura of menace about them.

Both groups spread out as they neared, and Lewis finally stopped Arete about five yards in front of General Agon. The others in his party did the same. Agon appeared somewhat surprised as his gaze took them in, lingering longest on Varaa and Leonor.

"It seems I met you all last night, in a manner of speaking—since we never actually spoke," Agon said loudly, in excellent if accented English. He gestured aside at a companion. "And *some* of you already met my aide, Capitan Arevalo." The officer he indicated, taller than the others, was staring intently, almost wonderingly, at Leonor, hand straying absently to his chest under his collarbone. Agon blinked and glanced around at the carnage, caused mostly by artillery down here. "Only last night," he said lower, then cleared his throat and glared at Lewis. "But now I know you quite well, even without words." He took a deep breath and let it out, glare shifting to a stiffly erect officer of lancers. "So. I believe we're now *fully* acquainted with one another's current dispositions. We can't know what reinforcements might be rushing to join each other, but it's clear what we have to fight with now." A hint of a smile touched the sharp line of his lips. "Therefore, since Don Frutos embraced this stimulating tradition of meeting before battle . . ."

"Perverted it into a treacherous attack!" Father Orno seethed loudly. Harkin put a hand on his arm, and Agon glanced at him before continuing.

". . . I found myself amazingly curious what *you* think we should do, Major Cayce."

"Interesting," Lewis ground out. "I was wondering the same about you since we *know* you have no other forces closer than Nautla, possibly even Campeche or farther. I'm afraid you'll have to make do with what you have—only what your men have in their cartridge boxes and haversacks."

"Which makes a strong argument for renewing the action at once and taking what I need," Agon countered. "And you!" He stretched out his hands to encompass the long crescent of the Allied line. "Despite your laudable performance and impressive display, you've no intention of mounting a general assault. Why should you?" He waved at the grand battery, then out to sea, where HMS *Tiger* lay some distance out, hove to at the moment. She couldn't linger like that off this lee shore for long, but Captain Holland had positioned her well for effect. "But if you mean to keep pounding me with your great guns, supposing I'll just stand and take it, I must disappoint you. I *will* attack and destroy you if it costs every man in my army."

"Well, considering the recent demonstration of your devotion to your men, it's clear what you intend, and you're only wasting our time," Lewis snapped, starting to pull Arete around.

"Wait," said De Russy, peering closely at Agon. "I can't believe you invited this meeting for no more purpose than this. But what are we to think? You invaded this land to subjugate and murder its people in the name of an abominable faith that would continue the process until all submit or die. You tried to murder us in our first meeting like this"—his tone grew incredulous—"and *did* murder hundreds—perhaps thousands—of your own men when they honorably withdrew, in remarkably good order, from an assault they couldn't complete. *That*, sir, is the most monstrous thing I've beheld in all the time I've been on this world *full* of monsters!"

Agon actually looked away. "I didn't do those things," he said softly, then met De Russy's gaze again. "No, I did. Some of them. But I wouldn't have taken advantage at the meeting or slaughtered my own men without orders." He gestured around him. "These officers and I have been soldiers all our lives, loyal to the Holy Dominion. The faith it requires is demanding," he conceded, "but we firmly believe our faith is the only engine that can secure this land and continent in a 'world full of monsters,' as you say." He frowned. "But the . . . leadership of our faith has changed in recent years, growing more adamant and strident, some might even say fanatical, than in the past. And the rise of the Blood Priests . . ." He shook his head. "You see none of them here, since all are dead or have followed Don Frutos in the retreat *he wouldn't allow* the soldiers I was ordered to destroy." He paused a long moment, regaining control of a flaring fury. "Our faith, our very souls require us to follow the orders of God, passed through the mouth of His Supreme Holiness and Blood Cardinals such as Don Frutos." He gestured behind at the mound of dead Doms his own soldiers made. "But since Don Frutos—ordered to command this campaign—has withdrawn, I can only take that to mean his army may do so as well—if it can," he qualified, then snorted. "You may note I extended that presumption to what remained of those others who retreated as soon as our commander did so."

"Such rigidity!" De Russy exclaimed. "And such . . . imaginative maneuvering within it on your part."

Agon bowed. "He is our 'leader,' after all. Are we not bound to follow him?"

Leonor started to say something, probably inflammatory, but Lewis beat her to it. "Am I to infer that you wish to be allowed to *retreat*, your army intact?" he asked doubtfully.

"It's hardly 'intact.' Nor is yours, I daresay. And I expect mine will be even less so by the time it straggles back to Nautla without supplies," Agon added bitterly. "But it can certainly fight *now*, if you want, and we can destroy each other entirely."

"Then why not?" Lewis asked.

Agon held up a finger. "Neither of us *gains*. Mutual annihilation might end our war for months, even years, but then it will all start again at the beginning." He gazed at the Home Guards, Pennsylvanians, 1st US and 1st Uxmal, the grand battery. . . . "You have made a good beginning, and even in my . . . withdrawal, I will have done so as well because I've faced you, met you, and know better how to fight you when we meet again. We're *destined* to be enemies, you and I," he told Lewis, suddenly enthusiastic, "destined to contend as proper soldiers should: as instruments of our countries and faiths for possession of this continent!" He looked at his officers. "Not all believe as we do, but our *foundational* faith, even now under assault by the Blood Priests and perhaps checked by those like Don Frutos on the surface, is still quite fervent and compels us—as soldiers—to fight and strive and suffer for God *as soldiers*. How can we do that without war? And such a war! A battle against respected peers, not filthy rebels in huts"—he glanced at Varaa—"aligned with demons, no less!" Varaa wisely kept her mouth shut. "But that makes it even better!" Agon proclaimed, warming to his argument. "The stakes couldn't be higher! What could please God more?"

"Good heavens," murmured Reverend Harkin. "My own argument thrown back at me." He frowned. "Quite twisted, of course. *My* God would have us stop fighting and live together in peace."

"The *same* God," Agon countered harshly. "Only your weak worship of Him makes Him seem different, and you misunderstand His requirements."

Harkin reddened, preparing a rebuttal, but Father Orno very earnestly shook his head at him.

Lewis cleared his throat. "Let me get this straight. You want to just stop fighting and leave."

"With our arms and flags, of course. You may consider it a victory if you like, but I cannot withdraw in defeat. Even the perception of that would ensure my officers and I would be subject to the same example we were ordered to make of the men who retreated earlier." He actually chuckled. "But since *Don Frutos* now leads us *away*, I'm duty-bound to follow him, am I not?"

"You can't take your cannon with you, not with all your animals scattered," Anson snapped.

Agon bowed again. "I fear you are correct. But I'll stand by my officers as long as they stand by me when I remind Don Frutos the animals would never have scattered and the camp never would have been taken if *he* hadn't ordered me forward, leaving so few troops behind." There was a clear tone of warning in his voice for his fellows.

Lewis looked at Anson, then Varaa. She glanced at Father Orno, who also wisely hadn't said a word, and then at Leonor. She alone looked angrier than surprised by all this. "We have to discuss it with the *alcaldesa* of Uxmal," Lewis said at last. "She's the only leader of our Allied cities present and will have to decide for them all."

"She?" Agon asked.

Lewis's face turned stormy. "Yes. Her husband was killed by treachery at our last meeting, so I've no idea whether she'll ask me to let you go or kill you."

Agon turned to look at the late-afternoon sun. "Very well," he said, "but do press her to decide quickly. I quiver with the precariousness of entrusting such momentous decisions to mere passionate females. We must resume our battle if she delays too long. I don't want to lose the light."

" 'MERE PASSIONATE FEMALES,' " Leonor spat as they trotted back to where Sira Periz and Samantha Wilde waited with Major Reed and Captain Beck in front of the 1st Uxmal. "I'll show him a 'passionate female' when I blow his damned head off!"

"Calm down," hissed Varaa. "You'll have the battle on again if you sway Sira, and I'm sure you will in your state."

"You want to let 'em *go*?" Leonor demanded, incredulous.

"Of course!" Father Orno declared. "Don't you see? We won! We were never going to destroy such a force entirely and were lucky to fight it to a standstill. As Major Cayce says, we won by not losing, and now we've won *time*!"

Lewis explained the situation to Sira Periz as plainly as he could while carefully withholding his own recommendations. That was largely because he was of two minds himself. On the one hand, all his arguments about winning by surviving were sound, particularly at this stage of what he feared would be a very long war. On the other hand, he'd brought his army here to fight, and a complete victory would earn them even more time. And if their losses had been worse than he'd hoped, his troops had stood strong, and morale was high. What's more, General Agon bothered him. He was just as fanatical as Don Frutos in his own way, and he wasn't a fool. Lewis doubted he'd had much control over the battle, but he'd clearly learned from it and would be harder to beat again. Lewis felt an almost overwhelming urge to destroy him while he could—but could he? That was the question—no doubt pondered by Agon as well—and he couldn't answer it. He decided he had to let Sira Periz choose. She and all the people of the Yucatán had the most to lose, in a way. Not just their lives, but their homes and families, their very identity as a people. That identity would have to change to a degree for them to win the war, but it wouldn't be exterminated by the Doms.

As it turned out, despite her personal feelings—almost exactly (and understandably) mirroring Leonor's as Orno foresaw—Sira Periz reluctantly came to the same conclusion as her other advisors; they must let Agon go.

"Colonel, if you would?" Lewis asked De Russy.

"And our terms?"

Lewis glanced at Sira. "Essentially as Agon outlined himself," Lewis replied, "with a few modifications. His men may keep the arms and flags they carry, but any that have fallen will remain where they lie. He has to pass back through the ruins of his camp, but he'll make no attempt to recover any animals or supplies that might've survived the flames." His voice turned harsh. "And he'll keep going past Nautla, at least as far as Campeche." They couldn't realistically shadow him farther. "If he does that, he has my word we won't harass his starving, weakening column on the march. If he doesn't, we'll know, and we'll pick him apart."

Captain Anson joined De Russy, calling on Teniente Lara and Lieutenant Joffrion to each pick a man and accompany them. He shrugged at Lewis. "The more fellas who know Agon by sight, the better." Together they rumbled back down the gentle, corpse-choked slope and Lewis, Reed, Leonor, Sira, Samantha, Harkin, and Orno all stood together, dismounted at last, watching the exchange at a distance. Two of Agon's officers broke away and galloped back to the regiments behind them, calling orders. Almost immediately, the Dom troops faced away from their enemy and began flowing from their battle lines back into a fat column, those first to do so already marching southwest toward the still-smoldering camp. Agon and three of his officers (including the tall aide named Arevalo) remained to converse with De Russy and Anson for a time, and though Lewis wondered what they were saying, he suddenly felt very tired.

"I still say we should hurry the devils along with artillery," Reed said darkly.

"No," Lewis said. "I should've seen it before. Crisp as they seem, the fight's blown out of them." He looked at the Uxmalo troops nearby, shifting

his gaze to the battered Pennsylvanians and 1st US Infantry, seeing the exhausted relief on their blood- and sweat-streaked faces as they slowly began
to relax. "Blown out of us too." He smiled sadly at Sira. "We were lucky, and
you made a wise choice."

"So she did," Varaa said with more energy than Lewis, voice suddenly
animated with as much disbelief as pleasure. "But you beat them! By the
heavens, you *beat the Doms*! King Har-Kaaska will be so amazed!"

"He didn't think we would?"

"Of course not!" Varaa gushed, then collected herself. "He hoped, of
course, but really, what were the chances?" She blinked benevolently at Sira.
"I think you'll find, with King Har-Kaaska more vigorously advancing the
cause among the other *alcaldes* as well"—she blinked apologetically at
Lewis—"and with the other cities now more secure, enthusiasm for this
great Union that Major Cayce, and indeed your late husband, proposed will
grow." She clapped her hands with glee and thumped Lewis on the shoulder. "You beat them!" she repeated once more.

"Damn right," Leonor affirmed, stepping closer to Lewis, even giving
him a strange look he didn't recognize as proud affection. "I was for killin'
'em all—but that's just my way, an' Sira chose right." She turned to look
where the little gathering was breaking up at last, De Russy, her father, and
the others galloping back, and Agon and his followers going to join their
troops. "They ain't runnin'," she said almost gently to Sira, whose strong,
pretty face was suddenly streaked with tears, "but they *are* leavin'. An' even
that fluffed-up General Agon knows Major Cayce made 'em."

Lewis shook his head and waved up and down the line at the still tired
but far more animated Americans, Uxmalos, and Ocelomeh. "*We* did. Together. And we have to get ready to do it again."

Anson and De Russy slid down from their horses as their escorts returned to their places, and as if they'd discussed it beforehand, both men
solemnly stood at attention and saluted Lewis. The men behind them exploded in a spontaneous cheer. Drums thundered, and fifes in the 3rd
Pennsylvania joined in, exuberantly playing the "Old 1812." Soon, the Uxmalos and 1st US were doing it as well.

"It seems we have a victory tune," Sira Periz said loudly, more cheerfully
over the racket.

"So we have," agreed Samantha somewhat ironically.

"What did you and Agon go on about so long?" Leonor asked her father.

Anson frowned, then shrugged. "Oh, the usual, I guess. Mutual expressions of esteem an' regretful descriptions of what we'll do to each other when we meet again. Pretty graphic on their part." He looked aside at Lewis. "Agon's mighty anxious to meet *you* again, he says. Was disappointed you didn't say goodbye yourself."

Lewis took a long breath, gazing at the carnage on the field, the battered enemy host now starting to enter the distant trees, the red sun dipping down toward the forest. *Tiger* was under way again, beating out to sea, sails a golden red as well. Turning to face his army, his cause, he raised his voice over the tumult. "The enemy general says he's anxious to meet us again!" He raised his hands to silence the hoots of derision, then bowed quite deeply to Sira Periz. Cheers exploded once more, even louder, the local troops ecstatic to see their beautiful, tragic *alcaldesa* so honored. She raised her hands in turn and, looking back at Lewis, cried, "The Doms *will* see us soon enough. And when we've built our Union of all the cities in the Yucatán and Major Cayce builds an army even greater than this—greater than anything ever seen—they won't have to come *here* to do it!"

Reverend Harkin, Father Orno, and many others nearby went down on their knees and clasped their hands before them.

"Praise the Lord for this, *His* victory, and the firm foothold He has granted us on purgatory's very shore!" Harkin cried out. "Let us now gird ourselves to press beyond it, confronting the demons and evil men of this whole land with His works and word!"

Father Orno intoned a prayer full of similar sentiments, met by more roaring approval, and Leonor leaned over and shouted in Lewis's ear, "Words an' works won't be enough. It'll be our blood an' bodies."

Lewis was already nodding back. "But spiritually inspired or contrived or not, we *do* have a 'cause,' Lieutenant." He paused, looking at her. "'Leonor' for the moment, if I may." She flushed and nodded and Lewis went on, "With no choice now at all, it's become our cause to make ourselves as 'good' as we can be"—he glanced at Barca—"in *all* ways, simply to survive the very real evil we've found. And I must agree with Sira Periz; the best way to do that is to go *after* it."

"On purgatory's shore" would remain a common description of their circumstances among the rank and file for quite some time. It was even somewhat appropriate as far as they could know since their earlier, by a century, perceptions of "this world" were even less informed than our own woefully inadequate understanding. We gradually accepted that not only have various prehistoric creatures been preserved largely unchanged in their adapted niches for millions of years; some of their descendants have advanced in unexpected, often shocking ways. Grik-like beings must be distant offspring of Dromaeosaurids, for example, and Mi-Anakka—whose small but important ongoing part in this tale (primarily revealed in surviving personal journals) has been otherwise largely forgotten, alas—might've originally been obscurely related to the giant lemurs of Madagascar.

But the "1847 Americans" couldn't know any of this, though it appears Reverend Harkin—of all people—had an inkling, stirred by wonder and the controversy surrounding the fossil remains of Iguanodon and others, his own intellect, and a few "evolutionists" of various sorts already lurking in the shadows. But Darwin wouldn't publish his famous work for another decade, and Owen only coined the term "dinosaur" less than a decade before. That word was by no means universally accepted or even known, virtually nothing was understood about the creatures Grant named, and there remained strong sentiment against the very notion of evolution and extinction, largely stoked by contention among some of the "lurkers" themselves! But the "1847 Americans" and their friends would learn much more, as we did, as they proceeded (allegorically) onward from purgatory, through ever deeper and darker levels of hell. . . .

Excerpt from Courtney Bradford's
Lands and Peoples—Destiny of the Damned, Vol. I,
Library of Alex-aandra Press, 1959

ACKNOWLEDGMENTS

The years 2020 and 2021 have been tough for everyone and I'm mostly thankful to my sweet wife, Silva, for not tearing my throat out during the extended time in which we were inseparably cooped up together and I had to write—and she couldn't escape. I escaped to the woods from time to time, and that's probably why I'm still living. I can only imagine how hard it's been for all my friends "up" in New York. Particularly strong in my thoughts are my wonderful editor, Anne Sowards, and great agent, Russell Galen. After writing the Destroyermen series for so long and starting "fresh" (sorta) with this, I'm especially indebted to Anne for helping me "get back to basics" here and there.

Otherwise, though I sometimes have a lot of people to thank for their direct technical assistance, that's not really the case this time, and there's nobody to take the blame for goofs but me . . . well, and Jim, as always. Jim's really the one to blame. I had a lot of *indirect* assistance from many sources, though, sometimes over many years. This might've been in the form of kicking ideas around for this very book or just things I picked up from them, or even came up with myself in their company. In many cases, their chief contributions to this book—and my life—have been their friendship and inspiration. If any of you see your name here and say to yourself,

"What? I didn't do anything!" Yeah, you did. In no particular order I must include here: Jim Goodrich, Dennis Petty, Eric Holland, Ron Harris, Dennis Hudgens, Mark Beck, Chris Fisher, Mark Wheeler, Dave Leedom, Robin and Linda Clay, Dusty "Crickett" Springfield, Don Herlitz, "The Ghast Boys," Dan Lawrence, Jim McNabb, Charlie Lara, Alan Hutton, Leo Bush, Dex Fairbanks, Michael Dunegan, Fred Fiedler, Gordon Frye, Kieran McMullin, Robert Norment, Gene Robinson, Steve Von Rader, Tony Hale, and last but not least (though I know I've forgotten so many), Bruce Frazier.

Thanks for the memories.